'You see,' Sweetwater said, putting a glass into Melville's nerveless hand, 'all we want to do is to make the transition as smooth and painless as possible.'

'You want me to hijack a Chinese communist general.'

'That's one way of putting it.'

'And you'll pay me 20,000 dollars?'

'Affirmative.'

'For a week's work?'

'More like a month all told.' Sweetwater hesitated. 'I'm not going to pretend that it'll be a complete stroll,' he said. 'The Tibetan border's sealed off; foreigners aren't allowed up there. Relations between Nepal and China are sensitive, so it wouldn't do to strain them by getting caught.'

'I won't do it,' Melville told Mr Yueh. 'I can't do it,' he told Sweetwater.

'Sure you can,' Sweetwater said.

'Quite apart from the moral objections,' Melville said, as if to himself, 'quite apart from the political implications, I'm just...' He punched his knee, beyond speech.

'Scared?' Sweetwater inquired. 'Perfectly natural.'

Melville raised haggard eyes. 'Even the thought of it makes me feel sick,' he said. He shook his head as though attempting to banish a foul vision. 'Oh boy.'

About the author

Windsor Chorlton was born in the north of England and worked for an international publisher in London before becoming a full-time writer. In 1981 he spent three months living in a remote Himilayan valley where he was able to interview Tibetans who had taken part in the guerilla war against China. *Rites of Sacrifice* is his first novel.

Rites of Sacrifice

Windsor Chorlton

CORONET BOOKS
Hodder and Stoughton

To Betty Walker

British Library C.I.P.

Chorlton, Windsor
 Rites of sacrifice.
 I. Title
 823[F]

ISBN 0 340 55102 X

Printed and bound in Great Britain for Hodder and Stoughton Paperbacks, a division of Hodder and Stoughton Ltd., Mill Road, Dunton Green, Sevenoaks, Kent TN13 2YA (Editorial Office: 47 Bedford Square, London WC1B 3DP) by Clays Ltd., St Ives plc.

BOOK ONE

Chapter 1

Chorphel paused outside the cave before going in. From up here the ageing guerilla had a god's-eye view of the mountains and the road swooping down to the frozen river plain. Some of his comrades were watching him from the slope below. One of them gave an impatient wave and Chorphel raised an arm in reluctant acknowledgement. He looked beyond them, searching the road as far as the shadows at the foot of the next range, and then, still hoping for a reprieve, he looked upwards. His eyes patrolled the shattered crest until they found the solitary figure of the lookout, hunched over his rifle. The man must have been watching him, because his hand described a slow, negative sweep of the horizons. With a grunt of resignation, Chorphel shouldered his Mauser and went into the cave.

In the gloom, Linka was as bulky as a bale of hides. All Chorphel could see of him was his shaven skull, bent in sleep or contemplation.

'General?' he whispered.

Slowly Linka raised his head. He looked past Chorphel with a melancholy smile, as though he had been listening to the voices in the wind.

Chorphel could hear them too – a disconsolate moaning. The thought that they had already told Linka the purpose of his visit stopped his tongue.

'You have something to report?' Linka inquired.

Chorphel cleared his throat. He was a man who lacked complexity in speech. This confrontation had not been his idea. 'Osher,' he began, 'the others . . .' His voice trailed away.

'Sit down, grandfather,' Linka said. 'No, not there. Where we can see each other.'

Chorphel lowered himself to the ground, hauling his Mauser across his knees. He avoided Linka's direct scrutiny. It made him feel slow and addled. He massaged the small of his back. The silence stretched to an intolerable length.

'It's fifteen days since we left Nepal,' he blurted. 'In all that time we haven't seen a soul.'

'That doesn't mean someone hasn't seen us,' Linka said. He yawned. 'Never trust a Tibetan skyline.'

3

As a former wilderness dweller himself, Chorphel knew how difficult it was for a man to cross nomad territory unnoticed. The Chinese had cleared the frontier zone, but had allowed a few nomads to return on condition that they reported any incursions across the border.

'I suppose that could explain why there hasn't been a convoy,' Chorphel mumbled.

'Unlikely. If they knew we were here, they would have sent soldiers.'

'Perhaps convoys can't use this road in the winter.'

Linka wagged a finger in friendly reproach. 'An old grey wolf like you should have learned to cultivate patience.'

'We've been waiting for six days.'

'We've waited longer,' Linka said, his eyelids drooping warningly.

'Not without the scent of prey,' Chorphel said, unable to mask his resentment.

'We'll give it three more days.'

'And go back with nothing to show for our pains.'

'Food's short; the weather could break. You can't expect starving men to cross that pass.'

'We could find all the food we need if we went north.'

'At the end of winter? In a famine year?'

'There's always food for the Chinese. Convoys use the big road every other day. We could be there in two days.'

'My mind is decided.'

Chorphel blew his nose with his fingers, clearing each nostril in turn. He wiped his hand on the floor and stared ahead with sullen anger.

'Old friend, trust me,' Linka said in the voice of reason. 'This was always meant to be more of a reconnaissance than a raid. We've been in our new base for less than six months. We don't know the strength and disposition of the Chinese in this region. We lack sufficient guns and ammunition, not to mention horses.'

'You have eighty men. They're all you have left. Unless you give them a success this winter, some of them will desert in the spring.'

'Better that than lose them all. No, our purpose this year is to observe the Chinese without being observed ourselves.'

'Our purpose is to kill them.'

'Only when conditions favour us. Those convoys on the big road are crammed with soldiers.'

'They won't be expecting an attack so far north.'

'Attack with what? We have less than fifty guns between us.'

4

'Then order the men with small hearts to give their weapons to the rest of us.'

'Ah,' Linka said, and seemed to relax. Idly he drew a shape in the dust. 'How many feel as you do?'

Chorphel hesitated. All the men were limp and despondent, but for different reasons. There were some who fretted at the inaction and wanted to ride north. Most, but not all, of these were Khampas – men from Tibet's eastern marches and therefore enemies of the Chinese by blood, tradition and personal grievance. The others were mostly refugees recruited at their old base in Mustang, four days' ride to the west. Their morale, never certain, had been sapped by the factional fighting that had forced them to flee the base. It had been eroded by the sickness that had fallen on the valley where they had established new quarters, and by the corroding sense that they had reached a dead end.

'How many?' Linka prompted, his voice hardening.

'None of the men want to stay here,' Chorphel muttered. 'Half want to ride to the big road; the rest are frightened of being cut off by a storm.'

'Half and half,' Linka said, balancing outspread hands. 'In such a situation, the task of a commander is to tip the balance the appropriate way.' He let one hand drop and the other rise. 'We return to the valley in three days.'

Chorphel hung his head. 'General,' he stammered, 'this is the first time I've questioned one of your orders, but you don't understand the problem.'

'Tell me,' Linka said in the gentlest of tones. 'You know how much I rely on you.'

Chorphel squirmed, pinned on his commander's stare. 'I only agreed to speak because of the bad feeling between you and Osher. He . . .'

'Do you imagine I don't know who's been gnawing on your loyalty?' Linka demanded, his eyes lacquered with anger. 'I knew the butcher's son had sent you the moment I saw your face.'

'Let him lead a group of volunteers to the big road,' Chorphel said quickly. 'It will give them heart, and a knowledge of conditions at the road will help us when we plan operations for next winter. Take the others back. Next year, when they have food inside them and proper weapons on their backs, they'll find their courage again.'

But the old guerilla had raised a demon, and Linka wouldn't be deflected until he had laid it to rest.

'I should have left him to rot in Mustang. I should have let . . .'

'He's too good a soldier,' Chorphel interrupted. 'If anything should happen to you, he would make a worthy leader.'

Linka blinked. 'Leader, is it?' he hissed. 'He's my lieutenant. He'll do what I tell him.'

Chorphel braced himself. 'No,' he said, 'he's come too far. That's what you don't understand. General, he intends to go with or without your permission.'

'And you?' Linka shouted, his eyes pits of black burning anger.

Chorphel's courage faltered. He took off his fur hat, fashioned from the pelt of a wolf, complete with snarling mask. Among Chorphel's clan, the wolf was a totem. 'Yes,' he said. 'Me and at least another twenty.'

Linka sucked in his breath as though he had burnt himself, but when Chorphel dared to look, his anger had been effaced and he was obviously thinking at a speed which Chorphel couldn't have kept up with even if he had been able to see behind those deep-set eyes.

'Let me tell Osher he has your approval.'

'Stop this pretence. Neither of you recognise my authority to command.' Linka slumped back and regarded Chorphel with a tolerant smile. 'So you think your commander has a small heart.'

Chorphel's eyes slid away. 'Osher says that you are considering seeking an amnesty from the Nepalese.'

Linka nodded in a detached way, his mind elsewhere. He did not seem to hear the faint cry from outside. 'Chorphel,' he said, 'how long have you ridden with me?'

'Eight years,' Chorphel replied, when he had worked it out. Linka's manner made him speak with caution.

'Eight years,' Linka repeated, and sighed. A frown slowly gathered on his face. 'Chorphel?'

'Yes.'

'Can you still remember why you're fighting.'

Chorphel had been trying to interpret Linka's mood. Surprise at the question and its moderate tone made him reach inside his robe for the scrap of paper that the Chinese officer had given him all those years ago. He stopped when he realised that Linka knew its contents as well as he did himself. It was a receipt for 120 sheep and the bags of salt they were carrying, requisitioned by the Chinese as an essential sacrifice to the cause of liberation.

'That's one mutton stew the Chinese have choked on,' Linka said.

There was another shout. Chorphel attempted to get up, but Linka seized his arm.

'Osher's right about the amnesty. Our military prospects are hopeless. We have no supply line, no chance of increasing our numbers, no way of returning to Mustang. Even if the Kuomintang send the guns they promised, we still have to cross that pass. We'll be lucky to mount more than one or two raids next winter. Maybe only one, because once the communists discover where our base is, all they have to do is wait at the pass like a fox outside a burrow.'

'One more winter may be all we need.'

'You're crazier than I thought. Forget Osher's nonsense.' Linka tightened his grip. 'Stay in the valley. I swear you'll have all the sheep you want.'

'That valley suffocates me. It's full of ghosts.' Chorphel tried to soften his rejection with a laugh. 'I'm not one of your Khampas. I'm a man of the plateau. Besides, I'm too old to go back to herding sheep.'

'At your age you should be playing with your grandchildren. You should be turning your thoughts towards death.' Linka's hand dropped from Chorphel's sleeve. His expression was listless. 'For me it's been fifteen years,' he said eventually. 'That's a long road to travel and be no nearer my goal. It's time I took another turning.'

'And Osher?'

Linka brooded, then gave a dismissive wave. 'When we return to camp, the council can decide if it wants him as leader.' Linka made sure he had Chorphel's eye. 'Until then, I remain your general.' He shifted his bulk. 'Well then, better find out what all the shouting's about.'

Chorphel clambered to his feet and stumbled out into the dusty yellow light. When the darkness had gone from his eyes, he saw that the lookout's attention was fixed on the plain. Another figure was descending from the ridge, almost falling, starting small avalanches of snow and scree. It was the boy from the valley who had begged to come along as their guide. Occasionally he stopped and jabbed his hand in the direction of the road, which remained empty as far as Chorphel could see.

'An army at the very least,' Linka murmured at his elbow.

Chorphel decided that even if it was a convoy, Linka had made his position clear beyond hope of recovery.

Osher was climbing up towards them, leaning into the slope with

7

long strides. Linka ignored him. Chorphel offered a silent prayer of thanks that the matter had been settled without bloodshed.

'Remember, he's not your general yet,' Linka said, as Osher approached.

The boy reached them first. His eyes were glazed with excitement. He doubled over to catch his breath. 'Trucks,' was all he could say.

Chorphel hauled him upright. 'How many?' he demanded.

'Not sure. Too far.'

'He's never seen a truck before,' Osher said, scrambling up the last few feet. 'It could be anything or nothing.'

Chorphel was relieved that he didn't express by so much as a glance any interest in how the discussion had gone.

'Everyone's ready,' Osher said. He cuffed the boy to send him on his way, then he climbed higher up the slope and half-lay, half-leaned on a slab of rock. He took out his ancient field glasses and squinted through the single functioning lens.

Chorphel sank to his haunches and let his gaze wander along the road. At the far side of the plain he detected a slow termite movement. The snow cover was patchy, making it difficult to keep the object in view or assess its importance, but it was definitely a vehicle of some kind. He looked up at Osher for confirmation of what he suspected.

'One truck,' Osher said.

'There may be more coming behind,' Linka said.

It took the truck half an hour to cross the plain and commence its ascent. The road behind it remained empty. Chorphel grimaced at Linka, who affected indifference. When the truck disappeared around the first bend, Osher began to make his way down.

'Tell the men to block the road,' Linka told Chorphel.

'For one truck?'

'It must be a very important truck to be travelling on its own.'

'The Chinese aren't stupid,' Osher panted, sliding to a halt. 'If it was carrying anything of value, it would have an escort.'

'Chorphel,' Linka said, in a warning tone.

'We didn't come all this way for one truck,' Osher shouted.

'I gave you an order, Chorphel.'

'Wait,' Osher demanded. He went up to Linka and stationed himself where the commander was obliged to face him. 'Let it pass,' he pleaded. 'It's probably engineers checking the road for a convoy.'

'In that case, our wait will have been worthwhile.'

'Take a look out there,' Osher said, pointing a hand that shook with rage.

Shadow had settled on the plain and the road across it was no longer apparent.

'It's too late for a convoy,' Osher said. 'Trucks wouldn't try to get through these mountains at night.'

'Tomorrow will arrive soon enough.'

Osher made an attempt to swallow his anger. 'The truck's probably expected at the next garrison tonight. If it doesn't arrive, they'll radio the convoy and send out a patrol before allowing it to leave.' He looked to Chorphel for support.

'Of course,' Linka said. 'I was forgetting that you used to drive trucks for the communists.'

Osher spat in disgust. Chorphel noticed that his hand was clenched close to his holster.

'The truck won't reach a garrison tonight,' he said, stepping between the two men. 'It must have broken down earlier. Destroy it and let's see what happens.'

He met Osher's glare with a warning shake of the head. After a furious, baffled moment, the Khampa whirled and slithered down to join the men.

'One day you'll push the goad in too far,' Chorphel muttered. 'We still have to share the same valley.'

In his nervousness, his hand had strayed to the charm packet he wore at his neck. Linka smiled in a way he didn't much care for.

'Remember when I gave you that? Well, you're under Osher's protection now. May you receive from him the reward that your service to me deserves.'

With a queasy sensation in his guts, Chorphel turned and left him. When he had arranged the ambush to Osher's satisfaction, he settled in the position he had selected days before. The truck climbed up at a determined crawl, passing in and out of sight. The grating of its engine carried on the wind.

Waiting for it to come into his sights, Chorphel had an uneasy feeling that the affair had not been entirely resolved. Linka had not told him what he intended to do when he relinquished command, but if he planned to remain in the valley it was hard to see how there could be an accommodation with Osher. Chorphel clicked his tongue with misgivings. They were both men of innate authority, and therefore mutual antagonism was to be expected. They were made of opposing elements, fire and ice, warring with each other in the depth of their hearts. Osher was a communist, a former student of the Chinese and, if the rumours were true, a collaborator who had given

9

evidence against monks and other reactionary elements. Chorphel remembered the day Osher had joined the Fortress of Faith. He had stood in front of Linka with a strange smile. 'Don't you remember me. I'm the butcher's son. I used to bring the meat to your monastery.'

The roar of the truck drowned Chorphel's anxiety. He nestled the Mauser to his cheek and waited for the truck to complete its climb.

Chapter 2

Aim Giver was exorcising demons in the Lucky Place.

He had summoned his protecting deities and laid out a feast for them on a small altar above the main chamber. There was a butter lamp for each guest, water for them to wash, skull cups full of cloudy beer, and conical barley cakes daubed with coloured butter. To gratify the senses there were smouldering pots of juniper and a bunch of plastic flowers arranged in a family-size Nescafé tin. The flowers had been donated by a pilgrim; the tin was salvage from a Spanish climbing expedition's abandoned base camp in the next valley.

Aim Giver addressed his guests in a hum, rocking on his throne, occasionally breaking off his chant to describe strange shapes with his hands and shake a brass bell and powerbolt at a black dough effigy of two riders arched backwards astride a horse, joined by a thick phallus.

Each gesticulation agitated the prayer scarves which shrouded the disintegrating features of Aim Giver's father, mummified behind the altar under a nylon pennant that carried a picture of junks and the legend SAY A BIG HELLO! SOUVENIR OF HONG KONG. The pilgrim again.

Trumpets blared, announcing the entrance of a hag with a crow's head and robes stitched from the flayed skins of corpses. She advanced on the altar with a swimming motion, holding an upraised dagger in one hand, a noose of intestines in the other. When she got close, she stopped, moving as though she was treading water, then she lunged in time with the cymbals, whirling the noose above the effigy. But it was only a feint. She gyrated away, her garments grey and vaguely transluscent, spinning to the edge of the circle before turning for a second stately approach.

Backwards and forwards, round and round. Satisfied with the way things were going, Aim Giver peered out into the pale, expectant sky. After a while, right on the edge of his vision, he sensed a presence, dark red, no larger than a tick, which plunged like a tethered horse each time the dancer threatened the effigy.

It was being jerked closer. Now it was almost in plain sight. Aim

Giver prepared to bring it into the circle as he would draw a single hair down through his skull.

Far away a horse screamed.

Aim Giver saw a cleft between mountains, one wall silver and the other black. A sickle of horsemen was riding out onto a field of moonlit snow.

The resonance went out of the music. The dancer lost rhythm. One or two guests muttered. Aim Giver lost his grip on the presence and it dwindled like a spark.

The horse screamed again.

Now they all heard it. They looked towards the north. The dancer cringed away from the altar, her dagger still raised high. Aim Giver ran to her and snatched the dagger and noose. He tried to mime her steps but his robes hampered him. Obstructions crowded in. His guests were getting up, their faces swollen with rage. They ignored his pleas. They were leaving him, going away, vanishing like mist sucked up by the morning sun.

He turned to find himself in a cave full of dust and ancient armour, with bundles of bones hanging from the roof and torn texts scattered on the floor amid stacks of spears and halberds. He found a way through the weapons and came to a stone altar. It was laid out with the ritual instruments, but the mirror was rusty and the silk stained; the skull cups sprouted hair and the lamps burned without shedding light.

Three figures sat on the other side of the altar, facing him. The one on the left had the head of a vulture, with knives for feathers and axes for hands. The one on the right had a face like a skinned ape and held a knotted sack that dripped a slow, thick liquid. The face of the one in the middle was covered by a tight leather mask. It was a martial figure with heavy legs splayed apart, one foot drumming. Its hands were spread wide in welcome.

'They thought you'd broken our vow.'

Aim Giver's father was standing in a corner. He pointed to an inscription chiselled in the rock above the altar.

'What does it say?' he asked.

'It wasn't me who disturbed them,' Aim Giver said in a child's voice.

'Now they're awake, you'd better feed them.'

There was a cloth-draped wicker basket beside the altar.

'I can't,' Aim Giver cried. 'It contradicts the doctrine.'

'These are the guardians of the doctrine,' his father said, indicating

12

the figures. 'Every valley its own Guardians; every Guardian its own master; every master his own doctrine. Don't tell me you've forgotten.'

'No, father.'

'Then you admit that an effective result sometimes depends on unorthodox methods.'

Aim Giver hesitated.

His father smiled and came closer. 'Consider the ecstatic union of guru and consort,' he said. 'It contradicts normal practice, but you can't deny that the joining of method and wisdom is coherent in result.' He tapped a knife on the rim of the basket. 'The offering of flesh contradicts normal practice, but that's a small price to pay for the protection of a strong, fierce Guardian.'

Aim Giver cowered.

His father glowered at him. 'How do you expect to keep this valley safe?' he demanded.

'I have my own tutelaries,' Aim Giver mumbled.

His father snorted. 'Illusions, masks – no more real than the visions of the dead.'

'You talk as though your Guardians are flesh and blood.'

His father turned to them and studied each figure in turn. 'Bird Rack, Dark Waters, Shalawoka,' he said tenderly. 'Let me show you.'

'I'm frightened, father.'

'Of course you are,' his father said, laying a hand on his shoulder. 'But remember that if blood and entrails are offered with a compassionate mind, no harm can befall you.' He led him closer. 'Go on. Look.'

He pressed the knife into Aim Giver's hand and stepped back.

Aim Giver knelt in front of the central figure. He peered down the tunnels bored into the mask. 'I can't see anything,' he said.

'If you want to know what lies at the bottom of the pool, you must lean over the bank.' The voice was faint and came from far away.

When Aim Giver turned, his father had gone.

Silence solidified around him, and then he heard a slow crepitation, a sigh as of pain or anticipation. He looked to find the eyes in the mask grinning at him with such malice that his very pores gaped in horror.

He tried to scramble away but the arms embraced him, swarming over his chest and pulling him close. He couldn't breathe. He was suffocating like the old woman he had seen put to death by salt diggers on the northern plateau. They had sewn her inside a soaking

13

yak skin and left her all day in the drying wind, so that the skin slowly shrank, squeezing the life out of her.

The hands lingered on his neck before moving lovingly upwards. Tendons clamped over his mouth and began to prise it apart. Bony fingers groped for his eyes.

'Father! Father!'

The hands went very still and seemed to listen, then stiffly, reluctantly and with a hollow sigh, they fell away.

He could feel his heart opening and closing like a fist. The walls of his chest felt as flimsy as parchment.

'Daddy!'

He could hear the lamps roaring in a draught.

'Please, daddy.'

He made a circle behind his eyes and in it constructed a symbol no larger than a thumbnail and as finely delineated as a silk thread. Concentrating on this, he repeated the appropriate formula two hundred times. At last he opened his eyes.

His daughter was kneeling in front of him, gnawing on her fist, her eyes shiny pools of fright.

He managed to raise a hand. His daughter sobbed and clumsily pushed a bowl to his lips, slopping some of the liquid into his lap.

'I thought you were dead,' she said. 'You were making such terrible sounds.'

He had his gums clamped on the bowl and could only shake his head. She watched him, with her head first on one side, then on the other. It wasn't just tears that made her face glisten. She had smeared butter on her cheeks and hung her mother's marriage beads around her neck.

'Why are you dressed like that?'

'They're coming back,' she said, her hands going to her neck. 'They must have crossed the pass in the storm. They'll need shelter.'

'Wolves must be content with the sky for a roof.'

She hung her head in disappointment. 'Can I watch them ride past?'

He examined her without affection, his gaze lingering on the marriage beads. A sour taste came into his mouth. 'Are you so desperate for company?'

'It's so long since we had visitors. I get so lonely.'

He held out his arms, like a baby reaching for its mother. She lifted him to his feet.

'I'm as frail as straw,' he said. 'If they decide to stop here, I can't turn them away. You'd better make ready to receive them. They won't be able to reach their camp tonight.'

'Oh!' She clapped her hands in delight. She noticed the effigy and giggled, thrusting out her pelvis in lewd pantomime. 'Is that how the Khampas couple – galloping on horses?'

'Go back to the house,' Aim Giver said, fumbling for his stick. 'They'll need food. Fodder for their horses.'

She bit her lip. 'Won't you come, too?'

'Tell them I mustn't be disturbed. Give them the old butter, the watery stuff from the spring pastures. And use the barley that was blackened by frost. Hide the seed grain.'

She climbed down the gallery steps, making the whole structure shake, and hurried through the temple as if pursued, shielding her eyes from the masks and statues that gaped down at her from the walls and pillars. At the door she paused.

'Daddy, did you destroy the demons?'

'The gods have conquered, the demons have been driven out. Now hurry. They'll need a fire.'

'Their leader was a priest. You never said.'

'Linka? He's a bandit – a renegade who scattered his vows in blood.'

'I heard it in the village. The Chinese made his abbot walk off the roof to see if he could fly, then they hung him by a chain.'

Aim Giver rapped his stick on the floor. 'Quickly! Quickly! They'll be here soon.'

When the door shut behind her he snuffed out the butter lamps until only one remained burning. He held up the guttering flame. The embalmer had done a good job. His father's soul rested in the universal absolute, mice nested in his robes, yet his expression remained a perfectly preserved reproach.

No doubting the effectiveness of his methods. While he was alive it had never been necessary to close the village gates at night, and the only time the valley's defences had been breached, the threat was not even discovered until the following summer, when a herdsman looking for a strayed yak found the bodies of a dozen brigands frozen on the pass, still hunched over their horses' necks, as if they had been struck down between one breath and the next.

Aim Giver tore open the web of coloured threads that enclosed the sacrificial effigy. He picked it up, avoiding the gleam of his father's remaining eye. There was a door at the back of the gallery. It was

15

frozen to its frame, and he had to hammer it with his stick before he could get it open.

He stepped out under the moon's glacial stare. Stars streamed in a cold, dry tide. New snow creaked underfoot. The storm had lasted two days, piling drifts as high as the eaves. Aim Giver shuffled to the edge of the roof and put down the effigy. He moaned as he fumbled his robe above his waist and aimed a curdled stream into the night. His piss crackled as it hit the snow.

The Lucky Place clung like a swallow's nest beneath a sharp crest overlooking a crossroads formed by four valleys. The valleys to east and west rose steeply and petered out in snowfields surrounded by hanging glaciers. The main valley zigzagged north towards a range that enclosed a peak as sharp and flawless as a blade of ice. The founder of the temple had chosen the site so that he could contemplate the mountain as the sun lit fires on its summit, and so that the villagers could look up from their huddled rooftops on the other side of the valley and take reassurance from the sight of the temple prayer flags offering defiance to invisible enemies. Now the banners were furled in ice and the houses stood empty. A month ago, after the New Year festival, the villagers had brought their valuables to the Lucky Place and then left for their winter settlement a day's journey to the south, before the first heavy snowfalls cut them off from the world.

Black specks twitched on the whiteness to the north. The Khampas would not reach the solitary place for another hour, but the night was so cold, so tightly stretched, that Aim Giver could hear the snicker of their horses and the *shush-shush* of hooves ploughing through the frozen crust. He picked up the effigy, broke it apart and threw it piece by piece to each corner of the world. By the time the last crumbs were scattered, the riders had reached the shrines on the village boundary. Aim Giver saw how the formation floundered, the riders slumped low in their saddles. If only the storm had lasted a few more hours.

He went back into the temple and climbed down into the main chamber, placing the remaining lamp on a large altar presided over by the flaking gilt statue of a pouting young man. Then he removed the gallery steps. His father made a pale blur in the darkness. Aim Giver took his prayer wheel and assumed a tranquil posture. His thoughts flew like sparks.

Relief at reaching shelter made the horsemen noisy. They cursed and laughed as their horses laboured up the path to the temple. There

16

were harsh slaps and ear-splitting whistles, the creak of saddles and the oaths of riders struggling to loosen frozen harness with numbed fingers, muffled thumps as they beat the cold from their chests. A door grated on snow. Aim Giver heard a gabble of voices next door, and the liquid pounding of tea being churned.

Steps crunched towards the temple door.

'Teacher?'

Aim Giver had his eyes closed, yet he sensed how Linka filled the doorway. Through the whirring of his prayer wheel he heard the Khampa negotiate the dark chamber without hesitation, sniffing the rancid smells as if they were memories. He stood close, his garments shedding chill, then sank to the ground in a creaking of frozen hides.

'This is an auspicious night for me.'

Aim Giver kept him waiting. When he finally opened his eyes, Linka was still kneeling, his shaven head pressed to the floor. Yes, he was a bull of a man, even allowing for his bulky coat of blackened skins. He raised his head and Aim Giver examined his face, probing for the points of weakness. It was as round and smooth as a water-stone, unmarked by wind or sun except for the fleshy mouth, which was cracked by cold and weeping. His eyes, tucked under heavy folds of skin, were acute and sceptical. Yes, Aim Giver thought, a priest.

Another man came into the light and threw him a perfunctory bow. This one was truly a barbarian – sharp, coppery features framed in a fox-skin helmet that was beaded with ice. His mottled robe was thrown back over one shoulder, exposing a heavy pistol at his waist. Its mineral smell caught in Aim Giver's throat. He leaned forward to get a better look at the Khampa's boots. They were cut from leather as heavy as wild yak hide and elaborately equipped with straps and buckles.

The Khampa spoke sharply in his own language. Linka ignored him.

'My lieutenant,' he told Aim Giver with an ironic smile. 'Osher Horkhang, deputy-commander of the Fortress of the Faith.'

'You know I don't allow visitors to disturb me in the winter.'

Linka bowed apology. 'We would have ridden past if we could have reached our camp, but the storm, that evil pass . . .' Linka's smile broadened.

'If a valley is reached by a dangerous pass, only the best of friends or the deadliest of enemies come visiting.'

Linka's smile appeared at full stretch. 'How could I resist the oppor-

17

tunity to prostrate myself before the lion of the snows who dwells on the summit of such perfected wisdom?'

Honey on a sharp knife, Aim Giver thought, unsettled by the flattery. Even though Linka was from the East, he spoke Tibetan as smoothly as a Lhasa abbot, while he himself had to grope for each word.

'Won't you bless me, Teacher?'

Aim Giver flinched before he realised that Linka was holding up a glinting scarf.

'I can't bless men who carry weapons. It contradicts the doctrine.'

'Our guns are the armour of the doctrine.'

The giant draped the icy silk around the lama's neck. Confused, Aim Giver laid a hand on Linka's skull. A warm pulse ticked under his fingers – obscene to someone whose own body had been stilled almost to the point of extinction.

Two men blundered through the door carrying a sagging bundle. One of them had a rifle slung on his shoulder, and when he bent to lower the corpse, the gun slipped. He grabbed at it, letting the bundle drop, then did a little dance of contrition, squeezing his hands under his armpits and hissing through his teeth to show that it was the cold that had made him clumsy.

Aim Giver spun his prayer wheel in outrage. 'What's the meaning of this?'

'Don't you recognise him?' Linka asked. He took the lamp and shone it on the dead man's face. 'It's Lhakpa.'

The eyes peered past Aim Giver with a look of surprise on the point of turning to fear, as if someone had led him to a door and he had opened it to find himself staring into a dark and empty room.

'Young men,' Linka said, with a shrug of apology. 'He was always hanging around our camp, begging to join us. We needed a guide for the pass, so . . .'

His lieutenant muttered angrily.

'Osher wants you to know that we left three of our own comrades up there.'

'Then why have you brought Lhakpa back?'

'Look,' Linka said, pulling open the dead man's coat. He put his palm on a wound large enough to take a fist. 'Still wet, see, although this was done five days ago. If it had been one of my Khampas he would have died within the day, but Lhakpa didn't want to die in a strange country, and then he begged us not to leave him to the demons on the pass. He waited until we came in sight of the Lucky

18

Place. "Now my lama will show me the way," he said, and his spirit left and flew ahead of him.'

'He doesn't need a guide to find the way to hell.'

'He had no illusions. He told me himself that his sins weighed like boulders, and he asked me to sell his best yak to pay for the special rites for raising the consciousness.'

The soldier who had dropped his rifle whispered to Linka.

'And he gives this man his horse. For his unselfish action.'

'How did he die?'

Linka hesitated.

The Chinese had stared stupidly at the road block. Two of them had guns and were shot as they scrambled out of the cab. The driver was weaponless, so the Khampas played with him, herding him this way and that until he was insensate with fear. They would have finished him with their swords, but Osher rescued him for interrogation. Meanwhile, Lhakpa had climbed the truck's tailboard. A soldier hidden in the back had shot him.

'He died in defence of the doctrine.'

Aim Giver half rose. 'Look well,' he said, addressing the dead man's eyes. 'All your life you were blinded by your karma, but now you can see where your crimes have brought you – to the bottom of the abyss, crawling on your belly with the last of the last.'

Linka massaged his skull.

As Lhakpa toppled back, everyone had fired into the truck. When their guns were empty they stood grinning slackly, not catching each other's eyes. Someone gave a nervous laugh and in the absence of any other sound it seemed to carry to the horizon. They must have heard the cries through the gunfire. Finally, Osher had climbed into the truck and pulled back the hood to reveal about ten Tibetans, tangled in chains on the floor. A road gang.

'Lhakpa told me there were disagreements between you,' Linka said. 'He mentioned a dispute about hunting in the sanctuary, a feud with a neighbour who caught him mounting his wife. Youthful folly, surely.'

Four of the Tibetans had survived the massacre. While Linka was treating their wounds, Osher came up to tell him that the road gang had been sent a day in advance of a convoy to repair a bridge. 'Tell the men to get ready to leave,' Linka had ordered, not looking up. 'We're finished here.' And then, sensing Osher standing stiff as a dog behind him, one hand on his holster, he had shouted the instruction to the waiting men. When he had done what he could for the Tibetans, he turned to see that less than half his force were in the saddle, with the rest clustered around Osher, who was squinting at a map through a cloud of cigarette smoke. Chorphel was among them and Linka

19

had nodded at him. Then he had walked to his waiting horse and led his silent followers away.

Linka was still smiling at Aim Giver, his outspread hands invoking compassion. His lieutenant shouted and chopped the air with his hand. Linka's smile slipped out of focus.

Osher had caught up soon after the storm broke and ridden past with seven fingers held up. Seven trucks, more than a hundred soldiers – a reasonable target for the whole force, but too many for Osher's band. 'Are they following?' Linka had shouted after his lieutenant. Osher had turned with a puzzled frown. 'The Chinese. The Tibetans must have told them what direction we took.' A gleam of contempt as Osher wheeled his horse into the blizzard. 'You killed them, too?' But Osher was gone, and there was nothing but the wind howling like a dog, reminding Linka of the terrible concatenation of cause and effect his mistake had unleashed.

Aim Giver saw Linka's anger masquerading as a smile. Thinking it was directed at him, he glanced away, agitating his prayer wheel. 'It's winter,' he whined. 'I'm alone except for my daughter. I'll set Lhakpa on his journey, but you must take his body back to his family.'

'I understand, Teacher. Solitude is the most cherished possession for a sage such as yourself.'

Or a sorcerer, Aim Giver thought, sensing something unwholesome behind the giant's unswerving smile.

Linka got up with a grunt and ordered the two soldiers to remove Lhakpa's body. He bulked over the lama. 'I have to see my men now. I'll come back later.'

'We have nothing to discuss.'

'On the contrary. There's the welfare of this valley to consider.'

That smile. It would draw the eyes out of a snake.

For twenty years the Lucky Place had been the centre and circumference of Aim Giver's world. Since his father died, he had left the valley only once – on a pilgrimage to Mount Kailas that ended ignominiously when his caravan was ambushed by bandits who attacked hanging under their horses' bellies.

And yet when he was alone in the long winter, Aim Giver often went travelling. Sometimes he just bounded from peak to peak or composed himself on the impeccable summit and inspected the four continents and outer ocean spread out before him. Occasionally his inward eye carried him down a broad river to groves of sandalwood where goddesses reclined under rainbow pavilions smoothing their skin with fine oils. Or it took him to palaces where he debated with masters of philosophy, or to rocky canyons and burning deserts where he duelled with demons. On one journey he was reunited with his mother, then eighteen years old and married to a wealthy merchant in Jomosom.

One day he would travel so far that the thread joining self and consciousness would snap, scattering him to the four corners of the universe.

Linka shut the door on the restless sounds of exhausted sleep and trudged back through the snow. Inside the temple he lifted his lamp high and made a slow circuit of the main chamber, inspecting the furnishings. There was the usual pantheon, crudely executed, some blissfully serene, most ferocious, trampling on copulating humanity, garlanded with hearts and skulls, twined in orgiastic embraces. He had expected something less orthodox. On the valley's trails he had seen many vestiges of the old religion – cairns and pillars with indecipherable inscriptions and arcane symbols. Here, the only item out of the ordinary was a mask shaped like the head of a blood-sucking insect, with huge mirrored eyes and a dangling proboscis.

It hung on a wall partitioned by pigeon holes, each one stacked with books. Reaching into one, Linka traced the title carved on the dusty wooden binding and caught a sad breath of childhood – the smell of birch paper, juniper, red robes, chanting, the clarity of print. He had a vision of himself as a boy of twelve on his first day in the monastery. He had stood in a room similar to this one while his teacher urged him to remember the fundamental precept. Apply your-self to meditation, for the time of death is uncertain.

He took a step back, impressed by the size of the library. Knowlege accumulated over six generations, he reminded himself, and felt a frisson of pleasure as he imagined exploring these treasures. He turned to address the repository of all this wisdom, but the lama's eyes were engaged with their own obsessions. Not quite, Linka realised, recalling one of the recluses in his monastery who had had himself walled up in a cell. As a novice, one of his tasks had been to take the hermit food – barley mixed with sand. Sometimes, looking through the grille, he would meet the hermit's eyes, cloudy as last winter's ice, but with a furtive gleam of watchfulness lurking a long way back in the skull.

Aim Giver's daughter appeared with tea. Linka insisted on pouring. He took a bowl for himself, filled it with tea, shook *tsampa* on it from a leather pouch, lapped at the floury heap until he reached the level

21

of the tea, then stirred the mixture to the consistency of thin porridge and drained it. Aim Giver wet his lips. The silence was almost companionable. The girl leaned forward to offer Linka more. He found himself exchanging a speculative glance, a mutual appraisal. She backed away, frightened, and then she smiled, stroking her cheek.

She would have been handsome, Linka thought, except that her features were curiously blurred, as though they had been shaped in clay and then casually squeezed before they had set. Impossible to judge her body under its layers of fleeces and skirts, but when she walked, it seemed to lag half a pace behind her. She had beautiful, wide-spaced eyes flecked with gold. Looking into them, Linka felt a thickening at his groin.

'Phat!' Aim Giver said.

Linka turned politely, sucking grease off his fingers. The girl left.

'I'm astonished that a man who took the vows of a virtuous beggar should concern himself with women.'

Linka interpreted this reproach, with its allusion to the carnal habits of his old monastic order, as a promising token of worldliness.

'I was only an ignorant novice,' he admitted.

'I was told that you studied the arts of prediction for ten years.'

Linka's head drooped in shame. 'My incompetence is a sore on the unblemished skin of my teacher's reputation.'

'That you can read the future in a wisp of smoke or a cracked bone.'

Linka swore that his skills were as counterfeit as those of the ragged itinerants who peddled fortunes at country markets.

'That you cast horoscopes before battle.'

Linka produced a hollow laugh.

'That my own people have started coming to you for charms and prophecies.'

'Ah.'

So that's it, Linka thought. What was it they said in this valley? Only room for one yak head in a tub of butter.

'Suppose I did have the skills you flatter me with.'

'Then you can tell me why so many children have died since you came to our valley. You can explain why our harvest turned black and why wolves have crossed the pass for the first time in memory. You can interpret the unpleasant sounds that fill the sky.'

'Disorder rules. It's the same in all the valleys.'

Aim Giver rattled his prayer wheel, making it plain that he wasn't concerned about the misfortunes of other communities. His responsibility extended only as far as the skyline. He fixed Linka with his occluded stare.

'I'll tell you what has caused our misery.'

'Your reputation for expounding and confounding has carried to the ends of the winds.'

Aim Giver peered at him as if he suspected insincerity, then he crooked his finger, drawing him close. He looked up, slowly swivelling his head, as though he was tracking a fly. 'There,' he whispered. 'Can you hear them?'

Linka risked a glance past the lama at the shuttered windows. Time was pressing. They would have to leave early, or the horses would get bogged down in the thawing snow.

Aim Giver's eyes came drifting back. 'They're everywhere now,' he said in a conversational tone. 'Waiting by the crossroads, hiding under bridges, curled up in the corners of houses. And who is it that's stirred them up?' He pointed a trembling but purposeful finger.

Linka shifted on his seat, feeling the going getting uncertain. 'We're not the cause of your misfortunes. When your children fell sick, I helped cure many of them. Your people may have lost their barley crop, but they eat rice twice a day with the money they've made from selling us mouldy grain and stinking butter.'

'What about the houses you stole?'

'Empty. Abandoned years ago.'

'And the fields where you spread your filth?'

'Fallow. No one has been robbed of a livelihood. There's not enough water to grow barley at our camp. The stream's been blocked by a fall of ice. Listen, we're digging a channel from the river. You'll see. We'll turn those fields into the most fruitful in the valley.'

'You think we can't dig a ditch as well as men who've never been closer to the soil than the back of a horse?'

'Then why leave good land unplanted?'

'Because,' Aim Giver said, averting his eyes, 'it belongs to the Guardians.'

Linka struggled to keep his irritation in bonds. 'It wasn't your Guardians who built the houses or turned the soil.'

Aim Giver seemed to have difficulty composing an answer. 'Strangers built them,' he admitted at last. And then, in a rapid, offhand tone he explained how strangers had invaded the valley many generations ago and offended the Guardians by polluting their temple. Roused to fury, the Guardians had destroyed them, every one. The houses had been abandoned and the fields left unworked.

23

Baffled by the confusion of folk memory and myth, Linka stopped listening. It was the wrong time to speak to the lama. Perhaps it would be wiser to leave him now and seek an audience another day. The problem was, he would have to return stripped of power, a poor supplicant. Tomorrow, when they reached the camp, he would formally relinquish his command to Osher. If he didn't, well . . . some of his men were still loyal, but they were like him; they had no more stomach for fighting.

Aim Giver's voice had trailed away. Wisdom came in different forms, Linka reminded himself. There was the wisdom acquired by method, and then there was crazy wisdom. Craziness too, he was forced to concede, seeing how the lama's papery lips fluttered and fluttered and never quite came to rest.

He made an effort. 'A tale to make the hairs of the faithful quiver,' he said, easing his cramped legs. In fact, a feeble lie. The villagers themselves had told him they had worked the fields until the death of Aim Giver's father. The marks of the plough were still plain to see. He brightened, clutching at the hope that the lama was after nothing more substantial than a hefty bribe.

'It's always wise to place yourself under the protection of a strong guardian. Tell me where this temple is hidden and what ransoms we should make.'

'Temple?' Aim Giver blinked in fright but managed to recover and look cunning. 'What are you prepared to give?'

Linka shrugged. 'Butter, curds, barley. Money – within reason.' There was a going rate for divine protection.

It took a while to identify the fibrous sound emanating from the lama as laughter.

Aim Giver picked up the lamp and swung it in an arc so that the flame dwindled to a point. As it flared up again, the statues and masks seemed to rush forward, menacing the little circle hollowed out of the night. 'Milk and cakes!' Aim Giver said, bobbing his head at something behind Linka. 'The stranger thinks he can buy the protection of the Guardians with milk and cakes!'

Linka's skull was hollow with fatigue. He managed to preserve his smile, but his scalp cringed when he turned and saw the pale figure on the gallery above him, leaning forward as if eavesdropping.

Aim Giver plucked at Linka's sleeve. 'You must take them away,' he pleaded. Next door, the Khampas were beginning to wake with hacking coughs.

24

'There's nowhere left to go,' Linka said.

'Return to Mustang. Rejoin your army.'

'A dozen factions who spend their days drinking and shooting vultures.'

'And what do you expect to achieve with your gang? Eighty men won't drive the Chinese out of Tibet.'

'We have allies.'

'Only a fool would trust your Chinese friends.'

'Nationalists, bitter enemies of the communists.' Linka gently unhooked Aim Giver's hand. 'You should talk to Osher about strategy. Last autumn he discussed the military situation with our Kuomintang supporters. One more winter, they told him. Just one more winter and then their armies will invade the mainland.'

Aim Giver conveyed scepticism with a sclerotic cough.

'Perhaps you're right,' Linka said. 'Taiwan's a long way from Tibet. But it's true that the communists are in chaos. In Lhasa generals take orders from conscripts, sons beat their fathers and dung collectors lecture on hygiene. They run this way and that, like rats in a plague.'

'Even if the Kuomintang beat the communists, it won't make any difference. The Chinese are like a tray of sand. Shake it . . .' Aim Giver suited action to words and pretended to study the result '. . . still a tray of sand. Still Chinese, still in Tibet.'

Linka gave an appreciative roar. Not such a wilderness fool after all. He wagged a finger in mock reproach. 'Have you forgotten the prophecy? China's armies will rise like a summer lake. They will outnumber the stars and Buddha's doctrine will become like a dying butter lamp. But just as a night full of stars looks bright until the morning comes . . .' Linka broke off, his smile warped. 'No,' he said, 'I can't delude myself any longer. Tibet is finished.'

From his sleeve he fished out a cloth-covered package. He unwrapped it and produced a hand-tinted photograph of the Dalai Lama. He rubbed the dross frame on his coat and handed it to Aim Giver.

'The war was lost when he went into exile. I was among the escort who conducted him to the Indian border. I watched him cross, and I knew that he had taken Tibet with him.'

'Yet ten years later you're still fighting.'

Linka took the picture back and frowned at it tenderly. 'His Holiness gave me it himself. Look, there's his seal. Which shows the vastness of his spirit, because when the Chinese first came, my own family was involved in a plot to overthrow him.' Linka grinned. 'We Khampas are like grit between millstones – China on one side, Tibet on the other, both trying to grind us down. Fighting's a way of life for us.'

'Because it's your karma,' Aim Giver said, brandishing his prayer wheel, 'like the wolf, like Lhakpa.'

Under the lama's disapproving gaze, Linka helped himself from a bowl of crushed juniper and sprinkled it on the incense pot. 'Noble teacher, what's the most consuming emotion a man can feel? Not love, nor even hate.' He looked up with an apologetic smile. 'Forgive me. I know that you don't allow such sentiments to cloud your vision. But as for me, the world still clings.'

He blew on the incense until it glowed. 'Revenge,' he said, with no particular expression. 'Hear how it resonates. The very sound of it makes wounds gape.' He fixed Aim Giver with calm eyes. 'I fight the Chinese because they killed the being I most revered.'

Suddenly he roared with laughter. 'A poor revenge, you must be thinking. I've been retreating for fifteen years – short rations, forced marches, a different valley every winter. It makes me giddy to think about it. If I mounted my horse tomorrow, it would be summer before I reached Kham. We've been chased to the end of the world. This is the last valley.'

'You swore to take your men away in the spring,' Aim Giver wailed.

'So I did. Unfortunately, the Gurkhas at the mouth of the valley won't let us leave.' Linka shrugged. 'Grit between millstones.'

'They'll let you pass if you hand over your weapons.'

'I didn't fight for fifteen years to end up penned in a refugee camp.'

'If you stay here the Chinese will destroy us all.'

'Not if we remain this side of the border.'

'You'll call a halt to your raids?'

'Our action in Tibet – it did not go as predicted. Morale was damaged.' Linka stirred the pot of incense. 'I can't speak for all the Khampas, but some of my men want to settle here and make peaceful lives for themselves. They were farmers and herders before the war. You'd be surprised – some of them owned more sheep than they could count in a day's ride. With your blessing they could restore the fortunes of this valley. The channel we're digging – I tell you, it will double the amount of land for planting. We could . . .'

'No!'

'You gave sanctuary to three nomad families.'

'Wilderness dwellers who pitch their tents close to the snowline, not brigands who pollute the soil under the very eye of the Guardians.' Aim Giver squinted in suspicion. 'As for you, I can't imagine you spending your days bleeding yak or guiding a plough.'

'Nevertheless, I have turned my back on Tibet for good.' Linka heaved himself to his feet. The shutters were outlined with grey. 'Think about what I've said, while I contemplate your noble summit.'

The world had grown rigid and inert. The stars glittered without energy, casting a gelid blue light. In the stableyard the horses stood motionless, heads drooping almost to the ground. Linka pushed between them. He took a knife from his coat and chipped snow from the notches in a log propped against the temple wall. On the roof he concentrated his attention on the slender pyramid that sailed between heaven and earth. Strange how this was the only spot in the valley where the peak could be seen.

His mind clouded with yearning. His tears made an aureole around the summit, and in it he saw, bright as a jewel, seated in an attitude of bliss, his beloved teacher. Apply yourself to meditation. Life is but a flash of lightning in a summer storm.

Immediately he knew what until now he had hardly dared hope. There was not a trace of uncertainty left in his mind. Every stage of his campaign had been part of a bitter pilgrimage fated to end here. How could he doubt it.

Something strange was happening. Here on the valley floor it was still night, but over the eastern ridge a pale seam was opening up. The summit was getting lighter, irradiated with its own energy, for stars still clustered about it, and the other mountains remained dark. Linka exhaled from the wellspring of emotion. The sun rose in a halo, striking sparks off the peaks, igniting fires that ran down the channels of ice. The horses shifted and snorted. A pair of ravens flew past, tumbling and barking.

Linka heard a furtive sound behind him and turned to see Aim Giver marooned at the top of the ladder. Filled with compassion, he lifted the lama onto the roof.

'You weigh less than my coat,' he said, shocked by the lama's appearance. His flesh did not so much look mortified as gnawed from within.

'You want my throne,' Aim Giver said.

Linka bowed in humility. 'I want you to take me as your pupil.'

Aim Giver grunted. He was pissing. 'So the wolf makes a necessity of virtue now that it has lost its teeth.'

'You're ill. Soon another visitor will knock on your door and you

27

won't be able to turn him away. Oh, I know you'll embrace death with open arms, but who will safeguard your people when you have departed to the immaculate fields of lotus light?'

Aim Giver watched the ravens hammering at the scraps of the effigy.

'Six generations,' Linka said, closing on him. 'Surely you don't want the line to end. Take me as your son-in-law. I'll give you an heir.'

Aim Giver produced a sickly laugh. 'Marry my daughter? Marry a witch? That's what they say, isn't it? That she rides through the sky on a drum and can see their shadows on a cloudy day.'

'Bad thoughts breed in darkness. You've turned away from your people. They lie there in their winter quarters, a dozen to each hovel, their minds writhing like snakes.'

'It's you who have poisoned their thoughts.'

'You can't blame me for their misfortune. There were sixty households in your father's reign; now there are less than forty. Your neighbours have broken off the old marriage arrangements. Women sell themselves to their neighbours' husbands and brothers lie with their own sisters.' Linka frowned. 'I don't understand why you allow them to remain in such an unhappy state. It's almost as though you wanted the community to die.'

Aim Giver eyed him blankly.

Linka shrugged the broad yoke of his shoulders as if reluctantly taking on a burden. 'They know they have wandered from the right path. Your own village council asked me to speak with you. They have invited me to be your successor.'

Aim Giver stared out at the icy bones of the earth.

'Can't you see?' Linka pleaded. 'It's meant.'

Smoke-blackened and greasy, knuckling their eyes and scratching, the Khampas emerged into the light. They pointed with exclamations at the mountain, then wandered away from the temple and squatted in a row. Osher appeared, yawning, his hair coiled in a braid. He had exchanged his robe for a leather jacket and had added a machine-pistol to his personal ordnance. He took a pack of cigarettes from a zippered pocket and lit up. Noticing the two men on the roof, he tapped his wristwatch.

'Is that the kind of man who will restore our fortunes?' Aim Giver asked.

Linka nodded slowly, as though he had misheard the question. 'He joined me two winters ago in Mustang. He was a deserter from the Indian frontier force – a mutineer who killed two of his officers.'

'A Tibetan?'

'From my own region.' Linka flashed Aim Giver a glance. 'A butcher's son. An outcast who grew up in a charnel house of bones and hides.'

Aim Giver laughed his graveyard laugh. 'You're afraid of him.'

Linka weighed the accusation. 'See that man there?' he said eventually, jerking his head at a middle-aged guerilla who was attempting to bridle a nervous horse. 'We've ridden together for eight years. Before each battle he brings me butter to bless and then smears it on his bullets so that they find their mark. That charm-packet he's wearing – I made it myself. Since he's worn it he's been wounded three times. And do you know what? Each time, he's kissed the amulet and sworn that if it hadn't been for my protection he'd be staked out on a mountainside in hell.

'Now observe Osher.'

The lieutenant was supervising the departure, legs braced, hands on hips.

'He can drive a truck and operate a radio,' Linka said. 'Are you familiar with the machine called aeroplane – the iron vulture? Well, Osher can jump out of such things. The Americans taught him the skill in their own country. Before that he was an enthusiastic communist. The Chinese cultivated young Tibetans like Osher. He studies their books on the craft of war and politics as you or I would study the sacred texts.' Linka's expression grew grave. 'In short, his consciousness has been formed in another world. You would not want him to remain in yours.'

'Your words are so much buzzing,' Aim Giver said, beginning to turn away.

'Wait,' Linka said. But when he had reclaimed the lama's attention he made no attempt to speak. His eyes brooded on the sacred peak.

'These mountains,' he said at last. 'Have you never wondered why the Chinese don't march across the pass and destroy our camps? They care little for Nepal's neutrality. No, the reason the Chinese tolerate our presence is because these mountains are all that separates them from India. If they invaded, the Indians would feel as though a huge wave was threatening to engulf them. It would lead to war.' Linka turned to face Aim Giver. 'Osher plans an action that will provoke the Chinese into crossing the border.'

29

The sun was pulling itself clear of the mountains. The Khampas were swinging themselves into the saddle.

Linka shrugged. 'Hard to see how he can achieve his aim with less than a hundred men. Nevertheless, while he may be only a trivial irritant to the Chinese, he's a major threat to your community.'

'I see a hook baited with fear. You hope to draw desperate words from me and store them behind that smile. Then, one day, you will return them to me, dipped in poison.'

'Accept me as your heir. In return I promise to rid you of Osher and his followers.'

'So certain. Tell me, is that the pledge of Linka the general or Linka the diviner?'

'The laws of causality apply to both. Results proceed from actions.'

'What actions?'

'I'll find a way. Osher can't mount another raid until the autumn. He's short of weapons and horses. He needs supplies from the Kuomintang. I'll find a way.'

'Ah, the sun has barely dawned on your new life, yet you can't wait to sacrifice the old.'

'An exorcism. A cutting off of the past.'

'A murder.'

Linka went to the edge of the roof and looked down on the waiting Khampas. At their head Osher saluted with a languid flourish.

Linka breathed a mournful but resigned sigh. 'Poor Osher. So many allegiances, so many betrayals.'

He observed a few seconds' silence.

'You believe then,' Aim Giver asked, 'that the result justifies the method.'

Linka bathed him in a grateful smile. 'With you elevated to the summit of your people's respect and me as your energetic servant, this valley can be restored to glory.'

In full view of the guerillas Aim Giver spat in Linka's face.

The Khampa's smile merely trembled at the edges. Ignoring the icy flecks of spittle, he bent to enfold the lama in his arms.

Pressed to the giant's chest, Aim Giver caught a whiff of corruption – like old rags and tallow, the odour that came off his embalmed father when the butter lamps were lit, the smell in the temple above the Khampas' camp, where the Guardians sat nursing their hunger.

The stench was still on his palate as he sat alone on the gallery, a whole set of correspondences juggling in his mind. Linka, the Guardians, Osher the butcher's son, blood and entrails. It was meant, the bull from Kham had said. Of course it was meant. Disasters of this magnitude didn't occur accidentally.

'You,' he cried, stumbling to his feet. 'It was you who sent him. Oh, how you always wanted a son like that one.'

His father's bolting eye ignored him.

'Pemba,' he called, suddenly aware of the resounding silence.

Water chirped on ice.

'Pemba,' he called again, rapping his stick on the floor.

He hobbled to his quarters. The hearth was empty. He imagined his daughter squirming under the giant's bulk.

An anguished bleating came faintly through the floor. He tottered down into the yard. Ice glared black in the sun. He slipped on snow stained yellow by the horses. The ravens flew up in tatters and sidled along the roof. The toggle securing the stable door was still in place. He undid it and the goats ran to him, butting his legs, pleading for relief. A solitary cow with staring ribs regarded him without hope.

He climbed to the roof again. She was walking back along the blue furrows, smiling at some pleasant private fantasy. As she came close she began singing a song she had learned from her mother.

If there are parents in the house, the children will be happy.
If there is a leader in the village, the people will be happy.
If there is a lama in the temple, the guardian spirits will be happy.
In this way the whole world will live in the light of the sun.

Noticing the goats, she spread her arms and swooped on them, calling their names.

Aim Giver remained on the roof for a while. Not a whiff of cloud. The sky was so blue that it curved into black, but the light had the brittle, glassy quality that always forecast a storm.

31

Chapter 3

'But seriously,' said the Englishman with the soft-boiled eyes, 'don't they scare you?'

Melville required a moment to work out that the Englishman was referring to the Japanese guests. They clung like limpets around the hulking *gaijin*, smoking as though their lives depended on it – head back, suck and expel, almost before the smoke could reach their throats. They smoked one-handed, while the other dealt with items of *cuisine bourgeoise* proffered by air hostesses on stopover dressed in chef's aprons and *tocques*. Above the room a banner said A TASTE OF FRANCE.

'I said, don't they scare you?'

'I wouldn't say that. A couple of weeks ago I was up in Yokohama, looking round a shipping company's headquarters. My PR man – young guy, spent a year at Columbia, into acid rock – showed me a padded room where a couple of junior 'xecs were beating shit out of dummies of the men on the top floor. Reduces stress, he told me, improves productivity, creates harmony. What about the bosses, I asked. Don't they mind? Ah no, says the PRO, picking up a stave and teeing off. Section heads and higher get to use the driving range on the roof.'

'Exactly what I mean,' the Englishman said. 'Bloody fanatics.'

He snapped his teeth on a belch. Frowning reproach at the nearest Japanese steward, he discarded the olive tart he had been sampling, putting it down as though it were an unexploded grenade.

'No,' he said, 'I know what we're up against.'

'In the war, were you?' Melville asked.

'I was reading this article,' the Englishman said. 'About this poetry competition the Japs hold every year – one of those traditional events with judges in long gowns and funny hats.'

'Yeah?'

'Well, according to this article, they had one right after the war, and guess who won it.'

'I give up.'

A panel of wall clocks behind the Englishman informed Melville that it was eleven-fifteen, 28 August, 1970. He took a sip of wine and then felt depressed, in mourning for a day wasted before it had hardly begun.

'The Emperor. Old Hirohito.'

'What was it about?'

'Pine trees. The pine tree gets covered by snow in the winter . . . de-dum de-dum . . . but when the spring comes – and this is the bit that made me sit up – the snow melts and the tree is still green underneath.'

Melville maintained a silence. He recalled the pines he'd seen outside a Zen temple in Kyoto. It was winter, and snow was cupped on the clusters of needles. They didn't grow that way by nature, Sumiko had told him. They were pruned, almost manicured, so that the needles grew upwards.

'Still the same, you see. What you have to understand is that the pine is a national symbol. That poem was written bang after the war – a sort of coded message to the Japanese people.' The Englishman turned his lymphatic eyes on the guests. 'I've been thinking about that poem the last few days. The Japs haven't changed their colours, believe me.'

'I guess you're here on business.'

'Insulators,' the Englishman said, nodding gloomily. 'Bloody coals to Newcastle.'

'Well, I think you're wrong,' Melville said. 'We blew the old Japan away. We turned it into a wholesale business and outfitted it in our own image. And the Japanese saw that it was good, but they also saw that they could make it better, and that's why seventy per cent of all the baseball gloves sold in the States last year were manufactured in Japan. Now, to you that might look like a step down the road to global domination. To me it's a touching demonstration of faith in the cultural superiority of the conquering nation.'

The Englishman appeared to look behind Melville, as though he might find a ventriloquist hidden there.

Melville took another drink, spilling a little. He checked the wall clocks, which were set to different time zones.

'Still yesterday in New York,' he said. 'Hey, maybe the Japs do so well because they get up earlier than the rest of us.'

Two patches of red blossomed on the Englishman's cheeks.

Melville made a placatory gesture. The booze was subverting him, he realised, and immediately the puritan streak in him registered a protest. Christ, it was hardly past breakfast. Why doesn't she show up, he thought, transferring blame to Sumiko.

33

'So you're in shipping,' the Englishman said.

'No. I'm an anthropologist. I teach a course at the university. The trip to Yokohama was fieldwork.'

'I thought anthropologists studied, you know, primitive tribes, puberty rites – that kind of thing.'

Dumb asshole, Melville thought. 'Some do,' he said, 'but the kind of tribal cultures you're thinking of have just about had it. I did my first work on aboriginals in Taiwan. That was twelve years ago. Last time I saw them they all rode Hondas and wore Bri-Nylon leisure-wear. Oh sure, there are still a few primitives here and there, but the competition's pretty fierce. Even if you do track down the genuine article, you find yourself standing in line behind the *National Geographic*, a CBS crew and some athlete for Christ from the Summer Institute of Linguistics.'

'In that case, what kind of anthropology do you do? If you don't mind me asking.'

'Urban anthropology. I suppose you could call me a sociologist who can afford an airline ticket. Right now I'm doing research into how traditional cultural values are incorporated into newly industrialised societies. I'm looking at the function of non-verbal ranking indicators in a medium-sized Japanese corporate structure.'

He laughed to show that amusement or even derision would be tolerated.

'I suppose you mean body language,' the Englishman said dubiously.

'You got it,' Melville said, 'only we like to Americanise the obvious. Now, body language, signals – they're very important to the Japanese. For example, have any of the buying managers you've been dealing with given you a straightforward "no"?'

'No, I suppose not,' the Englishman said, after pause for thought. 'I'm not sure.'

'That's because they don't like to refuse outright. Instead they use any of fifty ways of not saying "yes". It drives American businessmen wild. The ones I've worked for think body language is something spoken by a *Playboy* centrefold.'

'You speak it yourself, though?'

'What?'

'Japanese.'

'A little,' Melville said warily. 'I've been here less than two years.'

A waiter orbiting the reception proffered a tray of drinks. What the hell, Melville thought. One more and then leave. Sumiko wasn't going to show.

'Champagne,' the Englishman said, raising his glass in morose salute to one of the hostesses, who was trying to tempt the catering manager of the Tokyo-Kyoto bullet trains with a piece of smoked goose. 'I'll tell you one thing about the French,' he said, as if he were about to favour Melville with a privileged insight culled from a vast stock of Gallic lore. 'There's bugger-all the Japs can teach them about self-interest. Take cars. You won't see the Frogs driving around in those bloody rice sifters. Not like our lot. And they're doing very nicely in Japan, let me tell you. I was in a supermarket yesterday and saw all these cases of wine dolled up with ribbons. Know what was in them? Bloody *premiers crus*, that's what. Latour, Margaux, the lot. Way out of my league, I don't mind admitting. But it hurts, it really hurts to think of fine wine like that being used to wash down pickled fish and bean curd.'

While the Englishman was swilling his resentment around with his tongue, Melville scanned the room again. The only woman who didn't look like she'd stepped out of a Toulouse-Lautrec poster was a collegiate-looking stringer for the *Christian Science Monitor*. She was interviewing a chemicals baron whose factories had helped extinguish most of the vertebrate life in Tokyo Bay. The industrialist bowed and managed to disengage. The journalist rummaged in her purse, pulled out a mirror, puckered her mouth and applied fresh lipstick. As she set off in search of fresh prey, the Japanese parted in front of her, grinning in alarm.

Melville spotted Kamenev, dressed as usual in a plaid jacket and spotted bow tie – a combination that never failed to bring a lump of pathos to Melville's throat. How the hell had he managed to get himself invited? He didn't seem to be enjoying the occasion. He was examining an empty glass, turning it in his hands as though he couldn't work out its function. He was probably calculating how much he'd have to bribe the Vladivostok customs. He was returning to Moscow next month, and Melville had run into him outside a department store struggling with three identical hi-fi units.

Melville was about to make his excuses and go over when his attention snagged on something behind the Russian. Two figures, one very tall and one very small, were manoeuvring through a clone of Japanese businessmen. His stomach gave a lurch of apprehension. 'Oh shit,' he breathed, interrupting the Englishman's monologue.

'What's that?' the Englishman said in alarm. He had his teeth fixed

35

in Britain's decaying body politic. He was lamenting his country's bid to join the Common Market.

'Sorry,' Melville said. 'I just saw an old friend. Excuse me. I enjoyed talking with you. Really.'

'Hey,' Hubbard said, with his customary enthusiasm, 'look who I've got here.' He gestured at the big man. 'Charlie Sweetwater,' he declared.

'Walter,' said Sweetwater, switching on an incandescent grin and seizing Melville's hand. The combination of grin and bulk put Melville in mind of a backwoods senator whose name he couldn't quite remember. He tried to withdraw his hand.

'Nice to bring old friends together again,' Hubbard said.

'You're a hard man to track down,' Sweetwater said to Melville. 'I never figured you'd end up in Japan.' He let go of Melville's hand. 'So how's humanity?'

'You tell me,' Melville said. 'You people run the franchise.'

Hubbard gave a clubman's chuckle that he had been working on since adolescence. 'Good old Walter. He's the only anthropologist I know who doesn't like the human race.'

'Is that so?' Sweetwater asked. He hitched up his trousers and sniffed.

He was about six-three, built like a wall, and plainly didn't give a shit about the tube of fat relaxing over the buckle of his Navajo belt. In his presence Melville felt lightweight and loosely put together, though he was only a couple of inches shorter than him, and more than a head taller than Hubbard. In truth, by American measure Hubbard was a dwarf – a neat and nicely-finished mannikin with glossy hair brushed straight back, heavy hornrims and tiny bespoke shoes polished to an antique patina and sporting little acorn tassels. His suit of double-breasted linen was faintly foxed, as though it might have done service for an equally Lilliputian forbear who had carried the flag in hot climes. Probably it had; Hubbard was a sprig from a long branch of miniature blue-chip emissaries.

'It's true,' he insisted. 'Walter really *doesn't* like people. He has this wild theory about why the human race stays together. According to Walter, people don't get together in society because they like each other, but because they're frightened of the beasts out there in the dark. And get this. The reason people herd so tightly is not so they can protect each other; it's because no one wants to be the poor sucker left on the outside – the one the beast comes after.'

36

'Sounds like a tough assessment to me,' Sweetwater said. 'Sounds like the kind of smart, no-hope, shit-headed thinking kids get indoctrinated with today.'

'Well,' Hubbard said after a short interval, lathering his hands. 'Charlie's over here spearheading a sales operation. Office furniture. He's looking for some assistance on the ground, and since you rendered him some service in Hong Kong, naturally he thought of you.'

'Just orienting myself, Walter. Targeting the market. Hubbard's been telling me some good things about you. He says you've already learned the language. Chinese *and* Japanese. That makes you one in a million.'

'Hubbard's talking crap. I can barely direct a cab.'

'More than me or Hubbard can do. Trouble with us Americans, we're a nation of monoglots.' Sweetwater made it sound like a species of moral degenerate. 'Am I right, Hubbard? I mean, how many of your embassy colleagues can speak Japanese?' Sweetwater sighed. 'My business puts me in touch with a lot of State Department personnel, and I can tell you that things are not what they were. Hell, these days it's all ten-to-four, dope parties and telexes home if the iced-water fountain breaks down. Shit, I even heard they got Canberra declared a hardship post.'

'How about it?' Hubbard asked Melville, gamely hanging on to his smile. 'Think you can help out?'

'I hate to spoil your plans,' Melville told Sweetwater.

'Oh,' Hubbard said, 'I thought you were looking for work. Charlie's only asking for a few days. Term doesn't start for another month.'

'I decided not to renew. I've decided to leave Japan.'

'You never said anything to me about quitting.' Hubbard gave Sweetwater a fierce smile to indicate that this wasn't the first time he'd had to adjust to Melville's vagrant ways. 'So what's brought this on?' he demanded brightly.

'It's time I got back into the field.'

'Maybe I can help you there,' Sweetwater said. 'Did I ever tell you about my friends in the Christian Institute for the Study of Democracy?' He winked at Hubbard. 'The title's strictly for accounting purposes.' He turned to Melville. 'They're always looking to extend their Asia programme. If they like what you're doing, they'll set you down anywhere you choose – Thailand, Malaya, that other country down by Burma someplace.'

'I bet. And after a few weeks an assistant with a prison haircut and

37

an MA in political science shows up. No thanks, Charlie. I told you in Hong Kong: I'm not interested in playing the game of nations.'

'You told me fuck-all in Hong Kong,' Sweetwater said. 'You never even said goodbye.' He smiled his worldwide smile.

'Er, I guess I should leave you guys to thrash it out,' Hubbard said, eyes switching between them.

'That's okay,' Melville said. 'I've got a train to catch. I'm meeting Sumiko.'

'Ah, the exquisite Sumiko,' Hubbard said, straining to restore cordial relations. 'Walter keeps her to himself, in a cabin deep in the forest. He never invites anyone else. You know, Walter, I can't help fantasising about how you spend the time. You composing haiku while Sumiko plays on a stringed instrument.'

'Something like that,' Melville said, his eyes fixed on Sweetwater.

'Maybe I could come out and see you,' Sweetwater said.

'I don't think that would be a good idea.'

'I really would appreciate a chance to talk.'

'No!'

All three held a silence.

'Well,' Sweetwater said, massaging his jaw. 'Looks like there's nothing to be done.'

'I guess not,' Melville said.

He nodded determinedly but found it difficult to withdraw. Finally he punched Hubbard lightly on the arm and walked away.

'Glad I caught up with you,' Sweetwater called after him. 'By the way, Mr Yueh sends his bests and says he'd like it very much if you got in touch.'

The suggestion seemed to catch Melville between the shoulder-blades.

He had reached the door when Hubbard seized his elbow. For such a small man he had an impressive grasp. He didn't relax it, nor his clenched smile, until he had led Melville up to a landing on the marble stairs.

'What is it between you two? That was a very acrid atmosphere you created back there.'

'He gives me the chills.'

'You didn't like that beer salesman from Cincinnati – the one who was so curious about Japanese private parts. But it didn't stop you putting in a week's work for him.'

'Sweetwater doesn't want me to help him sell desks. And since when did you start working for the Chamber of Commerce?'

'Washington said to put him in touch with you. A lot of our businessmen pull strings at State.' Hubbard looked away, his eyes, magnified by thick lenses, shiny with embarrassment. 'Only, you know, working at the embassy, you get a smell for these people.'

'What people? Stop crashing around in the thicket and tell me which spookhouse Sweetwater crawled out of.'

'I was hoping you'd tell me,' Hubbard said. He spoke rapidly, as though doubtful of his legitimacy in such matters. 'You worked for him in Hong Kong. I heard you say something about the game of nations.'

'I had no idea what he was playing at. An old family friend asked me to do some translating for him. It wasn't on the level so I walked away. Hell, anthropologists are always getting propositioned by these guys.'

'Sure,' Hubbard said, still unhappy, 'only . . .'

'Only what?'

'Walter, are you intelligence?'

'The very embodiment.'

'Someone saw you with Kamenev last week.'

'So?'

'So he's the Soviet press attaché.'

'Come on, Hubbard. Kamenev collects cuttings from the *Asahi Times* and shows up at parties. He's the sociable face of socialism. He breaks the ice. That's what they call him – the Ice Breaker. Hell, he even gatecrashed the Swedish embassy when they gave a slide show on Lapp reindeer co-operatives.'

Hubbard blinked fast. 'Meeting Kamenev in a neutral environment is one thing, but the issue here is that you had lunch with him in the Spanish place. Claire saw you,' he admitted.

Claire was a foreign service lifer – a frump who wore kaftans and cluttered her desk with photographs of her schoolfriends' kids back in Marathon, Iowa. Melville dimly remembered having reduced her to tears at one of Hubbard's parties.

'Looks like you've got me cold,' he said. 'I met Kamenev carrying a stack of recording equipment. On inquiring what he intended doing with it, I was informed that he was off to bug your embassy and would I like to lend a hand.'

Hubbard placed his hands on the stair-rail and then rested his chin on his hands – an awkward position for such a small man. 'You should try out that terrific sense of humour on the new APO. Have you met Schiff – pinchy eyes, wears a hat indoors, glows in the dark? His last posting was Saigon.'

'First you ask me if I'm a spook, and now you seem to be implying I'm some kind of commie stooge. Oh, Hubbard. You have no idea how bad today is turning out to be. Look, I met Kamenev by accident. We'd talked a few times. He invited me to share a paella. Said it was his last month in Tokyo.'

'He told you he'd been recalled?'

'Just that he was going home.'

'So you said yes.'

'That's right; I supped with a hireling of the commie Antichrist. I quite like the guy. He arouses feelings of compassion. He's not afraid to show his emotions.'

'Chrissake, Walter! He's a party member.'

'Doesn't surprise me.'

'Oh, confide in me. Tell me what warm fraternal gossip you exchanged.'

'Nothing to melt the diplomatic wire. We started off talking about hi-fi, with me the passive partner.'

'That all?'

'Well, we had a bit of dialogue about Stalin.' Melville was beginning to enjoy himself.

Hubbard leaned back, trying to get Melville into focus.

'Strange, he struck me as such a sensitive soul, but it seems that he burns a candle for Uncle Joe. A bit of a barbarian, he called him, but a necessary barbarian, who got the war won for Russia. Naturally, I didn't let this assessment go unchallenged. I raised the matter of the Terror. Not a flicker – of guilt, I mean. He admitted that Stalin had slaughtered a lot of his countrymen, but insisted they were all guilty, all enemies of the revolution. He'd been putting the booze back and he turned eerie, very Russian – soul brimming in his eyes. If these people were innocent, he asked, why didn't they resist. After all, a lot of them were powerful people – generals, commissars, people who were used to standing on the other side of the firing squad. I said maybe Stalin didn't give them a whole lot of chance. Kamenev shook his head, as though I was being very obtuse. You don't understand, he said. We won the war because we're a very long-suffering people, and we're long-suffering because we're a very religious people, and communism hasn't changed that. For us, Stalin was God, and those comrades let themselves be slaughtered because they knew

40

they couldn't be innocent – because they knew that before God *everyone* is wrong.'

'What other homely topics did you discuss?' Hubbard said in a dull voice.

'Actually, Stalin came up because we were talking about China. Kamenev conceded that his hero had made a couple of bad mistakes there – first, assuming that the Chinese revolution couldn't succeed without Soviet help, and then failing to make sure that it *didn't* succeed. Kamenev is pretty scornful about Mao's brand of communism – two peasants sharing the same pair of trousers, that kind of thing.'

'Boy-oh-boy,' Hubbard said, moved to awe. 'I can't believe it. I can't believe you and this freaking little commie.'

'Try this, then. Kamenev not only worships Stalin; he also thinks our own president is a swell fellow. A man in tune with the realities of the age, is how he put it.'

Hubbard couldn't get his answer past a bolus of outrage.

'Go easy, Hubbard. I told you it was just a dialogue.'

'Let me tell you about the realities of the age,' Hubbard said, his voice starting high up in his throat. 'Two years ago the Chinese and the Soviets nearly went to war. There are still half a million soldiers outfacing each other along the Usurri River. Consider it from the Soviets' position. It can't be long before Mao departs for the celestial sphere, and there are a hundred factions competing for his throne. Mao hasn't managed to put the cork back in the bottle, so millions of his little imps are still running wild. Pure anarchy, right there in the Soviets' backyard. You think they get turned on by the idea of permanent revolution? Jesus, it's enough to give the politburo a collective hernia. They'd mortgage Lenin's tomb if they could swing things so that the Great Helmsman is replaced by someone who steered the Moscow road.'

'I don't doubt it, but what's it got to do with me?'

Hubbard paused for thought. He shook his head. 'All I know is that Soviet embassy staff don't lunch with American citizens so that they can sharpen their dialectic.'

'I'm just an anthropologist, remember.'

'Are you? No, no,' Hubbard said, fending off Melville's protest, 'I believe you. But look at it from Kamenev's perspective. You're an expert in the China field. You spent – what was it? – five, six years in Taiwan. You were in Hong Kong. You're seen around the embassy a lot. You spend a little time with me. And then there's Sweetwater.

41

Face it: in Kamenev's world there's only one class of citizen fits that profile.'

'Oh dear,' Melville said. 'This is a very tired genre.'

'I think he was putting down a marker.'

'Sure,' Melville said wearily. 'Kamenev chose me to launch a grand Soviet initiative. The Big Buck and the Red Terror team up against the Yellow Peril. Is that the way you want to write the script?'

'I know one thing, Walter. The golden rule of power politics. Three is always the sum of two plus one.'

'Hubbard, I'm going to miss you.'

Hubbard squinted in suspicion. 'Tell me why you're pulling out.'

Melville's laugh was a little sparky. 'Because my space is being invaded by fantasy artists, resentful spinsters, paranoid salesmen.'

'Seriously,' Hubbard said doggedly. 'I thought you were very enthusiastic about your project.'

'Wormwood and – soon as I can find a fire – ashes. It was journalism, not science – the kind of thing that gets you a niche on a campus where the dean blows weed and leads demos.'

'What about the teaching?' Hubbard asked, sticking to his task.

Melville's groan was authentic. 'I imagined facing next year's class – their grinding intensity, their inability to think for themselves. I tell you, Hubbard: if one of them had an idea, it would die of loneliness.'

'Er, Sumiko,' Hubbard said, masking his concern with diffidence. 'I thought you had something serious going.'

'A cultural exchange. Don't look at me like that, Hubbard. From the start we knew it wasn't the kind of relationship that leads anywhere. She's a terrific lady, but she's also married.'

'How's she taking it?'

'Fact is, she doesn't know. I guess that's why I'm a little abrasive. I'm going to have to tell her at the cabin.'

'I see,' Hubbard said, giving Melville the benefit of the doubt. 'So,' he said, determinedly cheerful, 'where to now?'

'Indonesia maybe. Christ! Look at the time. Sumiko's waiting by the station.'

'Right now, I happen to know that Washington finds sinologists very sexy. State's funding a long-term study on China. They've roped in your old professor to run the show. I know you and Wolfson didn't get on, but you've got all the qualifications. It's time you settled down and started using your talents. Home,' he added. 'Think about it.' Waiting for Melville to conjure up the appropriate images, he blundered into an uncharacteristic attempt at crude fellowship. 'Girls with legs up to here,' he said, 'and real tits.'

'Why the sudden interest in China?' Melville demanded. 'Did those assholes just find out that quarter of the world doesn't eat with knives and forks?'

Hubbard's face grew pale with thwarted friendship. 'Jeez,' he said, looking away, 'you really are a hard man to know.'

Poor Hubbard, Melville thought with shame. Poor Hubbard, with his Peace Corps enthusiasm, his dead men's clothes, his exorcised first name, the sad little wakes he held on the anniversary of Kennedy's death. These were not propitious times for the Hubbards of this world.

'I'm sorry,' he said quietly, 'but I don't think Wolfson would want me on board. I was a sad disappointment. All he asked of his protégés was that they go forth into the world and act as the instruments of his canonisation. As for working in Washington – how times change. I was working on my senior thesis when the John Birch society was founded. You know how many other white Americans were studying Chinese? Twenty – one for every fifty million Chinese. Course, that didn't cut any with those Birchite morons. Nuke Peking was the cry. Anyway, one night a guy I once roomed with dropped by and told me he'd had a visitor asking questions about me – vetting me for a government job I'd applied for. This visitor wanted to know who my friends were, what books I read, what views I expressed on the issues of the day. Hell, he even wanted to know if I played team or track. Seems that anyone who isn't on a team is likely to harbour unhealthy political tendencies. Of course I hadn't applied for any job.'

'A paranoid era,' Hubbard conceded. 'You must have expected that they'd check up on you.'

'Because of my father? Because he was a commsymp who put his money on Mao? Because he was listed? Listen, my father loathed all politics and all politicians. As far as he was concerned, they were the people who stopped him going where he wanted because of the lines they drew on maps.'

'I think you must be a lot like him.'

'Me? My father was an explorer. Give him a horizon and he was happy.' Melville laughed. 'I just thought of a neat little paradox. An explorer is someone who doesn't know where he's going – only how to get there.'

'That's what I mean,' Hubbard said. 'Where are you headed, Walter? You could have been the new Wolfson, but you've reached thirty without even making assistant professor. Since I've known you, you've torn up two projects. You use your gift for languages to pimp for salesmen. Walter, you're abusing your talents.'

'Pissing them away. Look, I appreciate your concern, Hubbard; but I'm entitled to go to hell in my own way. Anyway,' he said, mustering an encouraging smile, 'things are going to be different from now on.'

'I hope so. You want something, but I'm damned if I know what. You're always putting distance between yourself and the world, always on the edge of things.' Hubbard removed his glasses and appeared to examine them for defects. His eyes were bald in the bright light. 'Maybe your theory isn't so crazy after all – you know, people getting together because they're frightened of what's lying in wait out there in the dark. I was thinking about you and Kamenev and Sweetwater. Remember it's you who's the one on the outside, and when the beast gets hungry it's you it will be coming after.'

Melville felt the breeze of affection, almost a chill. 'Beware the beast, then,' he said. 'Which reminds me. If that crackerass wants to get in touch, tell him I can't be located.'

Hubbard listened to the clatter of Melville's shoes on the staircase. When he couldn't hear them any more, he inhaled deeply, shaking his head.

It was the end of summer and the sky weighed on the city like a dirty white rag. Melville's palms went slick the instant he stepped outside. He squeezed a handful of air, half-expecting fat blue sparks to streak from his fist. Typhoon Daisy – the Japanese had adopted the fatuous habit of giving girls' names to arbitrary acts of natural violence – was gathering her skirts a few hundred miles to the east.

Some of the people hurrying past wore respirator masks – not to keep the smog out, but because the morning news had threatened an outbreak of 'flu. The Japanese gave Melville plenty of room, noting with upward glances the agitation roving behind his eyes.

Hubbard had it about right, Melville was thinking. He was headed nowhere. Coming to Japan had been a mistake. This last year he had succumbed to a paralysing crisis of morale, a dead weight that rooted him to the spot. He had always prided himself on being one step ahead of events, but now he seemed trapped on the border between past and future, unable to shake off a dreary lethargy. Foresight had given way to foreboding; optimism was clouded by the first premonitions of failure. He was only thirty-four, and already he could see the slope falling away beneath him.

Pounding along the sidewalk, Melville embraced the idea of drink – the key, not too long found, by which he could briefly inhabit his old self. Projects laid to rest in the daytime miraculously revived when bathed with whisky, only to suffer a relapse during the hours of darkness, when the booze opened other doors filled with unwholesome images that crowded in on his sleep. He was getting seriously concerned for his equilibrium. He was beginning to entertain doubts about the efficiency of the systems designed to keep chaos at arm's length. Sometimes he would have to avert his eyes from the sight of an airliner crawling across the sky, so sure was he that somehow he would communicate his reservations about the laws that kept it suspended there, causing it to relax its hold on the air and drop like an anvil, spilling passengers onto the city. He could not bear to travel on the Metro. Newspapers left him convulsed with rage and fear.

Maybe he should be grateful to Sweetwater. Meeting him again had at least shaken him out of his apathy. The important thing now was to pick up momentum.

Walking with his head down, Melville almost collided with a refrigerator parked outside a high-rent apartment block. It was gleaming, pristine, obsolescent – abandoned to make way for this year's model. Marx had it wrong, he thought. Capitalism wasn't going to die of its internal contradictions; Japan was proof that it grew fat on them. A couple of months ago he had asked his help if she would take his kitchen knives to a sharpener. She told him that such a category of people no longer existed. Far out! A country where the sword was still a potent symbol, but where you couldn't get a knife sharpened.

He looked at his watch and speeded his pace, turning off the street into a half-hearted imitation of a European park, with a few acres of balding yellow turf intersected by a grid of pathways and dotted with a few clumps of gloomy conifers. On the grass old men were practising controlling their vital humours, or shadow-boxing in a cautious kind of way. Heavily amplified rock music drifted from the other side of the park.

Melville did not relish the prospect of three days at the cabin. He would have to tell Sumiko about leaving, and he would have preferred to do that in town, in a bar or restaurant – somewhere with bright lights and an international menu. The cabin was not the kind of place where you wanted to spend three days with bared emotions, particularly, Melville thought – casting an eye at the glutinous sky – if it was going to be raining the whole fucking time.

45

They had started going there because it was not easy to gratify their lust in the city. Sumiko, though separated, still lived in her husband's apartment and was sensitive about her neighbours. Melville shared two small rooms with a Swedish accountant who rarely went out. But it wasn't in the cabin that they had first slept together. Their relationship had remained chaste for longer than the moral climate demanded, partly because of lack of opportunity, but also because Sumiko was possessed of such an ethereal beauty that even to contemplate the possibility of sex with her seemed an act of violation. Finally, in a bar, drink had swamped his inhibitions – but he regretted the proposition when her hand flew to her mouth and she bowed her head, apparently overwhelmed with shame. He had writhed when she got up and went over to the barman. Was she enlisting help? The barman made a phone call. Calling the fucking cops! She had come back and sat down as if nothing had happened, except that she seemed to find everything he said inordinately amusing. Her giggles were beginning to get on his nerves by the time the barman signalled that their cab was waiting.

They hadn't spoken during the ride. It was a Friday evening – 'traffic jam' time for Tokyo's love hotels, which were doing a brisk turnover in salarymen and the pretty, mute functionaries they called 'office flowers'. Instead, the driver dropped them at an establishment which looked like a respectable rooming house, run by two elderly sisters. The only concession to wantonness was a mirror above the bed. It was badly positioned, so that instead of recording their embraces, it reflected a neon street sign advertising baby food which flashed the slogan NEW LIFE–NOW in chlorine blue. Sumiko demonstrated both adroitness and a kind of feudatory compliance; and the feeling that somehow he was engaged in plunder had made him precipitant, setting the pace for most of their future encounters.

The realisation that this would be their last weekend triggered an almost sexual pang of melancholy, but then a memory bubbled up that made him hunch his shoulders in shame.

During his Fulbright year in Taiwan, he had had an affair with an American archaeologist, Ruth – a twentieth-century witch given to muttering in her sleep and waking him to recount her dreams. Her arms were covered by a fine, dark down, and her pubic hair curled in silky black whorls as far as her navel. She was also brilliant, and Melville thought he was in love. When he found out his mistake, they had spent a whole night raking through the embers. They were still at it when the sun came up – Ruth in one of her damn yoga

46

positions on the floor, him sprawled in a chair, his head thrown back and his eyes closed, as if he had just run a long distance. He kept repeating: 'This is awful. I can't bear it.' Suddenly Ruth had sprung up and come over to him, her hand pouncing to grab his swollen flesh through a fold of his pants. 'Oh, you bastard,' she had whispered. 'You're really loving it, aren't you? You really get off on it.' *It* was never defined. Suffering – his or hers? – self pity, a perverse pleasure in misfortune, a secret self-destructive urge. Something like that. It had ended with a tearful, wet-mouthed contest on the floor.

There had been few American women since then. After more than ten years in Asia he was disconcerted by their gloss, their crispness – fruit designed for a long shelf life rather than consumption. He was drawn to women like Ruth; he was attracted to the worm in the flesh. The last he'd heard of her, she was employed by the Smithsonian and involved with a heavily-married congressman she had met while helping campaign for the re-election of the president. Ruth was the kind who would always collude in her own unhappiness.

Melville wondered how Sumiko would take the news of his leaving. He had been circumspect with his emotions. So had she. But you just never knew. It might be best to wait until they got back to the city before telling her.

All the while, Melville had been walking towards the sound of the rock music. Reaching the other side of the park, he saw that a section of boulevard had been sealed to traffic and invaded by several dozen teenagers dressed in drapes, crepes and suedes. They were split up into groups of four, each group identified by a martial-looking headband, and they were feigning epilepsy in their efforts to attract the attention of the judges of an Elvis Presley lookalike competition.

Chapter 4

Because he was late, Melville caught a cab. It was lined throughout with acrylic fur and the seat backs were protected by antimacassars. The driver wore white gloves and a mortician's gravity.

Melville stopped the cab half a block short of the station and walked down an alley until he reached a cafe sandwiched between a photographic store and a homeopathic pharmacy that specialised in snake medicines. Melville liked the cafe because you cooked the food yourself, on griddles that doubled as low tables.

Sumiko sat facing the door, talking to the woman who ran the cafe. The table next to her was occupied by five construction workers whose hard hats were placed on the floor beside them like samurai helmets. Their shoes were lined up by the door. That was something he always meant to ask Sumiko: why Japanese labourers wore flimsy cotton shoes that offered about as much protection as dancing pumps. Perhaps the possibility of dropping heavy objects was never entertained – Zen in the art of building construction.

Sumiko was listening to the other woman, and in the moment before she saw him, Melville had time to renew his wonder at the perfection of her face. It seemed to have been sculpted – no, too harsh – *caressed* into shape by water working slowly on a flawless piece of soapstone. A Zen painter would have studied it for weeks, and then rendered it in four or five brush strokes. After seeing her, Melville found that Western faces looked like sets of off-the-shelf bits.

It was only when you got very close that you saw the faint web around the eyes, only in the slack aftermath of passion that you noticed the pores between the breasts, the worm in the flesh. Sumiko was nearly ten years older than Melville.

The manageress bowed, Sumiko bowed, Melville bowed, the construction workers turned and bowed. Melville folded his legs and lowered himself to the matting, grimacing an apology for his gracelessness.

'Sorry I'm so late,' he said. 'I thought you were going to show up at the reception.'

Sumiko cast down her eyes in contrition. 'So sorry, Walter. My brother came to see me.'

'How is he?' Melville had never met Sumiko's brother – the head of the family and the boss of a small business fief that owned, among other things, the popular consumer magazine for which Sumiko worked. 'All well with the family? Business okay?'

'Oh, yes,' Sumiko said gratefully. 'Business is fine.'

'Good.'

Their hostess set down bowls of chicken and vegetables. She favoured Melville with the briefest of smiles. Somehow, he had the feeling they had been talking about him.

'What did he want then?'

Sumiko spread food on the griddle. 'Yamada-san went to see him last week.'

'Ahhh.'

Melville hadn't met Sumiko's estranged husband. The only significant thing about her remark was that she never mentioned him either – not since the first few weeks, when Melville had been naïve and curious enough to ask. It had been an arranged marriage, an economic merger rather than an emotional alliance. Their families had strong business ties. Yamada was working up north somewhere – something to do with electronics. Melville had formed the impression that he was queer.

'How is he?'

'Very well. He's been promoted.'

'Great,' Melville said vigorously.

'Yes, a great honour. The managing director himself came up to tell him. They spent the whole evening together.'

Melville could picture the scene: Yamada getting stoned with his champion in some company haunt under the admiring and jealous gaze of his colleagues. Melville had visited such places and been amazed by the febrile drinking of these sober-suited, hard-working salarymen. They said they got drunker than Westerners because they lacked some kind of enzyme that dealt with alcohol. Bull. They got drunk faster because they drank faster. Bars were where working alliances were formed, promotion discussed, resentments aired. An executive who lurched off the commuter train close to midnight was going places, or trying to, while the husband who got home sober and early enough to kiss the kids goodnight risked being stigmatised as a failure.

'I'm pleased for him,' Melville said. 'What's his new job?'

'The company is making a new range of instruments . . .'

49

Not electronics, Melville remembered. Measuring devices – gauges, micrometers, that kind of thing.

'. . . and Yamada-san will be director of marketing. They hope to export most of the instruments.'

Unaccountably, the trace of pride in Sumiko's statement aroused a thrill of jealousy, and that brought to mind their yet-to-be announced parting. He felt he was intruding in matters that didn't concern him, but at the same time he divined that he was somehow involved with Yamada's change of status. Unease stirred.

'Oh well,' he said. 'Another nail in the coffin of the Western economies.'

She wouldn't look at him directly. She pretended to be absorbed in the cooking, stirring the food with chopsticks. Her expression was masked under the serif curves of her eyelids. Once, he had surprised her peering into a mirror, propping up those graceful folds with her fingers – beside her, a magazine opened to an advertisement offering an operation that would turn her into a round-eye.

'I'm not sure where your brother comes into the picture.'

'It would mean living in Tokyo,' she answered without looking up.

'I see,' he said slowly. 'I see. I suppose this will affect us. I expect your brother thinks our . . . friendship . . . is a bit compromising. Does he want us to stop meeting?'

She raised her head then. 'Oh no!' she said emphatically.

She dipped her head again. Melville ignored the food she slid towards him. Vaguely he was aware that the construction workers were watching them. He turned, not really seeing them. Five bows in unison. One of the workers gestured at the untouched food and made enthusiastic eating movements. Abstractedly, Melville picked up a sliver of chicken.

'But there's a problem, right?'

He had to strain to hear her. 'It's a great honour for Yamada-san. A very important position. I'm very happy for him. There is so much for him to do. He will have to do a lot of entertaining – clients from many countries as well as Japan. He will need help. The managing director said so. He said that Yamada-san should have his wife with him. He made it clear.' She gave Melville a glittery smile. 'It's a wife's duty.'

'Dealing out smiles and crackers? Sumiko, are you serious?' Melville seized one of her hands, provoking intakes of breath from the construction workers. 'Sumiko, you've been separated for years. Do you want to go back?'

The desolation in her face rocked him.

'Well then,' he said. 'That's all there is to it. What did your brother have to say?'

'He says I must do what my husband asks.'

'Jesus!' Melville looked wildly about the room, seeking someone to share his outrage. 'Your husband doesn't own you. Your brother can't force you.' He stopped, brow furrowed. 'You said this wouldn't stop us seeing each other.'

Sumiko essayed a smile. 'My brother doesn't approve, but Yamada-san told him he is happy to let the arrangement continue.'

Arrangement? What fucking arrangement? Through his indignation and astonishment, Melville saw that the escape hatch was well and truly open. Share Sumiko with that dirtball of a husband? Righteous anger and an abrupt exit were the only decent response. Instead, without a moment's thought, but aware that here was a situation that looked like closing in on him, he went through a different door. 'Oh, Sumiko,' he said softly. 'You know I couldn't live with that. I'll do everything I can to help you get out of this mess, but there's something I was meaning to tell you. I was talking to an old colleague from Hong Kong. He's setting up a project in Indonesia and he asked if I would join the team. I said I'd think about it. But now . . .' He clamped a hand to his forehead and massaged it.

Sumiko's shame was hidden behind a fanned hand. 'Oh, how exciting! Please accept my congratulations. I'm so pleased. Forgive me.'

'Forgive you?' Her overwrought response made him curl with mortification. 'My work doesn't matter,' he said fiercely. 'It's you I'm concerned about. What's going to happen to *you*?'

'Please, not here.'

The construction workers had abandoned their own meal to view the drama. One of them was apparently whispering a commentary. The manageress was spectating from the kitchen door.

'Please, later.' Sumiko looked at her watch and made a little Japanese face of shock. It was a digital watch, one of the first. Melville was sure they wouldn't catch on. Time was relative. You couldn't easily tell how long before the train left by looking at a set of figures. You needed the conjunction of hands and numbers.

'Quickly,' Sumiko said. 'We'll miss the train.'

Melville unwound from the floor and massaged the backs of his knees. 'We'll talk at the cabin,' he said.

The manageress ushered them out. Her farewell to Sumiko was full

51

of concern, but for Melville her expression was rigid. He assumed she was annoyed because he hadn't touched the food.

The station could have been a set for an avant-garde version of a shogunate epic. Ranks of commuters surged across the concourse; amplified messages clanged off the roof like calls to arms. On the platform next to the one where Melville and Sumiko stood, a semi-circle of salarymen was bidding farewell to a captain of industry – the chairman, perhaps, off on a tour of inspection. Each subordinate bowed according to his rank and received in turn a nicely calculated inclination. The bigwig's wife was with him. They bowed to her, too; but she bowed lowest of all. One of them presented her with a bouquet, then she and her husband boarded the train and were politely clapped on their way.

Melville and Sumiko didn't talk on the journey. The coach was crowded, and a clerk sitting opposite kept them under close scrutiny. Eventually, Melville stared him down, forcing him to rummage in his briefcase for diversion. He brought out a comic, and as he turned the pages, Melville saw swinging swords, gouts of blood, heads rolling, bound and prostrate men, unoriental breasts skewered on lances. Back home, Melville thought, in some box two hours' commuting away, the clerk's wife would be bringing out the Manhattan Home Hostess Cocktail Kit and preparing to listen to an account of hubbie's day. Melville glanced at Sumiko, but she was staring out of the window at the denatured landscape.

At Matsumoto they changed trains, and after that they took a bus that laboured up into the mountains, threading long tunnels and skirting drowned valleys where the limbs of a skeletal forest reached out of the water. It was nearly dark when they reached the terminus and began the mile-long walk to the cabin. The track was just a gleam in the forest. Melville could feel the typhoon pressing close. 'Here,' he said, feeling for Sumiko's hand.

They walked in silence for a while, Melville concentrating on keeping pace with Sumiko's short stride. He had tried to come up with a solution, but he knew enough about Japanese conventions to be aware that, in their different ways, her husband and her brother did have proprietorial rights over her.

'When will you leave, Walter?'

He had already forgotten his lie. 'I'm not sure. I'm not even sure if I'll go. I want to make sure you're alright.'

They walked a little farther.

'Divorce him,' he said. 'You've got grounds.'

'It's very difficult.'

Melville grunted. Desertion, even cruelty, were not sufficient – at least, not in the wife's case. He considered raising the question of Yamada's sexual proclivities, but decided against it.

'Well then, simply refuse to go back. No one can make you. I know it might mean giving up the apartment.'

'It's very difficult. I would be going against my brother's will. If I refused, he would be ashamed of me. I would have to leave the magazine. You know how hard it is to find an apartment.'

'Get another job. You've got a good degree; your English is terrific. It's your life.'

She was silent for a time.

'Remember you once asked about *eta*?'

Untouchables, the bottom of the heap, relegated to an underclass even lower than that of Japan's Koreans. People used euphemisms when they mentioned them, or simply showed four fingers, representing legs – animals. Originally the *eta* were leather-workers, people who handled carcasses and bodies, cobblers; then the category was enlarged to include beggars, whores, circus performers and, of course, their descendants, whatever their occupation. They were not allowed to wear footwear; they were not allowed to leave their hamlets during the hours of darkness; in the company of humans they were obliged to get down on all fours before they could speak. Officially, the curse of *eta* status had been lifted at the Meiji restoration. Officially. Sumiko had denied that such a category of unperson existed, or had ever existed.

'You asked about the lists,' Sumiko said.

At least ten of them, listing the descendants of these outcasts. All Japan's leading employers – banks, insurance companies, teaching institutions, automobile manufacturers – kept a set handy for screening job applicants. Prospective in-laws hired private detectives to check for *eta* ancestry.

'You're not *eta*,' Melville said

'Of course not.' Quite sharp. 'But all companies investigate their employees' families. They would speak to my brother, and once he told them I had defied his authority, they would not take me. Maybe I could find a job somewhere, but in Japan they prefer . . . young women.'

Too old even to get work as an office flower. The slogan NEW LIFE—NOW flashed on his brain. He felt curdled by anger, and yet

53

he also felt the slow uncoiling of resentment. This wasn't the middle ages. Surely she could find some way out of the mess. She was holding back on him, waiting for *him* to show the way.

He stopped abruptly and took her by the shoulders. It was so dark under the trees he almost missed his aim.

'You must have thought about it, Sumiko. What do you want?'

He could sense her reluctance. Her face was half-turned.

'I thought, perhaps . . . America.'

'Do it,' he whispered. 'There's nothing stopping you.'

'I thought . . . You make me so happy . . . Sometimes, when you talked about going home. I thought . . . Walter-san, are you angry with me? You always told me, tell you what I think.'

'Yes, I did.' Oh God, he thought.

'Walter?'

'Yes.'

She had ducked away from his hands. He could hardly see her. Her voice was disembodied. This was ridiculous.

'I love you.'

She's got no right to say that was his indignant thought. To his ear, those three words sounded like a spell whose effect Sumiko was unsure of, but whose power she knew to be great.

'You don't have to say that,' he said gently.

He heard the hiss of her indrawn breath. 'I'm sorry.'

'Please,' he groaned, 'there's no need to apologise.'

She gave a little mew. 'Sorry.'

Melville laughed wildly. He felt like pounding his head on a rock. 'Where are you?' He groped for her and drew her to him, rocked her against his chest. 'Oh, Sumiko. What a bitch of a situation.'

The storm was his reprieve. It advanced in a whisper, like an army marching through long grass, then the trees creaked and bent overhead and it burst on them – a wind to suck the breath away, chased by a slanting deluge. 'Come on,' Melville shouted, dragging Sumiko by the hand.

The old man who let the cabin had left a cold supper which they ate for fear of giving offence. Afterwards they unrolled the sleeping mat and lay down, scrupulously apart. The storm made the cabin flex and tremble. Melville was wrung out. He knew that Sumiko was lying with her eyes open. When he reached for her, he found she had covered her mouth with her hand. She wouldn't let him remove it.

'It's just that I never expected to hear you say that,' he said. 'It came as a shock.' He laughed uncertainly. 'I guess you think Americans say it all the time, but it's not true. It's just too risky. What happens if you're wrong, or the other person doesn't reciprocate. "I love you, I think" is what people say. How do you say it in Japanese?'

No mistaking her hiss for anything but anger.

Melville hoisted himself on to one elbow. 'What can I say? You gave me no warning. I thought we were, well, good friends. I never considered that it might go deeper.' He pivoted so that his face, invisible in the dark, was above hers. 'Sumiko, whatever happens about us, I want to make sure you come out of this okay.'

It was as bad as he had feared. All next morning the rain confined them in each other's silence. When it got unbearable, they broke it with edgy solicitudes. In mid-afternoon, the wind tore a hole in the clouds and patches of mountain, streaked with summer snow, showed above the trees. Sumiko was working on an article about picnic ware. Pleading time to straighten his thoughts, Melville went out.

The old man farmed a few trout in a couple of ponds in front of the cabin. Melville followed the feeder stream until he came to a pool overhung by pines. The bottom was white gravel, in startling opposition to the black of the trees. As Hubbard had surmised, Melville had sat here on happier occasions trying his hand at haiku. Someone else, a long time ago, must have recognised that this was a good place to reflect, for there were two rocks by the water's edge, too well-ordered to be natural. Melville sat on one, heedless of the soaking seat, and uncapped a half of Suntory which he had had the foresight to bring.

He reviewed avenues of escape. He considered various projects he had outlined over the years, but ideas were radioactive: they had half lives. After a while the impulses they sent out weakened, and by and by the needles stayed on their stops. He allowed himself to consider Hubbard's suggestion. Maybe going home would be no bad thing. He even let himself contemplate the possibility of taking Sumiko with him.

After a while his thoughts began to idle. There were a few trout hanging in the current at the head of the pool. Every time water dripped from an overhanging tree, the surface shivered and the fish vanished, to reappear when the ripples died. Melville's mind attuned itself to the rhythm. A drop of water fell, the trout disappeared, the surface reformed. The pool was empty.

'Now you see them . . .'

Melville's heart flew up under his collarbone as a hand fell lightly on his shoulder. When he turned, he saw two silver swathes trampled in the soaking grass. A few yards behind Sweetwater a crop-haired Chinese man had arranged himself under a tree, his head cocked in the expectant expression of someone who is waiting to be recognised. He wore a suit with very wide lapels and flared trousers, sodden to the knees. His tie was a broad colourful statement, with a knot padded like a cushion. He was a long way from his natural habitat. In Taipei and Hong Kong Melville had seen many examples of the breed – muscular goblins who sat around brimming ashtrays in bolted restaurants at three in the morning.

Melville got to his feet. A muscle in his thigh kept on working.

'You remember Wang? Mr Yueh's driver,' Sweetwater said.

Wang advanced a few feet, rocking on his stacked heels, and gave a bony yellow smile.

'He's grown a moustache,' Melville said inanely. The two Americans took stock of Wang's growth. It made him look like a squat Chiang Kai-shek.

'I'd ask you in,' Melville said, looking anxiously towards the cabin.

'Better not,' Sweetwater said, jerking his head at Wang. 'Old enemies. He's still sore we didn't concrete Japan over and turn it into a parking lot.'

'What's the bug *doing* here,' Melville whispered.

'What we doing here, Wang?' Sweetwater called.

'Business for Mr Yueh. Very nice.'

Sweetwater shrugged. 'That's right. We're here as ambassadors of Mr Yueh's good-will.'

'This is fucking outrageous,' Melville said. 'This is harassment.' He pointed a quivering finger at Sweetwater. 'You'd better take care, Charlie. Hubbard got your number right away.'

'A good friend of yours, it would seem. Much concerned about your welfare and prospects.' Sweetwater looked around him. 'Ah, me,' he said softly. 'A beautiful spot. How can you bear it? These damn woods. Those mountains hanging over you. It would drive me bananas.'

'You're wasting your time. I won't have anything to do with your schemes.'

Sweetwater sat down on one of the stones, leaning forward, slope-shouldered and loose, like a football player taking his ease after a game. Scalp showed through the hair.

56

'You hear me?'

Sweetwater waved his hand as though he was deterring flies. 'Sit down, Walter, and stop looking like you've got your thumb up your ass.'

Melville sat. 'Admit it, Walter,' Sweetwater said. 'When you turned round and saw who it was, you thought we'd come to visit retribution. Right?'

Melville took a glance at Wang, who was holding a cigarette in an O made with thumb and forefinger. The way he sucked on it suggested the filter was blocked.

'What do you want with me?'

Sweetwater raised a hand and let it fall back. First things first. 'So why did you crap out?' he asked affably. 'Poor Wang spent two days looking for you.'

Melville stole another look at Wang, who let some smoke trickle between his teeth. His eyes were narrowed in a gecko's squint. Pure celluloid, Melville thought, but authentically scary for all that. He found the idea of Wang searching for him most unsettling.

'You know damn well why I left Hong Kong,' Melville said, packing in indignation. 'Mr Yueh told me I'd be translating for a journalist, not a goddamn spy.'

Sweetwater made his customary smile. 'A harsh term, Walter. All you did was put a few questions to some students. How many to a class; what courses they were following; what facilities they had; whether Mao's merry pranksters were giving them a hard time. Shit – hardly the kind of stuff that subverts nations.'

'They were illegal immigrants.'

'So? You think maybe we should have turned them over to those pink-kneed bobbies? You've been up to the border – seen the bits of cardboard where they climbed the wire, the rags marking the places where the Reds pulled off the ones who didn't make it. Next time you're in town, take a trip through the islands with the Coastguard. Count the inner tyres and fertiliser sacks you see floating about and work out what happened to the poor bastards who were riding them. Dissolving in a shark's gut is what.'

'They weren't all students,' Melville said. 'There was that guy from Shenyang, the freightman. Three days you had me interrogating him about rail traffic to the Mongolian frontier. How many trains; what were they carrying, freight or troops; what units; where had they come from; how long was the journey. You showed him pictures of tanks. A couple of weeks later I hear that the Chinese and Russians

57

are shooting at each other along the Usurri River. Don't tell me that wasn't military intelligence.'

'I'd say that was a grey area,' Sweetwater conceded. 'You know something, Walter? A distinguished ex-colleague of mine once said that the first thing an agent should do when he gets into town is make for the railway station. Assuming it's a big one, and that there's a war on, that is. You can pick up more Grade-A intelligence in a freightyard than you can in any embassy. True, but unromantic. Is that your problem? Did sweating in a flophouse with a railroad worker offend your sense of glamour?'

'Someone was following me,' Melville muttered. 'Same guy, twice. Once in the alley outside the rooming house, and again across from my apartment.'

Unexpectedly, Sweetwater did not receive this with derision. He merely said: 'You should have told me. Anyway, you weren't doing anything wrong. Hong Kong's still a corner of the free world. All we were doing was collecting a little information, shining a light on dark places. No more than any journalist would do.'

'You know that Hong Kong is crawling with agents from the mainland,' Melville said. He looked away. 'I could have been compromised.'

Sweetwater regarded him with astonishment.

'My father spent most of his life in China,' Melville said. 'I spent the first three years of my life there. Ever since I was a kid I wanted to go back. That'll never happen if I'm mistaken for a member of the intelligence community.'

Sweetwater shook his head sorrowfully. 'You mind?' he said, reaching for the bottle of Suntory. He took a pull, closed one eye and squinted at the label. 'Just goes to show what happens when the free flow of information is restricted. Look, Mr Yueh and me go back a long way. When he told me he had an American who spoke good Chinese, I thought I should take a look. Yeah, I thought maybe we could get together from time to time.'

'Why me? You people must have your own translators.'

Sweetwater waved the question away. 'Walter, your ass is sucking wind if you believe the commies are going to extend you an invitation. Ever since you came out here they've had you down as a wrong number.'

'Because of my father? Look, the Reds threw every American out of China.'

'Ancient history,' Sweetwater conceded. 'I'm talking about your dubious associates on Taiwan. Take Wang,' he said, pointing over his shoulder with the bottle. 'He used to drive you around, right? Well, back on the mainland Wang was an employee of the Nationalists' security outfit. The Bureau of Statistics.' Sweetwater poked Melville's knee with the bottle. 'A very robust organisation, Walter.'

Melville was not surprised to learn that Wang had been a member of the Generalissimo's gestapo, nor was he especially dismayed that his former mentor Mr Yueh had taken such a man into his employ. On Taiwan a lot of businessmen who otherwise were models of Confucist rectitude employed goons in case the ordinary rules of commerce broke down. On Taiwan, free enterprise was still in a very vigorous stage of development.

'And then there's Mr Yueh,' Sweetwater said. 'Don't get me wrong, Walter. I yield to no one in my admiration of the man. But I don't have to tell you what a good friend he can be. He took you into his home. You tutored his boy. You were practically family.'

Melville reached for the bottle. 'What have the Reds got against Mr Yueh?'

Sweetwater hung on to the bottle for a second, forcing Melville to meet his eye. 'Don't give me that "I don't know shit". Don't tell me you think Mr Yueh is just a big wheel in the rag trade and shipping biz.'

'I know he's fiercely anti-communist,' Melville admitted.

Sweetwater laughed merrily, relinquishing his hold on the bottle. 'Anti-communist! Shit, I could tell you things about Mr Yueh would make your scalp bleed.'

'I don't want to hear,' Melville said, tilting the bottle, now two-thirds empty.

'Fess up, Walter. You know damn well it was Mr Yueh who put me on to those refugees. And you sure as hell know that it's Mr Yueh who looks after those refugees.'

'I know he funds a welfare centre for people of his clan. You see, the Chinese believe that people with the same name . . .'

'Yeah, mutual friendship. Well, I guess that's right. Mr Yueh gets cheap labour for his sweatshops, a terrific percentage on the money he lends, and in return the poor bastards get a crash course in the way the Western world turns.'

'What's this got to do with me?'

'Some of the people in that flophouse. It was Mr Yueh who got them into Hong Kong. I'm not talking about the ones who swam across or climbed the wire. I'm talking about the grandfather or sweetheart they had to leave behind. For five, six hundred dollars, Mr Yueh can get them out. Some four-ballpen official in the Ministry of Frontiers and Immigration gets a warm overcoat or a pressure cooker and grandpa gets his exit visa. Now, Walter, people is not all Mr Yueh gets out of China. You want an update on Mao's health? A close-up of that interesting-looking cooling tower out in the middle of the Gobi? Mr Yueh's your man. You understand? Mr Yueh's got access. He has the kind of access that would give the CIA wet dreams.'

Melville sat with the bottle dangling from his hands.

'So,' Sweetwater said. 'Now you know why you'll never be welcome in the Great Hall of the People.'

'Why are you laying this shit on me?' Melville said dully.

'To avoid misunderstandings.' Sweeetwater stretched out his legs, at ease with his bulk. 'You seriously planning on leaving?'

Melville stayed silent.

'Fresh horizons. A tribe new to science. Hey, you hear about the guy who discovers this African tribe? The chief asks him what he does and the fellow tells him he's an anthropologist. The chief asks him how often he fucks. Naturally, the anthropologist is somewhat thrown, but he answers up, figuring it must be some kind of weird tribal custom. Then the chief asks him if he screws his cousins and a whole lot of other intimate questions. Finally, the anthropologist has had enough. "Look, chief," he says, "where I come from digging away at a man's sex life is considered very rude." The chief looks astonished. "No kidding," he says. "Only we had another an-thro-pol-ogist visit us last year and he went round the whole tribe asking those same damn-fool questions." '

'Ha, ha,' Melville said.

'I think it's time you went back home, Walter – share in the collective guilt. Out there' – waving a hand – 'beyond this little bastion of democracy, it's a war zone. Not just Vietnam and Cambodia. Indonesia, the Philippines – that's where the rival philosophies of our time confront each other in their most acute form. There's no place out there for detached observers, Walter. Besides, nobody's going to believe you're one.'

They both stared at the same invisible point on the other side of the pool.

'Tell me why you're here,' Melville said.

'You got money?'

'I'm not hurting.'

'How would you like to earn twenty thousand dollars?'

Melville turned slowly. He raised the bottle to his lips but arrested it when it was still short of the mark.

'I told Mr Yueh there was too much spin on you,' Sweetwater said, his eyes still engaged with something on the other side of the pool. 'Frankly, I told him you were unsound. We should find someone a little more executive.'

'What did he say when I left Hong Kong?'

Sweetwater shrugged. 'You know what he's like. If you cut one of his veins, embalming fluid would drip out. But he has a lot of feeling for you. He thinks you've got qualities. Maybe he's right.'

'Is he still in Hong Kong?'

'Bangkok. Some problem with his accountants. His son's over on vacation. Remember Bing. He's at MIT now. A whizz with numbers, his father says. He gives you the credit.'

'Me? All I did was coach him in English. Bing's a mathematical genius. I remember once . . . Oh, no. I see where this is headed.'

'You wouldn't recognise that boy now. His head's so crammed with numbers, he can barely communicate. Shit, he's practically a hippy.'

'Are you telling me Mr Yueh wants me to spend time counselling Bing?'

'No, no.' Sweetwater permitted himself a sigh. 'Look, Walter, Mr Yueh was explicit. He wants to discuss this business himself.'

'Chrissake, Charlie,' Melville said, moved to fellowship. 'You don't expect me to go to Bangkok without knowing what it's about.'

'Mr Yueh likes things formal. He's not going to let me discuss his business in the middle of a goddam forest.'

'Then we have a problem.'

Sweetwater turned to him. 'Suppose I told you, Walter. And suppose you still say no. Where does that leave us? I've given you something I didn't want to part with, and you're walking around with something you'd prefer you didn't have. Like I said: information's a powerful force. I'd hate to burden you with knowledge you had no use for. All the time I'd be worrying that you might get rid of it someplace, like it was an unwanted pup. But if Mr Yueh tells you. Well, that way you understand all the implications.'

'Implications? Oh dear, the whole thing sounds fraught with nasty possibilities.'

Behind them, Wang produced a raking cough and deposited a gob of phlegm on the ground. 'What do you think, Wang?' Sweetwater said.

Wang rasped his hand over his skull. Both Americans waited on the answer as though they were consulting an oracle.

'Can,' Wang said. It occurred to Melville that the pair of them must have rehearsed their moves.

Sweetwater bunched his shoulders. 'Ah hell,' he said ruefully, like a bazaar trader forced to accept a ridiculously low price. 'All Mr Yueh wants is for you to meet with a friend from the mainland.'

'Another refugee,' Melville said with derision.

'A legitimate vacationer. Got a two-week pass to visit his family. He has a story Mr Yueh wants you to hear.'

'And then you hand me twenty grand.'

'Mr Yueh said to tell you: "When you find a person worthy to talk to and you refuse to listen, then –" Shit! – I forgot the rest.'

'Then you have lost your man. Confucius. It doesn't really translate.' Melville looked sharply at Sweetwater. 'What man?'

'Hey,' Sweetwater said, impressed. 'You really do know your Chinese.' He leaned across and laid a hand on Melville's sleeve. His smile was glassy with secrets. 'Just come,' he said. 'It's a fucking dainty piece of business, Walter. You have my guarantee.'

Melville examined the ground without coming to any conclusion. 'I don't know,' he said. 'It sounds like a can of worms.' He faced Sweetwater. 'Why me?'

Sweetwater pondered this a while. 'Frankly,' he said, 'because you're a pointy-headed liberal who speaks good Chinese. And because Mr Yueh likes you.'

Melville nodded abstractedly, as if this was fair comment. 'I suppose I should have kept in touch. He was good to me.'

'You think you can fly over Monday?' Sweetwater enquired delicately.

'You're kidding! Today's Saturday.'

Sweetwater sighed. 'Well, these things sometimes drop out of a clear blue sky. Problem is, Mr Yueh's visitor works in a bicycle factory and has to be back punching the clock a week Monday. There are a lot of considerations to be . . . well . . . considered.'

'Now listen,' Melville said, thoroughly alarmed. 'The only reason I'd go is to pay my respects to Mr Yueh and remove from his head any notion that I'd lend myself to your cowboy schemes.'

'Sure,' Sweetwater said, as if this was entirely reasonable. 'You'll need this.' He pushed an envelope into Melville's hand. 'Someone will meet you.'

He got up, with that adolescent spring many American men preserve into middle age.

'The problem with you people,' Melville said, 'is that you suffer from arrested development.'

Sweetwater responded with a conspiratorial wink. 'See you in Bangkok,' he said. He turned to Wang, who extinguished his cigarette and dropped the butt among all the others. The two men walked away.

'Remember,' Melville shouted, 'I won't join in your games. Tell Mr Yueh that.'

Sweetwater turned. He raised his hand in a declamatory gesture. 'And *you* remember what the sages tell us,' he called. 'A journey of a thousand miles begins with a single step.'

Going away from him, his interlocutors looked comically ill-matched – Sweetwater throwing out his limbs as if he were crossing a prairie, Wang scuttling to keep up, barely in control of his platform shoes, his flares wrapping around his ankles. Melville opened the envelope and put his fingers to work. He shut it again as though it were full of vipers. Two thousand dollars for a few days in Bangkok? There was also an airline ticket – a return, he noted with relief – and a five-star hotel reservation.

He tried to get purchase on the facts but there wasn't much to hold on to. It was just foreplay. Apart from telling him about the visitor, the only information Sweetwater had laid before him was the revelation about Mr Yueh's connections in the People's Republic – which Sweetwater had said the CIA would dearly love to avail itself of, or words to that effect, as though neither he nor Yueh had any association with that agency. At the embassy he had mentioned CISD – a bunch of right-wing wackos whose strategy for dealing with the commie menace was to beam radio broadcasts on the theme of socialism as the tool of Satan to those Pacific-basin nations they had diagnosed as infected by the cancer of creeping liberalism. Melville could not imagine Sweetwater lending his talents to such an organis-ation – at least, not on a formal, paid-up basis. Behind that corporate smile, he had detected a runagate, mercenary soul. Oddly, he found this somewhat reassuring.

The only foothold Melville found as he scrambled among the possi-bilities was this: no one was going to lay twenty grand on him for a little translation work.

He realised he was scared, and he tilted his face skyward while he briefly reviewed the sensation. It wasn't the same as the low-grade anxiety and sense of foreboding that had disabled him these last months. It was healthy apprehension, a slight tightening of the gut, a whiff of adrenalin. It put an edge on him that had been lacking a long time. He resolved that he would indeed go visit Mr Yueh, as though the decision had not already been made. It would be an interesting diversion, a brief excursion down a by-way from the straight and not-so narrow, to which he would return as soon as he had satisfied his curiosity as to what skills or talents he possessed that could be worth so much money.

For the second time, Melville's heart went into spasm as he sensed a presence behind him. He whirled and then sagged, eyes shut, when he saw it was only the old man. He was carrying a pole with a net on the end. His other arm had been severed at the elbow. Something inside Melville always flinched when he encountered the old man. It was the way he walked, like he carried a stone in his belly, and the slow, speculative way he looked at him. Once, Melville had gone into his room to find him meditating, a sword laid in front of him, eyes fixed on a fading photograph of soldiers in puttees standing in the wreckage of a town.

The old man pulled a clown's doleful face and turned it in the direction of the cabin. Melville could just make out Sumiko at a window, looking out to where the forest dissolved in the weeping clouds. 'Oh, shit,' he said softly.

By the time he was inside, she was back at her work-table, turned away from him, watching television. Seeing her at the window, he had imagined she was wearing a kimono, but in fact she was dressed in blue jeans and an embroidered shirt. He kissed her on the nape of the neck and looked over her head to the screen.

A man in a suit was sitting at a desk, smiling into a blizzard: the mountains made for lousy reception. He announced the next programme, a tale of action and adventure for children, and then there was a break for commercials. He was back afterwards to tell the story so far, which was summarised in a series of clips showing horses dashing to and fro, men plotting in rooms and various melodramatic forms of death. The last clip showed a little boy and girl fleeing along a river bank from a horde of mounted warriors. They jumped into the water as their pursuers caught up. Break for more soaps and convenience foods. When the action resumed, the leader of the baddies had the boy in his grasp. One of his henchmen held the boy's face under the water while the chief cut off the lad's head. Cut to little sister, secreted among the roots of a tree. You could tell that revenge was uppermost on her mind. There was another commercial break.

Melville switched the TV off. 'That was the man I met at the reception,' he told her, not acknowledging Wang. 'After I left he got word his sponsor's going to be in Bangkok next week and wants to look me over. It's a pain, but I'll have to fly over Monday, so it means going back to town tomorrow.' He contrived annoyance with a click of the tongue.

To his surprise, Sumiko said she would stay on and work.

'You sure?' Melville asked, glancing out of the window. 'It can get pretty gloomy.'

She said she was. Melville examined her covertly. She appeared to be holding up. He nodded slowly, a bit reluctantly. 'I'll only be gone a few days. Maybe it's a good thing to have a while to think this thing through. We can talk properly when I get back.'

She looked away then, not quickly enough to conceal a dull blink of pain. When she faced him again, she was smiling brightly. She began to question him about the project, forcing him to extemporise wildly. One of his faults or virtues was his inability to lie convincingly or consistently, so he confused her by talking about doing research on the Karen people near the Burma border. She was too polite to embarrass him by asking him what had happened to Indonesia. They did not touch on the subject of her husband.

For Melville, calmed by most of a bottle of wine, the evening had a pleasantly elegiac tone. Outside the rain fell steadily. They went to bed early. Melville scrubbed himself with the aid of a bucket of hot water, then had a bath. Sumiko did the same, using a different bucket of water and the same bath.

Lying back on the sleeping mat, Melville watched her unrobe. Just as he could never hold the delicate cast of her face in his mind, so the plenitude of what was below always came as a surprise. Her body was full, with purple-crowned breasts too ample to be contained by a hand, and a long scooped-out back that curved from the vase of her hips. Out of some notion of gallantry, he did not let his attention linger on her legs, which were short and slightly bowed.

As she bent over to remove her sandals, he evoked the memory of a painting. A group of peasant women were stooped over the rice harvest, skirts hiked up to their thighs. Standing a little way apart from the others, a girl watched from under a shielding hand a band of horsemen in winged helmets passing by on the highway.

He was tumid when Sumiko slid to rest beside him, her skin still damp from the bath, but he maintained his distance. It was she who put her hand on his chest and ran it down his belly, where his penis jerked and crawled to meet it – a pup ingratiating its way to its mistress. 'How can I please you,' she whispered.

When he came, she did not release him with appreciative murmurings as she usually did, but clutched him tighter, bracing herself hard against him and moving with little oscillations that jarred. Confused, he hung on, rigid as a plank except for the bit that mattered. She began to mew on each indrawn breath and the sounds got coarser before she shivered and uttered a chesty cry. Even then she didn't stop.

Later, beached along her flank, Melville mumbled: 'I feel a fool. You should have told me before.'

She soothed his back and crooned to him. In an obscure way he felt she had revenged herself on him, and this excited him. He manhandled her round and mantled over her, spurred on by the image of the peasant girl watching the riders go by.

Sometime while they slept, he tried again – a slippery, inconclusive encounter, part of a bad dream attended by Wang, Sweetwater and other demons.

He woke up alone with a queer, light ache in his chest which he eventually identified as anticipation.

Rain was falling in hard straight lines when he left. Sumiko wanted him to borrow a set of oilskins from the old man, but he declined, knowing that there was little likelihood of him returning them. He stood holding one of Sumiko's hands in both of his, manipulating her fingers as if he were practising some obscure branch of palmistry. 'I'll call you,' he said, and looked her in the face when she didn't answer, hoping to see the smile that reassures. She managed it eventually. 'Sure you won't come back with me? Sure you'll be alright on your own? Well then . . .' And he produced his own smile, intended to convey regret, shyness, the inevitability of things.

He stepped into the downpour and was soaked by the time he reached the edge of the trees, where he turned and looked back. Sumiko was standing at the door with her hands clasped neatly over the spot where they had celebrated the end of their cultural exchange. They bowed to each other.

After walking for a while, Melville was struck by the feeling that today marked one of those rare, adventitious moments when you could sever yourself from the past and face life afresh, with optimism and a renewed capacity for action. He spread his arms wide and raised his face, letting the rain sluice away any lingering doubts. He felt euphoric and he felt favoured. The downpour was a silver jackpot deposited by a celestial fruit machine. Wang, Sweetwater, Mr Yueh shrank to harmless proportions. He felt as bold and purposeful as those riders galloping past the peasants. They were *ronin*, the lordless samurai who called themselves wave-riders.

Along the trail Melville met groups of Japanese hikers equipped with climbing boots, ice axes and golf umbrellas, leaving nothing to chance for a day's stroll in the woods. As he passed them, they moved aside, deferring to this tall, grinning citizen of the world, who covered as much ground with one stride as they covered in two.

Only for a moment did anything threaten his elated mood. At one point the track ran alongside the river, which was swollen and turbid, terrifying in its power. Above the roar of the water, Melville could hear the dull knocking of boulders being bumped and dragged along the bottom. For an instant he had an unbidden vision of Sumiko's face bobbing on the waves, but he shook it away and kept his eyes on the path for the rest of the journey.

Chapter 5

She knew that he was watching her, Gunn decided. The tight, streaky smile she threw at Annie each time she sealed a bag was a provocation aimed at him. He looked at the wall clock. Nearly half an hour until the end of the shift – another forty bags at least. He dug into the paper sack at his side and emptied a scoop of scampi onto the conveyor. They skipped and jostled before plunging into the batter dip, emerging subdued for the waiting women to seed them with Day-glo orange breadcrumbs.

Jessie laughed, and the sound set Gunn's nerves crawling. He thought he might be sickening. All evening a dull pain had been lodged behind one eye, which felt too large for its socket. Jessie laughed again, and coughed on her wad of gum. She had dropped a bag, and when she bent to pick it up, Gunn had to look away quickly, offended by her large rump straining against the slick stuff of her overalls. She picked up the bag and lobbed it in with the others. Even from where he stood, the ragged seal was obvious.

Oh, this won't do, Gunn thought with alarm. He pushed the switch and the belt clattered to a stop. The women, the ladies – and you styled them anything else at your peril – turned listlessly. All except for Mrs Livingstone, on her third part-time job of the day, who went on sprinkling crumbs; and Jessie, who sealed another bag, her shoulders trembling with the restraint she was imposing on herself. A radio you could only hear when the machinery wasn't running sang of baby love.

Gunn's determination wobbled, and he nearly succumbed to the temptation to say that the machine was clogged. By the time it had been cleaned it would be the end of the shift. Jessie kept her bun of a face turned away from him. Gunn got the impression that she was blown up with mirth. From the start she had mounted a campaign of attrition against him. At first he thought it was just hostility to his puny authority, but gradually he had sensed that the enmity was more personal. She hates me, he realised, with a jolt of astonishment.

He walked over, smiling at Annie.

'I'll just take a look at one or two of those bags.'

'Wha – ?' Jessie feigned amazement.

68

Gunn took a bag and examined the seal. It was burnt and incomplete. So was the next, and the next. He ran a finger along the jaws of the sealing machine. They were ridged with tarry plastic.

'This won't do, Jessie,' he said mildly. 'You know fine that the machine needs scraping off every half hour.' He picked up a knife and demonstrated. 'There,' he said, as if he were instructing a benign imbecile.

Jessie's features collected round her mouth – like a squid, Gunn thought, ashamed of his aversion. She couldn't be more than seventeen, but he could detect the woman she would swell into – the neighbourly vindictiveness, the brood of pasty, feral children, towed behind her on sorties to rent and social security offices. Gunn looked despairingly at the heap of bags.

'They'll all have to be repacked, I'm afraid.'

'Whit for? They're sweepings. Ah widna feed them to a cat.'

She had a point. The Sea Queen cold store processed three grades of scampi: Imperial, Crown and Princess. Imperial – large and of impeccable quality – were mainly exported to Germany. Crown were smaller and went to London. The bits that fell off these grades were scraped up, pressed into moulds and frozen, to emerge as Princesses, which were served up in portions of six to eight, depending on the rapacity of the local lunch-in-a-basket operators, at nearly ten bob a throw.

'Now Jessie, we can't have the customers getting food poisoning. Isn't that right, ladies?'

No help from that quarter. 'Best get on,' said Mrs Baird, the nightshift's unofficial shop steward.

Jessie's mouth pursed and unpursed. 'Here, I'll give you a hand,' Gunn said, tearing open a bag.

But she snatched it away and began to empty it herself. Irrationally, Gunn felt he had been reprieved, as if he had escaped a punishment that he, not Jessie, deserved. He went back to his station and switched on, smiling at Mrs Baird, who responded with a minute shake of the head. Still smiling, Gunn was confronted by the utter and irredeemable failure of his life.

'That's it, girls.' Mrs Baird was emptying the unused breadcrumbs into a sack. Gunn was startled to find that nearly fifteen minutes had passed.

'Where do you think you're going?' The words came unbidden, but when he saw Jessie start stripping off her overalls, his self-pity was transmuted into a rush of anger. Tonight he would not stay and make good her carelessness. He wasn't well.

'Away home, like all the rest.'

'You'll not leave until those bags have been repacked.'

Jessie maintained course for the door.

'Did you not hear?'

'They'll keep. Finish them yourself if you're that keen.'

'No, Jessie. I want them done tonight.' A muscle fluttered in his thigh. He knew that he was conspiring in his own humiliation.

'Oh aye,' Jessie said. 'Stick a broom up ma arse an' I'll sweep the floor as well.'

'I'll not have you speaking like that. Do you hear?'

'Away to fuck,' Jessie said casually. 'Just because you wear that daft bonnet doesn't mean you can tell me what to do.'

Gunn's white nylon trilby, insignia of rank, meant precisely that.

The women were watching him without sympathy. 'Give the lassie a break, Mr Gunn,' Mrs Baird said, offering him a way out. 'We'll do the bags first thing Monday.'

Jessie turned to her colleagues. 'He's always getting at me,' she whinged. 'He's always on about ma work, but it's him that's no able. You ken fine what he's like. Standing there talking to hisself. He's no normal. Whit for we couldna have a decent fellow like Dud on our shift?'

Dud was the day-shift supervisor, a tub of a man driven by a futile ruttishness, who maintained a steady stream of sexual banter and often busied his hands in his pockets.

'If you want to work days,' Gunn said, 'I'll have a word with Mr McKay.'

'I'll mebbe speak to him myself. It's no right us lassies working nights with someone that's mental.'

'It can't go on,' Gunn said shakily. 'Night after night I'm here cleaning up your mess. I won't have it any more, do you hear?'

Made cautious by his tightly wound behaviour, Jessie merely shifted her gum and blew a bubble.

'That's enough,' Mrs Baird said. 'Away home now.'

'No,' Gunn said, shaking his head as if clearing his vision. 'Jessie, I don't want you coming in again. I'll be seeing Mr McKay on Monday.'

'You giving me my jotters?' Jessie looked at the other women, whose mouths drew thin in solidarity.

Gunn didn't answer. He began cleaning the machine, his hands not up to the task.

'Whit for? Whit for? Tell me what I've done.' Gunn waited for the counter-attack, but instead, her face dissolved, turned to whey. Immediately a defensive formation gathered around her.

She wrenched herself away and took a step towards Gunn. 'See you,' she crooned. 'Wait'll I tell ma brother. He'll have you, so he will. By the time he's finished with you, you'll have tae shove your hand up your arse to clean your teeth.'

The other women shepherded her away, condemning Gunn with backward looks, but Jessie pulled herself free again and whirled on him, her face ballooning with wrath. 'An' I'll tell you something else. It's you that'll get your jotters when I tell McKay that you've been in the jail.'

When she had gone, Gunn stood dead still for a while, his hands splayed symmetrically on the work-table. Then he screwed a knuckle to his forehead, trying to still the pain.

'That was an awful daft thing to do, Alan. Why didn't you just give the daft wee bitch a good skelp?'

Gunn turned and saw Mrs Baird looking at him with remote concern, as if he were a traffic casualty viewed from a safe distance. She was the only woman who called him by his first name. Her husband had been killed a couple of years back when a pile driver burst apart a few inches from his head. She had a resourceful, gypsy face, planed to the bone by a lifetime of industry on many fronts.

'You've seen her working. She's useless.' He began clearing things away.

'Aye, but that's no cause to send her down the road,' Mrs Baird argued, with unassailable illogic. 'Just because you don't get along.'

'Don't get along?' Gunn laughed jaggedly.

'Aye, well,' Mrs Baird said judiciously. 'She's not over-fond of men right now. The daft cow has got herself pregnant. I don't know. She's like a dresser the way she lets lads go through her drawers. When her dad finds out, he'll murder her, so he will. They're all head-bangers in that family, and that brother's the worst of the lot. He's only just out of Peterhead for cutting one of they Norwegian boys down at the Palace.' She looked at Gunn with sympathy. 'You'll have to watch yourself there right enough.'

Gunn's mind filled with an image of his body being rhythmically kicked to mush in a dark close.

'What I'm saying is: mebbe you should reconsider. You should have seen Jessie upstairs – greetin' like a bairn. It's upset the other lassies.'

71

Gunn noted the hardening of her tone. 'They want me to take her back?'

'Well, she's been on the job a long time. Longer than you, Alan. She'll need the money for the bairn. Anyway, we're a team here. If that McKay hears there's bother down here, he'll start sticking his snoot in.'

Gunn felt helpless. 'You'll be asking me to apologise next.'

Mrs Baird considered the idea. 'No need for that.' She helped him clear up.

'Face it,' she said, slipping a bag of scampi into her coat, 'you're not suited to the job. Nothing personal, mind, but half the time you're standing in a right dwam. The girls like someone they can have a crack with.'

'Like Dud, you mean.'

'He's an awful coarse bugger, but he does make you laugh.'

Gunn faced her. 'So you think it's me should leave.'

'It's up to you. Mebbe it'd be for the best. This isn't your line of work, I can tell. Mind, you'll not find it easy to get another job like this one. Things being what they are.'

'Things being what?'

Mrs Baird was busy brushing down the conveyor. 'Well,' she said. 'Like Jessie said. You being in prison an' that.'

'Mrs Baird, Jessie doesn't know what she's talking about.'

'She heard what she heard is all I'm saying. She was in the office when that Margaret was on the phone to someone at the brew. About your stamps. And she was saying you'd been inside. For four years.'

'Mr McKay wouldn't allow me through this door if he thought I'd been in prison.'

Mrs Baird frowned, acknowledging that the boss wasn't the kind of man who interested himself in the rehabilitation of offenders. Nor was it easy to imagine Gunn committing Saturday night mayhem or rifling coin-boxes in laundromats. Still, there was something not right about him – a fugitive quality, the contagion of old guilt, the obsessional neatness of someone who has lived a long time in his own company. And Jessie had heard what she had heard.

'I'm not one for gossip,' she said, 'but if you have been in the jail, I think you should say.' She laughed a little wildly. 'After all, us girls are all on our own here.'

'It wasn't a jail,' Gunn said shortly.

'What was it then?' Mrs Baird demanded.

72

Gunn recalled with clarity the camp on the dusty yellow plain. 'It was called the Place of Flowers.'

'What kind of place is that?' Mrs Baird's eyes narrowed. 'Not a mental hospital, was it?' She checked the distance to the door.

'A Chinese detention camp.'

'Goodness. Whatever were you doing in such a place?'

Gunn emptied the unused batter into the sink. He turned the taps on full. 'Serving a fifteen-year sentence of corrective labour for illegally entering the People's Republic, fomenting rebellion, training terrorists, betraying the secrets of the revolutionary state to my imperialist masters in Wall Street and London.' He turned round, his expression as uninflected as his voice. 'And conspiring to assassinate an official of the People's Government.' He walked past Mrs Baird and put the batter pans away.

'Would you credit it,' Mrs Baird marvelled. 'Was it in the papers?'

'They reported my release. The Chinese let me go after four years.' Gunn looked over his shoulder, his expression odd. 'They wanted to hold out the hand of friendship to the oppressed masses of Britain.'

'My, my,' Mrs Baird said, much impressed. 'You really do have a past.' She closed in on him. 'And did you do all them things they said you did?'

Gunn gathered up the bags abandoned by Jessie and spread them on the table. 'No need to stay on,' he said. 'I'll finish up myself.'

'No bother.'

She stood silently watching him for a while, then went and laid a hand on his arm. He looked down at it uneasily.

'Let's have a drink.'

'The pubs will be shut,' he said, startled.

'There's some whisky my brother brought. Don't tell me a Highland man like yourself doesn't take a dram.'

Gunn's eyes cast about uncertainly. Mrs Baird tightened her hold on his arm. 'That's why your mind's never on the job,' she said. 'You're thinking about it all the time, that prison in China. You've never told anyone before, have you? Come on,' she said. 'We'll have a wee drink and a chat.'

'My last bus goes at eleven.'

'Aye, well.' She tossed her head – a gesture from vanished girlhood.

You daft old fool, she thought, not sure if she meant herself or Gunn. God knows, he was no oil painting. Shapeless build, baggy face, coarse, peppery hair. His voice was nice, though. Not that he spoke much – except when he muttered to himself. Mind, anyone

73

would be a bit odd after being locked up by foreigners. China. What kind of place was that? She wanted to hear his tale. He was alright, really. Just needed someone to take him on.

She attempted a flirtatious laugh, a desolate sound. 'You must think I'm terrible. Asking you home at this hour.'

'Not at all. It's just that . . .' He passed the back of his hand over his brow.

'Feeling poorly?' Her tone was curdled. A sense of her own worth asserted herself. Who did he think he was? Mind, he did not look like a well man. His skin was thin and susceptible, drawn and sagging. You bugger, she thought, making a snap diagnosis. A boozer.

'I'll be fine,' he said. 'Just a cold coming on.' Sweat gleamed under his hair.

'Best get to bed then,' said Mrs Baird sourly.

'I will,' he said gratefully.

On her way out she addressed him over her shoulder. 'I'll tell Jessie it's alright for Monday then. I'll tell her you weren't yourself. She can work on the batter. She won't be any bother.'

Gunn locked the processing room and went into the cold store, checking the temperature of the freezers. He opened a door and peered through an icy cloud into a gallery of dead meat. Dud claimed to have seen rats in there, at minus forty.

Upstairs, Gunn took off his coat and hat, dusted them off and hung them on a peg next to the splayed-out objects of Dud's fantasies. They reminded Gunn of the anatomical specimens he used to pin out for dissection at medical school.

When he went outside, he stopped still, turning his head in an arc. The city had assumed the intense reality of a dream. Malty vapour hung in coils on the surface of the harbour, but Gunn had the impression that the upper air, where late summer twilight still gleamed, was in a state of swirling agitation. On the dock opposite, a riveting gun hammered on plate steel. Acetylene flared in the depths of a workshop, lighting up giants in visored helmets and spacesuits.

Standing there, Gunn was oppressed by a peculiar sense of imminence.

Since childhood he had been cursed at intervals by – if not prescience – a slippage of identity during which the unseen assumed reality. Usually, these periods were marked by a profound sense of guilt and worthlessness. As a boy he had lived alone with his father in a lighthouse at the end of an Atlantic peninsula. His father was the kind of unreconstructed Calvinist who separates the roosters from the hens on Sundays and forbids smiling unless you're on your way to the kirk. Early on, guilt had become the grain of Gunn's being – undifferentiated and ineradicable. At night his father would read to him from black books, and in the daytime he would take long walks under chaotic skies and hear God's voice condemning him from the whirlwind. Naturally enough, these meaty symbols were seized on by the psychiatrist who treated him after his breakdown at university, where he was a fourth-year medic. He did not get far, and eventually diagnosed exhaustion. 'You boys from the islands – in the library until ten, six days a week, wearing yourself to sticks.'

The chaplaincy sent a visitor – Peter, a long-limbed, pipe-smoking divinity student who, two years earlier, had been fighting the Japanese in Burma and who still retained a military manner. 'Look here, old boy,' Peter said on his second visit, 'has it crossed your mind that these dreams may be God trying to come into your life?' Gunn had laughed wretchedly, his head twisting on the pillow. 'Babies coming alive in bottles? Blood flowing from books? More like the Devil.' Peter had seized his hand. 'You must find out. You must submit. Submit and be saved.'

When Gunn left hospital, Peter became a frequent visitor to his digs. One evening, sharing high tea, Peter had pushed his plate away and said: 'I say, Alan, does Mrs Beattock give you poached yellow fish every night?' Gunn admitted that this was the case; he had eaten yellow fish poached in milk every term-time evening for four years. 'But it's alright,' he said. 'I like it.' Peter had stared at him. 'My God,' he said eventually, 'we've got to get you away from here.'

So Gunn had moved into Peter's rooms. Peter intended resuming a military career, this time as a soldier for Christ: he wanted to return to the East as a missionary. 'Thing is, I've been blessed with something of a knack for ministering to men's souls, but when it comes to treating the ills of the flesh, I'm a complete duffer.' So Gunn, who could set broken limbs, perform an appendectomy – in theory – and amputate if necessary, never completed his medical training. No missionary society would sponsor them, but Peter was wealthy. They sailed for Shanghai on 23 October, 1947. Gunn was twenty-three, Peter nearly thirty.

During his years in China, Gunn suffered occasional relapses, but now his hallucinations were seen as divine inspiration. 'And what does the Old Man want us to do this time?' Peter would ask, sucking on his pipe – his relationship with God being that of a favoured subaltern with a general. They had plenty of need of guidance after 1948, as they retreated steadily westwards before the advancing Communists.

At the terminus a bus was waiting, breathing diesel. The conductor appeared to be asleep on the rear seats. 'Thought you'd never get here,' he said, without opening his eyes. They set off, careering through the industrial wasteland as if it were a dangerous frontier zone. A curfew seemed to have been imposed. Although it was before eleven, the only person Gunn saw during the first ten minutes of the journey was a drunk marooned on a street corner, swaying to the rhythm of invisible tides. Gradually, more of these appeared, and a few other passengers boarded the bus. They drove on through coolly classical squares and terraces that gave way to a wild gothic tableau of volcanic peaks and troughs crowned with spires and castles.

A clock was striking in restrained, protestant tones when Gunn alighted. He was in tribal territory – to the left, broken streets and corrugated iron; to the right, a high-rise reservation floodlit with sodium. Gunn went left, down greasy cobbles.

Halfway home, Gunn took refuge in the ruined doorway of a tenement. Down the long tunnel of the street, a knot of figures had lurched into view, ravelling and unravelling in a tribal dance, chanting a monotonous boast of invincibility. As they came close, they stopped singing, and Gunn feared that he had been seen. He cringed back, thinking of Jessie's threat. But the war party went past his hiding place – four boys led by a scarred cherub, all drunk to the point of near paralysis, reeling like cargo shifting in heavy seas, their eyes fixed ahead on some far distant landfall.

When they had gone, Gunn ran, keeping close to the wall, until he reached a shop grilled and shuttered for a long siege. A hand-painted sign, nearly obliterated by graffiti, proclaimed it to be a Scottish and Continental Grocery. He knocked on the piece of plywood where the shop window had been and put his head close. 'It's me. Mr Gunn. I've come for my order.'

Bolts were drawn and Gunn crossed the threshold into sixty-watt gloom. The door-keeper, in a fraying black cardigan and polyester saree, clicked knitting needles behind a baroque till. In the shadows at the back of the shop, her husband kept up a counterpoint with a machine for sticking price tags on the merchandise. The shop had the solemnity of a Hindu temple – a temple dedicated to a minor reflex

76

of money, the slenderest of profit margins, small change, 'Please do not ask for credit as a refusal often offends.'

Gunn went up the aisle, picking his supper at random. Pilchards in tomato sauce, a box of stale cup-cakes, three bananas. Every item had two or three price tags on it; each banana spoke for the bunch. *Clack, clack* went the machine, keeping pace with Gunn, who got the occasional glimpse of the proprietor's face through the gaps left in the stacks of tins and packets.

Back at the till, his order was ready – three unlabelled bottles of contraband whisky delivered after dark by a 25-year-old alcoholic who did his rounds of the city in a Ford Anglia that had been twice round the clock. Battery acid is how he described his wares, but that was a joke.

Propped against the bottles was a letter stamped with the gaudy parrot hues that betokened foreign origins.

Gunn paid, went out, and immediately turned hard left into his own doorway. He groped his way upstairs through the smell of stale curry and varnish. His rooms were on the second floor – fifty square yards of linoleum remnants and thrift-shop furniture. After placing the letter on the mantelpiece, with one of the bottles, he laid out his supper on a marbled formica table. He ate with the speed of the solitary, not looking at the food, his eyes fixed on the envelope.

In the months after his release, Gunn had received a fair volume of overseas mail from organisations with names like the Global Church of Christ, whose correspondents tended to underline key words, such as Faith, Truth, Freedom and Satan, and who invited him to lecture on same, with specific reference to his ordeal at the hands of Mao Tse-tung's agents of darkness.

Gunn washed up, poured half a tumbler of whisky, filled the other half with water and took the envelope in his hand. He drained most of his drink and tore apart the cheap paper. The address was a P.O. Box number in Bangkok. The letter read:

> Dear Sir, Teacher, Mr Alan Gunn,
> I am pleasure to write you now. I liketed the time we spent and never for getable it. Excouse me! I think you were dead, also your friend Peter too. I am sorry. My family is all killed, but I escaped for India. Now I am happy doing business in Bangkok.
> Also one thing to say you, well, can you come for visit. I don't no. Expensive, of course! But my friend here who finds you alive says maybe you would if he paid. Id you would not, That's o,key! Of course! But you ask to my friend. But you must not think I am

77

forcing for!! You know, If you do some great I never forget, If my friend think you blind I never believe.

Well that's it! Sorry my writing is not good. No practis!! But you no it is difficult to write what is in my head! Soppose you come! Well I shall do puja for you.

Thank you!!!!
Your sincere
Yonden Dhondrub

I hoped you remember me!

Underneath, in a Western hand, was written:

Write Yonden at this address and I'll fix your trip.

That message was unsigned.

Gunn did not dwell on the identity of this writer, or wonder why he did not explain how he had 'found' him, or why he hadn't taken the trouble to correct Yonden's English, or why Yonden gave no clues to his life in the twenty years since they had last seen each other. He had been vouchsafed a miracle. Yonden was alive.

Trembling, Gunn got up and filled his glass again. He read the letter once more, and then again, wringing out the meaning this time, searching for a note of accusation. 'My family is all killed.' Gunn closed his eyes and knocked back his whisky.

He carried the letter and the bottle into his bedroom and rummaged in a drawer until he found a mock-leather photograph album. Most of the pages were blank; the Communists had taken his unprocessed films and used them as evidence of his career of intrigue against the masses. He turned the pages until he came to a picture of three horsemen by a cairn on a plateau of shattered rock. There were a few snow patches visible in the background. His own face was blurred; his horse had moved as the shutter clicked. Peter was smiling ruefully, aware that he looked comical sitting on such a small horse, with his legs almost touching the ground. Yonden, dismounted, was standing ramrod straight, his arms stiff at his sides.

Gunn eased the photograph from its mounts and read the caption pencilled on its back. 'Thong-la, 17,400 feet. August 20th, 1949.' He looked from the picture to the letter. Yonden would be nearly forty now. Peter would have been over fifty.

The bottle was well below the level Gunn usually allowed, but he poured out another shot and sat at the foot of the bed, going over the letter again. This time he paid attention to the casual postscript, hearing an American accent, and for the first time he reflected on the nature of the writer. The brevity of the message implied certainty, the confidence of someone wise in the ways of men. Gunn imagined this unknown agent reading Yonden's chaotic script and saying: 'Send it. He'll come.'

Of course he would.

'I hope you remember me!' Gunn felt a thickening in his throat and stood up abruptly, staring at the wall until the emotion passed. To his dismay, he found that he had crumpled the letter. He straightened it and his eyes fell on Yonden's pledge to hold a rite of blessing on his behalf. The delusion that he was performing it right now, on the other side of the world, so wrenched his spirit that he fell to his own knees and began to pray, sobbing so much that his words would have been unintelligible to anyone except an almighty and all-forgiving God.

Chapter 6

Melville's buoyant mood kept them aloft even when the jets seemed to reverse thrust on the approach to Bangkok, pinning the plane at the top of a stall while the earth rotated round them. A waterlogged landscape slid past, then the city tilted into view – commercial grey and monsoon green, with saffron temples glowing in the shadow of a retreating rain front.

He went through immigration expecting to see Wang, but Mr Yueh had sent a cheerful moon-faced man with dentistry like a gold seam. The drive to the hotel was accomplished in silence. The driver said he would pick him up at nine.

A party of well-fed Germans in hothouse shirts had taken over the reception area. They stood guard over an immense pile of baggage, easing their shorts away from the tucks and folds of their crotches. Melville waited until they had dispersed. He subsided into a seat opposite a young man in designer combat fatigues who lay back with the overturned heels of his cowboy boots resting on a battered aluminium camera case. The man looked up out of his copy of *Ages in Chaos* and gave him a weary peace salute. There were Saigon stickers on his luggage.

Melville rode the elevator with a German straggler. When the doors closed, the attendant began calling his wares in a bored sing-song, as though he were announcing floors in Bloomingdales. 'You want all-night only twelve years. You like look mens fuck-fuck with girls? Maybe all girls. Hey, you want boys. Okay, no problem.'

Inside his room Melville dropped his bag and fell back onto the bed. It was a little after seven. He wasn't hungry, but the idea of drink kept stealing up to him. To rout it he took a long shower. Back on his bed he opened a copy of *Time*. The president, he learned, had declared the Moon-walk a triumph of Middle America. Good for the Big Sky folk, Melville thought, throwing the magazine into a corner. He himself had no wish to go out into menacing space. Not one small step.

As his mood congealed, he found himself questioning the wisdom of being here. From there it was a small step to ordering a whisky, and then another. He dozed until reception rang to say his car had arrived.

They pulled out into the demented traffic and cruised through a neon fireball, the driver patiently giving way to revellers who staggered with linked arms down the centre of the thoroughfare. Young men in black Dacron with metal combs sticking out of their pants' pockets stood outside the bars, bordellos and massage parlours. Some of them marked out their territory by performing stylised kung-fu routines. The night smelt of hot spices, raw perfume and electricity. Inside Mr Yueh's car, chauffered by Mr Yueh's driver, Melville felt safe.

Nevertheless, when they left the downtown area he felt an obligation to memorise their route. He soon conceded defeat. Although he guessed they were staying close to the river, he never actually saw it. The street lights grew sparse and then died out altogether. Eventually they turned off down a dirt road with shacks on one side and some kind of compound wall, overgrown by creepers, on the other. They stopped by a gateway and the driver killed the engine. Melville wound down his window.

Moths smacked and whirred against the headlamps. He smelt nightsoil, bruised fruit and the oily tang of the river. Frogs pulsed to the electric rasp of crickets, then they stopped as if a switch had been thrown, and the only thing he could hear was the distant hum of traffic and the thudding of his heart.

'This is Mr Yueh's place?' he asked. His voice sounded ridiculously loud.

The driver didn't answer. He let him out and indicated he should follow him. They went through the gateway. On the other side Melville couldn't see a thing. He stumbled along a broken pathway, resisting the urge to hold on to the driver's shoulder. At one point the driver took his arm and steered him around a well of blackness. Something heavy but agile scuttled over a smooth surface below him and clawed at a wall before dropping back with a thump. A rhythmic thudding came from ahead. Now Melville could make out a big, square shape like a hangar superimposed against the sky. He stopped.

'What in hell is this place?' he whispered.

'Hotel,' the driver answered.

He led the way up a shallow flight of stairs. If it was an hotel, it was strangely deficient in windows. The driver pushed open a big door and noise flooded out.

Blinking, Melville looked into a cavernous foyer walled with raw concrete. It was occupied exclusively by Chinese, some squatting in groups at the bases of pillars, others leaning against the walls in the economical stance favoured by chauffeurs. The clatter of mahjong tiles was like surf going out on a shingle beach. Naked light bulbs dimmed and brightened to the beat of an invisible generator. Two women in glittering sheath dresses were mounting a concrete staircase to the same rhythm.

Nobody looked at Melville as the driver guided him across the foyer to a door painted with women who combined compliant oriental faces with Hollywood breasts. On the other side was a hall as big as a church nave, lit by fashionably psychedelic strobes that ran over the bare concrete like oil. The room was occupied by US military. Melville knew they were military by their haircuts and the creases in their shirts, pulled from a suitcase that morning. He intuited that there were no officers among them. A few of the men were drinking at a bar, attended by girls in G-strings. A meagre audience was sprawled under a nimbus of marijuana smoke, watching two strippers. Most of the men were congregated at the other end of the hall, which was lit by conventional lights.

The driver motioned him to wait at the bar and then left. Melville slipped into a space next to a broad, red-haired man who was sitting half-turned away on a stool, talking to an etiolated black man and running a tatooed hand up the spine of a tall girl with heavily mascaraed eyes. The hand was curled in a pincer and every time it reached the base of her skull, it tightened, making her flinch without breaking the grip or her complacent smile.

The black man jerked his chin to indicate they had company. The red-head swung round and appraised Melville. When he resumed speaking, his voice was pitched louder than necessary.

'So I say to this wiggy browbar, "I'll stay here and cover your ass, sir, on account of there may be some other mothers out there." He's creeping up on the gook with his knife out and I'm standing way back behind a tree with my hands over my ears. The lieutenant sticks his boot under Charlie to turn him over – and Zap! Bits of him are flying every which way and his head's looking down from a tree.' The red-head sniffed. 'Shit, you could have sent him home in a Kleenex.' The red-head took a pull on his beer. 'No shit, I *smelt* that satchel charge.'

'Fuckin' A,' the black man said.

The red-head turned with ominous slowness. He fixed Melville with a loose smile.

82

'Why you eye-fuckin' me?'

Melville looked into space.

'You hear me, asshole?'

Melville bolted. He wondered if the red-head knew that his escort was a transvestite.

For a time he watched the strippers quietly arguing between themselves, then he drifted over to join the crowd at the other end of the hall.

The lights were trained on a square bamboo pen, about four feet high and floored with rough carpet. Two Thais in hillmen's loose trousers and baggy army shirts were standing at opposite ends of the enclosure, next to plaited baskets that gave the occasional rattle and shiver. 'Make way for the man,' someone called, and the crowd pressed apart to admit a big, rawboned man with a shy backwoods grin, who climbed into the pit punching the air with his fist, like he was a prize-fighter. He reminded Melville of the young Lincoln.

'You got some mean ones tonight, Tad?' someone called.

'Got some mean ones.'

There were a few whoops of pretended disbelief.

Tad raised his hands for quiet. 'Now most of you don't know beans 'bout cockin', 'cept,' he said, with his Huck Finn grin, 'what your mamas taught you. So I guess I'd better 'splain a few points. First off, though, we need a scrutineer.'

'Whassahellsascrutineer?'

'A scrutineer,' Tad said, 'is someone who scrutineers that the cocks don't have their spurs filed. Also, that there's no greasing, peppering, muffing or soapin' of the cocks.' He accepted the laughs and whistles as his due.

'Get your ass in there, Raczynsky. You're always playing with your cock.'

A man with the lop-sided smile of a natural victim was pushed into the pen.

'Since you folk don't know fightin' gamecock from Kentucky Fried, I better give you a few pointers make it easier to know where to lay your money.' Tad nodded at the hillmen, who opened the baskets and pulled out two struggling fighting cocks.

'Now you boys might be thinkin' this little darlin' is just a dunghill rooster,' Tad said, stroking the enamelled neck of a big bird whose iridescent plumage and jaunty tail bespoke health and confidence. 'But it minds me of a strychnine that was raised up by Otis Holly – best cocker I ever knew. Now that strychnine was one mean sonofabitch. It

83

heeled anything that came its way – rats, cats, it didn't care what. Once it caught a garter snake in the soak and beat it to pulp, then eat it up. I saw it win eight mains in a row, but it got hurt sore in the last one, and after that it began attackin' itsel', tearin' its wings and billin' its breast. Guess it was brain-damaged. That Otis, he loved his bird so, he had it stuffed and put it in his office, where I believe it still is – Holly's Body and Frame Shop, out on the Interstate between Rockfish and Lynchburg. Anyway, strychnines are strong and faster than a snake, and they're real mean with their bills.'

Tad turned his country-boy smile on the other bird. 'Shit, I know what you're thinkin',' he said.

Certainly, this one was no Chanticleer. It was much smaller than the other bird, and apart from its angry wattle and comb, the only colour it boasted were a few olive highlights on its plumage of jungle drab.

'Don't look worth a cold fart,' someone said.

'Well,' Tad said, 'looks don't mean much of anything. See these feathers,' he said, ruffling a handful. 'When they're all loose like that the other bird goes for the feathers, not the body. I've seen birds come out of the pit like they've been plucked, and not a mark on them.' He took hold of one of the legs and extended it. 'Take a peek at that. Strong as a pine. Nice and short, too, so I'd lay odds he's a shuffler, which means he'll let the other cock ride up on him and then go for his balls.

'Course,' he added, 'none of these cocks is what you'd call pedigree. These boys brung 'em up from up north, by Burma, and that's where fightin' cocks come from originally – ordinary peckers and scratchers too. Guess you boys didn't know that. So these are your genuine fightin' cock, straight from the jungle, meaner than shit, and I'd back them 'gainst any faggy, corn-fed, college-educated roosters back home.'

'Stop shittin' us, Tad, and show us the action.'

'We're fightin' by Red Lion rules, like where I come from,' Tad said. 'The cocks get to eyeball each other, then these boys set 'em down six feet apart. When I say "Go" the main starts. If either bird leaves off fightin', the boys will bring them together, touch their beaks and leave them go again. Unless one is blinded, which case the boys will set them down touching shoulders. The main ends when one of the cocks is killed or refuses to fight after six counts of ten. That means I'll count ten and say "Once refused" and on up to six. You got it? If they both get killed, the winner is the one that dies last.

Judge's decision is final. Now let's have that scrutineer so's you can lay a little money.'

Raczynsky slouched forth, winking at the crowd. 'What do I do?' he asked.

'Jes' check them spurs. See they're not filed so's they can slash.' Tad extended each armoured leg in turn.

Raczynsky peered dubiously from a safe distance. 'Take a real close look,' Tad said. The scrutineer did so, and Tad let go the leg, which jerked spastically, almost catching Raczynsky's face with its three-inch spur. The crowd laughed. 'Seems alright to me,' Raczynsky muttered.

A Chinese in a clean white shirt began taking wagers.

'Hell, I don't know. The only chicken I saw came in a carton with a scoop of French fries.'

'C'mon. I've seen you lay out fifty bucks to see fleas fuck.'

'I'll bet twenty on that fancy strychnine. Anything that kills snakes gets my money.'

'Here's a C-note says the parrot's gonna stomp all over that brown buzzard.'

'You don't know fuckin' nothing. Fifty at threes on the brown.'

'Ten against seven on the strychnine.'

A few latecomers drifted over, craning to get a look. A meaty silence fell. The hillmen brought the cocks to the middle of the pit, squirming and snaking their necks. The hillmen let them touch, then lowered them to the floor.

'Go!'

'Whooo-eee!' yelled the crowd.

The strychnine rattled its feathers and pecked at the carpet, first to the left, then to the right, as though it were feeding in a farmyard. The brown cock bobbed its head in agitation and set off in a comical lope. Still dabbing at the ground, the strychnine followed, neck held low. When it was almost up to the brown, it sprang, but the same instant the brown whirled and leaned back. The two birds came together with the sound of sticks meeting, rebounded and sprung again, whirring three feet into the air and striking half a dozen times before they fluttered to the ground, leaving feathers floating.

They moved so fast that Melville had only fleeting impressions of flashing spurs and serpentine heads going like hammers. Tad was right. The strychnine fought pell-mell, aiming high with beak and legs, while the brown stayed low and went for its opponent's breast and raked it from below when the fury of its attacks took it over the top.

'Strychnine's got a hold,' someone yelled. The strychnine had the brown by the first wing joint and was using it as purchase to hold the brown down so it could slash its head from above. 'The brown's bleeding!' A few drops of blood had flowered on the bamboo walls.

The cocks broke and circled once, then flew together and crashed wings. They recoiled and struck again, recoiled and struck. Ten times or more they collided – a whirring bound, a hollow crack as bone and pinion met. They moved in unison, but at last the brown seemed to miss a beat, and in that fraction of a second the strychnine was all over it, worrying its head, going for the eyes. A heave, and the brown had shaken its tormentor off, but one side of its head was torn and stripped. 'It's blind! The brown's blind!'

Most of the money had been on the strychnine, and the punters who'd gone for the good odds were trying to lay off their bets. Some brisk side-betting broke out on the strychnine's chances of finishing it in under two minutes. The brown was still on its feet, but it squatted low, like a partridge that sees a hawk overhead. It didn't try to counter-attack – merely weaved its head to dodge the jabs. Melville could see that one eye had indeed gone.

The brown managed to break free and it lolloped off with a rolling gait that incited the audience to laughter. The strychnine set off in hot pursuit. It closed and the brown managed to rise and meet it. There was an ominous crack, and when the birds separated, it was the strychnine's left wing that was hanging low. 'Goddam parrot's busted his wing,' said an amazed voice.

And now the fight began to slip the brown's way. Handicapped by its broken wing, the strychnine did not rise so commandingly, and its aggression seemed blunted. It stood up to the brown, but had to concede ground. Each attack drove a small puff of feathers from its chest. Something rattled like hail on the bamboo. 'Its crop's gone fercrissake. The fucker's all tore up.'

The strychnine fetched up against a wall and made a break, running round the pit, round and round, its bad wing dragging. Favouring its good eye, the brown stalked its opponent, keeping on the inside and trying to drive it into the wall. Checked by the bamboo, the strychnine bobbed its head this way and that, as flustered as the dumbest barnyard fowl. The brown hit it with all its weight, knocking it into a corner, then it sprang on top, gouging clumps from its iridescent neck. 'Stomp it. Stomp the fucker,' yelled someone who stood to gain. The brown needed no encouragement; it kept tearing away even when the strychnine was dead.

Tad lifted off the brown. Stunned, the crowd looked at the strychnine quivering on the carpet. 'Shee-e-e-ut,' whispered someone in the silence. 'That's the meanest chicken I ever seen.'

'Mr Yueh see you now.'

Melville looked down and saw Wang. He realised he'd been standing there for some time. He was wearing dark glasses, a dark suit, a dark shirt and a white tie.

'Pretty good,' Wang said. 'You like it?'

'I think it's disgusting.'

Wang laughed as though he didn't believe him. He took him up the hall, through a door and up a service staircase. Concrete was much in evidence here, too. The place was permeated by an unpleasant faecal smell. They went through another door, down a corridor where the smell was overlaid with but not masked by, strident perfumes. There were numbered rooms along the corridor. One door was open, and Melville saw a dozen women of two generations all wearing evening dresses and sitting around a perfectly circular, plastic-coated bed about ten feet in diameter. They were watching a television which was not in evidence from where Melville stood. When they saw him, they all gave little waves. 'Hiya,' he said.

Wang opened another door and ushered him into a passage painted and carpeted in different shades of turquoise. At the far end a man sitting on a chair got up and knocked on a door padded with fake leather. Melville's chest tightened. At the same time, he felt strangely sleepy. He had to stifle a yawn.

He went past Wang into a large room decked out in the same colour scheme as the passage and hung with paintings of sailing ships under full canvas. Mr Yueh was standing by a cocktail bar shaped like the front end of a ship, with bottles hanging from the bridge, mixers on the fo'c's'le and tropical fish mouthing O's of astonishment inside the portholes. Sweetwater was manning the bridge, glass raised in salute, flying his grin like a flag.

Chapter 7

Mr Yueh was pretty spooky – a tall, hollow beak of a man who looked like he'd been strung together from ganglia. Shock or illness had nearly decapillated him, leaving a few long black hanks hanging at irregular intervals on the circumference of his skull. He wore a suit of some expensive pearly material that shimmered blue and pink and lavender depending on the way the light caught it. His feet were shod with plaid carpet slippers.

'Water Marvel,' he said, his difficulty with liquid consonants elevating Melville to the stature of a mythical Chinese hero. His voice was papery, but he spoke English well enough. 'So glad you agreed to come. So glad to welcome you after so many years.'

His hands were clasped in front, his head slightly bowed. Depending on what business he was transacting, he would greet guests with poolroom bonhomie or the punctilio of an imperial minister receiving a Jesuit delegation from the court of Spain.

'The pleasure of seeing you again is almost more than my heart can bear,' Melville said in Mandarin.

Mr Yueh clapped his hands softly. 'Good. Very good. You haven't forgotten your learning.'

'Hey, let's have a little mutual comprehension here,' Sweetwater said. He stretched his arms wide. 'What do you think of Mr Yueh's new place? Used to belong to a pirate. A real pirate – lived all his life on a junk. He made a fortune running guns to the Vietminh, and when Uncle Sam decided to make Bangkok an R and R spa he put his money into the leisure industry.' Sweetwater shook his head. 'Fish out of water. He didn't know much about utilities and the contractors ripped him off cruel. You notice the bad smell? We got johns here but no pipes, light fittings but no electricity. It was an act of charity when Mr Yueh took the place off his hands and let him go back to living on a boat.'

Sweetwater's slightly overheated manner made Melville feel more confident of himself. 'Charlie told me you wanted me to meet a visitor from the mainland,' he said.

'Not until we've sketched in the background,' Sweetwater said, and Mr Yueh shut his eyes and nodded fast.

'Well then,' Melville said, looking from one to the other, 'what's it all about?'

'You'd better sit down,' Sweetwater said, as if he had bad news to impart. 'It'll take a bit of time. You want a drink?'

'Just a small whisky,' Melville said, breaking a resolve.

Sweetwater dispensed whisky and snapped open a can of beer for himself. Melville perched on the edge of a gargantuan couch covered in acquamarine Rexine and buttons. Mr Yueh sat in the middle of the room on a chrome-and-plastic swivel chair, his shins jutting like blades between his socks and the cuffs of his pants. Sweetwater came over with a thin folder. He took out two sheets and handed them to Melville.

The top one was a copy of a page from an army list, with one entry circled. It was in Chinese. The second sheet was a translation of the ringed entry. Melville skimmed it. 'General Liu Hongwen. Born Kweichow Province, 1912. True son of the proletariat . . . developed revolutionary consciousness at early age, joined the Party in 1926 . . . Veteran of the Long March . . . Hero of the war against Japanese imperialism . . . Fought in Korea against the US aggressors and their lackeys . . . Staff College 1961–64 . . .' A long and distinguished military career. Melville looked up before he had finished it.

Sweetwater was waiting with another sheet. It was a copy from another edition of the same list – the same page in fact, but none of the entries was marked, and when Melville checked, he saw that General Liu's biography was missing.

'From the official PLA list,' Sweetwater said. 'Worth its weight in gold.'

'What happened to Liu?' Melville asked. 'Did he die?'

'Ghosts and monsters,' Mr Yueh said.

In the silence that this provoked, Melville frowned a warning at Sweetwater.

'Listen to the story, that's all,' Sweetwater said soothingly, handing over some photographs.

Melville guessed that the top picture had been taken in the early 1950s, since none of the officers ranged in a beaming semi-circle with Chairman Mao was wearing insignia of rank. One man's face – Liu's presumably – was ringed, and the next photo showed it in blow-up. The picture was as grainy as porridge, but Melville made out a round-faced, jolly-looking character who looked as though he would be more at home behind the bar of some rustic inn than at the head of a revolutionary army. The last photo, wallet-sized and dog-eared,

89

showed a much younger Liu grinning stoically at the camera in the company of another man. Both were wearing Red Army caps and ragbag uniforms.

'The other guy is the one who came to see Mr Yueh,' Sweetwater said. 'His name's Zhang. Zhang Youmin.'

Melville felt the skin crawl over his ribs.

'Zhang Youmin was born in the same province as General Liu,' Mr Yueh said. 'At Maotai – you know, where the yellow wine is made. He was in prison when the Long Marchers took the town. The Reds emptied the jails and invited the prisoners to join them. Most did, but ran away after a few weeks or were killed. Zhang was one of the few who stayed to the end. During the march Liu saved his life – in the Grasslands. You know about the Grasslands?'

Melville, straining to hear, nodded.

'No, Water Marvel,' Mr Yueh said, 'you don't – any more than you know what hell is like.' Mr Yueh narrowed his gaze, as if viewing something a long way off. 'The sky,' he said, 'was the colour of mustard oil, with strange shapes in it – cities, armies, dragons. Nothing else to see. No birds, no trees. Nothing except that sky and the stinking swamp. I went into the Grasslands with thirty men and came out with fourteen. The man ahead of you would disappear into the earth and by the time you reached the spot there would be only a few bubbles bursting.' Mr Yueh's gaze came drifting back. 'Yes, I was there, Water Marvel, chasing the Reds. You look surprised.'

'I didn't know,' Melville said uncomfortably. 'You never mentioned it before.'

Mr Yueh gave the sour chuckle of reflection. 'Ghosts and monsters.'

Melville cleared his throat. 'You said Liu saved Zhang's life.'

'Zhang got sick in the Grasslands,' Mr Yueh said. 'He was left behind and Liu found him. He was a lieutenant then, in Lin Piao's First Army Corps. He nursed Zhang himself and shared his rations with him. Afterwards they stayed together all through the journey to Yenan. They served together in the war with Japan and fought the Kuomintang until . . .' Mr Yueh's lips went on flexing, unable to frame an acknowledgement of the Communists' triumph. 'At the end of the war,' he continued, 'Liu was a colonel. Zhang was only a sergeant. He left the army and went home to Maotai. Liu was promoted to general during the Korean War, but he never lost touch with his old friend. When he went home on leave they always met to talk about the past.'

'He was at home six weeks ago,' Sweetwater said casually.

As the silence lengthened, Melville realised that this was his cue. Fuck it, he thought. I'm not going to bite.

'Zhang tells us that Liu wants out,' Sweetwater said, in no particular tone.

'Out?' Melville said stupidly. 'Why?'

'He wants to go to the States.'

'But why?'

'Fifty thousand dollars for starters.'

'Fifty thousand dollars?'

'And a house. You know what they say – hearts on the left, pockets on the right.'

Melville took another look at the general's biography. 'His last posting was to the northern front, "presenting the unflinching face of true socialism to counter-revolutionary adventurers".' He put the sheet aside. 'This man isn't going to betray his country for fifty thousand dollars. Zhang must be trying to work some kind of con.'

'Zhang's on the level, take it from me,' Sweetwater said. He fell to pacing. 'Put yourself in Liu's place,' he said. 'Thirty-five years ago he was a guerilla hiding out in caves and eating chaff. Now he's a general in the world's biggest army. He's been on the winning side in three wars. What's the secret of his success?' Sweetwater about-turned. 'Order,' he said. 'Discipline.'

'Alright,' Melville said.

'So where's it got him?' Sweetwater said, resuming his pacing. 'First, Mao sets himself up as emperor and has all the kids singing songs about how the sun rises out of his ass. Liu isn't too thrilled, because he remembers Mao when his ass was hanging out of his pants. Still, so long as the sun continues shining on *him*. Then things turn a little sour with the Soviets, and instead of giving people like Liu more tanks and planes, Mao starts sounding off about people's war, preaching the everyone-a-soldier ethic. You think Liu likes the sound of that? Hell, no. He's a professional. The last thing he wants is to help run a part-time militia of five hundred million people.'

Sweetwater was into his stride. 'Okay, the Soviet scare dies down for a while. Things get so quiet you can hear people starting to mutter about Mao's crackerass economic reforms. I'm talking about building factories a hundred miles from the nearest road, sending bank clerks to grow radishes in the Gobi desert. The country's starving. Mao thinks that another dose of revolution will take people's minds off their day-to-day problems, so he says set the little devils free. Suddenly China's swarming with Red Guards.'

Sweetwater stopped pacing and faced Melville. 'Imagine what the Cultural Revolution was like for people like Liu. Everything stood on its head, everything you fought for put at risk by gangs of kids with spots and eyeglasses, all sorts of funny dudes giving your men ideological workouts after a hard day on manoeuvres.' Sweetwater strode over, picked up Liu's photo and flicked it with the back of his hand. 'Look at that big peasant mug. He's a general but he prefers to do his drinking with a bicycle mechanic. He probably farts in company and chews garlic by the bulb. That,' he said, prodding the portrait, 'is the face of a man who would tell those snot-nosed zealots where to shove their little Red Books.'

'And did he?' Melville asked, shifting on his seat.

'More than that,' Sweetwater said, still looking at the picture. 'Zhang was reluctant to discuss it; he's trying to save Liu's face. But Mr Yueh did some digging and came up with the story. Remember the Chen Yi affair?'

'The foreign minister?' Melville said, startled. 'It was the big story when I was in Hong Kong.'

'Another ghost,' Mr Yueh said, and gave a laugh like an ancient clock winding itself up. 'Chen Yi was another Long Marcher. Liu served under him when he was military governor of Shanghai. They were close associates.'

'Which automatically put Liu on the Red Guards' shit list,' Sweetwater said. 'After they'd finished with Chen they came after Liu. We figure he must have said something indiscreet about the treatment they handed out to his old friend. They grabbed him and gave him a public working over . . . what do they call it?'

'Struggle session,' Melville said.

'That's right,' Sweetwater said. 'Here's this guy, a hero of four wars, and the merry pranksters put him up on a stage dressed in a dunce's cap.'

'Accused of what?'

'You know the kind of crap the Reds lay on each other – opportunist, capitalist-roader, harbourer of bourgeois ideas, wrong thinker. Liu was invited to admit the error of his ways, but instead of bowing his head and taking all this shit, he told his accusers a lot of home truths, ending with the threat that next time they met it would be at different ends of a gun barrel.'

'Well, good for him,' Melville said.

'Bad, bad,' Sweetwater said. 'No matter how much the party bosses agreed with the sentiment, they couldn't ignore what amounted to a declaration of war on the people. Liu was hauled up before the Central Committee and sentenced to stay at home under what they call supervision by the masses.'

'An embittered man,' Melville said, studying Liu's picture.

'He blames the defence minister, his old comrade-in-arms Lin Piao. He's the man behind the little red devils. And,' Sweetwater added, 'he's the man who's tipped to take over from Mao. The future's looking pretty bleak for Liu.'

'For an honest soldier,' Melville said, 'he seems to have an unfortunate knack for making enemies.'

'He must have some friends at court,' Sweetwater said, 'because last fall he was partially rehabilitated. They handed him back his uniform and gave him a new job where he couldn't make any trouble.'

'But he still wants to defect,' Melville said. He turned to Mr Yueh. 'And he's asked you to help.'

Mr Yueh indicated yes with a fractional tilt of the chin.

Melville felt his stomach shrink. 'Do you think I could have another drink?' he said.

Sweetwater fetched him one and went back behind the bar. He and Mr Yueh waited in silence.

'It won't be easy smuggling a general out through Hong Kong,' Melville said.

'Impossible,' Sweetwater said. 'He's three thousand miles from there.'

'Oh?'

'Yeah,' Sweetwater said, scratching his scalp. 'The poor fucker's been posted to Tibet.'

There was a long silence

'You know anything about Tibet?' Sweetwater inquired eventually.

Melville gave a helpless laugh. 'Tibet. Let's see. A theocracy with one telephone. We used to have some kind of trade agreement with them. Wool, I believe.' Melville shrugged angrily. 'What would I know about Tibet?'

'I thought maybe your father had been there.'

'He walked all round it but never got inside,' Melville said. 'It was one of his biggest ambitions. To him Tibet was a geographical abstraction – the heart of the world.'

'Well it's sure as hell real to Liu.'

'What's he doing there?'

'Resolving contradictions among the people,' Sweetwater said, coming out from behind the bar. 'Keeping Tibetan asses in line.

Mainly he's there to protect a national minority from imperialist bloodsuckers – that's Indians to you and me. Specifically,' Sweetwater said, fighting with a large black-and-white map, 'he's assigned to HQ Himalayan Command based at Shigatse – here – west of Lhasa, not far from the southern border.'

Melville glanced at the map. The only commonplace item among the tightly packed contours and blank spaces was a notice warning that aircraft straying into the area were in danger of being shot down. He looked up and saw the eyes of the two men on him. His blood froze. He produced and swallowed a laugh. 'You're not kidding, are you?'

Sweetwater stepped back, leaving room for the protest he could see forming on Melville's face.

'Charlie didn't tell me why you wanted to see me,' Melville said to Mr Yueh. 'If he had, believe me I wouldn't be here. I came out of respect for you, Mr Yueh. I made that absolutely clear to Charlie. I suppose I should be flattered to think that I could play a part in this . . . in your activities . . . but honest to God . . .' Melville's voice trailed away. He studied his hands, entwined awkwardly between his knees. 'Mr Yueh,' he said in a barely audible voice, 'I think the best thing would be if we left it right here and I went back to Japan and forgot everything you've told me.'

Conversation stalled. Mr Yueh sat as still as a lizard on a wall. Sweetwater ambled back to the bar, poured himself a large cognac and contemplated it, his elbows on the counter. 'Out of all the people Mr Yueh could have asked,' he said quietly, 'he chose you. I went along with him against my better judgement, as you know, but it gives me no pleasure to find myself proved right.' Sweetwater raised his face. He was no longer smiling. 'This isn't the first time you've let us down, Walter; and far from trying to make amends, you don't even have the courtesy to hear us out. You sit there and tell us' – Sweetwater assumed a mincing tone – 'I think I should go home and forget I ever had this conversation.' Sweetwater drained his glass, pointed it at Melville and sighted over it. 'Fucking right you will.'

'Don't threaten me,' Melville shouted, indignation overriding fear. He was on his feet. 'I warned you at the cabin. I'm not getting messed up in your fantasies.'

'And I saw you light up and go "tilt" when I mentioned the money. Find out how you're going to earn it before you start parading that fine conscience of yours.'

'Keep your money. I don't want it.'

94

'Ssss!' Mr Yueh's upraised hand indicated there might be a middle way. 'I'm disappointed, Water Marvel. Not to speak to a man who can benefit from what you say is to let that man go to waste, but to speak to someone who is incapable of profiting is to waste words. I hope my words will not be wasted.'

'Frankly,' Melville said, subsiding with reluctance, 'Confucius must have had more elevated concerns in mind when he came up with that particular gem.'

Sweetwater, smile back in place, smoothed out the map. 'Let's take a closer look at Liu's problem,' he said. 'The general has a choice of borders to cross, but Bhutan is too far away and the Indian and Sikkim borders are crawling with Chinese agents. That leaves Nepal. Now look here – the main highway west of Shigatse. It forks at Lhaze. One fork goes south into Nepal, but Liu can't go that route because there are check-posts every few miles. The other fork goes way over to the west, and right here, north of Mustang – this bit sticking out into Tibet – it comes within fifty miles of the Nepal border.'

'That's a long way from Shigatse.'

'Liu does a lot of travelling. Garrisons to inspect, bridges and roads to be surveyed. At the beginning of November he's due to visit a new base a few klicks down the road from this town Saga. He'll stay a week to ten days. That's where he makes his break. From there he heads almost due south, aiming to reach the border here, at this pass. It's hardly ever used, so the Chinese don't guard it.'

'To reach it,' Melville said, pointing, 'he has to cross another road.'

'Yeah,' Sweetwater said, peering, 'I guess that's what passes for a road in those parts. Lucky to see one truck a week. He has to cross this river, too. The rest is bad-lands. Mountains and more fucking mountains. Just a heap of scenery.'

'He's going to walk out?'

'Ride.'

'He'll be cutting right across the grain of the country. He'll be lucky to cover ten miles a day.'

'I'd say that was a fair assessment. Five days to reach the border and another two to cross the pass.'

'A whole week,' Melville said, his voice a little drowsy, 'with the entire Chinese army chasing you.'

'If it goes like it should,' Sweetwater said, 'the Reds won't even know what's happened. Far as they're concerned, Liu will have stepped outside for a leak and simply vanished. Even if they do work out he's breaking for the border, they'll assume he's making for Mustang.'

'That's two ifs too many,' Melville said. 'They've got a week to find him. They'll have helicopters swarming over the area.'

'Helicopters can't operate at those altitudes. There may be planes, but that's real bandit country out there. You could lose a division in those mountains.'

'You'll certainly lose a middle-aged Chinese general. He'll never make it on his own.'

Sweetwater laughed, taking this as a sign that Melville was getting into the spirit of things. 'He won't be on his own,' he said.

Melville yawned – a convulsive breath from the pit of his stomach.

'Am I boring you?' Sweetwater inquired.

'Unpleasant intimations,' Melville said. 'You haven't told me what role you've dreamt up for me.'

'Don't worry,' Sweetwater said. 'No one's thinking of sending you into Tibet. The general will be picked up and escorted across the border by Khampas.'

'Khampas?'

'Tibetan guerillas operating out of Nepal. Their main bases are in Mustang, but the Reds have the place locked up and infiltrated, which is why Liu crosses the border further east. South of the pass there's another group. They call themselves the Fortress of Faith. They're the ones who'll bring the general out.'

Melville wished he hadn't had so much to drink. 'Hold it,' he said. 'Why should Tibetan guerillas risk their lives to help a PLA general?'

'Because,' Mr Yueh said, stirring on his chair, 'they are paid by the Kuomintang.'

'Let me fill you in on these people,' Sweetwater said. He paused in the act of striking a declamatory pose. 'You want another drink? No? Okay,' he said, 'Khampas, from Kham, which is Tibet's eastern province. Not all Tibetan guerillas are Khampas, but most Khampas are guerillas. It's in their blood. Off and on they've been fighting the Chinese for centuries, and since the occupation they've been the spearhead of Tibetan resistance. In 1960 about five thousand of them set up a network of bases in Mustang. I say network because although they're damn good fighters, they've never been able to establish an effective centralised command structure. They're too clannish, too easily distracted by internal feuds and personal vendettas.'

'Not a very reassuring proposition for the general, are they?'

'One cause of dissension among the Khampas,' Sweetwater said, ignoring Melville's interruption, 'is funding. Most of them are – or were – supported by American money channelled through the Tibetan government-in-exile in Dharamsala, but a few factions are sponsored by the Kuomintang.'

'Who claim Tibet is Chinese territory, just like the communists.'

'Right. Last year there was fighting between the rival factions, and one group broke from Mustang. Those are our people.'

'Without wishing to seem unduly sceptical,' Melville said, half-nodding, half-bowing at Mr Yueh, who appeared to have fallen asleep, 'they don't sound like anyone's people.'

'They're far and away the best of the bunch,' Sweetwater said. 'Not only are they well-led and well-disciplined, they're absolutely secure. Why do you think the general came to Mr Yueh instead of going direct to the Americans?'

'That was going to be my next question,' Melville said.

'There are three reasons. One,' Sweetwater said, counting with his fingers, 'Mustang is penetrated by Chinese intelligence. Two, the Americans have no direct access to the Khampas. Three, if you look at the map you'll see why. Mustang is at the head of one of the busiest trade routes in Nepal. It's a two-week walk from the border to the nearest road, and because the Nepalese are embarrassed by the presence of anti-Chinese guerillas on their territory, they've got the entire area sealed off by troops. The general would never get through undetected. Now look at our group's position. They have this valley entirely to themselves, and they can get down into the lowlands by any one of half a dozen routes.'

Melville tried to make sense of the map but the contours baffled the eye. 'I don't know,' he said unhappily. 'It's too involved.'

'It's dead simple,' Sweetwater said. 'Second week in November the Khampas cross into Tibet, pick up the general and hightail it back over the border. They hand him over at their camp, then we smuggle him into India in a truck and put him on a plane to Taiwan.'

'Taiwan? You said he wanted to go to America.'

'I did. He does. That's our only problem.'

'Our problem? My God, you have some fucking nerve.'

'Shut up,' Sweetwater said amiably. He pushed his hands into his pockets and stared at his shoes. 'Slice it any way you like,' he said, 'it's a weird situation. Here's a PLA general asking a staunch Nationalist to help him defect to the United States with the help of the Kuomintang-backed freedom fighters he's been sent to Tibet to zap.' Sweetwater raised his head. 'Be clear on one thing, Walter: the Americans know nothing about this operation, and they have no part to play in it. So why should Mr Yueh hand over the general to them? Wouldn't you say that he's entitled to get a little mileage out of Liu?'

'The political repercussions could be appalling.'

'No, they won't. Liu's not some hotshot strategist with the latest order of battle in his pocket. He's an old warhorse who's spent nearly two years locked in the stable. Since then . . . who gives a shit about what's going down in Tibet?'

'The communists do.'

'They're not going to broadcast the fact that one of their heroes has walked out on them.'

'The Nationalists will do it for them.'

'Nothing fancy, Walter. No ticker-tape reception or photo-calls with the Generalissimo. Mr Yueh will get to show off the general in influential circles; the KMT win some face and the commies lose some. That's the nature of the game.'

'Count me out.'

'Look,' Sweetwater said, 'if after a few months Liu still wants to settle in the States, no one's going to stand in his way. The Americans will have to pay, of course. It's only right that Mr Yueh should look for a return on his investment.'

'What you're doing is nothing short of piracy.'

'Private enterprise. Don't knock it. It's one of our cherished freedoms.'

'If your aim is to sell off the general for the highest price, why not do it now? Why not come to an arrangement with the Americans and let them handle the operation?'

'For the same reason that Liu sent Zhang to Mr Yueh's door. The Americans don't have the resources to get a man out of Tibet.'

'Then make it a joint effort.'

'A fuck-up, you mean. Forget it, Walter; we're not going to tell the Americans about the general until he's safe in our hands.' Sweetwater smiled nastily. 'As you might have gathered, my relationship with our countrymen tends towards the irregular.'

'I bet.'

Mr Yueh came alive with a brittle clearing of the throat.

'We have a lot of ground to cover,' Sweetwater said warningly.

'Water Marvel,' Mr Yueh said, 'I want you to deal with the Khampas in Nepal.'

A silence developed. Melville leaned back and shut his eyes. 'Why me?' he said miserably. He struggled upright. 'Why me?' he demanded of Sweetwater. 'You must know dozens of people who are trained to pull a stunt like this.'

'Not with your qualifications,' Sweetwater said. He went back to the bar. 'It has to be an American,' he said. 'When Liu arrives at the guerillas' base he'll expect to be met by a representative of his adoptive country – someone who speaks good Chinese and acts like he bears the stamp of government.'

'There's no need for deceit,' Melville said angrily. 'Tell the general what you intend to do.'

'He may give up the idea,' Sweetwater pointed out.

'Not if he's that desperate to escape,' Melville said.

'Well now,' Sweetwater said, 'Mr Yueh isn't in the business of second-guessing. The general may have strong objections to being flown to Taiwan. The communist old guard is funny like that.'

'But once he reaches Nepal he doesn't have any choice about where he ends up.'

Sweetwater nodded thoughtfully. 'You're right, up to a point,' he said. He frowned. 'Defecting puts a lot of strain on a man. It raises a lot of inner conflict. There's a period when the defector is in a kind of limbo, between worlds. In the case of General Liu, I anticipate that this transitional period will last six days, which is the amount of time it will take to get him from the camp to India. During that time I don't want him to have second thoughts. I don't want him to rush up to the first Nepalese soldier he sees and demand to be taken to the American embassy. No, I think that the right time to tell him is over a martini thirty thousand feet above the Bay of Bengal.'

Melville slumped back. Something rattled in Mr Yueh's throat.

'I think we're trying Mr Yueh's patience,' Sweetwater said.

'I will have that other drink,' Melville said.

'You see,' Sweetwater said, putting a glass into Melville's nerveless hand, 'all we want to do is to make the transition as smooth and painless as possible.'

'You want me to hijack a Chinese communist general.'

'That's one way of putting it.'

'And you'll pay me 20,000 dollars?'

'Affirmative.'

'For a week's work?'

'More like a month all told.' Sweetwater hesitated. 'I'm not going to pretend that it'll be a complete stroll,' he said. 'The Tibetan border's sealed off; foreigners aren't allowed up there. Relations between

Nepal and China are sensitive, so it wouldn't do to strain them by getting caught.'

'I won't do it,' Melville told Mr Yueh. 'I can't do it,' he told Sweetwater.

'Sure you can,' Sweetwater said.

'Quite apart from the moral objections,' Melville said, as if to himself, 'quite apart from the political implications, I'm just . . .' He punched his knee, beyond speech.

'Scared?' Sweetwater inquired. 'Perfectly natural.'

Melville raised haggard eyes. 'Even the thought of it makes me feel sick,' he said. He shook his head as though attempting to banish a foul vision. 'Oh boy.'

Mr Yueh levered himself to his feet. Haltingly, Melville did likewise. Mr Yueh came towards him, hands outstretched as if he intended an embrace, but stopped short and stood fighting for breath.

'Surely you can see I'm not the person you want,' Melville pleaded.

Mr Yueh smiled, showing false teeth. 'Do you remember how the Master answered when he was asked who he would choose for the three armies? He said he would not take a man who would try and fight a tiger with bare hands. He said that the best man to choose was a man who was fearful of failure.'

Mr Yueh pressed his palms together and went out of the door.

'With respect,' Melville muttered, 'screw Confucius.' He slumped onto the couch.

Sweetwater moved briskly to occupy Mr Yueh's chair. 'Well?' he said.

'Well what?' Melville snapped.

Sweetwater sighed, suggesting that his patience was not without limits. 'Zhang goes back Tuesday. I need to know if we have a commitment.'

'You're kidding.'

'Kidding?' Sweetwater straightened up, his eyelids drooping dangerously. 'Walter, this isn't the first time I've noticed your reluctance to get on terms with reality. What is it with you?'

'Students, merchant seamen, the occasional concert musician – they're the kind of people who defect, not heroes of the revolution.'

'Let me get this straight,' Sweetwater said pleasantly. 'Are you saying the general's playing us false?'

'I'm saying there's no precedent.'

'Precedents? The PLA's a fucking export industry. How about Colonel Chang? Paddled over to Quemoy in 'fifty-seven; now he's

100

the KMT's Deputy Chief of Staff. Or what about that cluster of brass who talked their way into Hong Kong a couple of years back? Okay, how about those four lieutenants who hiked out across the Himalayas?'

'Two died en route. That's a piss-poor precedent in my book.'

'They didn't have Mr Yueh's back-up.'

'Some guy, huh?'

'Just a businessman,' Sweetwater said evenly. 'A champion of private enterprise who happens to ply his trade in a corner of the world where the line between commerce and politics gets kind of blurry.' Sweetwater spread his palms about a foot apart. 'Like, Mr Yueh's concerns are represented in a lot of countries where the Nationalists don't have a diplomatic presence. Now, if some honcho in the Bureau of Foreign Policy Coordination wants to establish channels of communication with friends in these places, all he has to do is drop in at the Taipei Rotary after office hours and ask Mr Yueh to extend him the use of his trading network.'

'So the Kuomintang is involved in the operation.'

Sweetwater raised an admonitory finger. 'Ah, I didn't say that. In fact, absolutely not. Mr Yueh has no intention of seeing his general vanish among the paperwork – and take it from me, that's what would happen if those KMT types got to cock their legs on the enterprise. Vanish terminally, I mean. Problem is, the bottom-side of an open-house refugee policy is that you end up with a very porous security outfit.' Sweetwater heaved one thigh across the other. 'No, what I'm saying is that in return for enhancing Nationalist political intelligence, Mr Yueh can call on his compatriots in the military and ask them – discretion guaranteed – for the use of their facilities.'

'Such as a bunch of Tibetan guerillas.'

'Private armies are surprisingly easy to come by in these parts. You'd be amazed.'

Melville shook his head, unable to restrain a sigh at such cynicism.

'Anyway,' Sweetwater said, slapping his knees to discourage further speculation in this area, 'it's not as if Mr Yueh can't lay his hands on the necessary resources.'

Melville checked the door. He leaned closer to Sweetwater. 'Why's he doing it?'

Sweetwater pursed his lips a couple of times. 'Because he's a patriot, I guess. Because he believes that destiny is on the side of Free China. Frankly, I don't know. Maybe he's got political ambitions. Bringing home a commie general wouldn't do him any harm on that front.

You China-watchers are always talking about the coming war of succession on the mainland; you forget that Chiang's likely to fall off his perch before Mao.'

Sweetwater waited at his ease, watching the questions form up behind Melville's eyes.

'And you? Are you part of Mr Yueh's private army?'

Sweetwater smiled with half his mouth. 'I'll let you into a secret, Walter. When I first met him he was only a goddam sergeant – in the Yunnan Anti-Communist Army for National Salvation. I was in Burma to check out how parliamentary democracy was faring after the Brits pulled out. It was a freak show: white communists, red communists, the league of fascist boy scouts – all Buddhist. A very liquid situation. Mr Yueh's outfit was the only one which had its shit together.'

'He was with the Nationalists in Burma?'

'Right.'

'Jesus, what was that name again? The National Salvation Army? That's a pretty terrific title for a pack of bandits, opium smugglers, God knows what else.'

Sweetwater looked thoughtful. With his fingertips he tapped a rhythm on his bottom teeth. Melville ignored the warning. 'Just a sergeant, you said, and now he runs one of the biggest trading empires east of Suez. I'll tell you what I think.'

'Better not,' Sweetwater said. He jerked his head in the direction of the door. 'Far better not. I can see you making unhealthy associations. You hear? Unhealthy.' He smiled to show that he had Walter's best interests at heart.

Melville gnawed his lip and looked away. 'You're absolutely sure you're not government?'

Sweetwater made a rueful smile. 'Someone like me, their contract never really runs out. But no, I'm not on the payroll.'

He crossed his legs with a negligent flourish. 'I got bored living on my salary. After the Indonesia thing, they put me behind a desk. Clean white shirt every day, a monogrammed diary – shit, it was like working for IBM. I trained recruits, shiny young career officers.' Sweetwater's brow wrinkled. 'There was one guy, very smart, very ambitious.' Sweetwater looked blankly at Melville. 'He was a little cocksucker. He had this personal motto stuck on his desk. Know what it said? It said: "You must be proud, bold, pleasant, resolute. And now and then, stab as occasion serves." How about that?' Sweetwater shook his head in indignation. 'I knew the service was no longer for me. I had a lot of friends on the outside – people like Mr

Yueh. I went self-employed.' Sweetwater wriggled with amusement. 'That kid with the motto – the little fuck married his secretary. All those cold war recruits married their secretaries.'

Melville wasn't going to be deflected. 'If you don't have any official rating, how come you were able to contact me through the embassy?'

'An old friend returning favours.' Sweetwater pulled a contrite face and stood up. 'I'm sorry if Hubbard's gotten the idea you're consorting with spooks.' He wandered over to the bar. 'Don't worry. Nothing's going to show in the books.'

'What kind of favours?'

'The odd bon-bon.' Sweetwater gave a lethargic wave. 'Maybe I sent them the material we got in Hong Kong.'

Melville's puzzlement overode his resentment at being branded an accessory. 'Surely they have their own specialists for that kind of thing.'

'They do. Here, have another drink.'

Melville put a protective hand over his glass.

'Then why do they need you?'

'I fill a gap in the market.' Sweetwater propped himself against the bar. 'Look, we've always relied on the Nationalists for our dope on the Reds. I mean, our own penetration of the mainland goes no deeper than a mouse's pecker. Now until a few years ago there was a really close relationship between the intelligence communities in Washington and Taipei. They saw eye to eye on the desirability of harassing the commies.' Sweetwater laughed. 'They'd sit down and dream up all these far-out wheezes – poisoning the rice crop, flooding the Yangtse Basin, sending over balloons packed with plague-carrying rats or maybe just perfume and pantyhose, let the peasants know what they were missing. It's okay, Walter, this was just brainstorming, but enough joint operations were mounted to keep the yoyos on both sides happy.'

Sweetwater looked up sharply. 'You know what my old friends mean when they talk about BC?'

'I'm not interested in their puerile in-jokes.'

'Before Cuba.' Sweetwater shrugged. 'There was before Cuba, and then there was after Cuba. We decided we could no longer countenance the kind of positive action the Nationalists were demanding. They got angry. They started calling in our pledges, but we stopped answering the phone. So naturally they started having doubts about our commitment to Free China. They thought fuck it, why should we go on giving stuff away to these guys – and for free. It got so bad

103

that a KMT agent, if he saw one of our fellows on fire, he wouldn't cross the road to piss on him.' Sweetwater drained his glass. 'And that, Walter, is the way it still is.'

'So Mr Yueh gives you access to Nationalist intelligence which you peddle to the Americans.'

'Like I say, it's important to maintain a mutual exchange of views. Besides, who am I to stand in the way of market forces?' Sweetwater smiled sadly into his glass. 'But I have to confess, it's not really my style.'

'Oh, what would that be?'

Sweetwater transferred the smile to Melville. 'I'm not the dirk and back-alley type you think I am, Walter. I spent ten years in combat zones.' He looked away. 'Nothing epoch-making. Small wars, insurrections, footnotes in history. Yeah,' he said, looking heavenwards, 'if I wrote my life story, that's what I'd call it – An Historian on the Front Line.'

His face remained uplifted, wearing the rapt expression of someone listening to the faint melody of distant bugles. When the echoes died away he lowered his gaze and laughed.

'See your face, Walter. Like I was some kind of ogre. Well, maybe you're right. Ogres, historians – they're both attracted by the smell of blood.'

'You accuse me of being a man without ties,' Melville said cautiously, unsure what degree of affront would cause Sweetwater's good-natured mask to slip, 'but it seems to me that you're the one without allegiances.'

'I've got allegiances alright. I never let a partner down yet. No stabbing as occasion serves.'

He filled Melville's temporarily unguarded glass and raised his own as if in pledge. Melville looked for the smile that Sweetwater deployed when mockery was intended, but the man had assumed a senatorial gravity.

'When this is over, Walter, I'd like it if you came and visited me.' Sweetwater jerked his thumb. 'I live way up north, in a wood-and-bamboo house looking out over blue hills. Morning time, the mist sits in the valley so it's just the village and the clouds, like being on top of the world. I don't have a woman, I don't have children; I live like a fucking monk. But I've got allegiances alright. The kids calls me father and their parents call me uncle. I guess you could say I'm their guardian. It's paradise.' His faraway smile slowly contracted into a

frown. 'Hell no. It's better than paradise.' He moved his face closer.
'The world still beats a path to my door.'

Chapter 8

'Over here.'

Swivelling from the hip like an arthritic gunfighter, Lupus saw a hand with upraised index finger withdrawing below an intervening wall of greenery. On the other side he found Sweetwater sitting alone at a white wrought-iron table, ostentatiously reading a menu.

'I told you,' Sweetwater said, 'I have a plane to catch.' He looked up, a smile loosely tacked in place.

'Fucking traffic,' Lupus said, flopping onto his seat. 'One day this town's going to lock up solid.' He unfolded his starched napkin and wiped his glistening upper lip.

'I hope you like fish,' Sweetwater said, sliding the menu across.

Lupus glanced at it. 'I'm not all that hungry,' he said. 'What are you having?'

'I recommend the catfish,' Sweetwater said.

'Fine by me,' Lupus said. 'Just as long as it doesn't come with them rat shit chilies.'

'Beer?'

'Not for me,' Lupus said, patting his belly.

Sweetwater ordered in Thai. The waitress shimmied away on stilt heels, her buttocks massaging each other under her tight black skirt. Lupus' gaze wandered over the ornamental hedges, the vine-draped pergolas, the gilded spirit houses, and finally settled back on Sweetwater. 'This is nice,' he said. He rubbed his hands. 'Charlie, I have to say you're looking good.'

'I've become a student of Confucius,' Sweetwater said. 'Everything in its place, nothing taken to excess. It makes for a very tranquil outlook.' He was staring at Lupus. 'You should give it a try.'

'Even this guy Confucius would be lathered up after driving across town without air-conditioning in one hundred fucking degrees of humidity.' Lupus dabbed his forehead with his napkin.

'That reminds me,' Sweetwater said, 'how's the travel business?'

'Oh, you know. Up and down.' Lupus gave an empty laugh.

'Down is what I heard,' Sweetwater said.

'A temporary low,' Lupus said, running his hand inside his shirt collar. 'That's tourism for you.'

'Sure. Peaks and troughs. And you're six feet under.'

'What is this?' Lupus demanded. 'You bring me here to dance on my grave? I had a deal go wrong on me, that's all.'

'By the name of Chuang,' Sweetwater said.

Lupus crumpled his napkin and said nothing.

'I heard,' Sweetwater said, enunciating with care, 'that Chuang went and dissolved your partnership.'

'Keep your voice down,' Lupus said, his eyes darting from side to side.

'How bad is it?' Sweetwater asked, leaning forward.

'Not too good,' Lupus mumbled.

'He cleaned you out?'

Lupus examined his smeared napkin. The ridge of scar tissue along his jaw glowed redder than his hair. 'Down to the last fucking envelope,' he said at last. 'I've got six months' rent owing on the office. The airline's not been paid for the last tour. One of the hotels has been sending round a guy who looks like he goes down holes after small animals.'

Sweetwater tut-tutted sympathetically. 'The sharks in this town have three rows of teeth.' He leaned back and frowned at Lupus. 'What are you going to do?'

'If it takes me the rest of my days,' Lupus said, kneading his napkin, 'I'm going to find that scumbag and nail his balls to a pole.'

'Be realistic,' Sweetwater said. 'He'll be in Jakarta or Singapore by now.'

'Doesn't matter. I'll catch up with him.' Lupus threw his ruined napkin on the table. 'You know my record, Charlie.'

'Eleven targets, eleven hits.'

'Twelve.'

'Happy days,' Sweetwater said. 'But that was Korea.' He sipped beer from a bedewed glass. 'What are you doing to do?' he asked again.

Before Lupus could answer, the fish arrived. They were large and spiny.

'I don't mind telling you,' Lupus said, his eyes on the coagulated gaze staring up from his plate, 'I've been doing a lot of praying.'

'Are you sure that's enough?' Sweetwater inquired, squeezing a wedge of lime over his fish.

'I believe in just deserts,' Lupus said, his expression suddenly fervent. 'Good or bad, everybody gets what's coming to them.'

'I admire a man who can take the long view,' Sweetwater said, dissecting his fish along its lateral line, 'but how are you going to resolve present difficulties?'

Lupus thought for a few seconds. 'Leave town, I guess.'

Sweetwater nodded. He carefully prised a fillet away from the bone and impaled a piece on his fork. He raised the fork to his mouth, then paused. 'I might have something for you,' he said.

'By all accounts,' Lupus said hesitantly, 'you've become a pretty wild hombre. The last I heard, you were living up by the Burmese border, and I know what kind of activity goes on up there. I don't need that kind of trouble.'

'I resent your implication,' Sweetwater said, popping food into his mouth. 'Besides, I'd never involve you in dope. Every man to his trade.'

'Tourism's my trade.'

'Five minutes ago you were telling me about your career as a sharp-shooter.' Sweetwater took a folded sheet of notepaper from his shirt pocket and pushed it across. 'Weapons are your trade,' he said.

Lupus opened out the sheet and smoothed it flat. He scrutinised it as though it contained invisible writing. 'Christ,' he said.

'Can you supply?' Sweetwater asked.

'I don't know,' Lupus said, mopping the back of his neck. 'I mean, I don't know what to think. What do you want them for?'

'Export,' Sweetwater said, chewing.

Lupus took another look at the list. 'Christ,' he said again. 'Sixty M–16s, four 3-inch mortars, three M–60s.' He raised an anxious face. 'That is very heavy shit, Charlie. That's what they use on gunships. You can't dump a shopping list like this on me and not tell me who your clients are.'

'Just give me a yes or no in principle,' Sweetwater said, pointing his fork at the list.

'No,' Lupus said, 'not unless you tell me who and why.'

Sweetwater stared at him, his mouth full of food, his fork still pointing. Finally he resumed chewing. 'I recall you telling me you worked with the NVDA,' he said.

'NVDA, NVDA,' Lupus repeated worriedly. 'Give me a minute, will you? There were so many sets of initials.'

'National Volunteer Defence Army,' Sweetwater said, not prepared to wait. 'Tibetans.'

'Oh right,' Lupus said, his face brightening. It quickly dimmed. 'Tibetans?'

'Since I'm the one who's buying lunch,' Sweetwater said, 'it's me who gets to ask the questions.'

'I'm puzzled, that's all. I thought the NVDA was history.'

'Tell me.'

'Well,' Lupus said, prodding his fish with his knife, 'in 1958 – I'm pretty sure it was then – the gooks took over in Lhasa and the Dalai Lama . . .'

'Not the history,' Sweetwater said, waving his fork. 'Your own personal involvement. I understand you were an instructor at Camp Hale.'

'What happened,' Lupus began cautiously, 'is that there were all these Tibetan refugees who wanted to go back and fight the gooks. The Indians recruited some, the Kuomintang took some, and we shipped a few groups over to Colorado for training – weapons, radio, parachuting.' Lupus laughed with genuine pleasure. 'They were good, them Tibetans. They could pick up a Springfield and hit things most people couldn't see. They were good as me.'

'And you were the best,' Sweetwater said. He frowned. 'How did you get along with them?'

'I liked them fine,' Lupus said. 'They weren't the usual little brown people. They were big, tough bastards, but always smiling with it. They were Buddhist, right? Which means they weren't supposed to kill. Well, I never noticed any problems in that area. The ones I trained, they were people like you and me.'

'You saw them in action?'

'Not exactly,' Lupus said. 'The first time I visited this town, it was to arrange an arms drop for some NVDA people I'd helped train. This was back in '61.' Lupus scowled. 'It was a total fuck-up.'

'How's that?'

'Sending half a dozen barbarian longhairs to liberate a country as big as Europe? That has to be the crappiest enterprise ever,' Lupus sawed at his fish. 'There was a revolt planned for Lhasa,' he said, 'and an NVDA team was parachuted in to give it a bit of bite. They were supposed to radio when they got to Lhasa, and then we were going to drop them weapons. We waited six weeks and never heard a thing. Maybe they fell on a mountain; maybe their radios were no good; maybe they were picked up. We never heard what happened to them.'

'So they didn't get the weapons.'

'There was no point.'

'And after that?'

'After that I quit. They wanted me to train up an anti-Sukarno outfit in Indonesia.'

'But instead you went back to Bangkok. It must have been love at first sight.'

'It was a nice town then,' Lupus said defensively. 'No hippies, no sex tours.'

'Well,' Sweetwater said, arranging his knife and fork on his plate, 'now's your chance to make amends.'

'Amends?'

'Help me get the items on that list.'

'Charlie, tell me why the fuck you're running around with Tibetans. I mean, is it official business or what?'

'It's my own business,' Sweetwater said, dabbing his lips.

'What can I say, Charlie? Where's the basis for discussion? You haven't given me a price. I don't know where and how you want them delivered.'

'You deliver to me at the market rate,' Sweetwater said. 'All you have to do is come up with the source and handle the negotiations that end.'

'The pointed end,' Lupus said.

Sweetwater sighed and pondered for a few seconds. 'Have you heard of Mr Yueh?' he asked.

'He's got quite a reputation in Bangkok,' Lupus muttered.

'All over. Taipei, Hong Kong.' Sweetwater paused. 'Jakarta, Singapore.'

Lupus stiffened as the implication sank in. 'You saying you'll give me Chuang if I deliver the weapons.'

'Think of it as a bonus.'

Lupus pinched the bridge of his nose and laughed. 'I don't get it,' he said. 'I know you're close to the Nationalists, and if half what I hear about Mr Yueh is true . . .' He took a deep breath '. . . I don't see why you need me.'

'Old times' sake,' Sweetwater said. 'As soon as I started talking with the Tibetans, your name popped into my mind.'

'They're in town?' Lupus asked. 'Here?'

'Until the beginning of next week. I have to finalise the deal by then, and I'll be out of the country for the next couple of days – so . . .' Sweetwater indicated the list, '. . . yes or no?'

Lupus slumped back on his seat. A flight of swifts pushed close to the ground by the weight of impending rain slit the air with their thin squeals.

'I know this colonel,' Lupus said.

'Ah,' Sweetwater said, relaxing, 'where would we be without the colonels?'

'I met him ten-pin bowling. He works at a supply depot out by Chachoengsa. Since the Cambodian invasion they've been transiting one C–130 full of hardware a week.'

'Greedy?'

'The usual rear-echelon fatso. He plays dice and loses.'

'Start at eighty bucks apiece for the M–16s, whatever you think is right for the big stuff.' Sweetwater tossed a roll of money on the table. 'There's five hundred to buy him lunch. Two grand for you on delivery. Don't forget the ammunition. I know it's pushing it, but try to reach an arrangement by Thursday evening. That's when I have to talk to the Tibetans again. I'd like you to be there.'

'Do I have to?'

''Course you do. Dealing with an ex-instructor, they'll know the stuff has to be good.'

The waitress was hovering.

'You haven't touched your fish,' Sweetwater pointed out.

'It's too much,' Lupus said.

'Have a dessert.'

'You go ahead.'

Sweetwater ordered, then said: 'Did you run across an NVDA man called Yonden at Camp Hale? He was a radio operator.'

'Mostly I dealt with the ones who could shoot straight.'

'He's interpreting for the honcho I'm dealing with,' Sweetwater said. 'He speaks goodish English. He picked it up from a missionary – name of Alan Gunn. Mean anything to you? Well it did to me. Gunn was picked up by the Chinese in Tibet and spent four years in a camp. Yonden joined the guerillas. When he told me about Gunn, I checked him out and found he was alive and living in Scotland.'

'Quite a coincidence.'

'God works in mysterious ways.'

'So do you, Charlie.'

'I thought it would be nice to bring them together again. I've invited Gunn over. Unfortunately he flies in tomorrow, and I was wondering if you could call him up and bring him along to the reunion.' Sweetwater was writing in a notebook. 'Here's where he's staying, here's where you take him. Eight o'clock, Thursday. I'll join you back of nine.' Sweetwater handed over the addresses, his expression grave. 'Don't mention the weapons. Gunn's a civilian.'

'So am I,' Lupus said, casting an unhappy eye at the note. 'Won't you tell me what it's all about?'

'Definitely not,' Sweetwater said. 'Like it or leave it.'

The waitress arrived back, carrying Sweetwater's dessert at arms' length. It was a *durian* – a lozenge-shaped fruit with diabolical spikes, split in half.

'Jesus Christ almighty,' Lupus said, shoving his chair back from the table, 'no one eats those things.'

'Why not?' Sweetwater said, spoon poised.

'It stinks worse than anything I know . . . like a blocked drain . . . like dead meat.'

Sweetwater gave Lupus a tolerant smile. 'An acquired taste,' he said.

Lupus hurried crab-wise through the afternoon strollers, touching their shoulders and grimacing to convey the urgency of his mission. He came to an intersection and halted, anxiously bouncing up and down on the balls of his feet. In a cage opposite, a gibbon sat masturbating, teeth bared at a silent audience of schoolchildren. 'Hey,' Lupus yelled at their teacher, 'where have they hidden the elephants? Yeah, you. El-e-phants. Ah, shit,' Lupus said, and set off again. After a few yards he turned. 'Letting kids see that kind of thing. It's disgusting.'

A little later Lupus thought he had spotted his man, rounding a corner up ahead by the rhino pen. He pursued at a steady clip, slowing when he was a few yards off and creeping up until he was just behind. 'Alan Gunn?' The man turned, his face a question mark, and Lupus backed off, hands raised, smiling. 'Thought you were an old buddy.' The man smiled back, his hand automatically going to his wallet pocket, and walked away. 'Hey,' Lupus called after him, 'what have they done with the fucking elephants?' The man braced his back and accelerated.

Walking with less purpose now, Lupus went in the opposite direction until he reached an unpeopled part of the zoo overhung with trees and creepers. He paused irresolutely, buds of sweat on his brow. With all this growth and the animal sounds and smells it was like being in the jungle. A butterfly as big as a banknote fluttered onto his bare arm. He swatted it and looked with disgust at the mustard-coloured shit left on his skin. He hated the tropics – the indiscriminate lushness, the promiscuous growth, the way nature came creeping and crawling right into your house. Overnight, a pool of rainwater would turn into slime soup, plant a stick and three weeks later it would have grown into a hedge, switch on a light and bloodless lizards skittered away and squeezed into cracks. These latitudes were a breeding ground. It was time he pulled out. Australia, maybe. He imagined it as a big, clean island in an ocean encircled by gooks with patient mouths and chisel eyes.

Thinking of the attrition of his life's savings at the hands of the embezzler Chuang, Lupus groaned. He allowed himself a brief but heady daydream of the vengeance he would wreak when this job was over. Colonel Vichien had expressed a guarded interest in doing a deal, so that was alright. Now, Lupus thought, all I have to do is find this Gunn character. He checked his watch and experienced a swoop of alarm. It was after five. If Gunn didn't show, he'd have no choice but to try the hotel and arrange to meet in a bar. Once more he was diverted by a rush of rage for his dirt-ball of a partner. Out of all the hotels in town, Charlie had booked Gunn into the one that was threatening to fix his ass if he didn't settle forthwith an Australian tour party's bed and breakfast bill, plus breakages.

He decided to go wait by the gate until closing time. It crossed his mind that Gunn must be the only visitor to Bangkok who'd spent his first day mooching about the city zoo. The crowd was beginning to thin, but there were still a few idlers leaning on the parapets of a bridge over the lake, throwing bread to a stew of huge carp with armoured skin and little round mouths that sucked in the doughballs as though they were shelled eggs. Watching them made Lupus squeamish in a way he didn't care to examine.

Turning away, he saw Gunn immediately. No mistaking him – guy on the other side, dressed too warm for the weather, smiling stiffly at two soldiers in sloppy fatigues who were about to roll him. Lupus waited a moment, getting the measure of the man. He was about his own age and size – not big, but with those heavy arms and shoulders. By rights he should have been able to take those punks and jam their heads up their asses, but you could tell he wouldn't. Lupus' heart brimmed at the prospect of righting a wrong.

He walked over and clapped a hand on each soldier's shoulder, not looking at them, nor at Gunn, but smiling at the space between. 'Say, good buddies,' he said, 'mind if I join the party?' He adjusted his grip, caught Gunn's eye with a smile of welcome, and held it as he exerted pressure of nerve against bone. When the soldiers' knees folded and their mouths began to flutter, he cast them loose with a little flourish. They staggered back a few paces, clutching their shoulders, and Lupus smiled the smile of one who has achieved righteous ends by pure main force.

'Are you the gentleman who telephoned?' Gunn asked in alarm.

Lupus wrenched his gaze away from the retreating soldiers. 'Yes sir, I certainly am.'

'I'm afraid I didn't catch your name,' Gunn said.

Lupus told him. 'Say,' he said, 'a zoo without any elephants. How about that?'

'A keeper told me they were in the forest, working.'

'Working?'

'Pulling logs. It's like a holiday for them.'

'No shit?' Lupus marvelled.

'Perhaps,' Gunn said apologetically, 'it might have been easier to meet at the hotel.'

Lupus looked startled. 'You like the place?'

'It's very comfortable, thank you. The staff are very friendly . . . but some of them . . . they're always pestering . . . you know . . . I find it very embarrassing.'

'Alan, I know what you mean,' Lupus said firmly, 'and that's why I thought the zoo, out in the open, away from all that sex, sex, sex.'

'Are you a friend of Yonden's?' Gunn asked. 'I'm a little confused.'

Lupus considered for a moment. 'I've heard a lot about him from Charlie. Charlie and me go back a lot of years together.'

'I rather hoped Yonden would be with you,' Gunn said, looking about unhappily. 'Can we go and see him now?'

'The cab's right outside,' Lupus said. What a jerk, he thought, not unkindly. He looks like he doesn't know in from out. And that jacket. Tweed, for chrissake. Muggers would flock to him like flies to shit. I could take him over to Kenny's place, he thought, fit him out with a couple of lightweight safaris.

'How is he?' Gunn asked, as they began walking.

'Yonden? He's great, just great – really looking forward to seeing you again. What is it – nearly twenty years? I bet you nearly died when you heard he was still alive.'

'I expect I'll hardly recognise him,' Gunn said. He bit his lip. 'I don't know what to expect.'

Lupus chuckled fondly. 'Old Yonden hasn't changed.'

'He didn't say much in his letter. Neither did Mr Sweetwater.'

'Charlie was never much of a letter-writer,' Lupus said, and laughed to show what an incorrigible fellow his friend was. 'With all those

114

years to catch up on, I guess he thought it would be best to wait until we were all together again.'

'I'm sorry,' Gunn said, his face swept by sudden panic, 'I didn't mean to sound critical. I can't thank Mr Sweetwater enough – you too, Mr Lupus – for what you've done. Of course I'll repay the air fare and the money.'

'Don't even think about it,' Lupus said. 'Yonden's a valuable client, so when Charlie found out about you he thought it would be a nice gesture – a gesture of good will – to fly you out.'

'Yonden mentioned he was in business here. He didn't say what kind.'

Lupus laughed recklessly. 'You've got me there, Alan. Charlie didn't tell me either. He was in too much of a hurry to catch his plane. That's Charlie for you – always moving too fast to get a fix on.' Lupus gave Gunn a gingery smile. 'Kind of a mystery trip, huh?'

'I came to see Yonden,' Gunn said.

'Sure you did,' Lupus said. He cleared his throat. 'For he was dead, and is alive again. He was lost, and now is found.' Lupus cocked an eye skyward. Darkness was coming down. 'We'd best get a move on,' he said, 'else they'll lock us in for the night.'

The cab was gone. Lupus, his face an angry weather system, stared at the empty space and gave it a kick. 'You won't see another cab out here tonight,' he said.

'Isn't that one?' Gunn said, pointing tentatively up the road.

Lupus strode off, but when the driver saw him coming he wound up the windows, rested both hands on the wheel and stared into the remote distance. Lupus pounded on the roof, so incensed that he failed to see another cab approach from the opposite direction and glide to a stop by Gunn.

The driver beamed. 'Hey, you want nice fun?'

Gunn pretended not to hear. 'I'm with a friend,' he said.

'No problem. I know lots of good places for you.'

Gunn called feebly to Lupus, who was trying to pull a door off the other cab. He called again, more loudly, and Lupus trudged back, shaking his head at the world's slide into anarchy. He pushed Gunn into the car, squeezed in behind and shoved the address at the driver, who barely glanced at it before driving off.

They composed themselves in the meaty smell of their sweat. Lupus' failure with the cab had unsettled him, brought his doubts to a simmer. What in the name of fuck was Charlie doing selling guns

115

to the Tibetans? Charlie didn't get involved in lost causes. Lupus abandoned himself to speculation, but soon conceded defeat. You never could tell with Charlie – not until all the loose ends were in and he tied them together and looked at you with that smile which told you he'd been playing a different game from the one you'd imagined.

He took a sideways look at Gunn. Four years caged up by the gooks, Charlie had said. It showed. He'd seen that not-at-home look on quite a few guys who'd got caught in Korea. He felt a protective urge. A civilian, Charlie had said. Alright, Lupus decided, but I'll stay close enough to see that he doesn't land in deep shit.

The resolve soothed him. His breathing settled down.

'We get a lot of Tibetans through Bangkok,' he said. 'They're the Jews of Asia – getting into everywhere and everything. Mostly small-scale, though – tourist junk, souvenirs, that kind of stuff. What they do is, they buy maybe some Tibetan carpets and sell them in Delhi, then put the money into, say cutlery, which they trade in Bangkok for perfume. They sell the perfume in Hong Kong and with the profit they buy transistor radios, jeans, plastic shoes, and sell them for about a thousand per cent profit to the peasants back home. Then they buy another load of carpets and start all over again.'

'That doesn't sound like Yonden,' Gunn said.

'No?' Lupus said vaguely. He was hearing an echo of something he'd said. 'I got it,' he said. 'I remember Charlie telling me one time about dealing in musk. You know what musk is? They use it in perfume. They get it from a deer that lives in the Himalayas. It grows in pods on the belly, but only the males have them. You get maybe an ounce, an ounce and a half from each pod, but do you know how much one of those pods is worth? Go on, take a guess.'

'I haven't got a clue.'

'Hundred, hundred and fifty dollars, Charlie said. And that's before the middlemen get hold of it. It's like heroin. The dealers cut it, mix it with dried blood, dirt, all kinds of things, then move it on for five hundred dollars an ounce. By the time it reaches the end of the line, one of those pods is worth . . . God knows, a fortune.'

'I suppose that's why perfume is so expensive,' Gunn said.

Lupus looked for irony. Not finding any, he continued. 'Only problem is,' he said, 'the market is controlled by the Chinese, and they don't like hustlers getting in on the act. Charlie could do it, though. He knows a lot of big wheels in the Chinese community.'

'He sounds a very enterprising man,' Gunn said.

116

'Always where the action is,' Lupus agreed. 'I handle a lot of his transport arrangements and I never know what he's going to hit me with. This time it could be musk, last time it was . . . machine parts.'

Lupus suddenly found the subject taxing. Gunn wasn't paying attention anyway. His mouth was open, his forehead greasy with sweat. He looked to be on the verge of passing out.

'Pardon me,' Lupus said, 'you'd feel a whole lot more comfortable if you had proper clothes. I'd be happy to introduce you to my tailor.'

'I won't be staying long enough to make it worthwhile,' Gunn said. 'Thank you,' he added, too late.

'How long?' Lupus demanded.

'I'm not sure,' Gunn said, plucking at his knee. 'Probably a few days.'

'A few days, a few hours – it doesn't matter. If I took you round to see Kenny right this moment, he'd've run you up three suits like this one by breakfast.'

'Isn't that awfully expensive?'

'You kidding? This is the Third World. Kenny'll fit you out in full evening rig in silk for twenty dollars. We'll go tomorrow,' Lupus said with finality.

With just as much determination, Gunn shook his head. 'If possible, I'd like to spend tomorrow with Yonden.'

'Bring him along,' Lupus said. 'We'll make a day of it.'

'It's really very kind of you,' Gunn said, with a desperate smile. 'I need to spend some time alone with Yonden. We have a lot to talk about.'

Lupus breathed a sigh of resignation. 'Have it your way,' he said. 'You want to smell like a wet dog, that's perfectly okay by me.'

He looked about with a tight smile that vanished as through the windshield he saw faces bright with booze in the intermittent flicker of neon.

'Hey creep,' he shouted, snapping upright with the sound of bare skin peeling away from hot vinyl, 'where the fuck do you think you're going. We should be the other side of the river.'

Crouched over his wheel, just out of reach of Lupus' hands, the driver accelerated, keeping one eye on the road, the other on his irate passenger. He spun the wheel right, hard enough to send Gunn sliding into Lupus. They went down a ramp between buildings and slammed to a halt in an underground garage.

'You're gonna die for this,' Lupus yelled, pushing Gunn off him

117

and grasping for the driver, who flat-handed his door open and went through it without touching the sides.

'You like this place for sure,' he promised over his shoulder.

'Think we're some fucking tourists looking to dip our pricks in gook poontang?' Lupus roared, wrenching his door handle the wrong way.

By the time he had fought his way out, the driver was peeping between two thin, concerned-looking Chinese boys who rocked up on their toes and slapped their right hands to their waistbands in an unmistakably martial gesture.

'Give me him,' Lupus pleaded, his trembling hand outstretched towards the driver, whose smile, a permanent fixture, registered resentment more than fear.

'Are we there?' Gunn asked from inside the car.

Lupus put his hands on his knees and gave a single sob of laughter. He whirled on Gunn, his face boiled by frustration. 'Don't you know anything?' he shouted. 'We're in a whorehouse. Upstairs they've got big glass tanks with women in them who rub this grease all over and then lie down on you and squirm like snakes until . . .'

'Tell them we're not interested,' Gunn said. 'We'll be late if we don't look out.'

Lupus eyed him with astonishment for a moment. He staggered back to the car and slapped his hands down on the roof. 'Oh my,' he giggled. 'Tell them we're not interested. Alan, you're the naïvest man I met. You're wetter than I thought was possible.'

He straightened up, his expression going from benign contempt to consternation as Gunn got out of the car.

'Waddya doing? They've got blades.'

Haltingly, but with force, Gunn addressed the Chinese. They showed even more concern. They showed anger. They cuffed the grinning driver and then bowed and shook Gunn's hand. One of them offered him a cigarette. At their insistence the driver climbed back into his seat. As a gesture of appeasement he only partly ducked the blow that Lupus threw at him. It wasn't enough. Lupus felt humiliated.

'Now you know what this town runs on,' he said, as they drove back up the ramp.

'Every town's got brothels,' Gunn said shortly.

'Here's me thinking you couldn't find your way round the block,' Lupus said, 'and all the time you can speak Chinese. I guess you must have learned it in that camp Charlie was telling me about.'

'Keep your eyes on the road,' Gunn told the driver, whose attention was divided between the rear-view mirror and the address prominently propped on the dash.

Fuck it, Lupus thought. He spent the rest of the journey whistling morosely through his teeth.

The driver halted in an anonymous, low-rent district of family apartments with washing hanging from the windows. Lupus made him kill the engine. Noises leaked from the buildings – children's voices, the rattle of crockery, televised laughter. Lupus was seized by an inchoate suspicion.

'You'd think Charlie could have picked some place more in keeping with the occasion,' he said.

'We're late,' Gunn said, opening his door.

Lupus stopped him with a hand on his arm. 'You sure Charlie didn't tell you what it's about?'

'How many times do I have to tell you. I'm here to see Yonden.'

'Yeah,' Lupus said vaguely, scanning the dark street. The address they wanted was set back in an even darker courtyard. 'Listen,' he said, 'Charlie will burn my ass if he hears me talking like this, but I reckon you got a right to know what you're getting yourself into. Charlie's an entertaining fellow alright, but he isn't what you'd call overflowing with the milk of human kindness. He hasn't flown you round the world because it warms his heart to see you reunited with your Tibetan friend. Know what I mean?'

'You said it had something to do with his business activities.'

'Has to be – only, nothing that Charlie ever dealt in made the Dow Jones average.'

'Like musk?'

'Forget musk. Musk is bullshit.' Lupus considered telling Gunn about the arms, an impulse immediately displaced by a clear-cut picture of himself floating face down in a *klong*. 'All I'll tell you is this,' he said. 'Charlie's an operator. He jerks strings. He makes people dance. So if you want my advice, you'll go in there, say hello to your friend, have a few beers and talk about old times, and then get the hell out of town.'

'But you told me you were his friend. You said you worked for him.'

'From time to time, when I need the bread. Like now. Besides, I'm big and ugly enough to take care of myself.'

'Nothing you say makes sense. You work for Mr Sweetwater, but you don't know what kind of business he's involved in. Are you implying he's a criminal? Is Yonden in trouble?'

119

'I've said enough.'

'Enough to scare me.'

'Don't tell Charlie that,' Lupus said. He studied Gunn's troubled face. 'Ah hell,' he said, 'I don't want to spoil the occasion. What the hell. Charlie's probably got it in mind to offer you a consultancy.'

They went into the yard. It was overlooked on all sides by buildings, and one corner was occupied by a couple of beat-up trucks and a squadron of pedlars' bicycle carts. 'Over there,' Lupus said, setting off towards a modern block on the far side. At the entrance a group of men was playing a gambling game, throwing dice down with explosive cries. Their faces were broad and big-boned.

'Tibetans?' Lupus asked.

Gunn questioned them. 'Manangbas,' he told Lupus. 'From Nepal.'

'I know about them,' Lupus said. 'Gypsies.'

A man with expressionless Mediterranean features appeared in the open doorway and studied them. Gunn spoke to him in Tibetan. He said something and went away.

'He says to come in and wait,' Gunn explained.

They picked their way through the gamblers, who leaned aside lazily and looked up at them with leery grins. In the entrance hall, at the foot of a staircase, a woman was nursing a baby in a chair under an oleograph of the Dalai Lama. The building had the intense shabbiness of the new and gimcrack. In the eye-straining wattage of bald light bulbs, Lupus observed the ulcers on the plaster, the cracks meandering across the ceiling. Judging by the roar of portable stoves and the babel of radio programmes, it was heavily tenanted.

'What a dump,' Lupus said.

Down the stairs came the door-keeper. With no adjustment of expression he indicated that they should go to the top of the building. Lupus' chest tightened. The man was looking at him, not Gunn.

'You'd better not be shitting us,' he said, brushing past. He felt the door-keeper's eyes on him all the way up the first flight.

They laboured upwards. All the doors were open and each room was filled with transients. 'Crummy company your friend keeps,' Lupus said.

They were panting by the time they reached the top landing, where two men the wrong shape and size for their suits were waiting outside a closed door.

Gunn turned to Lupus. 'I don't want to seem rude,' he pleaded, 'but it's important that I speak to Yonden in private.'

120

'I was kind of looking forward to meeting him,' Lupus said. 'You don't know it, but in a way he's part of my history too.'

'Later,' Gunn said, 'when Mr Sweetwater gets here. Please.'

He looks, Lupus thought, as tightly wound as a man about to go into court for sentencing. 'Never come between buddies,' he said. 'You go on in there, and if I don't see you later I'll call you tomorrow. Besides,' he added, 'I've got my own appointment with the top man.'

One of the men opened the door at the full stretch of his arm and ushered Gunn through, keeping his eye on Lupus. He closed the door quietly and stood in front of it. He and his companion were considerably bigger men than the conscripts in the zoo, with honed faces that bespoke hard condition. Lupus smiled at each of them, unpleasantly conscious of the fact that Charlie wasn't due for another hour. 'Which one of you charmers is going to take me to your leader?' he asked.

They each seized him by the arm. He looked at their hands as if he were trying to work out a puzzle. 'Take your hands off me,' he said quietly, not looking up, beginning to pit his strength against theirs. Their grip tightened. 'I said take your fucking hands off me you slope-eyed fucks,' he shouted, struggling wildly. One of the men grabbed him round the neck. 'You think this is the way to do business? You think I'll get you the goods after this?'

He did not finish what he was going to say because one of the Tibetans jammed a plated .45 Colt automatic against his upper lip and placed a warning finger to his own. 'Motherfucker,' Lupus mumbled. 'Oh you motherfucker.'

He went limp and the Tibetan, still cautioning silence, released him. He tried to feel contempt for the sloppy way the man was pointing the gun. He nodded determinedly. 'My man,' he said, 'you are going to be number thirteen. Oh yes. You'd better believe it.'

The man waved him away. Hands uplifted, he complied, memorising the man's face, imagining seeing it through cross-hairs. The men matched his first backward step. 'No need to see me out, boys,' he said in a tremulous voice.

At the bottom of the first flight he turned to find them gone. He stared blindly at the wall, letting the tide of rage flood through him. When it subsided, he became aware that a change had occurred around him. He raised his head, listening. It was as if the building had been evacuated, as if it was holding its breath. He let his own go and started down the stairs, placing his feet sideways and pausing on each one in the hope of surprising a sound.

The tenants had shut themselves in their rooms. He went down three flights before he came to a door that was ajar. A bar of light showed in the opening. As he crept past, he heard a metallic rasp that he had no wish to investigate. As he stepped onto the next flight, someone said his name.

'Is that you, Charlie?' he whispered.

The grating sound came again, familiar but not from a gun. He knew all the sounds a gun makes. 'So help me, Charlie, if you're jerking my chain I won't forgive or forget.'

Silence. Anger returned. He'd done nothing to be scared of. He had the guns for fuck's sake. Who else could obtain a pledge of that kind of weaponry inside two days? Alan Gunn must have asked those meatheads to make sure he and his Tibetan friend weren't disturbed.

Swallowing the lump in his throat, he tip-toed forward and pushed open the door in a slow, controlled movement. The only light came from a fly-specked bulb above the door; the other side of the room was indistinct. A man was sitting there, at an empty table, juggling a bright object from hand to hand. The movement stopped. There was a flinty sound. A Zippo for fuck's sake, Lupus realised, and let the air rush from his lungs. The Zippo caught, sending shadows leaping up the walls and outlining the man's flared cheekbones.

He lit a cigarette, inhaled coarsely and placed the Zippo on the table, batting it back and forth between his hands like a kitten playing with a mouse. Lupus was reminded of the posture of one of his commanding officers when dealing with miscreants.

He advanced a couple of steps, stooping to see better. 'I know you,' he whispered.

The man took another drag, pulling on the cigarette until the tip glowed cherry red, then stood up. He was tall, a head taller than Lupus, with jet-black hair roughly cropped. His face was all planes and hollows. It was the damnedest thing, but Lupus couldn't remember his name. Fear had pushed it out of reach.

The man walked round to the other side of the table. In the attenuated light his eyes were golden as a wolf's.

'I thought you were dead,' Lupus whispered.

The man made no answer. Lupus wished to hell he could remember his name.

'How did you get out? What happened?'

The man looked at his cigarette.

'Did you make it to Lhasa? That pilot . . . Know what happened a couple of months after he dropped you? He flew into a fucking

122

mountain. Visibility fifty miles and he flew into a mountain. He was out of his skull . . . Remember him . . . ? Czech fellow . . . What was his name?'

The black-haired man with the yellow eyes listened patiently. He blew a stream of smoke and watched it coil upwards. Lupus decided that it was vitally important he remembered his name before he finished his cigarette. It was right there on the tip of his tongue.

'How about the rest of the team? They didn't get out. Ah, that's too bad. We waited, you know. We waited six weeks but you never called. It was those radios, right? I told them they were crap.'

The man dropped his cigarette and ground it out. He looked up with a slight frown and conjured a knife from his coat.

'Osher!' Lupus said, holding out his palms. The relief of remembering made him dizzy. 'If anyone was going to get out, it had to be you. Shit, I don't mind saying it, you were something special. Remember when you took fifty bucks off that prick Warren the time he bet you couldn't shoot a perfect score.'

'Guns,' Osher said.

'Guns?' Lupus queried. He tried to smile, but one side of his mouth was frozen.

'Guns.'

'Oh guns, right. I got 'em. Everything Charlie asked for except maybe the M–60s. There's a problem there about smuggling them off base. No sweat. We'll crack it.'

'Guns,' Osher said.

'I told you, it's fixed.' Irritation overrode his fear. 'Listen, why don't we wait until Charlie gets here.'

'I am here,' Sweetwater said behind him. He sighed. 'You've got your wires crossed, Lupus. Osher's talking about long-ago days. He's asking about the consignment you failed to deliver, the guns you sold off to start up in Bangkok.'

Osher presented the knife to Lupus' throat. Lupus was so indignant, so determined to clear up the misunderstanding, that he hardly registered the blade. 'He can't blame me,' he said, his eyes rolling round in his head, searching for Sweetwater. 'He was supposed to call in. We thought he was dead. We couldn't drop the guns not knowing who was going to pick them up. Tell him for chrissake.'

'He doesn't speak English,' Sweetwater said.

'Be serious,' Lupus pleaded, his voice skating up as Osher pricked his Adam's apple. 'Call the fucker off.'

123

'I'm not sure he'd listen. The way he sees it, you threw him to the dogs.'

'It wasn't my fucking operation,' Lupus squeaked. His eyes were on the ceiling, his throat laid bare. 'I told you what I thought about it.'

'It's funny the way things have come together,' Sweetwater mused. 'You and Osher down here, Gunn and Yonden upstairs. I was thinking that when you said everyone gets what's coming to them.'

'I can't think with this fucking blade digging into me,' Lupus said.

Slowly and stiffly, like a man in traction, he raised his right hand.

'Guns,' Osher said, and drew the knife across his throat, quick as a shiver.

'Sonofabitch,' Lupus marvelled. Gently he put his hand to his neck. Hardly daring, he looked at his hand. A thin red line was drawn across it. His throat felt cold. 'He cut me,' he said. 'The dumb fucking gook cut me.'

Sweetwater caught him as he tottered back and turned him round, holding him up at arm's length. 'Ah hell, Lupus, it's only a little bitty scratch.' He laughed loud. 'See your face, Lupus. See your goddam face.'

Chapter 9

The last time Gunn had seen Yonden, the Khampa had been standing, arm raised in farewell, at a turn in a path that zigzagged down slopes of biscuit-coloured clinker to a smudge of green occupied by drab trucks and waiting soldiers.

But the portrait that Gunn had carried in his head all these years framed Yonden in a more tranquil setting – sitting under an apricot tree in the family courtyard, reading *Heart of Midlothian* syllable by syllable, while his two sisters discussed a friend's dowry as they tended a flower-bed stocked with the Tibetan equivalent of geraniums. The lobes of memory had also enfolded a resin-scented wind, the distant clanking of yak bells, the unanswered cries of a herdsman, and the fervent gabble of Yonden's father at prayer, stocking up on merit after a lifetime of administrative skulduggery and outright banditry. Old men, Gunn remembered, make sacrifice of the devil's leavings.

Now, standing in a room as shabby as his own, he couldn't reconcile any of these images with the figure waiting to greet him. Yonden still had the short, slight build of a schoolboy, but in his canary-coloured beach shirt, loud checked slacks and Cuban heels, he was indistinguishable from the pimps who manned Gunn's hotel lobby around the clock.

As if to endorse this impression, Yonden slipped on a pair of sunglasses.

They mounted a painful silence while Lupus raged outside. Finally the building became still, but the atmosphere had been irrevocably corrupted.

'Tell me what's going on,' Gunn said, in a voice faint with fear.

'He's a bad man,' Yonden whispered back.

'He's an unhappy one.'

Yonden went to the door and listened. 'He's gone now,' he said, but went on eavesdropping a few seconds longer. He seemed to turn reluctantly, and with an expression of secret glee that had nothing to do with Gunn's presence. 'Welcome, my friend,' he said, bringing his hands together. 'Hey, you are very welcome here.'

His voice had acquired a confident yet ingratiating twang. With those clothes and the superfluous glasses, the effect was absurdly venal. He came forward, hands clasped like a bazaar trader, linked in a usurer's prayer.

Yet when he came close, Gunn saw that there was nothing urbane about his appearance. He was not merely slim but stringy as a juniper root, with weather-stained cheeks sunk under bony promontories that had been polished by wind and sun. When he smiled, baring teeth too large and numerous for his jaw, deep tracks fanned across his face, ageing him twenty years. His yellow shirt was patterned with nursery rhymes and characters: Jack and Jill, Hickory Dickory Dock, Three Blind Mice.

Raising his eyes, Gunn saw his blighted expectations mirrored in the reflective lenses. Full of shame, he realised that Yonden, too, must be finding it difficult to bridge the yawning gap between realisation and reality. It occurred to him that he had never been an objective figure to Yonden. With his medicines and his knowledge of the mechanical universe, he must have been a kind of symbolic incarnation, avatar of Western genius. And now, Gunn thought, the boy sees that he has overestimated my standing in the world.

Gunn fumbled apologetically at his jowls. 'I've changed, I expect. You must hardly recognise me. Nearly twenty years . . . seeing you again . . . it's like a miracle.'

His voice trailed away. Miracles didn't stand up to the light of day. Yonden took off his glasses and rubbed his right eye distractedly. A chill settled on Gunn's heart.

'How to fill in all the years,' he said. 'I don't know where to begin.'

'You one big doctor in Scot-a-land.'

'Oh, no. You have to be qualified. I'm not qualified, you see.'

'You don't treat sick people no more?'

'It's not allowed. No.'

Yonden sucked air as though he'd burnt his tongue. 'What kind of work you doing then?' His lips peeled back in a leer. 'Teacher, I think. Merchant.'

'No.'

'What then?' Yonden demanded, a shadow falling on his face.

'The truth is,' Gunn said, and then stopped, aware that the truth was too absurd and complex. 'I worked in a factory,' he said. 'I gave it up to come out here.'

'You don't have no job?'

'No.'

126

'Tssk.' Yonden's eyes narrowed, taking in more than they gave out. 'You not rich then.'

Gunn rubbed a fold of frayed cuff between his fingers and gave a half-baked laugh. 'I'm afraid not.'

He looked up quickly, his face swept by sudden panic at the thought that Yonden had brought him here to extort money.

'You got married?' Yonden asked, with mounting concern.

'No.'

'No children?'

'No family at all. No ties of any kind.'

Yonden clicked his tongue, surveying Gunn with evident dismay. 'What's wrong – educated man like you, good doctor?' He frowned. 'You got bad karma I think.'

'I've never really understood what that means,' Gunn said. 'I read somewhere that fate shuffles the cards and we play them. Is that karma?'

Yonden affected the sideways grin of a not-to-be-trusted dog. 'Better if you cheat a bit.'

'My problem is I don't know what game I'm playing. I don't think I'll ever know. In the end . . .' Gunn stopped, not knowing how to finish. In the end was a phrase that recurred often of late, meaningless as a snatch of birdsong.

'Yes?' Yonden's canine grin had vanished, replaced by a frown of inquiry.

'Nothing,' Gunn said lightly. 'In the end . . .' A mad gaiety seized him. 'You once told me a story about two old rogues who know they're both soon going to die. They calculate that each of them have accumulated so many sins that neither has a hope of a good rebirth. Remember?'

Yonden nodded uncertainly.

'They work out that if they add up their store of merit, there would be enough to ensure one of them a good rebirth, so they draw lots to see who will go to heaven and who to hell.'

Yonden's mouth was strained in a smile of incomprehension. 'Yes?' he said.

'Well, in the end, you can have whatever stock of merit I've earned.'

Yonden's smile collapsed. His face tightened with anger.

Gunn's stomach lurched. He knows, he thought. He already knows.

Yonden took hold of his wrist, his bony grasp seeming to serve notice of punishment to come. Gunn nodded acceptance.

127

'You want some tea?' Yonden asked.

Yonden installed Gunn at a table, then went to the door and shouted down the stairs until he woke an answering echo.

Above the table hung a picture of the Dalai Lama surrounded by pressmen on the steps of UN headquarters. A Tibetan rug with dragon motifs covered the floor in this part of the room, where a smell of incense lingered. On the table, next to a radio equipped with an impressive display of dials, lay a school exercise book open at a page of pencilled calculations.

Yonden came back rubbing his eyes, drew up a chair and sprawled out his arms. He was ill at ease, drumming his fingers restlessly, part of his attention on Gunn, part on the door. Whenever their eyes made contact, dim smiles came and went in a way that suggested faulty connections. Abruptly, Yonden pulled the radio towards him and began tuning it. Through the squealing of the airwaves, he said: 'Bloody communists kill Peter, yes?'

'Oh no,' Gunn said, shocked.

Yonden gave a noncommittal grunt. 'How did he die, then?'

Gunn felt the sheen of sweat on his brow.

He hadn't known that Peter was being kept in the same camp until one night he heard the strains of *Rock of Ages* rising in faint discord above the scandalised shouts of the guards. He had remained silent, frightened by the cracked tones in which Peter magnified his saviour's glory. After that Peter sang every night, sometimes breaking off to cry out, transported by rapture or pain. The man was mad; he would get them both killed. Gunn had screamed as much, pounding on his cell door until he became aware of a vast silence, broken at last by sobs. After that there had been no more hymns.

'He died of . . . a fever.'

'He gone to heaven, I think.'

'What? Oh, yes. I mean, I expect so,' Gunn said.

He had been woken one dawn by slamming doors and the sound of a pair of feet running. Later that morning the guards had searched his cell with scared faces. They had removed every scrap of furniture, drawing sharp breaths at the discovery of a nearly toothless comb. Even then, he hadn't realised that Peter had killed himself.

They never admitted it. His interrogator had offered him a cigarette and told him that Peter had died in hospital of a violent inflammation of the brain. The interrogator, a Kuomintang convert whose form of address swung between highly-wrought civility and violent political rhetoric, had been profoundly embarrassed, and as he registered this, Gunn had been charged with guilty hope. They wouldn't want a second enemy of the people to die on them.

Yonden had found an English-language station. A Thai youth was throttling an English pop song.

Gunn cleared his throat. His heart was thudding. 'Your parents,' he said. 'Lobsang and the girls . . .' His voice faltered '. . . All of them?'

Yonden picked up a pencil and jabbed at the exercise book. 'Maybe my sisters are alive someplace. The Chinese took them away.'

'There's something I have to tell you,' Gunn heard himself say. 'Something very bad that happened in the camp.'

'Fucking communists beat you,' Yonden said mechanically. 'Make you work on the roads for no food. Fucking bloody Chinese.'

'No,' Gunn said, shocked. 'There was nothing like that. The guards jostled me at first and shouted insults, but on the whole they treated me well.' He drew a shaky breath. 'The bad thing I'm talking about is something I did.'

Yonden frowned expectantly and Gunn knew that, after all, he suspected nothing.

'I had an interrogator assigned to me,' Gunn said. His cheek muscles worked stiffly and his voice sounded strange in his ears. 'Captain Ma was his name. He told me that I'd be treated leniently if I confessed my crimes. If not, I'd be . . . suppressed is the word he used. Ma questioned me nearly every day for four months. His assistants wrote down every word I said, but I didn't have anything of value to give them. I wasn't a spy. You know that.'

'Sure,' Yonden said, after a tiny but damning pause. He shrugged.

'He wanted to know everything about my time in Kham. He spent many days questioning me about you and your family. I told him how you'd taken me into your home, and about the journeys we made together.' Gunn's voice became slurred. 'I had to tell him it was you who tried to get me out of Kham.'

Lips pursed, Yonden was sketching a girl's round face. Into Gunn's mind came an image of his sisters. They had looked like twins, though they weren't. They had an identical laugh, which they deployed simultaneously, and the same apple-red cheeks. They had laughed when he had asked them what kind of make-up they used. The colouring was natural.

Gunn shook the picture away. 'One day Captain Ma showed me all the transcripts of our study sessions – that's what he called the

129

interrogations. They covered my entire life, not just my stay in Kham.' Gunn's face puckered in disgust. 'A record of one man's efforts to avoid reality, is how he described it. Then he warned me that I'd never leave the Place of Flowers unless I made a full confession. It wasn't a prison, you see. I hadn't been sentenced. A trial was only for criminals who'd shown by their confessions that they wished to be rehabilitated back into society. I wasn't even allowed to do any work; labour was too dignified for someone like me. Finally, Captain Ma told me he was stopping the study sessions. I'd be kept in my cell permanently. No one would be allowed to speak to me. That's what he meant when he'd said I'd be suppressed.'

Yonden drew a squiggly line through his drawing and pushed it aside with an irritated hiss.

'I began inventing crimes. At first Ma was pleased. He called in the guards and we all shook hands and slapped each other on the back. I felt . . . pleased, too.' Gunn bit his lip, looking at his hands hooked over the edge of the table. 'The next day,' he said dully, 'no one came to see me. Nor the next. The warders told me Ma had been sent on leave. I got the impression that he was in disgrace and it was all my fault. But then, two weeks later, I was taken to see him in the middle of the night. He was sitting at his desk with my false confession in front of him. He looked up. I'll never forget that look.'

Yonden peeped at his watch and glanced towards the door. When he looked back, he ducked his head.

'I told him to write out a confession for me. Anything. I'd sign anything. He flew into a rage. Didn't I realise that the only reason he'd spent so long on my case was because he believed I genuinely wanted to reform my thought. I'd tricked him, made a fool of him. It was obvious that I'd always evade my responsibilities. I'd deluded myself that my masters would get me released by bribes or threats. He was finished with me. Finished.'

Yonden looked towards the door openly, a little desperately.

'Oh, I know what you're thinking,' Gunn said eagerly. 'I was being brainwashed. You're right of course, but it didn't matter. The truth is, I did feel guilty. I begged Captain Ma to give me one last chance. He refused. As far as he was concerned I could spend the rest of my life alone with my delusions.'

Yonden smothered a yawn. He patted his chest. 'It's difficult for me,' he said, poking his exercise book. 'Not speak English too much.'

Gunn blinked, then slumped back in his chair, his eyes closed.

'That night,' he said in a flat voice, 'I realised how I could indict myself.'

'Why you telling me these things?'

Gunn's eyes snapped open, looking through Yonden. 'Remember Kenrab?' he asked.

'Sure,' Yonden said in a guarded voice. 'Fucking communist.'

'He came to your house. Your father told me he was working for the Chinese – a quisling.'

'Quisling?'

'Traitor. He was murdered on his way home, a few days after leaving your house. Bandits, people said.'

'Good riddance.' Yonden gave a cracked laugh.

'You and Lobsang were away from home when he was killed.'

Yonden studied Gunn with composure. 'What you saying? Listen, my friend. If we had wanted to kill that man, we would have put something bad in his food. One week later, one month later, he's dead, and no one knows why.'

Gunn shook his head wearily. 'I heard Lobsang and you discussing how you'd shoot him on that pass where the pilgrims had been killed.'

Yonden picked up his pencil and began to doodle. 'This is what you told your friend, the Chinese captain?'

'Friend?' Gunn frowned. 'Yes, in a way he was a friend,' he said, remembering Ma's reaction after the trial that followed his betrayal of Yonden's family. He had beamed at him across the courtroom as sentence was pronounced. He'd been as proud as a father at his son's graduation. Fifteen years. *I told you they'd be lenient.*

'And he was happy when you told him about Kenrab?' Yonden asked, leaning back with mock negligence.

'Not at first. He said it was another lie. He wouldn't let me fool him again. But at last he agreed to investigate my story. The study sessions were resumed. For a month I heard nothing, then . . .'

Yonden's eyes flicked towards the door, where an anxious-looking man hovered. Yonden waved him away.

'Your family had been arrested and they had confessed to the murder.'

Yonden's face wore a bright, unnatural smile.

'I incriminated myself, too,' Gunn shouted. 'I told them I'd helped plan the murder because Kenrab had threatened to have me expelled from Kham.'

Yonden emitted a high-pitched giggle.

'Don't you understand what I'm telling you, man?' Gunn shouted.

Yonden's face drained of expression. 'When did they arrest my family?'

'I don't know. Soon after Peter died. Six months after we were captured.'

Yonden nodded at length, rolling the pencil between his fingers. He began speaking in a voice so soft that Gunn missed the first few words. '. . . go to Lhasa. I knew that if the Chinese had cut the road to the east, they must be close to my house. I went back as quick as I could, walking for thirty hours without sleep.' He shrugged. 'The Chinese had come already. The horses were gone. My sisters were gone. My father and brother were tied together in the courtyard. My mother was in the house. Ah no,' he said, spotting the irrational hope dawning on Gunn's face. 'They were dead.' He dropped his pencil on the table and watched it roll towards the edge. 'The Chinese killed them many days before they caught you. So you see, my friend,' he said, raising his face to Gunn. 'Captain Ma likes to play crazy games with you.'

'I see,' Gunn said, hearing his voice coming out of the greyness within him. It seemed to him that his confession had been the last spark of a dying fire. 'I see,' he said, his voice a toneless echo.

Yonden signalled to the man at the door and jumped to his feet. 'Now we eat and talk,' he cried gaily, clapping his hands.

Gunn looked up. Three men were filing into the room, bearing loaded trays. At his savage laugh, they recoiled, bumping into each other with a rattle of dishes. They looked to Yonden for guidance.

'What's wrong with me?' Gunn shouted in despair.

'Please,' Yonden said sternly. 'Eat now.' He lifted a lid from a pot. 'Potatoes,' he said. 'Not easy to buy in this place.'

'Potatoes? Potatoes?' Gunn broke into wild laughter. 'I travel halfway across the world to confess my guilt, and all you can talk about is potatoes.' He shook his head. 'Why can't I get things right? I'm always out of step, going in the wrong direction.' He clutched Yonden's sleeve, a look of elation on his face, as though he had been vouchsafed some extraordinary revelation. 'Remember what widdershins means?'

'No,' Yonden said.

'Yes you do, man. Anti-clockwise – the direction in which the Bonpos walk round their holy places, the way their swastikas point. In my country it's the way witches dance, the way of bad luck. That's the way my life has gone.'

'Stop this bad talk,' Yonden shouted, banging down a dish.

There was a sudden, giddy silence.

'Not good to say them things,' Yonden muttered. He looked over his shoulder. 'I thought this would be a happy day for me, but you come here and talk about dying. You look backwards and see ghosts.'

Looking into Yonden's accusatory eyes, Gunn saw the confirmation of his guilt. He covered his face with his hands and wept.

Thin face drawn, Yonden stood by him, hand awkwardly patting his shoulder. The three other Tibetans watched with idiotic grins of sympathy.

'You still like Tibetan food,' Yonden said approvingly, watching Gunn wipe his plate.

'Yes, indeed. It's simple, like the food of my country.'

'I think you were happy in Kham.'

'The happiest time in my life.'

Warmed by the food and a glass of *rakshi*, Gunn realised that a residue of that happiness might still be his. Then he remembered Lupus' warning.

'In your letter,' he said, striving for a tone of casual inquiry, 'you said you were in business here. You didn't say what kind.'

'Import,' Yonden said vaguely, rubbing his right eye. 'Export. Nice goods for tourists. Carpets, masks, *thankas*. Hey, remember summer-grass-winter-insect. I sell that, too. Chinese pay many money for Tibetan medicines.'

'Lupus had an idea you might be dealing in musk.'

'Ah no,' Yonden said with regret. 'Musk is awkward for me.'

'This man Sweetwater,' Gunn said, his tone still light. 'Do you sell through him?'

'For sure,' Yonden said warily.

'He must think a lot of you to pay for my visit.'

Yonden's gaze wavered. 'He's very rich,' he said. 'American.'

'Yes, I know,' Gunn said, nodding seriously. His cheeks were stiff from smiling. He put his hand to his mouth and gave a small cough.

'Yes,' Yonden said with a sigh, 'he works for the American government.' His gaze wandered about the room.

He had always been an imaginative youth, Gunn thought, given to concocting whatever fantasies he thought you might like to hear, regardless of any contradictions in the telling. Gunn had found it a rather appealing trait, partly because the dishonesty was so transparent, partly because this creative interpretation of reality contrasted

133

refreshingly with his own rigid view. In the adult Yonden, however, the habit promised to be tiresome. Nevertheless, Gunn did not ask what an agent of the American government was doing buying Tibetan tourist wares in Bangkok. He knew that Yonden had discarded that fiction. By degrees a more serviceable version of the truth would emerge.

'What kind of work?' he asked, starting afresh.

'Helping refugees,' Yonden said, his gaze settling back on Gunn.

'Tibetan refugees?'

'My friends,' Yonden said. 'They live in a camp in Nepal. They're sick. They sent me here to find a doctor.' His expression was bright and open but unfocused, making it impossible to meet his eye.

Gunn found himself reaching for the bottle. 'What kind of sick?' he asked as he poured.

Yonden indicated his head, his stomach, his legs. Gunn nodded soberly. He studied Yonden's face for a few seconds, then slowly stood up, still peering. 'Come here,' he said. 'Yes, here, man.'

Wearing a worried smile, Yonden came round the table. Gunn took him by the shoulders and manoeuvred him into better light. He cupped his chin in his hand. 'How long have your eyes been like that?'

'Since winter.'

'Hmm. It doesn't look like snow blindness. Do you know what caused it? Did you injure your eyes in any way?'

Yonden shook his head.

Now Gunn understood why Yonden favoured sunglasses. Most of the iris of his right eye and part of his left were occluded by a subcutaneous waxy deposit the colour of old beef fat.

'Do they hurt?'

'Little bit.'

'Can you see alright?'

Yonden squinted through each eye in turn. He nodded.

Gunn uncupped Yonden's chin. 'Been to a doctor? Received any treatment.'

Yonden produced a small bottle from his shirt pocket. Gunn looked at the label, uncapped it and sniffed. 'God knows what this is,' he said, 'but it won't do your eyes a blind bit of good.'

'Will I be blind?' Yonden asked, alarmed by the unintentional play on words.

'Don't be daft,' Gunn said gruffly. 'I think you should get them looked at, though.'

134

Yonden was still braced for examination.

'Not by me,' Gunn said. 'I'm not a doctor and I know next to nothing about eye diseases. It could be a secondary infection, an indication of some systemic illness. The eye,' he said, peering once more into Yonden's diseased stare, 'is a very complex organ. As well,' he said drily, 'as being the mirror of the soul.'

Yonden obliged with a weak smile. He was still standing at attention.

'I told you,' Gunn said, and then stopped, frowning. 'Do you have any trouble with your . . . ?' Gunn's hand gyrated and finally came to a stop pointing in the general direction of Yonden's groin. 'Soreness? Discharge?'

'Some time, yes. Not any more.' Yonden's face crinkled in distaste. 'Bhotia women all got the love sickness.'

'Do your friends have similar symptoms?' Gunn asked. 'No, not necessarily their eyes.' Once more Gunn fell back on gesture.

'Ah yes, it's usual.'

'Don't I know it,' Gunn said heavily. 'Look, it's only a guess, but your eye problem could be a symptom of syphilis. You'll have to have penicillin injections. Remember those, Yonden? Hurt like hell.'

Yonden's face lit up. He darted to the table, flicked through his exercise book and presented it to Gunn.

'Penicillin,' Gunn read, picking out familiar names from a list that filled the page. 'Septrin, zinc sulphate, benzedrine. Benzedrine? Most of these I've never heard of.' He looked up. 'You have all these drugs?'

Yonden grinned proudly. 'Come to Nepal and make my friends well,' he said.

'Sit down,' Gunn said after a brief silence. He palped a fold of flesh on his jaw. 'Yonden, I'm not a real doctor. I haven't treated anyone since I last saw you. If I tried to help your friends, I'd probably do more harm than good. But even if I could cure their syphilis, they'd only reinfect themselves within a few months. You know what it was like in Kham.' Gunn was aware of other, potentially more serious objections which he did not think it wise to inquire into. At the same time, he felt bad – worthless. Just as Yonden's logic defied sense, so his own denial of medical skills must seem like a selfish evasion of the truth. He had, after all, gone as a doctor in Kham. He had supervised difficult births, stitched up sword wounds, expended hundreds of ampoules of penicillin in a vain assault on the endemic venereal diseases, delivered stern talks on hygiene both moral and physical. Why couldn't he do the same now?

Yonden's jaw was cocked at a resentful angle, his bottom lip over his top. He had switched on the radio. Gunn smiled sadly. For all Yonden's apparent sophistication, he was still an innocent.

'You used to look like that when you were a boy.'

'I'm not a boy,' Yonden said angrily, 'and it's not love sickness my friends have got.' He switched off the radio. 'This year six of them are dead – with bad pains here,' he said, squeezing his stomach, 'and here,' pressing his hands to his temples. 'Their shit's like water, with blood in it.'

'I hadn't realised,' Gunn mumbled. 'It sounds serious – cholera, possibly, or typhoid. Do you have a clean water supply?'

'Water is not the problem,' Yonden said contemptuously.

'You sound as if you already know the cause,' Gunn said.

Yonden faced him squarely. 'It's devils,' he said.

'Ha!' Gunn said, taken aback. 'Now who's being morbid?'

'Yes,' Yonden insisted, 'it's devils. I've seen them on the mountain.'

'In that case,' Gunn said, startled into levity, 'you don't need a doctor; you need an exorcist.' His smile faded under Yonden's disdainful stare. He nudged the exercise book. 'These drugs must have cost a fortune,' he said. 'You wouldn't have gone to all that expense if you truly believed that devils were the cause of your illness. It's germs that spread disease. Nasty little things you can't see.'

Yonden nodded, as if agreeing. 'Who sends these germs?' he asked.

'That's a very difficult question,' Gunn said. 'I don't have the answer.'

But Yonden did. 'It was the lama,' he said flatly.

'I'm lost,' Gunn said. 'You'd better start from the beginning. Tell me who your friends are, where they live.'

'The valley's near Tibet,' Yonden said, ignoring the first question. 'We came there last winter. The lama in the village was angry at us. We had a different general then. Linka Rinpoche.' Yonden looked at Gunn as if he expected him to recognise the name.

'I've rather lost touch with what's happening in Tibet,' Gunn admitted.

'Very famous man,' Yonden said. 'He was a monk before he joined the army of the Four Rivers and Six Ranges. In the winter the people asked him to be their next lama. The old lama's a crazy man. He told us to go away from his valley, and when Linka said no, he cursed

136

us.' Yonden shrugged as though further explanation was unnecessary. 'That's why my friends are sick.'

'I see,' Gunn said, and up to a point did. 'Isn't it unusual for people to go against the wishes of their lama?'

'They are . . .' Yonden hunted for a suitably damning epithet '. . . black.'

'Dark in colour, do you mean?' Gunn asked. Yonden could be intolerant in such matters.

'Black here,' Yonden said, tapping his head. 'They live in houses like caves and marry their cousins. They're always fighting. There is no *dharma* in the valley.'

'It sounds a troubled community,' Gunn said.

'Yes,' Yonden agreed. 'Even the lama's daughter is a witch.'

'Well,' Gunn said, deciding that they ought to return to firmer ground, 'the important thing is to find some way of helping your friends. How far to the nearest doctor?'

'Six days' walking, but no doctor will come to the camp.'

'I don't see why not. I mean, you have the money.'

'It's not permitted,' Yonden said. 'No one can come near the Tibetan border.' He rubbed his eyes, hissing as if in pain.

Gunn regarded him without sympathy. 'You said that Linka had been your general; you mentioned an army. Does that mean your friends are guerillas?'

'Soldiers,' Yonden said, looking up with bleary pride.

'And you?'

'I'm a soldier, too.'

Gunn's first reaction was one of stony indifference. In one evening, with no more than a token display of embarrassment, Yonden had described himself as an entrepreneur, a refugee relief worker and, now, a soldier. And then, as Gunn realised that this time Yonden was speaking the truth or a fair copy of it, and as the implications sank in, he found himself rising from his seat, his voice shaking. 'You, a soldier? But the war ended years ago. You're not still fighting the Chinese.'

'Sometimes, in the winter,' Yonden said offhandedly, as if war was a seasonal activity for amateurs.

Gunn wandered over to the photograph of Tibet's exiled former ruler. 'I don't know why I'm so shocked,' he said. 'I expected worse. I was worried that you might be involved in drug-smuggling.'

Behind him Yonden laughed.

'How many of you are there?'

137

'I think . . . two hundred.'

'Think?' Gunn said, turning.

'Two hundred.'

'Supported by the Americans – by Mr Sweetwater?'

Yonden nodded.

'I suppose he knows what he's doing,' Gunn said. He sat down again, picked up the pencil and drummed it on the list of supplies. Yonden watched him anxiously, his top teeth clamped over his bottom lip.

'You said no one is allowed to visit your camp.'

'It's not difficult,' Yonden said eagerly. 'I'll take you myself.' He hesitated. 'Another American is coming.'

'Not Lupus,' Gunn said in dismay.

'No, no,' Yonden said. He leaned forward with an expression of such sincerity that Gunn prepared himself for a lie. 'My friend, because we have a new general the Americans say they may stop helping us. Mr Sweetwater is sending a man to see for himself how well-trained we are.'

'To check on your military capability, you mean.'

'What?'

'Your fighting ability. Mr Sweetwater is sending someone to see how well you fight.'

'No fighting,' Yonden said. 'This man isn't a soldier. He just talks and asks questions.'

Gunn found it hard to frame any of his own. There were no appropriate questions; he realised, only a simple response – yes, or no. If he said yes, he knew he would be putting himself in harm's way, though it was impossible to tell from Yonden's flimsy explanation how much risk he would be running. And the alternative? It was clear-cut and soul-sickening: a life without hope of remission. Perhaps this was his last chance, he thought, and with that realisation his mind was made up. Whatever happened, he had nothing to fear. He was a man, he realised, who was in the position of having nothing to lose.

'Just tell me if it will be dangerous.'

'Not for you. I don't let harm happen to you.'

'I was thinking of you,' Gunn said.

'This year I don't go into Tibet,' Yonden told him. 'Maybe after this winter I go away from the mountains and start a business in the city. I have some big ideas I want to talk about.'

'I'd love to hear them,' Gunn said.

'Yes,' Yonden said with a sigh, 'when my friends are well again, I leave the mountains for ever.' He smiled sadly at the distant and perhaps unattainable goal.

'If I'm the only doctor you can find,' Gunn said, the words forming slowly but of themselves, 'I'll be happy to do what I can. It won't be much.'

Yonden frowned suspiciously. 'You'll come?'

'Yes.'

Yonden was still frowning. 'Don't you have no more questions?'

'What is there to say?' Gunn asked. 'I can never repay you for all you did in Kham. I'm in your debt. In your hands.'

There was a short, charged silence. Yonden tentatively reached out and touched Gunn's hand. 'You are my friend,' he said. 'All these years I never think bad of you.'

But when Gunn could bring himself to meet Yonden's gaze, it slid away, dull with uncertainty as though, having achieved his aim, he saw for the first time where it would lead. Gunn wanted to reassure him, tell him that whatever the outcome, there would be no blame. He was doing this gladly, of his own will. A great weight slipped from his mind.

Yonden stood up briskly. 'Now I get you a car.'

'We haven't finished talking,' Gunn said in dismay. 'I want to hear what you've been doing all these years. I want you to tell me about your plans, your big ideas.'

'Look how long we've been talking already,' Yonden said with a falsetto laugh, pointing to his watch. It was indeed much later than Gunn realised. 'Tomorrow, another day, we talk again and I take you to see Charlie.'

Gunn thought about going back to the hotel, the pimps dangling car keys and promises of sex in any permutation. He suspected the lurking presence of Lupus.

'I'd be quite happy to sleep here,' he said.

Again Yonden gave a high, synthetic laugh. 'No bed here. Not too comfortable.' He stole a glance at the door. 'It's awkward,' he muttered. 'Better for you to sleep in hotel.'

'Of course,' Gunn said, grabbing his jacket. 'Foolish of me.'

There was an interval. Yonden's eyes strayed around the room, anywhere but in Gunn's direction, and finally alighted with relief on his exercise book.

'What you think?' he asked. 'You think you can cure my friends' sickness?'

139

'Your devils, you mean,' Gunn said. He laughed. 'Well, with what you've got in that book, we'll certainly give them a fright.'

Chapter 10

They were in the middle of the Chao Phya river, hazarding a crossing in a wooden launch crewed by a pubescent girl and a boy whom Melville took to be her twin brother. A threadbare canvas awning rigged amidships diffused the sun without casting shade. Sweetwater sagged forward as if he was in a sauna, his scalp glowing through his hair. Behind him the waterfront was flat and distant against a tin-plate sky.

Melville looked away over the swollen olive river. The waves were showing their teeth, tripping over each other in their haste to reach the sea. Clumps of uprooted vegetation clawed at the launch in passing.

Melville blinked sweat from his eyes. Give it your consideration, Sweetwater had urged, and that's what he'd done, sitting alone in his room and in crowded eating places. But his thoughts had merely wandered over the surface, unable to grasp the reality of the situation. Thinking could do no good, since the basic proposition was unthinkable. That's all he needed to say – a flat rejection delivered from an unassailable moral stance.

But when it came to translating this resolve into action, he found that the dog of resolution had merely turned and whimpered in its sleep before once again stretching out its dead weight.

He sighed. He glanced secretly at Sweetwater's case, fantasising over its contents: a gun, Chinese documents, cipher books; bundles of currency – the whole arcana of the professional agent.

A tow of rice barges showing less than a foot of freeboard ploughed downstream, dragging a sullen wake that bludgeoned the launch to a stop, picked it up, smacked it a couple of times and dropped it facing the wrong way. Sweetwater called out in Thai to the boy, who was standing on the prow in a nonchalant J. M. Barrie attitude. The boy mouthed silent instructions to his sister, who strained her attention towards him, opening her own mouth the better to pick up what he was saying. She cocked her thumb, then leaned a skinny shoulder to the tiller. The boat changed course, skittered over a few crests and dug in stern first, shipping a spout of water that soaked the girl. She gave a gurgle of laughter and pulled her wet shirt away from her skin.

She wasn't more than fourteen, Melville guessed – a nice-looking kid, friendly and bright, not screwed-up by education. Her nipples showed through her shirt. He found himself recalling the feel of her small dry hand as she welcomed him aboard.

'You going to sit there nursing a hard-on over a dumb kid, or are we going to have a constructive conversation?'

Melville jerked as if he'd been slapped. He flushed with shame. Christ, he was coming unglued. He put the back of his hand to his brow, almost hoping for signs of fever.

Sweetwater was opening the case. 'Here,' he said, holding out a plastic tumbler which he filled with fruit juice from a thermos. 'Cool you down.'

Melville closed his eyes in gratitude as his tongue encountered the blunt edge of alcohol. The launch nosed into one of the *klongs* that branch off Bangkok's main artery. Get it over with, Melville told himself. You can be back in Tokyo this time tomorrow.

'How certain are you that the general will be in the right place at the right time?'

Sweetwater considered, his gaze lingering on a Thai woman who was soaping her husband's shoulders in the green shadows beneath a waterside stilt house. Melville's own disengaged stare was drawn to the couple.

'Fairly certain,' Sweetwater said.

'How certain's fairly certain for heaven's sake?'

'Nothing's nailed down in an undertaking like this. Liu could decide he doesn't fancy the deal; he could get another transfer. A lot of things could happen. My judgement is he'll be there right on cue.'

Melville gave a disjointed laugh. 'I have this crazy image – Liu sitting on a rock in some barren place waiting for a band of Khampas to ride by.'

'That's certainly a droll little picture.'

'You haven't told me when.'

'Second week in November.'

'That's more than a month off.'

'It's his only shot.'

'I'm thinking of the security aspect,' Melville said, frowning to show that he was being businesslike.

Sweetwater's mouth twitched. 'Glad to hear it. But the only people who know are Liu and Zhang, me and Mr Yueh, and you. Me and Mr Yueh,' he said, 'are as discreet as the grave.'

Melville wasn't happy about the implications. 'No need to worry about me,' he said stiffly.

'No,' Sweetwater said, after a pause for consideration.

'Aren't you forgetting the Khampas?' Melville said after a while. 'Don't tell me they're not in the picture.'

'Only the top man and his translator.'

'They can't be trusted, is that it?'

'Far as I can tell, this group is sound.'

'Far as you know.'

'Blow it out your ass, Walter.'

'Damn it, that's a legitimate concern. You can't expect me to go through with this not knowing what I'm getting into.'

Sweetwater hunched his shoulders. 'Walter, you're absolutely right. Go ahead, tell me what you want to know.'

'Now wait a minute. I didn't say I'd do it.'

'I'm sorry to hear it,' Sweetwater said heavily. 'For a moment there I thought we were moving towards an understanding.'

'Well I'm sorry if I've given you that impression.' Melville blinked sweat from his eyes. 'Charlie,' he said pleadingly, 'we're both deluding ourselves. You said yourself that I'm too half-assed for an enterprise like this. Why don't we drop it right now. Look, let me off here, okay? I'll find my own way back.'

'Wait,' Sweetwater urged, as if fearful that Melville might throw himself overboard. 'Wait,' he repeated softly. He made a penitent's face. 'I admit I said some hard things about you, Walter. I admit that I thought you were wasted effort. But Yueh said you were the right man, and the more I think about it, the more I find myself coming round to the same judgement.'

'I still don't understand why you don't look for someone with the right credentials.'

Sweetwater eased himself back on his seat, keeping a close eye on Melville, as though he still suspected an attempt to jump ship.

'You're an anthropologist,' he said. 'You've had experience dealing with primitives.'

'They weren't primitives.'

Sweetwater wasn't going to make a debate of it. 'That group you worked on in Taiwan. Mr Yueh says you got pretty close to them.'

'I like to think we had a sympathetic relationship.'

'And that's exactly the kind of relationship I want you to cultivate with these Khampas.'

'I wouldn't know where to begin.'

Sweetwater put aside his drink with care. 'The Khampa situation is a funny one,' he said. 'They're vital to the whole deal, but they're a bit of an unknown quantity. The group we're dealing with can't muster more than a couple of hundred men, probably less. No one's ever been up there to count them, not even their sponsors in the KMT. My guess is they exaggerate their strength so they can draw extra rations. I do know they've lost a few men through illness. Maybe they don't add up to more than a hundred or so. To add to the uncertainty, they've got themselves a new leader. Now the fellow he took over from had a proven record. Interesting character. He was a monk until the Reds blew up his monastery. He's been at war with them for fifteen years, but last winter he decided to quit, go back to staring at his navel. The guy we're dealing with used to be his number two, name of Osher.'

'You've met him? Here?'

'Yeah, I've met him. Couple of weeks ago. Not here.'

'You don't sound too impressed.'

'On the contrary. He's very purposive. A first-rate soldier. If Tibet had had a few more like Osher, maybe the Dalai Lama would still be on his throne.'

'But?'

'He's new to the job.' Sweetwater finished his drink. 'He puts it on a bit, makes out he's conducting some kind of military offensive, when all I want is for half a dozen hand-picked men to sneak into Tibet, grab the general and sneak out again. I'd like it better if the old monk was still in charge. Any guerilla leader who's still around to retire after fifteen years has proved he cultivates the art of survival.'

'Are you saying this Osher character's a gung-ho type?'

'Osher knows that if he goes in shooting from the hip, Yueh will have him cut off at the knees.' Sweetwater drew a deep breath and poured himself another drink. 'No,' he said, 'what we have here is more of a public relations problem. Most of the other Tibetan guerilla groups gave up fighting the Chinese years ago. The ones that still live in the camps get by on low banditry and the occasional KMT welfare cheque.' Sweetwater tenderly rescued an insect from his drink and flicked it away. 'Not Osher, though. Osher still goes raiding into Tibet. He's fighting a one-man war. Nobody's told him the cause is dead and buried.' Sweetwater was poised to take a drink. 'I mean that literally, Walter. Osher still thinks that one day Chiang's going to unleash his forces against the Reds.' Sweetwater took a tentative sip. 'Don't get me wrong, Osher's not loosely wrapped or anything.

144

But I guess that sitting around on a mountain has given him a rather narrow perspective on the international scene.' Sweetwater gulped without further ceremony. 'You see the problem. I need someone who can handle him diplomatically.'

'You want me to preserve the delusions of a fanatic.'

'Good old Walter,' Sweetwater said, smiling into his glass. 'Straight to the heart of things.'

'He's a wrongo, isn't he?'

Sweetwater leaned back and folded his arms. 'What gives you that idea, Walter?' He was half-smiling.

Melville stirred around with one foot. 'Just a feeling.'

'Well,' Sweetwater said after a silence. 'That's not a lot to go on. My own feeling,' he said, 'is that Osher and me made certain obligations. My concern is that we've only talked through an interpreter, and you know how it is. Wires get crossed. Now he's back in his valley, out of touch. No chance to tell him about any changes of plan. No way he can discuss his problems. No possibility of putting our heads together to sort out any glitches. So you see, I need someone in that camp not only to deliver a speech of welcome to the general, but also to sort out any misunderstandings that might arise. If you do it, you'll be representing Mr Yueh, which means you have full negotiating powers. Like if Osher comes to you and says his boys have been talking among themselves and they'll only go ahead for an extra fifty bucks apiece, feel free to say yes. What I don't want is for them to wake up on the big morning, see it's snowing and say fuck this, go right back to sleep.' Sweetwater looked offended. 'It happens.'

'He doesn't sound like the kind of man whose arm is easily twisted.'

'He'll go through with it.'

'Why should he risk his men for the sake of a PLA general?'

Sweetwater puckered his lips as if he were about to whistle. 'It's a lonely little war he's been fighting,' he said eventually. 'No medals or citations or media coverage. Just a hard slog through the mountains, blow up a truck if you're lucky, and run for home. Piss-ant stuff. Now he's got a chance to take the scalp of the guy who's been sent to zap him. If you were him, wouldn't you do it?'

'Only if there was no chance of getting hurt.'

'Osher doesn't anticipate any difficulties. He was in the pick-up area last winter and never even saw a Chinese presence.'

'This is different. Liu's going to be escaping from under the noses of his own troops.'

'If Osher says he can do it, I have to believe him. It's his ass that stands to get shot off.'

'I take it he speaks Chinese.'

'Like a native. He got his schooling from the commies.' Sweetwater's hand was reaching for the flask. It stopped an inch or two short. 'He knows a little English, too,' he said casually. 'A few Marine Corps oaths, the parts of an M–16.' Sweetwater's hand closed on the flask. 'I should have told you,' he said. 'A long time ago we gave him a few weeks' training.' Sweetwater looked up with a determined smile. 'Should make it easier to strike up a rapport.'

'He sounds like the last person I could get close to.'

'He's about your age,' Sweetwater said, as if this might help.

Melville nibbled his lip. 'What the hell do I know about handling guerillas?' he demanded. 'That's your line of work. You're the one who should be dealing with Osher.'

'You think I don't know it?' Sweetwater shouted, banging the flask down. He smiled blindly at the startled crew before continuing. 'Walter,' he whispered, 'you think I'd be feeling you up if there was any way I could get up into those mountains? Do you?' He subsided back onto his seat. 'Nepal's a small country and Kathmandu's a small town, which happens to be home for a lot of AID officials who don't administer much aid and a lot of Chinese merchants with no merchandise to sell. You dig? Someone like me shows up and right away these people start wondering about purpose of visit.'

Sweetwater had to shout again to make his final words audible over the din of an approaching water-taxi. The dart-shaped craft, powered by what sounded like an unmuffled aero engine, swept past in a mist of spray, through which Melville caught a glimpse of a line of mascaraed women, all clutching baskets of fruit and peering ahead with the fixed expressions of jockeys in the final furlong.

'That certainly puts my mind at ease,' Melville said. 'It's too risky for you to risk your ass, but it's okay to send me.'

'You're right,' Sweetwater said, 'I'm wasting my time.' His hand was poised to pour. 'Know what you are, Walter? A fucking voyeur. If you weren't getting off on what I'm telling you, you wouldn't be here still. It's time you pissed or got off the pot.'

He filled their glasses. Melville offered no resistance.

'No one in Kathmandu's going to take any notice of you,' Sweetwater said calmly.

'It's not Kathmandu that bothers me. It's what comes after.'

'You wouldn't be on your own. Someone's going in with you.'

146

'Who?'

'A doctor.'

'Expecting casualties are we?'

'You're a regular fucking joker.'

'The hell I am. As soon as I think I'm beginning to see the shape of this thing, you go and change it. Who is this guy anyway – some gamy old crony from derring-do days?'

'Never give a fellow the benefit of doubt, do you? He's an ex-missionary who spent a few years in Kham.'

'That's all I need. I hate missionaries.'

'He's not like that,' Sweetwater said. 'He didn't go to Kham to convert the heathen. He's a medic – not qualified, though. The only doctoring he did was in Tibet.' Sweetwater's tone, which had become defensive, grew crisp again. 'He couldn't be a better choice.'

'Where did you dig him up?' Melville asked. 'Or is he just another victim of circumstances?'

'Ah well,' Sweetwater said proudly, 'that's quite a story. Gunn's an old friend of a Khampa called Yonden, who turns out to be Osher's interpreter. They lost touch years ago, but I brought them together again.'

'You're all heart,' Melville said. He frowned. 'What was that name again?'

'Gunn,' Sweetwater said, his tone deadpan. 'Alan Gunn.'

'Gunn, Gunn,' Melville said. 'Don't I know that name?'

Sweetwater sighed. 'I'm afraid you do,' he said. 'Gunn was picked up by the Chinese and spent a few years in detention. That's how I was able to track him down.'

Melville stared at him. 'Oh that's good,' he breathed. 'That's pretty fucking good.'

'I can see you're not happy,' Sweetwater said, 'and you have my sympathy. Frankly, I could do without Gunn; he confuses the issue. If I'd known how Osher would react, I'd have kept my mouth shut. Osher's world view may be a little out of register, but when it comes to making a deal he's pin-sharp. He set quite a few conditions, including getting his men some proper medical attention. When he found out about Gunn, that was it.'

'A spy,' Melville wailed. 'How could you contemplate it?'

'He's no more a spy than your dad was,' Sweetwater said. 'He was a guy in the wrong place at the wrong time.'

'And now he's looking to do it all over again.'

'You talking about the general?' Sweetwater asked brightly.

'Who else?' Melville demanded. 'Doesn't it worry Gunn?'

Sweetwater stroked his cheek and grinned foolishly. 'Not to put too fine a point on it, Walter, I haven't told him.'

There was an appalled silence, then Melville punched his seat hard enough to skin his knuckles. 'You're crazy,' he shouted. 'You're out of your mind.'

'Simmer down, Walter. There's no point telling Gunn what doesn't concern him. His involvement's entirely personal. His only reason for visiting the camp is to treat sick Khampas. I discussed the issue with his friend Yonden, and he agreed we should leave the general out of it.'

'Because otherwise Gunn would run a million miles.'

'Maybe, maybe not. He's not dumb. I had to give him a line about you representing one of our more irregular foreign policy agencies and wanting to take a first-hand look at the Khampa set-up. He didn't seem put out.'

Melville gave an incredulous laugh. 'He must be nuts.'

'Gunn? Well . . . he's deceptive. Quiet, looks too slow to get out of his own way, but tenacious with it. Inner resources. Look on the positive side, Walter. He's close to the Khampas, speaks their language, understands the way their minds work. He might be a lot of help.'

'How the hell can he help when he doesn't know what's going on?' Melville jabbed an accusing finger at Sweetwater. 'First you lie to the general, telling him that you're arranging safe passage to the States, now you con this Gunn character into thinking he's off on a mission of mercy. What we have here is nothing but an exercise in the withholding of information, and I'm beginning to ask myself how much you're holding back from me.'

'I wouldn't do that, Walter. It's essential I put you completely in the picture, but Gunn hardly comes into the frame.'

'Crap! He'll be right in the frame if he's anywhere near the camp when the Khampas come back with the general, and fucking well you know it. No, Charlie, that just about does it for me.'

'Okay, okay,' Sweetwater said, putting up his hands in surrender. 'If it makes you happier, go ahead, tell him.'

'Me? He's nothing to do with me. You tell him.'

'He's already in Nepal. When you meet up, if you still feel the same way, that's fine by me.'

'You're getting way ahead of yourself.'

'Alright,' Sweetwater said, raising his hands again. 'On the *assump-*

148

tion that you accept the job, and if you *want* to give Gunn sleepless nights, put everything on the line for him. If he backs out as a result, personally I won't give a shit. But I think I ought to tell you, I gave my word to Osher and he won't be too thrilled to hear that the doctor's not coming.'

'What's that supposed to mean?'

'It means use your fucking judgement.'

Melville looked down, sucking thoughtfully on his skinned knuckles. 'One of the Khampas is Gunn's friend, you said, yet he's keeping silent about the general. To me that doesn't argue well for the Khampa character.'

'Don't ask me what goes on in a Khampa's head. All I know is that they're brave and keep their word. Oh yes, and they're into feuds. They're like Sicilians; they can keep a blood feud going for generations.'

Melville raised his head sharply. Reflections from the water rippled on Sweetwater's face, making his expression unreadable. 'Got any more rabbits in your hat?' Melville demanded. 'You said Osher had laid down several conditions.'

Sweetwater spread his hands to show his stock was all gone. 'A couple of personal favours,' he said. 'No big deal.'

A pair of butterflies as diaphanous as a cocotte's underwear rowed past in perfect synchrony. Melville tracked them until they had dwindled to dancing points of light, then dismissed them with a slow blink. The scenery looked blacker than it should have done. He felt light-headed and coarse-eyed, angry that once again he had succumbed to booze.

Sweetwater, who had drunk just as much, sat with his chin propped on his fist. He sucked in his cheeks to deny a yawn as Melville turned.

'We have to consider the political implications,' Melville said.

A look of pain disfigured Sweetwater's face. 'If you say so,' he said, not troubling to raise his head off its support.

'Peking's bound to see this as a hostile act, an American provocation. And then there's Gunn, a convicted imperialist agitator. In Chinese eyes it couldn't look worse.'

'Except Liu's going to Taiwan, which makes it a family squabble.' By a studied show of effort, Sweetwater sat up. 'This isn't about sides,' he said. 'It's about getting an individual out from under a system.'

'It's about losing face. When we gave asylum to that violinist, the

149

Chinese were so mad they walked out of the Warsaw talks. If they found out we had anything to do with the defection of a PLA general, it would be the end of Sino–American relations for a decade.'

'First, if Mao wants to turn China into an international basket-case, he can't complain when old comrades start heading for the door. Second, we don't have a relationship.'

They both turned as the boat's engine suddenly raced and cut out. Rousing himself from sleep, the boy came aft, stripping off his shirt. He lowered himself over the stern, held his nose and sank. A few seconds later he resurfaced, clutching a handful of mangled greenery. He dived again.

'Come on,' Melville said, turning back to Sweetwater. 'There's always some kind of . . . reciprocity.' He remembered Hubbard's political rule of thumb. 'Maybe we don't have a dialogue going right now, but neither do the Soviets. That's an unstable state of affairs. Some day the talking will have to start again, and who's to say that this time the partners won't be different?'

The boy came up again empty-handed, rested a few seconds, then had another try.

Sweetwater shook his head pityingly. 'We're not going to cuddle up to China while our boys are getting their asses burned just around the corner. Somehow I don't see the president trusting the voters to make the fine geographical distinction.'

'He might be able to swing it. Anyone else and the people would start yelling about closet communists; with him it would be hailed as pragmatism.'

'He's not capable of making that kind of accommodation. You're talking about one of the men who branded your own father a card-carrying red rat.'

Spluttering and shaking his head, the boy bobbed up again. His sister silently ordered him back into the boat. She took off her shirt and jumped in. A slick of water curled over her back and she was gone.

'Even so,' Melville said, looking at the spot where she'd disappeared, 'the administration would go crazy if they got to hear about private citizens messing about in the internal affairs of the People's Republic.'

'The people who matter will be delighted. I guarantee it.' Sweetwater moved as close to Melville as his seat would allow. 'An operation of this nature, I had to put out a few feelers. No details, no names,' he said quickly, cutting off Melville's protest. 'Just the general scenario played through to a select gathering of responsible, discreet insiders. They were very excited, Walter, and why not? They stand to get access to a prime source of intelligence without any risk of their own people tripping over their feet.'

Melville was distracted. The girl had been under a long time. Insects danced on the water. An unpleasant-looking swirl disturbed the surface some way from the boat and died away. Melville had an image of the girl down there in the soupy darkness, tentacles of weeds slyly taking hold of her legs.

'I don't know,' he said unhappily. 'It gets bigger and shakier all the time. It's a fucking house of cards.'

'I hate to inflict any damage on your self-esteem,' Sweetwater said. 'Your role's an important one, but it's a walk-on part. Liu and Osher are the main players.'

'Fucking hell!' Melville screamed as a dripping mass, suggestive of a long-drowned head, flopped onto the seat beside him. A moment later the girl's grinning face appeared over the side. Melville shouted at her.

'C'mon, Walter. The kid's only having a bit of fun.'

Melville rounded on Sweetwater. He was breathing fast and his hands were clenched. Sweetwater took his arm. 'Sit down, eh? Relax.'

Taking advantage of Sweetwater's intervention, the boy pulled his chastened sister aboard. They huddled together in the stern.

Melville had his hands over his face. 'Give me a drink, will you,' he said through splayed fingers.

Sweetwater silently obliged.

Melville shuddered as he drank. 'There's one possibility you haven't mentioned,' he said. 'I could get myself killed.'

'Let's keep things in perspective, Walter.'

'Nevertheless,' Melville said, 'I have to consider the objective risks.'

Sweetwater stared at him uncomprehendingly.

'Like getting caught,' Melville said.

Sweetwater's face bloomed with pleasure. 'Objective risks,' he said. 'I love it.' He snapped open his case and scrabbled among the contents, moving with the urgency of a door-to-door salesman who sees that he may yet break through a customer's resistance. He pulled out a map, smoothed it over his knees, placed his palms on it and looked up, ready to deliver his pitch.

Melville shrugged. 'How am I supposed to get to the camp?'

'You fly to Kathmandu the end of the month. We'll rent you a house. You'll be put in touch with Gunn and Yonden by an associate of Mr Yueh's.'

'Does he have a name? Just as long as it isn't Wang. I won't be party to any enterprise involving that bug.'

'This man will make himself known to you,' Sweetwater said. 'He's your ticket home, as well as your eyes and ears in Nepal, so you'd better be nice to him. Mr Yueh will settle up with him when it's over. I want you to handle the money for the Khampas.'

'I'd rather not get involved in exchanges of money,' Melville said.

'It establishes your credentials,' Sweetwater said irritably. 'Shows Osher who's paying his wages. I'm not talking sacks of gold. The Khampas get a dollar a day, near enough. Yeah, I know,' Sweetwater said, stilling Melville's indignation. 'There's no fucking justice, but there it is. Nobody ever became a guerilla for the money.'

Melville nodded. Sweetwater turned his attention to the map. 'Yonden will arrange your journey,' he said. 'The direct route to the valley's up this river. About five days' walk.' Sweetwater tapped his finger. 'It's a no-no. There are check-points every second village.' Sweetwater's finger slid westward. 'Here's your path. No military presence and not many villages. It should take six, seven days, walking hard.' He looked at Melville appraising him, his eyes coming to rest on the empty glass. 'Call it eight.'

Sweetwater's finger hurried along the trail, then circled and swooped. 'Fucking Gurkha garrison,' he said, 'right in the mouth of the valley. No way in except across a bridge, and there's a sentry post on that.'

Politely, Melville addressed himself to the map. 'I'm afraid it doesn't make much sense to me.'

Sweetwater flashed him a reproving glance. 'The only other way in is across a pass to the west, but it adds days to the journey, so use it only if Yonden says so. He won't, though. The Khampas have assured me that there's absolutely no problem getting you past those soldiers.'

'They seem to make a lot of untested claims.'

'They come and go all the time.'

'A week's a long time to be moving about in a restricted area. What happens if we're picked up?'

'On the way in, there'll only be the three of you. Use your imagination. Say you're a dumb anthropologist looking for a picturesque tribe. You're hippies doing the guru circuit. You're wackos looking for the abominable snowman. The Nepalese are always finding freaks wandering about off-limits. They throw them out of the country, that's all.' Sweetwater's finger began moving of its own volition, eager to be off again, while his face remained sternly fixed on Melville. 'But you won't let yourself get picked up,' he said softly.

'Okay,' Melville said. What's the use, he thought. He watched Sweetwater's finger resume its northerly progress and heard the man's voice as if it came from the middle distance.

'Once you're inside the valley, you're home-free,' Sweetwater said. 'The Gurkhas don't want a shooting war on their own border, so they leave the Khampas well alone. It should take you three days to reach the camp. I'd like you to be there no later than the twentieth, which gives you a clear week before Osher makes his run. Weather-wise, the timing's perfect – between the monsoon and the winter. With or without Liu, the Khampas should be back inside two weeks. If they don't show in three, get out. You'll know long before then if they've got the general, because they'll send someone ahead of the main party. As soon as you hear the news, get word to me through our associate. Yonden will bring you out the best way he knows, and I'll have transport waiting to take you to India. Whatever happens, don't go back to Kathmandu.'

Melville idly traced loops on the map. 'That means I could be stuck in the camp for a month.'

Sweetwater stared at him as if he'd just noticed his nose was missing. 'What is it with you, Walter? Are you worrying about how to pass the time?'

'No,' Melville said, still describing lazy circles on the map. 'It gives the Chinese plenty of time to do something about getting the general back.'

'They're not going to come marching over those mountains, if that's what's bothering you.'

'They could warn the Nepalese. Demand that they return Liu.'

'They could, but they won't,' Sweetwater said. 'That would be like telling Delhi. You have to understand, Walter, that Nepal's an Indian satellite, and the Indians would be partial to the general themselves. So assuming the Chinese know where Liu is headed, all they could do is crank up their agents to fetch him back. Now, these people are in the business of collecting gossip at embassy garden parties, not chasing after armed guerillas in the wilderness. The Khampas, on the other hand, have been smuggling men and weapons in and out of Nepal for nearly twenty years.'

Sweetwater checked to see if Melville was reassured. He decided

153

he wasn't. 'Yonden's a trained radio operator,' he said. 'He'll be in contact with Kathmandu. You'll get plenty of warning if the military come looking for you.'

'They've got helicopters,' Melville said. 'They could reach the camp in a couple of hours.'

Sweetwater shuffled through the contents of his case. He passed Melville a colour Polaroid. 'The camp,' he said.

Melville studied the snap from various angles. 'It's hard to make out anything,' he said at last.

'Because it's a fucking hole in the ground,' Sweetwater said. 'For a helicopter pilot it would be like dropping in through a skylight.' He plucked the picture from Melville's fingers. 'Believe me, I've gone through all the operational details with Osher and I have to say that the prospects look excellent. The fact that he's putting his own life on the line speaks for itself.'

'You must admit, though,' Melville said, enunciating with care, 'that getting caught isn't out of the question.'

'For twenty thousand dollars,' Sweetwater said gently, 'you can't expect it to be a total breeze.'

'I appreciate that. I just want to know what would happen.'

'Hoo boy,' Sweetwater said, rocking back on his seat. He pondered a while. 'Okay,' he said, 'the way I see it is like this. No one's going to shoot you or hand you over to the Chinese. The same goes for the general. The Nepalese will be pissed off at you, sure enough. They'll deliver a strong protest to our ambassador, who will have his period when he hears the news. Then he'll get in touch with Washington, and a bit later someone will get back to him and sigh and say, Mr Ambassador, I have spoken with those people across the river and they confirm that this is one of their operations. Yes sir, I too very much regret that they did not see fit to keep you informed of the situation, but you and I know that they are a law unto themselves, and it appears that in this case the security aspect overrode ordinary considerations of courtesy. Yes sir, this man will say, I know that it puts Nepal on the spot, but the general left the People's Republic of his own free will, and frankly, now that he's out, we insist, repeat insist, that he be allowed to go to the country of his choice, which as you know is the United States. Perhaps, sir, you would go back to our Nepalese friends, apologise for any embarrassment caused and tell them that we are reviewing our aid programme as a matter of urgency. In the meantime, we are sending a plane to bring home General Liu and agent Melville.'

Sweetwater spread his hands. 'You see, Walter. No way are our people going to pass up all that inside information, and no way are they going to dump you. Imagine what the public would say.'

'That certainly makes me feel a whole lot better,' Melville said, intending irony but conscious that to some extent it was true.

The seconds drifted past like coral fish. Insects clicked in an arch of trees. The launch nosed through a scum of pure chlorophyll. A kingfisher flew off like a striking match. They were on their way back. The sun was a phosphorous stain at three o'clock, its heat trapped under a chemical blanket.

'That's it?' Melville asked.

'That's about it,' Sweetwater said.

Melville puffed out his cheeks and blew. 'Suppose my final decision is no?'

'Nobody's got your balls in a vice,' Sweetwater said. He massaged his knees. 'It's too late to find someone else. I guess I'd have to take my chances.'

'I mean,' Melville said, 'what happens to me?'

Sweetwater looked perplexed. 'What the fuck do you mean? Nothing happens to you, that's what. Not a thing.'

Melville smiled shakily. 'Only, back in Tokyo you said you wouldn't burden me with knowledge I had no use for. I seemed to hear the suggestion of a threat. Well, now I'm weighed down with the stuff.' He drew a breath and squared his shoulders. 'That makes me nervous.'

'I'm sure I can count on your discretion.'

'Cowardice, don't you mean. Oh sure, I'm far too frightened to tell anyone. No need to worry about that.' A bright little smile came and went like a tic. 'But there's a puzzle here. Why would you try enlist someone you despise as a coward to an undertaking that obviously calls for cool nerve and – how can I put it – a certain lack of moral imagination?'

'No one said they despise you. It's in your own head. The only thing I've got against you is that you're a man of no purpose.'

'That doesn't mean you can fit me to yours.'

Sweetwater leaned back, his hands clasped behind his head. Sweat delineated the pads of muscle under his shirt. 'I knew kids smarter than you and with enough energy to turn the world on its head die in Burma, lying in a pool of their own shit. For them it was all risk and no choice, same as them boys at Mr Yueh's place.' He smiled a thin, sad smile at Melville, who avoided his eye. 'You, Walter, you've had all the chances you could ask for and pissed them away.' He snapped the case shut. 'But now time's running out,' he said softly. 'Drip, drip it goes in your skull. You're drinking too much, running a little to seed. You can see the future and it's not looking too bright.' He patted the case. 'Decision time,' he said. 'What's it to be? Go back to pimping for salesmen? Marry that Japanese doll? Teach?' He leaned forward. 'I'll tell you one thing, Walter. Life isn't a fucking rehearsal.'

Melville snorted with derision, but his heart was thumping. 'And what kind of alternative are you offering?' he demanded.

Sweetwater shrugged. 'A chance to climb out of the groove. An adventure, I guess you could call it.'

'An adventure?'

'I don't see the hell why not. How do you want to run your life? By the philosophy of risk or the philosophy of certainty? Either way we're all spinning on the wheel, and sooner or later it's going to come up zero. So why not make one good throw before all bets are off.'

Melville stared at Sweetwater. He really means it, he thought. 'It would depend on the odds,' he managed to say.

'That's what adventure's all about. A trial of one's chance, putting fate to the test. Look at your father.'

'The risks my father took were clear-cut. What you're holding out is a witch's brew with all kinds of funny ingredients bobbing about in it.' Melville hesitated. 'I have to consider the possibility that the cup might be poisoned.'

Sweetwater looked pained. 'Anything specific in mind?'

'As a matter of fact, yes.' Melville squared his gaze. 'It occurs to me that maybe the general's got no intention of defecting. It occurs to me that the whole production's nothing but a strategy to lure Osher and his guerillas into an ambush.'

Sweetwater ducked his head, smiling. 'Walter, you've been reading too many of those bleak, existential little spy fables.'

'I don't see what's so funny. That kind of thing isn't unheard of.'

'No,' Sweetwater said vaguely, 'I suppose not.' He pondered a moment, stroking his cheek. 'Only, in my experience the simple explanation's nearly always the one to go for. Right back when I was starting out, I realised that if I went round thinking everyone was out to blow smoke up my ass, I'd never get any work done. In this business, same as any other, you have to take people on trust.'

Melville made no answer.

'I'd like to hear you say you trust me.'

For a moment Melville looked blankly at Sweetwater's guileless smile, then abruptly he turned away, embarrassed by the note of pleading in the man's voice. 'Trust a cold-eyed intelligence veteran,' he said with a carefully judged laugh. 'You must be fucking joking.'

'I mean it, Walter. Once you're in the mountains, you'll feel completely at the mercy of events. That's when you need trust to carry you through the nights. That's why I want to hear you say it.'

'Okay,' Melville said, frowning. 'I do. Up to a point.'

Sweetwater sighed. 'Up to a point will have to do.'

Melville realised that for some time they'd both been talking about when, not if. He considered raising an objection, and then found he couldn't put any force behind it. Too late, too late, the warning voice inside him said.

'The twenty thousand,' Melville said, speaking loud enough to drown the voice, 'I take it that's on a delivery-only basis.'

'Seems reasonable. You get half if you reach the camp, whether or not the general shows. Okay?'

'Okay.'

'Any more questions?' Sweetwater said, looking at his watch.

Melville found he had none.

'Well then,' Sweetwater said. He divided the contents of the flask with precision and raised his glass. 'Do I take it we have a commitment?'

Confused and worn, Melville nodded.

Sweetwater unzipped his smile. 'There you go,' he said, punching him lightly on the knee.

Sweetwater disembarked at a *klong*-side pagoda, claiming that he had to get to Mr Yueh's place in order to arrange the meeting with Zhang. He walked away across the courtyard, threading a path through sightseers, his head turning from side to side in a way that suggested touristic zeal or the suspected presence of snipers. Already Melville felt abandoned, exposed to danger. Dejectedly he ordered the crew to take him back to the hotel.

It was a five-minute walk from the landing stage, across a street where six lanes of traffic sat cooking in its own hydrocarbons. Zigzagging between the cars, Melville saw two young Western men standing on the other side. One of them touched his companion's elbow and they both looked in his direction. Melville's stomach flipped. He began weaving a more erratic course, aiming for the hotel entrance,

157

but the two watchers moved easily to cut him off. When he reached the kerb they were stationed twenty yards down the sidewalk.

Melville slowed as he approached. His heart was thumping like a rabbit in a sack. There was no mistaking their governmental air. They were a boxed set, clean and athletic, with severe blond haircuts, blameless white shirts and light-grey, rather generously-cut suits with pants that stopped short of their ankles, revealing white socks and sporty black shoes. Melville lowered his head as he made to go past.

'Pardon me, sir. Can you give us a few moments of your time?'

'Who, me?' Wearing a goofy grin, Melville looked in diminishing takes from fixed smile to fixed smile. They weren't twins, but it was hard to identify at which line or parting their features differed. They had the same hairlines, the same snubby farmboy noses, the same pastel eyes and sanitised smiles.

'What's it about, fellas?' Melville asked. Hastily he erased his loopy grin.

'May we inquire your name?' the one on the left said.

'Sure. I mean . . . don't you know? Walter Melville.'

'Walter,' the one on the left repeated brightly. 'That's nice. Hey, Walter, you on your own here?'

'Afraid so.' Melville really had to concentrate quite hard to stop his face folding into another daft grimace.

'Oh, that's too bad,' the one on the left said. 'Say, Steve, wouldn't it be nice if Walter could share in our evening.'

'Sounds good to me,' the one called Steve said. 'How does it sound to you, Walter?'

For secret agents, Melville thought, they had a damn peculiar way of doing business. 'Aren't you going to show me some ID?' he demanded.

The one called Steve laughed. 'Oh wow,' he said to his partner, 'he's *so* suspicious.' He put his face close to Melville's. 'Walter, nobody's trying to pressure you here.'

'No way,' the one on the left said vigorously.

There and then Melville decided that nothing would be achieved by trying to hold out against questioning.

The one on the left put his hand on Melville's wrist. 'If you want to see our credentials,' he said, 'why don't you come along to our centre? It's only a block away.'

'If it's all the same with you people,' Melville said, 'I'd prefer to listen to what you have to say right here.'

He tried to free his arm but the one on the left tightened his grasp.

'Hey,' he intoned, 'you're so uptight. A lot of deep tension in there, Walter.'

'Take your goddam hands off me,' Melville said, pulling free. For a fraction of a moment something ugly stained the sterile environment of his persecutor's eyes. Holy shit, Melville thought with terror. A freak. A sicko who probably conducted interrogations with the aid of blowtorch and firetongs.

'Oh-oh,' the one called Steve said in mock alarm. 'Better give Walter the good news right away.'

'Good news?'

'How would you feel, Walter,' the one called Steve said, 'if I told you that today was the first day of the rest of your life?'

Melville received the banality at first with incomprehension and then with a faint dawning of hope.

'Right,' the one on the left said. 'Pretty exciting, huh?'

'You ever give much consideration to the future?' the one called Steve said.

'Your life,' his partner explained. 'Where it will eventuate.'

'Let me ask you something,' the one called Steve said gravely. 'Do you subscribe to any particular religion?'

Relief lanced Melville's fear. 'Strictly speaking,' he said, aping his interlocutors' nutty diction, 'no.'

The pair traded self-assured smiles. The one called Steve cued his partner with a nod.

'Then our message is tailor-made for you,' he said. 'Basically, Walter, we represent a new path in psycho-spiritual awareness. We're not talking religion here. What we offer is a scientifically designed programme guaranteed – guaranteed – to enhance personal growth.'

'That's why we'd like you to visit our centre,' the one called Steve said. 'We've got alpha meters there, diagnostic charts. It's a really scientific environment.'

'Shit!' Melville said angrily. 'I thought you were CIA.'

They blinked as though he'd thrown pepper in their eyes, but recovered fast.

'Oh boy,' the one called Steve chuckled, 'is it lucky you met us. Time to make a start on that paranoia.'

Melville barged past. The one on the left jogged alongside. 'Come on,' he pleaded, 'don't be like that. Let's make friends. Let's share a Coke and talk a little.' He tried to shove a card into Melville's pocket. 'Okay, you're busy now. I can see that. That's where you'll find us. Come by Sunday. Sunday a few of us get together for a game of softball. Hey, look at me, will you?' he demanded, a shard of hate bared in his voice. 'That's not a nice way to behave. What's your problem? You think we're going to rip you off? Jesus, we want to help. Psyche-wise, you're a basket case, you'd better believe it. Let's apply a little therapy to your problems, huh? Come on,' he said, pawing at Melville's sleeve. 'Don't blow it, man.'

'Get away from me,' Melville said, chopping the hand down. 'You android, you dingaling. I might be an atheist, but I'm a fucking protestant atheist.'

He strode away.

'I feel sorry for you, Walter,' his persecutor called after him. 'You are definitely sick. You are a time bomb waiting to go off. When it happens, remember I said it first.'

At the hotel entrance Melville turned and saw them standing shoulder to shoulder on the sidewalk, facing opposite ways, scanning the street with identical smiles.

Charged up by the encounter, Melville marched briskly past the doorman's snappy salute, through the receptionist's custom-painted smile and into the elevator. The attendant recited his well-worn litany, but Melville didn't hear. Reaching his apartment he went straight to the bathroom and scooped water over his scalded face.

Raising his head, he was confronted by his reflection. He was surprised, and even disappointed, to see how normal he looked. 'Aha,' he said, 'that's because you haven't heard the news. Today's the first day of the rest of your life. You'd better get used to it, because there are going to be a few changes in that department.' He sighed. 'I know what you're thinking,' he said. 'You're thinking folly, you're thinking irresponsibility. You want to know why?' He put his face close to the mirror. 'Because I'm sick of the sight of you.' He stepped back with a laugh that froze in an apprehensive snarl. Shame and anger assailed him. 'Fuck you,' he said. 'Who gives a damn what you think. As of now I don't need your hindrance.' His eyes stared back. He snapped out the light above the mirror. 'At least something's happening,' he said to his darkened image.

Melville had a drink, took a shower and then lay down under the air conditioning's striving. The night stretched before him and he was lonely. He would have liked to spend the evening with Sweetwater, discussing what swamps and thickets lay in his path. Wondering how to pass the time, he thought of Sumiko and was startled to find that he had already confined her to the deep past. He remembered that

160

he had promised to phone. Groaning at the prospect, he buzzed the desk and booked a call to Tokyo, then had another drink.

Someone tapped on his door and he jumped up onto the points of his elbows. For the foreseeable future, he realised, he would be living on his nerves. The door opened and a girl carrying a duster and wearing what looked like a lab technician's coat stepped into the room. When she saw him she apologised and began to back out, then stopped.

'You want massage, sir?'

'Can't you people leave it alone?'

'Only three hundred baht.'

'For a massage?'

'All over body, sir.'

She was not of the same race as the porcelain dolls whom Melville frequently encountered coming and going in the lobby. Her hair was coarse, her eyebrows heavy, her nose flat and tribal. Her dark skin bore the faint stipple of childhood smallpox.

Aware that scrutiny might find her wanting, she said, 'You like, I send some other girl.'

'I don't want a girl. I want to be left on my own.'

Her brows drew close. 'Why you like to be lonely? Not nice to be lonely.'

He felt a pang of self-pity. 'How much for an ordinary massage? No fucky-fuck. Understand?'

'Hunnerd,' she said, baring snow-white teeth.

She checked out the corridor before closing the door. Once inside, she proved to be in no hurry. She wandered about the room, examining his possessions, darting shy looks at him. Finally she halted at the foot of the bed and took his feet in her hands.

'Ow! That hurts,' he said, as her strong, aboriginal fingers probed a clump of nerves in the hollows of his ankles.

She climbed onto the bed and straddled his legs. Smiling thinly, she worked upwards in an even rhythm. She unbelted his *yukata*, parted it and dug her fingers between his thigh muscles. 'Take it easy,' he hissed, but felt himself stir. She sat back on her haunches. 'Ah, so much of you,' she said politely.

She peeled off her nylon coat. Underneath she was wearing only bra and pants. She took them off and stood in the beguilingly self-conscious pose of schoolgirls and Botticelli Eves, one leg slightly crooked, the thigh drawing attention to what it attempted to conceal.

'Come here,' Melville said, his voice thick. He looped an arm around

161

her shoulder and attempted to draw her face down to his, but she ducked under his embrace. 'Hunnerd no good,' she said, giving his penis a playful slap.

She accommodated him passively, looking down at him with the uninhabited smile of an idol. The intensity of his orgasm left him wrecked, mast falling, everything carried away.

The buzzing of the phone galvanised him into making one last spasmodic thrust.

Holding down the receiver as though it were spring-loaded, he disengaged the girl with his other hand. She went into the bathroom, leaving him wrestling with his robe; some malign imp seemed to have sewn up the sleeves. Taking a deep breath, he picked up the phone.

At first he heard only a faint sibilance, scratchy whispers speaking across deep space. Then there was a series of sharp clicks and the static cleared, leaving pure ether.

'Hai.'

'Sumiko? Hi, Walter here. Sorry I didn't call sooner. I've been so tied up, you wouldn't believe it. Look, things have got a little complicated here. I'm not sure when I'll be back . . . Sumiko?'

'Mr Melville?' a Japanese man's voice inquired.

Melville shut his eyes. Unbreathing, holding out the handpiece as though it were a bomb, he lowered it back onto the rest. Still unbreathing, he waited until he heard the connection break. In the silence it sounded like iron gates clanging shut.

The girl came out of the bathroom, and when she saw him sitting stunned on the edge of the bed, she took her duster and began polishing the dressing table, concentrating on the spot where his wallet lay.

'Oh for Christ's sake just take what I owe you,' he said.

After she had gone he poured a drink with trembling hands and took it to the window. He stood there so long that dusk stole in unnoticed and gathered behind his back. He tried to open the window, but it was stuck. He raised his glass. 'To explorers,' he said, acknowledging the invisible forces waiting for him on the other side.

As he downed his glass, a peal of pointless laughter came floating up from the poolside five floors below.

BOOK TWO

Chapter 11

Pemba bolted the animal pen and ducked into a gritty wind that came funneling down from the north. The long morning shadows were filled with drifts of hail. She rounded a corner of the Lucky Place and sheltered for a moment in a protected angle, holding up her face to the sun. She could hear the wind horses fretting on the temple roof. Against all reason she was suddenly delighted by the day's possibilities.

Across the threshold of the temple she paused again. 'Daddy?' she whispered into the dark.

Not getting an answer, she climbed the steps to the gallery. 'Shoo,' she said. 'Get away.' A smallish rat grooming itself by her father's throne lolloped off without haste. Mouth wrinkled in revulsion, Pemba watched it tunnel into the robes shrouding the mortal remains of her grandfather.

Pemba crouched in front of Aim Giver and passed a bowl under his nose. 'Milk,' she said. 'Freshly drawn.' She dipped a finger into the bowl and touched it to his lips.

He gave no sign of life.

Tongue clamped between her teeth, Pemba tiptoed over to a window and pulled one of the shutters ajar, then she crept back. She checked the bowl of *tsampa* she had left him for his supper. On the evidence of the droppings around it, she decided that rats must have eaten it.

She peered into his face, turning her head this way and that, as if she were trying to decipher a manuscript written in a strange language.

His eyes were fixed open. His matted hair straggled to his shoulders. A dirty wisp of beard clung to the slit of his mouth. His upturned hands lay on his knees like the claws of a dead bird. There was a book open by his side.

Although Pemba surveyed this apparition with apparent composure, her stomach fluttered with apprehension. One of these mornings, she knew, she would find him gone, his skinny fingers tangled in his lap, the lipless mouth frozen in a final condemnation of the world.

Not today, though. A sigh escaped her as she detected in his eyes a tiny point of light, no bigger than a mustard seed.

'Did you hear the hail?' she asked. 'Like pebbles on a drum. I couldn't sleep for worrying about the barley, but Buddha be praised, it was untouched. I could hardly believe it.'

Aim Giver's focus remained firmly inward.

Pemba removed the bowl of *tsampa* and replaced it with the milk. 'I'll have to spend the day in the fields,' she said. 'There's not much time to get the harvest in. It's terrible. Winter seems to come earlier each year. The snow's already down to the nomads' valley.'

Something rattled in Aim Giver's throat. His mouth trembled. 'Where scree and snow meet,' he intoned, 'the mystic finds warmth.'

Pemba tittered uncertainly.

'Where roads cross, he divines the goals of all travellers.'

'There, there,' Pemba said, tugging her father's robe across his shoulders.

Aim Giver's stare everted itself in the blinking of an eye. 'What are you doing in my cave? Why has he sent you here?'

'Who, daddy?'

'He won't leave me in peace.' Aim Giver shuddered and began to scratch himself violently. 'First he besieged me with rats and spiders, all biting and scratching, swarming over each other until their carcasses choked me.' Aim Giver clapped his hands over his ears. 'Then he threatened me with a blizzard of weapons that nearly split my skull with their din.'

'It was the hailstorm,' Pemba shouted.

Aim Giver's taloned hand pounced on her arm. 'But I made myself immutable as a powerbolt. His spears and daggers splintered like glass on the shield of immaculate virtue.'

'Hush,' Pempa pleaded, prising his fingers loose. 'Please hush.'

Aim Giver cackled in high glee. 'He sends thieves to steal my secrets. He thinks he'll find them here,' he said, patting the book, 'but they're locked away where he'll never get them.' He tapped his skull.

'Try and drink a little milk,' Pemba said, biting back tears. She looked around in despair. 'I *must* get the barley in.'

Aim Giver knocked the bowl aside, then squirmed backwards in disgust. 'What is it?' he screeched. 'Oh, you fiend! You'd poison me with his foul essence.'

Pemba sagged under the weight of the accusation. 'It's Pemba, daddy. Your daughter.'

He squinted at her for an appreciable interval. 'You're not my daughter,' he said finally. 'No, no.'

Pemba's mouth quivered in a childlike smile of shock.

A look of profound distaste swept Aim Giver's face. 'I never wasted my seed on that trull. I never wanted her here. Don't say she never told you.'

A bar seemed to tighten around Pemba's chest. From the boneyard of the past her mother's voice disinterred itself, its exotic accent compressed in a tight whisper that trembled between rancour and self-pity.

'A fine life, you promised me, and look what I've got. A husband with a thorn for a prick. A hermit who squats in his own dirt dreaming that he's perched on some pristine peak. You can't imagine what it's like for me, stuck in that place all winter. Ice for a roof, air for walls; that's all he wants. But I don't mind telling you . . .'

A murmur cut off the voice in mid-complaint. A busy silence intervened, broken by a coarse grunt of exertion and then her mother's voice again, sounding almost skittish. *'Ssshh, Pemba will be back soon. What would she think?'*

'Who was it?' Pemba asked in a colourless voice. 'Who was that man with my mother?'

But Aim Giver was preoccupied with his own visions. 'Do you think he's kept his promise?' he said, addressing the shrouded form above the altar. 'Is he offering flowers and water at the place of wet skulls, or . . .' Aim Giver gave a small-eyed giggle '. . . has he found something more to their taste?'

Dully, Pemba looked up, half-expecting to hear her grandfather answer. His rimless eye winked at her with a gay lustre.

'You were right,' Aim Giver was saying apologetically. 'I ignored them for too long. They grow hungry and our defences crumble. But it's not too late. This year they'll get their ransom.'

While Aim Giver unravelled the thread of his tattered speculations, Pemba stole away down the steps.

'I'll show that bull from Kham the meaning of sacrifice,' Aim Giver panted. 'The Guardians will feast on a butcher's shambles that will make his offerings look like a vulture's leavings. You'll see,' he shouted, his voice rising in grotesque exultation. 'You'll see.'

Pemba shut the door and went out into the delirious sunlight. Through her tears ghost images of the sacred peak glittered in prismatic colours. The cold wind blew, winnowing her confused senses to a single thought, reminding her that soon the villagers would go south to their winter quarters, leaving her trapped in her father's pain and visions.

Presently she wiped her face on the back of her sleeve and sniffed. The barley couldn't wait; the clear sky forecast an iron frost. She collected her basket and sickle and set off down the hillside.

Pemba had a child's capacity for effacing pain. A flight of swallows migrating down the wind was sufficient to lift her spirits. The smell of a herb that she picked and rolled between finger and thumb was like balm. Any day spent away from the Lucky Place was an adventure. Forgetting past rejections, she imagined herself accepted within the circle of the other women. She could hear them now, though an abrupt steepening of the valley hid them from sight. Brittle cries drifted up to her; mattocks chinked on stony ground. She broke into a trot.

When the bottom of the valley came into view, she sat down and smiled a smile of incomprehension.

Only a few women were working, their backs conspicuously turned to the rest, who stood immobile in the ruins of their labours. Pemba's fields and all the others on the far side of the river were indeed untouched, but on the east bank, invisible from the temple, the barley had been flailed into crooked swathes.

Pemba got up then sat down again, chewing her lip. She measured the distance to the only bridge across the river. Whatever path she took she would have to pass close to the women. At last, making up her mind, she stood up, left the track and half ran, half slipped down a shaley slope to the edge of the cultivated ground. She climbed from level to level of the terraced fields until she reached an irrigation channel. Face lowered, hands holding her basket's head-strap, she set off in the direction of the river.

As she came closer, she heard two women separated by the width of their fields arguing.

'If you hadn't stolen the stones from my wall, my barley would still be standing.'

'No one touched your stones, you silly bitch.'

'Oh yes? I was on the roof with my Dorje when I saw your son walking off with them. In broad daylight. I said, "Look, Dorje, at that thieving little Komi stealing our stones." And do you know what she said to me? She said, "They're all vultures in that family, mum. Cling to their own possessions like ticks to a blanket, but see anything lying about and they're away with it." That's what she said.'

'Vultures is it? Well the last thing we want is your trash. And that goes for that Dorje of yours.'

'Don't think you've heard the last of it. I'll get what's due to me, you wait and see.'

'Rivers will run backwards before you get so much as a goat turd.'

'You wouldn't dare speak to me like that if my husband was still alive. Your thieving brat would think twice about stealing stones if I had a man to protect me.'

'Chance would be a fine thing. At least my Komi's got a father.'

'But who? Your guess is as good as mine.'

'You're a fine one to talk. I haven't forgotten the winter you sold yourself for a cup of rice in every tea-house between here and Pokhara.'

'I've never heard anything so wicked in all my life,' the aggrieved party said, giving up the wrangle. She burst into tears. 'What about my stones?' she wailed.

'Stones? Are you still on about those bloody stones? I'll give you stones.'

Pemba heard the thrumming of a hard-aimed rock and then the crack of its landing, feet in front of her. Slowly she raised her head.

Little things caught her attention. Details imprinted themselves. A boy of at least six leaned like a straw doll against his mother, his damp, bone-white face clamped to her breast. Two small girls, square packages in their thick gowns, peeped out from each side of their mother's skirts, their dirty faces striped by tears and snot. An old woman sat stark naked on a yak skin basting her shins with butter oil.

Stone-thrower stood transfixed. She was a strong woman, handsome in a haggard, no-nonsense kind of way. She dropped the other stones she was holding and her hand went to the amulet at her throat. 'Popped out of the earth, I swear it,' she said, and Pemba saw the other women finger charms and heard whispered invocations.

She wrenched her gaze away and stumbled off, splashing along the channel, throwing panicky looks over her shoulder. The women didn't move. They were still standing there, watching, when she reached the far side of the bridge. They would still be there at sundown, she knew, her heart shrinking at the prospect of a two-hour detour back to the Lucky Place.

The wind worked its alchemy, turning the barley from base metal to gold. Pemba plucked a stalk, deriving satisfaction from the heft of the

169

seed head and the prickle of the guard hairs. She took a small phial from her sleeve and sprinkled milk on the juniper branch planted at a corner of the field. Taking her sickle from her basket, she set to work.

Soothed by the rasp of her blade, the shimmering breeze and the age-old rhythm of the harvest, Pemba constructed a daydream of domestic bliss, all the while humming a mantra that she visualised as a wish-fulfilling gem.

At midday the air grew still. It would stay calm now until the light began to rise from the ground and the mountains breathed in. Wiping her forehead with her dusty hand, Pemba straightened up.

'It's not natural.'

Pemba whirled and nearly toppled, dizzied by the crow-black line of women perched on the terrace above. Stone-thrower, armed with a sickle, held the centre with her light-fingered son, Komi.

They spoke as though she wasn't there.

'Look at that barley. I tell you it's not natural. Not with the summer we've had.'

'Ma,' Komi said, 'I thought you said she didn't have a shadow.'

'Yes, but what's that thing squatting on its shoulder? Anyway, you shouldn't look. Not unless you want the horsehair man to come visiting.'

'The invisible clings to the visible. No getting away from it.'

'It's the eyes give her away.'

'You can see it clear as day.'

'See what, ma?'

'Shut up and stop pestering me.'

'Her mother was the same. I always said no good would come of our lord marrying that outlander.'

'A poisonous flower, even if pretty, is not fit decoration for an altar.'

'You're so right.'

They brooded on this profundity.

'Anyone would think she was deaf.'

'Say something.'

'Maybe she can't. Maybe the demons have blocked up her mouth.'

'And something else, eh ma?'

'I've had enough of you. Wait until I get you home.'

'It's not the boy's fault. How can you expect our children to grow up decent when there's nobody to show them the way?'

'Nothing's gone right since he shut himself away.'

170

'My brother says he's like a corpse. Like a corpse.'

'Something's sucking his life away.'

'She stroked my baby and ten days later he was dead, a rat in his cot.'

The shrill counterpoint of their accusations merged in a despairing yet vicious threnody to sick infants and ruined livelihoods. Some of the women stamped the ground, raking their hair and pounding their breasts. Only Komi was unmoved. He watched Pemba with a slack grin, a rock secreted behind his back.

'Please,' Pemba cried, swinging her head in time with the invective. 'Please.'

'Witch!' someone shouted, and the accusation seemed to hang in the air and then fall as a stunned silence. Everyone except Komi was struck by paralysis. He looked slyly from side to side, produced the rock and gently lobbed it.

To Pemba it seemed planetary-sized. Centuries passed before it struck, splintering vision, bringing down curtains in fairytale colours, breaking off fragments of memory that raced to the surface and vanished like a stream of bubbles. Waters closed over her and receded. Murmurs from afar rose and fell. The women drifted into focus, bent like gleaners. They slipped away again, and when they reappeared, their arms were drawn back.

Years of rounding up errant livestock with stones had given their arms the force of slingshots, but none of the missiles hit her head and the rest bounced harmlessly off her robe and layers of under-clothes. The salvo jolted her senses. Before they could fire the next one, she had taken flight. Komi immediately jumped off the terrace after her. The women, constrained by a reflex observance of female daintiness, queued to climb down, chattering like weasels.

Pemba fled south, the only direction open to her. She ran clumsily, head back, unsighted by blood streaming from her head wound. There was a fierce ringing in her ears and the mountains swayed back and forth like pendulums.

Three fields away the cultivated land ended, leaving a quarter mile of shattered hillside to climb before she reached the path. Komi could have caught her easily, but he was well ahead of the others and he was enjoying the game too much. He ran at her side, sometimes one side, sometimes the other, thrusting his dolt's face close to her's and ululating like the men when they drove the yak down from the pastures.

The last few feet to the path were steep. Pemba crawled up and

171

just before she pulled herself over the top, her hand closed on a flint, nodular and weighty. Komi grabbed her by one boot. In an access of terror she shook him off. He found this so funny that he let himself slide down the scree. 'Wheee,' he cried.

She ran down the path, but within seconds she heard him slap-slapping at her heels. He caught up and held station by her right side, making mock lunges. She clawed feebly at him and he darted to the other flank, skipping sideways to humiliate, his mouth agape.

Pemba swung the flint up and round into his maw. It made a serious sound, akin to the crack that a block of rock salt makes when it is struck at a point of fracture. Legs shuffling frantically to catch up with his milling arms, he ran himself into the ground with a fleshy smack and a punctured gasp. His mother had just reached the path. She grinned like a mare and kept coming, backed up now by no more than four or five women who were picking their way up the hill, skirts upheld to the knee.

Pemba had no doubt that she was running for her life. She had no mark to aim for except the patch of sky wedged between the narrowing walls of the valley. As her breathing found a rhythm, it seemed that she would make it. Looking down, she saw the path sink away and dissolve beneath her flying feet.

Looking up, she saw the shrines marking the village boundary bob into view. The sight of them brought her down to earth. It was more than ten years since she had set foot beyond those spires. The winter settlement, a long day's journey south, would be closed to her. The rest was an unknown desolation. She was going nowhere, and as this inescapable truth took hold, her will drained away. Her wound throbbed and her mouth filled with a bitterness she couldn't spit out. A shadow pattered at her heels. She tripped and sprawled, splitting her lip and driving gravel into her palms. With the last of her strength, she crawled to the nearest shrine and clasped her arms around it.

When she saw Pemba fall, Stone-thrower stopped too and sank to her haunches, her head dropping to her knees. The sickle fell from her hand. Between gasps she mouthed curses, but they sounded frail and unconvincing. She was the only one left in the hunt and her passion was exhausted. Back in the fields, Pemba's death would have been frenzied, partaking of the nature of ritual, but out here, under a calm yet attentive sky, it would be cold-blooded murder. She blew each nostril in turn, wiped her hand on the ground and got stiffly to her feet. 'Go away,' she said dully.

After a pause Pemba's whimpering stopped and her shoulders

172

ceased shaking. She hauled herself round. 'Where?' she said, astonished.

'Away,' Stone-thrower repeated, her sickle describing a sweep of the south. 'It's harvest time. You'll find work. You won't starve. It's us who'll be eating husks this winter.'

'I can't,' Pemba said, with an incredulous smile. 'I can't leave my father.'

'We'll look after our lama,' Stone-thrower said. 'But he won't see another winter out. Next year we'll have another lama. There'll be no place for you here.' She hesitated, undecided between harshness and pity. 'Better go now, for your own sake.'

She began to back away. Still wearing a bemused smile, Pemba made as if to follow. Stone-thrower skipped back, flapping her hands as though warding off a threatening dog. 'Keep away from me,' she shouted. Watching Pemba every step of the way, she retreated to a bend in the path, then turned and ran.

Pemba let her outstretched arms fall. Absently she put a hand to her forehead and felt a ragged tear, a flap of skin. A few drops of blood had flowered in the dust at her feet. Overcome by giddiness, she sat down and hunted through her sleeves until she found the piece of polished aluminium that served as her mirror.

One side of her face was crusted with grey and ochre dust. Across the other, blood had drawn a bright red curtain that parted around a bolting eye. Her mouth was swollen in a lop-sided pout.

With a mew of revulsion, Pemba flung the mirror away.

She began a wordless prayer and immediately stopped, cowed by the stillness and emptiness of her surroundings. She looked about her dazedly. Even though she was so close to home, the familiar landmarks had vanished or altered their aspect to an astonishing degree. The village and the Lucky Place were hidden behind wasted hillsides. The peak that stood at the centre of her world had sunk into the earth. She felt crushed by the weight of sky, reduced to two dimensions by its hard light.

Beyond the shrines the path dived into a gorge. From the roof of the Lucky Place she had often plotted its labyrinthine course. She measured the angle of the sun and was surprised to find that at least four hours of daylight remained.

But she made no move. She sat, hunched over her knees, looking south as the day declined and shadows crept out from under rocks. Thorn bushes rattled in the returning wind.

At last Pemba stood up. She hesitated a moment more and a sigh

173

flew from her lips, then she turned and began to trudge back up the path.

She had no hope and no choice. The other women spent part of each winter peddling blankets or working the fields of the lowlanders, but she had never been out of the valley in her life. Better submit to the persecution of her own community than go alone among strangers or wander outcast with only wild beasts and silence for company.

As she walked, an insistent noise found its way into her consciousness. A pair of red-and-black birds were keeping pace with her, flirting from rock to rock, making a sound like pebbles being knocked together. *Tik, tik. Tikka.*

Her heart turned over.

Linka's camp was no more than half a day's walk away. The Khampas had animals; she might find work and shelter with them. No sooner had the thought surfaced than she tried to push it back under. And yet her heart went on beating fast. It was a possibility. No, more than that, she realised, recalling Stone-thrower's prediction and sentence. It was her only chance. As this reality sank in, her feelings towards Aim Giver took on a set that was strangely impersonal. The old man was going to die, and the imminence of his death left her unmoved, as did the fact that he was engaged in some kind of duel with Linka. All her life he had lurked in the dark like a spider, ravelling and unravelling his webs for the things that swarmed inside his own head.

Pemba blushed, aware that she was thinking in her mother's voice, and then some dim association made her face go even hotter as she recalled Linka's slow appraisal that night in the Lucky Place.

Before stepping over the village boundary, she spent several minutes looking for her mirror.

Kneeling at the river's edge, Pemba held her head under the water until her skull ached. She cleaned her punctured hands, watching the blood whisk away in the current. She tossed back her head and wrung out the ends of her hair, looking up at the sky, a jagged sliver that hardly kept the walls of the gorge apart. It was a gloomy place, a pale version of night. She took out her mirror. In the half-light her eyes were huge, dark eclipses. She touched the centre of her forehead. On the whole she was pleased by the transformation.

She hurried on as best as she was able. There was only one path but many versions of it – short cuts for the knowledgeable that brought her up against blind faces; detours around old landslides;

hundreds of false trails left by sheep and goats. The river was swollen by monsoon snow and the villagers had dismantled the more vulnerable bridges, so that several times Pemba followed a track to the water's edge to find a deep channel between her and the other side. Then she had to retrace her steps or make her own path, sidling along greasy ledges sometimes high over the river. Choughs side-slipped past her with frantic whistles. They swung up to their roosts, squeezing into crevices or clinging to the rock like blobs of black wax, peering at her along their thin red bills before sheering off with renewed squeals. At home on her windy ridge the aerobatics of the little crows delighted her. Down here, their crepuscular frenzy made her think of lost souls.

Realising that she wouldn't reach the camp before dark, she halted under a smoke-blackened overhang where other wayfarers had carved prayers and hung scraps of cloth to divert the country gods. She sucked a piece of dried cheese unearthed from a fold of her gown and dozed for a while. When she woke it was too dark to read the inscriptions by her head, but the strip of sky was still lavender and she knew that back in the village the population would be gathered on the west-facing rooftops, their shadows stretching the length of three houses. Stricken by loneliness, she keened for a while, then pulled her robe over her head and fell asleep.

Suddenly she was awake, straining into the night. While she slept, something unwholesome had crept up on her. She looked about uneasily and then sank back with a sigh of relief. It was only the river. At this time of night, before the streams of meltwater in the high valleys froze in their tracks, it was at its highest. The channel boiled and spouted, emitting dull knocking sounds and throwing up wafts of mineral vapours.

It made sleep impossible. Even though Pemba wrapped her robe around her head and held her hands to her ears, the noise stole in, approaching from different directions, coming close and then fading, like the blind quarterings of a dim-witted but persistent beast. She tried not to look. When she did, things gathered at the corners of her eyes, only to vanish when she confronted them directly. All her fear of the wilderness was confirmed. Every corner of it was inhabited by ghouls that shunned the villages and settled places but craved the company of humans above all things. Catching her breath, she fled from them.

She felt her way by instinct and thin starlight, concentrating so hard on the path that fear was pushed into the background. Time

175

passed. How much, Pemba couldn't guess, but when she saw a brightening of the sky to the south, she halted in puzzlement, sure that it couldn't be dawn. Wary as a traveller approaching a lantern in a desert, she edged round a corner and found herself looking into the swollen face of a yellow moon.

By its light the path was visible for quite a distance. Pemba remained where she was, convinced that down there in the vaults of the canyon a presence waited. Sure enough a long shadow detached itself from a pillar and stood facing her, holding its breath until her own burst from her lungs. Then it made a noise like an old man clearing his throat and came lurching towards her, sensing her through the hole where its nose had been. She pressed herself against rock, screaming silently. A cold grue struck into her bones as it swayed above her. It seemed to be trying to speak, pleading with her. She smelt the pall of terrible loneliness it trailed behind as it moved away, shuffling deeper into eternity, searching without hope for something lost a long, long time ago.

Climbing over a spit of smooth rock she looked up to find that she was in the maw of a giant whose lolling tongue was just about to move beneath her feet.

Running from one pursuing wraith, she floundered into the river, where water demons wrapped icy caresses around her calves and whispered salacious demands.

Soaked and bleeding, Pemba proceeded down the gorge in fits and starts. Finally her terror burned itself out, leaving her grey and shrunk, too exhausted for tears even.

Everything was grey. Dawn had crept imperceptibly across the abyss, driving the stars before it. Pemba took no comfort from it. She began moving again, with no idea where she was going.

The path began to meander upwards and the walls drew back a little. Pemba toiled on. The roar of the river receded to a hiss and then a murmur. She stopped and wearily raised her head. Contorted limbs reached down to her, but after one heart-stopping moment she recognised them as juniper trees overhanging the rim of the gorge. Shocked out of her stupor, she climbed faster, her nape alive to the touch she felt certain would fall on her and pluck her back. She covered the last few feet on all fours and fell with sobbing lungs onto grass.

It was just as she remembered it from childhood – a natural amphitheatre about a mile across at its widest, floored with wiry turf and walled in to stupendous heights. Chromatic beams glanced off the snowy crests, but where she lay there was only enough light to make out the outline of the Khampas' camp. It stood on a glacis at the centre of the bowl, its walls turreted like a castle, with sentries standing asleep on the battlements.

Pemba crawled into the lap of an ancient juniper and curled up over her knees, her hands gripping her ankles.

Fear came by night; doubts bred at dawn. He would turn her away. He was a soldier. They were all soldiers. Soldiers only took women when it suited them. She couldn't tell him about the women. He would send her away. Where could she go? How could she find food and shelter?

As her eyes closed and her head slowly tilted forward, she fancied some kind of answer hovered near, contained in a vision of her mother's bland, malicious smile.

The strengthening light demolished the Khampa stronghold, reducing it to a cluster of crude houses dug into the rubble of an old moraine, levelling its ramparts until only three keeps remained standing, manned not by soldiers but by clusters of ragged prayer flags.

Waking with a jerk, Pemba reached for her mirror. She let go of it, conscious of her bloated lip and crusted brow. Getting up stiffly, she wandered along the edge of the gorge in search of water. She grew increasingly desperate. Any moment the sky would burst into light, exposing her as a slinking cur to be driven off. On an anvil-shaped outcrop balanced a thousand feet over the river, she felt such despair that she poised herself at the tip. An updraught took her weight, blowing tears from her eyes. She opened her mouth to cry out and it filled her lungs. Taking another breath, she turned and set off towards the camp.

A few shaggy ponies cantered away on softly thudding hooves. Snow pigeons burst from one of the three towers and completed a circle on clapping wings. A blue haze of smoke hung motionless above the houses.

The only other sign of occupancy was a Khampa who sat cross-legged on his roof, mumbling prayers while he brushed his unbraided hair over his face with a bundle of twigs. It hung in a black veil to his waist, and either he couldn't see Pemba or else he chose to ignore her. For a moment she truly thought that she might be invisible, her form spirited away in the gorge.

'Linka,' she whispered.

Still praying, the man reached for the rifle propped by his side and parted the tent of hair, revealing hard bright eyes in a sooty face and white teeth as big as *mani* stones.

'I've come to visit Linka,' Pemba said.

The Khampa slowly swivelled his chin until it was pointing towards the tallest of the towers. Raw turquoise stood out against his dark throat. He dragged his rifle across his thighs with the same unconscious movement a mother makes to retrieve her baby. Pemba's interruption had not upset the even tenor of his devotions.

Linka's door was on the first floor, above quarters for the animals. The sounds of the warm crush below put heart into Pemba. The first storey, a single room, contained only a few sacks. A ladder led to the next, which was furnished with a sleeping board and blankets, a cold central hearth, a shelf for cooking utensils and another for texts and photographs, a crude wooden altar and another ladder that led to the roof. Pemba climbed it, biting her lip so hard that her wound bled.

Linka was sitting up in a nest of furs, his back bared to her.

'Has the lama sent for me?'

Pemba answered with a shake of her head.

Linka turned and stared at her. 'How did you hurt yourself?'

'I fell. In the gorge. I lost my way.'

He was thinner than she remembered. His shaven scalp was bristly, his skin a dark yellow. His eyes were small and heavily cowled.

'You must have an important reason for coming here. Not many people would care to travel that gorge by night. Well?' he demanded.

'There was a bad hailstorm,' she said in a small voice. 'It destroyed many of the fields. The women were angry. They've had so many misfortunes recently. All the children are ill, with eyes like curds. They won't eat. Some of them have died.'

Linka grunted, cutting her off. 'And they blame you.' His eyes were curious. 'It's a strange community where the people accuse their own lama's daughter of being a witch.'

Pemba's body felt as though it were enveloped in ice.

Linka climbed heavily to his feet, wrestling his coarse woollen robe over the yoke of his shoulders. He walked over to her and cupped her chin in his hand, forcing her head back. She submitted, knowing that this was a man who could peer into the dark heart of things, who could reach behind the surface and pull out a demon by the horns.

He let go of her roughly and went to the edge of the roof.

'Do you think I'm a witch?' she asked in a barely audible voice.

'Maybe,' he said morosely, staring out over the camp. 'Hostile

178

forces are very active here. Not only in your village, either. My own people have been sick. The channel we were digging was nearly finished when a landslide carried it away. That night I saw a column of lights on the mountain. Yes,' he said, 'there are signs.'

Everything within Pemba's field of vision began to recede and turn dark at the edges. The mountains fell away and the sky whirled past.

Linka caught her as she reeled. He said something she didn't hear, then she caught the word 'rest'.

'No, no,' she said, forcing open eyes that were already vacant. 'You must set me some work.'

'Sleep,' he said, in a voice that carried from the far distance.

Like all her people, Pemba had a constitution that was proof against all but the most severe forms of wear and tear. She woke up none the worse for her ordeal, if a little confused. Thin beams of sunlight pierced the cracks and knotholes of a shuttered window set deep into the walls. A bowl of milk had been placed beside her bed. She drank it, then took out her mirror to confirm what she had dreamt: Linka had bathed her face while she slept.

No sound penetrated the tower. She tiptoed over to the window. When she pulled back the shutter she had to avert her face and shield her eyes.

The eastern wall of the amphitheatre had metamorphosed into a burning fort, a dream citadel of curved and perpendicular forms carved out of a single mountain. Pemba made out gates and spires, a honeycomb of deep chambers and loopholes. Craning forward as far as she could, she could just see the summit of the monolith. Little breaths of cloud floated up from the rock, growing larger and more insubstantial until suddenly they sublimated into empty sky.

'Night falls early in this place,' Linka said behind her.

Embarrassed, she wriggled backwards out of the recess.

In the twilight Linka was a storm-coloured presence who seemed to fill the room. She recognised the patchwork coat of hides he had worn at the Lucky Place. He raised something shiny, a brass pot. 'Medicine,' he said. 'Come up to the roof.'

In the time that it took to climb the ladder, the mountain had burned down to a gargantuan ember, still glowing hot against a field of cold blue. While Linka laid out his instruments, Pemba looked out over the rooftops.

The Khampas were out in numbers. One was stretching a newly flayed hide, standing with his heels on one end while he tried to pull the other over his head. Another plaited a rope. Most were scattered in identical attitudes of repose, leaning with folded arms against the corner shrines, eyes shut to the sunset. A few of them were speaking to anyone in earshot who was bothering to listen.

The jangling of bells drowned their voices. A flock of lanky sheep came jostling towards the camp, stampeding before the vapours that were spreading out from the gorge. A woman darted back and forth beside them, shouting *ca-ca-ca, br-br-br* in an artificially high tone. She noticed Pemba and stopped. It was the time of evening when faces stand out like paper lamps, but Pemba couldn't tell if she was pretty.

Pemba stepped back, shivering. Linka patted his rug, inviting her to share it. Beside it he had placed the brass pot, a mortar and pestle, and a shabby cloth bag. Linka untied the bag and shook a piece of garnet-coloured stone into the mortar.

'How is the lama, your father?' he asked politely.

'He's very feeble. He doesn't eat. Everyone knows he'll die in the winter.'

'Then you should be with him.' Linka frowned. 'Does he know you've gone?'

'He no longer knows who I am. He says he hasn't got a daughter.'

'His is a greater awareness. You were wrong to leave him. Tomorrow you must go back. If you're worried about the other women, I'll send someone to speak to them.'

'I can't go back. I won't.'

Linka began pounding the crystal. 'Tell me the first law of right living,' he demanded.

'Not to take life,' Pemba said. She frowned in concentration. 'Put yourself under the protection of a strong god.'

'And how do you do that?' Linka asked. 'By following the counsels of a wise teacher.' He looked up. 'That's the cause of your people's misery. They've ignored the guidance of their teacher and sunk into a pit of corruption.'

'It's him who ignores them,' Pemba cried. 'They crawl on their knees to him but he won't listen.'

'Ah,' Linka sighed, shaking his head in admiration, 'it's a hard way that he's chosen. A hard way.'

'What do you know about it? You haven't spent your life walled up with him. You've seen the world.'

'Like the wind,' Linka said, smiling into the mortar, 'and like the wind I've raised nothing but dust.'

His gaze travelled around the amphitheatre. The mountain had grown cold and now appeared more shadow than substance, hollow like a cinder. The mist crawled across the turf, carrying the bitter smell of frost and dung fires. The silences from the other rooftops were growing longer.

Linka shivered. 'It gets dark here so quickly,' he murmured.

Pemba looked about her. The mountains massed close, but she felt safe within the huddled circle of the camp. She could hear the placid ruminations of quartered animals and the sounds of the hearth. It had been years since she spent a night in company. 'I like it here,' she said. 'I always loved coming here with my mother.'

'While I,' Linka said, just as dreamily, 'can't forget how your sacred peak came alight though the sky all about it was black.' He ground the pestle into the splinters of crystal. 'Did you know that the village council has asked me to succeed your father?'

'But you're a soldier,' Pemba said stupidly.

'So? It's a long road that has no turning.' Linka gave her a fractured smile. 'Unfortunately, I still have some way to travel. Your village council asked permission of the authorities, but they refused, so now your people plan to send a delegation to Dolpo. I understand the lama they wish to appoint has a reputation for restoring temple paintings.' His smile grew thin. 'I can't vouch for his ability to restore your good fortune.'

'Surely the soldiers will give you an amnesty.'

'That depends,' Linka said, working the pestle vigorously, 'on what I can give them in return.' He looked up, his face grave. 'Go home to your father,' he said. 'There's a bad winter coming. This isn't the place for a girl.'

'I'm not a girl,' Pemba cried, 'and the Lord Aim Giver isn't my father.' Her hands flew to her mouth. Her shocked eyes met Linka's amused gaze.

'Go on,' he said encouragingly.

'He isn't my father,' she murmured through her fingers, translating into words what she had never dared admit even to her secret self.

'Then who . . . ?' Linka said, tactfully letting the question die away.

'Aim Giver wouldn't take a wife,' Pemba said haltingly. 'It was my grandfather who contracted the marriage. He brought my mother from Kyrong.' Pemba looked about vacantly. 'She was so lonely here. She always talked of going home and taking me with her. There was a beautiful waterfall behind her house, she said, and forests of bamboo and rhododendron with birds like jewels.' Pemba bit her finger,

181

stifling a sob. 'She died when I was seven, the same year as my grandfather.'

'Your real father,' Linka said.

'Yes,' Pemba whispered. 'I found them together once, here – perhaps in this very house.'

'Well, what difference does it make?' Linka said energetically. 'Father, grandfather – you all spring from the same bone, issue from the same door of knowledge.' He slapped his knees. 'And that's why you must remain with Aim Giver until he reaches the goal of liberation.'

'You don't understand,' Pemba cried. 'I came here to warn you that he plans to kill you.'

Linka laughed from his belly. 'So his flame doesn't burn so low after all.'

'He's a dying lamp that spits and flares before it goes out.'

Linka peered at her. 'Why does he want me dead?'

'He's jealous. Soon his light will be extinguished, while yours burns like a brimming lamp.'

She lowered her eyes, hoping her blush would pass unseen in the dusk.

Linka dismissed her explanation with a tired wave.

'It's true,' Pemba blurted. 'He thinks you're going to steal his powers. He babbles about the place of wet skulls and threatens to make a sacrifice to drive you away.'

'The place of wet skulls?' Linka said, his head jerking up.

'A temple,' Pemba muttered, suddenly nervous, 'the throne of the Guardians.'

'Ah yes,' Linka murmured, looking up at the mountain. Under starlight it had assumed the form of a gigantic mollusc shell. 'Tell me about them.'

'I don't know,' Pemba said, turning away. 'Only the lama can go there. Even the other men aren't allowed into the cave.'

'Tell me,' Linka insisted. In the dim light his eyes stood out like spots on a die.

'Their king is called Shalawoka,' Pemba said haltingly. 'He was a great general.'

'Was it Shalawoka who built these towers?'

'Oh, no. Shalawoka lived here a long, long time ago, in the dark age. This settlement was built much later, but it was empty when our people came here. They suffered terribly at first. Wolves killed the sheep and the barley wouldn't grow. Bandits rode over the high pass every autumn. Things were as bad as they are now.' Pemba halted in confusion. 'I'm sorry. I didn't mean . . .'

Linka dismissed the apology with a smile. 'You're talking about the time of the first lama,' he reminded her.

'Yes,' Pemba said reluctantly. 'He divined the cause of the misfortune. In a dream he saw the place of the wet skulls with Shalawoka and all his army, so he transformed himself into a powerbolt-terror and lifted the mountain on the tip of his horns until the demon-general and his men ran out. Then the lama turned himself into a red fury and set their castle on fire. Shalawoka pleaded for mercy, but the lama showed no pity until the demon-general swore to put his powers at the service of the community. In return, the lama let Shalawoka withdraw into the lower part of the mountain and promised to bring them gifts after each harvest.' Pemba's voice faltered. 'I shouldn't be telling secrets to strangers,' she said.

'I expect I'd hear the same story in every valley within a month's ride.'

Pemba was scandalised. 'No one has Guardians as fierce as ours. That's why nobody but the lama can go into their cave.'

'But not Aim Giver,' Linka said with a condescending smile. 'He doesn't think it worthwhile to honour his ancestor's pledge.'

'Perhaps that's why we have so much bad luck,' Pemba muttered.

'Perhaps. There's nothing so vengeful as a god who's ignored.' Linka turned his gaze on the mountain. 'Your grandfather – your true father – didn't ignore them, though. Did he?'

'No,' Pemba said shortly. She didn't want to talk about gods and demons. This stranger with the small eyes and dry voice was beginning to frighten her as her father, with his well-worn gibberings, never had. When he asked questions, she felt he already knew the answers.

And then, recalling how this conversation had started, she was frightened for him.

'He can't really harm you, can he?'

'This is his valley,' Linka said absently, his attention still fixed on the mountain. 'They're his Guardians.'

'I don't believe it. He's a foul old spider who can't catch anything in his web.' She burst into tears.

Linka's cheeks bulged in a smile. 'I won't send you back,' he said.

Pemba was suddenly dry-eyed and cautious.

'You said you wanted work,' Linka said.

'Let me look after your flocks,' Pemba said eagerly. 'No one's more cunning with animals than I am. Ask any of the women. They'll tell you . . .' She broke off as she realised what the women would say about her uncanny way with beasts. In any case, Linka was denying her request with a good-humoured shake of the head.

'I want you to take me to the place of wet skulls,' he said.

Pemba bit her lip hard enough to draw blood. 'I can't,' she whispered. 'I don't know the path. It's secret. I told you, only the lama knows the way.'

Linka stared at her as though her thoughts were parading across a small stage behind her eyes. 'You said the temple was in a cave,' he pointed out. 'How do you know if you haven't been there?'

'I heard my grandfather talking about it to my mother.'

'They came here together, every autumn?'

'Yes.'

'Did they go to the place of wet skulls together?'

'I don't know where they went off to,' Pemba said in confusion. 'I was only a child.'

'But they did sometimes go off together, leaving you here alone.'

'Sometimes,' Pemba whispered. 'At night.'

'In the month of the harvest – this month,' Linka said quietly. He sighed. 'Now I know why the lord Aim Giver is happy to see the glory of seven generations end in the closing of an eye.' Linka picked up the mortar and peered into it. 'Tomorrow you and I will look for the path,' he said.

'Please don't take me with you,' Pemba begged. 'I don't know how to behave in the presence of gods.'

Linka frowned at her. 'With a lineage as glorious as yours? I promise, your comportment will be perfect.'

'I'll be frightened,' Pemba moaned, 'and then you'll be angry with me and send me away.'

'Not if you hold fast to the knowledge that the Guardians have vowed to protect your community.'

'But you're a stranger,' Pemba said.

'So was the first lama,' Linka said with a fat smile that wasted away as he looked once more on the mountain. 'Mind,' he said, 'we'd better make the proper offerings. They'll be hungry after waiting so long.'

Linka made Pemba eat, telling her that she must be strong for tomorrow. Afterwards he took the mortar and blew on it as though it were hot before tipping its contents into the bowl. The powdered crystal gleamed in the dark. Lifting the brass pot, Linka poured a thin

184

stream of bluish-white liquid onto the powder and stirred the mixture with the pestle. He cupped his hands around the bowl and raised it to her lips. 'Go on, drink,' he ordered. 'It's only *chang*.'

She shut her eyes and swallowed. The beer was vinegary and the powder bitter, leaving her mouth dry and puckered. Linka had a jar of water ready.

He got up, his head among the stars. 'It will make you sleep. You'd better go into the house.'

'Can't I stay here?' she pleaded. 'I'm not tired.'

For a few moments his shape remained impressed on the sky. As it dissolved, so did her consciousness.

She woke with a deep sigh and slowly lifted her arm, trailing her fingers down ghostly nebulae that drifted across the heavens like the flimsiest of prayer scarves. Her senses were magnetised, receptive to the faintest sound. A lynx coughed far down the valley. A flight of shooting stars hissed into extinction.

A slight tremor beneath her signalled Linka's return. Pemba caught her breath, her heartbeat matching the slow tread of his feet on the ladders. The trapdoor scraped back. He came and sat down beside her as if she didn't exist.

She plucked up the courage to speak.

'Will you let me stay if I show you the cave?'

She clenched her eyes and prayed wordlessly as she waited for his answer.

He didn't speak. He sat deep inside his own thoughts.

She lifted a corner of her blanket. 'It's so cold,' she whispered, her stomach constricting at her audacity. 'Won't you come to bed?'

He turned so slowly that she was able to imagine every kind of expression that his face might register, from contempt to utter incomprehension; but she could not have anticipated his gentle, somehow desolate smile. Tears started to her eyes when he laid his hand on her shoulder. 'Stay,' he murmured.

In gratitude her hand stole towards him, hesitated, and then settled cautiously on his thigh. Yearning filled her throat.

Linka appeared impervious to her desire.

With the panic of uncertainty Pemba undid one of the toggles on his coat and slipped her hand inside. He shied and in fright she tried to withdraw her hand, but his own trapped it as it fled. Slowly his grip relaxed, though she could sense the tension on his skin.

She worked her hand deeper, watching him in some puzzlement. He appeared to be in contention with some internal pain.

185

When her hand found the source, he braced as if to resist, then sagged and tilted, his bulk coming to rest along the length of her. She could hear his nasal breathing, like the nervous huffing of a high-strung horse as it stands under the halter.

It was so simple that she nearly laughed. By a touch she had tamed the beast, reducing him to straining acquiescence, closing his reason to everything but the pleasure absorbed through her fingers. With a crook of her hand she exerted her control, drawing him close, then clasped him around the neck and fell weightless back on the furs.

He leaned over her, frowning, and traced a line across her brow.

'I can look into one eye,' he said. 'Or I can look into the other. Not both at the same time.'

'Am I really a witch?' she murmured.

'I think,' Linka said, 'that you're your mother's daughter.'

Half smiling with the secret pride of power, Pemba unknotted her girdle. She sensed the enchantment of her eyes, cloudy abysses that drew him down.

He cupped his hands beneath her, lifting her as though she were a heavy vase.

She gave a little gasp, a quick squirm.

'A woman's lust is a thousand times stronger than a man's,' he whispered.

'No,' she panted. 'It's . . . oh! . . . aaah! . . . I haven't . . . I never went to the pastures with the boys.'

'How old are you?'

'Eighteen.'

'Then it doesn't matter if the gate stays shut a little longer.'

The silken ram was withdrawn a little. A red heat suffused her, spreading up her spine and scalding her breasts. She wanted him to invest her fully. Pressed against him, she tried to assimilate him through every pore, but while that sheerest of walls separated her heartbeat from his pulse, she felt removed from him. She gave a groan of entreaty and signalled submission by shaking her head. He remained at a distance, his drum beating time outside the undefended wall.

She looked beyond him at the sky.

The stars had thickened and solidified in a lake whose surface glistered and pulsated. Beneath it shapes came and went: dragons coiling and uncoiling, flowers that bloomed with soft explosions, conches issuing streams of different-coloured nectars.

Her fever cooled and a torpor settled on her. Her limbs weighed heavier than mountains. She was enfolded at the centre of a mandala, fixed at the unshakeable centre of things. It was her breathing that blew through creation.

Attuned to all rhythms, she sensed the current quicken within him. The moon was up, stamped on the sky like a shaman's seal, its gold face blurred by the vestiges of ancient ideograms. His eyes gleamed in its light like flakes of mica. The tide began to swell. His hands moved on her as though grasping for something insubstantial; they clutched as though he feared that in his moment of triumph she might elude him.

Pain stabbed to her heart. Arched on it, her throat bared, she hurtled through a spiral vortex, down scarlet and ivory cataracts into an indissoluble flow of pleasure that carried her far from land.

Waves lapped and died, leaving her adrift on a mirrored ocean.

Linka stirred. A breeze feathered the surface of the sea, turning it dark and opaque. She sighed, feeling her flesh congeal in the bitter air.

Linka pulled the blanket about them. She sensed his need for tribute. 'My master,' she whispered, stroking her face against his chest.

'My mistress,' he said sadly.

Chapter 12

For three days Melville's contact did not reveal himself. Melville wasn't put out. Since arriving in Kathmandu his sense of purpose had gone a bit fuzzy at the edges.

He was comfortably lodged in a spacious villa on the northern outskirts of town, well away from the haunts of hippies and the other seekers after emancipation. The house had been built for a Rana princeling whose portrait, in cricket whites and morning dress, framed windows that offered an almost Italianate prospect of wooded, civilised hills. Melville spent much of the time in the garden, under a pipal tree where a pair of lovesick scops owls, the birds of Athena, fondled each other's beaks. Two servants came with this little piece of Arcadia.

The previous tenants had been a husband-and-wife team of folklorists. They had moved out a month ago, laid low by hepatitis, leaving behind a stack of Fritz the Cat comics, a plate of dried-up hash brownies and a bicycle hand-painted with lotus leaves. Melville read the comics before feeding them to the fire, for the evenings could be cool. He threw the dope cookies to the piebald crows that hung about his breakfast table. The bicycle he decided to press into service when, on the afternoon of the third day, one of the servants gave him a hand-delivered note with a place and a time: *Tomorrow. 08.50. Bodhnath.*

A couple of miles outside town, when the chain jumped the sprocket for the second time, Melville regretted his impulse. The bike was of World War I provenance, a despatch rider's mount built on a prodigious scale, with double-crossbars in heavy-gauge steel and outsize wheels fabricated with Flanders mud in mind. Over the passing of the years the chain had stretched by a good inch, the sprocket teeth had worn to hooks, and the crank had accumulated so much free play that each arc of revolution between eleven and two o'clock was lost motion.

Melville hung the chain back and straightened up. The sun looked like a cigarette tip burning through layers of thin white cloth. The monsoon was late going. His only view of the Himalayas had been on the flight in, when his fear of flying had been temporarily quelled by the spectacle of snowpeaks racked up in the heavens a mile or so above the plane's cruising height.

Melville mounted up, watched by four Newar women harvesting rice. They elbowed each other and grinned as he went on his cranky way. Recalling his fantasy about warriors and mud-bound peasantry, he grinned back like he'd bitten into a mouthful of shit.

He reached Bodhnath ten minutes late. Hastily propping the bike against an alley wall, he went into the square and took up position at a corner of the giant white *stupa* whose lazy painted eye ignored the shopkeepers setting out their tourist wares around the compound. In the belief that less indifferent eyes would be watching him, Melville held his ground.

A row of novice monks filed past, idly spinning prayer wheels set into the base of the shrine. A reliquary housing the bones of Kashyapa Buddha, Melville read in his guidebook before he slipped out the piece of fibrous notepaper secreted under the cover and checked the pencilled message. The precise military timing was a little worrying, but surely his contact wouldn't have given up on him already. Shit, why couldn't he just drop in at the house and discuss things over a *nimbu pane*?

Melville had a moment of hope when an American in an Afghan helmet and baggy white drawers approached with an offer to show him the sights. Melville took in the guy's wispy beard and lobotomised smile and declined. The man backed away, his smile intact.

At 9.20, beginning to feel conspicuous, Melville set off on a circum-ambulation of the *stupa*. A group of women with tar-black hair and high, padded cheekbones were spinning wool at the entrance to a carpet workshop. 'Good morning,' Melville said in Tibetan, and then had to fend off a volley of unintelligible salutations. He'd only taken up the language a week before.

A fat shopkeeper in a business suit stepped out of his emporium and held up for inspection a small bronze buddha. Melville smiled no thanks. Next time round the dealer was rotating a hand-held silver prayer wheel.

Maybe all arrangements had been cancelled, Melville thought. It wasn't out of the question. The entire production had been mounted on the assumption that the general was happy with his lines, but he'd had plenty of time to rehearse his role, and the prospect of slipping his own troops and then giving himself into the care of a bunch of guerillas and . . . hell, nobody's nerves were bulletproof.

189

Come on, Melville growled. Give me a signal.

Rattled and dispirited, he began a third and, as far as he was concerned, final circuit. He would stay another week, he decided. Check out the ethnological opportunities. It would be a nice country to work in. Nice people. He'd arrived five years behind the rest of the caravan, though. Almost all titles had been assigned. Except in the border zone, of course. And that was another thing, he thought, his mind performing a back-flip. Charlie had implied that getting to the camp would be a stroll, but from what he'd been able to gather, the Nepalese were very serious about keeping people out of the restricted areas.

Melville groaned, thinking about the Khampa wages stashed back at the villa. He was meant to hand them over to Yonden. He stopped, his gaze swarming across the square. You want your money, you have to come and get it. And what about this Gunn fellow? He was supposed to be in town.

Christ, Melville thought, if I ever get to meet these people I'm certainly going to say a few harsh words about the organisational detail.

Punching his thigh, Melville continued on a diminishing circle.

This time the fat dealer was holding aloft a small white rectangle. He looked like a bored tour rep flagging down an unfamiliar passenger in an airport arrivals hall. In the forlorn hope that he was indeed being signalled, Melville went over.

'*Namaste*,' he said, baring a peaky smile.

The item proved to be a painting in gold on ivory of a courtly man and maid locked in gymnastic congress, watched by a pair of servants in hiding.

'You were so buried in thought,' the dealer said. 'I am wondering how to get your attention.'

Melville glanced at the sign above the shop. Ganesh Antiques. Shipping Worldwide. V.K. Sood. Melville assumed that Sood was an Indian. It *had* to be him, he thought.

'It is not quite the original,' Sood said, 'but you must agree it is charming.'

His voice was faintly husky and had the quality of complicity that Melville expected. His face, dark with darker sacs of subcutaneous ink beneath wily eyes, was composed around a small pink smile. He was an unpleasant-looking little prick, Melville decided.

'It's charming,' Melville agreed.

'Two hundred dollars.'

190

'But it's not what I had in mind.'

Melville let an opening develop that Sood declined to take.

'What I'm really looking for,' Melville said, speaking with emphasis, 'is an item with a Tibetan flavour.'

Sood laid a jewelled hand on his elbow and escorted him into the dimly lit shop, parking him in front of a wall given over to the usual collection of cottage industry prayer wheels, temple masks, statues of Buddha and Tara, ritual daggers, powerbolts, bells, incense bowls, charm boxes, hideous jewellery, tinderboxes and oleographs of the incumbent Dalai Lama. The air was a stale cocktail of smells – sandalwood, tarnished metal, raw jute, unwashed wool, Sood's hair oil. A radio was playing tinny music behind a closed door at the back of the shop.

'I don't mean something knocked out around the corner,' Melville said, gritting his teeth in a smile. 'I'm talking about a genuine Tibetan article. Something from Tibet.'

Sood inhaled through his nose at some length, as though he was warming up for a yoga exercise.

'How many times am I telling customers about the realities of that troubled but fascinating country.' He struck a pedantic schoolmaster's pose, head slightly bowed, index finger extended to tick off salient points on his chubby palm. 'Consider, please, the market situation. Most Tibetan refugees sold their treasures years ago to pay for bare necessities. The Chinese forbid the export of all works of art, and they have destroyed much of what exists wholesale. Wholesale,' he repeated, tapping his palm. He looked up gravely. 'With demand so vast and supply so small, how can prices be anything but astronomical?'

'How indeed? Look, surely you must have one item you can show me.'

'What particular item do you have in mind?' Sood said, his voice neutral.

Melville stared at him. The guy hadn't actually identified himself. What if he'd made a mistake?

Anxiously Melville looked out into the square. There were many figures now in the blinding, starchy light. One of them might be the real contact.

'No need to look elsewhere,' Sood said. 'You have come to the right place.'

Melville turned back, blinking light out of his eyes. 'That's what my colleague said. Charlie Sweetwater. He recommended you highly.'

Still Sood maintained his equivocal air. He pondered, outlining his mouth with the tip of his forefinger, studying Melville's face like a painter wondering what feature to draw first. At last he nodded.

'Since I am catching your eye with an amorous work, I think you are a gentleman smitten by the gentle sex. Wait here please.'

He backed away and Melville gave a vexed hiss.

The instant Sood was through the door he unreeled a string of Hindi that was matched in shrillness by a female voice. The radio cut out in mid-note. A door slammed.

Sood issued out of the door with the solemnity of a sacristan. He was carrying a large, squarish object wrapped in a blanket. He glanced out of the shop, both ways, placed the package on a counter and beckoned Melville over. He started to undo the wrapping.

'Have you been followed?' he said, his question pitched at such a matter-of-fact level that it took time to register.

'Followed?'

'Are you the object of attention?'

'Of course not. Why should I be? I've hardly set foot outside the villa.'

'In my experience, Tibetans are not the most discreet people to do business with. They like to get drunk, and then they become chatterboxes. Sometimes they chatter to the wrong people.'

Melville's heart sank. 'Are you saying the Nepalese know why I'm here?'

'If they do, you will soon find out.'

'I don't happen to find that particularly comforting, Mr Sood. Charlie assured me that nothing happened in this town without your knowing about it.'

'To my knowledge, nothing *has* happened. I am merely being cautious.'

'I'm all for caution, but no one's watching me. I guarantee it.'

'If they were, they might be wondering why you are showing no interest in this beautiful picture.'

Sood had pulled back the last fold of blanket and was looking at Melville as though his interest in the piece resided in the effect it had on the beholder.

Reluctantly, Melville gave it as much consideration as his mind would allow.

It was a *thanka*, a Tibetan temple painting, and although obviously old, the pigments were still brilliant under their patina of smoke and grime. The theme was coitus as an occult rite, portrayed with

192

conventional figures but undoubted technical skill. Adrift in a cerulean sky dotted with fluffy white clouds, a dark-featured man and a full-breasted woman were entwined in a carnal embrace on a throne of lotus petals. The man had assumed a joint-twisting but effortless meditative posture; the woman was seated on his lap, her legs wrapped around his waist. In her right hand she held a curved knife, in her left a skull cup brimming with blood.

'Very esoteric,' Melville said. 'Very Tibetan.'

'From a temple in Kham. I purchased it from the lama who smuggled it out. I can only guess, but I would say it is fifteenth century – an authentic work of tantric art. I take it you are familiar with tantrism.'

'Only the California school. You know, let it all hang out.'

'Nation must speak to nation,' Sood said indulgently. He put the tips of his fingers together. 'Some people would say that tantrism represents the flowering of Tibetan Buddhism, the ripening, perhaps' – his mouth formed a bud – 'the over-ripening. As a scholar, you will know that the tantric philosophy concerns itself with the identification of the self with the absolute, the microcosm with the macrocosm.'

'I'm no expert,' Melville confessed.

'Then my advice to you is: think of a ball.'

'A ball? Will a baseball do?'

'If you like,' Sood said, unprovoked. 'Now imagine that when you cut open this ball you find another one, and inside that another, and inside that one more, and so on and so on and so on etcetera, etcetera, ad infinitum until, at last, you open a ball and find . . .'

'Another ball?'

'The same one you started with. The same one.'

'Most instructive. Look, can we come back to this when we've settled the main business? First, I was expecting to meet up with these damn Khampas.'

'Soon, soon. I have sent word telling them you're here.'

'I've been here an hour, for chrissakes! You say you're worried about me attracting attention, but you let me walk round and round that *stupa* like I was in a showring. Mr Sood,' Melville said, fighting to keep his wrath in bounds, 'I'm not entirely happy with the way this is shaping up.'

Sood's cheeks dimpled in an inward smile.

'Now how do you reach this ball, this universal spirit that is in all and that *is* all? Not by lengthy study I am telling you. No indeed. In tantrism truth is experienced, not learned – experienced through every

193

kind of behaviour, including many that might seem indecent to modern sensibility East and West. Many people lacking your educational advantages are seeing this picture and thinking hanky-panky. They are missing the point. Look again. The man is a guru; the woman is his yogini. They are performing an exercise designed to achieve the union of opposites, a spiritual communion that transcends self.'

Try telling US Customs that, Melville wanted to say. He breathed a sigh of forbearance. String along, he told himself. You need this creep.

'Why the knife in the woman's hand?' he asked.

'Ah. Tantrism was a hotch-potch of many traditions. These figures are inspired by the Hindu gods Siva and Kali. As you know, when Siva is defeated by Kali the drinker of blood, he begs her to cut out his heart and unite with him so that he can absorb her terrible energy.'

'A kind of inverted ego trip.'

'Yes, you are correct. The heart is the ego. I am thinking that in this respect we of the East are a jump ahead of your Mr Freud.'

'Way ahead.' Melville studied the *thanka*. 'It must be worth a fortune.'

'Five thousand dollars. It is not everybody's cup of tea.'

. 'And then there's the problem about getting an export licence.'

Sood threw up his hands as though warding off bats. 'Please do not get excited over that question.' His eyebrows performed a shuffle. 'When it comes to cutting red tape, you will find me a tantrist. Action not words is my motto.'

'So if I pick up a valuable item that can't be taken out of the country by conventional channels?'

'I am at your service.'

'Any item?'

'Any item, any destination. When you have found what you're looking for, let me know as soon as possible.'

'Well good,' Melville said. 'I'm glad something's settled.'

Sood briefly engaged him in a supple smile.

'This item,' Melville said. 'I'm still waiting to get in touch with the people who can help me lay hands on it.'

A slight refocusing of Sood's eyes directed Melville's attention to the square, where a man in a black mock-leather jacket was lounging against the *stupa*.

'Your friends are waiting,' Sood said. He hesitated. 'Before you join them, please take some words of advice. Do not let yourself become too excitable with these people. They are only too excitable themselves.'

Sood began repacking the *thanka*.

When Melville realised he was being dismissed, he gave a startled cough. 'Before I go,' he said, 'I hope to hear a lot more advice than that. We've hardly started talking – if that's what you can call this pussyfooting around. I need to know about dates, ways and means. I expect to be briefed on the Khampa situation.'

'I cannot give you a shipping date,' Sood said, busy with the *thanka*. 'There are too many uncertainties.' He glanced up. 'You might not find what you are looking for. Transporting it through the mountains will be difficult. Provided that you can get it to me – preferably without damage – I guarantee its safe export. And yours, of course. But for reasons you will understand, I shall keep the ways and means to myself and alter them as necessary. As for the Khampas, there is nothing I can tell you that you won't soon find out for youself.'

'Hold it,' Melville said. 'You mentioned difficulty. Damage. As I understand it, part of the deal – part of the *contract* – is that you keep me informed about any untoward developments at this end.'

'You have me at a disadvantage,' Sood said. 'I am not being evasive; I do not have a full description of this item. How then, I am wondering, can I anticipate what difficulties may arise?'

'Nobody's asking you to anticipate anything,' Melville said tiredly. 'You have a line to the police and military. If, as and when you hear any stirrings in that area – anything that could affect our arrangments – just get word to the camp.'

'A messenger would take a week.'

'On the radio,' Melville said, drawing on slim reserves of patience. 'Through the Khampas' radio link.'

Sood squeaked with mirth. 'I don't know where you are hearing this nonsense.'

'From Charlie. From Mr Sweetwater, dammit.'

'He has not spoken to me about a radio,' Sood said, shaking his head decisively. 'I know who has been putting such fantastic ideas in his head. It is those Khampas. I told you. When they are drunk, they will say anything. In the mountains you cannot even hear the king broadcasting on Radio Nepal. You might as well be on the other side of the moon.'

Melville's stomach yawed. Plainly Sood was speaking the truth. Equally clear, he was a master in the art of covering his ass.

'Are you understanding me?' Sood said, with a concerned smile.

'Loud and clear,' Melville said savagely. 'But since I'm going to be out there on my own, I insist on making absolutely sure that you and I are operating on the same wavelength.' He took breath. 'The item I'm here to collect is not only fragile, it's explosive. Right? The previous owners haven't exactly given us their permission to take it. Okay? They'll do all they can to stop it leaving the country. Understand? Are you receiving me?'

Sood's face had gone blank.

'Mr Sood,' Melville said. 'I want to know beyond all doubt whether or not your definition of an exportable item includes important citizens of the Chinese People's Republic.'

'Please,' Sood said, his reticence massively affronted. 'Mr Sweetwater must have made it quite clear that I understand what a sensitive job I am undertaking. That is why I am not going around shouting at the mouth.'

'I just wanted to hear it from your own lips, Mr Sood. Because so far I have to say I find your attitude rather disappointing.'

Sood's mouth quivered like a tightly closed rose with a wasp trapped inside. 'And I'm not happy with the way you are carrying on inside my own shop. I know my business. Ask Mr Sweetwater. Ask anyone.' He snatched up the *thanka*. 'I will do my job to the letter, as agreed between myself and Mr Sweetwater and not with you. I am happy to give you the benefit of my experience while you are in Kathmandu, but I must ask you not to come directly to these premises. One scene is quite enough. Look at the crowd you have attracted.'

Two strollers were indeed watching out of earshot, the bars of their shadows reaching almost to the door.

'I'm sorry if I've offended you,' Melville said wearily. 'I'm sure you're the complete professional. Never make a move unless you know each step of the way. Only right now, I feel I'm just sleep-walking, hoping to God that someone in this place will keep me from falling off the path.'

Sood hid his alarm behind a puffy smile. 'If you deliver as planned, Mr Melville, I will have you safely out of the country in less than a day. The same if you have to leave earlier.' He was already forcing Melville to back-pedal towards the door.

'I was hoping for better than if, Mr Sood,' Melville said, glancing over his shoulder at the figure waiting in the square. The man pushed himself away from the *stupa* and brushed his hands on his trousers.

Melville halted his retreat so quickly that Sood would have rammed him with his paunch had the *thanka* not intervened. 'How would you rate our prospects?' Melville said, before Sood could step back.

At a safe distance, Sood found time to weigh his thoughts, his face finally settling in an expression that registered concern shading into pity. 'Mr Melville, that is not for me to say.'

'Bad as that, huh?'

By the time Melville got outside, the man in the leatherette jacket was thirty yards ahead. Still seething, Melville made no effort to close the gap. The man dived into an alley. When Melville rounded the corner, the lane was empty.

'I don't believe it,' he said aloud.

'Tsss!'

The whisper came from a doorway set into an institutional-looking wall. Melville entered it to see a monk in dirty yellow robes levitating across a courtyard at uncanny speed. He plunged after him, through a hallway and across a chamber where chanting novitiates followed his progress without breaking liturgical step. He went through a small room where two monks were putting the finishing touches to a bizarre piece of Tibetan patisserie constructed from dough and coloured butter. In the next room a thin man with unhealthy eyes and bad teeth received him with a hasty handshake.

'Is all this running about really necessary?' Melville panted.

The man was yanking him towards a door. He opened it and glanced left and right.

'Do you have the money?'

'Hell, not on me.'

'Bring it tonight,' the man said, shoving Melville into the street.

Breath labouring under the weight of his indignation, Melville stared blankly at the scrap of paper that had found its way into his hand. He did not unfold it until he had made his way back to the bicycle, and then the writing swam before his eyes. It was an address, pencilled in the same hand. The twist this time, the turn that wound him almost to the snapping point, was that it was in Nepali.

Lightly crumpling the message, Melville advanced on his bicycle and gave it a vicious kick. He kicked it a few more times before hoisting himself into the saddle and heading for home.

You can't get so low that there's no more down, Melville had reason to think a mile out of Bodhnath.

A yellow dog napping in the highway roused itself as he approached. It yawned, stretched each hind leg in turn, nuzzled a sore on its flank, then slid its lips away from its fangs, snarled and set itself up in the middle of the road. Failing to make contact on the first pass, it gave chase with demented barks.

As Melville balanced on one pedal, leg extended to boot the cur, the chain broke, throwing him violently down onto the crossbar. Fields of light sprang up; pain permeated every part of him, from toenails to teeth. Hands cupping his groin, he staggered at a crouch to the roadside and fell on his knees. Slowly he toppled onto his side. The cur whimpered and made off, belly to the ground.

For a while Melville lay like a monstrously developed foetus. When the pain settled into the pit of his stomach, he managed to sit up. He blinked the tears from his eyes and cupped his chin on his knees. His mind played him a snatch of Sweetwater at his most enthusiastic. 'This is going to be a very mammalian operation, Walter – small, nimble and highly directed. You'll be going up against a dinosaur – big, clumsy, with one pin-brain in its head and another up its ass, hundreds of miles away.'

Melville leaned to one side and spat bile.

A motor horn sounded with a polite *parp*. A rotund automobile of 'forties vintage free-wheeled past and coasted to a stop a few yards down the road. A hand beckoned from the driver's window. Taking it a bit at a time, Melville climbed to his feet and hobbled forwards.

'An accident?' a disembodied voice said. 'Nothing damaged I hope.'

'I haven't looked yet.'

'Transport in this country often proves unreliable.'

'So I gather.'

Bending gingerly, Melville looked through the window. The driver was a bookish-looking native of the region. He wore spectacles and a brown suit and was so small that his hands on the upper rim of the steering wheel were on the same level as his eyes. His voice went with his moustache, which was clipped and fastidiously presented. He put Melville in mind of certain shore birds that follow the edge of the tide without ever getting their feet wet.

'Can I offer you a lift?'

Melville hesitated, but it was more than five miles back to town. 'You can't imagine how much I appreciate it,' he said.

It took him a few seconds to work out that the front passenger door opened backwards. He slid with a sigh onto a dried-out leather bench and shut his eyes.

He opened them when he realised that the driver was making no attempt to get under way.

'Your bicycle. I regret to say that bad types will steal it.'

'Good luck to them.'

The driver angled his mirror so that he could see Melville's reflection. 'You are not serious, I hope.'

'I certainly am. Think of it as a gift to the nation.'

It was a crass thing to say, Melville realised, even before he saw the driver smiling tightly at the windshield. 'Really,' he said, 'I mean it. That bike and I don't get along too well. I don't know. Maybe someone can rig it up to run a generator, pump water.'

'Very well,' the driver said, manipulating the column shift.

The car took up drive with a gentle thump and proceeded slowly down the road.

'Your destination, please?'

'Anywhere near the palace will be fine.'

They drove at a funereal pace that inhibited conversation until the driver pointed towards a roadside grove of trees. 'When I first passed those trees, I saw a leopard dragging a goat.'

After studying the tranquil scene, Melville assumed that the sighting hadn't occurred earlier that morning. 'When was that?' he asked.

''Fifty-eight, 'fifty-nine. All this was forest then.'

The driver tooted the horn at a file of jaywalking hippies clad in mellow-yellow. They stepped aside reluctantly and peered into the car, resentment showing on their pale, boneless faces.

'You must have seen a lot of changes,' Melville said. He screwed round on the seat and looked through the dusty rear screen. He gave a cursory laugh. 'They don't seem too thrilled about reaching the end of the trail.'

'You sound pleased.'

'I don't care for easy answers. Eastern mysticism washed down with cheap dope never illuminated anything.' Melville wondered if he had caused further offence. He decided he might have. 'Sorry,' he said. 'You've caught me on a lousy morning.'

'Most people who visit Bodhnath find the atmosphere soothing. They leave refreshed in spirit.'

'I wasn't there to expand my consciousness. I went shopping. I got caught up in some unpleasant haggling.'

'With respect, I must disagree with you,' the driver said, after a slight pause.

Despite his snail's pace, he was concentrating so hard on the road ahead that Melville was able to inspect him more closely than politeness demanded. Small and prissy though he was, there was something about him – an air of self-containment, patience, an almost predatory stillness. Melville discarded his previous image. The way the driver sat, straight up and so close to the wheel that his hands were tucked under his chin, he looked like a goddam praying mantis.

'Yes,' the driver said. 'I cannot agree. A man should explore himself to the very limits, body and soul.'

'Or what's a heaven for?'

'A profound thought.'

'Not mine, I'm afraid. Robert Browning if I remember right.'

'I have never had the privilege of studying his work. I am an Indian from Dehra Dun, so not surprisingly the English poet I know best is Kipling. May I quote?'

'Sure. Go ahead.'

The driver's eyes narrowed in a declamatory squint. 'The wildest dreams of Kew are the facts in Kathmandu.'

Melville waited for more, but that, apparently, was that. Some stress on the word 'facts', an unpoetic inflection, struck him as sinister.

'What kind of facts would those be?' he asked.

'It may astonish you to know that Kathmandu is one of the world's most popular diplomatic postings. It is highly coveted by ambassadors who are approaching the age of retirement and want to spend the last years of their career away from the hurly-burly of international affairs.'

'Do you mind if I open a window?' Melville asked. He breathed deeply of the sluggish slipstream. 'It's certainly a peaceful country.'

'With staggering sights and colourful peoples.'

'That's why I'm here.'

'You are on holiday?'

'Working holiday. Kind of a reconnaissance. I'm an anthropologist.'

'Ah,' said the driver, in a tone that could have meant anything. 'And what is your field of interest?'

'Linguistics. I'm doing a comparative study of kinship terms in related language groups. I started on aboriginals in Taiwan, spent a couple of years in Japan, and now . . .' Melville produced a laugh that didn't come out quite right '. . . here I am in Nepal.'

'Americans,' the driver sighed. 'Always to to fro and fro to to. Where do you plan to pursue your studies?'

'Well, I've only just got here and I'm still reviewing the options, but I thought one of the Tibetan language groups. Maybe a Bhotia dialect, or Tamang. It depends on whether I can come up with an accessible group that hasn't already been worked to death.'

The driver nodded soberly. 'Unfortunately, the people you want live in the restricted areas and cannot be visited without a special permit. The northern border is very sensitive because of the guerilla activity. Have you heard of the Khampas?'

'Vaguely,' Melville said, breaking into a light sweat.

'Perhaps you saw some at Bodhnath. Sturdy chaps who look as though they rule the world, but there are bad elements among them, especially in their mountain bases. Only last year they murdered a German trespasser.' The driver was watching Melville in the mirror. 'Sad but true.'

'I'm not the adventurous type,' Melville said. 'I thought I'd give the Pokhara area a look.'

He was looking in that general direction now, seeing only endless road passing at an agonisingly slow rate. 'You're Indian, you said. What brings *you* to Nepal?'

'Lowly commerce. Visitors such as yourself are attracted by varied lifestyles and charming customs, but you demand the comforts of civilisation. I import the luxuries to which you have become accustomed: soft lavatory paper, toothpaste, whisky.'

'Must be profitable.'

'Not as much as you might think from the prices you are charged. All these things have to be imported from India and paid for in hard currency. Nepal has few resources of her own.' The driver laughed briefly but with gusto. 'There is her only export,' he said, pointing at a thinly wooded hillside slashed by the running sores of erosion. 'Herself – millions of tons of soil washed down to the Indian plains each monsoon. Everything that comes out of Nepal ends up in India.' The driver suddenly glanced at Melville with some concern. 'Are you alright?' he asked. 'You are not looking too chipper.'

'Bit shaken. Delayed reaction. If I could have a little more air.'

The driver unhurriedly wound down his window. 'You probably think that this exchange is one-sided,' he said. 'What, you might ask, does Nepal get in return?'

'What?' Melville repeated dully.

'Protection. This is what you anthropologists call a client-patron relationship, isn't it?'

'Let's hope it serves Nepal better than it did Tibet.'

'You are badly misinformed. India and Tibet had trade and diplomatic relations, not an alliance. Tibet chose isolation and paid the price. Nepal is not so foolish. *We* are not so foolish. We would not tolerate a threat to the territory of a country that looks down on the plain of Ganges. But such conjecture is academic,' he said. 'Whatever noises Peking makes, it has no hostile intentions against Nepal. She is the pygmy who keeps giants apart. That is why provocative elements must be kept away from the border.'

Melville strained forward like a mariner who thinks he's spied a reef dead ahead. 'Right here will suit me fine,' he said.

'We are still some distance from Kathmandu,' the driver pointed out.

Melville drummed on his knees. 'I need the exercise.'

'Perhaps you regret abandoning your bicycle.'

Melville scrambled out of the door and nearly collapsed as pain tied knots in his groin. He made it to the driver's side. 'Many thanks for the ride,' he said. By a huge effort of will, he forced his mouth into a smile. 'We never got round to introductions,' he said. 'Just in case you didn't know, I'm Walter Melville.'

'Major Jetha. Retired, of course. We Indians are devilish keen on titles and such nonsense.'

'I bet you earned it, Major Jetha. I've learned a lot from you in the short time we've been together.'

'I hope so. Kipling put it more briefly.' Major Jetha coughed and smoothed each half of his moustache. 'And the end of the fight is a tombstone white with the name of the late deceased. And the epitaph drear: "A fool lies here who tried to hustle the East." '

Melville found he had nothing to say.

'Very well,' Major Jetha said. 'Let us resume our separate journeys.'

The car eased off. Melville watched it go, his ghastly smile frozen in place long after it had disappeared.

'That's it, then,' he said.

Placing this conclusion ahead of him like a white flag, he limped homewards.

It isn't as simple as that, he told himself.

He was in a downtown restaurant, toying with an early supper. A bath, siesta and a couple of vodkas had worked miracles on his mauled system. He had examined his loins for signs of damage and found everything down there much as normal.

'It isn't as simple as that,' he repeated aloud, drawing a startled

202

glance from the only other diner – a pallid English girl who was eating buffaloburger and chips. She went back to reading a paperback edition of *The Third Eye*, raising her own eyes and sending them on an apprehensive circuit of the room as something scurried around behind the panelling.

Melville squeezed lime into his vodka. He was tipsy but lucid.

On reaching the villa, his only thought had been to book himself on the first flight back to Bangkok. He had been stayed by a premonition of Sweetwater's likely reaction. 'You were spooked by an importer of toiletries? You say he threatened you? In verse?'

At Melville's despairing bleat, the girl ceased chewing, then drew the book closer around her.

Melville knocked back his drink. He had determined on cool action. He would go to the meeting and tell the Khampas about Jetha. Hell, it was his duty to warn them. Their mission would be aborted. No guerillas, no general, no point. He could retreat with dignity.

He paid and stood up. He had to perform some rapid foot-work to keep his balance. He gave the girl a lop-sided grin.

'Do you think it's a rat?' she whispered, as the creature behind the walls came round on another lap.

'Mongoose,' Melville said. 'They use them to keep the rats down.'

Although dark, the sky had the velvety nap of a tropic evening; they were, after all, further south than Cairo. Hissing kerosene lamps outshone the few stars. Food vendors were doing brisk business. Women wearing silver and coral leaned over their carved balconys, shouting across the heads of rickshaw boys with straining calves who dodged through a sluggish procession of pedestrians. Shopkeepers stood in their doorways. A macedoine of spice and cow dung, fruit and leather, scented the air. It was a fairytale scene, and as he walked through it Melville saw himself as a figure of mystery and purpose.

Probably he was being followed, he thought, looking over his shoulder. It didn't matter. He hadn't committed any crime. He'd been a model tourist, free-spending and respectful of local tradition. With the help of his house-servants and a tempo driver he had identified the meeting place and cased it before eating. It was in a reassuringly touristic part of the Tibetan quarter – a street crammed with souvenir shops and cheap hostelries. Twice, touts begged him to sell his dollars. Even if he was caught in conference with the Khampas, he would admit to nothing more serious than illicit money-changing. The authorities could run you out of the country for that.

When he reached the address he held back, disconcerted by the number of people camped at the entrance. One of them, a street kid in blue jeans secured at the fly by a safety pin, said something to his friends and came over with what he imagined was a cordial grin. 'Hi American you wan' buy fuckin' nice piece Nepalese gold?' He tossed a foil-wrapped packet in his palm.

A tall young man burst out of the doorway, beat the kid about the shoulders and bulldozed him up the street. He came back dusting his hands, walking with the round-legged gait of a wrestler. He took hold of Melville's arm as if apprehending a felon and pulled him through the entrance and up a flight of stairs. At the top there was a shouted exchange through a door. Eventually the door was opened and Melville was propelled through.

Be sympathetic, he told himself, digging his heels in just long enough to run through a list of injunctions. Be professional. Be firm.

'At last we meet,' he said, putting on the best face he could for the two men who rose from a table to greet him.

Introductions were made. Yonden was the skinny fellow with cavernous cheeks and mossy teeth who had handed him the message in Bodhnath. He was wearing clear plastic sandals, bell-bottom pants and a denim cowboy jacket sewn from offcuts. The guy beside him was called Yeshe. He was thickset, with a primitive brow overhung by a Beatle-fringe so thick it looked like topiary. One side of his neck was swollen by goitre. He was dressed in what Melville thought was a needlessly flamboyant fatigue jacket. The two men were of a height, about five-seven. The man who had brought Melville up had followed him into the room. He was a head taller than his companions, and with his long hair and the graven features of a Plains Indian, he came closer to Melville's expectation of what a Khampa should look like. He was called Ngawang, which meant Eloquent, Yonden explained. Yeshe was Compassionate, while he was just plain Yonden. Everyone smiled agreeably, Melville baring his teeth at each Khampa in turn. Yonden and Yeshe. It sounded like a vaudeville act. Depression washed over him.

'You want some *chang* to drink?' Yonden inquired when they were seated.

'Why not? I mean, great,' Melville said.

Yeshe lit up a foul-smelling, hand-rolled cigarette. After taking a few puffs he passed it on to Ngawang. Melville glanced around the room. It was furnished with a couple of mattresses, a low table next to a stove and that was about all. A down mountain jacket hung on the wall above a pair of climbing boots.

Yonden maintained his wary smile. Furtive-looking individual, Melville thought, sipping his *chang* with appreciative noises. 'I was expecting to find Alan Gunn with you,' he said.

'He's not feeling good,' Yonden said, pulling a face and massaging his stomach. 'Later he comes.'

'That's too bad,' Melville said, 'but maybe it's better if we have a few words in private.' He nodded at Yeshe and Ngawang, who were following the dialogue with the intense concentration of lip-readers. 'Do your friends speak English?'

'Tiny bit.'

'Too much, I'm afraid,' Melville said. 'What I have to say is for you alone.'

'Yeshe's here to arrange transport.'

'For me?' Melville said in alarm. Yeshe, he had decided, was just about the most stupid-looking man he had ever seen.

'For supplies,' Yonden said. 'He has to buy food and pay for twenty mules. Did you bring money?'

'Later,' Melville said. He felt relaxed and in control. 'Right now, money's the least of our problems. I have to warn you that your plans are about to be upset.'

Eyes fixed on Melville, Yonden spoke to his friends and they made to leave. As Yeshe reached the door, Yonden called him back and held out his hand. Yeshe put his cigarette in it. Still staring at Melville, Yonden took a drag and handed it back.

It's just as well it's over, Melville thought. An outfit as ropey as this could never have pulled it off.

'Have you told them about the general?' he said, when the door had shut behind them.

'No.'

Diplomatically, Melville avoided Yonden's eyes. 'What about Gunn?'

As the silence threatened to become awkward, Melville looked up to find Yonden's gaze eluding him. 'I see you haven't,' he said. 'That's something else we should talk about.' He leaned back in his seat. 'Anyone else know about the general?'

'Only Osher,' Yonden said warily, 'and your friends in Bangkok.'

Melville nodded as if the answer had given him complete satisfaction. It felt good to be on top of the situation. He restrained the urge to put his feet up on the table. 'A few minutes after I left Bodhnath,' he said, 'an Indian picked me up in his car and warned me not to go anywhere near your camp.' Good, Melville told himself. You pitched it exactly right. Clear but not over-dramatic.

'What Indian is this?' Yonden said, an encouraging frown on his face.

'A former army officer,' Melville said, 'name of Jetha. Major Jetha.'

Yonden nodded like a mechanical toy, sucking air through his goofy teeth.

'You don't look too surprised,' Melville said, unease ruffling his composure.

'I know Jetha,' Yonden said. 'He was an officer with the Special Frontier Force.'

'I don't like the sound of that,' Melville said.

'It's a Tibetan army working for the Indians,' Yonden explained. 'Jetha was one of the officers, but he had bad trouble with some Khampas and had to leave.'

'Do you know what he does now?'

'He's a spy, sah.'

'A spy,' Melville repeated, looking at the ceiling, his hands clasped behind his head. 'I spend three days doing nothing, sitting in my garden, visiting a few temples, and then within minutes of making contact with you – bang! – an Indian spy grabs me.'

'What did he want?'

'Want?' Melville said, Yonden's complacency reducing him to parrot cries. 'He wants me out.' Melville rocked forward and rested his elbows on the table. 'Yonden, let me lay it out for you. The operation's blown. Jetha as good as told me that he knows about the general. He said something about everything that comes out of Nepal ending up in India.'

'If Jetha knows, he tell his friends in the police and next day they send you away.'

Melville hesitated. 'Maybe he thinks a discreet warning is enough. As far as I'm concerned, he's right.'

'I don't think so,' Yonden said, shaking his head with maddening slowness.

'I'd like very much,' Melville said, 'for you to share your thoughts with me. How come you know this guy?'

'Osher was with Jetha in the Frontier Force. He wasn't happy being sent to guard the Indian border, so he ran away and went to Mustang. I think Jetha is very interested in my commander.'

Melville gave a short, unhappy laugh. 'The Indians aren't going to excite themselves over a deserter.'

206

'He killed two officers.'

'Flaming hell,' Melville said, sitting upright.

'Afterwards Jetha was punished and left the army.'

Melville got himself under control. 'Well, okay,' he said, 'but what's Osher's colourful past got to do with me. I've never even met him.'

'I'll speak the truth,' Yonden said, inspecting his hands.

'I insist on nothing but.'

'An operation like this makes a wind,' Yonden said slowly. 'Although Jetha cannot tell what it is saying, he can feel it. He has spies in Bodhnath who keep their eyes on the Khampas, so when he hears we have been buying many supplies, he says yes, this winter Osher goes fighting in Tibet.'

'I'd like to remind you that this wind seems to have whispered my name in his ear.'

'It is a puzzle for me,' Yonden admitted.

'Not for me it isn't. A few minutes ago I was trading names with your two friends.'

'Yeshe and Ngawang don't speak to Jetha,' Yonden said scornfully.

'Somebody did. What about the crowd at Bodhnath – Sood, the guy who took me to the temple, the lamas?'

'Not them,' Yonden said. 'Jetha must have been waiting for you at Bodhnath. He must have known who you were before you got there.'

'Probably before I flew in,' Melville said. 'So much for secrecy.'

Yonden hesitated. 'To make the journey to the camp safe, it was necessary for me to tell some of my friends about you. They have to make arrangements. It is possible,' he conceded, 'that someone has opened his mouth and Jetha has heard.'

'Oh, is that all?' Melville said in an artificially cheerful voice. He sighed and fell listless. 'You'd better tell me who Jetha works for.'

'Maybe only for himself.'

'In other words we could be hit from any side – Nepalese, Indian, even the fucking Chinese.' He slapped the table angrily. 'It seems like every time I ask a question, every time I open a door, something nasty falls out.'

'Sah,' Yonden said after a delicate pause, 'don't be too worried by Jetha. I swear he has not found out about the general. Only me and Osher . . .'

'. . . and the wind,' Melville said tiredly. 'Yeah, we've been through all that. No point in beating our brains about it. I'm a marked man. My guess is that Jetha's a paid-up member of India's intelligence service. In fact I'd bet on it. He made a big deal about Nepal being an Indian puppet.' Melville sprawled back, drumming on the edge of his chair. 'I'll tell Charlie we had no choice but to cancel,' he said to himself. 'The thing is shot full of holes. We're drawing flak before we even get on the road.'

'What about the general?' Yonden inquired politely. 'It will be very sad for him.'

Melville stiffened, suspecting irony. 'At least he'll stay alive. He must know that his chances were never better than even.'

Yonden lowered his eyes as if to spare Melville embarrassment. 'When Osher makes a plan,' he said, drawing the words out.

'Yes?' Melville said, pulling himself to attention.

'. . . it is like an arrow in flight. I don't think he is frightened by Jetha.'

'It isn't a question of courage,' Melville said. 'It's a question of common sense.'

Yonden nodded gravely. 'You must tell Osher what has happened.'

'You tell him. I'm damned if I'm walking into hostile territory with the Indian secret service on my tail.'

For the first time, Yonden appraised him openly, his expression indicating that he was not entirely happy with what he saw. 'Okay,' he said, 'it isn't necessary for you to come to the camp. We will bring the general to Charlie by ourselves.'

'You don't seem to be able to get it into your head,' Melville said on a rising note of anger. 'There isn't going to be a general.'

'Osher decides,' Yonden said.

As they locked eyes, Melville came to a decision. He decided that he didn't like this Khampa. He could be forgiven his unprepossessing appearance, but not his slippery manner and lack of respect for logic. The idea that he could guarantee him safe conduct to the camp was preposterous. At the same time, Melville was forced to acknowledge, he had got himself into trouble. If by some chance the Khampas did go ahead, his own behaviour would look to Charlie like dereliction of duty – cowardice for short. He needed time to mull over the problem. He desperately wanted to consult Charlie.

'Did you bring the money?' Yonden asked for the second time.

'Of course I didn't bring the money,' Melville snarled.

'Bring it tomorrow,' Yonden said, and then looked up with a frown, as if a shadow had fallen across him. He glanced at the door and turned a shifty smile on Melville. 'No, better I think to come to your house.' He looked away again, running his tongue around his mouth. 'I'll come myself.'

The realisation that Yonden was contemplating skedaddling with his friends' wages induced a perverse sense of pleasure in Melville. It both vindicated his judgement and evened things up a little. 'Well now,' he said quietly. 'I'm not sure that's such a good idea. The last thing I want is to be arrested on my doorstep handing four thousand dollars to a Tibetan guerilla.'

'Charlie said you would give me the money.'

'Charlie hasn't encountered conditions on the ground. What do you take me for – a fucking bag-man? You can't ignore my advice and then expect me to hand over the money.'

'You make a big problem for me,' Yonden said in a monotone. He picked up a pencil and began doodling on the notebook that lay open before him. 'Soon it will be winter and we don't have enough food. Yeshe has hired twenty mules. He has to pay many people. Many,' he emphasised, directing a fierce look at Melville. He threw the pencil down and rubbed his eyes. 'If you don't bring me the money tomorrow, tell Charlie we don't do business any more.'

In a way it was the outcome that Melville had intended, yet as he considered the implications, imagined Charlie's reaction, a chill travelled the length of his spine. Calling off the show because of Jetha was one thing – and even that was uncertain if Yonden was to be believed – but wrapping it up because of a dispute about four thousand lousy bucks . . . the thought of incurring Charlie's dissatisfaction made Melville's mouth go dry. Self-preservation warred with self-respect, the former urging him to pay up, the latter grizzling what about me: are you going to let this runt with the thief's eyes walk right over me?

'Let's not get overheated,' Melville said. 'Nobody's trying to keep back what's yours. How much do you need in the way of immediate expenses?'

'Everything Charlie said.'

Melville moistened his lips. So much for the full negotiating powers conferred on him by Sweetwater. Yonden wasn't going to back down, that was clear. If only Gunn had been at hand, this ignominious encounter might have gone differently – except, Melville reminded himself, Gunn was not privy to the facts. Melville blinked. Gunn doesn't know, he thought with excitement. He ordered himself to calm down and consider his moves. Unlikely as it might seem, Gunn and this unpleasant Khampa were friends. Get this wrong, he thought, and there'll be nothing for it but to limp away covered with wreckage.

He smiled a big, easy smile. 'The money isn't important,' he said. 'What concerns me is the security aspect.' He stopped as if struck by a sudden thought and looked vaguely about him. 'I don't suppose there's any more of that *chang*.'

There wasn't, but Yonden dug out a half-full bottle of local vodka. Melville nursed his drink in both hands, contemplating it with a troubled expression. He tugged at his ear. 'I'm reluctant to come between friends,' he said, 'but all along I've been bothered by what Alan Gunn's walking into. I don't think it's right that he should be kept in ignorance.'

'Charlie said it's best for him not to know,' Yonden said, his face stony.

Melville gave Yonden a mellow smile. 'Some bad decisions were taken back in Bangkok, and that was the worst of them. Frankly, I'm surprised you went along with it.'

'It isn't necessary to worry him about the general,' Yonden said. 'That's not his business.'

'I'm aware that he has his own reasons for visiting your camp – humanitarian reasons, you could say. But I doubt if the Nepalese will see it the same way.'

'I never let harm happen to him,' Yonden said solemnly.

'Me too, I hope,' Melville said.

'I would never ask him to come if it was dangerous for him.'

From the dogged tone and slightly glazed expression, Melville decided that Yonden was being sincere. In his experience – his unprejudiced opinion – the oriental mind was perfectly capable of accommodating apparently incompatible convictions. Yonden was quite happy to hazard Gunn's life and liberty by keeping him in the dark about the general, while believing that he was acting in his friend's best interests. Of course for all practical purposes, it meant he had to be treated as a liar.

'Gunn must trust you a lot – with his life, even.'

Yonden didn't respond.

'Hell, let's hope it doesn't come to that,' Melville said cheerfully.

'What are you saying?' Yonden asked.

Melville leaned forward, all solicitude. 'He's bound to find out eventually, and when he does he'll wonder why you kept it from him.'

'You going to speak to him?' Yonden asked in a dull voice.

'Worried he might take the news badly?'

Yonden considered a while. 'It doesn't make no difference,' he said, with a shrug of what Melville took to be bravado.

'Aw, come on. A man who was locked up by the Chinese? Nobody's that foolhardy.'

Melville was gratified to see Yonden's face slacken with doubt. 'Then there's Jetha,' he said, and took a delicate sip of vodka. 'Gunn can't be so reckless as to ignore the threat from that direction.'

Yonden's face fell as much as a preternaturally thin man's face can fall.

Easy now, Melville told himself. Gunn's the only lever you've got. Talk to him on his own before deciding.

He set down his drink and shook his head, indicating that principle was at stake here, but also expediency. 'It's a fine judgement call,' he admitted. 'I'd hate to deprive your comrades of proper medical attention, and as you say, Jetha might only be sniffing the wind.' He sighed, coming to a difficult decision. 'I'll tell you what. We've got another week in Kathmandu. My feeling is we should seek Charlie Sweetwater's advice, wait on developments. No point in frightening off your friend unnecessarily.'

By the grain of malice in Yonden's narrowed gaze, Melville knew he had made an enemy; he considered it a worthwhile price to pay for his own self-esteem.

'Getting back to the money,' he said. 'Will a thousand dollars be enough? Let's say fifteen hundred.'

'You don't care about my friend one bit,' Yonden said.

'"Course I care.'

Yonden shook his head. 'You are a man with a small heart,' he said, in the solemn tone of formal pronouncement.

They were still pinned on each other's hostile stares when Gunn arrived in the doorway.

'I hope I'm not interrupting,' he said.

'Hell no,' Melville said, jumping to his feet. 'Great to see you. Come on in and grab a chair. We were just talking logistics.'

Chapter 13

An hour was spent discussing the journey.

Yeshe would drive his mule train to the valley along the busy trade route. Subject to the usual monetary considerations, the officials manning the check-posts allowed non-military supplies to reach the Khampas on the grounds that it deterred them from committing acts of piracy on the local population. Yeshe would also carry such items of personal equipment as Gunn and Melville considered necessary for their stay in the mountains.

Escorted by Yonden and Ngawang, Gunn and Melville would travel light on unmarked trails over the Himalayan outliers, having reached their starting point on the Pokhara road by Land Rover. They would sleep where night caught them, and in a couple of hamlets where the Khampas had reliable friends. Yonden was vague but reassuring about his tactics for smuggling them past the soldiers garrisoned at the mouth of the valley.

Since the discussion was academic as far as Melville was concerned, he let Yonden do the talking and concentrated on Gunn, whose own attention remained fixed on the patch of table where his hands rested. They were square, utilitarian hands, contributing to a superficial impression of a fairly stalwart character, but the face told a different story. The lines imprinted around Gunn's mouth were the mark of defeat accepted; the rheum about his eyes and the bloom on his sheer skin were the stigmata of the serious drinker. Melville, whose imagination had prepared him for an ex-colonial desperado or an out-and-out religious oddball, came to the only reasonable conclusion: a complete no-hoper. Whatever inner resources Gunn possessed, they were buried a long way down.

Melville became aware that Yonden had stopped talking and was expecting comment. 'Sounds straightforward,' he said, 'but I can't help wondering what the people we meet on the way will make of us. They'll know we shouldn't be there. They might report us.'

'No sah.'

'We'll be walking through Gurkha country,' Melville pointed out. 'Those people aren't simple hoers and tillers. Half of the male population has served in one army or another. We might run into soldiers returning from leave.'

'Mr Melville has a point,' Gunn said.

His voice was his best feature, Melville thought – a tenor lilt of surprising clarity.

'Call me Walter,' he said. 'You too, Yonden.'

'They think you're Tibetans,' Yonden said.

'Are you serious?'

'Yes sah.'

'Do I look like a Tibetan?' Melville demanded, struggling to keep his irritation in check. 'Does Alan?'

'In Kham,' Gunn said, 'I sometimes travelled disguised as a Tibetan.'

Melville gave him a long, cool look. If pressed to hazard a guess, he would have given Gunn's provenance as blue-collar Irish. 'At least you speak the language,' he said, 'but what about me? Whoever heard of a Tibetan with fair hair?'

'You'll see,' Yonden said, getting up. 'Wait here, please.'

A strained silence settled when he left. Gunn sat twisting his fingers as though they unscrewed at the joints.

'How is your Tibetan these days?' Melville asked at length.

'Oh,' Gunn said, apparently surprised to find Melville still in the room, 'it was never very good – just a smattering of Kham dialect mixed up with Lhasa Tibetan and Chinese. I haven't spoken it for years.'

'I expect it'll come back to you,' Melville said, his spirits scraping bottom. He laughed. 'Dressing up as Tibetans – it's certainly in the best Brit tradition. Very North-West Frontier, very Kipling.' He winced and pinched the bridge of his nose, as if afflicted with sinusitis. 'I wish I could share Yonden's optimism,' he muttered.

'He's very resourceful.'

'Imaginative, too,' Melville said, deciding it would do no harm to sow some doubt.

From Gunn's dejected expression, he decided that Yonden had already prepared the ground himself.

'Don't judge him by appearances,' Gunn said. 'When he was only a boy he helped me escape from China.'

'Must be quite a story. I'd love to hear it some time.' Melville allowed a damning pause to develop. 'But that was twenty years ago. People change – especially somebody like Yonden, somebody who's

213

lost everything. As a refugee in a grab-what-you-can world, all he's got to get by on is his wits.'

'I'm not sure that I care for this kind of talk.'

'I suffer from a modern malaise, too,' Melville continued. 'It's called pessimism, rational jitters. I worry about how easy Yonden makes it all sound; I wonder if he's telling us only what we want to hear.' Melville scratched his ear. 'I was thinking we should get together – just us two – and take a hard look at our position.'

'I'm sure there's nothing I can contribute.'

'You know the Khampas better than almost anyone. I'd welcome your advice.'

Gunn averted his face. 'I've no wish to interfere in your affairs.'

'I see,' Melville said heavily, getting to his feet. 'Same journey, same destination, separate business.' He offered the bottle of vodka to Gunn. 'Sure you won't have any? It's not bad; it doesn't have any taste.' He poured a glass for himself and swirled the liquid around. 'How much did Charlie Sweetwater tell you?' he asked.

'Only that your government was considering stopping support for the Khampas and had sent you to make a report.'

It's criminal, Melville thought with indignation. He nodded. 'What does Yonden say?'

'We don't talk about it,' Gunn mumbled.

'Never?'

'Not since the night we met,' Gunn said, blinking miserably.

Like an owl taking a shit, Melville thought, sympathy gone as he realised that Gunn knew perfectly well that he had been lied to. So why is he pretending otherwise, he wondered, and found himself speculating with some distaste on the nature of the relationship between Gunn and Yonden.

'Is there something else I should know?' Gunn asked.

'Come to lunch tomorrow and we'll talk at leisure. For now, though, there's no dodging the basic reality. We'll be marching into the border area without permits. Doesn't it make your heart go pit-a-pat?'

'Of course it makes me anxious,' Gunn said. He brooded for a few seconds. 'It's not as if I'm doing anything criminal,' he muttered, as if to himself. 'I wouldn't call what you're doing immoral.'

Melville was startled. 'What's immoral got to do with it? Isn't dangerous good enough for you?'

'It's no more dangerous for me than for you,' Gunn pointed out, 'and your government wouldn't have sent you if the risks were too high.'

214

Charlie has a lot to answer for, Melville thought. 'You can't anticipate every little thing that might go wrong,' he said. 'If we foul up, there won't be any cavalry coming over the hill. It's just you and me, Alan. No one else.'

'And Yonden.'

'He'll be on home ground; we won't.' Melville sat down and faced Gunn squarely. 'I don't have to draw a diagram of what will happen if the Chinese hear that somebody with your record has been messing with Tibetan guerillas right on their frontier. You're not the World Health Organisation, Alan; you're a convicted spy.'

Gunn swallowed the threat as if it were a stone. 'I don't understand why you're trying to frighten me off. Mr Sweetwater made it seem so straightforward. Are you worried that I'll get you into trouble?'

Tell him now, Melville thought. Get it over with. 'This is the proverbial grey area,' he said. 'Charlie may have played down the risks a little, told you only what he thinks you need to know.' Melville hesitated, glancing at the door. Yonden would be back any time; the prospect of a confrontation between Gunn and the Khampa was not a pleasant one. Tomorrow would be soon enough for the bad news. 'Look, it's getting late. All I'll say for now is that nobody will hold it against you if you decide to bale out.'

'I'm afraid Yonden would. I've given him my word, you see.'

'Wait until you have all the facts.'

'Facts?' Gunn said, as if they could only prove an unnecessary complication. 'There's only the one that matters.' He twined and untwined his fingers. 'I assume that Mr Sweetwater has told you about Yonden and me.'

Melville hoped this wouldn't be embarrassing. 'I understand that Yonden looked after you in Tibet.'

'Yes, he did. There was a war on, a revolution; hundreds of thousands of people were on the move. Life was very cheap; you could be killed for a pair of bootlaces. Without Yonden, I wouldn't have lasted a month. He protected me for two years, until the Chinese invaded. Nobody expected them to advance so fast. They were only three days away when we first heard, but instead of getting his family to safety, Yonden helped me try to escape to India. The Chinese murdered his whole family because of their association with me. Now he's asked me to help him. If you were in my position, wouldn't you say yes?'

'If I were in Yonden's position, I wouldn't put you on the spot like that. Asking someone for a favour they can't refuse and which could

215

cost them a lot isn't the action of a friend.' Melville was assailed by anger – anger at Yonden, at Sweetwater, at Gunn, at himself. The anger wearied him. He knocked back his drink. 'It's up to you,' he said. 'Just so long as you know the score.'

'In that case,' Gunn said, 'would you mind if we left it at that?'

Yonden came back with Ngawang, who had two black *chubas* slung over his arms. Yonden made an inquiring face at Gunn, who responded with a dilute smile. The exchange seemed to put Yonden into party spirits. He took one of the *chubas* and lobbed it over to Melville, who staggered under its weight.

'Gee, it must weigh all of thirty pounds.'

'Very warm,' Yonden said. 'Coat, bed, house – all in one. Now all you need is a pretty girl.'

He helped Melville robe up, demonstrating how the yards of harsh wool were gathered above the belt in a pouch capacious enough to cradle a sheep. He stood back and surveyed the effect. 'Good. Tall like Khampa.' He gave Melville a push. 'Walk,' he said.

'Like this?' Melville asked, taking a few hesitant steps.

'No, no. Tibetans walk like they want to shake the world.'

Ngawang showed how it was done, swinging round the room with a heavy, buccaneering tread.

'Looks too much like hard work,' Melville said. 'I'd never keep it up.'

He watched stonily as Gunn had a try. 'Forget it,' he said at last. 'The idea is *not* to draw crowds.'

Yonden clicked his tongue, conceding defeat. Everyone looked at each other helplessly.

'Okay,' Yonden said. 'First few days we walk at night. After . . .' he clapped his hands and glared about him '. . . we go bloody quick.'

Soon afterwards Melville left. The city had turned in for the night. At the end of the street a solitary rickshaw boy raised his head from his handlebars and peered at him with bleary eyes. Melville sent him back to sleep with a shake of the head. He needed ventilation. His mind was fogged with booze and foreboding, but it wasn't sufficiently blurred to blot out a frame-by-frame replay of the evening's sorry performance. He winced with shame when he came to the bit where he had taken Gunn hostage over the issue of petty cash, and he groaned aloud at the scene where he had delivered his equivocal

216

warning. Tonight, he realised, he had taken a significant turn from the path of virtue.

But what a flaky set of accomplices, he thought, deciding that the blame wasn't all one-sided. In a sudden, inescapable vision he saw how poorly provided he was for the job. If only I had a reliable partner, he thought, a friend I could trust. Sweetwater, he remembered, had asked for a pledge of trust – an odd request for a cold-war warrior to make. Up to a point, he had replied, which was a dumb thing to say. What point would that be? Would he recognise it when it came, perhaps the final apprehension of his life, as his eyes filmed over and rolled back in his skull?

No, by any reckoning he had overstepped the limits. He would send the news about Jetha to Charlie but he wouldn't stand by for instructions; he would take the first available flight home.

And yet as he lurched down the street, the resolve failed to give comfort. There was the difficulty of deciding where home was, the prospect of facing Charlie's contempt, and the nagging feeling that deep in his heart he would share that contempt. Irrational, of course; unceremonious flight was the only sensible course, but the situation and characters he was dealing with were notably weak on reason. The general was ignorant of the threat posed by Jetha and the Khampas dismissed it, which left Gunn, who gave the impression that the only thing that mattered was his obligation to Yonden. Melville found himself considering the unsettling possiblity that he had postponed the moment of truth with Gunn out of fear that the fool would ignore it.

Melville came to the crossroads and leaned against a corner, laughing weakly. He must have taken a wrong turn. Faced with a choice of directions, he didn't know which route to take.

He blinked. He was drunk enough for it to cost a degree of effort. The streets came into focus, dark, atrociously lit and deserted. Apart from the rickshaw boy, he hadn't passed a living soul. He checked his watch. It wasn't particularly late; there wasn't a curfew. It was as though the streets had emptied in response to some prowling menace that nobody had told him about.

Not empty, he saw with relief. In the middle of the intersection a pair of eyes were regarding him in a genial, uncomplicated way. They were deeply inserted under the white brows of an old beggar or mendicant who was relaxing on his bundle at the base of a stone water tank. They concentrated on him for a while, then moved away,

217

irresistibly drawing Melville's own gaze back down the street he had just travelled.

A long way off, at a distance of three or four patches of lamplight, a figure drew itself behind a slab of shadow. Melville turned with an inquiring frown to the beggar, who chuckled.

Melville had never come sober so fast. He walked unhurriedly around the corner and, as soon as he was out of sight, broke into a trot, running at less than full speed because of his bruised groin and because he had a lead of at least a hundred yards. Thank Christ for the old man. He had a general picture of where he was. He reckoned he was less than half a mile from safe ground. When he glanced back across his shoulder, it was purely a reflex action.

His heart popped into his throat. He stumbled and stopped.

The man was rounding the corner at a stroll, no more than fifty yards away. He halted, peering – a small, thin man, something that gleamed like pewter dangling loose at his side. The gleam changed hands as the man gathered himself for the chase.

Panicked by the uncanny speed with which his pursuer had closed the gap, Melville hared off. No longer complacent about his chances of winning a straight race, he took the first corner he came to, intending to lose himself by twists and turns.

He was in a lane parallel to the street where he'd first spotted the man. He needed to go right, dammit. The first opening was choked with shadow, a dead end. The next led left, into a tumbledown maze where his pursuer would have little trouble bringing him to bay. By now he must be back in the man's sight. He didn't look. He couldn't hear him. He couldn't hear anything except his laboured breathing, amplified by the echoing walls. There were people within feet of him. He glimpsed them in passing, caught in chinks of light, glowing windows, safe havens that were closed to him.

He came to a crossroads so narrow that he nearly overshot it. It was impossible. At the end of the lane to the left, his pursuer duplicated his motions, skidding to a halt, back-pedalling comically before turning and coming for him, blade winking as it swung. How the hell had he got there? The bastard must have been aiming to cut him off, chop him down from ambush. But he'd got it wrong. The gap had stretched again and the opening to the right offered a line of escape. He recognised the Hindu shrine at the far end.

He plunged into the gap. Yes, no doubt about it. The shrine was at the centre of a small market square he had crossed that very day. It was a hippy hangout with half a dozen routes radiating from it.

Only a short way down one of them he would come out into a main road where soldiers had been much in evidence. The hotel where he'd eaten was less than a minute away.

Headlong flight was no longer necessary and might prove disastrous. The ground was pot-holed and greasy, carpeted with rubbish. Economy of effort was the thing. Recover wind and hope the stitch knifing into his side would ease. Take it nice and steady as far as the square, while his pursuer bust a gut trying to recover lost ground, then a flat-out spurt to break clear, leaving the sonofabitch glassy-eyed and reeling in his wake.

Satisfied with his margin of safety, Melville slowed, gathering breath for the final effort.

The breath he had just swallowed was wasted in a sob of cold terror as a soft padding fell on his ears. It wasn't possible. It must be a trick of acoustics.

Lungs stretched to popping point, he listened. There was no mistake. Soft as they were, the footfalls were within thirty yards, nicely co-ordinated, the effortless stride of someone whose system wasn't furred up by booze and years of undemanding living.

The steady padding threw his own rhythm out. The bastard had made up lost ground as though he were standing still, yet now he was happy to dog his heels.

He tripped. Recovering, he looked back. There he was, no more than twenty yards adrift. No face, just a pair of legs that looked capable of maintaining the pace all night. And the flash-flash of the *kukri*.

His breath sawed in and out, too shallow, cramped by the pain wedged under his collar bone. His heart threatened to tear through the thin walls of his chest. He imagined it bursting, a splatter of pulp.

He shot into the square. On the shrine a moustached god and his bride sat wreathed in marigolds. He'd never seen them before. It was the wrong square. He wasn't going to make it.

His assassin had speeded up. He visualised the blade being transferred to the cutting hand, the arm go up, the blade slice down.

The lights went out as the supervisor at Kathmandu's electricity generating station threw a switch redirecting the plant's output to the southern part of the city.

An instant before the blackout Melville had seen the forked entrance to two alleys on the far side of the square. Holding that image in his head, he jinked towards it. There it was, a square darker than the night. It swallowed him. He was completely blind. Something, a piece

219

of timber, caught his cheek a sickening blow. He was thrown against a wall. His feet slithered helplessly and he fell, putting his hands into slime. On knuckles and knees he scrambled through the shit, deeper into the alley.

He could go no further. His heart was pounding for relief. He pressed back against the wall. Licking the corner of his mouth, he tasted blood. His lips curled back in a snarl as he heard soft footsteps.

But he'd won a few minutes. Even if his pursuer had seen which fork he'd taken, he'd hesitate before coming in after him. He groped around him, grinning with disgust as his hand encountered only more filth. The smell choked him – sweet and sulphurous, the stink of decayed vegetables and fruit left from the day's market.

His hunter was at the mouth of the alley, uncertain. He couldn't see him, but he could feel his presence. Eyes bulging with the strain, he held his breath. Now he could hear the man's unforced breathing.

Dimly he registered movement around him – small scuffles and quivers. He spared a reflex glance to one side as something dropped to the ground with a kittenish *plop*.

When he looked back, he experienced the slow haemorrhaging of hope. The man's shape was superimposed on the darkness, his face a fishy blur. As Melville's eyes adjusted to the night, other objects materialised – the market stall he'd run into, a hand-cart loaded with boxes, a guild supper attended by hundreds of rats, each group clotted on a pile of garbage.

They broke up with thin protests as the man stepped cautiously into the alley, turning his head from side to side, the heavy blade probing ahead of him. He halted and seemed to peer right at Melville, then casually turned his head, checking that the coast was clear. In panic Melville turned and searched the shadows behind him. The wall was only a few feet away; he was in a cul de sac. The man had not made another move. Melville was having difficulty keeping him in focus. He had faded into the dark again.

Sick with uncertainty, Melville waited, not sure whether the man had shrunk against the wall or retreated into the square, hoping to draw him out. The rats regrouped. In any case, he couldn't stay where he was. The man was very small; all he had was his *kukri*. If the first cut could be warded off . . . Melville began inching towards the cart with the boxes, provoking only a mild stir among the diners. He was almost there when the man came back. There was no hope of concealment. The man was staring at him and he was staring back, certain now of his killer's identity.

'Come out, please.'

'You don't want to do this, Yonden. There's absolutely no need. Tell Jetha or whoever put you up to it that it's finished. I'm taking the first flight out.'

'You come out now.'

'Be reasonable, will you? Think what'll happen if you kill me. I'm an American for fuck's sake.'

'Stop this bad talk.'

But Melville was beyond rational thought. 'Look, the money's not a problem. I've got it at the house. I don't give a damn what you do with it.'

'No more trouble now. I take you home.'

'Do we have a deal?'

'It's okay.'

'Alright. I'm coming out now.'

The runt, Melville thought, the murderous little runt. He saw the blade hanging at Yonden's side and his fear transmuted itself into a giddy, swollen rage. He imagined seizing Yonden's arm, locking it back and bearing down on it until the shoulder popped out like a chicken leg.

He swung wildly, grazing Yonden's cheek with his arm. 'Why you do that?' Yonden squeaked, skipping back. 'It's not me who chases you.'

'Not any more you're not,' Melville said, stalking him.

'You make crazy mistake,' Yonden said. 'Other man's run away.'

'What man? You hunt in pairs, huh?'

'The man who tries to kill you,' Yonden said, angry and bewildered. 'I ran after him.'

Comprehension flashed. Melville recalled his pursuer's supernatural turn of speed, the startling way he had appeared at the end of the lane. There had been two of them. Yonden must have been the one he saw first. His would-be killer must have been hiding only a few yards away.

'My God,' he said, 'he was going to kill me.'

'I think so.'

Melville wiped his hand across his face and smelt the rank sweetness of decay. He had a picture of himself sprawled in the alley, rats clumped on his belly, on his face. Yonden put a hand on his shoulder but he knocked it away and grabbed the Khampa high up on his throat. 'You still trying to tell me this is because of something Osher did all those years ago?'

'It's very bad,' Yonden managed to say, perched on the tips of his toes.

'It's disastrous,' Melville snarled. 'The Chinese have found out about the general and they're out to waste me. That's how bad it is.'

'Yes sah,' Yonden said. 'You must tell Osher.'

Melville dropped him and backed away, convulsed by silent laughter. He fetched up against the shrine and gazed up at the night sky. 'What am I doing wrong?' he pleaded. 'Why can't I get through? Yonden,' he shouted, 'after tonight I wouldn't go within a hundred miles of your camp.'

'It's very important you speak to Osher,' Yonden said, massaging his throat. 'You must tell him it's too dangerous to go into Tibet.'

'You've got me all confused,' Melville said, advancing on Yonden. 'Earlier you were telling me to get lost; now it's vital I risk my life going to your camp to state the obvious. No fucking dice.'

'I understand,' Yonden said, retreating. 'You're frightened.'

Melville laughed. 'You read me like a book. I'm frightened alright. I'm frightened now and I'll be frightened tomorrow and every day until I climb aboard that plane.'

'In the mountains you won't be frightened,' Yonden said, still back-pedalling.

'We have a failure of communication here,' Melville said softly, 'and that's because we're coming at the problem from different directions. I bet you anything you like that you'd share my way of thinking if it was you they had just tried to snuff out.'

'Yes sah, I'm frightened too. But not in the mountains.' Yonden had been forced back to the mouth of the alley. 'Jetha can't chase you there. You'll be safe with my friends.' He looked into the alley, where the rats made a faint agitation in the grain of darkness. 'It's not bad like the city,' he said. 'In my valley everything is . . .' he hunted for the word '. . . simple.'

Melville felt like weeping. 'Nothing's simple,' he said. 'Not me, not Gunn, not you.'

'It's true,' Yonden said eagerly, stepping towards him. 'You'll see.'

Into Melville's mind swam the vision he'd seen from the plane – immaculate heights piercing the muddy vapours of the lowlands. 'Ah, Yonden,' he murmured, 'if only I could believe it.'

Yonden came right up to him. 'I send Ngawang to stay with you,' he said. 'Not tomorrow but the next day, we can leave Kathmandu. One week and we'll be at my camp where no one can hurt you.'

'It's no use,' Melville said. 'Like you said, I'm a man of small heart.'

222

Yonden took hold of his elbow. 'You make me angry,' he said, although his tone was sympathetic. 'Always you're thinking about yourself. You say this is too dangerous for you, but what about my friends? It is not you has to go into Tibet for the Chinese general.'

'Nobody's going into Tibet,' Melville said tiredly.

'Easy for you to talk, but what shall I say to Osher? He will think I haven't protected you. He will think I have put bad ideas in your head.' Yonden's face creased in puzzlement. 'Why did Charlie not send someone else?'

'Bad judgement,' Melville said. 'I won't deny it.' He was beginning to hurt. His split cheek wept a thin, itchy lymph. He was sure that some small but vital component in the pit of his stomach had been irreparably damaged. 'I guess I cut a pretty poor figure,' he said. 'But when you've been hunted through the streets like a . . . like a . . .'

Yonden gave a defeated sigh. 'When will you go back?'

Melville sniffed. Nobody had given him a chance. His qualities had been set at nought. Rage kindled in him. 'I don't want to go back,' he said. 'I want to find who it was that tried to take my head off.'

'It's not important now,' Yonden said. He thumbed the tip of his *kukri* and grinned. 'Maybe one day I find this man.'

'Would you have killed him?'

'Oh yes,' Yonden said. 'You're my guest.'

His casual certainty confused Melville. He was also conscious of a great dissatisfaction with the way this had ended. He had nothing to show for it but his humiliation. Maybe Yonden's right, he thought. Jetha can't touch you in the mountains. Make it to the camp and you'll have discharged your duty.

Yonden was scanning the approaches to the square. Melville wrenched him round. 'Can you guarantee to get me in and out of the valley without trouble?'

Yonden gave it his consideration. 'It's not difficult for us,' he said. 'There is one small problem with the soldiers, but I wouldn't take you or Alan if it wasn't safe.'

'Shit,' Melville said. 'What are we going to tell him?'

Yonden shrugged, indicating that it was up to Melville.

'I don't know,' Melville said. He was already wondering if he'd made a rash decision. He would be on the trail for two weeks with a man he still wasn't sure of. Also, as Charlie had pointed out, Osher would be doubly unhappy if his men were deprived of medical attention. Gunn was not the ideal travelling companion, but he would

223

help keep the jitters at bay during the days ahead, and his appearance at the camp would help mollify Osher.

'Look,' he said, 'Gunn's been in town a few days and nobody's threatened him. We're going to have to say goodbye to the general, but there's no reason why your friends shouldn't get the treatment they were promised. It's me Jetha's interested in. My instinct is to keep Gunn out of it.'

Yonden wasn't sure what Melville was saying. 'You don't tell him about tonight?' he asked.

'Unless you have any objections.'

'No, no,' Yonden said, beaming. 'This is the best thing to do.'

'I suppose,' Melville said dubiously. 'I need to straighten out my head. I have to talk to Charlie.'

'No time,' Yonden reminded him. 'It's not safe to stay here.'

Melville exhaled a big sigh. 'Alright,' he said. 'As of now I'm happy to let you handle the arrangements.'

Chapter 14

'If you want to know anything,' Melville shouted, 'go ahead, ask. I bet I thought of it last night.'

'What?' Gunn shouted.

Melville opened his mouth. The Land Rover crashed over a corrugated section of unpaved road. 'Never mind.'

'Did you not sleep well?' Gunn asked, when the Land Rover had pulled itself onto more or less level ground.

Melville gave a hollow laugh.

'Nor me,' Gunn said, some moments later.

Seeing his own nervousness mirrored on Gunn's face, Melville twisted round, straddling the front seats with his arms. 'Can you believe it?' he shouted. 'This thing flies in the face of all automotive principles.'

Gunn smiled weakly, acknowledging the nest of disconnected circuitry dangling from the dash. 'It's a diesel,' he said. 'It doesn't have electric ignition.'

'No kidding?' Melville said.

The driver, a Tibetan smuggler based in Pokhara, spat through his window. He had spotted another vehicle approaching.

'Oh, fuck,' Melville said. 'Not again.'

The engine note hardened as the driver put his foot down, though there was no appreciable gain in speed. He moved to the crown of the road, holding that position by dint of constant steering adjustment. The oncoming vehicle flashed one headlight. It was a truck, loaded to twice its height and listing badly. The driver muttered a curse or a mantra, his voice rising to a pitch of ecstasy as the gap closed to yards. Melville shut his eyes. He felt the truck's wash as it swerved at the last instant, heard a faint but indignant yell. When he looked, the driver was adjusting his mirror, frowning into it. Satisfied with the way he had handled the truck, now hidden by a cloud of roadside dust, he carefully ejected another gob of spit.

'What did that poor guy ever do to him?' Melville shouted, tapping his head.

Gunn responded with an automatic smile, quickly dimmed.

Melville, Gunn and Ngawang jounced about on their bundles in the back. The Land Rover was a bottom-of-the-range model, with no rear seats or side-windows. Yonden had the only passenger seat – a position briefly disputed by Melville on the grounds that the military would be less likely to flag them down if they saw a dollar-spending face upfront. The issue had been resolved when Yonden pointed out that Jetha might have people looking for him.

In two hours they had covered less than fifty miles. The road was in poor condition after the late monsoon. The scenery – a river, always on one side or the other, green hills dissolved in mist – soon palled. Inside the vehicle there was a palpable air of racked nerves.

Melville shut his eyes, willing away the miles. The engine rattled like a bucket of nails. Changing gear was an effort of collective concentration as the driver stirred about for the next ratio, any old ratio, bottom gear, finally forcing the shift with the sound of cog eating cog into the gear he'd started from and trying again.

Hearing a noise that sounded terminal, Melville opened his eyes to find Ngawang watching him. Their mutual stare stayed in synch despite the joggling of the vehicle, then Ngawang's lips stretched in a stiff yawn. 'Alan,' Melville said, not taking his eyes off the Khampa, 'I think our friend isn't feeling too good.'

A moment later Ngawang effortlessly vomited. Hot liquid slopped over Melville's shoes and bundle. A corrosive gas filled the cabin.

Gagging, Melville hit the road before the Land Rover had stopped rolling. The river was fifty yards away. He ran for the margin and plunged his face into the water. When his nausea had passed, he sat on a rock, his back to the road.

A fish eagle sketched pot hooks over the river. It had an eerie, penetrating cry.

'We ought to be on our way,' Gunn said, coming up behind. 'It's all cleared up. Ngawang's cleaned your kit. He's very sorry.'

Melville indicated the bird with a loose swing of the arm. 'Do you ever get the feeling there's someone up there laughing?'

For the next hour no one attempted conversation. Melville's guts were wound tight with tension. Every few seconds he raised himself up to spy out the road ahead. It was always empty. Gunn would not meet his eye. Melville took a shaky breath. 'Must be nearly time to jump.'

A few minutes later Yonden hissed. Although the sound was not loud, everyone heard it.

'What is it?'

'Soldier.'

For a long moment Melville and Gunn locked eyes, then Melville scrambled forward to look.

The soldier was urinating by the roadside, sighting on them along his free arm, which was extended in a stop signal.

'Everyone got the story straight,' Melville said, fighting for calm. 'We're taking in the sights around Pokhara. Yonden's our guide. Ngawang, you're our porter. We'll be in the area a couple of weeks.'

The Land Rover went straight past. Melville glimpsed the soldier's face, his mouth open. He saw a rifle propped against a rock. 'What in hell are you playing at?' he shouted at Yonden, who was looking neither right nor left.

Melville whirled. Gunn had his face pressed to the filthy rear window.

'What's he doing? What's he doing?'

'A wee jig. Jumping up and down.'

'Oh Christ,' Melville groaned. 'We've really pissed him off.'

'Aye,' Gunn said. 'We have.'

'Here, let me look,' Melville said, pulling Gunn out of the way.

The soldier wasn't looking in their direction. He was staring at his fatigue trousers.

'Hell,' Melville said reverently. 'He's pissed all down his leg.'

In the general mirth, Melville strove for a note of censure.

'Yeah, I know, dead funny. But what if that soldier wires ahead and they pull in our driver friend? How does he explain where his passengers have disappeared to?'

A hiatus followed. Numbed by boredom, fatigue and the noise of the engine, Melville finally dozed. Gunn nudged him back to consciousness.

Yonden was leaning forward in his seat, one hand on the driver's arm, studying the right-hand side of the road. He twisted his face round just far enough so that everyone could hear. 'We're nearly there. Soon as we stop, run bloody quick for the trees.'

'Ai-yai-yai,' Melville murmured.

The Land Rover lurched onto the verge. 'Go!' Melville shouted, kicking the doors open.

He ran doubled up, as though trying to present a small target. It was easy to imagine muzzle flashes coming from the trees, a broken line sixty yards off across a cracked and stubbled dry paddy. There was a dike at the treeline. He flung himself across it, landing heavily, laughing. A few seconds later Gunn wheezed into cover, his face

227

blotched. Yonden and Ngawang were just starting their run, moving awkwardly, one each side of a large straw pannier. The Land Rover was pulling away with heavy grindings and a lot of black smoke.

The Khampas slithered over the bank and began checking the contents of the basket.

Melville glanced at his own bundle. In it were pills and ointments, a half of Black Label, a Tibetan dictionary and writing materials. He carried three thousand dollars in a belt strapped to his waist.

Gunn was still recovering his breath, panting in a way that did not bode well.

Melville reviewed his surroundings. Under a silky white sky the land was flat as far as the eye could see. Savannah trees delimited endless wet and dry paddies and half hid a clay-and-thatch hamlet half a mile off. Closer, a boy and girl stood together on a dike, watching them. They were holding hoes and wore dished hats. A pair of water buffalos basked in chest-deep ooze. Not a sound.

'Where are these mountains then?' Melville asked.

Still busy with the pack, Yonden pointed north. 'Two days if we walk good.'

When the load had been apportioned between the Khampas, Melville made no move.

'Quickly please,' Yonden urged. 'Not safe here.'

'In a minute,' Melville said.

When he was alone, he sighed. He looked at the deserted road, the silent children, the ochre-and-white houses – committing the point of departure to memory. He gathered a piece of red soil on his finger and drew a line on the smooth grey bark of the nearest tree.

His companions were a distant tremor in the heat haze. 'Hey, wait for me,' he called, and set off after them at a stumbling run.

They walked for an hour to get clear of the road, then lay up in a patch of woodland. At dusk a violet curtain rippled far to the north and the sky muttered. When it was dark they headed towards the sound.

Chapter 15

Shortly before noon on the sixth day, Melville and Ngawang breasted a ridge almost within touching distance of the cloud ceiling. On the other side forests of fir and rhododendron fell away into streamers of mist. Melville viewed the distant prospect without enthusiasm. More green diagonals intersecting at acute angles, the same pearly coverlet of sky. More of the same. His right knee throbbed in protest as he prepared to descend. He could not decide which was worse – going up or going down. Whichever you were doing at the time.

Ngawang checked him. He pointed down and traced a meandering shape.

'The river?'

Ngawang tapped his watch and displayed three fingers.

'Thank God for that. And the Gurkhas? You know – soldiers. Bang-bang.'

Ngawang nodded gravely and aimed an imaginary rifle at Melville's head.

Melville lowered himself stiffly to the ground. Ngawang asked for aspirin. He had an ear infection. He chewed the pills as though they were sweets, his face set in what Melville thought of as the thousand-mile stare. It was a look that often came on both Khampas. They would be talking animatedly by the fire, then simultaneously fall silent. A silence within a silence, the past.

Yonden came in sight, hands clasped behind his back, head bent, covering ground at his usual deceptive speed.

'Where's Alan?' Melville called. 'What's the story this time? Legs? Guts?'

'Sah?' Yonden said, when he was within ordinary speaking distance.

'I said I hope Alan's okay.'

Yonden gave a distracted smile and jerked his head at Ngawang, who rose to his feet. They moved out of earshot and began conferring.

Melville stretched out with a groan. Ten minutes passed before Gunn appeared, picking his way delicately, considering each step. Only fifty yards from Melville he looked up with the despairing expression of someone faced with a desert crossing. Melville shut his eyes. 'How you doing?' he said sleepily when Gunn drew close.

'Not too badly, thank you. Knees are feeling the strain.' Gunn grinned around him with senile incomprehension. 'Are we nearly there?'

'Three hours,' Melville said, with a languid wave. 'Unless there's another hold-up.'

'I don't think we've done too badly,' Gunn said, settling himself beside Melville.

'I was counting on being inside the valley by now.'

'Yes, well. I'm sorry about the delays.'

'Forget it,' Melville said, not opening his eyes.

Yonden pointed back up the trail, then down. He sketched something on the ground with a stick. Ngawang nodded. Yonden came over.

'Now you go together with Ngawang. You walk very quiet and easy. There's a place to wait near the camp.'

'Aren't you coming with us.'

'Later. We cross the river in the night.'

'Is that such a good idea?' Melville said, swinging himself up into a sitting position. 'I mean, if we have to hang around the camp until dark, I'd feel easier if we had you along.'

'Ngawang will show you the place. I'll meet you there soon.'

'Yonden, so far it's only been a stiff hike. Now we're at the sharp end. We can't take any chances when there are soldiers in the vicinity. Ngawang's a good guy, but he doesn't speak English. We need someone we can communicate with.'

'I can understand Ngawang fairly well,' Gunn said.

Melville stared at him for a moment. He clambered to his feet and, after another glance at Gunn, took Yonden's arm and led him away a little.

'What's the matter? You look worried.'

'No problem,' Yonden said stolidly.

'There never is.' Melville shepherded Yonden a little further. 'I wasn't going to say anything until we'd reached the valley, but I guess this is as good a time as any.' His tone was confidential. 'I know that Gunn finds it hard going. He has my sympathy, as do you. You've virtually had to carry him. Unfortunately, because Alan's in such poor shape, we've lost a lot of time.'

'You walk very good,' Yonden said, in an expressionless voice.

230

'That's not the point. We've been so strung out I haven't had any chance to sit down with you and talk.'

'Talk?'

Melville couldn't restrain a sigh. 'I'm not suggesting there's a conflict of interest, but you seem to have forgotten why I'm here.'

'To fix the business with the Chinese general.'

'To warn your boss about Jetha,' Melville said, trying to keep a smile going.

'That is for you and Osher to discuss.'

Melville's smile cut out. 'That's not the way I heard it the night somebody tried to murder me. We agreed I would go to your camp to call a halt to the operation.'

'Yes sah.'

'Bear in mind I've never met your commander. He's only a mental picture – brave, determined, not a guy who likes having his plans changed.'

'No sah.'

'So what I'd like from you is the benefit of your advice on how to present the disappointing news.'

'I don't know.'

'What do you mean, you don't know. You're his right-hand man, aren't you? You sat in on the planning sessions.'

'Only as interpreter,' Yonden said, obviously perplexed.

Melville struggled to bring his breathing under control. 'Whatever you are, Yonden, are you still planning to ride into Tibet after what happened back in Kathmandu?'

Yonden shook his head decisively.

'Thank God reason hasn't entirely flown,' Melville said. 'I'll be counting on your support when I sit down with Osher.'

'But sah,' Yonden said, 'I was never going into Tibet. My job is to look after you and Alan and the general.'

Melville closed his eyes. 'The general again. Are you telling me Osher could still go for it.'

'He listens, then he decides.'

When Melville opened his eyes, Yonden's shoulders were still hunched in a shrug. 'The hell with it,' he said, turning on his heel, 'I should have known better than to listen to you.'

'Sah?'

'I sure hate to lose all this height,' Yonden heard Melville say as the trio set off down the path. The Khampa watched them until they were out of sight then climbed back up the path. Burrowing into a bank of rhododendrons, he found a gap that offered a clear view of the ridge and hunkered down.

He permitted himself a massive yawn that made his eyes water. He disliked these journeys through the foothills, finding the repetition of low mountain spines wearisome and the heavy atmosphere something to be borne like an extra load. He must have walked twice as far as the others, going ahead to stop Melville taking too big a lead, retracing his steps to encourage Gunn.

It was worse than driving yaks, he thought. Gunn was the uncomplaining plodder, always at the back of the herd, while Melville was the strong and nervous beast, straining to get ahead but shying at every shadow. Yaks, however, were almost silent; a grunt was the only sound they made. Not like the American. Always he had to question, always his head was busy. Truly, Yonden thought, the mind is a monkey.

Then he laughed and smacked his knees, rebuking himself for being just as bad. His mind wouldn't lie still until they were safe on the other side of the river. With idle malice he contemplated the meeting between Osher and the American. That would be an encounter of opposites. The American was all thought and no decision; for Osher thought and action were one and the same.

Yonden's smile sickened as he imagined what his commander would do if he discovered that he'd tried to steal his comrades' money. A demon had entered him. It had looked out through his eyes and the American had seen it.

Was it guilt about the money, then, that made his skin crawl? No, that night with the American he had experienced a premonition of disaster, a warning that had made him want to steal the money and run away.

He stretched out and lay very still, watching the sun peering down from behind a pall of mist. The bad feeling came again, lasting for less than the beat of his heart, gone too quickly to be pinned down. Automatically his hand went to the rosary around his neck and he started to count off the appropriate magic formula. Before he had finished, he felt inside his *chuba* and took out a clear plastic envelope. Sitting up, he removed a letter from the Canadian High Commission in Delhi and read it through, although he knew the words by heart. They were formal but encouraging, referring to Canada's commitment to a multi-cultural society and assuring Yonden that, as a political refugee, his request to live in the Dominion and apply for citizenship would receive sympathetic consideration.

However the business with the Chinese general turned out, Yonden decided, he would leave the guerillas before the New Year. He would go when Alan left and not return. He would not tell Osher.

Feeling more tranquil, he lay back again, taking care not to look at the smouldering sun. The weather was beginning to clear. The cloud was lifting, baring fingers of snow that groped down from the sky. Yonden prayed that the overcast would remain until they had crossed the river. There would be a moon tonight, although he could not calculate how big it would be or when it would rise.

Suddenly he squirmed deeper into cover, stuffing the envelope back inside his *chuba*.

Preceded by the tap-tap of a staff, a saddhu clothed in dirty white came up onto the ridge. They had seen several on the journey – shuffling pilgrims with hot eyes whose blessings and appeals for alms rang like imprecations. Yonden took note of this one's upright stance and quick, alert gait, the way he halted and looked down the trail before continuing on his way.

Yonden gave him ten minutes to get clear, then started after him.

'It's weird,' Gunn heard Melville say. 'You can feel them, but you can't see them.'

'Soldiers?' Gunn said in alarm.

He'd been dozing, curled up on the spongy forest floor. Fragments of a dream about the sea were still lodged in his head. It must have been inspired by the fitful murmur floating up from the river five hundred feet below. He pulled himself to the edge of the outcrop, a natural window in the forest canopy, and looked down on the corrugated iron roofs of the Gurkha post. From this height it looked romantic and beleaguered, trees hemming in its stockaded perimeter on three sides, the river against the other. On the far bank, reached by a wooden cantilever bridge, a paddock of bright green grass sloped up to more trees pinched between the jaws of two vertical rock faces. The cliffs followed the curve of the river for as far as the eye could see, and because of the cloud there was no telling how high they were.

Gunn turned to Melville, knowing that he'd be confronted by the pained expression of a man who is forced to explain the obvious. 'I'm sorry,' he said, 'I didn't catch what you said.'

'Mountains. We've walked halfway across the Himalayas and I'm still waiting for the sight of a decent snowpeak.'

'Maybe tomorrow,' Gunn said. 'I'm sure the cloud's clearing.'

Again the response was too simple-minded, touching off the long-suffering look. Gunn cast about for a change of subject. 'Where's Ngawang?' he asked.

'Search me,' Melville said. His cheek muscles bunched. 'Who knows what they're up to? They slip off without a word and explain nothing. All the time we were on the trail I never knew when we were going to start or stop, or why we walked right through some villages and spent half the morning crawling around others. Every time I asked, all I got was a smile and a "no problem". Ngawang means eloquent, right? Well, I've had about six words from him.'

Gunn considered his reply. 'You wouldn't expect the pilot of an airliner to explain how he's doing his job.'

Melville guffawed. 'As an analogy, it's pretty far out, but it happens to be spot on. I'm up in the air with those two Khampas.'

'They're doing a job,' Gunn continued. 'They expect you to trust them.'

'I hear more of that word than I care to. All I'm asking for is a little feedback.'

'I must admit,' Gunn said, 'that I'm glad to have somebody else do the worrying.'

Melville was aghast. 'I hope to hell you can afford the price.'

'That sounds like another cryptic warning,' Gunn said, and saw Melville's self-righteous glow fade.

'Even if you're not worried for yourself,' Melville said, 'you must be concerned about Yonden. It's not as though his job carries a pension.'

'Money's got nothing to do with it,' Gunn said, and then wondered why he'd said it.

'I wouldn't bet on it,' Melville said. He dropped a handful of fir needles over the edge and watched them fall. He frowned. 'He doesn't come across as a freedom fighter. He's not a simple foot-slogger like Ngawang. He's travelled a fair bit. He's smart enough to know that the Khampas are pissing into a gale. I would have thought,' Melville said reprovingly, 'you'd be curious about his motives.'

'The guerillas are all he's got left,' Gunn said, wondering how to bring this conversation to an end. 'They're his family.'

'He could get himself killed.'

'I'm sure the possibility has occurred to him,' Gunn said, trilling his r's.

234

'And he isn't bothered? Why, has he got a fabulous reincarnation lined up?'

'Don't be daft, man. Yonden's no different from you or me. He wants to go to heaven, but he doesn't look forward to dying.'

'I didn't know he was a Christian.'

'Good Lord, whatever put that idea in your head?'

'I was forgetting that you weren't in Tibet to harvest souls,' Melville said. He rolled on to his back. 'Mind telling me what you were doing there?'

'Running away.'

'I'd like to hear. My father was an explorer, you know, and he tried for years to get into Tibet.'

Gunn rolled on to his back, too, and examined the dark tracery of the firs. 'It was pure luck,' he said. 'We'd reached a town called Qionglai, still inside Szechwan. We were stuck there a month before we found a caravan that would take us west. A few days before we were due to leave, a boy came to our inn and asked me treat his brother for a bad abcess on his elbow. They were part of a group of Khampas returning from Chengtu. The night we were due to leave, the boy came back and in a roundabout way told us that the caravan master intended to murder us. We had a lot of money and medicines. The boy asked us to travel with him.'

'Yonden?'

'You would have found him just as evasive in those days,' Gunn said. He chuckled. 'One morning, as we were breaking camp, I asked him how long that day's stage would be. Seven hours, he said, which surprised me, because we'd been woken at midnight and were ready to leave by three. Usually we didn't start until five or six. Well, ten o'clock came, then eleven. We stopped shortly after midday but nobody unsaddled, and after a drink of tea and a bite to eat we were on our way again. How much further, I asked Yonden. Seven hours, he said. We spent a total of fourteen hours on the move that day. I asked him why he hadn't told me and he said he didn't want me to worry about making such a hard journey. I tried to explain that what made it so hard was not knowing when it would end; the last two or three hours were purgatory. Later I found out why we'd made such a long stage: the last two caravans to cross that district had been massacred by bandits.'

'That's Yonden, right enough,' Melville said gloomily. 'I wonder what he's keeping from us this trip.'

'I never know when you're being flippant,' Gunn said.

Melville ignored the comment. 'There were two of you,' he said. 'Charlie told me your partner was a regular missionary. Was that the way you worked it – him ministering to the Khampas' souls while you took care of the flesh?'

Gunn was shocked – not so much by the casually insulting tone as by the fact that Melville had used almost the same words with which Peter had solicited his help all those years ago in the hospital.

'I find that offensive,' he said.

'Nothing personal,' Melville said. 'In real life I'm an anthropologist, and we don't get along too well with missionaries. We're competing for the same territory, but unless we combine roles we don't mess about with hearts and minds.' Melville sat up and brushed fir needles from his legs. 'Frankly, I've always been dead against the idea of anyone setting himself up as king of a far country.'

'You don't know the Khampas very well if you imagine that I could have played that role.'

'Tell me about them.'

'You can't categorise an entire people,' Gunn said. He paused for thought. 'All I can tell you is what the Tibetans themselves say. They say Lhasa for religion, Amdo for horses, and Kham for men. You find yourself thinking about them in clichés: good friends and bad enemies, clannish but hospitable, courageous but full of bluster.' Gunn frowned. 'I suppose they're a bit like the Highland clans of three centuries ago. Who's like us, they used to say. Damn few, and they're all dead.'

'Bloody-minded, huh?'

'Doomed by an unshakeable belief in their own worth.'

Melville sighed. 'I have the feeling that treating with Osher isn't going to be a helluva lot of laughs.'

He fell into a reverie and Gunn took the opportunity to study him. Superficially he looked the part – tall and well set up, cutting a fine figure in the *chuba* that he'd mocked back in Kathmandu but now wore with a freebooter's swagger. At rest, though, the fear showed through. It kept breaking out in contractions of the jaw, dry flickers of the tongue, intakes of breath.

Unaware that he was being watched, Melville obliged by sitting up and looking dazedly about – as though, Gunn thought, he was wondering how he had got here.

'Anything wrong?'

'What? Oh, no – tired of waiting, is all.' Melville summoned a smile. 'Go on about Kham,' he said. 'I guess that was a good time for you.'

'I was happy to be doing something useful.'

'Saving lives?'

Gunn ducked his head. 'Ah, you've found me out,' he said. 'Yes, with my box of medicines I was a king. I was more god-like than any incarnate lama.'

'Is that why you're here?' Melville asked.

'To play God? You ought to know, Mr Melville. In the kind of work you do, you must have learned a great deal about men's motives.'

Once again Melville lay back and shut his eyes. 'You don't say much about your partner,' he said after a while.

'No,' Gunn said. 'I don't.'

He rolled onto his side, facing away from Melville, and dug his hand into the carpet of needles. The top layer was crisp and springy, grading down through brown mulch into a fine black tilth. The carcasses of the trees that had added to these layers littered the hillside, frail hulks rotting down, clothed with violent green mosses. Dark parasitic wracks hung from the branches of the living trees. Gunn scooped up a handful of soil and breathed in its clean smell. He found his thoughts turning towards death.

Quickly he rolled onto his other side. 'There's something I want to ask you.'

Melville tensed. 'Anything you like.'

'Have you ever been to Canada?'

Melville was pinned to the ground by soundless heaves of laughter. By a supreme effort he managed to twist his head round. 'You really break me up, Alan. Here we are about to cross the point of no return, and you're thinking about Canada.'

Gunn looked away with a small, bright smile.

Melville swung into a sitting position and hugged his knees. 'I went to Canada once,' he admitted. 'It was Sunday and they'd taken the sidewalks up.'

'Never mind,' Gunn said.

'I thought you had something else on your mind,' Melville said, and paused. 'Hey, don't close up on me,' he said, turning on a boyish grin. 'I'm always outsmarting myself. Fact is, Canada's a fine place. I have an uncle – old Loyalist stock – in New Brunswick. I used to go there in the fall. Being Scottish, you must have relatives there too.'

'Thousands, I imagine. I grew up in a parish with six families where there had been more than fifty at the beginning of last century. Most of them went to Canada.'

'You planning to visit?'

Gunn hesitated. 'I was considering emigrating.'

But Melville's attention had slipped. 'You'll love it,' he said vaguely, peering down at the fort. Suddenly he punched the ground. 'It *is* him,' he cried.

Gunn drew himself forward. It took a while to identify the foreshortened figure approaching the bridge as Ngawang. Two soldiers came out of a guard-house and blocked his path.

'In-fucking-credible,' Melville said. 'The dummy's trying to walk straight through.'

Gunn caught his breath as the sentries halted Ngawang. While one of them searched his pannier the other frisked him, then all three withdrew into the guard-house. The seconds ticked off like hours. At last Ngawang came out, followed by the soldiers. He shouldered his load and walked across the bridge, up the paddock and through the mouth of the valley. Gunn and Melville blew simultaneous sighs of relief.

'There you have it,' Melville said. 'Surely it wouldn't have hurt to let us know what he was doing.'

'Someone else coming,' Gunn said, before Melville could develop his displeasure. It was a figure in white, carrying a staff.

'One of them holy men,' Melville said.

The saddhu spoke at length to the soldiers, who pointed across the river. Gunn got the impression that they were shaking their heads.

'Admission refused,' Melville said as the pilgrim turned away and retraced his steps. 'They must have put him wise about the Khampas.'

He kept up his surveillance. 'I don't see it,' he said after a few minutes.

A detail of Gurkhas was walking across the paddock with lengths of timber on their shoulders, a dog frisking behind. Not wishing to provoke, Gunn said nothing.

Melville clued him in with a wave that embraced the fort, the approach to the valley and the walls of rock on either side.

'The bridge is out, and I don't see any other way.'

'The less conspicuous the better,' Gunn said.

'Look at those cliffs. They drop right down to the river either side of the entrance. Wherever we cross, it has to be within a couple of hundred yards of the garrison. Then there's the open ground. I've been keeping my eye on it and it's like Times Square. See that smoke on the left there? Charcoal-burners' huts, and they've got dogs. Say we make it to the gap. It can't be more than fifty feet wide. If the garrison commander really wants to keep people out, all he has to do is post a couple of sentries inside.'

'Ngawang is there to warn us,' Gunn pointed out.

'What will you do if we're caught?' Melville asked abruptly.

'Tell the truth I suppose.'

Again, Melville seemed to be on the point of saying something, but again the light in his eyes dimmed and he turned away with a grim shake of his head to continue staring at the problem.

Gunn looked at him and for a split second saw Peter. He jerked his eyes away, but an after-image remained, changing form – Peter prostrate with altitude sickness, Peter insisting that they leave Tibet for India, Peter spilling out his resentment the morning that Yonden told them they were trapped inside a Chinese pincer.

A breeze feathered the tree-tops.

'Looks like you're right about the weather,' Melville said. 'Could turn out a perfect day.'

The sun had brightened to an angry white blister, boiling away the fog, leaving thin wisps snagged on ledges. Secret forests emerged, clasped in the knuckles of fierce crags. The valley went on deepening, its walls separating only narrowly. A vaporous blue window opened in the clouds and through it Gunn saw a snow peak where he would have expected only sky. He constantly had to revise his ideas of scale and perspective as the clouds rolled back, laying bare the route to the north, revealing the valley to be a mere hairline crack in the fabric of a tectonic city. Overhead, a huge circle of travel-brochure blue had opened up, Far to the north, shafts of light flared between cloudbanks over a waste of livid mountain blocks and green-black glaciers.

'This time the good guys win,' Melville declared, his fears dispersed in the blue yonder. 'How about that beauty?' he said, pointing to a bland ice dome that capped most of the horizon. 'Must be twenty thousand feet plus.'

'If you've got something you want to tell me,' Gunn said, 'now's the time.'

Melville went on gazing at the mountain, his smile wasting away.

'From the start,' Gunn said, 'you've been dropping veiled warnings and making unpleasant insinuations against Yonden.'

'You're a hard man to get through to, Alan. You're so starry-eyed about Yonden, you can't see how he's been leading you on.'

'He's not the only one, is he?' Gunn said, his voice hardening.

'I offered you a chance to pull out,' Melville said, matching Gunn's anger, 'and you told me to drop the subject. I've given you plenty of openings and you've declined to take them.' His shoulders sagged. 'Ah shit,' he said, 'you're right. Neither of us has been truthful with you. We thought it was the right thing to do.'

'Does this have anything to do with our unscheduled departure?' Gunn asked.

'Yeah,' Melville admitted.

'I'm listening.'

Melville jerked his head and Gunn saw Yonden traversing towards them, negotiating the steep slope with the ease of a monk strolling through a cloister.

'You certainly pick your moments,' Melville said. 'Do you want it now, or on the other side of the river?'

'Will it make a difference to the way I feel? About going on, I mean.'

Melville snorted. 'I should damn well hope so.'

'You aren't turning back, though.'

'Not yet,' Melville said with a martyred smile. 'Like it or not, I have to see it through.'

'Even though you're frightened.'

Melville's smile sickened. 'Even if that gap over there leads right into the jaws of hell.'

Gunn plucked at the end of his belt. In the arboreal gloom Yonden looked pale and drawn, no bigger than a boy. What does it matter if he lied, Gunn thought. Nothing's changed. The debt still stands.

Yonden was close enough for Gunn to hear his feet stirring the forest litter.

'I'd prefer to wait until we're across the river,' he said.

'As you wish,' Melville said. 'I'd better warn you that it isn't pleasant.'

They began their descent as the last band of daylight withdrew from the upper heights. Beneath the trees the dark was marbled with the sickly glow of moulds and fungi. The dimness and uncertain relief made the going awkward. Several times Melville lost his footing on the loose earth. Sliding into a stump he jarred a knee that was already bruised from too much walking. Gunn had to be nursed down by Yonden.

As they neared the bottom of the slope they saw a homely light playing hide-and-seek among the trees. Yonden used it as a beacon, leading them to the path a little way below a tea-house and traveller's rest. The fort was about half a mile up the valley, hidden behind a bend. They crouched down a few yards back from the path and waited.

The air was cold and moist, bitter with leaf mould and mist. An owl delivered a quavering hoot and was answered by an inflected screech that set Melville's neck hairs bristling. Snatches of domestic clatter carried from the tea-house. A lanterned window cast a yellow glow on the trees. Melville thought yearningly of bed and board. It had been three days since he had eaten hot food. Whenever he shifted position, his right knee twinged. Yonden had said they'd have to put some hard walking between themselves and the garrison before they could sleep.

Stars began to fill in the inky hollow of the sky.

Gunn muttered to himself.

'Knock it off for chrissakes.'

Gunn pretended to cough. 'It's the damp air,' he said, patting his chest.

Melville's own chest prickled with a rash of bad temper. What a bozo. Blisters, diarrhoea, leg cramps, piles – and now he threatened to blow it because of a little night air. Some of the dumb things he said. Melville snorted, remembering the moment on the third night out – fourth night? Christ, already the days were a blur – when he'd looked up to see Gunn about to walk off a cliff. Snatched from the brink, he'd looked around and said: 'I must have dropped off for a second.'

Gunn's face was pale as a moth. At intervals he blinked, and that little tic made Melville's hands clench. It's not my fault he's been left in the dark, he told himself. I practically told him to go home. The idiot's so insulated against reality nothing touches him.

And there's the one who wants to keep it that way, Melville thought, stealing a look at Yonden. What's in it for you? Money, I bet. You wouldn't be hanging in with the guerillas unless it paid. You're creaming off fighting funds. I've seen you at work on your numbers, the shabby exercise book you keep close to your chest.

I'm the only one who's coming at this thing straight, Melville told himself with self pity.

Yonden reached over and punched him lightly on the arm. Time to move out. A second or two in the open, then they were in the trees on the other side, listening. A dog yapped maddeningly from the direction of the camp. It had been barking since dusk.

Melville's nerves were stretched as thin as piano wire as they filed off, Yonden leading. Although the trees were well-spaced and the slope gentle, they kept bumping into each other. Twigs crackled under-foot, but soon the heavy note of the river drowned the sound, and as they got close the noise made ideas about stealth laughable.

From their perch in the forest, the visible sections of river had looked like slow trickles of quicksilver, but no allowance for distance could have prepared Melville for the force of the torrent. Standing twenty feet back from the edge of the gorge, he could feel its power striking up through the soles of his feet. The din billowed on gusts of spray that tossed clumps of ferns and made the tops of the trees bend in deference. Melville approached and craned forward. He jumped back. 'Oh my good God.'

It was a boiling pot fed by an ice-green race that plunged down a smooth chute and then, as if sensing the trap it had fallen into, beat itself into foam in its efforts to get free. The outlet was a crack where the water was backed up to a height of five, six, seven feet. It was difficult to tell, for the surface was in a state of eruption, detonating in thunderous spouts of spray that banged against a slick black wall where Ngawang, clinging to a twisted tree fifteen feet above the cauldron, grinned across at them. Melville's chest went pulpy with terror as he saw the rope between the banks.

'You said a bridge,' he shouted at Yonden.

Yonden cupped a hand to his ear.

Melville put his face close. 'No way are you going to get me on that.'

Yonden laughed.

'We have to look for a safer place,' Melville yelled at Gunn, pointing downstream.

Yonden gripped his arm and mimed a body dropping down a series of cataracts. Before Melville could make any further protest he led the way down a slippery gulley to a ledge a little above Ngawang's level.

It was only a couple of feet wide and Melville felt as though he were standing on marbles. He held onto the rope for support, its vibrations setting his fingers atingle. A plaited hemp sling hung from it with two lines attached, one of them held by Ngawang.

'This is madness. The fucking thing's made of straw.'

'It's the only way,' Gunn shouted.

'So help me, one more half-assed remark and it'll be your last.'

Gunn smiled woodenly, not hearing.

Ngawang was gesticulating, his mouth framing soundless instructions.

Melville wiped spray from his forehead. 'Who goes first?'

Yonden prodded himself in the chest. Melville and Gunn were too heavy for Ngawang to pull across single-handed. Gunn would go next. Melville last.

Suddenly Melville was impatient. 'Let's do it,' he shouted.

Yonden steadied the sling, climbed into it and hailed Ngawang, who braced himself against the tree. As the Khampa flung himself off, Melville's stomach went with him and he shut his eyes. When he dared to look, Yonden was wriggling in the sling, reaching up for the rope. He got hold of it and, without any assistance from Ngawang, swarmed across. Safe on the other side he turned, gave a casual wave and made winding motions with his hand. Melville hauled the sling back.

Gunn got stuck with one leg through the halter. He hopped up and down. 'Watch it!' Melville yelled. 'You'll have us both off.'

At last Gunn was ready. He teetered on tippy-toes.

'You want me to send you on your way,' Melville asked, 'or are you going to stand there all night?'

Gunn smiled mournfully, lifted his feet and shot down the rope like a sack of sand. Spray flew off the rope as it twanged taut, and Melville was dismayed to see how much it stretched. Gunn bounced up and down, his feet coming within inches of the water. Tightening the safety line, Melville felt the dead weight of him. If the rope broke, he realised, he would have no chance of holding him. He would be pulled off himself. His mind flashed him a detailed picture of what would happen. A gasp cut off as he was sucked into the centrifuge, whirled round and round, caroming off the walls of the pot before it spat him out chewed up and half digested.

Melville uncoiled the safety line from around his arm and held it loose in his hand. He did it without conscious thought.

Inch by inch Gunn was being hauled up. It seemed an age before Yonden, held by Ngawang, reached out and caught hold of him. They grappled briefly, then Gunn was home.

Don't think about it, Melville told himself as he retrieved the sling. One step, nothing to it. Mechanically he tackled up and prepared to jump.

He made no move, mesmerised by the din. It was white noise, a sensory overload.

A tug nearly unbalanced him. Ngawang was making short, angry gestures; Yonden was stabbing his hand upwards. Melville had forgotten about the Gurkhas. He looked to the clifftop, not much caring whether there was a squad of soldiers ranged there.

243

He smiled ruefully at his companions. A short impasse followed, broken by Yonden and Ngawang yanking him off the ledge.

He fell in a vertiginous swoop, down and down until the rope took the shock and gave and gave and . . . *nghhh*, he grunted as the sling cut into his midriff. His feet smacked into the foam, then they were pointing at the sky, then dangling in the water.

In panic he tried to kick it away. It was up to his knees, pushing him sideways, resisting the Khampas' efforts to drag him clear. He drew up his legs and it gobbled and spat at him. 'Get me out of here!'

Slowly and lumpily he was dragged up to the waiting hands. They grabbed him. He fell out of the sling and cuddled the tree, his back to the maelstrom. 'I'm fucking soaked,' was all he said.

After a short silence Ngawang and Gunn started climbing. Yonden gave Melville an urgent shake. 'What's all the panic?' he demanded.

'Look,' Yonden hissed.

Twisting around, Melville saw the moon painfully hauling itself clear of the tree-tops. The spray was luminous with its phantom light. A massive ice face accounted for half the sky to the south – the presence that Melville had sensed as he waited in the forest.

He shivered. Yonden was trying to untie the rope, muttering because the knot was tight and wet. Melville felt for his knife, a compact kit of tools designed to meet any backwoods emergency. The blades were razor sharp, unused. 'Here, let me,' he said.

Yonden nearly lost his balance lunging for the rope as it snaked out of reach. He looked at Melville as though he might burst into tears.

'Hey, we're across, aren't we?' Melville said. 'We made it.'

'How do you think you go back?' Yonden demanded.

'One step at a time, Yonden.'

Skirting the open ground, they took nearly an hour to reach the mouth of the valley. They hugged the base of the overshadowing cliffs like mice creeping towards a chink in a cathedral door. The lights of the fort dropped out of sight.

Ngawang called a halt on a grassy slope outside the entrance. They sat exposed to the glare of the great ice face and as Gunn contemplated it, he too felt its power – incommunicable secrets encased in a white silence.

'Big bastard, isn't it?' Melville said, flopping down behind. Then he laughed as the mask slipped a little and the sky trembled.

The man was impossible, Gunn thought. Now he was bubbling

with good spirits. His moods rose and fell with the unpredictability of a ping-pong ball on a column of water.

Yonden rousted them up.

They insinuated themselves through the valley entrance on a bar of moonlight, stealing along with upward glances, as though worried that their intrusion would be detected and the gateway would slam shut on them. Even when they were well inside, their footfalls muffled under the hiss of a stream, they held their silence. The mood of the place had infected them. It was like walking through a sculpture gallery after hours. Among ragged firs rose cool, dichromatic shapes – erratics smoothed and hollowed by forces working with all the time in the world.

At the tail of the column Gunn shied and spun as a bird burst up behind him and went rattling away through the trees. Too big and clumsy for a night-bird. A pheasant most likely. Gunn stared until his eyes watered. All was still as a crypt. He blinked, and blinked again, unable to dislodge from the periphery of his mind's eye the impression of movement flitting between shadows.

He hurried after the others. When Yonden noticed him, he fell back.

'I think someone's following us.'

Yonden clicked his tongue in vexation and Gunn realised he wasn't surprised.

'Do you know who it is?'

'Nothing,' Yonden said, with the distracted air of someone searching for a taxi in a busy street. Reaching a decision he took Gunn's arm and propelled him onwards. When the others came in sight he ran ahead. By the time Gunn caught up, Ngawang had managed to detach himself from the group and disappear.

A little before midnight they reached a clearing and halted at a log lean-to half-filled with hay. If Melville had noticed Ngawang's absence, he was too weary to comment on it. He collapsed into the hay like a puppet whose strings have been cut.

Gunn prodded him. 'Mr Melville. Walter.'

'It'll keep,' Melville mumbled. 'I'm out of it.'

Gunn lay down and in a few seconds sleep closed over him.

At some incalculable time of night he was woken by a horse snorting at a distance. Looking out, he saw two dark smudges gathered around a cigarette glow.

'Yonden?' he whispered.

One of the shapes got up and rustled through the grass. 'Go back to sleep, my friend,' Yonden breathed.

'Who was it?' Gunn whispered.

'Only some saddhu.'

'We saw him talking to the sentries. They must have warned him about the Khampas. What's he doing in this valley?'

'He's come from Patna to visit the lama.'

'Where is he now?'

'Gone back.'

'A man who's walked all the way from India isn't going to turn back within a day or so of his goal.'

Yonden's voice came closer. 'Ngawang made him go away. If he sees you and the American he might talk to the soldiers.'

'But he must have seen me. He's bound to tell them.'

'No. Ngawang gave him money.'

'He sounds a rather worldly holy man.'

Yonden understood the tone if not the words. 'This man is very greedy,' he said.

Gunn wished he could see his face.

'I know what you're thinking,' Yonden whispered. 'The American has been putting bad ideas in your head.'

'No, Yonden. Bad ideas grow in the dark. Mr Melville wants to let some light in.'

'I don't care what he tells you.'

'I'd rather hear it from you.'

'Better you talk to him, then you don't have to worry about me telling you lies.'

'Och, Yonden. There's no need to take that attitude. You could have explained everything in Bangkok. You know I'd still have come.'

'You don't trust me.'

'Of course I do, only . . . faith doesn't imply an absence of doubt, Yonden.'

Melville ground his teeth and gave a deep sigh.

'Listen,' Yonden whispered, 'the American wants to go back but is frightened on his own, so he thinks he'll make you come with him.'

'You're wrong. He told me he's going on, come what may.'

'You'll see,' Yonden whispered.

'Is that all you can say? I'm sick of hints and innuendo.'

'Ho,' Melville muttered sleepily, 'do I hear sounds of a falling out?'

There was a painful pause, then Yonden squeezed Gunn's shoulder and was gone.

*

246

Hearing wistful chimes, Gunn imagined they were part of a fading dream. Seeing frosted grass and a watery sunlight, he assumed it must be a little after dawn. Yonden and Ngawang were outside, heads cowled against the cold, hands cupped round a little yellow fire. Yonden pulled back his *chuba* and grinned. 'Sleep good,' he said.

Gunn looked at his watch. It was nearly ten. He dragged himself to the entrance. Rock ramparts shot up on each side of a gentian sky. A flock of tiny birds flitted through black needles, trailing a string of tinkling bells. Ten yards away, its pattern plain to see, a fat grey spider gyrated on the end of its thread. Gunn smiled, his doubts forgotten. It was years since he'd woken with an unburdened mind.

Melville sneezed and crawled into the light. The cut-glass morning made no impression on him. 'Was I dreaming,' he asked, 'or did I hear a gunshot last night?'

'A gunshot?'

'How about you guys?' Melville asked the Khampas.

'Hunters maybe,' Yonden said, stirring a pot of water with a clasp-knife. 'Lots of musk deer near here. The men from the village shoot them.'

'In the middle of the night?'

'It was very bright,' Gunn said, looking at Yonden.

Melville gave him a neutral stare, then transferred it to Yonden. 'Something going on I ought to know about?' he inquired.

Gunn felt sick. He caught Yonden's sideways glance of warning. 'I was asleep,' he said. 'The devil and all the coaches of hell could have ridden past and I wouldn't have noticed.'

The horse had gone, he noticed.

Melville grunted, idly scratching his stomach. He stiffened, his expression passing from wrinkled puzzlement to grimacing distaste. Rapidly he unbelted his *chuba*, parted his shirt and peered at his stomach.

'What is it?'

'A tick,' Melville said in a stunned voice. 'Big as a fucking dime, right on my belly button.' He swallowed. 'Ngawang, give me that cigarette.'

Ngawang unstuck the brown butt from his bottom lip.

'Shall I do it?' Gunn asked.

'I can manage,' Melville said, holding the tip close to his belly. The tick waggled its legs pathetically but didn't let go. Melville winced as the cigarette scorched his skin. He applied it half a dozen times.

247

All four peered at the problem with varying expressions of concern. 'It's dead,' Gunn pronounced.

'Oh shit!' Red-faced from being doubled over, Melville looked imploringly at Ngawang. 'You must know how to deal with these little fuckers.'

Ngawang exchanged puzzled looks with Yonden. He shrugged. Reaching out, he plucked off the tick, popped it between his fingers, wiped the blood on the grass, retrieved his cigarette and took a deep drag.

Melville inspected the result. When he looked up, his eyes were as hollow as his voice. 'The head's still in. It might go bad. I could get blood poisoning. Alan, you're supposed to be the doctor. Please get this crud out.'

Gunn tweezed out most of the debris. He anointed the tiny wound with antiseptic. 'I'll take another look tonight,' he promised.

Melville bent to look. 'A tick in the navel,' he said bitterly. 'Can you contemplate it?'

Chapter 16

All day they climbed under a faultless sky, filing past waterfalls that dropped in slow motion from hidden cloud-forests, criss-crossing the stream on cantilever spans and rope suspension bridges that swung in three planes at once. Lizards panted on boulders that were warm to the touch, but the gravel bars were salted with ice and in places where the sun never reached there were banks of corroded snow.

Leafless birches and twisted junipers succeeded the firs as autumn gave way to winter. Gradually the valley walls moved apart and the path struck away from the river, still climbing.

Yonden was somewhere far ahead. He had set out at his own pace before Gunn could question him. Melville was beginning to suffer from the effects of altitude and, for the first time, Gunn was able to keep up with him.

The day still had a little way to unwind when they hauled themselves over the edge of a grassy basin ringed on high by deserts of stone and ice. Melville did a slow turn, hands on knees. 'Too much,' he panted. 'Out of sight.' He sank down, broken-winded, dizzied by the excess of space and form.

Harmonious chaos – broken-backed ranges backlit by the failing sun; sections of ancient ocean floor warped up and laid on edge; the dreadnought prow of the massif they had seen by moonlight cutting through petrified breakers; the sugary dome, close up as convoluted as a brain, plumes of spindrift dancing along the crest and fading like ghosts in the quiet sky.

Melville tried to get his bearings from the map, but the contours cancelled out any features of significance. Gunn guessed that the cluster of low buildings over in the centre of the basin was the villagers' winter settlement, still vacant. Yonden and Ngawang had given it a wide berth. They were specks making for the rim of the river canyon. Gunn and Melville followed. Livestock had cropped the grass to the quick and in places gales had rolled back the turf like threadbare carpet. It felt odd to be walking on level ground.

'I can't tell if I'm moving,' Melville said. 'It feels like someone else has got the use of my legs.'

They came to the edge of a wide hollow and stopped, looking

down at a massive, stepped *chorten*. The sun was hull down behind a splintered ridge. Yonden and Ngawang had set down their loads by the shrine and were gathering firewood among the junipers that encircled it. They were hard to see in the murk of shadows that had gathered under the trees.

Melville kneaded his cheeks. 'Cosy little spot,' he said.

'Those trees remind me of black-hat dancers,' Gunn said.

In the dusk the junipers did seem to be racked in solemn pirouette.

'They assist at rites of exorcism,' Gunn explained. 'They represent the protecting deities summoned to expel evil spirits.'

'That *chorten*'s a very sober piece of architecture,' Melville said. 'I wonder what it's doing stuck out here.'

'It probably commemorates a lama.'

'Judging by the size of the trees growing out of it, I'd say the folks hereabouts stopped paying their respects a long time ago.'

'It could have been built by earlier settlers who moved away.'

'Pre-Buddhist, do you think?'

'Possibly. Tibetan nobles used to be interred in *chortens*.'

'Along with a few loyal retainers, I bet. There's a strong whiff of that old-time Bon religion about this pile.'

'People talk a lot of nonsense about Bon.'

'There's no truth in the blood sacrifice and black magic stories?'

'Historically, yes – in the same sense that you could describe Christmas and Easter as pagan rites. But for the last thousand years the Bonpos and Tibetan Buddhists have followed parallel paths. The people in this valley certainly don't make a firm distinction.'

'I thought they were Buddhist.'

'Both, according to Yonden. They're not interested in the abstruse metaphysical distinctions. All they're concerned with is the manipulation of the forces that govern their world.'

'Strange we haven't run into any of the locals,' Melville said, glancing back at the settlement.

'They're shy of strangers. Not many people come through the valley. It's a dead end.'

'So they're likely to have kept more old shamanistic practices than their neighbours,' Melville said. 'Did you notice those standing stones along the trail, and the inscriptions carved into the cliffs? Look at that juniper growing out of the roof. It looks like a horse's head stuck on a pole. Yep, I'm definitely picking up vibrations.'

'You don't mean that,' Gunn said.

'A backwater like this – who knows what you might find? It's bound to reward some anthropological digging.'

Gunn looked around him. A cold exhalation was rising from the turf. He could hardly distinguish Yonden and Ngawang against the mass of the *chorten*. He shivered. 'Let's get into camp,' he said. 'Tonight will be bitter.'

'Tonight I could sleep on a clothesline,' Melville said.

In an hour either side of sunset the temperature fell thirty degrees. Melville and Gunn lay fully clothed in their sleeping bags while Yonden cooked supper over a druidical blaze.

Melville broached his half of whisky and Ngawang produced a bottle of *rakshi*. Turning his back to the fire, Gunn watched the massif to the south assume its mask. A single planet hung over it. By the time he had finished his drink the sky was knitted together with stars.

Supper was served. 'Already I'm having food fantasies,' Melville said, scooping up a mess of rice with a hunk of buckwheat bread the texture of pumice.

Ngawang was lining his boots with fresh hay. He rested his bare feet on the rim of ashes.

'When you die,' Melville told him, 'I hope you donate them specimens to a geology museum.'

Ngawang grinned and passed over his bottle.

'Good guy, that,' Melville told Gunn, implying an openness lacking in Yonden, who was just a glitter of eyes on the far side of the fire.

The flames grew low. The cold tightened around them.

Melville drained his glass and subsided on to his back. 'Listen,' he said.

'I don't hear anything,' Gunn said after a few seconds.

'Loudest silence I ever heard,' Melville said.

Gunn gazed up. The sky was incandescent with burning gases.

'Remind me,' Melville said. 'Is the universe exploding or imploding?'

'I don't know. I've never been particularly interested in space.'

'Heresy. That's man's density – shit, destiny – out there.'

'Mr Melville, at this altitude I'd go easy on the drink. You'll have a terrible head on you tomorrow.'

'Got to celebrate breaking through.'

'You said you wanted to talk.'

'I do, I do. That's what I'm doing. And call me Walter, for chrissake.'

Gunn settled back resignedly.

'Maybe I am a little pissed,' Melville said drowsily. 'Or else the world really is turning.'

Gunn checked and saw stars sliding over the horizon.

'There's one going the wrong way,' he said.

Melville spotted the little light drifting against the current. 'Satellite,' he said. He imagined the blinking eye bouncing its images over the curve of the earth into the neon hum of an empty white room.

'It can probably read small print,' he said. 'Imagine being ID'd from four hundred miles up. Crazy little old world. Nowhere left to hide.' He took a thoughtful pull on his bottle. 'A couple of years back, in the New Hebrides, the French were running a road into the interior and one of the local shamans got worked up because it cut through his spirit trails. So he went into town in his warpaint and busted a few heads, then ran off chased by the gendarmes. Know where they picked him up? In the museum of ethnology, hiding in a dinky reconstruction of a grass hut, alongside the drums and masks. He claimed immunity as an endangered species.'

'You must have led an interesting life,' Gunn said.

'That wasn't me. This is the first time I ever went anywhere you couldn't reach by taxi.'

Yonden and Ngawang rose stiffly to their feet. After feeding the fire, Ngawang retired to a cell-like chamber attached to the *chorten*. Yonden hovered with an adolescent's awkwardness. 'It's alright,' Gunn told him, and he withdrew with a muttered goodnight.

'He knows we want to talk,' Gunn said.

'He doesn't win any merit points from me,' Melville said, pouring himself another drink.

'Why are you trying to turn me against him?' Gunn asked.

'I wouldn't waste my time trying. He saved your life at the expense of his own family. That's a rich lode of guilt to mine.'

'I can hardly keep my eyes open,' Gunn said. 'I'll wish you good night.' He rolled onto his side.

'Hear me out,' Melville said, leaning over. 'Whatever you owe him, you have a right to know the rate of interest.' He offered Gunn the bottle.

'Not for me, thanks.'

The fire was a bed of coals. The moon was just up. The junipers, the barbaric pagoda stood out against the mountains and frosted grass with the clarity of photogravure.

Melville's mouth was on the point of forming words when a

252

bubbling cry of high-spirited dementia sounded from the other side of the river, growing louder and more manic and then terminating with cut-throat abruptness. From the opposite side of the basin came a hollow chuckle.

'What in the name of God was that?' Melville breathed.

'A noise.'

Melville swivelled to face Gunn. 'Has anyone ever remarked on your amazing tendency towards the simplistic?'

'You'll hear plenty of inexplicable noises in these mountains,' Gunn told him. He yawned.

'Be not afraid, for the mountains are full of weird shit,' Melville said, lying back. He belched into his drink. 'You must be wondering why someone as jumpy as me is mixed up in a crazy stunt like this.'

'I expect that when you get round to telling me what you're doing, I'll know that you've got a lot to be nervous about.'

'Right,' Melville said vaguely. 'Right.' He blinked in the sidereal glare. His chest heaved as he took a deep breath. 'I'm here to arrange the defection of a big-wheel commie,' he said in a flat voice. 'A PLA general to be precise. Yonden's friends are going to run him across the border.'

Gunn's face appeared above him. He contrived to stare through it. 'You might say something,' he said at last.

He heard Gunn flop down beside him. They both looked into the heavens.

'Is Yonden going into Tibet?' Gunn asked.

'No, he's supposed to wait at the camp and then help me smuggle the general into India. At least, that was supposed to be the idea. The operation's cancelled.'

'What's made you change your mind?'

'I told you the truth wouldn't be pretty,' Melville said. 'The day we met, a Major Jetha, former Indian officer, late of the Special Frontier Force and now working for we don't know who . . . well anyway, this guy advised me to quit or else. He must have thought I hadn't got the message, because that same night, right after I left you, some punk, identity unknown, tried to waste me in an alley. He would have done too if Yonden hadn't chased him off. Hence our hasty departure.'

Gunn sat up and stared into the fire.

'Say something, will you?'

Gunn looked at him. 'Why did you ignore the warning?'

253

'Personality failing. I don't so much step back from problems as run away from them – usually in the wrong direction.'

'I don't understand. If you've given up the idea of rescuing this general, what are you doing here?'

'To give the bad news to Osher in person.' Melville looked away and sighed. 'Maybe it was a mistake. I don't do this kind of thing for a living.'

'Your government . . .'

Melville waved his hand. 'There is no government. I told you, it's just me.'

'What about Mr Sweetwater?'

'Ex-government, now an agent of fortune. Behind him there's a Kuomintang fixer, name of Mr Yueh. None of us has any official clout.'

'So you're doing it for money.'

Melville laughed. 'What other motive is there?' He watched the world go round and then breathed a sigh as of boredom. 'No,' he said, 'money's only a part of it.' He frowned. 'I was doing alright. I got by. I had work, the love of a . . .' He broke off as a vision of Sumiko in all her soft complexity pierced his drunkenness. 'Anyway,' he said angrily, 'I had no particular worries. And you know what?' Melville rolled his head and fixed Gun with one eye. 'Every morning I woke up feeling dread.'

'Worse than the fear that's on you now?'

'Different,' Melville said.

Gunn made a sound of exasperation.

Melville drank and sagged back, his glass balanced on his chest. 'Shall I tell you what really scared me – what pushed me into this lunacy more than the money, more than anything? It was something Charlie said.' Melville held up a declamatory finger. 'Life, he said, is not a rehearsal.' Melville slowly shook his head. 'How about that? I tell you, man, it terrified me. I mean, I'd never thought of it like that. I bet most people don't – or only when it's too late to make any difference. There I was, wasting time, and all the time, time was wasting me. Time's a real bitch, don't you find? One day you're pushing it ahead of you like it was a rock, and the next you're chasing after it like it was a . . . flyaway kite or something. I was always out of synch, never engaged. I never . . .' he struggled to say, patting the ground. 'I never seemed to get . . . to be . . . in contention.'

As he closed his eyes, his glass slid off his chest and spilt on the turf.

'And would you say you're in contention now?' Gunn demanded in suppressed fury.

Melville's eyes snapped open, making him look remarkably alert. 'At least I'm out of my puddle,' he said, performing a brisk sit-up. 'The Russians say you don't drown in the sea; you drown in a puddle.' He looked for his glass with an expression of faint annoyance.

'The Russians know bugger-all about the sea,' Gunn said.

'Metaphor, Alan. Take a look at a puddle that's been standing a few days. Tooth and claw, fang and pincer. Death on a small scale, but you end up just as dead. Where's my drink?'

'I grew up beside the sea,' Gunn said. 'My father was a lighthouse keeper. Believe me, you drown in the sea.' He shook his head as though to rid it of the lick and chop of waves.

'You're full of surprises,' Melville said, still groping for his glass. 'Christ, this ground is frozen.'

Gunn found the glass for him and placed it in his hand. 'I'd hate to be you when you meet yourself in the morning.'

'Tell me something,' Melville said. He paused to decant another measure with hands that could hardly feel. 'Forgive the grossness, but you used to drink a lot yourself. Am I right?'

'More than you.'

'Wow. What's the secret?'

'Secret?' Gunn said, startled.

'Of giving up.'

Gunn couldn't restrain a glance before he averted his eyes. 'I never touched the stuff before I came back. My father was a temperance fanatic. Drink would take you straight down the path to black, burning hell, he used to tell me. Then when I came back I found drink helped me forget.'

'Yeah,' Melville said, 'but then you stopped.'

'I never drank in Tibet. I used to preach the dangers of drink to Yonden.' Gunn halted for a while, and when he spoke again his voice was stiff with misery. 'Hearing that he was alive was like a . . . second chance. I didn't want him to see what I'd become. I wanted to go back to what I used to be.'

'Oh God,' Melville breathed, 'what an awful mess.'

A pall of loneliness settled on the two men.

'You must think I'm an awful fool,' Gunn said.

'All things considered,' Melville said with caution, 'you're **acting** very cool.'

'Why did you lie to me?'

255

'I'm not sure I did lie.'

'You told me you were doing a report on the guerillas,' Gunn shouted, rounding on him. 'Now you suddenly tell me about a Chinese defector and a murder attempt.'

'That's right,' Melville shouted back. 'A murder attempt. I was practically unstitched with shock. If I'd been thinking straight, I wouldn't be here.' He pointed shakily at the *chorten*. 'What's his excuse?'

'Answer for your own behaviour,' Gunn shouted. He swallowed. 'Why have you waited until now?'

'Alright, I lied,' Melville admitted. 'You're an easy man to lie to. You almost invite it.' He banged his glass down. 'Call it cowardice, call it what you like. I didn't want to come up here on my own. I figured that since the operation is off, you wouldn't come to any harm. I thought you being here would sweeten the pill for Osher.'

'I don't follow you.'

'Look,' Melville said, 'you're a clause in the contract, a condition laid down by Osher.'

'Osher?'

'Osher, Yonden – what does it matter. No doctor, no general; that was the deal.'

Gunn held out his hands to the embers.

'Anyway,' Melville said, 'now you know.'

Gunn gave a bleak laugh.

Melville hesitated. 'It's still not too late to turn back.'

Gunn stared past the *chorten* towards the north. 'You're right,' he said eventually. 'I didn't come this far by accident. I'm not as gullible as you think. I knew the night I met Yonden that he was lying to me. I think he wanted me to know, so that I would have an excuse for refusing to help. But then I thought of my obligation to him, and I knew that it would outweigh any misgivings I had.' He shrugged. 'It still does.'

'You must have other obligations.'

'No, none at all,' Gunn said. He reached for the bottle and swallowed an impressive quantity without wincing.

'A lighthouse keeper's son,' Melville said, shaking his head. 'You've hardly told me a thing about yourself. I don't even know what line of work you're in.' He detached the bottle from Gunn and took a swig.

'I was a supervisor in a cold store.'

'Beautiful,' Melville said choking on his drink. 'A cold store super-

256

visor and an amateur anthropologist.' He wiped his chin, his expression suddenly sober. 'Let's fuck off out of here.'

Gunn gave him a disturbing smile.

'So,' Melville said, 'you're still in the game.'

'You've abandoned the idea of rescuing this man – the general?'

'Seems that way.'

'In that case,' Gunn said, 'I'll stay for a few days.'

'Well,' Melville said, 'I don't mind admitting it – I'll feel a bit easier with you alongside when it comes to dealing with Osher.'

'I know it's partly my own fault,' Gunn said slowly, 'but I can't forget how you duped me.' He looked at Melville. 'You'll have to handle Osher yourself.'

Melville rubbed his hands above the ashes. 'Fair enough,' he said. He knocked back the last of the whisky and then inverted the bottle with melancholy satisfaction. 'The pure and simple life from now on.' He yawned and stretched out, facing away from Gunn, and pulled the hood of his sleeping bag up.

'I'm afraid not.'

Melville slowly hoisted himself up on one elbow. A few seconds went by.

'Last night,' Gunn said. 'You heard a shot.'

'A rock splitting or a branch snapping. A dream.'

'The saddhu we saw at the bridge followed us into the valley.'

'Hang on. We saw the Gurkhas turn him away.'

'Think back. Ngawang crossed the bridge, then a few minutes later the saddhu arrived and talked to the soldiers.'

'They were putting him wise about the Khampas. They were explaining why he couldn't go into the valley.'

'I don't think they'd stop a holy man.'

'But we saw him head back down the trail.'

'Only as far as the tea-house. He must have crossed the bridge after dark. I saw him a few minutes after we entered the valley. He was right behind us.'

Still swaddled in his sleeping bag, Melville crawled over. 'You dumb shit,' he said. 'Why didn't you tell me?'

Gunn averted his face from Melville's whisky breath. 'By the time we stopped, you were out on your feet, and then this morning you were distracted by that damn tick. You're easily distracted, Walter.'

'Are we talking about a genuine saddhu, or what?' Melville demanded.

'Apparently the man was on a pilgrimage to see the village lama.'

'Answer the goddam question.'

'There's no reason to disbelieve Yonden,' Gunn said miserably. 'Except . . .'

'He didn't seem surprised when I told him.'

For a moment Melville continued staring at Gunn, then he pushed himself back on his knees. 'I wondered why he was acting so cagey on the ridge,' he said. 'He was gone the whole time we were waiting in the forest. This saddhu might have been on our trail even then.'

'There's nothing sinister about someone taking the same route as us.'

'All day, maybe,' Melville said. 'All fucking week.' He peered around. 'He might be out there right now.'

'Ngawang gave him money to go away.'

Melville laughed harshly. 'Here you are mister holy man. Here's a hundred rupees on condition you don't tell the soldiers you've seen a couple of foreigners creeping around after dark near a guerilla base.' Melville's eyes widened. 'I heard a shot.'

'You said you weren't sure.'

'Oh, right – just one of those inexplicable sounds. Chrissake, Alan, you're the one who brought it up.'

'Neither of them have guns.'

Melville caught the uncertain tone. 'Spit it out,' he demanded.

'When Ngawang came back, I heard a horse. In the morning it was gone. There must have been another Khampa near the entrance to the valley.'

'Right,' Melville said, struggling with his zip, 'let's have those jokers out here.'

Gunn grabbed his arm. 'Let it rest until morning,' he pleaded.

'You're nuts,' Melville cried. 'This is our last night, our last chance.'

'Threatening will do no good. We're in their territory now.'

Melville wrenched his arm free but made no attempt to get up.

'Please,' Gunn said. 'Let me go.'

He walked over the crackling turf. When Melville heard slow footsteps returning, he cupped his chin in his hands. He did not look up as Gunn squatted by the fire.

'Gone?'

'Aye, the two of them.'

'That clinches it,' Melville said, trying to kick his way out of his bag. 'Going-home time.'

'You're not going anywhere in that condition,' Gunn said wearily. 'Neither of us are. We can't find the way back on our own.'

Melville gave a little laugh of astonishment. 'I underestimated him. Your buddy's really quite a prime mover. He's set us up so it doesn't matter if we jump or hang on. Either way we stand to get burned.'

'He told me you'd try to turn back.'

'Because he knows that half the intelligence services of Asia are crawling over my ass.'

'The man was only a saddhu,' Gunn muttered as though reciting an article of faith. 'Ngawang gave him a fright, that's all. Let's get some sleep.'

'And wake up with my throat cut? Where's the protection we were promised?'

'He must have a good reason for leaving us,' Gunn said fretfully.

'I have never met anyone so industrious, so fucking diligent, in the pursuit of self-delusion. Yonden didn't invite you here to relive the carefree days of youth. He's a guerilla. He kills people.' Melville fell back. 'Time you got to grips with the facts.'

'And it's time you stopped acting like a sahib dealing with treacherous natives,' Gunn cried. He laid himself down like an old man. 'Why can't you just let things be?'

Chapter 17

Melville surfaced with no sense of place, only the feeling that he had been here before – wrenched from free-floating depths into arcing light and pain as sharp as surgical steel. Birth? he wondered in the first moment of consciousness. No, the last time he had experienced pain as insistent as this was when he came round after an op to saw out a deeply-impacted wisdom tooth. Clamps and augers, his mouth full of broken crockery and his brain – shrunk to the size of a walnut – pickled in hot brine.

He buried his face in the crook of his arm and concentrated on breathing, not taking his viability for granted. Behind his sealed eyelids globular clusters drifted from left to right – parasite cultures migrating to fresh feeding grounds. On an experimental basis he opened one eye. *Flash.* He shut it again.

Rough hands had hold of him, preventing him from going back under. 'For heaven's sake, man, wake up,' a voice said.

He took a swing at it and sat up in one unconsidered movement. The light went black and his mouth flooded with saliva. He gripped his ankles until the nausea passed.

'How do you feel?' Gunn asked.

Melville was forced to take stock. Numb and parched, his guts boiling, fish-hooks in his eyes.

'Good as new,' he tried to snarl.

'You don't look at all well.'

'I'm telling you,' Melville croaked. 'Death holds no mysteries.'

'I did warn you,' Gunn said.

Melville attempted a look swollen with malice, but Gunn didn't notice. His well-rested eyes were engaged on other matters. Melville was distracted by the left sleeve of his *chuba*, which had turned white. He touched it to find that it was rimed where his breath had frozen.

Behind him someone laughed.

He hauled himself around like a beached sea mammal. His neck seemed to have fused into his spine.

Silhouetted against the brutal sun, a figure looked down from a shaggy pony. Melville raised his hand, partly to shield his eyes, partly out of fear – the atavistic dread of the earthbound for the man on the horse.

'This is Dorje,' Gunn said. 'He's going to escort us to the camp.'

The Khampa chirruped and his horse sidestepped into a less intimidating position. He grinned, displaying an absence of teeth. Dirt inked in the lines on his spare face. His hair, worn in an untidy bun tied with a grubby red ribbon, glistened like tar. A weighty chunk of turquoise dangled from one ear. He was dressed in pepper-and-salt homespun, the trousers tucked into felt boots with upturned toes, the *chuba* gathered at the waist by a depleted cartridge belt. In spite of the cold, his chest and right arm were bare, the empty sleeve hanging like an elephant's trunk. Across his saddle he carried a carbine with a scarred stock.

'Nice to meet you, Dorje,' Melville said, his voice slurred. 'If you'd care to step down off your high horse, we were about to take some coffee.'

'We ought to be on our way,' Gunn said. 'Dorje claims it's a five-hour journey, but you know what that means – more like eight or ten.'

'Look at me,' Melville said. 'What you're witnessing is a triumph of mind over matter. Unless I get a fix of caffeine, I'm gonna die.'

Shaking his head, Gunn went off to perform his toilet, carrying – to Melville's scorn – a neatly folded hand towel.

Melville gave Dorje a smile and levered himself more or less upright. 'So cold,' he crooned, 'so goddam cold,' shrinking before the bitter air and the horseman's scrutiny. He crammed his feet into unlaced boots and hobbled off. The Khampa's attention unmanned him, making him exaggerate his infirmity – clownish gestures of appeasement. He went behind a juniper and pissed, glumly contemplating the fluted ice walls of the massif. There was too much scenery this morning. It taxed his mind like a problem in advanced trigonometry.

He couldn't get a fire started. His lighter spat raw fuel and the horseman's unblinking interest made him clumsy. 'Shit!' he yelled, hurling the useless implement away. 'Damn and shit!'

Iron clinked as the Khampa slid off his horse. On foot his centaur grace deserted him. He advanced with heavy, rolling tread, retrieved the lighter and crouched in front of Melville, clicking his tongue in a deprecating way. The stink of untanned hide, horse, smoke and animal fat made Melville blink. The Khampa rummaged in his *chuba* and withdrew a tarnished silver box, then he rearranged the mess of twigs and bent over it. There was a flinty knocking, and when he

261

straightened up, a flame – hardly visible in the sunlight – was crawling up the fire.

'See that?' Melville called to Gunn, who was walking back looking pink and bonny. 'A guerilla with a tinderbox.'

'That's not a flintlock on his saddle,' Gunn said.

Dorje held out the lighter, snapped it a few times to show that it worked then, when Melville reached for it, dropped it into his *chuba*.

While the water heated, Gunn talked to the Khampa in Tibetan, using what Melville sourly regarded as excessive gestures and exclamations. He felt excluded, relegated to the status of passenger, and he had the uneasy impression that the balance of their relationship had shifted in favour of Gunn.

'Dorje's from the same region as Yonden,' Gunn said, beaming. 'His father met me several times. Isn't that amazing?'

'Sensational. Look, when you're through with old times remembered, how about asking him what happened to the saddhu.'

Gunn turned back, ignoring him.

'Who was the saddhu who was following us?' Melville asked in Chinese.

'He doesn't know,' Gunn said quickly. 'He's just arrived here from the camp.'

'Riding all night?' Melville said. He frowned. 'I didn't know you spoke Chinese.'

'Four years in prison,' Gunn said.

Melville ran his fingernails across his scalp. 'Screw it,' he said. 'I ought to dump the whole mess in your lap and go home.'

Dorje looked from one to the other, sensing antagonism. He said something to Gunn, whose answer made him laugh and clasp his head.

'I told him you had a bad hangover,' Gunn said.

'Were you the rider who came by our camp two nights ago?' Melville demanded of the Khampa.

Dorje glanced for help at Gunn, then produced a smile which he held until Melville was obliged to follow suit. They stayed like that for several seconds, grinning like foxes, nodding politely in mutual recognition of the other's mistrust.

'Coffee's ready,' Gunn said. 'I only hope it puts you in a better humour.'

The first tepid mouthful made Melville gag. Cheeks bulging, he struggled to contain it. Gunn and Dorje looked on in consternation, balls of rice arrested in the act of being popped into the mouth. Unable

262

to hold it back, he stumbled away, hand clapped over his mouth, until he rounded a corner of the *chorten*. He vomited until he felt he had turned himself inside out, then leaned weakly against the shrine. He felt better, although not up to any enterprise, let alone one that called for a ten-hour hike through serious mountain terrain. Two or three days, he told himself. Two or three days and you'll be shot of it. He took a deep breath, wiped away the tears and mucus, drew himself up and marched back to the fire.

'Anything I can do?' Gunn asked. He and Dorje no longer appeared to be in a hurry.

Melville picked up his mug and emptied the coffee on the fire. Dorje was dismayed by such prodigal behaviour, Gunn resigned.

'Right,' Melville said, 'let's get this circus back on the road.'

After an hour's walking, Melville's nerves consented to lie flat and line up in the same general direction. His mood, however, remained vile, poisoned by doubts that circled on an endless loop. He stopped and squinted down the empty trail. Yesterday the mountains had exalted; now they loomed, shapes stabbing into void. The sun beamed down from the clarion sky in a way that he found wearisome. This was a journey into the absurd.

He and Gunn plodded in the Khampa's train like spoils of war. The path circumvented the dripping snout of a glacier, then the valley narrowed, hemmed in by pastel cliffs folded into startling arabesques. In places the trail had fallen into the river, leaving sickeningly steep scree slopes that had to be crossed on a rut one footprint wide. The Khampa set his horse at these places in a rattle of shale, while Melville and Gunn tip-toed after with a lot of balletic arm movements.

At the peak of the day the path squeezed down into a gorge with walls so steep and unconsolidated that it seemed a single pebble removed from their base would bring down a mountain. The sun slid away and the sky closed to a slit, leaving them in twilight. An hour later, the river vanished into a tunnel formed by an immense flake of rock that had spalled off and come to rest at an alarming angle on the opposite wall. There was no way round it.

'Now what?'

Dorje had dismounted and was placing a stone on a cairn at the base of the slab.

'He says the path gets difficult from here,' Gunn explained.

Dorje remounted, turned as if retreating, then whirled with a shout and drove his horse straight up the canted rock. Its momentum ran out before it reached the top and for a moment it hung on its hind legs, front legs flailing air, its rider squeezing its flanks and flapping his elbows. Then the hooves found purchase and horse and rider disappeared over the top as though plucked by a cord.

Without catching each other's eyes, Melville and Gunn followed on all fours. Sweat started from Melville's pores when he looked down through his legs and saw how high he was, so high that the surface of the river had solidified. He completed the climb with his eyes fixed on the rock directly in front of his face.

The upper ledge of the slab marked the start of a vertical maze, a path that served no logic but its own. It went clockwise and anti-clockwise, around pinnacles and turrets, through doors and along walls, scaling heights of gothic fantasy. Melville felt as though he were climbing round and round inside his own skull.

A high-pitched wail sounded from several directions at once. Searching for the source, Melville located Dorje leading his pony up a crooked chimney a hundred feet above his head.

'He's singing to keep the demons away,' Gunn said, and Melville nodded as though dismissing the obvious.

One foot in front of the other – that's what was needed. One-step, two-step. Round the rugged rocks the ragged rascal ran. Round the ragged rocks the rugged rascal ran. Round the . . .

Blind walls, staring caves, corkscrew towers reeling round the patch of sky. He had been here in dreams.

One-step, two-step. His heart palpated, his eyes went stiff in their sockets as he sidled along a ledge on a perpendicular face, grazing his cheek on the stone. He felt the mountain pushing him outwards.

One-step, two-step . . . the earth opened at his feet. Two birch logs spanned a crack fifteen feet wide and so deep as to be bottomless. Gunn was on the other side, removing a boot.

'Dorje couldn't have taken his horse over that,' Melville whispered.

'He must have gone a different way,' Gunn admitted.

Melville examined the problem.

'It's not too bad if you don't think about it.'

'Okay, okay,' Melville said. He spread his hands over his face and drew long breaths. 'Okay.'

He lowered himself astride the logs and began to pull himself forward. Halfway across he stopped. 'I can't move,' he said – a flat statement of fact.

'Don't be daft. You're nearly there.'

'I'm telling you, I can't move.'

264

The bones had been withdrawn from his flesh. He was a blob of protoplasm.

'Relax. You're clinging too tight.'

Melville managed a sob of laughter. 'I am relaxed. I'm fucking deliquescing.'

'Don't look down. Look at the logs.'

Melville couldn't take his eyes off them. They were wet with rot and bored by insects. The river gave a faraway sigh. He pictured his body pinwheeling into purple depths.

The bridge shuddered. 'No,' he yelled. 'It won't take both of us.'

'It's alright,' Gunn said. 'I've got you.'

This was nonsense, since he was balanced on hands and knees, with nothing to anchor himself by.

'Get back,' Melville said through gritted teeth. 'I don't need your help.'

Gunn reversed and Melville came after, dragging himself like a wounded sloth.

On reaching solid ground he rested with his head between his knees. A fit of ague shook him. 'My body gave up on me,' he said, amazed and indignant.

Gunn probed a blister. 'It's a strange thing, your strength going when you need it most.'

'No it isn't,' Melville said. 'It's nature's way of letting you know you're in a jam.'

'Not much help if you don't have the means to get yourself out,' Gunn said, pulling on his sock.

'That's what I mean. You shouldn't have got yourself there in the first place.'

'Aye, well,' Gunn said, rising to his feet. He gave Melville a grave look. 'A damn awkward place to find you have no head for heights.'

'Alan,' Melville called as Gunn moved off, 'do you mean it about going your own way when we reach the camp?'

Gunn halted but didn't turn. 'I'll wait for you at the top,' he said eventually, and walked away.

Melville remained slumped on the ledge, ignoring the clammy chill on his back, indifferent now to the half mile of air beneath his feet. Alone, deserted. Anger scoured him as he watched Gunn's squat figure trudge upwards.

'This isn't a jaunt arranged for your benefit,' he shouted. 'You're not here on a pilgrimage.'

. . . *image, image*, the booming walls flung back at him.

*

Dorje and Gunn were waiting on a windy shoulder planted with a clump of shredded prayer flags. The Khampa dozed over his horse's neck; Gunn was sprawled against a rock. 'Careful, man,' he murmured, and Melville obediently halted at the edge of a two thousand-foot drop.

They stood at the brink and stared down.

As Sweetwater had claimed, the Khampa stronghold occupied a hole in the ground, completely immured except where the river made thin incisions north and south. The sun rested on the western wall, firing the upper half of the cliffs on the other side, but around the camp the light was already beginning to clot. Melville could just make out a flock of sheep dotted on the turf like lice.

A squadron of griffon vultures swept past, big as bombers, close enough for Melville to hear the wind moaning through their slotted wing-tips. One of them gave him a blank, invertebrate glance in passing. His eyes followed them as they banked and lost height, dropping in giant steps, sunlit motes abruptly extinguished in shadow.

Dorje fired his rifle. It made a puny sound and woke no echoes. He spurred his horse over the edge, lying back on its tail. It slid twenty yards, all four legs braced, then Dorje wrenched it round and they vanished behind a knuckle of rock.

It was growing cold. The prayer flags chattered in the wind. Gunn and Melville had no choice but to follow the Khampa down.

Chapter 18

They halted like big, broken toys in front of a three-man welcoming delegation.

Yonden, dressed in a padded Chinese army jacket, stepped forward and hung white nylon scarves around their necks. He ignored the promise of a reckoning distilled in Melville's stare. Next, a man called Chorphel gave them bowls of sour beer. To Melville he looked a bit long in the tooth for hit-and-run warfare, but he cut a fine figure nevertheless – tall, belted into a patchwork coat of animal skins, with the untamed locks and beaky nose of a Judean prophet. Osher was even taller – a fierce angel wearing an aviator's jacket over a blouse of parachute silk, with a holster at his hip. Melville drew himself up to receive his fleeting handshake.

Ceremony concluded, Osher led the way into his base. Melville followed on rubber legs, looking down on his feet as from a height of several thousand feet.

Imposing at a distance, the camp turned out to be a collection of hovels dug into glacial debris. Imported detritus littered the alleys – polyester rags and condensed milk cans, soap powder and cigarette cartons as gaudy as the day they left the factory. There were heaps of human and animal excrement in the corrals between the houses. In the cold sterile air nothing degraded quickly. A raven skipped ahead, dragging a hank of hair attached to a flap of pink tissue, and bounded into slow flight. Gun tut-tutted at the squalor.

Wolf-faced, silent, wearing soot like a second skin, the guerillas watched from the rooftops. They were dressed in a ragbag assortment of hides, *chubas* and the uniforms of half a dozen foreign armies. Their head-gear included fox pelts, bobble hats, trilbies, proletarian caps flaunting the red star or badges of the Dalai Lama, and baseball caps stencilled with the names of Thai beach resorts. A few of the Khampas carried weapons; one had a short sword thrust through his belt. They greeted the strangers with bony grins, flat stares, dropped jaws. Truly, Melville thought, we have fallen among barbarians.

Slipped through a warp, he thought, as Osher stopped under one of the camp's three medieval keeps. It was a tall building, its height exaggerated by walls that sloped inward towards the roof. To Melville it seemed to pierce the sky. All the light was fled there now, a pink glow tracing the circumference of this nether world.

Osher showed them to a first-floor room ventilated by a single window eighteen inches square. Smoke from a dung fire burnt their eyes and throats. The Khampas crowded in after them, bobbing their heads in awkward introduction. Osher sat down, yanking his holster over his crotch, and invited Gunn and Melville to take the places opposite. Chorphel sat at his right side, a young man with a bland face and hostile eyes on the other. The rest of the company arranged themselves where they could. The room was full of teeth and eyes.

Osher delivered a long speech of welcome.

A woman in a black gown and candy-striped apron came in and began working a plunger in a wooden cylinder. Noticing that the slurping noises had caught Melville's attention, one of the Khampas inserted a finger into an O made with his other hand and plied it vigorously. Melville smiled weakly; the woman laughed like a drain. She transferred the contents of the cylinder to a blackened kettle and then poured the emulsified liquid into bowls. Tea was served. A man with a septic lip pressed a bowl into Melville's hands. Tightening his throat, he drank, straining the liquid through his teeth. It tasted somewhat like chicken broth. He lip-smacked his appreciation and declined more.

The woman was watching him, scratching her breasts. Absently she put her hand to her mouth and brought her teeth together on something small and brittle. A flush spread over Melville's ribs.

Osher spoke to Gunn.

'He wants the rest of the money,' Gunn said.

The commander's features had settled in a polite smile.

'How many men did you say you had here?' Melville demanded, his voice pitched to carry to Yonden, who was ostentatiously lounging against the wall behind Osher.

Yonden muttered and scuffed his foot, playing the company fool. He got a laugh.

Osher requested a translation. He said something that provoked more mirth.

'Give it to him,' Gunn warned.

'Look around, Alan. Two hundred Khampas, Yonden said. This dump can't hold half that.'

'What does it matter?'

'The truth matters. I'm sick of being fed bullshit.'

'Hand it over. You're in no position to refuse.'

Smile intact, Osher stretched out his arm and rubbed finger and thumb under Melville's nose.

Safe for the moment behind his own smile, Melville refused to back down. 'All I want to know is their real strength.'

'Fifty or five hundred, it's all the same.'

'Not to me it isn't. Look, I thought you were going to stay out of it. Just get me that one fact and I'll take it from there.'

Gunn put the question and Osher answered, his smile threatening to grow weary.

'He says two hundred and ten. Satisfied?'

'This is nothing but a shakedown,' Melville said, feeling for his money belt.

He had to inflict on himself the indignity of half disrobing before he could undo the belt. Osher raised it above his head to a murmur of approbation. He looked at Melville and his smile twanged shut.

'Half my duty done,' Melville muttered to himself. He let Gunn tell Osher about the journey. Fatigue and altitude had done for him. His eyes felt as though they were being struck from behind by rubber mallets; the tendons in his neck were pulled as tight as cables. The Khampas were speaking, their voices running together and seeming to speed up like a tape on fast forward, their faces floating in the fog like carnival masks.

'We'll leave you to sleep now,' Osher suddenly announced in fluent but oddly accented Chinese.

Melville found that he had slumped sideways against Gunn. 'Forgive me,' he said, straightening up. 'If I'd known you spoke such excellent Chinese, I would have addressed you directly.'

'Yonden tells me you have bad news for me,' Osher said.

Melville pulled a face to convey regret.

'Urgent news,' Osher said. He stood up and the rest of the Khampas did likewise. 'Report to me in two hours.'

'Two hours,' Melville agreed, 'and then I shall be delighted to present myself at your headquarters.'

Osher initiated the move to the door. Within a minute the room was empty. Melville collapsed onto the boards of a sleeping platform.

'Can you imagine old General Liu putting himself into the hands of that badass rabble?' he asked.

'They're well-disciplined enough,' Gunn said, holding out water bottle and aspirin.

'Osher's an imposing character,' Melville conceded, accepting the pills. 'Did you ever see a more beautiful man?'

'Bright angel of the morning, how art thou fallen?'

'Huh?' Melville squinted up at Gunn, his headache making him see stars.

'I'd watch yourself there,' Gunn told him.

'Glad to hear a cautionary note,' Melville said, feeding the pills into his mouth.

Gunn went over to his own pallet. Melville sensed unspoken concern.

'I expected you to be more blithe now that we've reached journey's end.'

'How is it that you didn't meet Osher in Bangkok?' Gunn asked, rooting through his pack.

'He was never there,' Melville said. He was going to tell Gunn about Osher's problems with the Indians, but thought better of it.

'Yonden was,' Gunn said. He turned round, his expression indeterminable in the fug. 'So was I.'

'Gone before I arrived,' Melville said. Privately, he was bothered by the way Sweetwater had scheduled everyone's visits so that they had failed to coincide. Worry made his head thump.

'Who's Lupus?'

'Never heard of him.'

'He does business with Sweetwater. He was the one who took me to see Yonden. He said something about Yonden being part of his history.'

'Sorry, can't help you.'

'Aren't you concerned?'

'I call that pretty rich,' Melville said, struggling to sit up. A cruel homunculus seemed to be clamped to his skull. 'Last night, when we still had a chance, you didn't want to know. Now it's questions, questions.'

'Our last chance went the night we crossed the river.'

'That's right,' Melville said. 'We're here now, and talking isn't going to change that.' He lay down again. He was tired of explanations, tired of his fears.

'I've been thinking,' Gunn said.

'You heard what Osher said. I've got less than two hours to get my head together.' Melville shut his eyes. Presently he heard Gunn cross to the trap-door. 'Where are you off to?' he mumbled.

'To see my patients.'

Detecting an uncharacteristic note of sarcasm, Melville opened one eye. Gunn was on the ladder, peering from corner to corner.

'Piss-poor facilities for doctoring,' Melville said.

'At least we have the house to ourselves.'

'You must be fucking joking,' Melville muttered, scratching his ribs.

In a two-room building that served as storehouse and infirmary, Gunn straightened up, concluding a ritual as old as military history. Mouth set in an apprehensive smile, the next Khampa in line stepped forward.

'What's his problem?' Gunn demanded.

'Love sickness,' Yonden said.

'Tell them again,' Gunn said, massaging his forehead. 'Only serious cases tonight.'

Yonden berated the crowd by the door. One man shuffled in and sheepishly held out a bandaged arm. Gunn unbound the filthy dressing, exposing a forearm gashed from elbow to wrist.

'How did this happen?'

'Cutting wood,' Yonden replied. The Khampas laughed.

Gunn examined the gash. What at first he took to be a suppurating discharge proved to be a compound of rancid butter and dye.

'Who put this filth on?'

'Linka,' Yonden said, glaring at the casualty as though it was his fault.

'Why in hell didn't he clean it? It's a miracle this idiot hasn't got gangrene. What does he expect me to do at this stage? It's too late to stitch.' Gunn broke off. He shook his head as if to clear it, and squeezed the bridge of his nose. Then without a word he began redressing the wound, using the same rag. 'I'll look at it when the supplies arrive. Another few days isn't going to make a difference.' He turned away, leaving the patient still holding out his arm, and sat down on a sack of barley at the back of the room. He cupped his face in his hands. 'Get them out of here,' he ordered.

'Sah?'

'You heard me.'

Yonden shooed the Khampas away, lashing out at the dawdlers. When the room was clear, he came back and took up a wary stance.

'It's not quite what I expected,' Gunn said.

Yonden sighed as though he had expected complaint.

'Why did you bring me here?' Gunn asked, raising his face. Exhaustion was stamped around his eyes and mouth.

'To help my friends,' Yonden said, his eyes flickering doorwards.

'One suspected TB case, the usual pox, a few minor gut infections and a sword wound. You said your friends were dying.'

'They died before I left. They died in the summer.'

'They'll die every summer in this cesspit,' Gunn cried. 'You of all people should have more sense.'

'There's no stream here,' Yonden told him. 'It takes two hours to bring water. We know about bad water. We're not stupid peoples.'

'I'll go along with that,' Gunn sneered. 'You're not stupid by a long way.'

Next door the TB patient was racked by feeble coughs. Gunn waited for the seizure to end.

'Your only serious case, and there's nothing I can do for him.'

Yonden sat down next to Gunn and composed his hands in his lap. 'I knew you'd be angry,' he said softly, staring straight ahead.

Gunn laughed, after a fashion. He was close to hysteria. 'Whose idea was it to lure me here?'

'Lure?' Yonden said, giving him a sideways glance. 'I wrote you a letter when Charlie told me you were alive.'

'I have it on me still,' Gunn said. He fished out the creased note and read it. He looked as though he was smiling, but he wasn't. He handed it over to Yonden. 'You seem to have left a few things out.'

Yonden studied it with a frown, his finger combing the lines. Suddenly his face brightened as though he had discovered the crux of the misunderstanding. 'You mean the Chinese general.'

'I mean the whole bad business,' Gunn shouted, snatching the letter back. In the face of Yonden's complacency he felt robbed of power. Slowly he tore up the note. 'Last night,' he said, struggling to keep his breathing even, 'Walter told me that someone tried to kill him.'

'I would have told you,' Yonden muttered, fiddling with a strand of sacking, 'but the American wouldn't let me. He's frightened all the time.'

'You mean to say you sided against a friend,' Gunn said, shocked into an unconsidered response.

'You would have gone home,' Yonden said, winding the thread round his fingers, 'although the general is none of your business. And then the American would have gone away too.'

'Would that have been such a loss? Walter's only here to warn Osher.'

'Osher said it was important to bring him.'

'At any cost?' Gunn said, feeling a stirring in his guts.

272

Yonden shrugged. 'He gave me money.'

'How much?' Gunn asked, in a tone calculated not to alarm. He wanted to pummel the self-satisfaction out of Yonden's face.

Shyly, not entirely certain, the Khampa reached beneath his shirt and pulled out a wad of notes. 'Five hundred American dollars.'

For a moment Gunn was bereft of breath, then he jumped up, knocking the money out of Yonden's fist. 'Walter's right,' he panted. 'Money's the only thing you care for. You've risked both our lives for a few filthy dollars. You've lied and cheated from the day I met you. Even as a boy you could never tell the truth.'

'I'm not some bloody fucking boy,' Yonden cried, pawing at the notes. 'I'm a soldier.'

'You don't have to use barracks language to prove it.'

'Same as Ngawang, same as Osher,' Yonden shouted, slapping the ground in a gesture of displaced anger.

'Cut it out.'

Yonden looked up at him and smiled. 'I wish I was with the American now. One bad word to Osher and . . .' Yonden whipped his hand across his throat.

Gunn realised that he had seen Yonden smirk like that once before. He sat down as though he had been pushed.

'Osher was in Bangkok, wasn't he?'

If anything, Yonden's lips unrolled even more, but he was no longer smiling.

'All the time we were talking, he was in the same house. That's who Lupus was going to meet.'

Yonden bent down to retrieve the last few notes. Gunn watched him dully. 'He said you were part of his history.'

'Not me,' Yonden muttered. 'Osher.' He straightened up and did not avoid Gunn's eye. 'One time Lupus sent Osher into Tibet and didn't give him any guns. He sold them for himself. This made Osher very unhappy. When Charlie told him Lupus was in Bangkok, he decided to make his revenge. He pretended to be a ghost. He gave him a fright.'

'The same kind of fright that Ngawang gave the saddhu?'

Yonden's face set as sharp as a knife. 'It's not important,' he said, stuffing the wad of notes back under his shirt.

'You're right,' Gunn said. 'Your loyalty is to Osher.' He stood up.

'You want to go back to Kathmandu?' Yonden muttered.

With a shock as severe as pain, Gunn suddenly saw how far he had wandered away from the course he himself had set. The pledge he had made in Bangkok had been unconditional, but like so many promises he had made, it had not stood the test of reality. It seemed to him that he stood in the wreckage of broken vows and friendship.

'Can't you see?' he cried. 'I'm doing no good here.'

Yonden nodded with sullen resignation. 'Tomorrow I'll talk with Osher.' He turned and left the room. After a moment, Gunn followed.

They went out into the frozen alley and walked to the house without speaking. The moon wore a thin halo. The house was empty. Yonden followed Gunn into the room and stood looking out of the window.

'It's this place,' he said softly. 'It makes you see the wrong way round.'

'Back to front,' Gunn said, mouth askew. 'Widdershins.'

'I don't like that word,' Yonden said, looking over his shoulder. 'Not here.' Yonden resumed his watch. 'Look at the ring round the moon,' he said eventually. 'That means a lama will die.'

Gunn came and peered through the window. All he could see was a mountain mass against diffuse starlight.

'Are Linka and the lama still fighting?'

Yonden glanced at Gunn. Finding no scorn in his expression, he nodded. 'Linka has taken Aim Giver's daughter away by magic, and the lama has cursed them both. While I was away, my friends saw the lights of a whole army on the mountain. Yes,' he said 'one of them will die this winter.'

'Where is Linka? I thought he'd be with Osher.'

'Up there,' Yonden said, jerking his chin. 'At the place of wet skulls. He goes there for many days.'

Gunn experienced a peculiar, unfocused excitement. He was too exhausted and troubled to sleep, and he knew that bad dreams waited for him.

'Take me to see him.'

'Now?'

'It's only right that I should introduce myself. He's been treating your friends. He might resent my interference.'

Gunn's voice sounded magnified in his ears. A crawly sensation moved over his insides. Although the light in the room was feeble, objects stood out with hallucinatory sharpness. He recognised the onset of mania.

'Ah no,' Yonden said, backing away. 'You're not allowed.'

'I'm not frightened of anyone's demons but my own,' Gunn said, following him.

274

'Osher would be angry with us. He doesn't want Linka to know about the general.'

'That's not what I want to talk to him about,' Gunn said, although he had no idea where his compulsion would lead. 'I'm only going to ask him about the epidemic. Please,' he said.

Yonden unhooked Gunn's hand from his shoulder and took a step back. 'Now,' he said, staring straight into Gunn's face, 'I think you believe about demons.'

So far, Melville thought, partway through his account of events, it could be worse.

It was hard to tell, though. Osher's good looks went with a studied absence of emotion, and Melville made it doubly difficult to gauge his mood because he couldn't bring himself to meet his eye. Instead he directed his tale at Chorphel who, being unable to speak Chinese, relied on a whispered commentary from Tsering, the young lieutenant with the aggressive eyes.

Melville faced the guerillas across a crudely planed table. The rest of the furnishings were equally spartan – a couple of cheap tin chests, a camp bed, a shelf of books in Chinese, with the plastic spine of Mao's red thoughts conspicuous, and – affixed to the wall by sticking plaster – magazine portraits of Ho Chi Minh and his veteran military chief, Vo Nguyen Giap. Osher smoked steadily. A pack of cigarettes, a Zippo and an ashtray were to hand next to a plastic pouch of the kind handed out to junior delegates at sales conferences. The only other object on the table was a pair of compact and expensive binoculars which Melville had presented at the beginning of the meeting.

'Finally,' he said, 'there is the mystery of the saddhu who followed us into the valley.'

'A pilgrim,' Osher said, fanning smoke away from his face. 'A wayfarer whom Ngawang set on a different path.'

'But he saw Gunn, and probably myself.'

'In the dark. If he had reported you to the Ghurkas, I would have heard by now. I have my informants in the garrison.'

'That still leaves Major Jetha.'

Osher stubbed out his cigarette, giving Melville the chance to adjust his position. He was perched on a pair of PLA ammunition boxes whose edges cramped his circulation. His poise was further affected by altitude sickness. His scalp felt a size too small for his skull.

Osher and Tsering were conferring – or rather, the lieutenant was speaking in a rising tone of discontent while his commander brooded, feeling for a fresh cigarette. Chorphel picked up the binoculars and attempted to focus them on Melville. At last Osher delivered his verdict.

'The Indian is not a serious threat.'

Melville hung on to his seat. 'I confess you have me at a loss.'

'Next spring,' Osher said, blowing a lungful of smoke, 'the Nepalese plan to expel us from this camp and resettle us in India. Major Jetha is advising them on the operation. We are completely safe here until then.'

'That's news to me,' Melville said.

'I have my spies in Kathmandu,' Osher said, inclining his head at Tsering.

'Have they found out why Jetha attempted to murder me?' Melville demanded.

'You have no proof that it was him,' Tsering said. 'Perhaps the man who attacked you was only a thief.'

'Perhaps isn't good enough. Jetha warned me in the clearest terms.'

'And you have delivered the warning personally, for which I owe you thanks.'

'It was my duty.'

'Your advice, too.'

'I'm sorry, could you repeat that?'

'I have the impression that you are against us carrying out the operation.'

'I'm against the pointless sacrifice of men's lives.'

'Pointless?' Osher said, tapping ash from his cigarette. 'My objective is to capture a Chinese general and bring him here to you.'

In the face of Osher's imperturbability, Melville felt spaced out and ineffectual. An inflamed pulse throbbed in his temple. He wished the meeting could have been postponed until morning.

'Sir,' he said, trying a different tack, 'your heroic struggle against overwhelming odds has won the admiration of . . . everyone who has heard of it. Although small in numbers, your army is a symbol of hope to all Tibetans, an inspiration to supporters of freedom everywhere. My point is this,' he said, seeing impatience break through Osher's reserve. 'You have very few men. In the circumstances, can you afford to risk them?'

'War always entails risk.'

'Only if the goal justifies it. General Liu isn't worth the destruction of your entire force. As you know,' Melville said, deciding to take a risk himself, 'I have been empowered to speak on behalf of Mr Yueh. I'm sure that he would agree with my decision.'

Osher took a thoughtful pull of his cigarette. 'I see,' he said. 'You're no longer interested in the general.'

'We'd love to have him, but we must be realistic. Perhaps there'll be another chance.' Melville leaned forward. 'Confucius said that want of patience in small matters confounds big plans.'

'If I followed the advice of that old hypocrite,' Osher said, his tone still pensive, 'I'd be sitting here when the Gurkhas march in next spring.' He pointed his cigarette at Melville to forestall protest. 'You must understand my reluctance to accept your decision. I've been put to a lot of trouble. I've had to buy horses, and good horses in these mountains cost a fortune. Even as we speak, I have men in Tibet searching for a secure route to the rendezvous.'

From Osher's uncertain tone and the way that Tsering was glaring at him, Melville felt that he had recovered somewhat from the initial setback. His own tone became expansive.

'I need hardly tell you that your efforts on our behalf will be generously rewarded. I mean, if it's a question of compensation . . .' He limped to a halt, alarmed by some small but threatening rearrangement of Osher's features.

'What's the date, Mr Melville?'

Melville was forced to the unsettling conclusion that he had lost track.

'In eleven days,' Osher told him, 'General Liu will arrive at the rendezvous.'

'Unless he's been exposed and interrogated. He may have been executed.'

'Tsering is certain that Jetha has heard nothing about the general. Nobody here could have told him. Therefore the chances that the Chinese know are remote.'

'But they can't be entirely discounted.'

'Then we would be going to our deaths.'

'It's a possibility.'

'Would you also agree that we would be entitled to a prize proportionate to the risks?'

'It desolates me to point out that dead men don't collect prizes.'

'Neither do cowards,' Osher said, grinding out his stub. He looked at Melville. 'Since you don't want the general, we'll keep him for ourselves.'

'I'm afraid I may have overstated my position,' Melville said, breaking into a sweat. 'I was merely offering my opinion of the risks. If you consider them too high, you have my complete support for calling off the operation. If not, the arrangement you made with Mr Yueh still stands.'

'The Americans would give me ten times more than he's paying me.'

'In view of the altered circumstances,' Melville said with desperation, 'I'm sure that Mr Yueh would consider any request for more money favourably. I would be happy to lay such a request before him as a matter of urgency.'

A smile slid back along Osher's jaw. 'The Indians would give me even more. General Liu knows the entire disposition and strategy of the Chinese forces along this border.'

'Sir, I beg you not to contemplate making a deal with any other party. Mr Yueh would be most unhappy. You would find his reaction . . . disappointing.'

Osher's smile, stretched beyond the bounds of humour, collapsed abruptly. He smashed his fist on the table. 'First you crawl, now you threaten. Yonden has told me of your want of resolution. I've met Mr Yueh and I know that he's not the kind of man who would give up the general.' Osher slumped back on his chair. 'My agreement with him will be honoured in full.'

'Your determination and courage command my profound admiration,' Melville muttered, conscious of having suffered a total and devastating loss of face.

'On the contrary,' Osher said, selecting another cigarette.

'I only wish I knew why this man is so important to you,' Melville blurted.

Osher brooded over his unlit cigarette. 'Before we came here?' he said at last, 'I was in Mustang. From Mustang it is not easy to cross into Tibet by horse, therefore we were obliged to walk to our targets, carrying six weeks' supplies. We did not walk back, though. We ran, day after day, with the Chinese chasing us, racing to cut us off.' Osher took hold of Chorphel's sleeve. 'Now you must understand,' he said, 'many of my comrades were not young men. They would do this three or four times and then their hearts would burst. More men died that way than were killed by the Chinese.'

'Terrible,' Melville said. He wondered where he might acquire a drink.

'Last winter,' Osher continued, 'we travelled eight days to attack a convoy on the Lhasa road. Instead, we destroyed a single truck, and do you know what was in it? Tibetans.' Osher leaned forward, no longer reserved. 'I want this general,' he said. 'I want him because our struggle will soon be over and I need something to show for it, something for all those men who ended up in a vulture's belly.'

Melville shifted uncomfortably. 'All the more reason why this operation should be flawless.' He gave a little cough. 'Might I be permitted to know your strategy?'

'What do you wish to know?' Osher said, composed once more to the point of detachment.

'Well, how many men will be involved.'

'Fifty.'

'Isn't that rather a lot?'

'Less than I would like, but our resources are limited.'

Tsering laughed. Melville smiled bitterly. Osher removed a ballpoint from the selection in his blouse pocket. He unzipped the pouch and slid out a pad similar to the one carried by Yonden. He opened it and tapped a page scribbled with Chinese writing. Tsering craned to have a look. Chorphel went on staring at Melville as though he was a source of wonder.

'Horses are essential,' Osher said, 'but we have two difficult passes to cross. The worst is a day's ride to the north. We lost three men and half our horses on it last winter. This time we will send yaks to clear a trail going and coming back. Six men will be required for this purpose. Another six will be deployed as scouts – two ahead, two on each flank. Inevitably we will lose some horses, so fresh ones will be left at two stages – another four men.'

'Leaving more than thirty to escort the general.'

'To defend ourselves.'

'I'm not a soldier, but the way I see it, your only defence is to escape detection, and that is best achieved by keeping your numbers small.'

'You are not a soldier,' Osher agreed, 'and you don't know Tibet. Across the border a hundred men who are familiar with the country can avoid detection as easily as five. The Chinese move their troops by road. When they leave them they are obliged to travel in groups no larger than my own force. Although an encounter with a patrol can't be ruled out, it needn't be disastrous.'

'Let's hope you're not put to the test.'

'To minimise the chances of pursuit, I intend to create a diversion. A few men will be sent back by a different route, making the Chinese believe we are heading for Mustang.'

Melville nodded approval. 'You're the man in charge,' he said gratuitously.

Chorphel said something to Osher.

'He wants to know if you'll be riding with us.'

'It would be more than my life is worth,' Melville said, flushing with shock. 'The Chinese would treat my intrusion as a gross violation of their territorial interests – however false,' he hastened to add, 'their claims may be.'

Osher charitably intervened. 'I only told him about your mission last night. Apart from Tsering and Yonden, no one else knows about the general. They believe they're going on an ordinary raid. They won't be told until the last moment. So you see,' Osher said, 'your fears about security are unfounded.'

'Not while Jetha's interest in me remains unexplained.'

'I would be misleading you if I claimed that everyone in my camp is trustworthy. There are fools who think that the Nepalese will grant them an amnesty.' Osher flicked ash. 'I can only assume that one of them found out about your visit and informed the Indian.'

'So he knows I'm here, even if he doesn't know why.'

Osher assented with a wave of his cigarette. 'No one is allowed to leave the camp without my permission. For your part, you mustn't satisfy my soldiers' curiosity. Is that understood?'

'Absolutely. But why rely on half measures? My continued presence here can only prejudice your chances. In the interests of your safety, the most prudent course would be for me to leave Nepal and make new arrangements for the general's crossing into India.'

'How you get him over the border is none of my concern,' Osher said.

'Can I assume then,' Melville said with caution, 'that I am free to leave.'

Osher looked at him absently. 'We'll discuss it when the weapons arrive.'

'Weapons?' Melville gave a fatuous laugh. 'Are you sure?'

He swallowed on the shock as if it was a wad of horsehair. The blood pumping through his temples almost drowned Osher's voice talking of a flight from East Pakistan, now worryingly overdue.

'Nobody mentioned anything about weapons to me,' Melville said, up on his feet. 'They're no responsibility of mine.'

'You represent Mr Yueh and Sweetwater,' Osher pointed out.

'Much as it embarrasses me to admit it, they haven't been entirely open in their dealings with me. They may not have been completely honest with you. It's conceivable that there are no weapons.'

'I can't go into Tibet without adequate guns and ammunition,' Osher told him. 'Your friends understand this.' He shrugged. 'No weapons, no general.'

A dreary lethargy forced Melville back on his seat. 'Do I take it that you are holding me as indemnity for these guns.'

'The weather's been unusually poor for days,' Osher said, 'and this place is hard to find. Now the sky is clear. We still have a few days. I'm confident things will go as arranged.'

'Very well,' Melville said, forcing himself to his feet. 'Against my will and judgement I consent to stay until the matter of these weapons is resolved.' His head felt like a blood-swollen bladder. 'I must retire now.'

Chorphel and Osher rose. Tsering remained seated. Chorphel took Melville's hands in his own and shook them warmly.

'He's never met an American before,' Osher said drily. 'He's not a Khampa; he's from the Chang-Thang.'

Osher himself bent from the waist, bringing his hands to his chest in a gesture that Melville found out of character. He glanced at the portraits of the North Vietnamese leaders.

'You seem puzzled,' Osher said.

'Curious. I mean, these people are on the wrong side, aren't they?'

'Was this man on the wrong side when he fought with you against the Japanese?' Osher asked, rapping his knuckles on Ho Chi Minh's face. 'Was he on the wrong side when he threw the French imperialists out of his country? Is he,' Osher asked, with an elastic smile, 'on the wrong side now?'

'It was naïve of me to talk of sides,' Melville mumbled.

'History,' Osher said, his smile gone and his eyes opaque. 'That is the only side to be on.'

Cloud had come up under cover of dark, and from time to time thin snow seeded down, brushing across the rock face with a scaly rustle. The camp was somewhere below, swallowed up in the maw of night, and as Gunn stumbled after the darting beam of Yonden's flashlight, he had the uncomfortable sensation of being in only precarious touch with solid ground. Compulsion had relaxed its grip. This climb was senseless and perilous. One false step and he would end up smeared on the rocks below. Several times he called on Yonden to slow down, but the Khampa was sulking and pretended he hadn't heard.

Without warning he bumped into Yonden's back. They seemed to have reached a broad shelf. The torch beam slid across a smooth fall of rock and out into the dark.

'I never imagined it would be so far,' Gunn panted. 'Let's go back.'

Yonden switched off the torch.

The moon appeared fleetingly, dragging ragged clouds. A faint, rhythmic dissonance shivered the silence. When the moon disappeared, Gunn could make out the suggestion of light at the end of a squarish opening in the cliff.

'What kind of place is it?' he whispered.

'A *gon-khang*,' Yonden whispered back. 'Where the lama hides his special gods.'

'Then Linka has no right to be here.'

'Aim Giver's daughter showed him where it was hidden.'

Gunn made to step forward. Yonden hung back.

'Aren't you coming with me?'

Yonden shook his head, slowly for emphasis.

'I'm not sure I blame you,' Gunn said, with an attempt at a laugh. He peered into the fissure. As he tried to penetrate the darkness, he was overwhelmed by the sensation that in its depths a sombre presence awaited him.

Yonden was whispering something, warning him to keep quiet about the general, but Gunn was too distracted to pay attention. Moving like a sleepwalker, he felt his way forward, outstretched hands brushing the wall. With his first step, the outside world was banished.

He could recognise the noise now – the sour clash of small cymbals marking the pauses in a droning litany. The passage was about twenty feet long, and at the far end was an entrance framed by juniper trunks polished as smooth as glass. Although there was no door, access was obstructed by a screen of banners, grey and threadbare with age. Gunn halted, his mouth dry. There was something on the other side – a squat hairy shape silhouetted against a tremulous light. Gunn jerked at the curtain and recoiled with a whimper. The cadaver of a bear hung in the opening, revolving slowly at the end of a chain. All around it, dangling like the remains of a spider's larder, hung other carcasses – wizened apes and bald wildcats, moulted birds of prey and shrunken lizardy things.

Gunn looked back down the passage. The darkness was total. In front of him the hanging carrion turned with the slowness of eternal motion. Swallowing his disgust, he ducked under them, their imagined touch making his short hairs stiffen.

Straightening up, he found himself in a dusty pocket about forty feet square, illuminated by a buttery glow that didn't reach into the corners. The light came from around Linka, who was hidden behind a tent-shaped stack of weapons – enough spears and pikes, bows and arrows to equip a company of medieval warriors. On a frame of poles beside them hung three suits of armour, comprising jerkins of liver-coloured hide, skirts of chain-mail, and helmets of iron and leather.

Gunn held his breath. He had visited *gon-khangs* in Kham; unlike this place, they had been crammed with statues and frescoes of demon kings swollen in an orgy of metaphysical rage. He had found them repellent, but their passion had left him unmoved. They belonged to an alien cosmography, someone else's nightmare. They had no place in his internal landscape.

This place did, though.

It was the cupboard under the stairs where he had once hidden during a childhood game and then, crouched among the oilskins and gas masks and broken umbrellas and bolting-eyed rocking horses, found he had taken refuge in a domestic chamber of horrors . . . *ninety-eight, ninety-nine – Coming!* It was the abandoned croft across the headland where poor Murdo Sinclair's teddy bear sat, one buttony eye hanging by a thread, stuffing spilling out, cocooned against a cracked window pane by layers of spider web. *Murdo's not coming to school today. He's awful poorly with the 'flu.* It was the lantern chamber in the lighthouse where his father hanged himself in his Sunday suit. *My days are swifter than a weaver's shuttle, and are spent without hope.* It was the musty recesses of his own mind, the graveyard of memories visited only in his dreams.

They rose up to stifle him. He put his hand to his forehead and found it was drenched in sweat.

Linka's chanting drew him forward.

The Khampa was seated over a text. Round and hairless, his head swayed back and forth like a Chinese lantern. His eyes were shut, and in the feeble light Gunn believed that his entrance hadn't been noticed. He choked back a cough. Dust. It lay thick and fine on the floor. It settled on his palate and collected high in his nostrils.

Against the wall behind Linka stood a painted screen, its icon-ography obliterated by time. It blocked off a recess about ten feet long and half as high. In the wall to the right there might have been another opening, but the chamber was so choked with shadow that it was difficult to be sure.

Linka's chanting stopped. Silence crept out from the walls, and in that silence Gunn felt utterly exposed, the object of hostile scrutiny, though Linka's eyes were sealed.

Just when he thought he must scream, the chanting resumed and the awful feeling was gone, leaving him dizzy and trembling. He forced himself to listen to the litany, and gradually he began to disentangle its meaning.

Linka was reciting the rites for the salvation of the dead, describing the terrifying visions that would try to distract the soul from the narrow white path leading to judgement and liberation. Gunn caught references to crow-headed ghouls, cannibal monsters – the terrors of the unknown that would try to keep the soul wandering world without end in the rounds of birth and death.

To one side of Linka was a wicker basket draped with a heavy green cloth. Gunn couldn't understand it. Why hadn't Yonden told him that one of the Khampas had died?

Linka's cadences were growing louder. His voice was cavernous. He was urging the departed spirit to ignore the terrors that beset it. They were self-constructed fantasies, projections of its own fears.

As the voice resonated in his head, it seemed to Gunn that the light changed quality, becoming sickly and addled. I must get out, he told himself. I'm ill. I was crazy to come.

He began to back away. Linka picked up a small drum shaped like an hour-glass and twirled it. Its clappers gave a dry rattle. Silence fell, cold and resentful, trapping Gunn like a thief.

Linka's head was downcast. Transfixed, Gunn watched as he stretched out a hand, took a pinch of incense from a bowl, rubbed it beneath his nose, and dropped it onto a lamp. Under cover of its sputtering, Gunn took a backward step.

'You are Yonden's friend.'

Gunn yelped in shock.

'Well?' Linka said, lifting his head.

Tongue-tied, Gunn could only bow. He had a ceremonial scarf in his hands. He made to move forward, but Linka checked him with an upraised palm.

'He did wrong to bring you here. He knows how dangerous it is.'

'He warned me about the demons,' Gunn said. The shock was wearing off. He felt foolish.

Irritation showed on Linka's face. 'I'm not talking about demons. It's lucky you didn't slip to your death.'

'It was my fault,' Gunn admitted. 'He didn't want to bring me. I made him.'

'So soon after completing a long journey?'

'I felt I owed you that courtesy at least,' Gunn told him. His breathing was nearly back to normal.

'Of course – you're the doctor. Yonden's often talked of you. But as you must have seen, your medicines are no longer needed here. The sickness has been driven out.' Linka spread his hands to show where the credit lay.

Gunn could not help glancing at the wicker basket.

'An accident,' Linka said, without shifting his head. 'A poor unfortunate who broke his neck hunting.'

'Forgive me,' Gunn said. 'I would never have trespassed if I had known you were conducting a funeral.'

Linka held up a hand. 'Since you've risked your own neck climbing here, you might as well stay a little while longer. Come into the light where I can see you properly.'

Gunn approached. He placed the scarf around Linka's neck, then sat in front of him. He felt dwarfed – not just by the Khampa's size, but by his massive composure. The Khampa's even stare made him uncomfortable. Those tiny eyes must have been watching him from the moment he entered, he thought. They were as hard as an auger – a sharp contrast to the indulgence implied by the fleshy lips. There was a hint of humour in Linka's expression, the wry cast of someone who has seen much of human folly and knows he is not exempt from it.

To escape Linka's inspection, Gunn made a show of examining the chamber. 'When I first came in,' he said, 'I could have sworn there was someone else here.'

'Give me your hand,' Linka said, with no change of expression. He took Gunn's wrist and felt the pulse. 'You have a fever.'

Linka's gentle touch made Gunn aware of his wretchedness. 'I'm tired,' he muttered, 'worried sick.'

Linka's lips pursed in polite inquiry.

'Yonden and I had a quarrel,' Gunn blurted.

'Dissent is an ever-present companion on a long journey,' Linka told him. One brow arched a fraction. 'Money?'

'That's part of it, I suppose.'

'Always a weakness of Yonden's,' Linka said, nodding in

285

sympathy. He took another pinch of incense and inhaled its scent. 'What else.'

Dimly Gunn recalled Yonden's warning outside the *gon-khang*. His eyes slid away from Linka's polite, undeviating stare. 'Just money,' he mumbled.

Linka exhaled a patient sigh. 'That was only part of it, you said.' He rolled thumb and finger. 'Part of what?'

'I can't tell you,' Gunn said in sudden panic. 'I must go. Poor Yonden's waiting. I promised I wouldn't be long.'

Linka restrained him gently. 'You had a quarrel and now you're sorry that you exchanged harsh words. It wasn't only the money. That's why you came to see me. You need someone to talk to.'

'I can't tell you,' Gunn said, stricken with misery.

Linka's laugh filled the cave. 'I've been expecting you. I know all about you and the American. I know that you're here to help Osher.'

'It's got nothing to do with me,' Gunn cried. 'That's why I'm leaving. I only found out about the general last night.'

'The general,' Linka said. He smiled. 'What general is that?'

Gunn passed his hand over his eyes. 'You're right,' he said. 'I'm sick. I don't know what I'm saying. I think I'm going mad.'

Linka took his arm in a fierce grip. 'To cultivate ignorance is a sin. You're not a sinful man.'

'Yes I am,' Gunn shouted. 'Yes I am.'

Linka's hand shot out and clamped itself to Gunn's skull. 'There's a demon inside you,' he hissed. He held Gunn, rocking and muttering, and then his hand fell away. He looked on Gunn with compassion. 'Now you can tell me.'

And Gunn poured out everything. He couldn't see for tears. Afterwards, there was a long silence.

'What should I do?' Gunn whispered.

'Stop tormenting yourself,' Linka told him. 'Go back to your own country. Forget Yonden. You've repaid the debt ten times over.'

'But I can't simply desert him.'

'Then take him with you.'

'He won't come. He worships Osher.'

A spasm of annoyance crossed Linka's face. 'Offer him money, and then you'll see where his loyalty lies.'

'And there's the American. I'm worried about what will happen to him.'

'He came here of his own choice, didn't he?'

'He doesn't know what he's doing.'

286

Linka's laugh sounded unpleasant. 'You're wriggling,' he said, 'unable to decide whether to stay or to go.'

A great weight of sadness settled on Gunn. 'It's not as if I have anything to go back to. I don't know which way to turn. I'm utterly lost. Finding Yonden was my last chance to return to the path I lost all those years ago.'

'There's no going back,' Linka said, and for a moment he seemed to share Gunn's sadness. He tapped the text he had been reciting. 'To read a book, you must turn the pages forward.'

Gunn tried to smile. 'I've been stuck on the same page for twenty years. In the end . . . Well, there always has to be an end. That's some kind of consolation.'

'You're like that man,' Linka declared, pointing towards the corpse, 'clinging to the past, distracted by ghosts, frightened to go forward.'

'I've left it too late.'

'Twenty years is nothing. Look at me. Last winter I was still a soldier – a murderer like Osher.'

'But you both fought for a cause.'

Linka smoothed his robe – an angry gesture. 'I fought to save the doctrine. Osher makes war because it's his karma.'

Gunn gave a feeble laugh. 'Yonden says I have bad karma.'

The flames of the lamps lay flat under the force of Linka's merriment. 'By which he means unlucky.'

'Well, in that respect, he's not wrong.'

Linka's expression grew restive. 'What does that rogue know about karma?' he muttered. 'So many determinants are interwoven that no mortal can assign a just weight to them all.'

'But to put it simply,' Gunn said, 'a man's fate is determined by the actions he commits in his life. They're entered on a kind of balance sheet and at the day of judgement he is held accountable for them.'

'Suppose it is so,' Linka said. 'You look puzzled.'

'I was wondering,' Gunn said slowly, 'how it could ever be possible for a wicked man to be saved. If wickedness is part of his nature – a nature conditioned by the deeds committed in previous lives – then he can no more help acting wickedly than a wolf can stop being a wolf. The way ahead can only lead down.'

Linka tugged violently on his robe. 'Even the darkest sinner has the potential for good. It may take him a thousand existences to realise it, but if he finds the clear light of Buddha's doctrine, he may realise it in a single lifetime, a single moment.'

The rapture that dawned on Linka's face as he was speaking only

287

made Gunn aware of the gulf that separated him from any hope. 'In my church things are much simpler,' he said. 'You're either damned or saved.' He realised how tired he was. His long disclosure to Linka had left him drained. 'You've been very kind,' he said, 'but it's time I left you in peace. Yonden must be frozen.'

'Stay a little longer. I rarely have an opportunity to speak to a stranger. I would like you to tell me more about this church of yours. Let me bring you tea. I have something that will cool your fever and help you sleep.'

Gunn's head was swimming with fatigue and he was no longer sweating, but Linka's insistence was overpowering. The Khampa left him and went out of the light, disappearing into what must have been an ante-chamber in the wall to the right. Gunn closed his eyes.

He came back to consciousness with a jerk. Something had changed. The chamber seemed to have grown smaller, closed in on him. His breathing stopped.

'Is that you?' he whispered, sure that outside the circle of lamps someone was watching him.

His skin took on the texture of suede as he heard, close by, a dry clerical rustle.

'Who's there? What do you want?'

Heart hammering, he picked up a lamp and rose to his feet. Shadows came to life on the walls. Over by the entrance the carcasses rotated with infinite slowness.

He spun round with a sob. Straining into the darkness, his eyes registered the tendency of one shadow to move independently of the others. It was gone in a blink.

He found that his eyes were concentrated on the aperture behind the screen, and he realised that he was not looking at it so much as into it – as if he was trying to see beneath the surface of a dark pool.

Holding the lamp high, he began to walk slowly forward. He reached the screen and still he couldn't see what lay behind it. The darkness was unfathomable. It stretched deep into the mountain. He lifted the lamp.

There was some kind of inscription carved into the rock. It was hard to make out. The lamp was beginning to die. He looked at it and grunted in disgust. The light it shed had assumed the quality of fur.

When he looked back into the aperture, the space was no longer vacant. Eyes were upon him, peering under the ragged edge of his soul.

'Get away from there!'

Linka charged out of the gloom and almost hurled Gunn away from the screen. He was beside himself with anger and fright. 'What do you think you're doing?' he panted.

Gunn rubbed his eyes. He felt light-headed. The memory of what he had experienced had the lucidity of a dream. 'There was someone there.'

Linka stared at him with concern. 'You could have come to great harm. The Guardians are merciless to strangers.'

'Guardians?'

'The gods of this place.'

Gunn looked around him in a daze. 'Bon gods,' he murmured. 'The place of wet skulls.'

'Old gods,' Linka said. He glanced at the screen, then stared at Gunn with mingled anxiety and curiosity. 'What did you see?' he asked.

'I don't know. I thought I heard something, so I got up, then . . . I could have sworn that something was watching me from behind the screen. Things . . . I don't know.' Gunn shuddered.

'Are they watching now?'

Gunn forced himself to look. The darkness was empty. The lamplight was clear. 'I must have been dreaming,' he said.

Linka's face was grave. 'Come and sit down,' he said.

'Wait,' Gunn said. 'Something was written on the wall. What does it mean?'

Linka studied the inscription at some length. His face when he turned back to Gunn was expressionless. 'It says: May all violators of the oath meet the same fate.'

'A curse?'

'A warning.'

'To whom? What oath?'

'The oath sworn by the lamas of this place.'

'What do they swear?'

'To make the appointed offerings.'

Gunn caught a gust of putrefaction from the corpse. A sickening suspicion took hold of him. 'What kind of offerings?'

'I've answered your questions with patience, but there are some secrets that can't be revealed to strangers.'

'Aren't you a stranger here yourself?'

Linka had regained his composure, and it remained unruffled.

'I didn't mean to sound discourteous,' Gunn said. 'Yonden told me about your disagreement with the lama.'

'I ask for nothing more than to sit at his feet.'

'But he refuses.'

'Our differences will soon be settled,' Linka said. He took Gunn's arm. 'Let us return to the discussion we were having earlier. The tea is . . .'

'No,' Gunn said, pulling himself free. 'I really must go.' He had an overpowering need to be out in the fresh air.

Linka shrugged.

Mouthing courtesies, Gunn began to back away.

'When does Osher go into Tibet?'

Linka's question stopped Gunn in his tracks. He was appalled by how much he had given away. He was held on Linka's gaze.

'I don't know,' he managed to say. 'The American thinks it will be too dangerous.'

Linka's eyes probed and seemed to accept what they found.

'The American is right. I advise you to leave the valley as soon as possible.'

'I will,' Gunn said. He began to retreat again. He was desperate to get away.

'When will you go?'

'I have to discuss it with Yonden. In three or four days – when the medicines arrive.'

'In that case, I would ask a favour of you.'

Gunn forced himself to stop. Linka's face shone like a planet.

'Visit the Lucky Place. Tell the lama I've kept my side of our agreement.'

Gunn made a gesture of incomprehension.

'He'll understand what I mean,' Linka said. 'Tell him that next summer he'll have a son and heir. Tell him . . .' Linka paused, weighing his words '. . . that I have found a way of cutting myself off from the past.'

'I'll try,' Gunn said, and blundered backwards into something that laid a scabby caress on his neck. He lashed out and barged through the scarecrows at the entrance, leaving them trickling dust.

Outside he inhaled draughts of icy air. Yonden clambered stiffly to his feet, his scowl of resentment turning to a worried frown when he saw Gunn's face.

'I told you not to go in there,' he said.

'You were right,' Gunn panted, throwing his arm around Yonden's neck. 'Next time you warn me about demons, I'll take your word.'

'You saw them?'

'No, Yonden. They saw me.'

Yonden peered fearfully at the opening in the cliff. 'Better not to come near this place again.'

'Never,' Gunn vowed, and let Yonden lead him down to the camp, visible now by the light of the declining moon.

'No need to crash about in the dark,' Melville said drowsily. 'I'm not asleep.'

Gunn lit a lamp and laid out his sleeping bag in silence.

'You were gone a long time. It's after midnight.'

'I went to see Linka,' Gunn said, climbing into bed.

'I hope you didn't tell him about the general. Osher trusts him as far as he can spit. Apparently, the old guru wants the Khampas to lay down their arms and take up the pastoral life.'

'Yonden told me.'

'Right.'

'I'm not sure that it's possible to keep anything secret from Linka,' Gunn said after a while. 'When he looks at you, you get the feeling that he knows what you're thinking better than you know yourself.'

'Far out. I could use some of that insight myself. Osher's going ahead.'

'I had a feeling he would.'

'Everyone's a fucking clairvoyant. Well, since you're so smart, you'll already be wise to the latest wrinkle. Osher's holding me until he receives an arms drop courtesy of Charlie fucking Sweetwater.'

'Didn't you know?'

'Did I hell.'

'He doesn't seem to have told you much, does he?'

'Just the odd fact to keep me guessing.'

'It's so pointless. He must know you'd quit when you found out.'

'I suppose.'

Melville watched the shifting pattern of lamplight on the ceiling.

'How did your meeting with Osher go?' Gunn asked.

'Apart from being made to look like an ignorant errand boy, hard to say. I can't work Osher out. He's some kind of homespun Marxist – refers to the dynamic of history and all that crap – yet his speech is full of straight-arrow terms like honour and obligation. Chorphel, the veteran guerilla who gave us the beer, and Tsering, that guy who

291

looks like a student activist, were in on the meeting. I figure them for counsellor and hatchet man.'

'Tsering used to be a monk.'

'You can see it in his eyes – kind of doctrinaire. Is Linka like that?'

'Far from it. He gives the impression of being . . . it's hard to describe . . . self-indulgent.'

'You must introduce me. I could use the services of a diviner.'

'He warned me – us – to leave. I think he's expecting trouble.'

'No shit. Even I could have forecast that. By the way, speaking of phenomena unknown to science, dig the light show.'

The ceiling was dappled with amber, reminiscent of the play of sunlight in peaty water, yet the lamp burned with a constant flame.

'Walter.'

Melville saw that Gunn was looking at the floor. Around the hearth a swarm of cockroaches was massed, their shiny carapaces so closely packed that the formation had the appearance of a bronze shield.

Chapter 19

'Going for a walk?' Gunn asked.

'Thought I'd collect our mail, ride into town, take in a meal and a movie.' Melville yanked hard on his bootlaces.

'There's no call to take out your resentment on me.'

'Four days in this hole,' Melville said, standing up. 'It's driving me batshit.'

'It's a foul place.'

'It's certainly somewhat lacking in ambience,' Melville said, stomping a roach. He reached the trapdoor and turned, his jaw tightening. 'You look like shit,' he said. 'You going to fester there all day?'

Gunn didn't react. He lay flat on his back, his arms held straight by his sides. His depression hovered above him like a black balloon.

'Some partner you've turned out to be,' Melville said, swinging himself onto the ladder. 'Your nightmares kept me awake half the night. I'm going to ask for a different room.'

'Walter, do you believe in God?'

Melville stopped and glanced behind him before peering back. Gunn hadn't adjusted his posture.

'A little early in the day for theological speculation, isn't it?'

'What about the devil?'

'Sure – the devil and all his works.'

'It's not a laughing matter.'

'Who says I'm kidding?'

Gunn didn't respond.

Melville hesitated, then with a groan of exasperation he climbed back into the room and went halfway over to the bed. 'Alright, tell me what's wrong.'

'Do you remember the night we camped by the *chorten*?' Gunn said eventually.

'I try not to. I was out of my mind, babbling about time the destroyer and drowning in a puddle.'

'You were sober enough when we arrived. You were struck by the unpleasant atmosphere. You suggested that people might have been entombed in the shrine.'

'And you knocked the idea on the head,' Melville reminded him.

Out of the corner of his eye he saw the cockroach he had stepped on lurching back to its hole.

'In a backwater like this,' you said, they might still practise pagan rites.'

'Okay, so?' Melville said, deciding to humour the man.

Gunn heaved himself into a sitting position. 'You were right,' he said. 'Something vile is going on in that *gon-khang*.'

'You have evidence?' Melville asked with pretended lightness. 'You never mentioned it the night you visited.'

'The name for a start,' Gunn said, swinging his legs over the edge of the bed. 'The place of wet skulls – a Bon name, old Bon. There's a curse inscribed above the altar. May all oath-breakers come to the same end.'

'Tibetan religions bristle with blood-curdling curses. They're one big horror show. Nobody takes them seriously – not even the Tibetans.'

'Yonden explained its significance. It scared him silly. It's an ancient Bon vow of allegiance sworn to their kings and priests. It was sealed by blood sacrifice.'

'Human?'

'Animal usually – horses and dogs. But yes, I expect people were sacrificed too.'

'Back up,' Melville said, his patience drawing thin. 'You're talking about long-ago times, not the here and now.'

'I'm not sure.'

'So you don't have any proof,' Melville said, breathing through his nose.

'All I can tell you is what I felt.'

'Alan,' Melville pleaded, 'for God's sake don't turn funny on me. I need you.'

'You felt it yourself at the *chorten*, and I was wrong to dismiss it. Even where I grew up, people still had pagan superstitions. No fisherman would turn his boat widdershins while he was in harbour. There were crossroads where you said a prayer before passing, and standing stones that you never dared set eyes on at night. Some of the crofters laid out food and drinks for the souls of the dead.'

'Like you said, superstitions.'

'There are three of them,' Gunn said, frowning. 'Yes, three of them, behind the screen.'

'Three what?' Melville demanded almost shouting.

'The Guardians,' Gunn said. He stared in haggard wonder. 'It's them I see in my dreams.'

His eyes made Melville flinch. 'Great,' he said, 'we're in the realm of dreams now. Look, before it gets any heavier, think back to the night in question. You were completely ripped, same as me; and when *I* was sitting in here with the guerillas, my mind was throwing up all kinds of weirdness. Okay, so you have a showdown with Yonden, then risk your neck climbing to a cave full of stuffed animals and a deceased party in a basket. The state you were in, I'm not surprised you hallucinated ghouls and goblins.'

'Ask Yonden if you don't believe me.'

'Yonden's a pathological case, for chrissake, while you're not exactly . . .' Melville stopped abruptly, pinching the flesh on his forehead. He sat on the edge of his bed and examined his hands. 'You're under a lot of strain,' he muttered.

Gunn appeared not to hear. 'Yonden explained what's happening,' he said. 'Aim Giver will soon die, and Linka's determined to take his place. He's got the support of the villagers and he's seduced the lama's daughter. She's expecting his child, but even that won't make Aim Giver accept him. Last winter Yonden saw the lama spit in Linka's face. They're involved in a duel, and the key to the outcome is in the *gon-khang*. The Guardians are the protectors of the community. Whoever gains control of them will win.'

Melville gave a miserable bleat. 'You really do believe in them.'

'They're real enough to Linka and Aim Giver.'

'And flesh and blood to you. Are you suggesting that Linka is feeding them tit-bits of meat – dogs and horses, the occasional stranger?'

Gunn's head jerked up. 'That's what Linka told me: they're hostile to strangers.'

'Stop right there,' Melville ordered, jumping up. 'I don't know why I'm listening to this. If Linka and the lama choose to slug it out on the astral plane, I don't give a shit. Linka can make terms with the devil for all I care. It's the deal struck between Osher and Sweetwater that keeps me awake nights.'

'You think I'm mad,' Gunn said.

Melville walked over to the window. 'Alan, listen to me and listen good,' he said. 'This trip has not been good for you. It's stirred up a lot of sediment in your head. You're conflating all kinds of shit from the past – what happened to Yonden's family in Kham, the years in prison, the death of the friend you never talk about. Oh yes,' Melville said, turning his head, 'I know about him. And something else. You mentioned seeing three of these Guardians in your dreams. Well, I happen to know that cases in the People's Republic are judged by a tribunal – three, right. You don't have to be a shrink to work out who you're really dreaming about. And then to top it all, you're having to come to terms with Yonden's duplicity.' Melville turned fully around. 'The sooner you're out of here the better.'

'I know,' Gunn said, dragging his hand across his stubbled face.

'Five days,' Melville said. 'That's all we have to wait. After five days Osher can forget about the weapons; he'll never make it to the rendezvous in time.'

'I don't think we should wait until then.'

'Osher might have something to say about that.'

'I have no intention of telling him.'

'Sneak out?' Melville whispered. He was astonished. 'Alan, this is one hell of a turnaround.'

'I can't face another day,' Gunn told him, 'and if you're honest, you'll admit you're out of your depth.'

Melville faced away. He saw bleached rock through the window. 'One look out there is all you need to know there's no going home without Osher's say-so. I've walked all round this pit and the only way out is the same way we came in.'

'Yonden could find a way.'

'After his double-dealing,' Melville said, whirling. He snorted. 'You are mad. He'll go running straight to Osher.'

'He's unhappy about the operation. He wants to start a decent life, but he needs money.'

'If he goes along with what you're suggesting, money won't buy him any kind of life. Osher will kill him dead. That's the kind of man he is. Make an agreement with Osher, he expects you to stick to it.'

'You agreed to wait for the general,' Gunn said. 'Osher will hold you to that.'

'I know it,' Melville said, 'knew it all the time.' He came and hunkered down by Gunn's bedside. 'I might be out of my depth,' he admitted, 'but I reckon I'll find my feet. Usually when I feel the bottom falling away, I flounder back to shore. Not this time, though. I guess I'm in it for the duration.'

'What's made you change your mind?'

'Lack of choice is a pretty good reason. Also . . .' Melville slowly stood. 'Sitting there with Osher and the others, they made me feel like I'd never done a thing in my life.' He gave Gunn an embarrassed smile. 'I'm not ready to go back to my puddle yet.' He rubbed his hands. 'Hey, let's grab some of that good mountain air.'

296

Gunn shook his head.

Melville hesitated, then reached out to squeeze Gunn's shoulder. He did not quite make contact. 'Hang in there,' he said.

As soon as he was outside, he threw back his head and ventilated his lungs. A stiff breeze held the prayer flags taut. The sun stood at the eastern edge of the sky, but it was later than it seemed, for the cliffs were high enough to rob the camp of two hours' daylight. Although the sun could still mount a brave rearguard action, soon all the hours would belong to winter.

Picking his way down a lane mired by piss and melted snow, he saw a girl approaching, her eyes downcast, absorbed in a world of her own. She only noticed him when he stood aside, giving her right of way, and then she stopped, baring small white teeth, before edging past, her back brushing the wall. A few yards off she halted and inspected him. Her eyes were almond-shaped and set far apart. There was something unfocused about them, a fey quality. She made him think of some shy, crepuscular creature from off the main evolutionary track. He found her not unattractive.

So that's Linka's consort, he thought. A thousand to one it was her creeping about in the *gon-khang*. Poor Gunn, he thought. Poor bastard was coming apart at the seams. I'll ask Osher to invalid him out. The resolve pleased him. It proved he was finding his way, learning to cope on his own.

Five minutes' walking over open turf brought him to a huge prow of rock sticking out over the gorge. On the other side of the gulf was a gutted mountain, with great ribs curving up to a broken spine.

As was his daily ritual, he forced himself to stand within a foot of the edge, toeing the thin line between fear and fascination. So far he hadn't been able to lean far enough to plumb the depths of the gorge. He always shrank back at the moment when his descending gaze met the point where twilight deepened into pitch dark. Heavy stones dropped into the abyss fell without a sound. Occasionally it gave out a murmur.

Today wasn't going to be the day he got to the bottom of it. His knees quaked and he retreated, fixing his eyes on the slopes opposite until his head stopped spinning. He noticed a greyish stippling high above, visible only because it was moving. It was a flock of wild sheep traversing a scree channel, moving slowly up in search of pasture. In the afternoon they would head down again, turned back by some impending change in the light. He watched them until they receded into the landscape.

Sitting against a juniper, he tried to apply himself to the rules of Tibetan grammar, but after half a page he put the book aside with a tuneful sigh. His mind wouldn't settle. These days, the simplest mental exercise defeated him.

What price adventure. Resigned to staying, he now saw the days stretching ahead of him like a desolation. He had hoped for action, an adrenalin purge, and instead here he sat in fixed orbit, prey to vacant unease.

He lay on his back and stared at the disc of sky. It had darkened to the colour of new jeans, with brilliant white clouds parading across it. Everything except him had direction. He thought with envy of Osher, and with dread of the long wait while the Khampas were in Tibet. If only . . . His stomach tilted like the bubble in a carpenter's level as he realised where his thoughts were leading.

He exorcised them by sitting up quickly and shying a splinter of rock into the chasm.

Like a genie summoned from the depths, the damndest-looking bird floated up out of the gorge and stabilised itself at his level, rocking slightly on a nine-foot span. It was some kind of vulture, but it had little resemblance to the bald-headed, weak-chinned griffons whose tea-tray silhouettes turned and turned over the camp. This bird was fully feathered, with angular wings drawn to points and a long cuneiform tail. It was an original, an ambitious prototype that might have been designed by a pioneering aeronautical engineer heavily influenced by the gothic. Red-rimmed eyes regarded him from behind a black mask that extended down on each side of its beak to form a stiff little tartar beard. There was something hieratic in its aspect, an impression heightened by the convocation of choughs that hung in its train. Looking into its eyes, Melville fancied he encountered a primitive knowingness, as though it had been around since the beginning of things and would be there at the end.

Its buoyancy was remarkable. Unruffled by the breeze, it remained pinned in the same spot, not flapping its wings, merely flexing the tips of its primaries as it fine-tuned its relationship with the air. It rested for a minute then, like a shark, it slowly sank back, trailed by its retinue. Dropping onto hands and knees, Melville crawled to the edge. Down it drifted, sable back glinting against reefs and grottoes, until it vanished into the depths. Melville remained where he was. Presently the choughs came eddying back up and swirled aimlessly about with querulous squeaks. Melville realised that he was leaning out further than he had ever dared before, and suddenly he was sweating, a muzziness in his head and a fluttering in his right arm, which was taking most of his weight. Shutting his eyes, he transferred the strain to his other arm and prepared to push himself back.

Simultaneously there was a sound like tearing calico and a rush of wind over his head. He opened his eyes to glimpse a shape elongated by speed that stopped almost within its own length. The bird was back. It swung up and pivoted round, facing him head on, its ferocious eyes sighting on him down a beak as thin as a blade of obsidian.

He uttered a wild laugh, defying it, and it tilted away before anchoring itself atop another column of air. The choughs bobbed around it, skinny claws dangling. He heard his name called. Gunn was alternately walking and trotting towards him.

When he looked again, the vulture was gone.

'Did you see it?' he cried.

'See what?' Gunn asked, coming to a breathless stop.

'Mean-looking vulture with a beard.'

'Oh aye, I used to see them in Kham. They always turn up for a funeral.'

'Mine, if it had its way. I swear to God it nearly had me off.' Melville was exhilarated by the encounter and did not grasp the significance of what Gunn was telling him.

'Linka's performing the rites of the air for the poor soul I saw in the *gon-khang*. I thought you might find it interesting.'

'Feeding him to the vultures?' Melville said. 'You bet.' He was relieved to see that Gunn had shaved and looked altogether less peaked. He risked a sly grin. 'I guess that means the Guardians can't be too hungry.'

'I owe you an apology for the way I carried on this morning.'

'Absolutely no need,' Melville said with vigour. Gunn looked sedate enough, but his calm might have been chemically induced and only skin deep.

'This journey *has* stirred up bad memories,' Gunn told him. 'Especially about Peter.'

'Maybe you'd rather not talk about it.'

'He hated Kham, you know,' Gunn said, looking vaguely about him. 'It bored and frustrated him. The lamas wouldn't let him preach his mission, so he never attempted to learn the language or get to know the people. Within days he was looking forward to leaving.'

'Whereas you loved the place.'

Gunn smiled. 'It was spring when we arrived. I've never seen such flowers. It wasn't like here, all dried up and confined. It was more like Switzerland, except that the mountains . . . well, they seemed to climb to heaven. And then I had my work, of course. I was far too absorbed and happy to pay any attention to Peter's warnings. He'd been a soldier, and he knew how quickly the Chinese could cut us off. But like the Khampas themselves, I believed that it would take months for the Chinese to reach us. In fact, by the time we heard about them, they had already cut the only route to India.'

'Fortunes of war,' Melville said. 'Not your fault.' The banality of his response angered him.

'After we were captured, I never saw him again, even though we were kept in the same camp. But I often heard him, singing hymns in his cell.'

The grim little nod that accompanied this induced a chill in Melville.

'I suspect he looked on imprisonment as a challenge,' Gunn continued, 'a test of faith. He refused to co-operate with the Chinese.'

'What kind of co-operation were they looking for?'

'There was no organisation to appeal on our behalf. Nobody knew we'd entered Kham. As far as we knew, our government had no idea we existed. Our only hope was to make false confessions which the Chinese could use as propaganda.'

'But Peter wouldn't play ball.'

'He wanted martyrdom. I began to think he would ruin our chances of ever being released.' Gunn looked skyward, where the clouds were slanting fast across the blue. Each time one passed through the sun, the wind cut to the flesh. 'I wished him dead,' Gunn said, as if he still couldn't believe it. 'I prayed for it.' He turned his incredulity on Melville. 'And my prayers were answered.'

'Do you mind if we walk as we talk?' Melville said. He didn't wait for a reply. When Gunn caught him up, he said: 'Peter didn't die because you wanted him to.'

'He'd be alive today if I'd heeded his warning.'

'The guy who makes it back across no-man's land often feels guilt at surviving. It's a familiar syndrome.' Melville slid a glance at Gunn. 'Sometimes he has to be restrained from turning round and heading straight back in.'

'No-man's land,' Gunn said, coming to a halt. 'The *bardo*.'

'If memory serves,' Melville said, wondering what he'd said to

300

excite Gunn, 'that's what the Tibetans call the intermediate state between death and reincarnation.'

'A rite of passage lasting forty-nine days.'

'Like Pilgrim's Progress, only tougher.'

'As I walked through the wilderness of the world,' Gunn recited, gazing about with a sour little smile. 'It was one of the few books my father allowed in the house.'

'You were telling me about the *bardo*,' Melville reminded him.

'Linka says I'm like a man who's trapped in it.'

'Makes sense,' Melville said, after he had given it his consideration. 'And his advice is pretty sound too. You'll never be able to put all this bad history behind you while you remain here. Talk to Osher. He won't hold you against your will.'

'What about you?'

'I'll be fine,' Melville told him. He shifted his weight to his other foot. 'I'll speak to him myself if you like.'

'I'll spare you any more,' Gunn said. He touched Melville's elbow. 'I'm very grateful. I know how this kind of conversation makes you writhe.'

They went on. The mules that had brought the supplies were complaining behind the camp. Cloud shadows raced across the turf. Two figures could be seen at the base of the cliffs.

'I ran into Aim Giver's wayward daughter earlier,' Melville said. 'She looks a little spacey.'

'A witch, according to Yonden.'

'I wonder what they get up to. *Yin* embracing *yang*, awareness getting it together with compassion, insight opening up to knowledge. Cosmic sex.'

'Missing your creature comforts?'

'I'd settle for a steak and salad.'

A cry made them face to the rear. Yonden was running after them. He stopped thirty yards off.

'Where are you going, please?'

'To a funeral,' Melville shouted.

'Come back please. It's not allowed.'

'Nobody ever objected in Kham,' Gunn called.

Yonden threw a look towards the camp. 'Tsosang needs some medicine for his arm.'

'I dressed it before coming out.'

Yonden thought for a moment. 'Sah, Osher wants to see you. Look, there he is waiting.'

'It's an insult to the intelligence,' Melville said to Gunn. He made a trumpet of his hands, as though he was conducting a battlefield parley. 'Tell him I'll drop by later,' he shouted.

'Okay, okay,' Yonden said, skipping up, 'but you mustn't sit close. You must show respect.'

'What's got into him?' Melville asked as Yonden cavorted ahead.

The site for the disposal of the corpse was a boulder-ringed circle about fifty feet in diameter, close to the base of the cliffs where the *gon-khang* was hidden. Linka was seated outside the far perimeter, under an arch of three stone slabs resembling a Celtic dolmen. He was tapping a hand drum in time to the liturgy. A trumpet fashioned from a human thighbone was placed before him, and at his side stood a cake of coloured dough. The corpse, still doubled up in its basket and shrouded with a dark green cloth, occupied the centre of the circle. The ritual butcher was bent over next to it, sharpening a *kukri* on a stone. Two ravens perched on a boulder, their heads sunk into their necks.

At a cry from Yonden the butcher straightened up and acknowledged their arrival with a cheerful flourish of his *kukri*.

'Bloody hell, it's Ngawang.'

They took up positions opposite Linka and settled down to wait. Ngawang's blade chimed on the stone. Linka's obsequies droned on the wind. The clouds went by.

'He couldn't have been very popular,' Melville said.

'Sah?'

'We're the only mourners.'

'His friends have already said goodbye.'

With no further preliminaries, Ngawang whisked back the shroud and tipped the corpse onto the grass. It was pale and naked, swollen and sexless in death. Melville stood up to get a better view, but Yonden tugged him down, wagging his finger in admonition. 'Very bad to see a dead man's face,' he whispered. 'He might haunt you.'

At a trumpet note from Linka the ravens flew barking round the circle, their wings stroking the grass, and alighted on the dolmen.

Ngawang felt the edge of the *kukri*, hefted it, offered it to the corpse's neck, turned and brandished it at the mourners, then, shuffling his legs for balance, brought it down in a shining arc, severing the head at a stroke. It rolled away and Ngawang bounded after it, marshalling it into a convenient position with the flat of his blade. Twice the *kukri* rose and fell, leaving Melville with a subliminal image of a quartered melon. Next, Ngawang chopped off the arms and legs.

A decisive stroke unseamed the torso from sternum to groin. Reaching into the cavity, Ngawang drew out the cold blue coil of guts and hung them over a rock. He rolled up his sleeves, blew out his cheeks and then systematically proceeded to chop up the corpse into bite-size pieces, scattering them within the circle.

'Do you find it grisly?' Gunn asked.

'It's sobering to see a man turned into pie filling.'

'I prefer this method to ours. I hate the idea of rotting in the ground.'

'There's always cremation. That way you cheat the worms.'

Ngawang finished his butchery, wiped his forehead and took a seat next to Linka, who began breaking up the cake. When this was done, they shifted their position a few yards.

Human flesh was much darker than Melville had imagined. His eye kept returning to a mucilaginous glob ten feet away. He was fairly certain that it was an eyeball. He felt cold in the wind and moved closer to Gunn. The procession of clouds had grown ragged, almost a rout, and high above them in the jet-stream a frosty whiteness was spreading. Of the vultures that were usually to be seen, there was no sign.

Nothing much happened in the next half hour. Although the ravens had the feast to themselves, they seemed to have no appetite. They pecked in a desultory way at the smaller scraps, often flicking the food away. Then a flock of choughs flew down, jostling in the air like rowdy student witches barging into a refectory. They ignored the flesh and applied themselves to the cake crumbs.

Melville cloaked his head with his *chuba*. 'Never a vulture around when you need one.'

'Soon,' Yonden said.

'What happens if the guests don't show?' Melville asked.

'This man has an unhappy birth – maybe even a *yi-dag*.'

'Tantalised spirits,' Gunn explained. 'Always hungry, always thirsty, always craving for the impossible.'

'Assuming you're not destined to be a rat or a lizard in your next life,' Melville said to Yonden, 'which sphere of existence do you fancy?'

'The land of the gods,' Yonden replied without hesitation.

'I thought the goal of all Buddhists was nirvana,' Melville said. 'I thought that the aim was to become one with the universe as the dewdrop dissolves in the ocean.'

'Boring,' Yonden said. 'In the land of the gods there's many women, many money, many happy things.' He smiled in anticipation, then his expression grew sober. 'Maybe in one million years I become a Bodhisattva,' he announced. 'Help poor suffering people.' He gave a determined nod, as though fixing the resolution in his mind for all time.

'With your record,' Melville said, 'you'll need a million years at least.' He turned to Gunn. 'How about you?'

'Having an infinite number of lives sounds like hell to me.' He looked away. 'I rather like the sound of that dewdrop. What's your ambition?' he added quickly.

'I don't believe in the transmigration of souls,' Melville said, staring off across the circle, 'but for the sake of argument . . . ah no, what the hell; I'll settle for the same life – only next time I'll get it right.'

The silence of introspection. There was more cloud than sky now, and in the intervals between the sun the wind was rigorous.

Linka blew a flourish on his trumpet.

Following the direction of his gaze, Melville saw a shallow inverted V gliding towards them. He shielded his eyes and recognised the falcate outline and diamond-shaped tail of the vulture he had seen at the gorge. Behind it, following so close that it seemed to be attached by an invisible towline, came another, and behind that trailed a wisp of choughs. The vultures cruised over the circle very slowly, their heads turning this way and that. They made several passes, then tilted out and up, rising like kites to alight on a ledge close to the gon-khang.

'Not hungry,' Melville said.

'They don't eat until the end,' Gunn said. 'They come for the bones.'

A squall of hail blurred the cliffs to the south. Through the gaps in the clouds the sky was brilliant.

'I know it's in bad taste,' Melville said, 'but I could use some lunch.'

Yonden sucked in his breath and pointed.

Along the escarpment griffons were sailing in line astern. Another echelon appeared from upwind and the two formations converged exactly above the circle, forming a round of their own.

'The company is met,' Melville said.

But the vultures maintained their height, the square-rigged shapes going round and round in an accelerating rhythm.

'What's keeping them?' Melville asked.

'They're waiting for the king of the vultures,' Yonden told him.

He put a finger to his lips, enjoining silence, and Melville saw that he was rapt – no longer a spectator but a participant, an initiate awaiting the unfolding of a rite.

The wheel in the sky spun like a carousel. A gust of wind boomed against the cliff and the sun sprayed through the clouds. Melville saw something falling away from the wheel, dropping at a speed to baffle the eye. His scalp tingled and he felt hollow and weightless – the sensation he had experienced as a boy standing at the side of the railroad, waiting for the express train to rush through. The bolt assumed a form. The vulture was plummeting with its wings folded into its body, its legs extended in front. It fell free until Melville could hear the wind-whine of its descent, then, when it seemed as though it would plunge into the ground, its wings opened with a *whoosh* and it parachuted down to land as light as a sigh in the centre of the circle, where Ngawang stood waiting to receive it with a chunk of flesh held in his outstretched hand.

It ignored him. It lifted its head and bobbed it at the mourners, and Melville, before he knew what he was doing, bobbed back. As though satisfied with his comportment, it waddled towards Ngawang, stopping a yard short. Slowly it extended its neck, opened its beak, snatched the meat and swallowed it in a throat-bulging gulp.

A soughing filled the air as the rest of the guests dropped in. In a matter of seconds the feast had degenerated into a feeding frenzy. Even though the food was distributed throughout the circle, the griffons fought for particular morsels, leaning back on their tails and grunting and hissing in disturbingly human voices. Melville saw one of them clop its beak on the yolky eye. Above the vultures dozens of choughs swooped and whistled, while on the margins the ravens, appetites sharpened by competition, took turns to sneak in and grab what they could.

In less than twenty minutes the corpse had been devoured – every bit. After a brief wait to settle the food in their crops, the griffons departed in twos and threes until only one remained. Melville was sure it was the king vulture. Sated, it perched on a boulder, its head drawn into its ruff. Finally it roused, hung out its wings as if drying them, folded them again, cocked its tail and squirted a copious dropping. Then, stretching and twisting its neck, it regurgitated part of its meal.

The circle begins again, Melville thought. The merry-go-round keeps turning.

The vulture looked at its vomit with stupid eyes and gave it a feeble peck. Melville's gorge rose. He shook his fist and the griffon flopped off its perch, pedalled over the grass and lurched into flight. On ponderous wings it flapped away until the wind took the strain and bore it into its element.

Linka and Ngawang had already packed up and were going their separate ways – Linka without a backward glance at the spectators, Ngawang with a wink at Yonden, the customary butt pasted to his lips.

'He was on very familiar terms with the king vulture,' Melville said.

'They have met before,' Yonden said, and snickered.

'C'mon, I'm cold,' Melville said. The sky threatened hail.

'Don't get up,' Gunn said in a wooden voice. 'Stay where you are.'

Caught in the act of sneaking off, Yonden stopped, his mouth frozen in a sickly smile.

'What's up?' Melville demanded.

'Did you notice anything unusual about that man?' Gunn said, nodding at the circle as though he could still see the corpse.

'He was dead.' Apprehension sprouted beneath Melville's ribcage.

'He was small – smaller than Yonden. Too small for a Khampa.'

'All dead men look small,' said Melville, who had never seen one before. He couldn't take his eyes off Yonden. He had the impression that the Khampa was wasting away behind his smile.

'Oh, use your head, man,' Gunn said. He sounded more tired than angry. He looked with sorrow at Yonden. 'Tell him.'

But there was nothing left of Yonden except teeth and gums.

The tumour in Melville's chest burst. 'Answer up you little punk, and unless I hear the ring of truth, a dime to a shitload of bad karma you'll be spending all eternity in the coldest corner of hell.'

'It was the saddhu,' Yonden's disembodied voice said.

'You killed a fucking holy man?' Melville shouted.

'I doubt that,' Gunn said, climbing stiffly to his feet.

Melville's anger was a rocket that blew up on the launch pad. He reeled into the circle, staring about with bemusement. He stopped in the centre and did a slow turn, but there was nothing left except a few smears of blood and mucus. With trembling hand he pointed at one. 'Jetha?' he asked faintly.

'One of his spies,' Yonden said. He had materialised again. He was scoring a line on the turf with the toe of his boot. 'I don't know his name.'

'You bloodthirsty bastard.'

'Maybe it was the man Jetha sent to kill you,' Yonden retorted. 'Yes, I think so. Did that man stop to talk to you?' He resumed his

306

footwork. 'It was necessary for Ngawang to kill him. He saw you. He was running away. He would have reported you.'

'We're accessories to murder,' Melville marvelled. 'You've fucked us up in spades.'

'He didn't speak to the soldiers,' Yonden said. 'They don't know who he is. They don't know you're here.'

'Jetha does, you cretin. When his man doesn't report in, he's going to come looking for him, and when he finds him . . .' Melville walked in a little circle, punching his palm. 'My God, they'll put us up against a wall for this.'

Yonden laughed. He opened his hands and raised his eyes with theatrical slowness from the empty circle to the thin air. 'Nothing to find.'

Melville was experiencing difficulty breathing. 'When you're freezing in hell, Yonden, someone's going to be there plucking out your guts and stuffing them back in again. And so help me, that person's going to be me.'

'Enough of that,' Gunn ordered.

'You going to stand there defending a murderer?'

'Osher's watching us,' Gunn said.

Melville registered the fact that the commander had them under observation with his new pair of field-glasses.

'If Jetha's advising the Nepalese army,' Gunn said, 'why didn't that man identify himself to the garrison.'

'Because Osher's got informants there,' Melville answered. 'Forget that. I want to know why this scumbag kept us in the dark.'

'He didn't want to lose his bonus,' Gunn said, and looked miserably away from Yonden.

'Bonus?'

'Osher paid him five hundred dollars to deliver you. That's a small fortune in his terms. No,' Gunn said at the question in Melville's eyes, 'nothing for me.'

Melville gave a vacuous laugh. 'What makes me so special?'

Yonden chose to remain silent.

'Dammit, I swear to God . . .' Melville said, running at him. He stopped short. The Khampa's willingness to kill had induced respect verging on awe. He rounded on Gunn instead. 'For chrissake, someone tell me what's going on.'

'Osher doesn't trust Americans,' Gunn said. 'They haven't served him well in the past.' His apologetic shrug indicated that present company was no more reliable.

At the truth of the accusation, Melville felt the force of his anger diminish. He wandered away, his eyes panning over the mountain walls. 'Is this the first time he's received an arms drop here?'

'We've had no guns since we left Mustang,' Yonden said.

'And he's not going to get any now,' Melville said. 'A pilot could fly within a mile of this hole and never see it. Like I told you, Osher's holding me as surety.'

Gunn ignored him. He went up to Yonden, who came to attention, chin up, rocking back on his heels.

'Take us away.'

Yonden took a pace backwards.

'You must,' Gunn said, following up.

'I'll ask Osher,' Yonden said, leaning so far back that he threatened to topple over.

'Secretly,' Gunn cried. 'Not a word to a soul.'

Yonden cringed. 'There's only one path and it's always watched.'

'I saw another trail across the gorge from the *chorten*,' Gunn said.

'That must be the alternative route Sweetwater mentioned,' Melville said, 'but Osher would catch us up before we were halfway there. Put it out of your mind, Alan. We're stuck.'

Gunn stepped back and looked helplessly at the ramparts to the south.

'Wait until the guns arrive,' Yonden begged.

'And if they don't?'

'Osher will let you go. He won't hurt a friend of mine.'

'I'm not your friend,' Melville said.

'You're Mr Yueh's friend,' Yonden said in a wheedling voice. 'Charlie said to look after you good.'

'You're doing a terrific job so far.'

'Walter's friends aren't in control,' Gunn said. 'Osher is. Look at him. He wants us to know.'

Melville checked and found that the commander still had them in view. He sat down on the nearest boulder. He was having difficulty keeping any train of thought on rails. 'Slow down and take a grip,' he said. 'Jetha's man was killed a week ago and there hasn't been a whisper from the Gurkhas. However, we have to assume he left word of his whereabouts with Jetha. Okay, the major knows where we are, but there's nothing he can do short of sending in the army to storm the camp. Even if the Nepalese were prepared to go along with that, Yonden's right: to prove murder, you have to have a body. There isn't one. It's metempsychosed into vulture shit. If Jetha's asking questions, he's asking them in Kathmandu. Right now, this is the safest place to be.'

Gunn snorted. 'We can't stay here indefinitely with a murder charge hanging over us.'

'Only until the deadline for the guns passes. We're in so deep, another few days won't make any difference.'

'I won't remain a hostage to fortune.'

'Alan, Alan,' Melville said, 'what we're facing here is nothing compared to what will be waiting for us when we set foot outside. We can't go back to Kathmandu. We're going to have to ask Charlie to pull us out.' His anger rekindled as he sounded the depth of their predicament.

Gunn looked at him for a few seconds, then marched up to Yonden. He hesitated and essayed a smile that made Melville's toes curl.

'Yonden, you promised not to lead me into danger. I'm asking you – pleading with you – to keep your word.'

Melville couldn't bear to watch. He was sure that Gunn would break down and start pawing Yonden, appealing to the spirit of friendship and loyalty. It didn't bother him that the Khampa was a liar and a murderer. All he wanted was a token, a little something that might yet rehabilitate his faith in the man.

'It's not as if you're the one Osher's holding to ransom,' Melville said. 'All you have to do is ask, and he'll let you leave by the front door.'

'With what I've learnt?' Gunn demanded.

The scorn in his voice stung, but Melville couldn't deny he had a valid point. Both men looked at Yonden. Under their combined scrutiny, he hung his head.

'There's a path from the village,' he said. 'It goes to Mustang.'

Melville laughed. 'All roads lead to hell.'

'Two days west,' Yonden continued, 'another path goes south and joins the big valley to Pokhara. I don't know the way. It's difficult.'

'We could hire a guide in the village,' Gunn said. 'I could go tomorrow. Linka asked me to take a message to the lama.'

'To Pokhara it's two weeks' walking,' Yonden said. 'Every day we will have to go past checkpoints.'

'You'll find a way,' Gunn said. He turned excitedly to Melville. 'Won't he?'

'Frankly, I think it sucks,' Melville said. He registered Yonden's face appealing to him over Gunn's shoulder. He noted the even more desperate plea on Gunn's face. 'No harm in checking it out, I suppose,' – adding, for Yonden's benefit, 'I'd be surprised if it leads anywhere.'

Gunn stood back. He looked dizzy and his legs were unsteady. He took several steps in the wrong direction before turning and stumbling back to the camp. Melville watched him go.

'You did a bad thing bringing him here,' he said.

'Osher will shoot me,' Yonden said, limp and abject.

'No medals for self-inflicted wounds.'

'Guerillas from Mustang use the path,' Yonden said, raising dazed eyes. 'The valley is their main supply route. They have made an affair of blood with all Khampas who take money from the Kuomintang. They all know who I am.'

Basically, Melville was not unsympathetic to Yonden's situation. 'Go through the motions,' he told him. 'Give Alan time to come to his senses.'

Yonden made no sign that he had heard. He walked off, slack in the legs, looking from behind like an unfairly whipped schoolboy. After he had gone a little way, he started a bitter dialogue with himself, thumping his hip and occasionally kicking the turf. Melville formed the impression that he was railing against fate.

'Never mind,' he called after him. 'Think of it as a down-payment on that place in paradise.'

Left alone, he found he was too fatigued to move, although black cloud was drawing a curtain across the cliffs. One side of his mouth twitched in a smile as he recalled the rub-a-dub lines with which Jetha had threatened him.

'And the end of the fight is a tombstone white with the name of the late deceased. And the epitaph drear . . .'

He stopped. As an epitaph, the verse was not entirely appropriate. He heard cries. Lurid against the approaching squall, the guerillas were driving their animals into shelter. He ran, not comprehending the need for urgency until the cloud caught him just yards short of the camp, bombarding him with icy marbles big enough to planish steel.

Chapter 20

Early next afternoon, Gunn and Yonden reached a parting of the
ways. To the left a path braided by use coiled round an outcrop
shaped like a giant termite mound. On the roofs of the dun-coloured
houses that capped it, trollish figures kept watch. To the right, a
single track zigzagged up to the Lucky Place. Ahead, another trail
wandered away past tiny watermills towards a waste of peaks on
the Tibetan border. Against the inflexible grey sky, the mountains
resembled cut-outs. There was little snow. The ranges behind had
robbed the air of moisture, and the slopes around the village were
bare and treeless, shattered by frost and sun.

Yonden made a last attempt to steer Gunn from his course. 'Osher
will ride after us. He'll find us wherever we hide.'

'I've told you,' Gunn said. 'There's no need for you to come.'

'Osher will drag me behind his horse for cheating him.'

'I swear I'll forget what I've learned,' Gunn said. He was confused
and sick, his mind fouled by the residue of last night's dream – alone
in a room with all the chill in the world, a fugitive stumbling across
rubble outside, running down broken corridors, rattling the doors of
locked rooms and calling his name with increasing terror as the leather
dolls closed the gap.

'You'll tell the soldiers everything,' Yonden shouted, 'just like you
told the Chinese about my family.'

Silence laid a shadow on Gunn. He could hear the beating of his
heart. And yet he experienced no shock – only relief as the accusation
lanced something close to the core of his being.

'I knew you blamed me,' he said.

Yonden did not avoid the hand Gunn put on his shoulder. His
head drooped as though in submission to the forces that had linked
him to one so ill-starred. 'I wish I had never heard your name again,'
he said, before turning towards the village.

Gunn plodded up the opposite slope. The gritty wind conjured up
an endless succession of dust devils. He heard the vibrato of the
temple prayer flags and the plangent chiming of wind-gongs. The
same wind blew streamers from the icy spine that slowly emerged
from the clutter of mountains to the north.

Reaching the shoulder on which the Lucky Place stood, Gunn gazed on this spectacle for a minute, then turned to see a man in a wine-red *chuba* peering at him from the temple steps. He called out a greeting, knowing he would get none back, and walked over, past a line of *chortens* like miniature ziggurats and a long cairn of weathered *mani* stones. The man pretended he hadn't seen him. He began turning a squeaking prayer wheel as big as an oil drum. Gunn imagined the hundreds of invocations released by each spin of the wheel, picturing them flying down the wind and falling among the rocks.

'Are you the sacristan?' he asked.

The man started in fright. His hair was bound in a pigtail and his skin was the colour of pemmican. He had the hunched shoulders and attenuated gaze of a man who toils underground; the blackened silver box charm tied to his waist might have been beaten from ore that he had dug from the earth himself.

'I wish to offer my respects to the Lord Aim Giver,' Gunn said.

At mention of the lama's name, the sacristan sprang back and spread his arms to deny passage – a dwarf guarding its precious lode. In impenetrable dialect he made it clear that entry was forbidden.

'I have a message for him – an important message from Linka.'

After a few seconds Gunn realised that the door-keeper had switched to a garbled form of Tibetan. Aim Giver never received visitors. He was close to death. He was preparing for a ritual. Unpredictable forces were involved. To disturb his holiness would be dangerous. With a small, explosive gesture the man indicated that the lama might fly apart like the workings of a clock. The universe might come to pieces.

'I've travelled here from across the sea,' Gunn pleaded.

The door-keeper was adamant.

'Then allow me to admire your fine temple,' Gunn said, holding out a ten-rupee note.

The man skirted the money as though it were bait in a trap before snatching it at the full reach of his arm. He held it up to the sky, examining it from a distance of two inches, then snapped his fingers for more. Gunn peeled off another note. The man demanded his boots, his watch, his sweater. Finally, for thirty rupees and Gunn's mittens, the man stood aside.

Gunn went up the steps, between a pair of recumbent stone lions, and through the half-open door. He held his breath, but there was nothing sinister here – no unnatural light, nothing to disturb the lumber of his mind. It was a plain and simple temple of the Nyingma sect, laid out on conventional lines, with a tawdry image of a petulant and effeminate-looking Padma Sambhava, subduer of demons, in pride of place.

The sacristan tip-toed ahead of Gunn, glancing anxiously at the gallery while he showed off flaking gilt statues of Buddha and carved wooden masks of the lamaist pantheon. Among the faded *thankas* above the altar hung a pennant advertising Hong Kong's floating restaurant.

On a shameful impulse, Gunn sidled off as the sacristan stopped to admire a fresco of a tantric saint, and made for the ladder. He was on its bottom step before the sacristan noticed, and then he ignored the hiss of outrage and even lashed out with his foot as the man tried to claw him back. When he reached the gallery, he looked down and whispered reassurance. The sacristan was too stunned by this act of sacrilege to do anything but cover his face with his hands and twitter like a bird whose nest has been pillaged.

Aim Giver, clad in soiled and faded yellow, sat as still as any statue and more insubstantial. One shake, Gunn thought, and he would crumble into dust. His eyes were filmed and sunken. There was more vitality on the waxy face of the mummy that winked down at Gunn from above the altar.

Father and son, Gunn realised, looking from one to the other. He peered closer at Aim Giver, struck by some correspondence with his own life. It seemed to him that he had seen that face before, in a different incarnation – the same unyielding droop of the mouth, the lines that mapped out an inner desert of one whose chosen purpose is to mortify the senses. It was the face of a man who condemns this world and shows no pleasure at the prospect of redemption in the next. It was, in essentials, the face of his father.

Down below the sacristan's squeaks had dwindled to a frightened crooning. Gunn stood up, knowing that Aim Giver was beyond the reach of any earthly message. If he wasn't already dead, he was standing on the edge of dissolution.

Laying a prayer scarf on the altar, Gunn climbed down. The sacristan had gone. Gunn went out into the wind and found the man swinging the wheel with both hands, toiling to undo the harm that the stranger's impiety had caused.

'I had to see him,' Gunn said. 'Even to come near him is to stand in the pool of perfect knowledge.'

The man went on churning out prayers, adding his own verbal imprecations to the formulae painted on the wheel.

Gunn held out money. It looked like the sacristan would knock it from his hand, but poverty won and he grabbed the notes, whining for more. Slightly mollified, he put his head on one side and asked Gunn where he came from.

'From Britain. Across the sea.'

'Pilgrims used to come from as far as Calcutta,' the sacristan boasted.

'Before your lama became ill?'

'In his father's reign, nearly twenty years ago. We haven't seen the sun since he died.'

'Doesn't the Lord Aim Giver look after you as diligently as his father?'

'He's a saint,' the sacristan said, his tone implying that Aim Giver was too unworldly for the village's own good.

'A recluse.'

The sacristan nodded. 'From the beginning of the first month to the middle of the fourth, we have only our clan leaders to teach the doctrine.'

'He stays at the Lucky Place while you're in your winter settlement?'

'Ever since the death of his father.'

'Then he no longer worships at the *gon-khang* above the Khampa camp.'

'There is no *gon-khang*,' the sacristan said, shutters falling on his eyes.

'The *gon-khang* where his father made offerings,' Gunn said, seeing in his mind's eye the conspiratorial leer of the mummy above the altar.

The sacristan's dumbness was an impregnable defence evolved by generations of mistrust towards strangers.

'Who will succeed the Lord Aim Giver?' Gunn asked quickly.

'Our prayers will be answered.'

'By Linka?'

'Nothing good ever came here from the north,' the sacristan said, and spat.

'I understood that your village had asked Linka to be your next lama.'

Judging by the sacristan's spittle-filled answer, it was not a decision that he endorsed.

'The message I have to deliver,' Gunn interrupted, and then hesitated, sensing that it would not be well-received. 'Aim Giver's daughter is expecting Linka's child.'

He was crowded off the steps by the force of the sacristan's invective. 'Wait,' he called, skipping backwards. 'Wait.'

The sacristan halted, one eye shut, the other peering in suspicion. In his hand he held a stone. He made to throw it as Gunn took a step forward.

'A ritual, you said. You said your lama was making preparations for a ritual.'

The sacristan still had one eye shut. Behind him the wind chimes gave a sudden peal.

'What kind of ritual?' Gunn asked, fumbling in his jacket.

'An exorcism,' the sacristan replied at last, watching Gunn's hand.

'To cast out what?' Gunn asked. He had to raise his voice to make himself heard over the buzzing prayer flags.

The sacristan shrugged as if to say, take your pick. He began to approach by a rather devious route, eyeing with great care the money in Gunn's hand.

'Only if you tell me about the exorcism,' Gunn said, pulling the notes out of reach. 'I've visited the place of wet skulls. I know it has something to do with that.'

For a fraction of a second a current of understanding sparked between them.

'He wants to drive Linka away,' Gunn said.

'He wants to cleanse the valley for his successor,' the sacristan said. He turned his attention back to the money.

'Take it,' Gunn said. 'Give it to your lama to use as he wishes.'

As the man counted and recounted the notes, Gunn wondered what had possessed him to make such an expensive gesture. The feud was nothing to do with him, and in a few days he would be gone.

When the sacristan had established the amount of Gunn's largesse, he begged for more. He came after him thrawn-necked, one hand extended, the other cupping his elbow. He had lost his barley and his yaks were nearly dry. His only son had vanished in the high pastures five summers ago, and he had no daughters to care for him in his old age. His suppliant whine nagged at Gunn until it finally merged with all the other unanswered prayers carried on the wind.

Yonden was coming straight down, ignoring the path, slaloming from one patch of scree to the other, starting small landslides. Watching him, Gunn saw the exuberant teenager he had known in Kham. Twenty yards off, Yonden slowed to a dejected walk and Gunn effaced his smile of welcome as though it were something obscene. He's acting, he thought, pretending that no one will take us.

Wordlessly Yonden flopped into the lee of the rock. He accepted the proffered meal of tinned fish without thanks and began to chew savagely. He knocked ash from a chunk of stale bread and crammed his mouth. 'Did you see the lama?'

'I couldn't speak to him,' Gunn said. 'He's very near the end.'

Yonden grunted, chomping the bread into submission.

'The sacristan showed me round the temple. Nothing good ever came here from the north, he said.'

'Nothing good ever came here from anywhere,' Yonden said, and spat out a piece of grit.

'They're wary of outsiders. I don't suppose you had any more luck than I did.'

Yonden paused in mid-chew. 'Ten days to the big valley,' he said, 'then six until we come to the road. Many soldiers in the valley.' He chased a scrap of fish around the can. 'They'll see us for sure.' He shrugged. 'Up to you.'

It took a moment to sink in. 'You found a guide?' He looked away. 'You could have told me that nobody would help and I'd have been none the wiser.'

'He wants two thousand rupees,' Yonden said, banging down the empty can.

'That's a huge amount.'

'The price of one yak calf,' Yonden said. He stood up, holding out a hand. 'Give me all your money. He wants half now.'

'I don't have it,' Gunn said, patting his pockets. 'I gave it to the sacristan. Can't the man wait a day?'

'Crazy stupid,' Yonden squeaked. 'He has to buy rice for the winter. I told you these people only help if they see money.'

'Does that mean he won't take us?' Gunn asked, abject with misery.

Yonden's expression suggested that it would be no more than he deserved. He turned, stuck two fingers in his mouth and gave a whistle shrill enough to split rock. Presently a man came slithering down from the village, taking more or less the same line that Yonden had chosen.

'Maybe you'll have to give him your watch,' he said.

'How soon can we go?' Gunn asked.

'Three days,' Yonden said, watching the figure on the scree.

Gunn closed his eyes.

'Why did you give the sacristan your money?'

'It wasn't for him,' Gunn said. 'It was a donation to the temple.'

Yonden's stare demanded that he say more.

'Aim Giver's carrying out an exorcism. I'm sure it has something to do with the *gon-khang*. Since he's been lama, he's never visited it, and now Linka's there with his daughter, stirring up God knows what.'

'You want the lama to chase away the demons you saw.'

'I didn't see *them*. *They* saw me. I came to their attention. I want them put to rest.'

Yonden made fists of his hands. 'This is an affair between Linka and Aim Giver,' he said. He brought his fists together and held Gunn's eyes, not quite smiling. 'It's not wise to stand in the middle.'

Gunn shivered. 'Everything about this valley gives me the creeps.'

Yonden watched the approaching guide.

'Do you think Linka will become lama?' Gunn asked.

'It's very important for him,' Yonden said. 'Next spring the soldiers will come.' He grinned. 'It's very hard to put a lama in prison.'

'Not all the villagers want him. The sacristan doesn't. You should have seen his reaction when I told him about the child.'

'Because the mother is a witch,' Yonden said, scraping lichen off a rock.

'In that case, Linka hasn't improved his chances by taking up with her.'

'Look at this monkey,' Yonden said, nodding at the villager. 'Linka can make these people do what he wants. He can always make people do what he wants.'

'Except Osher.'

Yonden nodded.

Fear came on Gunn, insidious as the foul aftertaste of the fish he had eaten. 'Could Linka have been the one who told Jetha about Melville?'

Yonden opened his hand and watched the wind carry the lichen dust away. 'I think it's best for you to shut your mouth.'

'Far out,' Melville said, as a shower of meteors underlined their last brilliant moments.

'We're wasting time,' Gunn told him.

'They're wasting precious wood,' Melville said, staring down at the beacon fires on the floor of the basin. He pulled his *chuba* about him

317

and took another drink. The night was shaggy with stars and fiercely cold.

'Now is the perfect time,' Gunn said. 'Nobody's around to see us. What are you waiting for?'

'The prognosis is lousy,' Melville said. 'Ten days' hard slog, living on crusts and sleeping out in temperatures that would harden flesh to metal. Another week playing hide-and-seek with the Nepalese army. No thank you.'

'You're a damn weathercock.'

'Cool it, Alan. I didn't say I was getting out at any price. I agreed that Yonden should check it out, and that's what he's done, and the odds are stacked against us.'

'Then why are you packed and ready to leave?' Gunn hissed.

'Because you've got me jumpier than spit on a pan,' Melville said. He threw back his head as another flight of shooting stars streaked to extinction. 'What we're witnessing tonight, folks, is the heat death of the universe.' Some of his words slid sideways under his tongue.

'You're drunk,' Gunn said in disgust.

'Anti-freeze,' Melville said, holding up a bottle of Yeshe's white lightning. 'And damn me if it don't taste surprisingly fine.'

'You'll ruin everything,' Gunn moaned.

'Let me run the facts past you,' Melville said, suddenly sober. 'Our chances of making a clean break are worse than evens. If Jetha links us to that murder, we're looking at twenty years jail minimum. Then again, if Yonden is recognised by the Mustang guerillas he says we're likely to bump into, he's a dead man. Think on that.' Melville paused, glancing at the dim shape of Yonden, who appeared to be asleep against a corner shrine. 'Set that against the alternative,' he continued. 'Another three or four days of freezing our butts off, eating food that tastes like the inside of a pillow, and then we say goodbye.' He waved his bottle in the direction of the fires. 'Osher can forget about his guns.'

'He'll still have us.'

'He isn't interested in you, and the worst he can do to me is charge for my release. If he does, Charlie will just have to cough up. He'd better, because I could blow him out of the water with what I've got on him.'

'A man like that wouldn't think twice about paying Osher to throw you into the gorge.'

'That's a shitty thing to say,' Melville said, his voice shaking. 'A shitty thing.' He went to the edge of the roof and stared at the dying beacons. 'I'll tell you this,' he said. 'I prefer to take my chances with Osher. At least I know where I stand with him. Since I agreed to stay, we've had several amiable discussions.'

Gunn snorted with contempt. 'I suppose he paid Yonden the five hundred dollars so that he could have someone to chat with.'

Melville swivelled round. He glanced at the silent figure of Yonden before crouching down in front of Gunn. 'Well now,' he said softly, 'I asked him about that, and do you know what he told me? He told me that he'd offered Yonden the bonus so as to lessen the chances of him scramming with his friends' wages. I was there, and believe me, it was a close thing.' Melville stood up abruptly. 'You go if you like,' he said. 'Speaking Tibetan, you stand a better chance on your own.'

'Osher would shake the truth out of you inside five minutes. No, Walter – we both go or we both stay.'

'I guess that's it, then,' Melville said slowly. 'Sorry, partner.'

'Ssh,' Yonden said.

'We're keeping your friend from his sleep,' Melville said.

'Shut up, please,' Yonden told him, scrambling to his feet. He peered up into the sky.

Melville listened. If he could hear anything, it was only the stars humming to themselves.

Sparks billowed as the Khampas tried to kick life into the fires. Horses whinnied.

'It's the plane,' Gunn murmured.

Collective hysteria, Melville thought, then heard the faint drone of a prop-driven aircraft. It swelled to a throb, faded, came back again, dwindled once more. Some idiot fired a rifle.

'He can't see us,' Melville said.

'He must be circling,' Gunn said.

'Ssh,' Yonden repeated.

In a little while Melville heard the plane again. He could not see it. It made a distant hum, now to the south, now to the north. He massaged the constriction in his throat. He did not know what he wanted. The hum of the plane deepened. It seemed to be nearly overhead. He could not understand why it was invisible against so many stars.

There was a crack and white light seared his retina. Another flare popped. He saw them swinging down on their parachutes. Their light plated the cliffs silver, etched every contour on the floor of the pit, outlined black riders galloping on black horses towards the southern wall. The note of the plane faded.

'It's now or never,' Gunn said. 'He's got his weapons. He's going into Tibet.'

'So everyone's happy,' Melville said, his voice pitched too high.

'You're forgetting the Khampas who don't want any more fighting. It must have been one of them who tipped Jetha off.'

'Pure supposition,' Melville said, clutching his chest.

'They're Linka's men. They'd do anything for an amnesty.'

'They wouldn't sell out their own people.'

'It's that or a refugee camp.'

'If this is another of your crazy notions . . .' Melville warned.

'It's as real as those guns out there. That's why Linka warned me to get away.'

'What did you say to him up there? How much damage have you done?'

'I didn't have to tell him anything. In a few days he'll see Osher leaving for Tibet.' Gunn seized Melville by the arm. 'Can you face another month here – day after day, not knowing what's happening?'

'Lay off, will you,' Melville cried, shaking himself free. 'Stop crowding me.'

The flares were low now, their hissing audible. Cries came from the Khampas. Melville's brain raced without reaching any answer. The conflict within him was choking. He pulled open his robe to ease his breathing. Jesus, why had he had to go and get drunk.

'What do you think, Yonden?'

'Up to you.'

'Think we could make it?'

'He wouldn't be here unless he did,' Gunn said.

'Give me a minute.'

'Now or never,' Gunn repeated.

'I don't know what to think. There are just too many fucking things beyond my control.'

'You'll come?'

Melville hadn't meant that. He hadn't decided anything. In the absence of any clear-cut solution, the construction Gunn put on his words decided it for him.

'I'll come, soon as the lights go out.'

Hardly had he spoken when the flares died. For a few moments their after-images were scrawled on the sky like snail tracks. The brilliance of burning magnesium and phosphorus had sent the stars into hiding.

'Show's over,' Melville said. 'Let's do it while they're still unwrapping their toys.'

They clambered down and slipped through the alleys. There was no one around to challenge them. On the open turf they broke into a half-run, often glancing back. The stars had emerged from eclipse, but the camp screened the fugitives from the guerillas gathered in the dropping zone.

Melville flung himself flat, clawing at the turf as gunfire racketed behind him.

'They're not shooting at us,' Gunn panted, dropping to his knees beside him.

The shooting became indiscriminate and then stopped, silenced by a series of quickfire concussions that Melville felt through his guts. Up and over the mountain rim a stream of tracer described a parabola.

'Some toys,' Gunn said. 'Come on.'

They staggered on. Yonden's shadow disappeared among the junipers that stood at the approach to the gorge. Melville found himself on the path, his feet jarring on loose stones. 'Slow it down,' he called after the fleeting shape of Yonden. 'I'll look pretty dumb if I turn an ankle.'

He ignored his own advice. When he came round the next corner, he was going too fast to avoid colliding with Yonden, who had halted in the middle of the trail. The Khampa was knocked forward onto the muzzle of a carbine pointed at his stomach.

'Good thinking,' Melville said, recognising the man at the other end of the gun as Ngawang. 'Having him along will improve our chances no end.'

He said it even though he could see that Ngawang's expression was somewhat deficient in the way of welcome. Nevertheless, he was constrained to respond with a grin. 'Why are we all standing around?'

Yonden reached up and detached Melville's hands from his shoulders. He walked forward until he was standing next to Ngawang, but he didn't turn round. His shoulders were shaking. Melville took a step in the same direction. Ngawang jerked his gun up and Melville raised his hands. 'This isn't very friendly,' he said, and gave a gusty laugh.

Behind him he could hear Gunn wheezing. 'You talked me into it,' he said. 'Now talk us out. Offer them money. Appeal to their greed.'

Getting no response, he intensified his smile and took another step towards Ngawang. 'How do you like the idea of making two hundred dollars?'

Without straightening his elbows, Ngawang swung the barrel of the carbine into Melville's face. Nobody had ever hit him like that before. It shocked as much as it hurt, and it hurt plenty. He found himself on the ground, fingering his torn mouth. 'That was one helluva bright idea you had,' he mumbled at Gunn.

Gunn went on staring at Yonden, his eyes like unlit lamps.

Ngawang stirred Melville up with the point of his carbine. Yonden turned his palsied face to him.

'I had to do it. We would have all been killed unless I stopped you.'

Melville grinned, blood running down his chin. 'You've got my word, Yonden. Eternity's going to be too short for what you've got coming.'

At a prod from Ngawang, he began retracing his steps, brushing past Gunn. As he reached level ground, he heard a howling from below. He experienced the most marvellous sense of detachment. Fear and booze and an intuition of what was coming made a potent cocktail. He felt incredibly – almost literally – high, as though the laws of gravity had been relaxed in his favour and he was gliding along with his head in the stars.

Gunn shambled in his wake, feet slurring on the frozen turf.

Swallowing to ease the dryness in his throat, Melville waited for Osher to speak. The commander appeared to be in no hurry. He seemed to have a lot on his mind. As usual he fiddled with his Zippo. Finally he reached down by his side and produced a bottle of Yeshe's moonshine and a glass.

'You like to drink,' he said.

'At moments of crisis,' Melville said, 'I find it settles the nerves. Someone once said he was born two whiskies below par.' He was aware that his hands were shaking, and he trapped them between his knees. The bottle was out of his reach, and he did not dare stand to move closer.

Osher filled the glass to the brim and slid it across. Melville knew he would spill a lot; it seemed important that he shouldn't.

'Aren't you going to join me?'

'It sends the mind to sleep,' Osher said, and lit a cigarette.

'Someone else said never trust a man who doesn't drink.'

Osher laughed. Laughter doesn't suit him, Melville thought.

He took the plunge and picked up the glass, slopping only a small quantity. He was not able to prevent his teeth chattering on the rim of the glass. His face twisted as the raw spirit burnt his wounded mouth and took its fiery course. Osher's own face contorted in sympathy.

'Like watching a man swallow live scorpions,' he said.

'Smoking does more damage in the long run,' Melville said.

Osher studied his cigarette, letting the smoke crawl up his hand and coil round his fingers. 'Everyone is allowed one vice,' he said. He fanned the smoke away. 'You have many more than one. You are treacherous, dishonourable . . .' He leaned forward and his voice rose on a note of interrogation '. . . chickenshit? That is what you Americans say?'

Melville nodded to corroborate Osher's use of English. 'An unfortunate lapse,' he said. 'It won't happen again.'

'You gave me your word that you would remain here until our business was settled.'

'That was my intention, believe me. Ask Yonden. I succumbed to Gunn's unfounded fears in a moment of weakness. He's not well,' Melville said, tapping his head. 'He suffers from irrrational misgivings, and I foolishly allowed his doubts to infect me.'

'Because you were drunk.'

'Because I was drunk,' Melville agreed gratefully. Osher's reasonable tone gave him the confidence to put a question of his own. 'Yonden exposed our ridiculous plot. Why did you let us go through with such a charade?'

'I wanted to see what you would do.'

'Words can't express my shame.'

Osher waved his hand as though he was beginning to find the subject trying.

'You have your weapons,' Melville said. 'I'm more than willing to keep my side of the bargain.'

'Our agreement is ended,' Osher said, with a casual finality that froze the alcohol in Melville's guts.

'Your agreement isn't with me,' he said quickly. 'I'm merely the representative of Mr Yueh.'

'Then he deserves to go empty-handed,' Osher said. 'If he has such poor judgement in his choice of agents, it is probably unsound in other areas.'

'He did send you the guns,' Melville pointed out.

'At the last moment,' Osher said, and rubbed his eyes as though

323

Mr Yueh's tardiness had occasioned sleepless nights. 'He can have his general,' he said in a throw-away tone.

Surreptitiously, Melville let his breath go.

'We leave in three days,' Osher said, juggling his lighter.

'What are you going to do with me?' Melville asked. The question couldn't be put off indefinitely.

Osher's eyes glazed slightly. He blew a stream of smoke and watched it as it eddied up out of the lamplight. 'You are a liability,' he said, in a vexed tone.

'There will be no more lapses on my part.'

'If I leave you here, you will try to escape again.'

'Not me.'

Osher grunted.

'I give you my word.'

Osher leaned forward. 'You are a man easily deflected from his promise. Like so many of your decadent kind, you fear the possibility of adversity more than you fear adversity itself – which is why you and your bourgeois friends will fail the test of history, scattered before the winds of your own cowardice.'

'There may be some truth in what you say.'

'I will confront you with real fear,' Osher said, stubbing out his cigarette. 'You will meet it face to face. Who knows? You might not be so frightened as you imagine.'

Melville felt he was already looking it in the eye.

'You came here to escort the general,' Osher said, sitting back comfortably, 'and that is what you will do. You will ride at his side the entire way. I am taking you into Tibet.'

Melville's stomach careened down like a roller-coaster. 'That would be a grave provocation to the Chinese.'

'The graver the better.'

'It might incite them to severe acts of retaliation.'

'You have an inflated estimation of your importance.'

'If I fell into their hands, they would make political capital out of it.'

'They won't capture you.'

'I could be wounded. You might have to leave me behind.'

'We don't leave our badly wounded behind.'

'I applaud such noble behaviour, but I'd hate to be the one who slows you down.'

'We shoot them.'

While Melville gathered his wits, Osher lit up a fresh cigarette.

'It's years since I've ridden a horse,' Melville said. 'I doubt if I could stay in the saddle.'

Osher squinted in suspicion. 'All Americans can ride,' he said. 'I saw many films of this at Camp Hale – warlord armies massacring defenceless peasants, like the Chinese in Kham.'

'We're not all cowboys and indians and slave-owning capitalists.'

'Fear is a good teacher,' Osher said. 'You will learn to ride because there is no alternative.'

'Suppose I refuse to come?'

Osher unbuttoned his holster and drew his pistol. 'We can end this in a moment,' he said.

'Mr Yueh would be deeply saddened to hear news of my death.'

'These mountains are full of pitfalls for the unwary,' Osher said, pressing the muzzle to the bridge of Melville's nose. 'As you have seen, vultures do not make good witnesses.'

Melville uncrossed his eyes and languidly pushed the gun barrel aside. 'Alright,' he said.

'I expected you to offer more resistance,' Osher said.

'One submits to the inevitable.'

'See, already you are less frightened.'

'Wait until the drink wears off,' Melville said, taking another swallow. 'What about Gunn?'

'He stays here.'

'Let him go. The man is being driven out of his mind.'

'He has seen and heard too much, and he is not a man who would remain silent under questioning.'

Melville nodded. In Osher's place, he would have done the same, and in his own new and vulnerable position, he was glad that Gunn wouldn't be at large to incriminate him. 'After tonight's episode,' he said, 'he might do something drastic. He can't cope with Yonden's deceitfulness.'

'Both of you have demanded too much of Yonden,' Osher said, rising in anger. 'He's not your servant; he's a soldier under my command. You didn't think of that when you bribed him to desert, and as a result I have had to punish him.' Osher subsided again, still glaring, and gathered his cigarettes and lighter to him as though they were important documents. It was a gesture of dismissal. 'Sleep and eat as much as you can,' he said. 'You won't do much of either once we're in Tibet.'

Melville stood up and attempted a salute. Those who are about to die. He made it to the door, head erect, then did an about-turn, headed back to the table, turned to the door again and left, dangling the bottle by the neck.

He was drunk almost to the point of insensibility when Yonden arrived and stood at the foot of his bed, poised for flight or retaliation.

'Don't worry, Yonden. Even if I could move, I wouldn't waste the effort getting up to tread on you.' He was glad it wasn't Gunn. He couldn't face the old man tonight.

'I had to tell him,' Yonden said. 'We could never have done it.'

'Pity you didn't make that clear at the outset,' Melville said. He struggled up into a sitting position, and after a couple of attempts he made it. 'Did Osher put you up to it?' he asked.

Yonden shook his head with an air of distraction. 'Because I waited so long to tell him, he was very angry with me. I thought he would shoot me.'

'He said he'd punished you.'

Abruptly, Yonden sat down on the bed. He looked stunned. 'He says that I can't be trusted to guard Alan,' he said.

'That would be punishment enough.'

'He says I might help him escape again, so he's ordered me to come to Tibet.' Yonden turned to Melville, wide-eyed and fearful. 'Why are you laughing?'

'I'm not really laughing,' Melville said, wiping his eyes. 'I'm not laughing at all.'

BOOK THREE

Chapter 21

They came crashing out of the clouds, looking as if they had been created that very dawn. Curtained flanks tossing, they barged into camp, a solid mass pivoting around a single point. Behind them darting figures in red and black emerged from the overcast. They lassoed the yaks and wrestled them to the ground, jeered by the Khampas spectating from the rooftops. The yaks grunted as the herdsmen pierced their nostrils with daggers and threaded wooden rings through the holes. Before drifting back into the murk, their owners pinned red tassels to their ears and gazed on them with sorrow.

On his roof, Melville waited, wrapped in clammy cold.

Four hours later he was still waiting, watching the guerillas lash down loads with lengths of braided rope. Chorphel was supervising the departure, his *chuba* tucked into his breeches, a scarf knotted round his head corsair style. Osher was somewhere about, organising the stowage of weapons. The yaks should have arrived yesterday, but they had been delayed by the weather. Snow like beads of polystyrene packing slanted down on a breeze that couldn't dislodge the clouds. Snow and cloud merged into one less than fifty yards from the camp.

A yak that had patiently submitted to being loaded bucked off its panniers and stampeded round its corral, dragging one of its handlers who had hold of a horn. In the next pen Ngawang laughed.

'What a way to go to war,' Melville said. 'One look at this sorry crew and the general's going to wish he'd flung himself on people's justice.'

He spoke for himself, to keep the jitters at bay, not for the benefit of Gunn, who had just joined him. He had seen little of Gunn the last two days; in such cramped quarters, avoiding him hadn't been easy to arrange.

He shook snow from the folds of his *chuba*. 'I hope Linka's a better fortune-teller than he is a weather-forecaster.'

The night before, he had sat in on a scapulimancy session. A ram's shoulder-blade had been baked in embers until its surface crazed in a kind of proto-Chinese calligraphy that spelled out, according to Linka, a successful mission and a safe homecoming.

329

'What did he predict?' Gunn asked.

'Fair winds and clear skies all the way,' Melville said, watching Yeshe feed a coil of blood sausage into a sack.

'About the outcome, I meant.'

'A few gems of fortune-cookie wisdom. Right thought and right action will see us through. Burn a dozen lamps to Buddha to be on the safe side. After the build-up you gave him, I have to say I'm disappointed.'

'I expect he tells people what they want to hear.'

'Well, he certainly set my mind at ease. My future's looking A-OK, rosy as far as the eye can see.'

Linka had calculated his horoscope, shuffling a crystal of quartz over a cloth chart painted with a tortoise and cryptic combinations of broken and unbroken lines that represented the various regions of the Tibetan universe.

'He had it all worked out. I'm going to live till I'm ninety, have three wives and a tribe of kids, and when I die I show up again as a tax collector. Thing is, I think he might have got my date of birth wrong. He calculated I was born in the year of the Iron Sheep, but I checked and I reckon I'm Water Ape. It makes all the difference.'

'I seem to remember that Tibetans date birth from conception.'

'How the hell can they do that?'

'Or else from the first birthday. I'm not sure.'

'That makes it worse. That makes me Water Bird or something.'

'Did he give you that?'

'Oh, yeah,' Melville said, looking at the charm packet he'd been fiddling with. 'Cast-iron protection against everything from dog bites to massed air attack.' He tucked the amulet into his collar. 'Can't be too careful.'

Osher walked down the lane below, stopping at each corral, consulting his watch like a time-and-motion man. Melville checked his own watch for the tenth time in an hour. He groaned as Osher ordered a tightening of the cinches on a yak carrying one of the 3-inch mortars. The day after the drop, he had familiarised four teams in their ballistic eccentricities. A waste of ammunition, in Melville's opinion, since the sky was closed right down, making it impossible to sight on a target, let alone observe where the shells landed. Each time he heard the *twang* of a shell leaving the tube, he had cowered into his *chuba* until the whistle of its descent terminated in a harmless thud somewhere on the far side of the gorge.

He looked at his watch again. 'The boss might as well stand us down. Dawn, he said, and it's gone ten already. He can kiss goodbye to the idea of reaching the pass tonight.'

'He'll be wanting to get as far as he can.'

'I have one consolation,' Melville said, slipping Gunn a look of cold dislike. 'At least I'll be spared your unerring instinct for the banal.'

'Below the pass there's an icefall. If I were him, I'd want to tackle it first thing, while the horses are . . .'

'But you're not him,' Melville snapped, 'and I can do without armchair strategy from someone whose sole contribution has been . . .' Melville's voice trailed away. He wiped his mouth with the back of his hand.

'Would you prefer to be left on your own?'

'Thanks to you, that's exactly where I am.'

'You know what I mean.'

'Suit yourself,' Melville told him. He gave a shuddering yawn.

'Russians used to spend a few minutes in silence before setting out on a journey.'

'It's my fucking journey and I'll spend my last hour how I want.'

'Sorry.'

Melville began to whistle Dixie through his teeth. Soon he stopped. He waited, isolated in his foreboding, while the snow went on falling and his hands and feet turned numb. In the pens the final loads were secured. The yaks bore their burdens phlegmatically, crazy highlights in their eyes. Idly Melville noted how shiny their coats were, how well-groomed they kept themselves, not a hair in their plumed tails out of place. They looked like soft toys except for the vicious horns.

Someone came up on the roof and stood behind him. He put his mitted hand to his mouth and bit the ball of his thumb hard enough to bruise. Time. It always caught you unprepared.

'Horses are ready,' Yonden said in a subdued voice. 'Sah, it's better for you to wear mountain jacket. *Chuba* is awkward for you.'

'I listened to your advice once before,' Melville said brightly, straightening his shoulders, 'and look where it's gotten me. Everything was going to be simple in the mountains.' He turned his head. 'Well lookee here, the complete guerilla.'

Yonden was outfitted for war. Over his quilted jacket he wore webbing harness hung with ammunition pouches. He was insulated from the weather by a leather and fur helmet, climbing boots and gaiters. A pair of snow goggles dangled over a military scarf.

'I'll show you your horse,' he said to Gunn, ending a short, awkward interval.

'Riding along with us a ways?'

'I'll just check that the medicines have been properly packed,' Gunn said, clambering to his feet.

Slowly Melville's stare travelled up, taking in the heavy boots and pants, the mitts and duvet jacket. Dreadful confirmation of Gunn's intentions was provided by his gormless smile.

'Oh no you're fucking not.'

'Everything's settled. I spoke to Osher while you were with Linka.'

'Tell him you've changed your mind. Tell him you're sick.'

'You know I can't stay behind after what I've done.'

'The Chinese will crucify you. They'll nail you to a pallet and carry you through Peking with the TV cameras running.'

'It's the same for you.'

'The difference is that I'm being dragged along against my will.'

'You'll be glad to have me near if you break a leg.'

'Speak to him,' Melville begged Yonden. 'Can't you see he's raving. He doesn't know what he's doing.'

'I'll wait with the horses,' Yonden said, making his escape.

'Everything's going to be alright,' Gunn said.

'Alright?' Melville cried, dashing tears from his eyes. 'It's a crock of shit. It's positively gruesome.' He uttered a savage laugh. 'This has got to be the ultimate fucking guilt trip. Twenty years on you're replaying the same scene that got you four years' thought reform. I'm telling you, those Chinese couldn't have been trying.'

'I don't care what you say. I'm going.'

'Listen to him,' Melville jeered, inviting the gods to bear witness. 'He'd rather go up against the PLA than face bye-byes.'

'I'd rather die than spend another night here.'

The words lodged in Melville's skull and rang like a curse. 'Stay away from me,' he panted, his voice clotted with fear and disgust. 'Leave me out of it. I've got all the bad luck I can handle without getting messed up in your regressive hang-ups.'

He stormed down into the alley and grabbed the reins of a small, untidy pony from Yonden. 'What do you call this – a fucking Newfoundland?'

He mounted up and waited. Gunn came down and got on a horse behind him. The snow continued to fall – not heavily, but with a monotonous intensity that made Melville rub his eyes every minute or so. His anger was not pure enough to resist it. Now that it was happening, it seemed to him that all events had led him inexorably to this moment, and though he could not yet make complete sense of the pattern that had emerged behind him, he knew in his heart that Gunn wasn't the only agent of fortune that had fucked him up so comprehensively.

Osher strolled down the line, his cloak of parachute silk whipping in the wind. He inspected Melville with a slight frown, as though he had criticisms to make but didn't know where to begin. He moved on to the next man.

'It's your *chuba*,' Gunn said. 'Yonden's right. At eighteen thousand feet it will weigh like a suit of armour. Fall through a frozen river and it will drag you under.'

'Can it,' Melville told him without force.

'As you wish, but I'm warning you – the margins of survival out there are closer than you imagine.'

'In that case, let's make like the Russians and say our prayers.'

Osher swung himself into the saddle. After a last glance behind, he pulled his horse round and ambled off to the north. The others took up his pace. Melville's horse twitched into slow motion, nearly throwing him over its tail. With staccato cries the yak handlers goaded their beasts into life. On the rooftops the remaining Khampas called farewell. Linka was among them, his hands knitting an invisible web over the passing men.

Cloud closed round Melville and there was only the hiss of snow sliding past, covering tracks.

Down in the gorge, with the wind rifling between the walls, Melville fought for control of his crazy, shit-headed horse. Its strength and will had grown enormously since first acquaintance. A half-hearted attempt to make it face the right direction made it break away and go careering down the track, striking sparks from boulders glazed with ice. Heart in mouth Melville watched it skid on a corner over a drop, somehow get round and stampede all the way to the bottom. When he caught up, it plunged into dead ground booby-trapped with holes that threatened to snap its legs like bread-sticks. He stalked it, cursing it in a soothing voice, and it bolted again, galloping with trailing reins until it reached a bridge. Here it balked. Melville took in the rickety scaffolding, the black lacquer pool below, and decided he was not up to the situation. He smacked the horse's rump, trying to drive it across, but it reared round and brushed him aside. When he picked himself up he saw it wall-eyed and sweating on a ledge forty feet above the river.

Yaks began wandering past, chewing reflectively. Their handlers viewed the problem with curiosity. Gunn and Yonden had stopped, but chose not to intervene.

Melville, one shoulder wrenched, his *chuba* unbelted and flapping about his ankles, sat down. 'That's it,' he declared. 'Tell Osher it's me or the horse.'

Without a word, Yonden recovered the pony, tied it to his own, and led the way over the bridge.

There were chemical springs in the gorge that belched gusts of sulphur and acetylene. The river ground its teeth and the walls leaned in. Melville experienced a tangible easing of weight as the path began to climb. Above the gorge conditions were worse, the wind driving a ground blizzard that met him face-on. He stumbled on Gunn, almost unrecognisable in an arctic moustache and Santa Claus eyebrows.

'It could keep up for days,' Gunn shouted, gulping as the wind forced the breath back down his throat. 'Stay close to Yonden.'

By two in the afternoon they had only got as far as the village, its proximity signalled by a child in rags with derelict eyes who sat clutching a goat in the lee of a shrine. Not much later, at some incalculable place, Melville found himself alone. He peered into the blurred whiteness, then looked back the way he had come, though he knew that even the lumbering yaks had overtaken him. The snow flowed over his boots, drifting fast enough to wipe out prints in the interval between one man's passing and the next. Nobody would miss him if he turned back. The village couldn't be more than a mile away. He dismissed the possibility of taking refuge there even before it formed.

He refused to be alarmed. He was on the track – well, fairly sure he was. Gunn couldn't be far ahead. He called and heard a cry. He broke into a clumsy trot and soon saw a fleeting shape. No matter how hard he tried to catch up, it stayed the same distance ahead, and eventually he realised he was pursuing a phantom. Immediately after that disappointment, he became aware that the wind, which had been blowing from due north, seemed to have shifted to the western quarter. Also, the path had taken a steep turn downhill. Maybe it wasn't the path after all. He must have strayed, taking the line of least resistance. He retraced his steps until they petered out.

Work it out, he told himself, quelling the first prickings of panic. But the snow cancelled out all bearings; every direction was the same, each prospect as confused as television static. He was losing time and the wind was against him. Soon he would be completely out of touch. Without considering his moves, he struck out directly upwards and found the way barred by tiers of rock. He tried in another direction, only to flounder to a halt in a drift. Backing out, he forced himself to push straight into the swirling whiteness, cursing himself for not having done so earlier. Soon, though, it blinded him and he had to shield his face from it.

'Help!' he called. He had never had recourse to the word before, and his first attempts sounded ridiculous. His last efforts merely sounded puny.

Several times he thought he saw figures approaching, but they were apparitions that altered shape as they danced past. Miserably he sank to his haunches and hugged himself. Occasionally he raised a hand, making the slow insect movement of a man clearing a misted windshield. After performing this gesture a few times, he saw that a shadow had materialised against the white-out.

'Yonden, is that you?' he said, the cold making him slur his words.

'Alan sent me,' Yonden said, sounding as though he would not have bothered had it been left to him.

'Where am I?'

'Lost,' Yonden said. 'Freezing on a mountain.' He turned away.

'God, am I glad to see you,' Melville called, struggling after. 'Wait. Not so fast. I can't see a thing. Where's that goddam path? I thought it was up.'

Yonden hurried on without answering. He had gone a very little way – perhaps no more than a hundred yards from where he had come upon Melville – when he halted by two tethered horses. There was no indication that they were on a path.

'You take good care from now,' Yonden said. 'Next time I might not find you.'

It sounded like a threat.

For the rest of the stage Melville walked with a hand fastened on to his horse's tail, his view confined to its clenching anus. The wind settled to a quiet roar that nullified thought, whittling down the brain to its primitive cortex. He hung on and he walked, mechanically lifting each leg in turn and setting it down again. Each step was the same as the last, obliterated by the next. Moving with the blind precision of a somnambulist, he made a faultless traverse of a giddy cliff path, balanced on an ice-sheeted diagonal drawn a thousand feet above the river.

He lost balance when his horse broke step, straining to get ahead. Apathetically he raised his head and slowly focused on other horses and men. They were gathered beneath an overhang beside a couple

335

of broken-down animal pens. Down-slope the snow flakes seethed over a small tarn swept clear by the wind and whorled by successive advances of ice. The Khampas, plastered white, were disposing the loads for the night. Osher was in the thick of it, his cloak ballooning about him as he dragged a heavy machine gun off a yak.

Mustering what strength remained to him, Melville tottered into camp. He had reached that geographical abstraction, the middle of nowhere. It was a little after five in the afternoon.

'We're still well short of the ice-fall,' Gunn yelled, grappling with a bundle of firewood. 'Here,' he said, kicking a sooty pot, 'fill it with snow.'

He seemed elated.

Two tents of a sort were rigged up by tying tarpaulins over one of the enclosures. Loads were stacked at the entrance to form a wind-break, and Yeshe, the company cook, lit a fire in a brazier. The last of the light was squeezed out of the clouds. The wind blew without remission.

Crammed like a beast in a stockyard, Melville swallowed his sudsy tea at a gulp. He wolfed his portion of rancid sausage and dry *tsampa*, his eyes darting as he chewed, and used the grease to salve his skin. Already he was a creature of gut responses, living close to the bone.

After eating he lay next to Gunn in the pungent crush.

'We'll be on our way before light,' Gunn told him. 'Hard day tomorrow. Seven hours to the pass, five down.'

'I don't like the sound of that ice-fall.'

'They lost a couple of men in it last winter, but that was in a blizzard.'

'What do you call this?'

'Och, just a wee bit of a blow.'

'Come wind and weather, huh?'

Someone was already snoring. A Khampa started a wistful song but stopped when no one took it up. The hum of a mantra under-scored the wailing wind. Men swore at Ngawang as he used their bodies as stepping stones on his way to relieve himself. Melville needed a piss, too. He stayed put. Nothing could induce him to face the storm again. The cold soaked up from the ground and he shifted from side to side. He had forgotten what it was like to be warm.

Sleep was a veil passed tantalisingly before his eyes and then whipped away on a rising note of the wind. It wouldn't settle at a constant pitch, but cycled up and down eerie chromatic scales. A corner of the tarpaulin broke loose and thrashed about. Someone got up and fixed it, but a few minutes later it tore free again, and this time nobody could be bothered. Snow poured through breaches in the walls, drifting against the men on the outside and insinuating itself into sleeping bags. Some of the Khampas gave up the attempt to sleep and squatted round the remains of the fire, feeding it scraps of wood as though it were a dog and holding out their hands for a lick.

'What are you thinking about?' Gunn murmured.

'I was thinking about all the nice people back home – guys putting on clean shirts for their dates, having a last martini before dinner, saying goodnight to their kids.'

'I wonder what General Liu is thinking.'

Melville put his mind to it. 'He's never really existed for me, you know.'

'But he's the only reason you're here.'

'Reason?' Melville said, as though he found it a novel concept. 'He's part of it, I guess – necessary but not sufficient.'

'For his sake, pray that the storm blows itself out.'

'The noise it's making, who's listening?'

'Are you hoping we'll be forced to turn back?'

'Depends.'

The wind slammed against the shelter, drawing a collective twitch from its occupants.

'Depends on what?'

'Alan, do you think Osher set me up?'

'Is that why you weren't angry the night we tried to get away.'

'I was angry. I was too drunk to express it.'

'You were angry this morning.'

'Fucking furious. It scares the shit out of me when you talk as though we're on a one-way ticket.'

'Are you angry now?'

Melville sniggered. 'We sound like a couple of faggots.' He listened to the buffeting wind for a while. 'I keep turning it over in my mind, and it always falls the same way. The five hundred bucks he paid to Yonden, the business with the funeral, letting us go through with that pathetic escape attempt. It was the excuse he needed. He fixed it so that bringing me along would seem like a reasonable thing to do, but he wouldn't have burdened himself with baggage unless he had a use for it. You saw my antics with that fucking horse. I nearly got lost today – five hours out and I nearly lost myself. He must have something in mind for me.'

337

'Why not me?'

'Yonden, for one thing. For another, you're not American. He has a chip on his shoulder about us. He's always sniping at our military prowess. God knows, we're not covering ourselves with glory these days, but to hear Osher tell it, America at war is Sergeant Bilko. At the same time, I can't help feeling he's looking for our approval.'

'He certainly gets it from you. Your admiration for him is obvious.'

'The French thought a lot of Napoleon, and look where it got them. Anyone who believes he has an appointment with history should be worshipped from afar – preferably from the other side of the grave.'

'He's only a guerilla leader, Walter. He's not marching on Moscow.'

'This is his last ride,' Melville said, speaking slowly. 'Next spring Jetha and the Gurkhas will pull the plug on him. The Indians want him for murder and he can't go back into Mustang. What else is there?'

'Another valley. There are bands of Khampas scattered all along the border.'

'Petty thieves and rustlers. Robbing the peasantry isn't Osher's style. He's the only man I've met who isn't frightened of turning his dreams into reality.'

'Honestly, you romanticise him too much,' Gunn said. 'Meeting the general and getting safely back across the border are all he dreams about.'

'Picture it,' Melville said. 'An American China-specialist, known associate of a KMT warlord, penetrating a hundred miles into Chinese territory in the company of a gang of counter-revolutionary terrorists and a convicted imperialist spy.'

'I wish you wouldn't speak like that,' Gunn said.

'Reality time,' Melville told him. 'You've been so lost in delusions, you've forgotten who the real enemies are.'

'How will the Chinese react?'

'I'll tell you one thing. Wars have been started for less.'

'They'd need proof of our involvement.'

'A body ought to do it.'

'Oh, man,' Gunn said, shocked.

'Preferably alive and talking.'

'Oh, man,' Gunn said again. 'He wouldn't. I know he wouldn't.'

'I think,' Melville said, enunciating with care, 'that he's planning to use me as the signature on the operation.'

Outside, the wind scaled new heights.

'In Tibet,' Gunn said after a while, 'there are tantric masters who can chant on three chords simultaneously.'

'Did you ever hear them?'

'No.'

'Well then.'

'Walter,' Gunn said.

'I'm still here.'

'Your Nationalist friend . . . Mr Sweetwater.'

'I was hoping you were going to say something reassuring.'

'Without you, they won't get the general.'

'They don't need me. Osher can clip me or dump me and they wouldn't be any the wiser. He can deliver Liu himself and tell them I fell off a cliff. I don't have a contribution to make, Alan. I am, as they say, expendable.'

'That's quite enough. You're getting worked up over nothing.'

Melville affected a laugh. 'Everyone to his own fears,' he said, and then stayed quiet, listening to the wind play on his nerves.

He lay in the dark, torpid as a lizard, waiting for the remnants of his brain to reinstate themselves. Cigarettes glowed and men grumbled. A flashlight played across his face. He checked the luminous dial of his watch, tapped it and held it to his ear. The evidence was irrefutable. It was shortly after two in the morning and the wind had gone away.

All around the Khampas were waking to the same bad dream. They hawked phlegm and blew their noses in their hands. Someone passed him a can of tea. He felt for his boots and eventually found them, frozen hard and filled with snow. Low ebb, he told himself, rock bottom. He lay without moving until everyone else was up, then levered on his boots and went out on a spasm of shivering.

His torch glared back from slowly drifting mist. The snow was crimped by the wind and frozen hard. Men were squatting in it, but some vestigial observance of nicety made Melville take himself off behind the pen. With useless fingers he undid his *chuba* and waited for the message to get through to his strained bladder. When it finally did, the snow buckled and heaved before him. A yak levered itself to its feet, cracking open a white shell. It regarded him placidly, ruminating on an ice cube.

Soon after four the yaks moved out, nostrils blowing steam. Today they would be breaking trail. An hour later the men and horses followed. By seven they were in the ice-fall.

For Melville the passage between the seracs and crevasses happened with the inexorable slowness of nightmare. Cloud chasms breathed stagnant vapours and green walls with the gleam of winter entombed in them slid down into a black nether world. Freakish shapes loomed down tunnels and floated past in windows of mist. From above came a crash like heavy furniture toppling over in an attic. The Khampas trudged upwards at the solemn, processional pace of mourners following a catafalque.

On the other side they came to virgin snow ploughed by the yaks. As they climbed, slabs of the crust slithered away, cracking and humming as they disappeared into the slaty clouds. Melville was unable to rid his head of a fatuous tune. *When the red, red robin goes bob, bob bobbin' along – along. When the red, red robin goes bob, bob bobbin' . . .*

Cries from overhead – an accident, someone slipping back.

But it wasn't. It was the shouting of men breaking out, paying tribute to the pale band of daybreak across an ocean of white billows and spectral bergs. Far away and below spread the dark stain of the lowlands.

Turning from this remote vision, Melville saw the yaks curving up to a notch in the skyline, strung out like beads on a necklace.

With gratitude, he accepted a plastic mug from Yeshe. At this altitude, in this cold, the clear liquid it contained could only be alcohol. He took a swig and his eyes widened with shock. The Khampas exchanged shrugs as he sprayed the liquid out. Yeshe reclaimed the mug and finished off the cooking oil at a gulp. He thumped his chest.

'Give me another minute,' Melville pleaded as the caravan got under way.

'In a couple of hours the snow will be like porridge,' Gunn told him. 'Where are your goggles?'

'Shit – I forgot. They're in my pack.'

'Bloody idiot.'

He made a vain effort to outclimb the sun. Behind him the peaks and clouds flooded with light; stray rays flashed through gaps in a ridge to the east. But the sun was gathering its strength unseen, setting up reverberations that suddenly splintered the skyline into a thousand pieces. No matter where he looked, the glare struck him with jagged strokes. A wind sprang up and made the snow seethe, raising frail columns of spindrift that clawed him in passing. The crust softened and gave way in unpredictable places. Bogged down, he wrenched one foot out of the slush and fell, sliding helplessly for a

340

hundred feet. He lay spread-eagle on the snow and watched high clouds sail through the indigo.

'I'm done for,' he told the black crabbed shape bending out of the sky.

'Now will you get rid of that ridiculous *chuba*?' Gunn said, hauling him upright.

Up on the trail again, Yonden offered him goggles and down jacket. He refused the jacket.

Heart thumping in his ears, chest squeaking, he made it to the ridge. It proved false. Beyond it lay a shallow col, almost snowless, with the vitrified surface of a dead star. It was after midday when he came up to the yaks, bunched in a glossy mass and motionless as only yaks can be. The guerillas were sprawled like victims of a gas attack at the base of a cairn crowned by the skull of a wild yak with a blue swastika picked out between its immense spread of horns. Melville collapsed among the Khampas and dozed, one side freezing, the other baking.

When he woke, his head felt like a bloody membrane. The light abraded his eyes. Yeshe was crouched in front of him, holding out the same mug. He turned his face away, although his mouth was dry as a grate.

'Good,' Yeshe said, smacking his lips.

'What is it?' Melville said, eyeing the drink with suspicion. It was inky black and steaming slightly. 'It's not blood, is it?' The day before he had seen one of the Khampas tapping a vein in a yak's neck.

'Coffee.'

He took a cautious sip and stiffened. Scooping up a handful of snow, he tried to scour away the taste of iodine.

'They use one tin to a pint of water,' Gunn said. 'It keeps them going. God knows what it does to their hearts. I've got some Benzedrine if you need it. It'll be night before we stop again.'

'I'd say I'm high enough.'

'That's the spirit,' Gunn said. 'Ready for your first look at Tibet?'

At the second attempt, Melville made it to his feet, moving as though he was manoeuvring in a confined space. He followed Gunn across the border and stopped at a corniced edge.

In the dustless air the land was without depth or bounds. An endless series of ridges – brown and copper, pink and yellow, capped with baby blue – floated on mauve shadows. Melville knuckled his eyes. He had never been exposed to such clarity before, yet the very sharpness of definition made it unreal – a reflection in still water. The stillness. Although there was no wind on this side of the pass, even a Khampa's harsh laugh or the pawing of a horse failed to dent the silence, vanishing into it as if it were another dimension.

'The heart of the world,' Melville murmured.

'What was that?'

'Nothing – it looks like broken biscuits.'

'Look how clear it is. Nothing hidden.'

'What is there to hide?'

Gunn nodded slowly. 'The first European to cross Tibet from north to south turned right round when he reached India and went back. He was sure he'd missed something. He was worried that someone else would find it before him.'

'Find what?'

'He never said.'

'It must have existed only in his mind. Look at it. It's so *old*.'

'Actually, it's relatively young.'

'Dead bones,' Melville said. 'Extinct.'

Osher was leading the men out. He halted at the cornice, conning the way ahead, then swung his arm to embrace everything as far as the eye could see. 'My country,' he said, and kicked his horse forward through the scalloped edge. Behind him the snow flew away in crystals.

A horse fell off a ledge onto a glassy slope. Landing on all fours it hurtled down in an uncontrolled gallop, hit a rock and cartwheeled, spilling its load as it turned end over end and crashed into boulders at the bottom of the gulley.

Arriving a few minutes later, Melville was impressed by the peculiar horror of the scene – the petroleum sheen of ice under a wasted moon, the Khampas bending over the scattered load like battlefield scavengers, the smashed horse struggling to raise its head.

'Isn't anyone going to put the brute out of its agony?' Melville demanded, as the guerillas started back up the slope.

'Its back is broken,' Gunn told him. 'It won't feel any pain.'

'They're not going to let it freeze to death,' Melville said, as the guerillas began apportioning the load.

'They're Buddhist,' Gunn said.

Melville gave an exorbitant laugh. 'They'll shoot their own men rather than let them fall into PLA hands, and they won't kill a poor fucking *horse*?' He spun round and Yonden backed away from him. 'Give me your gun.'

'Leave it, man,' Gunn pleaded. 'A shot might be heard.'

Melville's bay of laughter had the quality of derangement. He reeled across the path, his arms spread wide. 'Ho,' he called. 'Anyone out there? Anyone listening?' He cupped a hand to his ear and waited. The bluffs and ice flows absorbed his cries without a ripple. 'You see?' he said quietly. 'Give me your gun.'

Instead of unslinging his rifle, Yonden dug into his pack and produced a clumsy-looking revolver. 'Right,' Melville said to himself, biting his lip and nodding. 'Right.'

He slid and scrambled down to the horse. 'Good horse,' he said, his heart racing. Gunn and Yonden were watching from the track. Where did you start when it came to killing a horse? The eye, for certain, but he could not bring himself to blow out that lustre. He aimed at a spot halfway between eye and ear. He was shaking so much that he had to use both hands to keep the muzzle on the mark. He jerked the trigger. The safety was on. The horse was watching him. He fired with his eyes shut, then fired again. A tremor passed down the beast's neck; slowly its lips curled back from its teeth.

When he regained the trail, Gunn was gone. He held out the pistol to Yonden, then withdrew it and stood staring at it.

'How much do you want for it?'

'Ah, no.'

'For personal use. I can't let myself be taken by the Chinese.'

Yonden fretted his lip.

'Fifty dollars,' Melville said. 'How can you refuse?'

Yonden examined the empty trail in both directions. He nodded.

Alone on the path, Melville examined the revolver. Yonden had done well out of the deal. It was a vintage piece – a .38 British army-issue Webley with three bullets in the chamber, their cases green with verdigris. Melville spun the chamber and held the barrel to his head. One for me, he told himself; two for contingencies.

Like figures on a Chinese screen where perspective is indicated only in terms of height, they straggled by random ways and frozen rivers over the trans-Himalayan range. There were fewer of them now. The yaks had been left with their handlers in a cave on a valley bottom below the pass, and where the mountains ran down towards the broad spaces of the Tibetan plateau, another two men fell out to warn of any patrol that might try to cut off their retreat from the east, where a military road came down to the border.

They threaded a badlands' maze and followed a fossil river across

343

stony barrens dotted with tumuli. It was an inert, mineral world, the sun suspended in the monochrome sky like a tiny orange kite. Day and night they froze, scourged by flurries of dust and snow that forced them to ride hooded and lop-sided in the saddle. One man wore jaunty ski goggles under a bearskin helmet. Osher wore aviator glasses that reflected fish-eye images of his company when he rose and turned in his stirrups to check that they were still with him. Melville no longer brought up the rear. That position was taken by a snowblind Khampa who peered out from a slit in a filthy bandage.

Melville was pulverised by so much emptiness, flattened by the weight of the sky. The insides of his thighs were rubbed raw, his lips black and blistered. He suffered from violent stomach cramps and constant back pains. At the end of each stage he had to be lifted from his horse. There were times when he desired nothing more than to be left to die. He could envisage no end to this journey. He was a *rolang*, the Tibetan standing corpse condemned to wander the plateau world without end.

And there were times, when the company advanced like the leading edge of a wing, when he was exhilarated beyond reason. Looking down the curving line he saw himself as one of Tamurlaine's irregulars, a grey dog-wolf bent on plunder, scalps tied to his belt, stinking of gang rape.

Day by day the black and white contours of the ranges they had crossed slipped lower beneath the horizon. On the fifth day out, creeping shrubs appeared, hung with icicles that tinkled like cut glass as the riders pushed their way through. They came upon bones and met their first ravens since leaving base. A pair of burnished eagles took off from the skeleton of a wild ass and flew escort for an hour, trailing their hunger across the sky. Two silver darts inched along under the stratosphere – Chinese fighter jocks going home to breakfast after a border patrol.

Crumpled in the saddle, Melville breasted a low ridge to find the guerillas bunched and uneasy, staring across a massive gorge to a pasture dotted with small but important shapes. He rubbed his eyes and kneaded cheeks stiffened by wind and sun. Yaks and sheep. Among them, spaced out with the regularity of formal arrangement, he saw the bat's-wing profiles of nomad tents.

A group of mounted men followed by baying mastiffs were wheeling towards the far side of the gorge. Reluctantly, Osher detailed a party of Khampas led by Chorphel to parley with them.

They reined in a furlong apart as the raven flies and bawled greetings. One of the nomads discharged a rifle.

Yonden translated the exchange.

'What kind of men are you?' the nomad spokesman called.

'Pilgrims – returning to our homes in the Chang-Thang.'

'Ah. *You* sound like an honest man of the north, but your friends look like Easterners.'

'Kham isn't the only province that raises tall sons.'

'Ah. You're right. Look at my own untamed sons here. And what do you think of our dogs? Have you ever seen bigger-boned mastiffs? They love Khampas. One sniff of a man from the East and they'd pull down a horse to get at him.' The nomad hurled a stone at one of the dogs. 'Come away from the edge there. Those aren't Khampas.'

'We don't need dogs for protection.'

'Ah. So I see. Pilgrims with guns. Where are you coming from?'

'Kyrong.'

'Ah. Where are you going to?'

'Lunggar.'

'Ah. You must be lost. The path you want is three days to the east.'

'We're frightened of Khampas too. Have you seen any?'

'Not since last winter.'

'What about Han soldiers?'

'They come and go.'

'When was the last time they came this way?'

'After the harvest.'

'Then we can go on our way with light hearts.'

'We'd ask you to share our hearth, but to get from where you stand to where I stand takes two days.'

'Maybe another time. Oh, a favour from you, father. We're travelling without permits. Better if the Chinese aren't told.'

'Such dedicated pilgrims. Buddha and all the good spirits protect you.'

'And you.'

'Go slowly.'

'Go slowly.'

The two parties disengaged. 'Will they report us?' Melville asked as they rode away.

'*Drokpa* don't like Chinese,' Yonden told him. 'They take their animals and don't pay for them.'

'That's alright then.'

'Khampas steal their animals too,' Yonden said. 'But they get money from the Chinese for telling them they've seen us.'

'Ah.'

The wind died early and for the rest of the stage Melville felt naked, exposed to a sky that he imagined bristling with radio traffic. So he was alarmed when Osher halted his force in daylight, and on open ground commanded by two ridges. While the guerillas unloaded, Melville was sent to gather thorn scrub for the fire. It burnt with a short-lived crimson flame and clouds of oily black smoke that rose high into the still air.

Taking his cue from the others, Melville gave the appearance of relaxing against his saddle. As he conducted his daily body-count of vermin, he studied his companions.

Yeshe, talking to himself as he cooked, had the uncertain temperament of many great chefs but none of the artistry. His distinction in that field was his ability to produce tea and *tsampa* on a few chips of dry dung in a full gale. His ambition was to open a guest house and restaurant in Pokhara. He liked to play the simpleton, yet under that heavy fringe was a shrewd entrepreneurial mind.

In another world Ngawang would have been a corporal, busted from sergeant, in a para-military police force feared for its energetic and unrefined interrogation techniques. He was the company bully, incapable of greeting a friend without twisting his wrist or cuffing the back of his head. In his relaxed moments, he cheated at cards or sank into melancholy. The grievous things the Chinese had done to his family were alluded to but never described.

They weren't all Khampas. Besides Chorphel, there were two Goloks from Amdo, Tibet's north-eastern province. They were the company scouts and looked like survivors of a medieval barbarian irruption, with shaven pates, long plaited pigtails and ivory wristbands. Their boots were stitched from felt dyed in primary reds and greens, with prow-shaped toes. They came and went like cats and always sat a little apart from the others. Osher and Chorphel were the only guerillas they spoke to.

Tsering was not, as Melville had supposed, Osher's Marxist-Leninist soulmate. He was a former seminarian from Lhasa who still studied sacred texts morning and night, re-reading some passages as if to extract every last bit of merit from them, rocking and groaning with a depth of fervour that struck Melville as more Islamic than Buddhist. He was held in awe for having slit the throats of a PLA patrol he had captured single-handed. Of all the guerillas, Melville liked him least and feared him most.

Chorphel he admired in the sentimental way one admires the last representative of a fierce, dying tribe. He was sixty-three and not a guerilla through any ideological conviction. Eight years earlier, driving a flock of sheep packed with salt from the pans and flats of his native Chang-Thang, he had run into a PLA unit near the Nepalese border. They had confiscated sheep and salt, claiming he was a capitalist bloodsucker, so when they let him go, clutching the scrap of paper they had given him as a receipt, he went back to where he had hidden the old Mauser he still carried, shot two of the soldiers from ambush, then walked on into Nepal with his two sons and a daughter. They had died of measles in the lowlands. After that he had joined the National Volunteer Liberation Army in Mustang. His age was against him, but his marksmanship was exceptional and he knew every salt trail and caravan route between Everest and Ladakh. His wife still waited for him at home, provided for by her other husband, his brother; polyandrous marriage was a natural solution to the problems of coping in a society where men traditionally spent up to six months of the year away on trading journeys. One night, Chorphel had shown Melville a letter he had received from his wife two or three years before. It was a short note, only a few lines expressing the hope that he would return soon and bring with him plenty of matches, which were in short supply since the Chinese had curtailed travel. In the spring, Chorphel had said, he would go home.

Briefly Melville surveyed the rest of the force. Their faces were drawn with fatigue, their eyes even at rest narrowed as if they were contending with pain. Many, in fact, were not well; Gunn was kept busy at each halt dispensing pills for internal disorders, severe headaches, a whole range of psychosomatic ailments. Bad diet, poor hygiene, shot nerves. God knows why they'd volunteered. Not for the money, and not for the winning of spoils or glory. They still believed their task was to impress their sponsors by blowing up a convoy or taking out a patrol. They were from different backgrounds and mutually antagonistic regions, and though they talked of fighting for the cause of nationalism, they admitted it wasn't there for the winning. The rank and file worshipped the Dalai Lama, but they obeyed the Buddhist precepts imperfectly and had all taken life at least once. They had no future. Outlaws then, in no one's service but their own. The conclusion left Melville open to fear. Misfits they may be, but at least they had their own fellowship, while he was alone, a long way from home and no hope of finding his way back.

Automatically his eye went to Osher, who was speaking quietly to the Goloks. That was what kept the guerillas together. Without his leadership, the men would have given themselves up to the Nepalese. Without his figure going before them, their momentum would dissipate within a few yards. Surely a man who inspired such loyalty was incapable of injuring anyone who rode at his side. Holding this thought to him, Melville slept.

He started up at the sound of violent crackling. Sparks flew up from a bonfire; he thought he saw coppery faces stealing back into the dark. 'Don't leave me,' he managed to cry, before a hand clamped over his mouth.

'No noise,' Yonden's voice said. 'Some peoples might be watching us.'

Still dopey with sleep, he got up and followed Yonden, skirting the firelight. The Khampas were leading their horses out. Half a mile from the camp they mounted and rode silently away. Draped across his horse's neck, Melville found he had slept for less than two hours. He looked back and saw the fire still burning – a dragon's eye in the cave of night.

They rode until dawn, when they halted by a ruined monastery that overlooked a great downwarp with silvery threads running along its base and the patchy imprint of cultivation on the faraway slope. They lay up until after sunset, sleeping and worrying about crossing the valley.

That night Melville had a dream that he crossed a road – Tsering standing in the middle of an unmade highway, hissing at him to make speed and holding out his arms as though he expected an unlit truck to come thundering down on them. Later he dreamt he stood at the edge of a pale jade river with rafts of ice grating between shingle banks. It took gasping contact with the water to persuade him it was real. On the other side they climbed again, not stopping until they had put a new horizon between themselves and the lights of a few scattered homesteads.

The sun was pouring itself back into a crack in the earth as they set out on the next stage. In four days' time the general was due to leave his garrison. The men's voices died with the light; the muffled chinking of harness and the shuffling of hooves was soporific. There was no moon, but the stars pulsed energetically, tiring the eye with shadows. As he picked his way on foot across a boulderfield, Melville heard a subdued cry of pain behind him. It was the snow-blind victim; his horse had kicked him as he hung asleep on its tail. Gunn diagnosed a broken kneecap, and Chorphel ordered him to go back and wait until they rejoined him at the river. Melville wasn't sorry to see him go. He was unlucky, and bad luck was contagious.

It was a short stage that seemed to end nowhere in particular. So far as Melville could tell, they were at the edge of an escarpment, the view down the other side hidden by an abrupt steepening of the crest. A new range of mountains lay pale and quiet to the north. Another block of high land stood off to the east. Too tired to investigate, Melville swilled the dust from his mouth, found a space between boulders and laid himself down to rest.

He came awake to find Yonden crouched down in front of him. It was still dark. The stars looked like chips of chrome. There was no sign of the other men and horses.

'Where is everyone?' Melville asked. He was strangely calm.

Yonden jerked his chin at the ridge.

'How much further?'

'We're there now,' Yonden said.

He, too, seemed quiet and resigned, and Melville had an urge to make his peace with him, to tell him that he harboured no hard feelings. But before he could speak, the Khampa was moving away. Melville got up and scrambled after.

Under the black night, dawn was breaking in bands of acid blue and green. Along the ridge the Khampas were sharp silhouettes, their attention bent on an illuminated square in the narrowest part of a plateau rift. The facility was unmistakably military, with huts regimented inside a floodlit perimeter. Just behind it stood a *dzong* – a traditional Tibetan fortress erected on a rock boss, topped by the winking lights of radio antennae. From a pass to the east, a highway looped down like tangled string before straightening out as it approached the base. Farther west it divided, one branch meandering away down the valley, the other forking south. Melville judged the fort to be about a thousand feet below, maybe a mile distant.

'Is that it?' was all he could say.

'That's it,' Yonden said.

'General Liu is in there?' Melville asked on a high note of incredulity.

'I think so,' Yonden said. He rolled his eyes in warning towards the other guerillas.

'Hasn't Osher let them into the secret yet?'

'They think they're here to attack the fort.'

Melville glanced with some concern at the Khampas. There was something rapacious in their attitude, the hungry intensity of predators scouting a sheep-fold from the shadow of a forest.

'Boy, they're in for a shock.'

'So is the general,' Gunn said, startling Melville by his presence. 'Meeting you in Nepal is one thing, but coming to Tibet is going to seem like the height of recklessness. How will you explain that?'

'I'll have a word with Osher. I'll tell Liu we're part of the service.'

Gunn's sombre expression was unsettling. 'I asked Yonden to . . . you know . . . try and find out Osher's intentions.'

'And?' Melville said, venting his fear with a laugh.

Yonden shook his head. 'Osher is too busy thinking about the general.'

'That's right,' Melville said, his relief palpable. 'Now that I can see what he's here for, I realise he doesn't need to put on any sideshows.'

Infuriatingly, Gunn's eyes remained murky pools of doubt.

Chapter 22

At fifty-eight, his body padded by disuse and army food, General Liu Hongwen had taken to starting the day with a few simple calisthenics performed at the funereal tempo of *The East is Red*, which was transmitted by Radio Lhasa and relayed through the camp via loudspeakers.

This morning, he was halfway through his routine of knee-bends when he was convulsed by the sight of two figures sneaking along inside the perimeter. Still in a squatting position, he gripped the window-ledge, like a man whose discs have slipped. Shock melted into anger as he saw the shapes slip into the men's dormitory. His anger was directed partly at the miscreants who felt at liberty to go on copulating until reveille, but mainly at himself for imagining even for a moment that they had been Khampas.

Still gripping the ledge, he straightened up and raised his gaze to the plateau. He went on staring as the cliffs began to take on the tawdry colours that would oppress the eye until nightfall.

There was no one out there. They weren't coming.

Down in the compound the road gang was shuffling out of their quarters, but he didn't see them. There were worse postings, he told himself, trying to reconcile himself to failure. He could have been put in charge of a borax mine on the northern plateau, where the wind blew a gale one day in three, making any activity, even sleep, impossible. But he didn't feel lucky. His knuckles whitened as he contemplated the dead-end of his career, buried in the graveyard of military ambitions.

Tibet had ruined more important men than him. It gave him a crumb of solace to reflect on the fate of General Zhang Guohua, the republic's military overlord, sent scuttling back to Szechwan by rebel gangs. Small comfort. Zhang had courted the rat pack and deserved to pay the price, whereas *he* had warned what would happen if those delinquents were allowed to swarm through the countryside. But those self-serving bastards on the Central Committee weren't going to acknowledge their error or compensate him for the humiliation he had suffered. The hypocrites hadn't even given him a role in the counter-attack on the Red Guard. Too intemperate, not enough of a diplomat.

And that judgement, delivered to him by an aide of the defence minister – Lin Piao being too much of a diplomat himself to see his old comrade personally – had been the last straw.

They weren't coming.

At a cry from below he looked listlessly at the Tibetans, who were being herded into some semblance of order. His expression had no more emotion than if he had been contemplating a swarm of flies.

Some of his compatriots expressed sympathy for them, but he soon put the milksops right, telling them a story that informed his entire conception of the land and its natives.

In 1936, he and his fellow Long Marchers had struggled through the Tibetan Marches, fighting a running battle with the barbarians. It was a rare day if the man at the rear of the column reached camp that night. The men used to bet on his chances of survival – five to one against, he seemed to recall. Those Tibetans were the only people we liberated who refused to sell us food, he told his officers. The bastards drove their livestock into the mountains and burnt their fields ahead of us. Do you know what kept some of us going? Butter. Stinking butter which we licked from their devil idols in the temples.

Anyway, next time you start feeling sorry for those animals, remember this. Once, I was sent to search for an overdue foraging party. Two days later I found them. They were in a nomad tent, seated round a cold fire, still holding bowls of tea. Every one of them was dead, and not a mark on them.

There's a man who understands Tibetans, he would say, turning, just as he did now, to the portrait of Chairman Mao on his wall. The Red Army always pays its debts, our leader promised when we reached Yenan, and foremost of our debts is the one we owe to the Tibetans. That's why we're here, comrades – to repay old debts.

Last year he had been reprimanded for his views, which had been reported to his superiors by the Tibetan representatives on the Preparatory Committee for the Autonomous Region. His remarks didn't assist the process of assimilation.

Looking at Mao's portrait, he allowed himself an acid smile of reflection. Friends used to remark on the resemblance – the same moon face and square brows, the shrewd, deceptively humorous eyes, the thick tonsure. Cast in the same peasant clay. But it had been a long while since his attention had been drawn to the likeness; you didn't compare a mortal to a god.

352

At 09.00 Peking time, 07.00 local time, General Liu finished his breakfast of soup and dumplings and went next door to his office. He looked for the night's batch of signals. There were none. He summoned the duty officer.

'Nothing from Headquarters?'

'Not since 11.00 yesterday.'

'Is that usual?'

'Usually we receive three or four messages overnight. Routine stuff.' The duty officer was about to shrug, then stiffened to attention as he gauged Liu's expression. 'Are you expecting something important, sir?'

General Liu didn't know what to expect. Over the last three months his nerves had been worn thin by fear of exposure. Zhang Youmin was the only man in China who knew of his plans to defect, but Zhang was exactly the kind of suspect the Public Security snoopers would pull in for questioning – a man born under the old regime, with relatives in Hong Kong, and therefore liable to harbour dangerous bourgeois ideas. His trip to Hong Kong and Bangkok would make him doubly suspect. At least he didn't have any children; it was the kids who did the denouncing these days, encouraged by their teachers.

The waiting duty officer cleared his throat. 'Sir?'

'No news is always good news, eh?' Liu said, with the faint, sick feeling he remembered from dawn attacks in Korea. 'Dismiss.'

Major Hsu Tsung-pi came in for the daily briefing. A grain convoy was due through about midday, but no other traffic was expected until tomorrow. Two shovels and a pick had gone missing, and Major Hsu requested permission to withhold half a day's rations from the labour force. Permission was granted, although Liu wondered why he was being bothered on such a trivial matter. Perhaps Hsu, a tall, lugubrious man from Shansi who was the fort's commanding officer, hoped to drive his superior away through sheer boredom. Liu knew perfectly well that Hsu couldn't understand why he had chosen to waste ten days in his fort, and that he couldn't wait to see the back of him.

'By the way,' Liu said, 'I was disgusted to see two of your men shambling out of the Tibetans' dormitory with their trousers still unbuttoned.'

Hsu swallowed. 'I'll double the watch, sir.'

'You're not expecting an enemy attack. Just tell your men that all

353

leave is cancelled the next time one of them can't keep away from the labourers.'

'It already is, sir, but that's the trouble. These men haven't seen a woman in over six months. They'll risk anything.'

'Anything?' Liu said dangerously.

'I mean, sir,' Hsu said, 'syphilis.'

'Your men have got syphilis?' Liu said very quietly.

'Two cases,' Hsu said, looking as though he would prefer to be dead.

'I trust they've been dealt with.'

'Yes, sir.'

'What charge?'

'Contravening the spirit of the socialist revolution.'

Liu fell back in his chair. 'I don't want to hear any more,' he said. 'This is your command. But remember this when I leave you in three days: discipline, and with it morale, crumble from the top down.'

'I will, sir.'

Hsu went away. He wasn't a bad soldier – a bit of a dullard, but hard-working and loyal to his men, old-fashioned.

'Captain Chen Feng, with your permission.'

General Liu delayed the moment of confrontation with the new face of the PLA. He pretended to be busy with paperwork.

'It would appear that Headquarters has forgotten us,' he said, not raising his head.

'We're easily overlooked here,' Chen said.

'Would you care to explain that remark?' Liu said, stopping writing.

'With the class-cleansing campaign in progress,' Chen said, 'it's understandable that the road-building task should be given a lower priority.'

Slowly Liu looked up. His eye went straight to the Mao Tse-tung Thought Propaganda Team badge on Chen's otherwise plain uniform. In his breast pocket was the square shape of his *vade mecum*, the Chairman's collected quotes. His face was smooth and shining – a confident, urban face. Whenever Liu pictured the cadres who had engineered his disgrace, it was Chen's face he saw. It wasn't paranoia. He was certain that Chen had been sent to spy on him, that he recorded his criticisms and sent them back to the internal security unit in Lhasa. Suspecting this didn't make Liu more cautious in what he said. Something about Chen drove him to intemperance.

'What you mean,' he said, slowly raising his head, 'is that you can't understand why we're kicking our heels in this blighted hole.'

354

'With so many urgent claims on your attention,' Chen said stiffly, 'I'm sure you have excellent reasons for remaining here so long.'

'Indeed I do,' Liu said with a carefully calibrated smile. 'Road construction is one of our most vital tasks. You can't reach the hearts of the people if you don't have channels of communication.'

'Yes sir,' Chen said. 'But there aren't any people here.'

'No revisionists, you mean. No reactionary cliques and rightist conspirators for you to get your teeth into.' He bared his own teeth, a gesture of intimidation he made increasing use of now that he had a false set. 'You should apply for a transfer to the Public Security Bureau, since that's where your heart lies. It hasn't escaped my notice that your reports are almost devoid of military significance.'

'The workers and the People's Liberation Army are inseparable,' Chen said, his hand straying towards his breast pocket. 'We don't stand apart. Our strategy must always be to support the broad masses of the left in all their endeavours.'

'Yes, yes,' Liu said. 'We must organise revolutionary committees and set the curriculum in schools, not forgetting to manage opera troupes and ballet companies. And when we've done that, if we still have any fighting soldiers left, we might be allowed to defend ourselves against an Indian invasion.'

'The gun alone will not bring about the fruition of the socialist revolution,' Chen said, patting his breast pocket to make it clear on whose authority he spoke.

'I know you're a great advocate of unarmed struggle,' Liu said, making it cuttingly clear that he was referring to the struggle sessions at which counter-revolutionary elements were denounced and beaten up, 'but when you eventually see combat with an enemy who can fight back, you'll find that a gun will give you more comfort and security than a book of great thoughts.' Liu broke off, breaking into a sweat as he realised how this remark would be interpreted by the government in Lhasa. 'Now much as I enjoy listening to your ideas on military strategy,' he said quickly, 'I assume you have a practical purpose for calling on me.'

'We've received a report of bandits near the Xungru road,' Chen said.

Liu received the news in the pit of his stomach. 'Renegades or Tibetans?' he asked, amazed to hear how calm he sounded.

'Khampa guerillas, sir. One of our activists among the nomads reported them to Observer Post 8.'

'Have they investigated?'

'It's too large a gang, sir. Twenty or thirty, all mounted.'

'Those nomads will say anything for a few sacks of barley.'

'We trained the activist ourselves, sir. He's been reliable in the past.'

'Show me where this alleged sighting took place,' Liu ordered. He needed time for his mind to start working again. He had rehearsed this possibility many times, and now that it was happening he didn't know what to do.

'Here, sir,' Chen said, pointing at the large map behind Liu's desk. 'Right in the middle of our sector. It's close to the spot where a truck was ambushed last winter. This far east, it can only be Linka Rinpoche's group.'

'When was the sighting?' Liu asked, putting his hands behind his back to conceal their trembling.

'Three days ago,' Chen said. 'They must be planning another attack at the same spot.'

Liu couldn't help darting a glance towards the window. Three days ago. They could be here, within a few kilometres, looking down on the camp.

'Do we have any counter-insurgency units in the area?' Liu asked, knowing that they didn't.

'As you will recall, sir, most of them are deployed along the Mustang border. Three of them are patrolling near Kyrong.'

'Answer my question.'

'Sorry, sir. The answer is no. The nearest unit is four days' away.'

'What bad luck,' Liu said. 'Very well, leave it with me.'

Chen appeared reluctant to give it up. 'Sir, I was thinking we might call in one of the rapid reaction groups.'

'Were you indeed? The trouble is, Captain, there's nothing to react to except an unconfirmed, three-day-old sighting. You know we catch most of these gangs *after* they've made their attacks.' Liu clapped his hands in relief in seeing his way out of the dilemma. 'That's it. We'll keep all traffic off the Xungru road for the next couple of days.' He rubbed his hands, favouring Chen with an unusually warm smile. 'The next convoy that goes down there will look as though it's carrying grain, but there'll be an infantry platoon from Zhongba riding in it. I'll go over the details with Colonel Pi.'

'In the meantime,' Chen said, 'the CIUs from Mustang had better be brought east to cut the guerillas' line of retreat.'

So ingrained were Liu's soldierly responses that he almost found himself in the disorienting position of ordering his own life-line severed. The experience left him light-headed. Then he remembered that it was the prerogative of command to issue baffling directives. 'Leave them where they are for the time being. It would take them a week to work their way to the guerillas' rear, and you know what will happen if we move them: one of the Mustang groups will choose that moment to break out. No, let's wait until we know what this gang is going to do.'

'Spotter planes?' Chen said, persevering to the last.

'They could be anywhere by now,' Liu said. 'Linka – if it is Linka's gang,' he added quickly, not liking the way the name had come so familiarly to his tongue, 'might even be planning a raid somewhere along this road.' There was a madness in him, Liu realised, that made him scatter self-incriminating clues.

Chen had given up. He saluted and made for the door.

'Remember the informant I told you about?' Liu asked. 'He might arrive today.'

'You mentioned such a person,' Chen said, 'but you gave me no details – not even a name.'

Liu contrived to look worried. He went over to Chen. 'It's a delicate matter and very painful to me personally. This man has been investigating a rebel faction that has been attempting to foment sedition among . . .' Liu's voice dropped to a wounded whisper '. . . soldiers of my own command. Naturally, I don't want word to get out.'

'But it must be investigated,' Chen declared, scandalised. 'I beg you to take me into your confidence.'

'Ah,' Liu said, giving Chen a mournful and fatherly smile, 'I wish that I could. But you see, Captain, the targets for these traitors are . . .' he fingered Chen's MTTPT badge '. . . hot-blooded young socialists not unlike you in background and sympathies.'

'Never, sir,' Chen cried, standing as though a pole had been stuck up his arse. 'I'm your Intelligence Officer, sir.'

'And I'm your General,' Liu said breezily, throwing an arm around Chen's shoulders. 'But since they abolished badges of rank again, it's hard to establish the function of any soldier.'

As soon as Chen had gone, Liu hurried to the window. The wind was up, chasing dust across the compound. Under cover of the greyish-yellow fog the plateau had drawn nearer. He half-expected to see the dull wink of metal on the skyline. Resting on his knuckles, he tried to consider coolly the choice before him. There was no hope now of slipping away without trace, vanishing into thin air; the guerilla sighting, his half-hearted response to it, and his decision to waste ten days at a construction site – they were bound to make the connection. Yet if he stayed and the guerillas were captured, he was finished anyway. Go or stay? Action was always better than inaction. Bent over the window ledge, stricken by a sudden stomach cramp, he knew that he didn't have the nerve for it.

'Sir?'

Liu pulled himself around and stared blindly at his signals officer.

'The order you were expecting, sir,' the man said. Dimly Liu was aware that the man looked pleased with himself.

'What order? What are you talking about?'

He read it at a glance. The sky is falling, the sky is falling, kept going through his mind.

'You'll be pleased to get back to civilisation for a few days,' he heard the signals officer say.

'Who else has read it?'

'Just me, sir.'

'Not a word to anyone.'

'Your escort and driver will need a day's notice.'

'Not a word,' Liu shouted, coming out of his trance.

'Sir.'

'And until I leave, no signals are to be sent without my approval.'

'Understood, sir.'

Liu went back to the window, the message crumpled in his hand. No reason had been given for the order to present himself before the regional commander in Shigatse within the next seventy-two hours. It might have meant a divisional shake-up, a transfer, promotion – anything. But in the circumstances, Liu didn't have any intention of finding out.

Fending off the wind with outstretched hand, Melville scurried over to Osher as soon as he had finished briefing his men. He was sitting against the flat-topped boulder that served as his command centre, eating a meal of cold rice.

'I must talk to you.'

When Osher blinked, one eye opened slower than the other and the lid went on fluttering. Dust dulled his features and matted his hair. He still looked like a million-dollar film property.

'Make it quick,' he said, chewing hard.

'First,' Melville said, collecting himself. 'I must congratulate you. Only one man injured and three horses lost – remarkable.'

Osher, whose jaws had ceased moving during this tribute, set them to work again. 'Getting here is the easy part.'

'Quite. I mean . . .'

'You're wondering how we get the general.'

'Precisely. He's down there and . . .' Melville uttered a foolish laugh '. . . we're up here.'

'Tsering!'

The former novitiate trotted out from behind the rock and came to attention. He was dressed in boiler suit and sneakers, a model of proletarian zeal. At an order from Osher he unbuttoned a pocket and handed over two cards which Osher passed to Melville.

One of them identified the bearer as a resident, designated top class, of Shigatse. The other stated in red print on recycled card that he was a cadre in the Fiery Spark Snake Hunting Corps, empowered by the regional secretary of the CCP to travel freely in the search for bourgeois factionalists.

'A Red Guard,' Melville said. 'I don't understand.'

'A member of the Great Alliance which is collaborating with the PLA in their war against the rebels.' Osher's teeth grated on a piece of grit. He put the unfinished meal aside, swilled water around his mouth, rubbed his teeth with a nicotine-stained finger and spat. 'Until last year,' he explained, tapping a cigarette from a battered pack, 'the PLA's main military effort was directed against the Red Guard extremists. More Chinese died in the fighting than we killed during the uprising.' Osher pushed strands of tobacco into the cigarette with his fingernail. 'Most of the rebels have been crushed, but a few groups are still active outside the towns, sheltered in some cases by sympathisers in the PLA.' Osher hunched himself around his cigarette and applied the Zippo. 'Tsering is going into the camp to give General Liu information about a new rebel offensive.' Osher plucked Tsering's identity cards from Melville's fingers and handed them back. Tsering trotted away. 'Is anything wrong?' Osher asked Melville. 'Don't you approve?'

I think it's the most crackpot scheme I ever heard of, Melville wanted to shout. 'Truly audacious,' he murmured. 'Tsering's a very brave man. I was merely wondering about the consequences should his identification be recognised as a forgery. Alliances in China change from day to day. The group Tsering claims to belong to might have fallen from PLA favour.'

'The general might have changed his mind. He might have been arrested or transferred. The nomads might have reported us. At this moment an entire division might be blocking the river crossings and the road.' Osher spread his hands. 'At a time like this, suppositions aren't very helpful. They inhibit action.'

They were inhibiting Melville's powers of speech. 'Fine,' he managed to say. 'Let's not think of what could go wrong. Tell me how General Liu can leave the camp without being detected.'

Osher rose and strode away up the slope, crooking his finger for Melville to follow. On the crest, hidden beneath an overhang, the two Goloks squatted as still as gargoyles. Their gaze did not shift from the *dzong*.

It looked very white in the dull metallic light. Movement was visible in the compound and a mile or so down the highway, where a pair of dumper trucks was ferrying surfacing materials along a stretch of new road to the south. In the opposite direction dust hid the highway before it reached the top of the pass. All that could be seen of the high mountains were the icy tops gleaming through the murk.

Osher raised his binoculars. One of the Goloks murmured to him.

'He's there,' Osher said, focusing the glasses.

'Does he come out with Tsering?'

'By himself, after dark,' Osher said. He rolled onto his side, facing Melville. 'This is a general. He can do what he wants.'

'He can hardly claim to be taking an evening walk,' Melville said.

'No one will see him,' Osher said. 'Take a look.' He handed over the binoculars. 'The *dzong* is outside the perimeter. Only one of the guard towers is manned.' He grinned. 'If the man in charge of security can't escape, who can?'

Melville adjusted the focus and the base leapt up at him. He drew a sharp intake of breath as the ants became armed soldiers – real communist Chinese soldiers not more than a mile away. His field of view trembled with the thought. One corner of the compound was a vehicle park. Among the trucks were two armoured cars and two hardened troop carriers with machine guns affixed to the front. The muzzle of another machine gun poked out of the guard tower, which overlooked an inner compound with two rows of prefabricated huts.

'At a rough estimate, I'd say there were three hundred people in there.'

'Only half of them are soldiers,' Osher said. 'The rest are Tibetan slaves. Their huts are the ones fenced in by barbed wire.'

A soldier was crossing towards the vehicle park. He stopped a little distance away, hands on hips, and a moment later three more soldiers dropped from the back of a truck and saluted.

'A general is rarely left on his own,' Melville said. 'He's always surrounded by aides, asked for orders. Liu's absence could be discovered within minutes.'

'It's a brave soldier who wakes a sleeping general,' Liu said. 'Tonight he will retire early. I want him away from the camp well before midnight.'

'What about the floodlights?'

'There's a fuel shortage in Tibet, so the only ones in use are aimed at the Tibetans' compound. When the general leaves, he will walk up the road to that small bridge across the gulley . . . there, just before the road starts climbing. A party led by Chorphel will be waiting to meet him.'

But Melville's hands were shaking too much to bring the glasses to bear.

'With luck he'll be in our hands by ten,' Osher said, 'and we'll be back across the road and river before they discover he's gone. Even then they won't know where to start looking for him.' He held out his hand for the glasses.

As Melville leaned across, he tensed and half rose, his eye caught by a flash in the direction of the pass. Osher pushed him flat and wriggled round.

'A convoy,' he said at last.

'One of those driving past at the wrong moment could prove awkward.'

'General Liu is notified of all traffic passing through his command,' Osher said, his attention on the highway. 'He knows the disposition of all troops in this sector, including the anti-guerilla patrols. Why do you think we haven't seen any? The general must have sent them all to Mustang.' He shot a quick look at Melville, who could have sworn that he winked. Maybe it was only his tic. 'Satisfied?' he asked.

'Sir, I do believe it might work.'

'Might?'

'These things seldom go as smoothly as you hope. Actually,' Melville said, his tone careless, 'I was wondering how Liu will react when he finds me here. He'll be most distressed to learn that I was brought against my will?'

Osher pinpointed him with his stare. His lazy eyelid slid up and flickered.

'But there's no reason why he should,' Melville said quickly. 'I'll tell him I volunteered.'

Osher grunted and turned back to the convoy. 'You've done better

361

than I expected,' he said. 'Given time I could make a guerilla out of you.'

'When word of my involvement gets out,' Melville said, pleased by the compliment, 'there won't be any other opportunities left to me.' He smiled sadly at Osher's back. 'I don't expect you to believe me, but before Gunn persuaded me to run away, I did consider volunteering.'

'Why?' Osher asked, watching the convoy's downhill crawl.

'Hard to explain. I've spent my whole life trying to stay uninvolved. For once . . . I thought that . . . I could be part of something, sharing the risk.'

'And do you feel you are?'

'Sharing the risk, certainly. As for feeling I belong . . .' Melville looked at the dirty sky '. . . no, I can't say I do.' He shook in a gust of wind. 'Listen,' he said, 'have you considered the possibility that Liu is the bait in a trap?'

'I told you. The time for doubts is past. I considered all the risks when I met your friends Mr Yeuh and the American, Sweetwater.'

'For me they're only just beginning. I can't help wondering why Mr Yueh didn't let me meet you in Bangkok and discuss the operational details.'

'You were never meant to be part of them,' Osher said, and again he seemed to wink.

'If the object is to cause maximum embarrassment for the Chinese – maximum provocation – you couldn't do better than bring me along.' Melville shook his head and hissed, as though trying to rid himself of doubts. 'The reason I can't feel I belong is because I can't shake off the feeling that I'm being used as the instrument of someone's political ambitions.'

Osher gave him consideration. 'You're here as a consequence of your own weakness, nothing else.'

And Melville had to make do with that, because the convoy was down on the valley floor, drawing close to the camp, the leading vehicles dull gleams at the eye of a dust storm. The Goloks were chattering like crows. One of them spoke to Osher, looking down at the trucks as though they were a species of game.

'They think it's a tempting target,' Osher said. 'The camp, too. General Liu has left its defences wide open.' He saw Melville glare at the scouts. 'They'd rather attack the camp than capture a general. To them he's nothing but dead weight.'

Melville found himself dwelling on the phrase.

'. . . sixteen, seventeen, eighteen,' Osher said, counting off the trucks as they rolled past the camp. 'Good, I was worried they might stop.' The last vehicle went past. 'A food convoy. Tibetan food for Han mouths.' He tracked the convoy until it was swallowed up in its own dust, then turned the binoculars on the road gang. 'In five years,' he said, 'the Chinese will be able to drive to Mustang.'

'A monument to your struggle, you could say.'

'The Chinese aren't building that road to squash a few guerillas. It's for the war with India.'

'You think it will come to that?'

'Who do you think those people are?' Osher said, pointing his binoculars at the road gang, then handing them to Melville.

He brought the tiny figures into focus. Many of them were women, recognisable by the aprons they wore on their backs. Chinese soldiers stood at ease at twenty-yard intervals.

'Slave labour, I suppose. People with bad class designations.'

'Conscripts in the War Preparation Army,' Osher said, feeling for his cigarettes. 'Conflict with India is inevitable. China is encircled by enemies and unstable elements. Skirmishing has already begun with the Soviet Union in the east, and the Soviet Union is an ally of India, which will soon possess its own nuclear weapons.' Osher put a cigarette to his lips. 'Did you know that Tibet has a bomb?'

'What?'

'A Chinese bomb,' Osher said, ducking down and turning his back on the wind. He flicked his Zippo. 'Over there,' he said, blowing smoke in a north-easterly direction. 'On the Chang-Thang north of Lhasa.'

For a backwoods' guerilla, Melville thought, Osher had a disturbingly broad picture of international stress points. His unease expressed itself in an intestinal gurgle. Instability in that region had been threatening all day. 'Do the labourers get paid?' he asked for distraction.

'Not enough to grow fat. There's another famine. There have been famines ever since the occupation.'

'Yet you're a communist,' Melville dared to say. 'You're not fighting to restore the old order.'

'All you foreigners think Tibet was a paradise before the Chinese came.'

'At least people had enough to eat.'

Osher forgot about his cigarette. 'In Kham I lived below a monastery with two thousand monks. They owned all the land for a day's ride in any direction, and what they didn't own they taxed. There were

363

taxes on yaks and sheep and dogs. The monks taxed barley and butter and *chang* and potatoes. They taxed wool, salt, fruit and flowers. We even paid tax on hides and bones.' Osher remembered his cigarette and sucked on it. 'The Chinese came,' he said. 'They abolished taxes and sent the monks to work in the fields. Now there was plenty of food, but the Chinese put it in trucks and sent it away to their Han brothers. Tibetans who had once harvested enough barley to fill their storehouses to the roof walked the pastures, breaking open clods of horse shit for undigested seeds. You didn't pay taxes on hides and bones any more, but that didn't mean you could afford them. You couldn't buy them at any price, because the Tibetans had eaten them. They ate their own boots and died shitting out their guts inch by inch.'

'There was a priviliged category, though,' Melville said, aware that he was taking a risk. 'Poor Tibetans who were considered ideologically sound and therefore suitable for positions in the new administration.'

'Yes, provided we kept our place,' Osher said, watching his cigarette burn unevenly in the wind. 'Think of us as your elder brothers, the Chinese told us. While we looked up to them, deferred to them, they were happy to see us improve ourselves. As soon as we looked on them as our friends and equals, they showed their true attitude. In my case I was sent to work in a slaughterhouse.' He took a drag and opened his mouth to let the wind suck the smoke out. 'My family were butchers,' he said, and looked up quickly, as though trying to catch Melville's expression by surprise.

'Of low status, I understand.'

'No status,' Osher said. 'None at all.'

'You've suffered a lot of disappointments with people you trusted – the Chinese, the Indians . . . us.'

'All of you wanted to use me as your tame hunting dog,' Osher said. 'No more. Today I run with my own pack in my own country.'

'And tomorrow? Do you think you'll ever see Kham again?'

'Kham's a long way away,' Osher said.

'And God's too high above. It's what the people of another oppressed country say,' Melville explained.

'Well, they're right,' Osher said, grinding out his cigarette. 'You must build the future with your own hands.'

'Whatever happens,' Melville said, 'it's been a privilege to know you.'

'You're a sentimental people,' Osher said, 'and therefore not to be trusted.' He laughed at Melville's crestfallen expression. 'No, that's

not entirely true. I have great faith in your weapons. Look at this
Zippo,' he said. 'American. Guaranteed to light in a storm.' He held
it out in the wind, flicked it, and it did.

Partly reassured by his conversation with Osher, Melville craved more
talk to speed the passage of time, but Gunn was busy teaching the
rudiments of first aid to a group of Khampas, and of Yonden there
was no sign. He was probably with the horses, which had been led
to the rear, out of sight and sound. Melville got into his sleeping bag
and waited for the interminable afternoon to unwind.

Some of the guerillas were asleep. Some sat in a loose group around
the flat rock, their weapons propped between their knees, wrapped
in blankets to protect them from the dust. The men were sensitive to
the slightest movement – a man scratching his ear, fingering a charm
package – but they wouldn't catch one another's eyes. Melville's chest
tightened.

The wind goaded him. Whichever way he turned it found him out.
He lashed out at it. Finally he cocooned himself in his bag so that
only his nose was exposed and pulled himself into a ball. As the light
began to drain from the sky, the wind moderated and he slept.

He woke to an apocalyptic sunset, the horizon the colour of blood
and egg yolk. The wind had died completely and the dust had settled.
With a shock he saw Osher standing on the flat rock, surrounded by
the Khampas, who were split into three groups, all armed and ready
to go. Among them was Tsering, dressed now for combat. Cursing
himself, Melville scrambled out of his bag and staggered over.

He listened in a fever of impatience as Osher finished addressing
his men, assigning them to different tasks. One group was burdened
with the heavy machine guns. The second had the mortars. Chorphel's party was the most lightly armed. There was no sign of Gunn
and Yonden.

At last Osher finished. He jumped off the rock and came towards
him, smiling.

'You were sleeping so soundly, it would have been a shame to
wake you. It's good. You'll be riding all night.'

'Is he coming?' Melville asked, bouncing up and down with
excitement.

'He's coming.'

'Wonderful, marvellous. Where are Gunn and Yonden?'

'Minding the horses. When it comes to fighting, that's all Yonden's good for; and I want the doctor to be ready to leave the moment General Liu arrives.'

'Fighting, you said. Why should there be any fighting?'

'If anything goes wrong,' Osher said with a soothing smile.

'What do I do?' Melville said, suddenly at a loss.

'Wait here. We should be back by ten – eleven at the latest.'

Melville checked. More than three hours to go. It wasn't to be borne. 'Couldn't I go with Chorphel?'

'We don't want to give Liu too much of a shock. Let's wait until he's well away from here before he meets you.'

Melville saw the sense of it. 'Well, all I can say is good luck and may all the gods be with you.'

'With us,' Osher said, accepting Melville's hand. He turned to his men and gave the order to go.

Relieved that the waiting was over, they chatted softly and even laughed as they filed off up the slope. Melville envied them. Once again he was a spectator. When the last silhouette had gone over the crest and the stones dislodged by their feet had come to rest, he turned away.

There was someone standing by the flat rock. The light had nearly all gone. A man outlined against the sky would have been visible from fifty yards or more, but a man standing against a shadow was part of that shadow.

'Who's that?'

A chill moved along his spine as the figure came towards him. 'What are you doing here?' he whispered.

Grinning and nodding, Ngawang sat down, laid his carbine across his lap and drew up his knees. Melville sat down too and watched the Khampa watching him. His stomach made a noise like a drain emptying. He needed food. He'd eaten nothing all day except for a handful of rice. He put his hands in his pack, feeling for the remains of a chocolate bar. The first thing they encountered was the Webley, wrapped in a torn shirt. His eyes jerked up, colliding with Ngawang's interested stare.

'Fancy some chocolate?' he asked, rummaging deeper. He found the chocolate and divided it between them. He left the pack open.

No sooner had he eaten than pain knifed into his guts. Dysentery, he thought. Clutching his stomach, he stood up and indicated that he needed to shit. Ngawang followed and watched him from a polite distance.

Back in his place, his stomach restive but manageable, he was consumed by the desire to get his hands on the revolver. He tried to tell himself that it would do him no good, that there was nothing to be afraid of, but as the minutes dragged by his faith in Osher ebbed away and he found himself replaying their conversation, putting a sinister interpretation on every remark made by the Khampa. If only he had left him with Yeshe or Yonden. His stomach went into another spasm as he wondered why Osher should want to separate him from Gunn and Yonden. This, above all times, was when they should have been together.

Ngawang looked at his watch, stood up, stretched and, after silently enjoining Melville to stay where he was, climbed to the ridge. Without thought, Melville felt for the gun, unwrapped it and slid it into his *chuba*. The move left him shaking. He looked up. He could see Ngawang silhouetted against a field of stars. Cautiously he climbed to where he was sitting.

Five yards short, Ngawang heard his approach and turned lazily, his eyes barely registering his presence before moving back to the fort. Melville hauled himself alongside, lying so that his right hand was inside his *chuba*. He couldn't remember if the safety was on and he was scared that if he made a sudden move he might shoot himself in the belly.

'Ngawang,' he whispered, 'what's Osher going to do with me?'

The Khampa shook his head, absorbed by the small illuminated rectangle in the valley bottom.

Under artificial light the garrison had the ramshackle air of a car lot on a desert back road. The square *dzong* stood above the vehicles and huts like a giant hoarding, the red lamps on its rooftop radio antennae flashing an incomplete slogan. Melville fancied he could hear generators purring. He couldn't see any movement within the perimeter. The road looped emptily away between mountains that shone with the ghostly glow of objects lit by a black and white television screen.

He kept looking at his watch and forgetting the time he had just read. His breathing was so fast as to be ineffectual, and at intervals he was obliged to raise himself on all fours and make a determined effort to squeeze air past the straitjacket clamped around his chest. The doubts crowded in.

The new moon came up, the thinnest of parings.

No, he told himself, you're getting excited about nothing. Osher's a straight arrow. He's here to collect General Liu. If he gets him, he doesn't need to put on a sideshow.

Somehow ten o'clock came. Now, surely, something must disturb the peace. He waited for dogs to bark, guns to go off, sirens to wail, but it was quarter past and the square below remained as static as a TV test card.

He shut his eyes. He may even have dozed, because suddenly Ngawang was shaking him, hauling him back down the slope.

Someone was coming – more than one, and in a hurry, with no concession to stealth. Ngawang tightened his grip. Melville heard harsh breathing and feet sliding on loose stones. He thought he saw a knot of figures, but the light was deceptive, for only two came out of the dark – Osher and Tsering, grinning like hunted wolves.

His own lips rolled back from his teeth. 'What happened? What went wrong?'

'Nothing,' Osher panted. 'It went perfectly.'

'Then where is he?' Melville asked, looking behind the Khampas.

'With Chorphel,' Osher said. He laughed. 'He's not ready to see you yet.'

The laugh infuriated Melville. It made him feel like the butt of a joke. 'He's going to have to see me sooner or later. Let's go before they find him missing.'

Osher was doubled over, gasping for breath. 'No time to talk,' he said, and looked up, exultant. 'I'm going back to attack the camp.'

'You're crazy. You'll ruin everything. Let's get away while we still have a chance.'

'It makes no difference now,' Osher said. 'The nomads reported us. By this time tomorrow the Chinese will have a whole division hunting for us.'

Melville struggled to break Ngawang's grip. 'We're wasting time. An hour could make all the difference.'

'Calm down. We can destroy the camp and still be across the road before the Chinese cut it.'

'You know I'll never be able to keep up.'

Osher laughed again at the expression on Melville's face. Then he stopped laughing. 'You'll leave when I say so, American. You're going to stay here and see how Khampas can fight.'

'I don't want to,' Melville sobbed. 'Please.'

Osher shook his head in disappointment. 'I thought you wanted to share the risk.'

'For something worthwhile. The general's the only thing that matters. Why are you doing this to me?'

But Tsering was pulling on Osher's arm, and they were already fading back into the dark. 'I'll come for you when it's over,' was the last thing Melville heard from Osher.

Before any of it had sunk in, Ngawang was hustling him up the slope, a knife in his free hand, his carbine on his back. Going down the other side he was more solicitous, showing Melville where to place his feet, clucking like a mother hen when he made too much noise. Melville just went where he was pointed. About a half mile east of the fort and a couple of hundred yards back from the road, Ngawang pushed him down in a little circle made by boulders and squatted down facing him, one hand resting in friendly fashion on his shoulder, the other holding the knife under the angle of his jaw.

Now all his doubts were back, and this time they didn't flock randomly. The money paid to Yonden for delivering him to the camp, the escape attempt allowed to go ahead so that Osher would have an excuse to bring him into Tibet – these were merely the last links in a logical sequence of deceptions that went back much further, to the moment when Charlie Sweetwater had smiled his universal smile and talked of retribution. He followed the chain link by link, through Bangkok, where he had been kept in the dark about the arms and denied the chance to meet Osher, and found that it led to only one possible conclusion. He knew with sick, cold certitude that Osher, with Sweetwater's blessing, was going to kill him and dump him in the road for the Chinese to find. It had been their intention from first to last, just as it had always been Osher's intention to attack the base.

Ngawang's face was as inert as a totem. Melville wondered how he could ever have thought him sympathetic. He gave a whispered groan and the Khampa laid the blade of his knife to his lips, then backed away a few feet to sit on a rock. He was intent on the fort, facing towards Melville, who remembered the pistol in his *chuba*. Even if he could get it out, killing Ngawang would do no good. He was about as far from friends as it was possible to be.

Listlessly he turned his head. The base still looked lifeless and there was no sign of the guerillas. They could be within yards of the fort, hidden among the rocks that littered the valley sides. He looked back at Ngawang and stiffened. Squares of matt blackness were coasting down the road. He rubbed his eyes, but he wasn't mistaken. It was a convoy free-wheeling without lights.

His shock communicated itself to Ngawang. The Khampa must have been blinded by the brightness of the fort because it took him several seconds to spot the vehicles. Then he flung himself flat on the rock, gibbering in panic.

With a faint squeak of brakes and a crunching of gravel, the vehicles came to a stop, like big primitive animals that have sensed danger ahead. Melville estimated that they were about as far from him as he was from the fort, and therefore invisible both to the garrison and the besieging Khampas. He fancied he could see the snout of an armoured vehicle in front. So far as he could tell, nobody got out. There was no sound.

It was creepy and inexplicable. The general was kept informed of all traffic, and even Osher wouldn't be so rash as to mount an attack when a convoy was due through. He had said that the Chinese knew about the Khampa incursion, so it was probably a relief column. But why in hell was it riding without lights, and why had it halted out of sight of the fort?

Ngawang was also having difficulty making sense of it. He was making sounds like an aviary. Remembering the immediate threat, Melville slipped the pistol from his *chuba* and held it out of sight.

Immediately the Khampa swung round, but he was looking towards the base, obviously worried that the guerillas were oblivious to the menace. His eyes switched back and forth and Melville could tell he was wondering how he could get down there to warn his friends. In a moment he would decide, Melville thought, and then he would be confronted with the problem of what to do with *him*. Really, there was only one solution, Melville decided, easing up the safety.

Just as he had anticipated, Ngawang turned his face towards him, and the doubt went out of his expression. Perhaps he was alerted by the look on Melville's face or the awkward way he was sitting, with his right arm held stiffly at his side. Maybe he caught a glimpse of the revolver. He rose in a half crouch and came at him with his knife held low and straight out.

Melville didn't know if there was a round in the chamber or whether he had switched the safety on or off. He didn't think about these things. He just jerked the trigger twice.

The flat ugly noise made Ngawang step back one pace and stand up to his full height. He took another step and seemed to search for something, his pendulum gaze swinging from side to side, before his legs folded up and he fell face down, hitting the ground with a sickening smack. One of his legs wouldn't stay still.

When Melville finally wrenched his horrified gaze away, he saw spidery shadows spilling out of the vehicles. A radio squawked and whistled. An engine fired up. From the other direction came a subdued burst of automatic fire, followed by deeper, punchier notes repeated very quickly. Another machine gun opened up and the noise ran together. Two shallow arcs of tracer converged on the base from front and rear. Melville heard the tinny report of mortars and the crack of the shells landing.

A light popped on overhead, turning the valley into a snowscape. He cowered down like a burglar surprised by an irate householder, then risked another look as he heard the rattle of machine guns from the road almost directly below. The shadows were speeding down on either side and he heard their voices as they advanced. Ahead of them went the armoured car. It fired and hit the *dzong*. Someone should stop this madness, Melville thought.

One of the lines of tracer was playing like a hose on the trucks parked in the compound. The other fired unvaryingly into the barracks. A truck skipped into the air. Melville's diaphragm fluttered as fuel exploded and the flame mushroomed above the base. By its light he could see figures running inside the perimeter and thought he heard screams. He watched aghast as intersecting lines of tracer sketched in the situation. The Khampas were shooting at the base, the base was shooting back, and the soldiers from the convoy were firing at both sides.

Balls of tracer floated towards him and then rushed past. A stray bullet ricocheted off a rock and droned into the sky. Then he realised it wasn't a loose shot, because several more rounds hissed overhead, fired from below at figures traversing towards him, moving too quickly on the broken ground to be anything but Khampas. Around the fort the fighting had died down, although one of the heavy machine guns was still hammering away in short, selective bursts. He saw shadows below beginning to move up towards him.

He stood up, not knowing where to turn. Everyone was his enemy. There was no way out. A Khampa bounded over the rocks above, followed by a couple more. Whatever Osher intended, it was preferable to being captured by the Chinese. He could hear their voices on each side.

Without a glance at Ngawang he fled. A Khampa overtook him and grabbed him, hauling him over a rock and then disappearing ahead with a whoop. A couple more came past and he cringed away. He ran tensed for a bullet in the neck. Soon, though, he was on his own, stumbling and falling up the hill, not knowing how close the Chinese were. The Khampas didn't have to shoot him. They would leave him behind.

Another flare went off and he saw figures on the ridge and heard horses' hooves. A voice called his name. It was Yonden. He was alone, trying to hang on to four maddened horses.

'Quickly,' he cried.

'What's the fucking use? Osher won't let me get away.'

'Oh hurry, sah.'

'Didn't you hear?' Melville yelled. 'He wants me dead. I'm his ticket to glory.'

'He's down there behind the *dzong*,' Yonden shouted.

The barracks and Tibetan quarters were fiercely ablaze, beginning to buckle on their frames and fall in. The crackling flames made a steady counterpoint to the tappeting of small-arms fire from somewhere in that quarter. Another truck erupted in a slow billow of infernal red that lit up three armoured cars drawn up along the road outside the base, their guns firing at the opposite side of the valley. Whoever was trapped there had little chance of making it back.

'Who else is in on it?' Melville demanded. 'What about Tsering?'

'He's dead,' Yonden said. The horses were tugging him about. 'Where's Ngawang? He was supposed to look after you.'

Melville gave a wild laugh. 'The dumb shit collected a stray bullet.' He realised he was still holding the revolver. 'Don't look at me like that,' he yelled. 'It wasn't me who started this.'

Yonden was pulled over as the horses shied away from a volley of bullets splattering amongst nearby rocks. As Melville went to help him a Khampa leapt over the top, turned and swung his M–16 in an arc, using up the rest of the magazine. He laughed savagely, bounded over to the horses and grabbed one, knocking Melville out of the way. He vaulted into the saddle and galloped off, shouting until he was lost in the dark.

'If someone else comes,' Yonden said, suddenly calm, 'there will be no horse for you.' He held out the reins. 'Chinese very close now.'

'I don't have any choice,' Melville said, taking the reins.

Yonden tied the remaining horse to a rock and they left. 'What a fucking waste,' Melville said, taking one last look at the pyrotechnics. 'Why didn't Osher ask Liu if there was another convoy expected tonight?'

Yonden looked at him oddly. 'Those soldiers were coming for the general,' he said. 'Someone has told them he was going to run away with us.'

After that they didn't speak, but concentrated on keeping up a fast pace. Behind them the fire-fight spluttered on a little longer and bubbles of light swelled and dissolved, then everything went quiet again and there was nothing to show the way but stars and the thin moon. They caught up the main party four hours later, shortly before it reached the road. Melville hung back, but when the Khampas saw him they seemed pleased to find he was still alive. Gunn gave him a long interrogative look to which he could only shake his head in a way that suggested it had been a close thing. The only person who really seemed pissed off to see him was General Liu Hongwen. Melville thought he had every right.

Chapter 23

Bugs, Gunn thought, looking up the straggling line of horsemen. Bugs crossing an empty floor, all their senses attuned to danger. As they go they scan the edges of the world – a slow sweep through all the points of the compass, and then a cowed inspection of the sky. Nothing. But what the bugs fail to appreciate is that *they're* moving, crawling across a place where movement is contrary to nature. They pause often, antennae waving, and make frequent shifts of direction, but just when they think they see a haven ahead, the half-indifferent giant who has been following their self-important odyssey, abstractedly computing speed and course, stands up, yawns, takes a single step and . . . *crack*.

In the hungry silence of the mounting sun the survivors rode south, their long shadows gliding over drifts of rock and snow. Of the thirty or so Khampas who had reached the fort, Gunn had counted eighteen. It was more than he had expected. They had forded the river without incident and crossed the road a few minutes ahead of probing lights. Later, as the sun struggled clear of the mountains, they had heard ragged gunfire to the rear.

General Liu was at the head of the column, shielded from the bleak outlook by a screen of horsemen. Melville had detached himself from this group and was riding back down the line. Behind Gunn were the only wounded survivors – one of the Goloks, who had been shot in the abdomen, and a Khampa who had lost most of one foot. Yonden was at the tail of the column, a long way back.

Gunn raised himself in his stirrups and squinted to the east. He subsided slowly, knowing that no matter how much he braced himself for the inevitable, the first sight of the Chinese would stop his heart like the touch of a hand in an empty house. The thought he had tried to suppress since dawn could no longer be contained. It was happening all over again.

'See anything?' Melville called. He was halted twenty yards ahead.

Gunn shook his head. As he got close, what he had taken for a rictus of exhaustion turned out to be a sheepish smile.

'How do you feel?' he asked.

'Pretty much as you see me,' Melville said, falling in by his side. 'You?'

'Coping.'

Melville gave him a keen, glancing look, then nodded at the wounded. 'What are their chances?'

'None for the Golok,' Gunn said. 'The other one . . . he'll be alright while he stays on horseback, but from the direction we're taking, I think Chorphel means to walk out.'

'Hump over that lot,' Melville said, eyeing the ranges. 'Old Liu is going to love it.'

'Have you talked to him?'

Melville laughed, after a fashion. 'We rode side by side, him gaping at me as if I was a poison toad, rubbing his eyes and hoping when he looked again I'd have gone away.'

'What did you tell him?'

'What's there to say? Sorry about the aggravation back there, general. The boys got a little out of hand.'

'How did you explain our presence?'

'Told him I was worried something like this might happen.'

'Did he believe you?'

'Who cares?'

'It sounds as though you didn't hit it off.'

'He's a pill,' Melville said, after a pause for consideration. 'He's a total pain in the ass. The way he's bitching, you'd think he'd been kidnapped.'

They stopped at a cry from behind. The unwounded Golok was lifting his companion from his horse.

'I'm amazed he got this far,' Gunn said.

As they rode back, Yeshe overtook them. By the time they reached the dead man, he had been laid out and stripped of his ivory bangles and silver charm box. His companion said a prayer, then stood up and looked around him, as if searching for something. He tied the spare horse to his own, swung into the saddle, muttered to Yeshe and then pulled his horse round and rode slowly towards the northeast. All along the line a hollow jeer went up.

'Backwards head,' Yeshe said, tapping his own.

'Where the hell does he think he's going?' Melville asked.

'Home,' Gun told him. 'Amdo.'

'How far's that?'

'A month, two months.'

'Will he make it?'

Gunn looked at him sideways.

'Only asking, dammit.'

They watched the Golok grow small. Yeshe shouted abuse after him until it was no longer possible to hear his one-word response. It took a long time for him to disappear completely, and even when he was engulfed in space, his image continued to play on the mind.

They rode a little way in subdued silence.

'Not a very encouraging sign,' Melville said.

'He won't be the only one to drop out,' Gunn told him. 'I heard Dorje and some of the others talking about finding somewhere to hide for a week or two and trying to get into Mustang. It makes good sense. Mustang is the only sanctuary open to them.'

'They're certain it was Linka who blew the whistle.'

'The timing suggests it had to be someone from the camp.'

'Don't look so sick. Seems to me it could have been anyone – the nomads, most likely, or that guy with the broken knee. He never showed up again.'

'Whoever it was,' Gunn said, 'we can't return to the valley.'

'Do we want to go to Mustang?' Melville asked.

'We haven't been invited,' Gunn said, 'and even if we had, it's the last place we want to be. It's blockaded by the PLA on one side, by the Nepalese on the other. And in the middle there are half a dozen Khampa factions.'

'Shit,' Melville said. He studied the faraway mountains. 'So tell me the alternatives.'

'There might not be any. The Chinese have at least four days to find us. They'll send spotter planes up, and then all they have to do is parachute troops in front of us.'

'Horses can't use parachutes,' Melville said. 'If we can get off this plateau, lose ourselves in broken country, travel by night, I'd say the odds are with us. Some of these boys have been running rings round the PLA for the last fifteen years.'

'Not with a general and two useless passengers in tow.'

'No, listen,' Melville said. 'A few years back Chorphel was in a raiding party that took out a convoy not far from where we picked up the general. When they went through the wreckage, they found they'd killed the head of Tibet's western command and all his staff. They walked back to Mustang without a scratch.'

'Dead generals are one thing. Dead generals can't give away their country's secrets.'

'Wrong. Chorphel took away all his papers too. Battle orders, troop positions, the lot.'

'The Chinese will move heaven and earth to get Liu back. By now every anti-guerilla unit in southern Tibet will be converging on the border. Even if we find a way through, the Nepalese will be waiting for us. The Chinese must have identified us by now. They'll put pressure on all the frontier countries to hand us over. Unless . . .' Gunn's voice faltered.

'. . . they've gone ahead and invaded Nepal,' Melville finished for him. 'Ai-yai-yai, how does it feel to be the cause of World War Three?'

'Stop that!'

'You have to hand it to him,' Melville said after a while. He looked back to the north. 'Boy, I bet he's laughing all the way to hell.'

'How can you credit a man who tried to murder you?'

'I don't think it was personal. It was his way of earning a footnote in the history books. I reckon he's earned it. Don't you? Yeah.' Melville shook his head in admiration. 'I still can't figure if it was his own idea or a twist dreamt up by Charlie and Mr Yueh.'

They rode on, their shadows shortening. The day continued breathless. Wind would have been a welcome diversion.

'Look at it from the Chinese end,' Melville said. 'They'll be coy about admitting one of their generals has walked out on them. They won't let word get out while he's still in Tibet.'

'You're whistling in the dark, Walter.'

'I'm trying to get ahead of the game.'

'The Khampas may simplify our predicament,' Gunn said. 'They may decide that the general is more trouble than he's worth.'

'Kill him?' Melville cried, reining in. 'They can't. He's our ace.'

'Not to them he isn't.'

'He knows how the search operation will work. He'll know if there are any holes in the net.'

'That would explain his remarkable good humour.'

'We have to stick with him,' Melville said. 'Our people will fall over themselves to get their hands on him. If we can reach Nepal, they'll pull us out.'

'The reckoning might be too much even for them.'

'For chrissake, Alan. China's a hostile power. It's nobody's fault but their own if they're careless enough to lose one of their commanders. All we have to do is find a place to lie up in while we get word to the right people. I have this friend in Tokyo.'

'What happened to Sweetwater and Mr Yueh?'

377

'Fuck them. They've cheated me seven ways from sundown. They sucked me in without telling me the rules. From now on, I'll play it my way.'

'Play it any way you like, but there isn't anywhere to hide. No village would take us in. It's the middle of winter, man. Where will we find food?'

'For once, Yonden can exercise his guile in a good cause. Chorphel can take us across the border, but no further. Yonden's going to find us a cave or a hermitage and food to keep us going while we wait to be picked up.'

'Please keep him out of it. Please. On his own he stands a chance.'

'You're a total gas,' Melville said, his voice cracking. 'I know what your problem is. You're suffering from a bad case of *déjà vu*. Well, call it what you like; call it karmic necessity, fate fucking us up, we're in it together and I'm going to use Yonden how I like.'

'Use him? What's got into you, Walter?'

'A compelling desire to live. Last night I rehearsed dying a hundred times, and I was no better at the end than I was in the beginning.'

'It's something we have to face up to,' Gunn said. 'There'll be very little time when the Chinese catch up with us.'

'I know it,' Melville said. He spurred his horse forward.

'Walter.'

Melville reined in.

'We agreed we couldn't let ourselves be captured,' Gunn said.

Melville didn't say anything or turn around.

'Do you still have your gun?'

'There's only one bullet left,' Melville said. 'You'll have to ask Yonden to help you out. I'm sure he'll make a better job of it than me.'

'Promise me . . .' Gunn began.

'You're spooking my horse,' Melville cried, fighting the reins. He brought the horse under control, and when his own breathing had quietened he gave Gunn a smile that was meant to be encouraging. 'We'll sort out that problem when it comes,' he said. 'In the meantime, this is what we're going to do. We're going to be a team. I'll look after the general and fix up a deal with the Americans. Yonden's going to take us to a place of safety, you're going to make sure we stay in sound health, and the general . . . he'll do what he's told. Same as you.'

Yonden was asleep on his horse when a plane ripped open the sky above his head. He found himself sitting on the ground, still holding the reins, watching the plane go straight away from him. It went out of sight behind a swelling horizon and a few seconds later threw up over the column. Yonden waited for the bursting of bombs, but there was only the chatter of the Khampas' weapons. The plane made height and began to circle. Yonden shook his head to clear it. There were about three hours of daylight left. He reckoned the distance to the great scarp to the south, allowing for the clearness of the light, which brought the most distant ranges within a day's ride, and he decided they should reach it with time to spare unless the Chinese already had bombers in the air. He yawned and waited for the plane to go away.

Rolling onto his other side, he checked the plain to the north. Even healthy, well-rested eyes would have been confused by the repetition of insignificant features. He took out the little bottle of medicine that Alan had given him, put his head back and squeezed two drops into each eye. He blinked and opened his eyes wide. The drops made his vision fuzzy at the edges and sharp as crystal in the middle, where he thought he saw something extraneous to the landscape. He blinked again and it was gone.

The light made him want to shut his eyes; the droning of the plane made him sleepy. He dozed, letting his mind play over a fantasy. He was a businessman in Canada, the owner of a car, a house and a television. At last the plane came back, close enough for him to see the pilot, not close enough to be worth a shot. When it had gone he hoisted himself to his feet.

Half in, half out of his saddle, he tensed, his blood tingling. This time he couldn't dismiss it. There was something out there that didn't belong, although he could not tell precisely where it was. The trick was not to look too hard, but to let the eye surprise itself – like searching for a flea on a blanket. He let his gaze roam at will until it halted of its own volition on an animate note. Time passed, and he was able to identify it as a horse, ambling in his direction. He thought it must be one of the pack animals they had left behind, but gradually it became clear that the hump on its back was a wounded man. The rest of the Khampas were out of sight. He was all alone. No one would ever know if he were to ride away. He waltzed around on his horse, unable to choose a course, then with a throaty moan he trotted back.

His horse came close and splayed out its feet, whickering and tossing its head. The other came on, placing its feet with care, its rider lurching paralytically at each step. Yonden was overcome by dread; the rider was a dead man – a ghost come to haunt him for his sins. The horse came right up to him and halted.

Slowly, with a bubbly sigh, Osher raised his head. All the blood in his face had drained into his mouth. Yonden's own mouth filled with saliva.

Osher's eyes came into focus from a far place. 'Yonden? Is that you?'

'I'll fetch Gunn-la,' Yonden said, fighting the urge to spur away at once.

Osher shook his head. 'Help me down,' he mumbled.

He was a dead weight, and Yonden's grip slipped on his blood-sodden jacket. He dropped to the ground and made slow, broken movements before Yonden managed to haul him to a rock and prop him up. He turned his face away from Yonden's water bottle and feebly stroked at his zippered pocket. Clenching his teeth, Yonden extracted the Zippo and a pack of cigarettes. They were unsalvageable, but Yonden selected the most complete one and put it in Osher's hand. He stood back, frightened and useless, and stole a guilty look south, where he expected to see soldiers coming up over the edge of the earth.

'Please, sir.'

'Not long,' Osher mumbled with the half of his mouth that still worked. 'Tell me who's left.'

Yonden told him. He left out Melville's name.

'More than I expected,' Osher said. 'Fancy that convoy showing up like that. They must have come to arrest the general. Do you know which fool fired the first shot?'

'No, sir.'

Osher gave a gurgle, then, with an access of strength that made Yonden despair, he sat up a little straighter, his left arm and leg stretched out.

Yonden looked in panic at the southern horizon. He saw fidgety movement there, veiled in dust.

'They're coming, sir.'

'Alright.'

'I can't leave you.'

Osher opened one eye. 'Shoot me.'

Yonden whimpered.

'What's wrong?'

'I can't, sir.'

'Superstitious fool.'

'It's a sin,' Yonden moaned. He cast a frantic look at the advancing Chinese.

Osher leeered at him. 'A sin? You've been robbing me for years. I'll tell you what. There are three thousand dollars in my belt. Two thousand is for the company; the rest you can have if you shoot me. No cheating. Promise?'

'Promise.'

'Go on then.'

Yonden's eyes stung. He began to cry. 'Sir, I lied to you.'

'Of course you lie. You try to keep too many people happy.'

'The American's still alive.'

Osher smiled with one corner of his mouth.

'Do you want him killed?'

'Killed?' Osher seemed to ponder the question, his eyes narrowing as if in intense concentration. He began to snore.

'Sir,' Yonden said, wringing his hands.

'Of course I don't want him killed. The longer he stays alive, the harder the Chinese will chase you – all the way into Nepal this time.'

'But he said that Ngawang took him down to the road.'

'To show him how Tibetans can fight.' Osher turned his head. 'Are the soldiers close?'

'Very close,' Yonden said. He didn't need to look.

'You'd better get it over with, or you'll be shaking too much to hold the gun straight.'

Yonden swallowed and began to unsling his rifle.

'Not with that. Use your revolver.'

'I lost it,' Yonden said, his teeth chattering.

'Use mine,' Osher said, his hand creeping towards his holster. 'It makes a bigger hole. I don't want them to recognise me. Let them think I'm still alive.'

Eyes fixed on the Chinese soldiers, Yonden clawed at the holster. He fumbled out the heavy automatic and pointed.

'Not like that. The back of the head. That's better. Wait. Which way is Kham?'

'Behind you.'

'Turn me round.'

Yonden did so. Osher sighed.

'How many soldiers?' he asked.

'Hundreds. A battalion at least.'

Osher smiled. 'Go slowly, Yonden.'

381

Yonden pulled the trigger and half of Osher's face blew away in a gust of spray, leaving a bloody blank above a dreamy smile.

The Chinese were temporarily hidden in a fold. Yonden's hands busied themselves at Osher's waist. He found the belt and unbuckled it. He considered taking the binoculars and decided against it. There was still no sign of the soldiers. He dropped the Zippo into his pocket, wiped the belt in a patch of snow, strapped it on beneath his shirt, cleaned his hands as best he could and ran for his horse. He galloped away and did not look back until he had gained the skyline.

Empty – empty in all directions. In all that expanse Osher's body stood out like a punctuation mark on blank paper. Yonden rode on.

Dusk was rising like daylight's dying gasp when he came to a thin slash in the scarp. Dorje was waiting just inside.

'Have they found our trail?' he asked.

'No sign of them.'

'I thought I heard a shot.'

'I fired at a hare.'

The canyon was part of a massive, reticulated system with many branches which they sometimes took and sometimes ignored. They heard planes several times. It was dark when they caught up with the main party, but they went on for an hour before Chorphel called a halt at a cave. By then exhaustion had cauterised Yonden's emotions. If it hadn't been for the belt that he touched from time to time, he would have been inclined to think that Osher had been part of the same mirage as the Chinese army.

'I give up,' Melville said, getting to his feet. 'I'm not asking for a vote of thanks, but I would have expected a military man to show a little more pragmatism.'

'My sympathies are with the general,' Gunn told him. 'All along I thought that you were a fool, but honest in your way, and now I find you were prepared to con this man into going to Taiwan.'

'I owned up, didn't I. I'm offering him what he wants.'

'Sleep is what he wants.'

Sitting with his back to the wall of the cave, the object of contention looked from one to the other with the wary glitter of a trapped animal. In the space of a day, his military bearing had deserted him. He looked overweight and middle-aged and scared. Occasionally he glanced towards the mouth of the cave, where the Khampas were gathered. Two of them were sorting through the remaining supplies, deciding what to discard, but their attention was on the group arguing around the fire. It was clear that they had split into two camps.

'If we don't put our act together,' Melville told Gunn, 'we're going to end up playing along in someone else's.' He looked down at Liu. 'Forgive the lack of elementary courtesies, but this may be the last chance to talk before we reach the border.' He sank onto his haunches. 'General, in spite of the unhappy circumstances, your objective is still within reach. You asked for safe passage to the United States, and that's what I'm offering you.'

'It's not within your power to offer me a thing,' Liu said. 'You are not an agent of the American government. You're a criminal who would even try to swindle your accomplices.'

'I don't need any lectures on treachery from you,' Melville said in English. He smiled nicely. 'You'll get everything you asked for. House, money – everything. In fact, I always thought your original demands were far too low. The more you ask for, the more seriously the people we'll be negotiating with will take you.'

'I would like to hear how you intend to negotiate with the Americans from a cave.'

'Quite,' Gunn said.

Melville gave him a melancholy smile. 'Why don't you shut up,' he said. He turned back to the general. 'Don't you worry. I'll take care of things.'

'No,' Liu said with testy finality.

Melville blew a sigh. 'Am I overlooking something? There are only two ways out of Nepal – my way and Mr Yueh's. You've rejected both.'

'India,' Liu said.

Melville and Gunn exchanged looks.

'Three days after crossing the border,' Liu said. 'I could be safe in India.'

'General,' Melville said, 'how would your government react if India gave you asylum?'

'They would lodge a protest.'

'Great,' Melville said to Gunn. 'The general of an army that's on a war footing with India surfaces in Delhi and all Peking does is write them a stern note. General,' he said, 'I think your leaders would threaten severe retaliation – so severe that the Indians might be obliged to hand you back.' Melville squirmed into a more comfortable position. 'The Chinese, as you know, are not in a position to put pressure on my government.'

383

'We don't know how anyone will react,' Gunn said. 'We're completely out of touch with the world.'

'And you seem determined to throw away our only ticket back,' Melville told him. He stared into the general's face. 'I don't owe this man a thing,' he said. 'If he won't play ball, we may as well dump him.'

'I won't have you talking like that!'

Yonden came hurrying over. With a glance at the general, he drew Gunn and Melville aside. 'It's decided,' he said. 'Dorje will go to Mustang.'

'How many does that leave with Chorphel?' Melville asked.

'Eight, I think.'

'Why don't the others want to go with Chorphel?' Gunn asked.

'The Chinese will be waiting at all the passes,' Yonden said. 'Chorphel knows one place, but it is difficult, and there will be Gurkhas on the other side. Dorje knows many ways into Mustang, and once he is there he says he will be safe. It is better for him.'

'Not for us, though,' Melville said. 'The question is, will Chorphel take us with him – plus General Liu?'

'Yes, he has agreed.'

'But?'

The Khampas had fallen silent. They were looking on, attentive and unsmiling.

'They are very unhappy,' Yonden whispered. 'They must find another place to live, but without money it is very difficult for them. I told them we can get money for the general. Dorje said it's too dangerous; kill him. Chorphel said no, he comes with me and we exchange him for money.'

'Who from?' Melville asked.

'I said we must do what Osher wants and give him to Mr Yueh. I said you would ask for many dollars to share among them.'

'Are they convinced?'

'I think so,' Yonden said. He giggled. 'One man wants to sell him back to the Chinese.'

'Jesus.'

'So much for your grand ideas,' Gunn said.

General Liu's eyes had been switching from face to face. 'Since you can't agree on the best way to get the calf to market,' he said, 'perhaps you could let it get some rest.'

Melville stared blindly at the Khampas for a moment. He nodded at them, then turned back to Yonden and gripped his arm. 'Okay,

Yonden, for now it's back to business with Mr Yueh. You go back to your friends and tell them we're going to do just what they want. Tell them we're going to ask Mr Yueh for whatever round figure excites them. Tell them anything you like, so long as it makes them believe the general's life is worth saving.'

'You make him sound like a commodity for barter,' Gunn said.

'He is,' Melville told him. He sat down in front of Liu again and parodied a smile. 'It grieves me to tell you that the Khampas have been debating whether to slit your throat or ransom you.'

Liu's mouth tightened.

'Avarice has prevailed, I'm pleased to say. Unfortunately, they think they'll get the best price from the Kuomintang. They want me to keep my agreement with Mr Yueh.'

'I'm not going to live in that dung heap,' Liu insisted.

'Calm down,' Melville told him. He jerked his head at the Khampas. 'They're in a volatile mood. Ten of their friends dead, a traitor in their own camp, no leader and no place to go. We'll talk about final destinations later. For now, though, I'd welcome your professional opinion on our chances of giving your patrols the slip. The Khampas are splitting up, and we're going with Chorphel and half a dozen others. He's an honourable man and he knows every pass between here and Sinkiang.'

Liu's face split in a scornful smile. 'You can't control a few bandits, but you swear you can get me to America.'

'Money talks, we say. The Khampas will listen, don't you fear.'

'I know another of your corrupt sayings. Money has no smell. These barbarians would be just as happy with Indian money. I'm going to talk to them.'

'I'd much rather you didn't,' Melville said, restraining Liu with one hand.

The general's face went blank. He began to exert pressure. With his other hand, Melville reached inside his *chuba*.

'General,' Gunn said quickly. 'Mr Melville and I can't have anything to do with the Indians. One of their army officers tried to have Mr Melville killed when he was in Kathmandu. He followed us into the valley.'

'I wish you hadn't done that,' Melville said, his eyes still fixed on Liu's.

'What officer?' Liu said. 'Does he know about me? Why wasn't I told?'

'We never had a chance to ask,' Melville said. 'The Khampas murdered him.'

The general folded up. Melville nodded.

'You see,' he said. 'If I could find a way out of this maze on my own, I'd let you go where you choose. But you're the only reason why anybody would rescue us, and the only people I want to be rescued by are the Americans. For me India means prison, maybe worse. So,' he said, climbing to his feet, 'if you try making your own deal with the Khampas, I'll shoot you dead. Have I made myself clear?'

Liu nodded dazedly.

'Good,' Melville said. 'Now we can go forward in a spirit of compromise. I'd get some sleep if I were you. We leave in five hours.'

An hour later he was still lying wide-eyed in the dark. 'Alan,' he said softly.

'No more.'

'The PLA must be a cheerier outfit tonight. Hard to imagine that Liu was once a hero – an idealist.'

'People change. People lose hope or get corrupted.'

'We'll have to keep an eye on him.'

'Would you really kill him?'

'If it's him or me.'

'*You've* changed, Walter. For all your faults, I never thought of you as a villain.'

'Out here there are no heroes and no villains. There are only survivors and victims.'

Climbing in mauve shadows, Melville envied Dorje's party inching up the sunlit slope on the far wall of the basin. The Khampas had separated a couple of hours ago, taking opposite sides of the canyon just before it opened out into a wide cirque. The parting had taken place with little ceremony, and in the dark Melville had hardly noticed it. Judging by their superior height, the men bound for Mustang were having the easier time. They were already two-thirds of the way to a smooth ridge that suggested good going beyond, whereas on this side the angle got progressively steeper towards a tumbled skyline. Fans of frozen scree and slabs sheeted with ice made the going hard and sometimes treacherous.

At least Melville wasn't handicapped by his horse; with several others it had been left to die at the camp – no thought of putting it out of its misery. Freed from that responsibility, he was able to succumb to the monotony of motion, climbing on the fringe of consciousness. At frequent intervals he stopped and frowned around him, like an old man who has the dimmest idea of where he is and where he's going.

The faintest of cries woke him. Across more than a mile of thin air, Dorje and his companions made a tiny frieze against the unblemished sky. They lifted their hands then, one by one, sank from sight.

Melville didn't meet the sun until he reached the top an hour later. It was small reward, its warmth cancelled out by a freezing wind. He found the lee of a rock and looked impassively at what was yet to come. They were at the angle of two ridges. Between them, precipices shot down on each side of a crooked defile that was so narrow as to be little more than a chimney. The view beyond was forbidding – ranges aligned in no particular direction, with raw-edged summits standing straight up from bowls of snow and glaciers striped with debris. In the opposite direction Dorje's party were back in sight, dotted like fly specks on a snowfield that climbed away in soft folds.

Yonden manhandled his horse up the last few feet and gazed with satisfaction at the wastes ahead. 'Chinese never find us in there,' he said.

'I hope there's a way out,' Melville said.

'Ah, I hope so,' Yonden said, collapsing beside him.

'It's uncanny. Two days and not a sight of the PLA. What's keeping them?'

'They'll be waiting at the border.'

'A million of them,' Melville said, 'a human chain stretching from Sikkim to Ladakh.' He nodded at the Khampas grouped around Chorphel, who was pointing across the mountains to the promised land. 'What will your friends do when they reach the other side?'

'They know some Khampas who work as shepherds in another valley.'

'Do we cross directly into this valley?'

'It takes three, four days to walk there from the border.'

'I had a nasty feeling it might.'

'Sah?'

'Would strangers be noticed in this valley?'

'I've never been there. Chorphel says there are some villages.'

'Yonden, you don't intend to spend what's rest of your life as a shepherd.'

'Soon as this trouble is over, I leave the mountains and go back to the city. I'll learn to be an accountant and start my own business.'

'You'll need money.'

Yonden smiled.

'Ten thousand dollars – would that get you started?'

Yonden's smile turned sad.

'Unless I can get Liu to America, Alan and I are dead.'

Yonden's smile stiffened. 'Charlie will get you out.'

'Charlie's the bastard who got me in. It was probably Charlie who persuaded Osher to leave me as his calling card outside the *dzong*.'

'That is not the truth.'

'Huh? What makes you so sure?'

Yonden avoided his eye.

'Well, never mind that,' Melville said. 'Say we reach this valley. It will take at least a week to send a message to Mr Yueh and another week for him to arrange a getaway. We'll never escape notice that long – not surrounded by villagers, with every Chinese spy in Nepal out looking for us. Face it, in Nepal Alan and I will be a bigger handicap than we are now. The general's worth clinging on to, but I couldn't blame your friends if they decided to ditch us.'

'I'll take you out of the mountains myself.'

'I appreciate it. But then what? Like Jetha said, everything that comes out of Nepal ends up in India. We can't leave overland. The only way is by private plane, but no one's going to send a plane unless we have the general to put on board. Do you understand what I'm saying?'

'You want me to cheat my friends.'

'They'll get what's owed to them, I swear.'

'You must speak to Chorphel,' Yonden said, attempting to rise.

'He's not a man of the world like you,' Melville said, holding Yonden back. 'He can't see the big picture. Help us slip away when we get over the frontier. Help us find a place to stay while you contact a friend of mine.'

'This is unlucky talk,' Yonden said.

'Luck's an item we've been pushing for weeks. This way we don't leave it all to chance.'

Yonden stood up and looked away across the basin, his teeth nagging his lip. Melville stole an anxious glance at the Khampas.

'Ten thousand,' he said.

Yonden took a couple of steps forward, in an absent-minded kind of way, then crouched like a diver.

'What is it?' Melville asked.

At Yonden's shout, the Khampas grabbed their guns and ran up

388

to the crest. Melville held out his hands to ward them off but they went past him. Their voices died. Melville pushed his way through them.

Even from this great distance the figures of Dorje's party stood out pin-sharp on the snowfield. They were heading back – retreating before a stippled crescent. There was no sound of gunfire; the wind was against it. They simply vanished, one after the other. They were there; then they weren't. Wiped out. The crescent came on, losing shape, breaking up into clusters.

'How long have we got?' Melville asked, after a decent silence.

He didn't really have to ask. It was after ten, some four hours since they had separated. It would take the Chinese soldiers at least seven hours to reach this spot, which effectively meant they had a one-day lead. But the soldiers now knew where they were and what direction they were taking, and they had at least three days to close every chink and loophole in the wall ahead.

Chapter 24

The weather turned wrathful. Three days after the death of Dorje's group, a wave of cloud rolled over the mountains, pushing a band of hail the size of bantams' eggs. It was the leading edge of a blizzard that blew for two days and nights. The survivors sat it out in a cave, certain that nobody else could move in such conditions, and the next afternoon they were able to make a little progress, although they had to abandon the last of the horses when they got bogged down in the new snow. That evening the sky turned red. Dawn came up as a blue and ginger stain, the colour of ripe meat, lanced by beams of light that picked out patches of mountainside like cuirasses. By mid-morning the cloud blanket was complete – low enough to hide every summit, high enough to show the formidable scale of the range they had to cross.

They were working their way along its base, following a stream bed up a steepening valley, climbing frozen waterfalls and ice-covered boulders. It was sweaty, painful work, but preferable to forcing a passage through the deep snow on either side. The frequent tremors of unseen avalanches reduced them to silence.

After two weeks they were in poor shape. Yeshe had a fever caused by an abcess in his ear, and three of the others had frostbitten toes. The dry air had inflamed the general's throat, making breathing an effort and speech painful. Gunn often staggered like a drunkard and had to be fetched back to the correct line by Yonden, whose eyes were crusted with an unpleasant yellow discharge. Melville's guts felt as if they had been tied in a knot. His teeth felt loose in his head. Falling apart, he thought. Although he had lost a lot of weight – he couldn't say how much, because it was weeks since he had seen himself in the flesh – he had little appetite. Nowadays, the stuff of his daydreams was a spotless bed and a fragrant bath. He smiled often – the kind of smile that would have made a stranger give him a wide berth. He had words of encouragement for himself, although he was not conscious of muttering them. They were mainly curses.

Morale was deteriorating. Each time Chorphel came to a snowfield and examined it for clues only he could recognise, the rest of the company slumped where they had stopped, careless of the sweat

390

freezing on them. As the morning wore on it took longer to get them moving again, and they began to resist Chorphel to the point of jostling him. He grew anxious, his gaze sliding about in search of something to latch onto, his answers becoming evasive and then drying up altogether. Hope rose when he halted at the foot of a snowfield that rose clear of obstructions into the clouds. It fell when he shook his head and they moved on, to find the valley blocked by vertical, ribbed walls of ice. They trooped back and Chorphel studied the snowfield again, then issued instructions. They would wait a night, hoping that the sky would clear. Two men would go back down the valley to search for shelter. After eating, he and one other would climb the snowfield to check its condition.

Yonden lit a stove and melted snow. The Khampas chewed singed horsemeat. Melville forced himself to eat. He assessed the problem. The snowfield took the form of a slightly dished fan with a bulge, almost a step, in its centre. Its surface was fretted by the wind and in places he detected the wicked gleam of ice. He concluded that it wasn't beyond him.

'We've come through worse,' he said to Gunn.

'There could be another five thousand feet hidden in the clouds,' Gunn said.

'That's my ray of sunshine,' Melville said.

'It's not just me, Walter. Look at the men.'

'They'll be fine after a night's rest. We don't have to rush at it. Nobody could have followed us through the storm.'

'This may not even be the right valley.'

'I'm backing Chorphel's judgement.'

'We passed a snowfield very much like this one a couple of hours ago.'

'So what do you want us to do – flip a coin?'

'We might have reached a dead end.'

'Boasting or complaining?'

'I don't know what you mean.'

'Oh for chrissake, Alan. Ever since we started heading back you've been acting like a man who's ready to curl up and die.'

'I'm only trying to be realistic.'

'Realistic – you? The only reason you're here is because you were scared of the bogey men.'

'I don't expect you to understand.'

'I understand, all right. This is another futile exercise in squaring your conscience. I don't need it. Yonden doesn't need it. Look where it's landed us.'

'You're upsetting the men.'

'No one's paying a blind bit of notice. They've got their own problems.'

Gunn got up, his face blenched, and moved away twenty yards. He sat down, his back to everyone.

'Yeah, well,' Melville said. His squall of anger had brought tears to his eyes and left him shaking.

Chorphel and the Khampa he had selected started up the slope. Melville concentrated on them fiercely. They grew small very quickly. It always surprised him how fast the landscape reduced the human figure to insignificance. A man could die of it, he thought. Of exposure. Annihilation by space.

Half an hour went by. The cold gnawed at him. The two Khampas were the size of flies on a shopfront window. They weren't quarter of the way up it.

Melville heard faint popping sounds. He sat up apathetically. 'They must have found tonight's lodgings.'

No one paid any attention. The Khampas were getting to their feet, reaching almost absently for their guns. They were all looking down the valley. The pair on the mountain had stopped.

'Wasn't that the signal?' Melville asked. His guts fluttered.

A short way below them the valley kinked. Nothing was moving. The silence became intolerable. At the same moment everyone looked at the two Khampas on the mountain. They were making slow come-hither signals.

Melville swallowed saliva.

Yonden straightened up from a crouch, as though relaxing. 'Soldiers,' he said.

Like a film suddenly restarted, everyone was in motion at once, running different ways, grabbing packs, dropping things.

'We don't even know if it's the right mountain,' Melville cried, carried along with the rest. He was fumbling his pack over his shoulders, floundering after the Khampas, his breathing already unequal to the effort.

'Your ice axe,' Gunn shouted behind him.

'Move it, move it,' Melville shouted, his eyes on the turn in the valley. He took the axe at arm's length, frantic not to lose an inch. Yonden was hanging back, arms spread wide, shooing his little flock out of harm's way.

Fear pushed Melville past his usual limit, but when at last he was forced to stop, he saw that he had climbed no more than the height of a modest house. The Khampas were already out of touch, pulling themselves up with long, low strides. He could hear them exchange the occasional word. He looked back to see that Gunn and the general and Yonden had hardly made any height at all. Yonden was hauling the general up by the front of his jacket. Gunn was resting every third or fourth step. It's everyone for himself, Melville thought.

He resumed climbing, taking it easier, husbanding his strength for the moment the Chinese appeared.

He almost missed them. They were lower than he would have dared hope and inconspicuous in winter camouflage. They were climbing as a unit – a grey caterpillar. Melville wiped the sweat from his eyes and tried to count them. About thirty. Thirty against ten, of whom eight were armed. But the Khampas weren't going to make a stand. They were going to save their own skins. Already they were as high above him as the Chinese were below.

Gunn and Liu were catching up. He could distinguish the general's high, piping breathing from Gunn's harsher note. In a few minutes the Chinese would have them in range. It would be like shooting fish in a barrel. He decided to give up. It was as simple as that. He sat down to wait. The revolver was in his *chuba*, but he knew he wouldn't be able to use it.

Yonden was waving him on. So was Gunn.

'I'm tired,' he called down. He was impressed by how calm he sounded. He felt calm, too.

Gunn tried to stand up straight and fell over.

'Climb . . . one . . . minute,' Yonden managed to get out.

'No point. Your friends are running out on us. You'd better join them.' He looked around at the mountains. It occurred to him that he was probably the first Westerner to have set foot on this mountain.

'They . . . wait . . . there.'

Chorphel and his partner were out of sight above the bulge; the other four Khampas were starting to climb it. The Chinese formation was growing ragged. It couldn't be much fun for them either. They looked so puny, so ill-adapted to the effort.

Liu got within a few feet, then stalled, his face blue and bulging.

'Give me your pack,' Melville said, sliding down to him. 'Come on, come on. Get your fat ass up there.'

Dragging the general's pack, he set off again. Immediately beneath the bulge the angle relented, then inclined up so sharply that he had to climb on all fours, kicking toeholds. A fizzing sound made him lie flat, trying not to slide back. It came again and lingered. He looked up and saw that the path made by the bullet was still imprinted on the air.

He pulled himself over the step to find the Khampas relaxing behind their weapons. Chorphel was adjusting the sights on his Mauser with the squint-eyed concentration of a watchmaker. Melville lay down next to Yeshe, who patted him on the back. When he was able, he wormed his way to the edge and peeped over. Gunn and the general were at the bottom of the bulge, with Yonden still behind them, walking backwards so that he could keep an eye on the Chinese, who were close enough to be picked out as real flesh and blood beings. An officer climbed to one side of them, forcing the pace, shaking his fist. Melville bit his lip at the thought of putting so many people to so much trouble.

Hands reached down to haul Gunn and Liu up. The general began to retch. Yonden scrambled over the top and lay on his back, his arms crossed over his face.

A cry was heard. The soldiers had stopped, the sheen of exertion on their upturned faces. A small group was setting up a machine gun. The rest were spreading out behind it. Some of them sat down, and when the officer noticed he yelled and shook his fist harder than ever. He shouted up at the Khampas, calling for a peaceful surrender, but the way he had to gulp air between each syllable robbed the demand of power.

Breathing grew quiet and sweat chilled. The group behind the machine gun had gone still. The rest had formed two lines, parallel to the bulge, about ten yards apart. Knowing what was going to happen, Melville put his hands over his head and flattened out.

'That was decent of you,' Gunn murmured in his ear.

'What?' Melville said, looking at him through the crook of his elbow.

'Staying back like that.'

'I was going to surrender.'

'You took the general's load.'

'Self interest.'

Gunn's response was blown away in a rush of bullets. Where they went, Melville had no idea. The firing went on for a long time, stopped and then resumed. This time he heard the soft impact of bullets hitting the snow below. Between the hammering of machine gun fire came the crackle of lighter weapons – co-ordinated at first, then growing fitful. The machine gun fell silent and Melville risked a

394

look. The two lines were advancing in turn, covering each other. It looked rather orderly, but though Melville was no expert, he knew that even a company of crack shots had next to no chance of hitting almost invisible targets at a range of more than two hundred yards up a thirty-five degree slope – not when their brains were so starved of oxygen that even lifting a rifle to the shoulder and staying upright required conscious effort.

Chorphel raised his head and seemed to sniff the air. He cuddled up to his Mauser and fired without effect. He shot again – another miss. Melville could see the machine gun crew working on their weapon. The officer was leading his men. He turned, saw a man hanging back and pointed his gun at him. Chorphel fired and shook his head irritably. Yeshe murmured something across Melville's back and his neighbour nodded and pulled a face. Chorphel missed once more, hissed with displeasure, and made a small correction to the sights.

The soldiers were close enough for features to be inferred. The officer was a thin, olive-skinned young man. The soldiers in the leading line raised their weapons. One or two found it hard to keep their balance. Their gaping mouths made holes in their faces. Chorphel fired and a soldier fell over backwards. The man next to him turned to look and a bullet knocked him sideways. At Chorphel's next shot, the officer took two or three steps back, sat down and began to slide through the lines. Someone grabbed him but was pulled over, and they both went gliding away, spinning slowly.

Wriggling into a fresh attitude, Chorphel squeezed off one more round, raised his head and pursed his lips. He ducked a fraction of a second after a burst of machine gun fire whacked into the top of the step. The Khampas waited until the machine gun was being reloaded before dragging themselves forward. They began firing single shots, taking time over each one. The machine gun opened up again and they continued firing.

Melville's ears were ringing. He heard commands and someone shrilling in pain. The Chinese were retreating, glissading back to the level of the machine gun, leaving six, seven bundles in the snow – no, eight; the officer had slid a long way down the mountain. One of the bundles was moving, leaving a smear of red. Two of the soldiers stopped, hesitated and turned back. All the Khampas fired at almost the same instant and the wounded man lay still and the two soldiers slipped down to safety.

In the space of thirty seconds, Melville's emotions had gone through fear, indifference, excitement and disgust. It was disgust he was left with, and when he turned to General Liu he expected to see the same expression on his face. Instead the general, his composure returned with his wind, looked as though none of this had anything to do with him.

'Those are your soldiers,' Melville said. He hadn't meant to say it.

Liu's expression turned peevish. He tried to speak and failed. He made another attempt. 'If they had been my soldiers,' he said in a strangled whisper, 'we'd be dead.'

'They've lost a quarter of their strength. Maybe they'll call up reinforcements.'

'Unless they have mortars,' Liu said, 'they'll do what they should have done in the first place.' His eyes switched from one side of the snowfield to the other.

It was about half a mile wide at this point, bounded by sharp, snow-wrinkled ridges. Anyone keeping to the edges would be beyond effective range. The Khampas might kill a few, but most would get past the step, reversing the position.

'Do we sit and wait?' Melville asked.

Liu appraised the situation. He tapped Yonden on the shoulder. 'Can we climb higher without being seen from below?'

Yonden nodded.

'We must leave as soon as possible,' Liu said, indicating Gunn and Melville. 'Tell your friends to wait until the soldiers have reached the cliffs before following.'

Melville thought that Chorphel might have his own ideas, but the elderly guerilla nodded agreement.

As the general had predicted, the soldiers were moving off left and right, leaving behind a group of five or six dug in around the machine gun. Its crew loosed off short bursts to keep the heads of the Khampas down.

Melville rolled over. Fanged ridges converging on a dreary sky. Snow threatened. It would be dark in a couple of hours.

Out of the corner of his eye he saw Yeshe rise on one knee, taking aim at a tail-ender. Bullets *swish-swished* past. There was a solid noise – *thwock* – like a bar striking a wet sandbag, and Yeshe's head changed shape. Something flew off. Before Melville could look away, he registered the fact that Yeshe no longer wore a luxuriant fringe – an indelible impression. Gunn wormed over and pulled the Khampa's hood over what was left of his head.

The machine gun fell silent and the Khampas' shooting became perfunctory. A radio squawked below. The leading Chinese had gained the margins, their uniforms hard to spot against the rock and snow. Melville calculated that they would reach the level of the step in twenty minutes at most.

'What are we waiting for?' he muttered. The question had no force. His adrenalin had been squandered in the fire-fight; his feet and hands ached with cold. What did it matter? The choice was between freezing and frying.

Yonden was touching him on the ankle, looking at him as though he knew the choice was a hopeless one. The other Khampas' eyes flicked up at him. He hesitated, wanting to say something suitably valedictory. Nothing came to mind. They'll come through, he told himself. These guys are in their element. Yonden was tugging at him. He crawled.

In this manner he climbed about fifty yards, then Yonden stood up and he cautiously did the same. The group around the machine gun were out of sight below the bulge, but the soldiers on each side of the snowfield had them in sight and raised a shout. Seconds later machine gun fire fizzled overhead.

Now the soldiers were in a dilemma. If they continued creeping up below the ridges, where the going was slow and uneven, they had no chance of catching up. If they moved back to the centre, they risked being shot by the Khampa rearguard. Even as he took in the situation, Melville saw the Chinese leave the cliffs and begin heading back towards the bulge. If the Khampas withdrew now, the Chinese would have the advantage. If they hung on too long, they would be cut down from both sides.

Don't think about them, Melville told himself. Get into the cloud.

With this resolution fixed in his mind he leaned into the slope, not pushing too hard. The snow was soft but not mushy; it compacted nicely, accommodating itself to his feet. He was making steps for the others to follow, and he even found a kind of satisfaction in the repetition of basic moves. He sensed the cloud getting closer, and he knew he would make it.

A clatter of shots signalled that the Khampas were retiring. Gunn and Liu were making progress. The two lines of Chinese were coming together in the shape of an arrowhead pointed at the knot of guerillas. Where Melville stood the snowfield was only a couple of hundred yards wide. If the Khampas could get this high, they could command the mountain. And they were going to do it. They were almost running up the slope. The Chinese knew it. They were shooting aimlessly as they climbed.

Melville sat down. Up here the mountains were wrapped in a massive calm. He viewed the scene below with relative detachment.

A moment later he was on his feet, alerted by some primitive reflex. From behind, above the wavering edge of cloud, came a strange sound – a feeble mewing, like a basket of kittens. He had never heard such a sound before, yet he knew immediately what it signified.

Gunn and the general were still climbing. Yonden had stopped and was looking up.

'Avalanche!'

The snow puckered, swarming past with an unpleasant susurration. It took him by the knees and pushed him back, slewing him around. As he fell he glimpsed the general, his legs pumping like a man trying to run up a down escalator. Gunn was sliding head first on his back, helpless as a capsized beetle. Yonden was scrambling out of his field of vision.

Melville fell on his side and gasped as snow poured down his neck and pressed an icy poultice to his back. He tried to get up, failed, tried again and found himself running and sinking at the same time. He was dimly aware of hearing a soft detonation, like the explosion of untamped gunpowder, and then a painful, drawn-out grating.

He had stopped moving.

He was on his knees, recording what was happening though not making sense of it. Not far below him the snow had fractured along a front about thirty yards wide. Everything below the break was sliding away, gliding at first in a cohesive mass and then buckling into blocks and floes that accelerated with a deepening roar. It didn't seem to be moving fast until he saw the figures below, scattering in hopeless flight. It swallowed them, first the Khampas, then the soldiers, and raced on over the bulge. A bass rumble rose on a cloud of white powder and drifted down in angry mutters.

The avalanche had cut a swathe as broad as a six-lane highway.

Some loose snow slithered away from the fracture zone and went singing down the slope.

The general was sitting down.

Gunn had disappeared.

Yonden was on all fours, scrabbling at the snow. He was whimpering.

Melville waded over to him, certain that Gunn had been swept away. It was difficult to know where to look first. When he had last

398

seen Gunn he had been above him and the general. Now he was well below Liu.

It was Yonden who spotted the scrap of cloth poking out of the snow. Gunn's knee. Yonden dug away the snow above it, but Melville remembered that Gunn had been sliding head-first, and he dug below. He found one of Gunn's arms and pulled. They both pulled. The snow had him fast. They dug some more and uncovered Gunn's face. It was deathly grey, with icy coins over his eyes. He was still wearing his pack and they had to ease him out of it before they could sit him up. His head lolled.

Melville laid him on his back, stuck a finger down his throat and put mouth to mouth. Yonden was massaging Gunn's hands in a useless way. Melville grabbed one of them, feeling for a pulse, but he had lost one of his gloves and his fingers were too numb to feel anything even if there had been anything to feel.

'He's dead,' Yonden said.

'Stop snivelling and try get his heart started,' Melville shouted. He demonstrated how.

As he worked, he saw how close they had all come to death, and how precarious their position still was. They were near the edge of a tongue of frozen slurry that had been left behind when the slab avalanche broke away. Trickles of snow were still coming down. Night was close. There were so many frightening considerations that he couldn't consider them.

'Help me turn him over,' he told Yonden.

The general was still sitting, stupid with shock.

'Haul your ass down here,' Melville yelled. 'Take Gunn's pack.'

As the general lumbered down, Gunn coughed frothy pink sputum.

'Get yourself over there,' Melville told Liu, jerking his head towards the western ridge. 'Find shelter – safe shelter, not the first hole you come to.'

He and Yonden rolled Gunn onto his back again. His face was the colour of gunmetal, his eyes open but glassy.

'He's taken snow in his lungs,' Melville said.

'Is he going to die?'

'How long was he buried?'

'I don't know. Two or three minutes.'

Two or three minutes? Melville would have guessed thirty or forty seconds.

Gunn coughed again, dribbling froth, and mumbled. Melville went on kneading his chest until he began to rock his head from side to side.

'Can't do more here,' Melville told Yonden. 'We have to move him before the rest of the mountain goes.'

The general had traversed halfway to the cliffs. In the dusk his clothing looked black. Melville was worried about a lost mitt. Gunn's ice axe was missing. They searched for them without success. When they lifted Gunn to his feet, Yonden hesitated, looking back down the mountains.

'Maybe someone else is alive,' he said.

Clean sweep was the phrase that came to mind. 'Nobody else got out,' Melville said.

Still Yonden went on looking.

'I saw all of it,' Melville said. 'They didn't have a hope.'

But as he moved off, he took with him a nightmare image of a hand reaching out of the snow, straining to make contact.

Gunn was semi-conscious, his legs moving in a reflex gesture at walking. It took fifteen minutes to reach the general, who was huddled miserably in a rocky fissure, blowing on his hands. 'Great help you've turned out to be,' Melville said. He could no longer feel his own hands and feet, but before he could start worrying about that, there were other concerns to be met. He fumbled Gunn's pack open, drew out his sleeping bag and spare clothes and, with Yonden's help, got Gunn into them. Gunn was conscious, his skin white and oily, black circles under his eyes. 'Stove, stove,' Melville cried, terrified that they had no means of cooking. Yonden held up a Primus and a bottle of fuel. Melville snatched it and thrust it at the general. 'Do something,' he said.

He opened his own pack and took out his sleeping bag and down jacket. He stripped to the waist and put on every item of clothing he had, then he worked his boots off and got into the bag. He drew his knees up and clasped his feet. Dead meat.

'Give me that,' he said, losing patience with the general. As Yeshe's assistant, he had familiarised himself with the stove's quirky behaviour, but his hands were too numb to operate the screws. He handed it to Yonden, who had it primed and purring within five minutes. The general offered up a pot of snow as though fearful of rebuff.

Time to take stock. Melville leaned back against the cliff, his left side pressed close to Gunn, who was breathing in short, shallow bursts. Situation not good, Melville thought. Situation bad as bad can be. No real idea where they were, no shelter, weather closed in on them, food for only a couple of days, a sick – possibly dying – man on their hands.

'Where do we go from here?' he asked Yonden, who was feasting his eyes on the blue flame of the stove.

'Over the mountain.'

'Did Chorphel give you directions?'

Yonden shook his head. 'We see where to go from the top.'

'We won't see anything in this shit,' Melville said, looking up at the clouds coiling around rock, 'and we can't sit it out here. General,' he said, 'tomorrow we'll go back down. Maybe we'll find some food, maybe even a tent.'

'Tomorrow more soldiers will be here.'

'They'll assume we're dead.'

'Dead men don't leave tracks.'

'It might snow.'

Liu snorted.

'Either we freeze here,' Melville said, 'or we . . .' He was unable to come up with an alternative.

Gunn mumbled something.

'Welcome back to the land of the living,' Melville said.

'. . . others?' Gunn managed to say.

'You rest that throat,' Melville said, his smile beginning to ache.

'Are they down below?' Gunn asked.

Full fathom five. Melville's eyes stung with tears. 'Only us four left,' he said, looking away.

Gunn looked at Yonden, who pretended to be busy with the stove. 'Where are we?'

'Between a rock and a hard place,' Melville told him. 'We'll work something out.'

He was spared further effort by the water coming to the boil. Yonden stewed tea, loaded it with sugar, and poured out four equal measures. Melville drank his in one draught, not wanting to waste one calorie of heat. He watched anxiously as Gunn put his mug to his mouth, but he got it all down and held out his mug for more. Yonden hesitated, then gave him his own drink, his eyes meeting Melville's.

'How much fuel do we have?' Melville asked softly.

Yonden picked up the bottle and shook it. The sloshing sounded hollow. He put more snow in the pan and relit the stove. Melville watched it like a hawk, thinking of the fuel ebbing away.

'It's funny,' Gunn said suddenly.

401

Melville viewed him with caution. It was clear that he hadn't grasped the nature of their predicament. Perhaps he had been under so long that a part of his brain had died.

'Funny's a funny word to use.'

'Us surviving. It's not fair.'

Fair was a funny word, too. Nevertheless, Melville could not deny that he had no right to be alive and all the others dead. He saw the hand again.

'How bad do you feel?'

Gunn touched his chest. 'Sore inside . . . hurts to breathe.'

'Cold or warm? My fucking feet are frozen.'

'Warm,' Gunn said, as though surprised.

'How many fingers?' Melville said, holding up three.

'Oh don't be daft, man.'

'Well I don't know,' Melville said. 'You were like a corpse when we pulled you out.'

'I can't remember. I haven't even thanked you.'

'No need,' Melville said. He was unable to suppress the thought that it might have been better if Gunn had died. Digging him out had only put off the inevitable.

Yonden doled out four portions of half-cooked rice and horseflesh. Melville ate ravenously. When he had finished, he felt sensation beginning to return to his fingers and toes.

He sat back and waited, clamping his jaws against the pain he knew must come. It started as a distant tingle that grew into an itch that swelled to a bloated throb. His fingers felt as if they had been injected with ground glass and then squeezed in a vice. The pain came in colours – black and red, black and red, alternating with each beat of his heart as he rocked over his knees. He inspected his fingers, expecting to see them swollen to twice normal size, the skin splitting like peel and the flesh curling away from the bone. They were merely a little discoloured and slightly puffy. The lightest touch was agony.

Eventually the pain ate itself up, leaving him nauseous and light-headed. He looked at the others and realised that they hadn't noticed his distress. Gunn was lying back, eyes half closed, trying to get air past the obstruction in his throat. Yonden and Liu gave every indication of being asleep. Marooned with strangers, he thought. Trying to retrace the stages of his journey, he only succeeded in making the world he had left recede like an object viewed through the wrong end of a telescope. He hungered for it, looking across space and silence, the blank indifference of snow and rock. Indifferent? The

402

mountains held them fast and would never let them go. 'Bastard,' he whispered, tears squeezing out of his eyes. 'Bastard.'

He slept and was woken around midnight by Gunn's coughing. Hack, hack, he went. Hack, hack – and then a mumbled apology.

Confused sleep and a cold awakening. The air was knife-sharp. Pale constellations swirled in the sky. The overcast was retreating eastward, leaving behind a single cloud shaped like a flying saucer. The mountains of Tibet stood out with the chill fluorescence of a morgue. Melville's stomach contracted as he saw that the snowfield rose smoothly to a gap-toothed summit. It was one-forty.

Gunn's face was as slick as plastic, but he was still breathing, hacking in his sleep. At exactly the same moment, Yonden and Liu struggled into a sitting position. Their gaze travelled up, and back, settling on Melville with an expression of nervous inquiry. Why should it be down to me? he wondered.

Liu spread his hands with a fat-faced smile. 'Do you still swear to take me to America?' he asked. His voice was stronger this morning.

'Give it an hour,' Melville said.

'Who is this man?' Liu asked, eyeing Gunn with disdain. 'He speaks Tibetan as well as Chinese?'

'Imperialist spy,' Melville said. 'He was a guest at one of your thought reform camps and he liked it so much he came back for more.'

'Delinquents,' Liu said. 'Kuomintang hooligans.'

'That's something I wanted to ask you,' Melville said. 'Given your dislike of the Nationalists, why did you call on Mr Yueh to help you defect?'

'No one else could organise an escape from Tibet.'

'The Indians have recruited Tibetan guerillas, too. You'll know more about it than me, but I understand that they organised them into a commando group called the Special Frontier Force. As a matter of interest, the Indian killed by the Khampas served with them.'

'Indian security is a joke,' Liu said. 'The generals tell secrets to their wives, who gossip to their cousins, who tell their brothers, who broadcast it in the bazaars. Believe me, there is very little that is decided among the Indian Himalayan Command that we don't hear about within a week.'

'I'll take your word,' Melville said. He accepted a mug of melted snow from Yonden and drank greedily. 'You must have allowed for the possibility of the Kuomintang taking you to Taiwan against your will.'

Liu banged down his mug. 'You convinced Zhang Youmin, a friend whom I trust implicitly, that you and the other American . . .'

'Mister Sweetwater.'

'. . . were senior officials representing your government.'

'People will say anything to get what they want. What do *you* want?'

'That is a very foolish question in the circumstances.'

'I would understand,' Melville said, 'if you had taken measures to make sure that you didn't spend the rest of your life among people you despise.'

'I don't despise the people of Taiwan,' Liu said. 'They have been brainwashed by a gangster clique.'

'I wasn't talking about the Nationalists,' Melville said. He made himself stare Liu in the eye. 'You don't strike me as a man who could settle easily in the land of the free. If you were, you would have demanded much more than fifty thousand dollars. That always bothered me.'

Liu stared back, then burst into laughter. 'You think I want to defect to India . . . to live with *Indians?*'

When he laughed, Melville thought, he looked like the jolly, twinkling captain in the photograph Sweetwater had shown him. A man who'd been through what he'd been through would have evolved into a highly complex organism, hedged in and mined with defences in depth. He wasn't going to give anything away under mild questioning on a frozen mountain.

'You make me nervous, that's all.'

The general's laughter had woken Gunn. 'Glad to see you still with us,' Melville said, and meant it.

Yonden served the same dish they'd eaten the evening before. As Melville ate, his eyes kept straying up the snowfield. Each time he looked, the food jammed in his throat. Why look for death, when death was looking for you?

Gunn ate half-heartedly and put down his share unfinished. General Liu gobbled his portion and scraped his bowl clean. Yonden brewed more tea. By the time it was finished, it was past three, and there could be no reason for delaying longer.

'Time we were rolling,' Melville said, not stirring. Everyone was waiting for someone else to make the first move.

Yonden unzipped his bag. He had hardly spoken since the avalanche. Melville yawned, then his face brightened. 'I know,' he said. 'We could pop a couple of bennies.'

404

Gunn found the benzedrine tablets and gave them to Melville, together with some other bottles.

'I don't want all these,' Melville said.

'I'm not coming with you.'

'The hell you're not.'

'I'm finished, Walter. Can't you see?'

'You think I'm raring to go?'

'I've got fluid on my lungs. I couldn't keep up.'

'We're wasting time,' Liu said, rolling his bag into his pack. 'We must be off the snowfield before it gets light.'

'Hear that?' Melville said.

'It's no use,' Gunn said.

'What are you arguing about now?' Liu demanded, stomping his feet.

'My partner prefers to die here.'

'Get up,' Liu said, bridling in soldierly fashion.

Gunn paid no heed.

'In a few hours,' Melville told him, 'the PLA's going to be swarming all over this mountain.'

'I've got something I can take,' Gunn said, patting his pack.

Melville recoiled. 'That medicine's for keeping us alive.'

Gunn shook his head with a faint smile. 'Sometimes you're so naïve.'

'And you're a self-obsessed son of a bitch. While you're drifting off down here, one of us could be lying up there at the bottom of a crevasse with the bones sticking out of our thigh.'

Gunn stifled a cough. 'I couldn't help you any more than I was able to help the Golok.'

'Four stand a better chance than three.'

'Not when one of them is being carried by the others. Walter, I'll be lucky to last the day.'

'So there's no problem. You want to die? Fine – come along with us. Freezing's a good way to go, they say.'

'Leave him,' Liu said, swinging his arms across his chest.

'He doesn't give a damn about you,' Melville said, 'and if I was to break an ankle he wouldn't give a damn about leaving me.' Melville hunkered close. 'I know we haven't always got along too well, but I'd rather go out with you than him. Also,' he said, lowering his voice, 'there's a conflict of interests, and I need you to make sure his don't come out on top.'

'You know I don't want any part of that.'

405

'Talk to him, will you?' Melville called to Yonden, who was idly scuffing at the snow.

'He understands,' Gunn said.

'I get it,' Melville said.

'He shouldn't be here,' Gunn said.

'He's not the only one.'

'Remember the journey to the camp?'

'What about it?'

'How long do you think it would take a very fit man?'

'Four days. Who cares?'

'Yonden has done it in two. If there's a way off this mountain, he could reach a village by nightfall.'

'You're fucking nuts,' Melville said, his voice sliding up the scale. 'You think I'm going to let him go?'

General Liu had ventured out onto the snowfield. He managed a few steps, and then his feet went from under him as though they were mounted on castors.

Melville sat down and hugged his knees.

Gingerly, looking shaken, the general came back. 'The surface is frozen,' he said. 'We must rope ourselves together.'

'No rope,' Melville said, not looking up. 'You're on your own.'

'What are you doing?' Gunn asked after a minute.

'What does it look like?' Melville said. 'I'm staying. If I were to walk out on you, I'd have nightmares the rest of my life.'

Several minutes went by, then Gunn swore in what Melville guessed was Gaelic, ripped off his sleeping bag and stuffed it into his pack.

Wisely, Melville said nothing. Nightmares or not, he had decided to give Gunn fifteen minutes to come to his senses. After that – good riddance.

By the time Melville came out of the gap and began the final push, the sun was halfway up the flat blue sky. He moved with obsessional slowness, his eyes searching for holds, his feet following sluggishly. Often he looked up to remind himself of the goal. It seemed to be no nearer: it might be seven minutes off or seven hours. More like the latter, he thought, as he registered a curious phenomenon. Where he was, there wasn't a breath of wind, yet the summit was feathered with spindrift. Deciding not to think about it, he went on, and on, climbing at first on the points of his crampons as the slope steepened, then on the balls of his feet as it levelled off, and then . . . this wasn't making sense. He was tottering downhill, the summit high above and as far away as ever. He pushed up his goggles and peered through spread fingers. It took a while to reconcile the conflicting signals, but when it finally clicked into focus he couldn't understand why he hadn't seen it immediately. He had reached the top. He was on a smoothly cambered ridge, looking across a snowfield thousands of feet below to a windswept dome thousands of feet above.

There was no way off to the east; the ridge ended against a wall of rock stacked straight and tall like giant crystals of pyrites. In the opposite direction it swelled in a voluptuous curve that hid the view to the west. Refusing to panic, Melville went forward. A section of the ridge came into profile, rounded above and . . . he stopped, eyes popping, waiting for the crack, the sensation of the elevator starting down. He was standing on a cornice. Heart in mouth, he backed away.

He sat down with his back to the ridge. Thousands of square miles of Tibet were spread before him like exploded confectionery. He peeled off his remaining mitt and inspected his hands. They were faintly mottled with brown and were tender to the lightest touch.

To his surprise it was Gunn who appeared first.

'Spot of bother,' he said, giving the thumbs down.

Gunn looked in all directions. 'It can't be west,' he said. 'West would bring us back to the Khampas' valley.'

'East is out. So is south.'

'We passed several gulleys that might have got us above the cliffs,' Gunn said.

'Any particular one you fancy?' Melville said, and hurled a snowball.

'Let's wait for Yonden,' Gunn said.

Melville looked at him side on. 'For a man on his last legs, you're remarkably spry. What's keeping the others?'

'The general's sick,' Gunn said. 'We have to get him to a lower altitude soon.'

'Beautiful,' Melville said. 'You tell him from me, we don't carry our wounded.'

'With all the cloud we had yesterday,' Gunn said, 'Chorphel couldn't get his bearings. We have to consider . . .'

'I don't want to hear it,' Melville said, pulling himself up on his ice axe. 'This has to be the mountain.' He took a drink from his water bottle and pulled his goggles down. 'I'll take a look at what's behind this heap,' he said. 'The ridge swings north higher up and I got a glimpse of some kind of valley down below.'

The sun was near the middle of the sky and the crust was softening, giving way unexpectedly. His crampons worked loose and hampered him, but he didn't have the patience to take them off. He plodded on, eyes fixed on the hard line separating snow from sky, feeling as if he was working his way over the rim of the world. A shadow fell on him and he ducked as the vulture he had seen in the gorge wafted past, heeled over so that one wing seemed to stroke the snow, scribing an invisible line for him to follow. 'What are you doing up here?' he demanded. 'Nothing for you here.' The vulture vanished.

Sharp crests emerged, brown smudges beneath. Heart drumming, he forced himself up the last few feet. The world leapt up.

An angry sea under a sheer fall of sky, the ridge dropping straight as a plumb-line under icy crenations.

He sank to his knees and howled into the black core of the sun.

Gunn came up behind him, breathing as though his lungs were in his throat.

'I know where we are,' he said at last. 'The domed peak is the same one we saw from above the Gurkha barracks. That curved wall over there is right above the *chorten* where we camped. We're only a few miles from the valley.'

'And some nights the moon looks close enough to touch.'

'The ridge continues round to the north. We don't know what it's like on the other side.'

'Fuck it. I've seen over enough horizons.'

'Don't give up now. You seemed so confident.'

Melville stood up and stretched. 'Peaks and troughs. If I had the chance, I'd never leave level ground again.' He stook a step nearer the edge. 'How high do you reckon we are?'

'Higher than the pass out of the valley. Nineteen thousand feet, I'd say.'

'Probably higher than anyone else in the world. How about that? Stuck on top of the world, all those people down there going about their business.'

'How does that make you feel?'

'Lonely.'

'We'll find a way down.'

Melville yawned. 'We've left it too late. Sun will be down long before we are.'

Yonden and Liu joined them, the Khampa leading the general by

408

the elbow. Liu's cheeks were leaden and his lips blueish. Melville sketched in the situation with a casual sweep of his arm. Yonden took it in at a glance, let go of Liu and trudged on.

'He's being very quiet,' Melville said.

'There isn't much to be said.'

There wasn't. They waited without speaking. Melville spent some time retracing part of the route that had brought him to the valley. A mile or so away, a cornice broke off and fell like a severed wing.

'Yonden's calling,' Gunn said at last.

The Khampa was a tiny black star on the pillowy snow. He was waving both hands slowly above his head. Gunn and Melville got slowly to their feet. When he saw he had their attention, Yonden pointed downwards.

'He must have found a way,' Gun said.

Melville grinned. 'That's my boy.'

'Yonden will always find a way,' Gunn said, smiling back.

The first three or four thousand feet were easy – technically easy, that is. All they had to do was keep their balance on a ramp of snow as true and steep as a ski run. To begin with, Melville applied caution, using his ice axe for each step. As he got the feel of it he began to coast, sometimes on his feet and sometimes on his back, using his axe as a brake, not really in control but unable to hold himself back against gravitational force. In the process his boots filled with snow, and he knew he would regret this later when warmth slipped away with the daylight. Already the sun was in his eyes.

He reached the bottom a few minutes after Yonden, who had schlussed down as though equipped with an internal gyroscope. They had to wait twenty minutes for Gunn, who came down on his heels, and nearly an hour for General Liu, who descended on the sides of his boots, like a geriatric on a fire escape. By then the sun was setting on the next ridge and Melville had exhausted all possible avenues of escape.

They were trapped on the balcony of a huge natural theatre, looking down over a horseshoe-shaped precipice into an icy cockpit that opened out into a broad, relatively snow-free valley. To one side of the valley – the north – there was a finely chiselled, triangular peak which Gunn said he had seen from the Lucky Place. Yonden agreed that the temple must be over the pass at the other end of the valley, several miles away, another day's journey distant. All this was academic, Melville shouted, since the cliffs were unclimbable. They were several hundred feet high, broken and taxing to the eye, crowded in by mountain walls. Yonden went off to search from a different angle.

'The wisest thing might be to wait until morning,' Gunn suggested.

'They won't shrink during the night,' Melville snapped.

'We could find ourselves trapped halfway down.'

'We're trapped where we are. Unless we get down tonight, some of us won't see tomorrow.'

'We'll still have to spend another night in the open.'

'Better than two nights. Who knows what the weather will decide to do next? Get down now, and we can sleep at the temple tomorrow.'

'What do you say, General?'

'Nothing that could make any difference. I think we have used up all our luck getting this far.'

'I agree,' Gunn said.

'Hopeless bastards,' Melville said. 'Out here you make your own luck.'

Inwardly he quaked at the prospect of setting foot on the cliffs.

Yonden wandered back, purse-mouthed, and pointed away to the left. 'There is a . . .' his hands described a couloir. 'Halfway down it joins another, not so steep. After that it is not so difficult.'

'And before it?'

'A little,' Yonden said. He studied each of them in turn, his bottom lip sticking out, as though he was deciding which of them he was looking at for the last time.

The sun was cupped in the bowl of the pass. The few high scraps of cirrus had turned rosy. Melville stamped to show he was cold. 'Now?' he asked.

'Yes, sah,' Yonden said, turning to lead the way.

Melville's first reaction was that it was impossible. The line proposed by Yonden – what little could be seen of it – seemed more severe than most of the others he had considered and rejected. But the Khampa almost sauntered over the edge, slithered down a smooth slab, stopped, turned and held up his arms to receive Melville. Now or never, Melville thought. His legs were wobbling, his mouth parched. He sat and rowed himself down a few inches at a time. Yonden took hold of him, although it wasn't necessary, because he was secure on a fairly broad ledge. Yonden caught the others in the same way, then led the next stage.

That is how they continued – Yonden taking the initiative, pointing out the holds and obstacles, leading them by hand past the dicey bits.

There weren't too many. This part of the cliff was a ramshackle staircase for those with eyes to see. Melville began to wonder what Yonden had meant by difficult.

He found out when the couloir came in sight. It was a slipway of solid ice, about forty feet wide, jammed in a gulley that shot down at a daunting angle and then vanished between the main face and the sheer end of an outcrop. The outcrop was vaguely sail-shaped, aligned roughly parallel to the face and connected to it by a rock bridge. On the left of the bridge – the vertical end of the outcrop – was the ice gulley; on the right a snow-filled chute that slanted down diagonally between the side of the outcrop and the main cliff, all the way to the bottom. The problem was that the bridge was still a good hundred feet below, and Yonden was patrolling up and down the ledge where they had assembled, leaning out and peering over like a cat stuck on a roof.

Melville blew on his hands, looking anxiously at the pink shadows creeping across the snow. In an hour it would be quite dark.

Finally Yonden acted. Turning his face to the cliff for the first time, he lowered himself out of sight. A minute later he was back. He tried in another spot. Melville heard a rock go clattering down and he massaged the constriction in his throat. Yonden appeared again, looking tired. No one spoke to him. He disappeared once more, and this time was gone for a long time. Occasionally he called out, his voice waking hollow echoes. It sounded as if he was working his way left. At last Melville spotted him, emerging at the edge of the gulley. He looked around, apparently quite collected, saw Melville and signalled that he would cross the ice and descend on the other side until he was in a position to spy out a route. It took him five minutes to make his way to the other side of the gulley.

'That's sheer ice,' Melville said. 'He doesn't even have an axe or crampons.'

'He'll be alright,' Gunn said.

'God, I can't bear to look,' Melville said.

But he couldn't tear his eyes away as Yonden commenced his descent, keeping off the ice as much as possible, swinging from hand to hand, using opposing forces to keep himself stuck to the wall. It was like watching a different species, Melville thought. He could no more have emulated Yonden than flown.

The Khampa stopped. His head turned slowly and tilted back, moving from side to side as he searched out a line. His upturned face was white in the gathering dusk. He jabbed upwards with one hand,

411

hanging on with the other. Melville moved to the right. 'Here?' he called. Yonden guided him into position.

'What's it like?' Melville called.

Yonden's response was unintelligible.

'You'll have to come back across, help us down,' Melville called, pausing between each word.

'Difficult for me,' Yonden shouted, leaning out and pointing at the ice.

'You got across alright.'

'If he says it's difficult,' Gunn blurted, 'he means it's bloody impossible.'

'Cool it, okay?' Melville said, making downplaying gestures with his hands. 'What will you do?' he asked Yonden.

The Khampa looked up and down. He might have shrugged. 'You . . . climb . . . down. Not difficult.'

'Oh my God,' Gunn said, 'he's stuck. Quick, you must help him.'

'I can't,' Melville shouted down.

'You must,' Gunn yelled.

'I wouldn't last ten feet. You saw me come apart on that bridge – on a bridge for fuck's sake. I'm just not up to it.'

Yonden had got the message. Without saying anything, he lowered himself onto the ice. He stood perfectly still for a few moments, then moved an inch to his left, paused, another inch, and another. In this way he reached the middle of the gulley, where he halted for a long time. Eventually he adjusted the position of his hands and with great care stretched out his left leg. His foot searched about for a hold, found one, and he let go with both hands. He began to slide, flung up his hands and stopped at the full stretch of his arms.

'I'm going to throw up,' Melville said. He could see Yonden's gloveless fingers bunched like claws. 'Can you move?' he shouted.

Yonden raised his face and shook his head.

'Some of us make their own luck,' Gunn said, 'and some of us rely on someone else's.'

'You telling me this is my fault?' Melville said, rounding on him.

'Out of my way,' Gunn said. 'I'm going down.'

'No you're not,' Melville said, shoving him back. There was a moment of indecision, ended by a blind, probably fatal, impulse on Melville's part. 'Ach,' he said, 'I'd only have to risk my neck saving two of you. Give me your crampons.'

He strapped them to his hip with his own and hung his ice axe on his wrist. 'Can you talk me down?' he called, craning out. 'Okay, don't go away.' He swung his legs over, gave Gunn a hopeless smile and looked over his shoulder at the ghostly oval of Yonden's face. 'Where to from here?'

'More right. A ledge. No, further. Yes.'

Gunn was repeating the instructions.

'Shut up,' Melville shouted. 'Leave it to Yonden.'

Bit by bit, hold by hold, Yonden guided him down, sometimes changing his instructions, once obliging him to regain height and start in another direction, but always able to conjure up a toe-hold here, a crack there. And then the instructions stopped.

'What now? My hands are frozen.'

'Ledge to your left,' Yonden said after a lengthy hesitation, sounding unsure.

'I see it,' Melville said. It was too far below to step on to, and there were no handholds he could use. 'No good.'

'Left hand,' Yonden said.

Melville patted the cliff and went on patting until he had pushed out his arm to its full extent. 'Nothing there,' he shouted, panic starting.

'Little further,' Yonden said. He sounded very calm.

'Wait,' Melville said. He checked the hold he had with his right hand, saw that it was secure and let go with his left, arching back. He saw it, an icy handle way beyond him. 'Isn't there any other way?' he called.

'It's difficult,' Yonden admitted. He did not speak again.

Melville shifted his weight and tried to the right. Nothing. He felt directly below him and his boot skidded over soapy rock without finding a place to rest. He looked down and everything began to rock, like choppy waves in a harbour. He shut his eyes and jammed his cheek to the rock. He found he had bitten his tongue. The terrible weakness was in his legs. 'Are you alright?' he heard Gunn ask.

'You still there, Yonden?' he called.

'Yes.'

'Okay, be honest. Is that the only way?'

Long empty interval. 'Yes.'

Melville clung where he was, growing weaker, bones and muscle liquefying.

'Sah? Walter?'

It was Yonden, sounding scared. Although faint, his voice carried clearly. 'I think I fall soon.'

'I'm trying my best,' Melville cried. His eyes and nose were running.

No you're not, he told himself. You're a spineless jelly, a blob of protoplasm. There's not a thing you can do. It's nature's way of telling you you're in the wrong place. He shook away his tears and studied the hold again. About six feet away, he calculated. He had a good foothold. It was his hands that bothered him. He couldn't feel them. He wasn't sure if they were up to the job. 'I'm coming,' he said.

Gathering himself, he let go with his hands. In the instant of committing himself, he snatched them back, aware that there was no force behind his effort. He would have simply toppled over sideways. One chance, he told himself, so you may as well put everything into it. He straightened his right knee and jumped.

In that moment he saw himself from the outside, frozen in mid-air, apparently with all the time in the world.

His hand clutched the rock and held. He dangled a moment and fell, and in the act of falling grabbed another hold, lost it and slid six inches onto the ledge.

The rest of the descent was easy.

Getting to Yonden wasn't. He was well out of reach, stuck to the ice by little more than friction.

'It'll take a minute,' Melville told him, buckling on his crampons. It took much longer, because his fingers were as dead as sticks. 'How are your hands?' he asked.

Yonden had to look at them to make sure they were still there.

The first step was the worst. The ice had shrunk away from the walls, leaving a gap four feet wide, much more under the surface. Melville bridged it, hooking his axe in, clawing with his boots. He brought the other leg across. Each step had to be bitten out. Splinters of ice bounded away. 'Tell you what we're going to do,' he said in a conversational tone, chipping away. 'Can't put crampons on you, and you can't hold an axe – right?' Yonden, an X pinned to the ice, moved his face slightly. 'No problem. I'm going to cut out a nice big step for your feet, and when I say the word, you ease down into it. I'll be holding you.'

He kept up a chatty monologue as he chiselled away. 'Hard bit's over for us. Be down at the temple this time tomorrow. Ideal hidey-hole. Villagers should be in their winter settlement by now. Still got to get the others down, but we'll come up with something. Always do.'

And so on, until he was at Yonden's side, where he nailed the points of his crampons into a step he had already cut, hacked out a hold for his left hand, leaned down and began chipping out a notch

414

below Yonden's left foot. It was like working with an artificial limb. His senseless right hand could barely control the axe, which bounced and sometimes jarred from his grip and would have fallen if it hadn't been attached by a loop around his wrist. 'If I come out of this with ten fingers and toes,' he told Yonden, 'it will be a miracle.' He worked on in silence.

'Should do,' he said at last, taking stock. Dark had come up by surprise. It was just him and Yonden, the others somewhere he couldn't see. He transferred the axe to his left hand, hooked it into the anchor point, bent forward and took Yonden's left wrist in his free hand. 'Nice and slow now.'

Yonden turned his head. His face looked as transparent as wax paper, the bones showing through.

'It's right there,' Melville said soothingly. 'Let yourself go. I've got you.'

Yonden raised his palms a fraction and slipped with shocking suddenness.

'Easy, fella. Gone past it. Stay where you are. Don't even think of moving. I'm going to pull you back up.'

His tug was weaker than it should have been, and Yonden slipped again, slewing slightly to the right, away from the step, which was now at the level of his thigh.

'Don't want that to happen again,' Melville said, fighting for calm. He filled his lungs a few times. 'One big heave,' he said. 'Try and find a little grip with your feet.'

He was leaning far down now, unable to exert much leverage with his feet, most of his weight on the axe. He pulled, Yonden wriggled, and the axe sprang out, leaving him teetering on the front claws of his crampons, Yonden's weight dragging him sideways and over. Maybe he let go; maybe his hand didn't know what it was doing; maybe he just couldn't take the strain. Yonden was loose and sliding, clawing at the ice. He stopped ten feet below and Melville did not move a muscle, scared that the slightest vibration would set Yonden off again. 'Got it all to do again,' he said.

But Yonden panicked. His right hand came up like a swimmer's, his left leg bent like a frog's, but whatever hold he was striving for was already beyond his grasp when his hand came down. His upturned face remained still as his limbs fought and scratched the ice. He stopped struggling as he began to slide. He slid quite slowly, his face white and tiny, his eyes a cord between himself and Melville that snapped as he slipped into the dark. He went without a sound. Melville listened and didn't hear a thing.

'He's gone,' he shouted up at the cliffs. 'I had him, and then I lost him.'

'Why didn't you hold on,' came Gunn's anguished cry.

Melville sidestepped back to the bridge. 'Listen,' he called up after a while. 'I'm going down to look for help. If I don't find any . . .' His voice fell to nothing '. . . I'll be back.'

It took another hour to descend the snow gulley and find Yonden's body. He was lying face down, one leg resting flat on his back, the side of his boot on the nape of his neck. Melville forced himself to straighten it out. Yonden's midriff was exposed, and Melville saw the belt. He touched it and recognised the greasy, synthetic feel of the belt he had handed over to Osher. In one of Yonden's jacket pockets he found the Zippo. He did not find Yonden's plastic envelope with his exercise book and letters because he couldn't bring himself to turn him over. None of the things he had discovered excited much curiosity. He was beginning to freeze, the cold tightening around his brain stem and his blood beginning to thicken.

'Found him,' he called up at the cliffs. 'He's dead.'

The cliffs repeated it.

'I know,' Gunn's disembodied voice rang out, '. . . know, know . . .' Coming from all directions at once.

Freezing wasn't too bad – just as they claimed. Scary at first, and lonely with only him and the black rock and white snow. But then a little bit of a moon came up and sailed at his side and he didn't feel too bad. No, freezing was a cinch because – and this was the killer – you didn't feel cold at all. On the contrary. You felt deliciously warm – the wonderful amniotic warmth you experienced in the half-waking moment before you drifted back into deep sleep. Too warm really, even with your jacket unzipped and no hat or mittens.

He fell over, and found it so comfortable that he decided to stay where he was, relaxing in a bed of feather-down while the moon held station over the triangular peak. It was waiting for him – waiting to ferry him over the channels of ice. Where to, he wondered, and decided on Tibet. He was sad, now, that he had left it without a parting glance. Maybe he'd missed something after all.

'Look at it,' Gunn told him. 'Nothing hidden. There's your answer.'

'Fine, now what was the question again?'

Gunn went away.

There was something he must do. He couldn't remember what. 'Not yet a-while,' he told the moon, pushing himself up.

Presently he saw Charlie coming towards him.

'Hi, Walter. How's humanity?'

'Pretty small from where I'm standing. How the hell did you get here?'

'Dematerialised. It's an old trick I learnt.'

'Can you teach me?'

'I'd like to, Walter, but it takes years of practice.'

'You know, Charlie, I ought to kill you.'

'No question but you have the motive. Where are you headed?'

'How do I know until I get there?'

'And where are you coming from?'

'The heart of the world.'

'What's it really like?'

'Same as anywhere else, only emptier. Except for the ghosts. Lot of ghosts.'

'C'mon, Walter, you can tell me.'

'Life's a ball.'

'It surely is.'

'No, you don't understand. It's like a ball, see? Open it up and what do you find but another ball, and inside that another one, all the way down to the last, which is the same as the first.'

'Sounds crazy to me.'

'Charlie, that was a shitty trick you and Mr Yueh played.'

'Not me, Walter. I never stabbed a guy when he wasn't looking.'

'You said I was like part of Mr Yueh's family.'

'Most murders are committed within the family.'

'Why me? Why me?'

'I guess he blames you for the way things are going.'

'You've got to get me out.'

'I'll have to take instruction on that one.'

'I don't want to die on my own.'

'What about all your friends back there?'

And damn me, he was right. There they all were. Osher riding along in his biker's jacket, applying his Zippo to the inevitable cigarette. Chorphel swinging along beside him, his Mauser held across his shoulders like a yoke. Ngawang walking with Yeshe, holding him in a companionable headlock. Yonden mooching behind, working out the accounts for a contemplative order. The whole rascally crew minus Gunn and Liu.

'I've got news for you. The general's planning to do a disappearing number on us.'

But Sweetwater had abandoned him.

Melville was no longer lonely, though. He was part of things now. Chin held high, spine straight, he marched stiffly on at the head of the procession.

The dog was disturbing his peace. Its barks were heavy and threatening, deep as a locomotive building up steam. There it was, coming out of a tunnel. No, it really was a dog, as big as a foal and a lot more ferocious, hurling itself against its chain. Down boy.

This was nice. They'd laid on a reception. He counted a party of four outside a tent with little pennants on its guys. They seemed surprised to see him, but they made an arresting sight themselves. Here was Genghis Khan in his dotage, rheumy hooded eyes and a droopy wisp of moustache. By his side stood Granny Khan, wearing wire specs with discs of ice where the glass should be. Young master Khan was pointing a gun at him. Most amazing of all was the beautiful Amazon with the thick coil of hair over her shoulder, and one heavy breast naked in the moonlight.

He began to address them in the language of the country, telling them that he was a stranger passing through who had lost his way. Something else he had to tell them. Halfway through remembering what it was, the old man dragged him into the tent and insisted he lie down.

Chapter 25

December 2, Melville wrote.

He paused, not sure if he'd got the date right. He began counting back. Eight days since he reached the camp, six – or was it seven? – days on the journey out of Tibet. Which made it . . .

His drifting attention snagged on the vision of Nyima. She was milking the goats. They were tethered in two lines, facing each other shoulder to shoulder in interlocking rows, which gave the illusion that the head of each animal was growing backwards out of its neck.

Although he was sitting inside the tent, he could see Nyima through the loose weave of the fabric, and the mountains behind her. It created a beautiful textured effect, like a landscape painted in oils that have worn away until the canvas shows through.

He thought what a wonderful structure the tent was. It kept him in touch with the world, but at a safe distance. And it was warmer and cleaner than his lodgings at the Khampas' camp. It was such an efficient design, it remained waterproof despite the open mesh. Komi had told him that the yak wool swelled when wet, effectively sealing the holes. It was like a second skin.

Theoretically, he wrote, *a drokpa tent is ageless, infinitely renewable. This one is made up of eighteen panels, two of them added this year, the rest up to eight years old. The oldest ones are at the base of the walls, and when they rot they will be discarded and new sections let into the roof, so that the tent is being constantly renewed from the top down. It is like an animal that sloughs off its dead skin.*

Writing was a chore with crippled hands. He flexed his bandaged fingers and touched his cheeks. His mind went into a glide, lulled by the rhythmic chirping of milk squirting into the horn that Nyima held under the goats' udders. Gunn and Liu were outside in the sun, wrapped in blankets. The old woman was sitting at the entrance, chuckling over her prayer beads. Komi and young Tashi were away gathering brushwood.

Melville read what he had written and sighed. He stood up, crossed to the corner where the old woman slept, and picked up her broken mirror, angling it so that light fell on his face.

It had fallen in on its foundation. His lips and the tip of his nose were black scabs. The skin on the crowns of his cheeks was grey and lifeless; around his eyes it had the unnatural gloss of a burn victim's graft. His eyes stared out with boiled blue clarity – a lucid stare which he associated with shock or pain. A piece of newsreel clippage played through his mind and was gone. For reasons he didn't try to fathom, he found himself thinking of the old man at the cabin in the Japanese Alps.

He replaced the mirror and returned to his notebook.

New tent panels don't come cheap. Komi has to buy the wool from the villagers because they won't allow him to keep yaks of his own. When a son gets married, his father usually gives him a new tent, but since Komi is so poor, Tashi will have to make do with this one. Komi is saving the money for Nyima's dowry – hard to credit that he should have to pay someone to take her off his hands. With the money I intend to give him for our keep, I guess he'll be able to afford both a new tent for Tashi and a husband for Nyima.

Food, shelter, sex. When you get down to it, what else is there?

His hand strayed to his money belt. Undoing it, he pulled out the Zippo and weighed it in his palm. Osher had told him it would light in a storm. He gave the wheel a flick and stiffened, his eyes darting towards Gunn. It was such a distinctive rasp.

Gunn hadn't heard. There was nothing to listen out for, except the voices in his head. Melville knew that Gunn heard them by the answers he was forever giving. What with him and the old woman, who also spoke to herself, it was like being banged up in the booby hatch. Melville was not unsympathetic to either of them. It was just that he feared for his own sanity.

He found he was still holding the Zippo. He looked towards the cliffs and shook his head in bewilderment. How Yonden had come to be in possession of the lighter and money belt was a mystery to which he had no answer.

Tears came without warning. These days, they often took him unawares. Through the blur he commenced to write quickly.

Komi and his son recovered Yonden's body three days ago and we held the funeral right away. The awful thing is that the vultures didn't come for him, and we had to leave him out on the mountain. I keep remembering how I cursed him.

Melville saw him slipping out of reach without a word. That was the truly awful thing. Another was the cutting of the rope after they had crossed the river by the Gurkha post. Telling himself that Yonden could have got another, and that it wouldn't have made any difference, didn't make him feel better or stop the bad memories from coming back.

December 11

The bad snows are due any day now. Yesterday we moved a mile or so further down the valley and pitched the tent in the entrance to a cave where the animals will be kept when the weather gets really tough. It's a relief to be out of sight of the cliffs where Yonden fell.

From here we can see the way up the pass into the main valley. Komi says it isn't difficult. By now everyone must have written us off, but none of us is ready to face the world yet.

December 13

It would be best to stay dead another month, but we ought to consider making a move because Komi doesn't have enough food to see us through into the new year. Unfortunately he can't tell us how much of a storm we've raised. None of the family has been over the pass since the end of October.

Liu and I are in reasonable shape. Gunn's chest is a bit better. I wish I could say the same about his head. He speaks if spoken to, and that's about all. I can't help feeling he blames me for what happened to Yonden. He blames himself too. I don't think he wants to get out. It's shaping up to be a big problem.

December 16

Last night we discussed what to do. Alan didn't join in. We had to lay everything on the line for Komi. I offered him a round thousand if he would help us out. I hate to involve his family, but what other way is there? I have searched my conscience about this and I told Komi that he was free to turn me down if he considered the risk to his family was too great.

The upshot is that he's agreed to help. In a couple of days Tashi will go down to Kathmandu and wire Hubbard to arrange a rescue. It was a hard decision to make. Several times I have thought about picking up the pieces of the original plan. What stops me is a) the prospect of dealing with Sood, and b) the feeling that Mr Yueh and Charlie planned all along for Osher to take me along with him. Events are beginning to blur, but one thing stands out in my mind. When the PLA officer was calling on us to surrender, he used my full name and also Gunn's. I can't believe that Linka or any other of the Khampas who might have informed on us could have given the Chinese our names, so where else did they get them from? Maybe they checked back when they heard Osher was riding with foreigners. I'm not prepared to bet my life on it.

Komi refused to go to Kathmandu himself. Tashi is only fifteen, and though he's a bright kid and independent, he's never set foot in a town in his life. On the plus side, he speaks some Nepali, having lived in the lowlands for a few years when his parents were working as field hands.

There are quite a few pros and cons to keep me from sleeping during the two or three weeks it will take before Hubbard receives word.

The PLA might have invaded the Khampa valley.

No, we'd have seen planes.

The Gurkhas have occupied the camp.

Probably, but they're not going to haul in a nomad kid for interrogation.

Maybe Tashi will walk up to the first soldier he sees and give us away.

His father could have turned us in right at the start.

Liu is remarkably laid back about the plan. I laugh and say, it's okay for you, General; if Tashi screws up, there's always India for you. For me and Gunn, it's goodnight. He laughs at that. We both laugh. Ha-ha – skirmishing laughter. I don't like him, I don't trust him, and I don't know why. That makes it worse.

Melville paused as a shadow blocked out the entrance. After a few seconds he resumed writing.

Nyima has just come back. She has been washing her hair outside. The ends are white and stiff with frost. Untied, it falls to her waist. She kneels in the sunlight coming through the tent flap and tosses her hair forward so that it trails in the dust like a black curtain. Then she proceeds to dry it by beating it with a switch of twigs. She's watching me. I can see her dark eyes through a gap in the curtain. She doesn't know I can see them. If she did, she would look away. She's very shy. She's twenty-two and as tall as me, but she's as awkward as a sub-teen in my company. She's looking at my hands. She often does. At first I assumed she was wondering about their sorry state, but now I think she's fascinated by their whiteness. Her own are as dark and tough as seasoned rawhide.

She has brought back water for the next meal.

Frowning, Melville laid aside the notebook and dipped a hand into the pot.

'It's warm,' he said to Gunn, who was sitting in his corner. 'This water's warm.'

He looked expectantly at Nyima.

'The water,' Melville said in laborious Tibetan. 'Where did it come from?'

Nyima pointed uncertainly over her shoulder.

'Do you keep a fire going in the cave?'

She smiled, displaying the gap between her top teeth. Melville guessed that the gap was the result of chewing sinew for thread to sew leather – a chore that often occupied her evenings. She pointed again.

'She must mean a hot spring,' Gunn said, without interest.

Melville stared at him. 'Hot running water,' he said, his mind having difficulty getting around the concept. 'This I have to see.'

He pawed through the contents of his pack until he found a bar of Japanese soap still in its wrapper. He held it in triumph. 'For those moments of your precious dreams,' he said, translating the copywriter's promise. He held out the soap to Nyima. She sniffed it warily. A beatific smile spread over her face and she reached for it.

'Not unless you lead me to paradise,' he told her.

As they left, the mastiff came at him with a rattle of rusty chain. Just in time he skipped behind Nyima, who whipped her arm round and sent a half-pound rock thudding into its ribs. It nuzzled its flank as though faintly puzzled, then went back to its stone kennel. Melville gave Nyima an adoring smile. 'No kidding,' he said, 'I'd marry you for nothing. I'd pay for the privilege.'

About two hundred yards from the tent, close to the base of a cliffy outcrop, she caught his arm and bade him listen.

He heard a sound that he had almost forgotten – the urgent trickle of water under the snow. Nyima ran ahead and shyly pointed to the source.

It was a grotto dissolved out of the rocks, its entrance almost sealed by layer upon layer of ice. Steam drifted from a runnel that issued from the opening and vanished a few feet further on down a sinkhole in the snow. Melville tested the water. At its lowest point it was tepid. He tried nearer the source and found it to be warm. He looked at the girl in wonder and squeezed head and shoulders through the opening.

Inside, stalactites hung down over a bubbling, tub-sized spring. The water was hot. On one side of the spring there was a smooth ledge. He laughed for joy. Nyima smiled. He grabbed her and kissed her cheek. Still smiling faintly, she rubbed the spot.

Since the idea of a bath seemed alien to her, he decided to let example serve.

While he undressed, she sat at the other end of the ledge, watching with a frown, determined not to miss whatever trick he was about to perform. She giggled when he got down to his underwear, and contemplating his near-nakedness he had to concede a self-deriding laugh. Secretly he was appalled by his wasted state. He was a forked

423

stick, peeled white, thin and knobbly. Out of shame as much as modesty, he turned his back and slid into the water.

It was delicious; it was bliss surpassing heaven. He let out a whoop and she laughed aloud. In words and mime he tried to persuade her to join him, but she shook her head quickly and looked away. She turned back as he began to work up a lather. She held out her hand. After a moment's hesitation, he gave her the soap.

She took off her boots and hiked up her skirt a few inches. Her ankles and shins were as black as candle smoke. Putting her feet into the water, she applied the soap. It seemed to have little effect; the dirt was engrained over a lifetime. She raised her skirts a little higher, baring knees as pale and smooth as alabaster.

'Let me,' Melville said.

Pausing, her neck and back gently curved, she pushed a strand of hair away from her eyes and looked at him. In the aqueous light her face was as delicate as a cameo. He took the soap from her hand and put a finger to his lips to quell the wrinkle of protest forming on hers. Gently he washed her legs, then, carried away by a great weakness, he laid his head on her knees. He was not certain what he intended. All he wanted was a little comfort, a moment's ease in a world of pain. He found he was tearful again.

He let them come, while she combed his hair with her fingers. When he glanced up, he saw that her face wore the abstracted, enigmatic expression that he had only seen on women. There was no telling what she was thinking – the meal that was going uncooked, a goat whose milk yield was down, particle diffusion.

Reaching up, he kissed her on the mouth. Her lips betrayed no reaction; his own registered none. Without anger she pushed him away and wiped her mouth with the back of her hand. Her frown seemed to express a question rather than disapproval.

Madness, he thought. Folly heaped on folly. Old Komi would be within his rights if he came after him with a gun. The nomad had a rifle that he oiled every day after breakfast. He didn't have to go to such an extreme, though. He could simply send him away, back into the wilderness.

'Nyima,' he said. 'I love you.'

Easy to say, since they were speaking different languages. Nevertheless, in that moment he meant it, and she seemed to intuit his heartfelt emotion because she ducked her head so that her chin was tucked into her throat, her eyes suddenly serious.

His hands found her girdle. Next moment he was up against the opposite wall, ruefully rubbing his head. It wasn't much of a defence, but he could truthfully tell Komi that, in his depleted condition, Nyima could hold off his advances with one hand tied behind her back.

Shamefaced, he began to apologise. His protests trailed off as she untied her belt. Holding him at a distance with her eyes, she unwrapped her robe. Underneath she wore a shift of lamb's wool, and under that a lot of petticoats that got increasingly ragged as she worked down to the skin. At last she was unconfined.

'Nyima,' he said, sounding as if he was speaking through a throatful of blood.

She was proportioned like a warrior queen, her hips an amphora, her breasts bombshells. She untied her hair and it spilled down. Not since he was a kid had he felt so clueless. In desperation for something to do, he splashed her. She kicked water in his face. He splashed her back. Things became rowdy.

The one-sided contest was ended by her pinning him against the side of the grotto. Their laughter stopped at the same moment; they swallowed simultaneously. Her eyes had lost their shellac brightness and clouded over. Her mouth was parted and he could see a pulse throbbing in her neck. Her breathing had harshened. A fierce joy possessed him. Burning boats. Ride till you crash.

As he took hold of her she shrugged him off and turned away, crouching on all fours. She gave him a luminous smile over her shoulder and waggled her rump.

'Not like that,' he said, bringing her back to him. They kissed, and this time, though her lips stayed curiously immobile, his tongue found the gap between her teeth. He pulled her veil of hair about him and shut his eyes.

Finesse was not possible in such cramped surroundings. He rode and he crashed, pumping out in a few seconds the accumulated misery of weeks.

'If it were to end right here,' he murmured, 'I'd die happy.'

Gently she disentangled herself and dressed. He made no attempt to stop her. She left, taking the soap with her. As she backed through the entrance, she paused, fingering her lips, rubbing them back and forth and looking at him with faint puzzlement, as though he was a new taste that she couldn't decide if she liked.

Since he was not immediately struck down by a stroke of lightning, Melville forgot his pact with death. Thinking on what he had done, he felt stunned and a little frightened. He waited without daring to move, listening for the crunching of snow that would tell him Komi was coming for him. After half an hour he decided that he wasn't going to be punished, but he stayed in the pool for quite a while longer, constructing fantasies about Nyima that grew increasingly daring and hopeless. At that stage, though, he knew they were only daydreams.

When at last he stepped outside, the huge temperature drop almost made him swoon. Weaving a drunkard's course back to the tent, he wandered within range of the mastiff, which knocked him flat and would have pulled his face off had Nyima not dashed out and driven it off with a weighted rope's end. Smiling dopily at her, he limped at her side to be confronted by a gamey grin from Komi and the blank indifference of the others.

December 24

Sometimes, like now, I find that I have stopped writing to listen. Listen to what? It's hard to describe. If I strain too hard it goes away. It sounds like toneless music. Imagination? Then why did Nyima stop sewing and Komi look towards the door at the same moment I put down my pen?

That's not all I've heard. At any time of day the mountains may give a crack or groan, and a few nights ago, when the temperature was about absolute zero, we all sat up at a noise I can only describe as being like a stadium full of people all talking together miles and miles away. Komi said it was the mountain gods, and that will do for me. Now that I think of it, I remember how the Khampas would all go quiet as they were riding through some place that looked like any other. They would all be talking, then suddenly stop, in mid-sentence sometimes. A couple of minutes later they would start talking again, picking up where they had left off, the same sentence. Like the Zippo, it comes into the category of insoluble mysteries. Gunn is right, though: these mountains are full of strange noises.

In a couple of hours it will be Christmas. If Gunn knows the date, he's not letting on. We talk more now, but there are so many painful subjects to avoid that we have very little to say. I've tried to find out what his intentions are – whether he aims to go back to Scotland or maybe emigrate to Canada, which I believe I heard him mention as a vague possibility. So far I've got nothing out of him except a reassurance that I needn't worry. I do worry, though. If I press him, a guarded look comes over him and he tells me he hasn't decided. It's hard to tell if he's rational or completely out to lunch.

He'd better make up his mind soon. Tashi has been away five days now. Thinking about what he might be up to makes me go up in smoke. Liu takes it all very calmly. He's full of questions about the States, and though I do my best, I tell him it's been so long since I was back home, even I've forgotten what it's like, so God knows what a commie general will make of it. He has no family there or anything like that. The other night I asked him straight out if he had reservations about going, at which he laughed and said not any more. All the fuss he made earlier was due to hearing his own base being blown up – not to mention the jolt he received when I owned up about sending him to Taiwan. Remembering what Charlie told me about the strain defecting puts on a man, I have to give Liu the benefit of doubt. Besides, he gave full backing to the plan to wire Hubbard, and he's not going anywhere without Komi's help. I just wish I liked the guy better.

It annoys me that I can't remember Hubbard's first name. It's bad enough that I had to make the message so cryptic, but there was nothing to be done about that because the post office is like a public reference library. The staff and anyone who takes a fancy open all international mail. They open the outgoing to find the requests for parental hippy relief, then they wait for the incoming and lift the cheques.

All I could come up with was I'M ON THE OUTSIDE AND I WANT TO GET BACK IN THE MIDDLE – and then my name and Tashi's contact address. I hope Hubbard recalls our last conversation together.

Melville broke off to scratch himself. Regular bathing hadn't reduced his bug population – merely incited it. Five minutes after getting out of the water, he felt dirtier than before he took the plunge. Nyima hadn't come back to the hot spring. Twice he had made love to her in the cave, among the sheep and goats. Sometimes he couldn't help wondering if she just used him to – well – scratch an itch. He was besotted with her.

He studied her as she ground salt on the other side of the hearth. *I'm crazy about her,* he wrote. *I'd take her with me if I could.*

He crossed it out.

His heart gave a kick as the dog began to bark. It barked rarely, and only in the presence of the unusual. His eyes sought out Komi's. The nomad was rising to his feet, picking up his rifle. He stooped through the entrance and went out into the night. After exchanging an anxious glance with Liu, Melville followed.

To his huge relief, the mastiff was facing up the valley, away from the pass. It was throttling itself at the end of its chain, struggling with a ferocity that should have broken its neck. Strings of saliva glistened on its black coat. Giving it a wide berth, Melville joined Komi, who was crouched by the pen where his two horses were corralled. They were badly spooked, skittering around with the whites of their eyes bulging. Some predator must be on the prowl. Komi pointed to a line of paw prints.

'Wolf?' Melville asked.

Komi said something he didn't understand.

'Snow leopard,' Gunn said behind them.

The nomad straightened up with the infinite care of the rheumatic and looked on the mountains. The young moon held the shadow of the old in its arms. The starlight was strong enough to read by. Komi called out and shook his gun above his head, issuing a challenge. He listened for a while before turning back. He spoke to his dog and it went and lay down outside its stone kennel, whimpering quietly, watching.

'I've never seen that before,' Melville said, looking at the moon. 'Appropriate, isn't it? The old year giving birth to the new.'

'A new decade,' Gunn said.

'I guess we'll see some changes. An end to revels,' Melville glanced at Gunn. 'You'll get over it,' he said.

Gunn gave him a pitying smile.

'I miss him too,' Melville said. He looked down, kicking at the snow.

'I thought you couldn't stand him.'

Melville drew a shuddering breath. 'Say what you like, he was always around when we needed him.'

Narcotised by the cold, Melville opened one eye to find Komi still sitting in the position he had taken up when they arrived. The old man was jammed into a crevice at the back of the ledge. His rifle lay across his lap, wrapped in a piece of blanket. His slow blinks showed he wasn't asleep.

Pain like a hot wire shot down Melville's thigh as he adjusted his position. Sciatica. Too many nights sleeping on frozen ground. Still two hours before dawn. Across the valley the slender peak was dormant. On the glassy blue snow the carcass of the goat was a small black shape. Melville wished himself back in the tent.

He wondered why Komi had invited him along. Perhaps he thought of it as some kind of initiation, a test for a prospective son-in-law. In any case, Melville thought, he had no wish to kill the snow leopard. Drawing himself into a knot, he went back to sleep.

Next time he woke the peak was alight and a yellow wash was spreading down from its lower slopes. It would be mid-morning before the sun struck this side of the valley. In the spectral light a pair of ravens was up and about, hammering at the goat's frozen paunch. On the cliffs behind it a vacant wind licked at the powder snow. Komi was still sunk in the folds of his coat. Without taking his eyes off the crags, he handed Melville a few curls of cheese. Melville flexed his legs to restore the circulation. His eyes probed the cliff without any expectation of seeing anything.

Some change in Komi's attitude summoned him out of another doze. As he lifted his head, the nomad pushed him flat, unwrapping the rifle with his other hand. He was fumbling the task because he was intent on keeping the cliffs under watch.

'Did you see it?' Melville whispered, excited now. He scanned the ledges and secret places without success.

Komi had squirmed into a firing position, but now he looked unsure, his eyes panning up the rock and snow and down again. On the crest the random wind raised thin coils of snow. Imagining things, Melville thought.

At last Komi relaxed. He rubbed another dab of butter on the barrel of his rifle and lay still, his eyes vacant but receptive. Melville was beginning to feel bored. He faced the other way, watching the valley fill up with sunlight. Stifling a yawn, he anticipated the moment when it would reach him

'How long are we going to wait,' he whispered a few minutes later, hearing Komi stir at his side. The nomad hissed. Melville turned to find that he was back on the alert. While the old man stared elsewhere, Melville indulged himself in a dream that he might not have to part from Nyima after all. With the money he got for the general, he could take her whole family to America. Montana, perhaps. Buy a ranch. Turn it into a Tibetan community. Such schemes weren't unheard of and, with the current demand for exotic truths and other-worldly insights, often turned a handsome profit. He yawned.

A bubbling, chuckling cry startled him. There was a flurry in the snow behind the bait. A pair of pale birds – some kind of large Himalayan grouse – burst up from the rock debris at the foot of the crags. They rocketed off like loosely wrapped parcels driven by rubber bands that suddenly cut out, leaving them swaying and heeling on set wings until they disappeared across the divide between sunlight and shade. Some snow leopard, Melville thought, rubbing his eyes. He sent Komi a resentful glance.

The old man wasn't at home to collect it. His gaze was still fixed high on the cliffs. Melville followed it and saw a flock of choughs corkscrewing down the face, eddying around an overhang.

'Is it there?' he asked. 'Show me where it is.'

Komi put all his excitement into his trembling finger. Search as he might, Melville couldn't see a thing. The choughs were still swooping at the same spot. His eyes began to tire and objects blurred. He shut them tight for a moment. When he opened them something was not quite the same.

He sensed it rather than saw it – a pale wraith, too insubstantial to keep in view. Stupidly, he blinked and lost it, then picked it up lower down, a wisp of smoke streaming over rock. It vanished again and this time he could not find it. He felt a terrible frustration at the idea that he might miss it. Komi was making noises like a rubber toy, too excited to direct his attention to the right spot.

It clicked into place, silencing the nomad. It appeared out of nowhere, standing on a ledge about twenty feet above the snowfield. Melville saw it lift its head to test the small breeze. Its tail was swishing in slow disdain for the choughs checking at it.

'She's out of this world,' Melville breathed, unconsciously attributing its beauty to femaleness.

Using her tail as a rudder, she glided down and padded out into the open. The snow was as fine as talc and she sank deep. She was re-enacting the ritual of the hunt, stalking and freezing, her glacial stare frozen on the goat. Fifteen yards from it she halted, gathered herself, then exploded forward in puffs of snow. At the last instant the ravens sprang up.

Couched beside the carcass, one heavy paw resting on its neck, the snow leopard seemed to be looking straight at him. He was close enough to see the burrs of ice in her ruff and the snow that powdered her dark rosettes. He was so overwhelmed by her presence that he momentarily forgot he was here to witness her death. When he remembered, he felt physically sick.

'You mustn't shoot her,' he whispered to Komi. 'I'll give you twice what she's worth. Don't,' he said, grabbing for the gun.

Out of the corner of his eye he saw the snow leopard twitch a split second before the rifle fired. He had the impression of disjointed movement racing towards the cliff, then he was fending off the nomad's anger. Still haranguing him, Komi heaved himself to his feet and struggled off through the snow. Melville picked himself up and plodded after.

A few spots of red had blossomed near the carcass. Komi examined them briefly, grunted, then set off up the leopard's trail.

Blown it, Melville thought. Disgraced. He felt rancid with misery.

From beginning to end, all he'd had to offer was money. Out here that didn't take you far.

The shot had robbed the valley of sound. His ears rang in the silence. He slumped down. He lay back, his eyes wide open. Choughs were spiralling up like burnt leaves. High above them griffons cut perfect circles out of the blue sky. Why hadn't they come for Yonden?

Very clearly he knew this was no place for him. Even the predators lived on the knife-edge of survival, and he was no predator. It was time he returned to his own, time he went home. It was such an unfamiliar word, such a distant notion.

Behind him Komi gave a whoop of triumph. He came sliding down a slab of rock with the snow leopard slung around his neck. Melville managed to summon up a congratulatory smile as he laid the trophy at his feet.

In death it was smaller than he had imagined. Its eyes were closed to slits and one long fang was hooked over its lower jaw, which gave it a silly, drunken expression. There was bloody froth on its ruff and a small black hole in its shoulder. Looking at it, Melville could not escape the feeling that there was a hole in him too, and that whatever virtue he possessed was draining out of it.

On the way back Komi, restored to the best of temper, kept up a cheerful flow of hunting tales. Although Melville was resigned to losing Nyima, his heart still gave a lurch when he saw her waiting outside the tent, shielding her eyes against the glare. Komi raised the leopard above his head and Melville made himself look glad on his behalf. Home is the hunter. Nyima did not smile back. Melville saw his notebook in her hand.

'What's wrong?' he asked. 'Where are the others?'

She pointed towards the pass.

Chapter 26

Knowing what he must do in the first moment of consciousness, General Liu did not betray his intention by any sudden movement. He gave the throaty moan of a man awakening. Tightening his grip on the knife in his right hand, he flung out his left. It encountered rock. He rolled over to find the space beside him empty.

He laughed aloud in disbelief. He could have sworn that Gunn was lying beside him. Still clutching the knife, he scrambled to his feet.

A dark wind threatened snow. Down in the bottom of the gorge the cold cut like a blunt saw. Liu shook as he peered around, expecting to see Gunn relieving himself or collecting sticks for a fire. He called softly and his own voice startled him. Snow flopped off a ledge and he spun round, feinting with the knife. Gunn might be only yards away, watching him from the wreckage of a landslide across the frozen river. Liu swore at himself for not finishing it last night – not acknowledging the fact that he hadn't wanted to be alone in this place during the hours of darkness. Now the air of menace that had seemed to recommend the spot seemed to have solidified around himself. He stared nervously at the ledge where they had spent the night, unable to rid his mind of the impression that someone had been at his side as his hand felt for the knife.

Trembling with indecision, he looked up the empty gorge, trying to convince himself that Gunn must have changed his mind and gone back for the American. The nomad had agreed to detain him for at least a day, but as the American had said, money talked louder than promises. He might be close behind – perhaps around the next corner.

Conscious that he was wasting time, Liu searched for Gunn's tracks. They led down to the river, then turned south. Panic took hold of Liu. Gunn had told him that the Khampa camp wasn't much more than an hour away. By now he might be there. The soldiers could have sent a radio message to Kathmandu. Liu broke into a clumsy trot and slipped almost immediately, falling heavily on his wrist. The pain shocked sense into him. He forced himself to continue at a pace that allowed him to think through the changed situation.

Unlike the American, Gunn had neither the means nor the motive to stop him reaching his goal. Then why kill him? Because the very fact of him being alive and in Nepalese hands meant ruin. India would never admit such a man, and whatever the Nepalese did with him – put him on trial, hand him over to the People's Republic, repatriate him – there would be diplomatic exchanges that must expose his own arrival in Nepal. Liu groaned. If news had already reached the Nepalese foreign ministry, some indignant fool might at this very moment be protesting to the British and American ambassadors. No, Liu decided, the Nepalese stood to lose more than anyone. A moment's reflection on their part would bring them to the same conclusion he himself had reached. Gunn's existence must never be made known. Killing him was the only way to prevent a political explosion. The American, too, but because his government knew he was alive his fate was less of a foregone conclusion.

Liu glanced anxiously behind him. Twenty-four hours was all he needed. Provided the nomad boy had contacted Jetha as arranged, he could be out of the country before the end of the day.

Sooner than he expected, Liu reached the path leading up to the camp. With a thrill of trepidation he saw that Gunn's trail had got lost among the prints of many army boots. At every turn he expected to meet a squad of soldiers coming down to look for him. They didn't appear, and when he gained the top his soldierly eye told him at once that the camp wasn't on alert. He detected leisurely activity among the houses. Outside a group of bell tents pitched near the settlement, Gurkhas were warming themselves at a fire. They weren't expecting him; Gunn couldn't have reached the camp.

He swung round. There was no one there. Once again, though, he had to shake off the feeling that he wasn't alone. He was reluctant to go forward. Looking back into the gorge, he came up with the answer. Gunn might be sick in the head, but he must have anticipated what the Nepalese were likely to do to him. He may even have divined his own intentions. Almost certainly the man had gone straight on down the gorge, by-passing the camp on the frozen river, hoping to rejoin the path near the mouth of the valley. Liu shook his head as he pictured him down there. His own way would have been kinder.

After adjusting the remnants of his uniform, he marched towards the camp, exaggerating the limp he had acquired in Korea. Although nervous, he was looking forward to being in the company of proper soldiers again, and enjoying in prospect the astonishment that his appearance would elicit.

Gunn felt a weight slip from his heart as he saw the general give himself up. And now, he thought, his breath catching in his throat, it's my turn.

'Who is that man?'

'The Chinese general,' Gunn said, savouring Linka's bafflement.

'You brought him here on your own?' Linka asked in amazement.

'Only through the gorge. I left the American at a nomad camp near the Lucky Place?'

'Who else?' Linka demanded, coming to stand behind his shoulder.

'No one else.'

'Tell me what happened. I've heard nothing except rumours. They said you were all slaughtered by the Chinese.'

'Some were,' Gunn said. He didn't want to talk about it, but it was right that Linka should know. 'A few died the night we met the general. Dorje and a dozen others tried to reach Mustang and rode into an ambush. Everyone else was swept away by an avalanche. Except for Yonden. He fell as we were climbing down into the nomads' valley.'

'Osher?'

'You needn't worry about him.'

Linka stepped past Gunn and gazed upon the camp. He had become quite gaunt, his well-nourished mask grown thin.

'I warned him,' he said, after observing a few moments' silence.

'Liar. You told them they would return safely. You promised success.'

'If someone is determined on a fatal course,' Linka said, 'there's no point telling them what perils lie ahead. I gave Osher and his followers a little hope to cling to, not a map of the future.'

'You knew they were going to their death,' Gunn cried, quaking with anger.

Linka gave a fastidious smile. 'You flatter me with skills I don't possess.'

'I'm not talking about your fortune-telling. The Chinese were warned we were coming. They were waiting for us.'

Linka's smile collected at the corner of his mouth. 'They must have been extraordinarily incompetent to allow so many to get away. Only minutes ago I watched the general walk into the Gurkha camp.'

'You betrayed us.'

Linka's smile withered away altogether. 'Next, you'll be accusing me of arranging the avalanche and encouraging Dorje to go to Mustang. No doubt you imagine I caused Yonden to slip and break his neck.' He pointed at Gunn. 'Those men were volunteers. You yourself chose to accompany them, although I warned you to leave. None of these misfortunes are my responsibility.' He turned back to the camp. 'Why aren't you with the general?'

'We have different destinations,' Gunn said. His outburst had left him too exhausted to explain.

'Is the American too ill to travel?'

'I'm not a lucky travelling companion. He stands a better chance on his own. He has friends who can smuggle him out of the country.'

'You should have stayed with the nomads until the soldiers left,' Linka told him.

'Did they attack the camp?'

'There was no fighting. They took the Khampas to a refugee camp near Pokhara.'

'Everyone except you.'

'This place is hard to find.'

'Perhaps they weren't looking.'

A spasm of irritation crossed Linka's face. 'You slander me with accusations of treachery, then expect me to help you.' He looked away, his manner suddenly less certain. 'I'm not sure if I can get you to safety. There's another army post at the winter settlement. It might be impossible. All I can suggest is that you return to the nomads and wait until spring.'

'I didn't come here for your help. I'll be on my way before dark.'

Linka stepped close, his eyes narrowed. 'Aren't you frightened I'll report you to the soldiers? There is a reward for the capture of anyone who went with Osher.'

'You have all the reward you need,' Gunn said.

Linka followed the progress of a Gurkha detachment as it marched two abreast towards the gorge. 'Did you leave a path for them to follow?' he demanded.

'As far as they're concerned,' Gunn said, 'I've vanished from the face of the earth.' A fit of coughing bent him double. He hawked phlegm.

'You're in no condition to travel further,' Linka said, hurrying to him. 'Come inside and rest.'

'I am tired,' Gunn admitted, letting Linka take his arm. 'It's been such a long journey. We hardly slept the last two nights. We tried to take shelter in the Lucky Place, but it was locked and shuttered.'

'The Lord Aim Giver died ten days ago,' Linka said, leading him down the passage.

'Then you have everything you want,' Gunn said, and his laughter brought on another convulsion of coughing.

'Your mind is out of balance,' Linka said, dragging him on. 'Sleep is what you need.'

Gunn tried to pull away when he came up against the barrier of cadavers.

'There's nothing to be frightened of,' Linka said, parting the bundles of skin and bone.

'No,' Gunn said, slowly looking round like a traveller who has returned home after a long absence.

Outwardly the chamber was exactly as he remembered it. Even the silence was stagnant. The air in here can't have changed for a thousand years, he thought. There was no cloying light and no carnal smell. Part of Gunn was disappointed. The fusty atmosphere irritated his throat, producing another fit of coughing.

Quickly Linka guided him through the temple and pulled back a heavy blanket. Behind it was a fair-sized chamber that must have been ventilated by an unseen flue in the rock. Pemba was at the hearth, blowing a fire into life by means of a wooden tube. She got to her feet and pressed her fingers together at her breast. Her eyes were huge and timid.

'It was her all the time,' Gunn said.

Linka didn't respond. He led Gunn to a sleeping platform and gently forced him to sit. Pemba busied herself with the fire.

'It was you I heard,' Gunn told her. The transition from arctic cold to merely chilly made him sweat. He sat at the edge of the platform and couldn't keep his hands still.

The girl took care not to catch his eye.

Across the fire Linka seated himself in one businesslike movement and smoothed out the skirt of his patchwork coat. He picked up a prayer wheel and twirled it. Gunn sensed that he was not at ease.

'By coming back I fear you have put yourself under sentence of death,' Linka said.

A gust of laughter escaped Gunn. He couldn't suppress his mood of excitement.

'Are you so careless of life?'

'It's life that's full of care,' Gunn said. 'You yourself told me that.'

'Why did you come back?' Linka demanded.

He had arranged the lamp so that his eyes were blacked out, but Gunn could feel their narrow scrutiny. He was glad that Linka could see his thoughts. It made explanations so much simpler.

'There is a story which I have always thought would appeal to the Tibetan temperament,' he said. 'A man is walking to town when he meets Death on the road. Death looks startled to see him; the man is terrified. He flees as far and as fast as he can, sailing across the sea to a city where he is certain Death won't find him. On the day he arrives he goes to the marketplace and there, smiling at him, is Death. "I have an apppointment with you here," Death tells him. "That's why I was so surprised to meet you on the road in your own country. I seriously doubted whether you'd be able to get here in time." '

Linka's mouth puckered. 'You're like a dog returning to its vomit. You won't find death here.' He stood up and came to Gunn. The harshness left his face. 'After the ordeal you've been through, it's only natural that your feelings are disordered. Lie down now.'

'I'm not ready for sleep,' Gunn insisted. Although he had seen nothing in the *gon-khang* to play on his fears, he remained flustered with the sense of being on the verge of revelations. In his ears was a noise like the whine of a mosquito.

'I'll prepare something to make you calm,' he heard Linka say.

'First let me look behind the screen.'

Linka stepped back, his lips clamped in a stern line. Gunn sensed a warning signal pass between him and Pemba. The girl had backed away to a corner, her hands crossed at her throat.

'I've told you,' Linka said. 'Strangers mustn't set eyes on the Guardians.'

Gunn struggled to his feet. 'I'm not frightened to face them,' he panted, wriggling in the Khampa's huge grasp. 'Don't you see – it's only the *thought* of them that makes me afraid. Seeing them will set my fears at rest.'

Linka held him in one hand. His tiny eyes were piercing, but they did not seem to have found what they were searching for. He released Gunn and appeared to relax. 'Go at your own risk.'

Gunn went out of the chamber and walked through the temple. He halted a few feet short of the screen and turned. Linka was behind him, the wry set of his mouth indicating that he disclaimed any responsibility for what might happen. Pemba was watching from the chamber, clutching the curtain in both hands. She seemed to be braced for a shock.

'The one in the middle,' Gunn said. 'Is he a soldier dressed in armour and some kind of leather mask?'

'How did you know?'

'I dream about him.'

437

Linka nodded without surprise. 'His power can be felt throughout the valley. He was a general who retired here in defeat.'

'Just like you,' Gunn said, with a snuffle of laughter. 'No one could serve him better.'

Linka smiled without mirth. 'Judge when you have seen.' Casually he waved Gunn on.

With faltering heart, Gunn stepped around the screen.

It wasn't the three wizened dolls behind the stone slab that made him lurch in horror. It was the small corpse seated on the other side with its hands held out in entreaty.

He crashed into the screen and it collapsed, coming apart at the hinges. He fell with it, smashing it to flour. Dust choked him and tears spangled everything with points of light.

'Beast,' he gasped. 'Foul murdering beast.'

'I warned you not to meddle,' Linka said, his voice nourished with satisfaction.

'Beast. Isn't the sacrifice of Osher enough for you?'

'Aim Giver came here himself,' Linka snapped, coming closer.

Gunn tried to squirm away. 'Do you expect me to believe that? It's impossible. He was at the point of death when I saw him.'

'Don't ask me how. All I can tell you is that he was here, just as you see him now, when Pemba and I returned after hearing that the Gurkhas were marching up the valley. Some of the villagers might have brought him. He might have flown here.'

'He never visited this place. The sacristan told me he hadn't left the Lucky Place in years.'

'Not since his father died, and for the same reason as you. Because he was afraid of the Guardians. And like you, he forced himself to confront his fears.' Linka studied the corpse. 'And exorcise them,' he added.

Gunn wiped his eyes. 'I don't believe you. Where are the ritual instruments?'

'The true adept doesn't need such toys.'

'Where are the offerings?'

Linka smiled. He pointed at the lama. He dropped to his haunches beside Gunn, his expression rapt. 'There is a rite of exorcism which only the greatest of lamas dare practise,' he said, the words spilling out. 'Such a genius offers his own body to the devouring spirits, but when they are gorging on the feast he assumes the form of his own tutelary deities and traps the demons. He rolls them up in his own skin, he binds them with his own entrails and then dashes them to

438

destruction.' Linka's excitement cooled. He stood up and offered Gunn a helping hand. 'It is a rite fraught with danger. Imagine the consequences should the exorcist lose control. Ah no,' he said, intercepting Gunn's shocked glance, 'see how calm he is. As I said, as I knew the moment I set eyes on him – a true adept.' Linka exhaled a melancholy sigh. 'If only he could have perceived my devotion and accepted me as his pupil.'

'He perceived what kind of man you are,' Gunn said, looking at the corpse reaching out to the scarecrows. Death had not softened the lama's expression. The grooves on each side of his mouth suggested that his death had been no great loss – that his life had been a small thing, something lived within brackets.

Gunn turned his attention to the Guardians, wondering how he could have feared them. They were bloodless, desiccated objects, no more menacing than the dried-up remains turning on their chains by the entrance. Then why had they forced themselves into his dreams? He made himself look at each mask in turn, holding his breath for a distant echo, a tremor of recognition. Nothing. They had lost interest in him.

'Bird Rack, Shalawoka, Dark Waters,' Linka said, watching Gunn as he studied the figures.

'Demons, you called them, yet they're meant to be the protectors of the community. Why would Aim Giver exorcise his own Guardians?'

'Subjugate rather than destroy. Tame rather than banish.' Linka slipped a glance at the curtained chamber. Pemba had withdrawn behind it. 'When the blessed Padma Sambhava carried the sacred doctrine into these mountains, he didn't annihilate the old gods. He subdued them and appointed them defenders of the holy law. The lamas still rendered them their due, but they had to satisfy their hunger with barley cakes instead of meat, and quench their thirst with beer and milk instead of blood.'

'Not here, though,' Gunn said. The name of the *gon-khang* recalled some of his fear. 'Not in the place of the wet skulls.'

Linka nodded complacently. 'In a few dark corners the unenlightened continued to worship the old gods in the old way.'

Gunn stared at the altar. It was hewn from a single leaf of stone, smooth at the edges, with a shallow trough at its centre. His lips parted in revulsion.

'I found bones in a near-by cave,' Linka told him. 'The skeletons of children. They were very old.'

'How can you bear to remain here?' Gunn cried.

'I also found animal bones,' Linka continued. His smile seemed to mock. 'They were not so old. They were the sacrifices made in Aim Giver's own lifetime.'

'By his father,' Gunn said, seeing the leering eye in the Lucky Place.

'And by all his fathers before him, right back to the beginning of the line and even earlier, to the time of the first clans.' Linka faced the lama and gave a sigh as of admiration. 'But the Lord Aim Giver was a man of pure *dharma*; he refused to observe the old rites.' Linka's gaze sparkled with what Gunn took to be humour. 'Alas, you can't starve a god into submission; you only swell its appetite. When the lama broke the vows made by his fathers, the Guardians withdrew their protection and the fortunes of the community suffered.'

'He knew you would restore those disgusting rituals,' Gunn said. 'That's why he wouldn't accept you.' He couldn't tear his eyes away from the basin in the altar. 'All these months you've been here . . .'

Linka's laugh pealed through the cave. 'You think I've tried to satisfy their cravings. Listen,' he said, clamping his hand on Gunn's shoulder. 'They aren't dogs that will lick your hand if it throws them a few scraps of meat. It takes time to form an alliance with gods as fierce as these. Months, years of preparation are necessary. Approach too hastily and . . .' Linka showed his teeth '. . . they will bite the hand that feeds.'

'But you would have,' Gunn said. 'You still could.'

Linka's hand fell away from his shoulder. 'By his last act, the Lord Aim Giver glutted the Guardians and made himself their master. They serve the community on his terms now.'

'Then he's defeated you. All your efforts have been wasted.'

'The villagers still need a new lama,' Linka said, walking away.

'Do they still want you?'

'They haven't learnt of Aim Giver's death. When the soldiers leave, I shall go down to the settlement and give them the news. It's for them to decide.'

'But you'll agree if they ask you.'

'Perhaps,' Linka said, stopping in the centre of the *gon-khang*.

'Why the doubt?' Gunn demanded. 'It's what you set your heart on.'

'They hate Pemba,' Linka said, 'and I won't be parted from her.'

'The baby,' Gunn cried. 'I'd forgotten. She's carrying your child.'

Linka turned slowly, the sparks in his eyes betraying the fires within. 'She lost it the night we found the lama. He made certain that he would be the last of the line.'

'So it was all for nothing. Fifty men dead, and for what?'

'You abuse my hospitality, stranger,' Linka bellowed.

'Who else could have told the Chinese where to find us?'

'Since you left I haven't set a foot outside the camp,' Linka shouted.

'You could have sent someone else.'

Linka's anger fell away in an instant. 'Enough of this,' he said, coming up and taking Gunn by the shoulders. 'You have heard enough, seen enough, talked enough. Stop hunting for ghosts.'

His touch laid a great weakness on Gunn. His bones swam in his flesh and he would have fallen if Linka hadn't got hold of him. 'I know you did it,' he managed to say. Linka's face had swollen to massive proportions. He wrenched his eyes away and searched for the curse above the altar. He looked back to find confirmation of Linka's guilt in his sad smile.

'Ah yes,' he heard the Khampa say. 'But whose vow and whose guilt? Yours or mine?'

When Gunn regained consciousness, he found Linka's face still floating before him, issuing soothing noises. Eventually it slid away and he realised that he was lying on the platform in the sleeping chamber. Gunn struggled to move but his muscles had dissolved in sweat. He groaned and rocked his head. Once again his strength had deserted him, his purpose failed. In the end . . . would he never hear the end of that refrain? In the end, Yonden could have what merit he possessed. It wasn't much, but it might be enough to tilt the balance. The balance is upset. The balance of my mind is upset . . .

'What are you saying? Speak Tibetan. Better still, don't speak at all. Here, drink this. It will drive out the fever.'

He felt Linka's arm lift him from the pillow, then tasted the bitterness of aloes. He spat it out and closed his mouth against more.

'I have my own remedy,' he mumbled. 'Water is all I need.'

Icy meltwater was trickling into his mouth, easing his parched throat. He drained the bowl and held it out to be refilled. His mind had become cooler.

In the end it was simple. Almost without having to think about it, he slipped from his pocket a small bottle, uncapped it and broke the seal. Sipping and swallowing alternately, he finished off the contents.

'What kind of medicine is this?' Linka asked, picking up the discarded bottle from the floor.

Gunn laughed at the suspicion in his face. 'Strong medicine,' he replied. 'For conditions that are incurable.'

He slumped back on the pillow and closed his eyes. He couldn't avoid feeling guilty, but that was the state he had lived in all his life. Besides, he had had a month to examine all the alternatives. It seemed to him that all of them would be no more than different routes to the same end. This way guaranteed a minimum of fuss. All his life, it seemed, he had caused people a great deal of fuss.

As his consciousness began to drop away he tried to frame in his mind's eye the view from Yonden's house, paying particular attention to the inconceivably bright summits. It wouldn't hold. As he slipped further down, the picture dissipated and he found himself stranded on a wind on a beach in a wind that made the sand swarm at his feet like a plague of mites. Watching the sea's oily swell, he detected shapes beneath and tasted nausea. Offshore, a black freighter swung at anchor, trapped in a cone of ugly light. A squall was drawing towards him. He waited at the water's edge to meet it, and when it struck, he held his face to the cold lashing rain. At last it passed, leaving an evening sky washed clean and a sea that was alive in an entirely innocent way. The freighter had pulled up anchor and was under way, its black hull shortening as it swung round and steered a course between the dragon-backed reefs of childhood, heading for the clear light over the horizon.

As Linka prayed over the snoring shape of Gunn, he brooded. His thoughts wouldn't lie still. The stranger's return had unsettled him. What he had said ate into his self-assurance.

The wind moaned in the rock chimney and the flames of the butter lamp trembled. Outside, the storm had broken.

Asleep by the hearth, Pemba uttered words in a foreign voice. She jerked on the blankets as if she was being tugged by invisible cords. Her mouth opened in a sharp grin and her eyes stared. Without hesitation, Linka went to her, ready to quell this latest mischief. It wasn't the first time there had been disturbances, nor the first night that Pemba had ground her teeth in her sleep and cried out in another woman's voice.

He held her until the spirit that had entered her left. Slowly her eyes changed focus.

'It was her,' she whispered. 'She says it's not too late.'

'Not too late for what?'

Her tongue flickered. He knew she was listening to the droning of Gunn's snores.

'Give him to them.'

'Who?' he whispered. He knew perfectly well, but he wanted to hear it from another mouth.

'The stranger.' Her eyes were dreamy. She was in a waking trance.

Hearing her articulate what he had hardly dared think, he experienced a visceral excitement that was all the thicker for being based on fear. How else could he explain the return of the stranger, blown back by karmic winds to die in the place of wet skulls?

Frustration gnawed at him. He knew why Gunn disturbed him. The stranger had witnessed at his first visit what had remained hidden from him all these months. Pemba had seen it too. Looking into her sleeping, waking eyes, he sensed the shallowness of his own vision. Oh, it was acute enough in the world of men, but she saw from within another dimension. Hers was the real perception, the gift of a perfect union. His excitement quickened. If only he dared harness his will to her insight, he might yet find the source of the power that Aim Giver had denied him.

'Stay here,' he told Pemba.

Her eyes closed. He waited beside her. Gunn's breathing had become faint and ragged. Presently, Linka heard from the direction of the *gon-khang* a noise like the claws of a bird scrabbling on bark. Taking a deep breath, he picked up a lamp and went through the curtain.

As soon as he entered, he sensed the presence of a host. Some of them were hostile. Most of the lamps he had set around the lama had blown out, leaving areas of blackness between them, and the light from the others was being pulled this way and that, making the shadows of the Guardians dance on the walls.

He had the impression that they had put on weight and substance. Bird Rack had fledged up, Dark Waters was as squat as a barrel, and Shalawoka was sitting straighter and taller, more alert. It was hard to see, though. The nearer he reached, the vaguer they became. It was as if they were retreating into pockets of shadow. He raised his lamp higher and a gust of wind snuffed it out. All the lamps were out. He stood in the darkness with the curse he had glimpsed incised on his brain. *May all violators of the oath come to the same end.*

Close by he heard the slow drip of viscous liquid falling on dust. Spilt butter oil, he thought, his scalp tightening. His senses were dislocated by the dark. He crouched on one knee and fumbled for matches. His hands shook so much that he upset the box and had to feel around in the dust. He cringed at whatever his groping hand might encounter. Match after match that he struck went out. At last

443

he succeeded in lighting the lamp, but though the flame burnt evenly, its light had congealed.

Within its small circle he saw a black stain spreading out from the base of the altar. He held the lamp at full stretch. Drip, drip, drip. The source could only be the sack that Dark Waters clutched in his left hand.

Only a dream, he told himself, mind phenomena – yet it took every fibre of will to stand up.

Look well, he told himself. Don't be afraid. If you can face this, you will see deeper and further than any dream. He raised the lamp.

'I've waited for this moment.'

Shalawoka remained an obscure presence, but it was his voice that Linka heard.

'Come closer.'

Linka approached the altar.

'Kneel.'

Linka knelt, his hands grasping the edge of the stone.

'Closer.'

Linka almost disobeyed. His fear was trying to drag him back. He could feel Shalawoka's malevolence. And yet he was so close now. He mustn't retreat. He leaned as far as he could, his head right over the altar.

Ice encased his bones as the Guardian began to come alive behind the mask. Down the holes in Shalawoka's helmet he saw eyes approaching him. They were as bright as varnish and stared at him with a vicious, unblinking intensity. The leather nose-guard jutted like a muzzle; the slot beneath was filling with a slashing grin.

'What do you want?' he whispered.

The mouth moved, and in the instant before it spoke, Linka knew. 'You, you, you,' he heard as he flung himself back. 'I've come for you.'

A sob of terror was squeezed from his throat as he hit the floor. The impact extinguished the lamp, leaving him with the image of all three figures rising to their feet. He screamed and held up his hands to ward them off.

Pemba ran to him. He babbled a warning, striking out at the shapes. 'He's come back.'

'Who?' she shouted, her eyes darting to Aim Giver.

'The one in the middle. The butcher's son.'

Her lamp almost blew out as she whirled round. By its pinched light he saw the Guardians shrink back behind the altar. She cupped

444

her hands around the flame until it caught. The Guardians were shrivelled puppets, frail enough to crumble at a touch.

'It was Osher,' he said in a voice too small for him. 'I saw him. He spoke to me. He's come to take his revenge.'

She stepped over him. Sprawled at her feet, one hand still shielding his face, he knew how pathetic he must look.

She scowled at the lama. 'He brought him back. He took my child and now he wants to destroy you.'

Linka lay in the dust and understood for the first time the unassailable power of the man he had had the temerity to challenge. Aim Giver was a man who had stripped himself down until he existed only as a living antenna, an organ refined and developed solely for the purpose of communing with the invisible.

Linka climbed heavily to his feet. His mind was dull, his body a blunt instrument. 'You'll have another child,' he told Pemba, 'but not here.' He sensed a stirring among some of the unseen host. There were those who did not want him to leave.

'The stranger's dead,' she told him.

'Then there's nothing to keep us here.'

'Not even the lama's throne?'

Linka's eyes went to the curse in stone, then settled on Osher. That is always how he would see the chief Guardian. Behind the mask Osher was waiting; he would always be waiting. Linka raised a self-mocking smile as he recalled his excitement when Pemba identified the parallels between Shalawoka and himself – an echo returning down the ages. The correspondence between his former lieutenant and the general who had retired here in defeat all those years ago had never crossed his mind. He bowed low before the armoured figure, acknowledging the rightness of the succession. Osher would make a formidable Guardian.

'Let someone else take the throne,' Linka told Pemba. 'I'm not the rightful heir.'

'You seemed so certain.'

Linka breathed a desolate sigh. 'My beloved teacher used to tell me that your destination shouldn't be where you're going, but where you are. Fix your eyes on the horizon and it will always recede before you. The night I came to the Lucky Place, I was sure I had reached my final goal.' He shook his head sadly. 'I was wrong. A path brought me here, and now it leads me away.'

'Will you take me with you?' she asked timidly.

'To the very end,' he said, bathing her in his most tender smile.

Chapter 27

The snow fell in Christmas card plenty. Only when an occasional shift in the attitude of the wind gathered it in pleats could Melville see the three towers of the camp. He had his back to a rock near the edge of the gorge. Nyima had been gone too long for comfort.

He blew on his hands and re-read Gunn's letter.

Dear Mr Melville . . .

Rage quickened his blood. *Mister* – after all the grief they'd been through?

I know you will be angry with me, but I have decided not to go back with you. I hope and suspect you will understand. You will find it harder to understand why I have left with General Liu, so let me explain if I can. Your suspicions were right. He is going to India. This was his intention from the moment he decided to defect, and he made the arrangements with Major Jetha before he approached your friend Mr Yueh. I'm afraid to say that he bribed Tashi to go to Jetha instead of sending your message. You have done your best, but he is determined not to live in either America or Taiwan, and if you had tried to take him against his wishes I think he might have done you serious harm. Let him go. It's what he wants.

Stay with the nomads until spring comes. Enjoy the happiness you have found with Nyima. She is more important than any general. You needn't worry that you will be found. Believe me, I will never give you away. As for General Liu, he is extremely anxious to avoid any diplomatic ructions and has sworn to tell the authorities that you died in Tibet.

I hate to take my leave like this, but it's for the best. You have my word on that, so there is no reason to worry about me. I wish you a safe journey home and all the good luck you deserve in the future. You are still a young man with your life ahead of you and many things can change. I have seen how much you have changed since I met you. Looking back on these last two months, I am not as sad as you might imagine.

Yours, Alan Gunn

The asshole, the perfect fucking asshole. He couldn't even write his own suicide note without condemning someone else to death.

He screwed up the letter and stared into the falling snow. It settled with hypnotic slowness. Nyima had been gone too long. The soldiers must be questioning her. He no longer cared He was assailed by weariness.

It was the end of the line, as near as made no difference. He had chased after Liu with homicidal intent, and then, when the storm made a mockery of that resolve, he had clung to the slim hope that he might be able to get word to the embassy before the general could leave Nepal, while he was still within reach. Some hope. By now he would be receiving five-star treatment in Delhi. God, how he must be laughing.

All that remained was surrender. Sometimes he thought that if only he could get out of this valley, away from the restricted zone, the less hard it would go for him.

Nyima appeared out of the snow. She stood before him like a gawky schoolgirl.

'How many?' he asked, pulling himself to his feet.

Her hand made a quick negative gesture. She had spoken very little since they left the camp.

'Deserted?' He laughed in disbelief. 'Don't tell me those bastards have kept their word.'

The news confused him. Perhaps he should follow Gunn's advice and return with Nyima. The thought of retracing his steps was abhorrent. He was too cold to think properly.

'Alright,' he said, 'let's get to shelter. I'll make a decision tonight.'

She shook her head and the refusal infuriated him. 'One more night, that's all I'm asking.' His anger blew out. He went to her and laid his cheek against hers. Stiff as ice. 'One more night,' he murmured. 'Our last night.' He placed his hands on her shoulders and looked into her eyes. 'I love you,' he said. 'I want you to know that.'

For answer she took hold of one of his hands and ran her finger down the large vein on the back. She looked at him from under the fringe of her fleece helmet and he saw moisture on her cheek. A melted snowflake. Before he could say anything, she kissed him quick and hard, a clumsy meeting of teeth and lips. Then she lifted up her skirts and ran. For a brief moment after she disappeared, the snow retained a whirligig impression of her.

Behind him he heard a rifle bolt snapping to. As he fingered his smarting mouth, he found that it had composed itself into a kind of smile. He raised his hands with relief. 'I give up.'

The soldiers seemed a little scared of him. They herded him into camp at the points of their guns and manhandled him through a trapdoor into a windowless basement. Two of them with an officer came in after him and removed his boots and tied his hands. When they left, they pulled some heavy object over the trap. The idea that he might attempt an escape struck Melville as ludicrous.

An hour or so later the weight was dragged off the trap and the same trio descended, carrying a lamp. The officer introduced himself in English as Captain Kamal Gurung and ordered him to explain himself, which he was prompt to do. Captain Kamal Gurung listened without interrupting, his manner never deviating from civility. Melville concluded with a plea that the American embassy be informed of his predicament right away. The captain left without a word, taking the lantern with him. A short time later two different soldiers came with a meal, the first of several that broke the monotony of his confinement over the next two days.

The sound of guards stamping to attention woke him from a thin sleep. He had dreamt he was the only survivor of an avalanche listening to a search party going past the place where he lay buried. The trapdoor grated back, exposing a square of withering sky. Captain Kamal Gurung's face appeared, polished by the cold. When Melville tried to comply with his order to come out, he found that his legs were as pliant as cardboard. He had to be carried to the roof and propped between guards until his senses had unscrambled.

It was a glorious day. Nothing stood between him and outer space. Not far from the camp a work detail was clearing a circle of snow. They stopped and leaned on their shovels when they saw him. He tried to face the possibility that this was the last day of his life.

Assisted by his guards, he was taken to his old room, where a basin of warm water had been prepared for him. He washed and shaved. Looking into the little mirror that one of the soldiers held for him, he saw that he had slipped down the slope into middle age. He couldn't even plead youth in mitigation.

He refused the plate of goat stew and lentils which they offered him, but accepted some rice and a mug of instant coffee. His throat closed and he heard the *thocka-thocka-thocka* of a descending helicopter. Captain Kamal Gurung rose and straightened his uniform. Before making for the door, he pushed a pack of cigarettes at him. 'As bad as that,' Melville said, shaking his head.

The building trembled under the din of churning machinery. As the rotors flop-flopped to rest and the motors whined to a halt, the guards pinioned his arms. They held him like that until the captain returned. Before he could speak or even catch the captain's eye, he was led out.

The helicopter was hidden behind the buildings. He could smell the stink of its exhaust and hear its expensive componentry pinging as it cooled. The soldiers escorted him to Osher's old headquarters.

Inside were two men identifiable as Americans by their fur-lined parkas, ski resort sweaters and brand new outdoorsman boots. The smell of their aftershave made his eyes smart. Hope rose and sank, deflated by the stare of the man standing by the window, nursing a tin mug in his hands. He was the older of the two, a hard-faced, closely razored individual with a thinning widow's peak and an unforgiving mouth. He was the kind of hardass you saw just out of camera focus behind presidential shoulders. Everything about him bespoke professionalism. Melville could not imagine this man letting the general make an idiot of him.

The younger one was seated, contemplating a small statue of Buddha contemplating him. It was a mass-produced tourist item and its owner was frowning slightly as though he suspected a rip-off. His frown intensified when he allowed Melville to come to his notice. He looked clean and athletic and happy in his calling. Melville formed the impression that under his fair, cornbelt skin he was packed with some kind of highly compressed elastic material. He looked like a living testimonial to one of the military academy-style colleges advertised in the pages of *National Geographic*.

No meeting of minds with this pair. If they were embassy people, they were not from the front office.

'Walter Melville?' the older one asked.

'Are you here to take me out?'

'Just answer the question. Are you Walter Melville?'

Melville admitted it. He experienced difficulty keeping his face in order. The lower part moved independently of the upper.

'What happened to your nose?' the older one asked.

'Frost bite,' Melville said, touching his nose before he could stop himself.

'Identify these individuals,' the younger one said, spinning a photograph onto the table where Osher used to play with his Zippo.

He leaned away, crinkling his nose, as Melville approached.

It was a snap taken at a party at Hubbard's place. Boozy faces, his own among them, looked carelessly up into the flashlight. It was an incriminating and demoralising picture, corresponding not in the slightest to the self-image which he cherished.

449

'That's me,' he confessed. 'I'm Melville. I'm the one you want. I'd deny it if I could.' He was conscious of running over at the mouth. He drew a steadying breath. 'Do I get to know who you are.'

'Esposito,' the older one said, pointing a thumb at his chest. 'Kraft,' he said, pointing it the other way.

Melville had a moment of hope. 'You've been in touch with Hubbard.'

'He helped compile your profile,' Kraft said. He gathered up the picture and examined it. 'A featherweight, an amateur. Amateur anthropologist, amateur hustler. No fucking judgement. Immature.'

'Hubbard should know,' Melville said, roused by the betrayal. 'He's been fifty-five ever since I met him.'

'A wise guy,' Kraft continued. 'A clever prick who never put together a week's work in his life but always had the answers.'

'I dispute that. I'd like to point out that I nearly delivered you a Chinese general.'

'Your fucking diddy-bopping around Tibet put two nations on fucking war alert,' Kraft roared.

Melville cowered. 'Am I in bad trouble.'

'A world of trouble,' Esposito said.

'It was never meant to be like that,' Melville whimpered. 'I was never meant to go any further than here. Things just happened.' He clutched his head.

'You lost control,' Esposito suggested.

'That's it,' Melville said, startled. 'Events got away from me. If there's any way I can put it right.'

'That's why we're here,' Esposito said. 'To make good the damage.'

'You've got to get me out of here,' Melville said. He held out his hands to Kraft. 'I need treatment. Unless I get to a hospital I'm going to lose my fingers.'

Kraft inched his chair back. Esposito breathed on his coffee to attract their attention. 'We have to be out of this crater before dark,' he said, 'carrying a line-by-line deposition from you.' He placed a portable tape recorder on the table and switched it on.

Shock sparked along Melville's nerves as the connection was made. 'You mean I'm not coming with you,' he whispered.

Kraft snorted. 'The only way you'll leave here is if we bag you out.'

Esposito sent him a look you could have strung beads on.

'Tell me what you're going to do with me,' Melville cried. 'Tell me what's happened to Liu. I have a right to know. I demand to be heard by the proper people.'

'We are the proper people,' Esposito said, adjusting the volume of the recorder, 'and you don't have any rights.' He stopped the tape and played back the exchange. Melville's fear was too powerful a signal for the little machine to handle.

'You can't make me incriminate myself.'

'In that case your situation goes from very bad to much worse.'

'Worse is what the people we're expecting would like to do with you,' Kraft explained.

Again, Esposito shot him down with a look. 'Better co-operate,' he said.

'Alright,' Melville said. His legs were about to buckle. Kraft noticed and got him a seat.

'How many more of you are there left in the woodwork?' Esposito demanded when they were settled.

'I'm the last.'

'What about the other crazy – Alan Gunn?'

'I don't know. He's the nut who let Liu get away from me.'

'He was supposed to come in with the general,' Kraft said.

'With the general?' Melville repeated, surprise hanging a loose smile on his face.

'Liu woke up a few klicks from here and Gunn was gone. No idea where.'

'Try asking harder,' Melville said. 'He must have murdered him.'

'The soldiers picked up Gunn's trail close by the spot where they took you in. Then it vanishes. He was on his own. We figure he's hiding out. Any idea where? Did he have friends he could call on?'

Melville laughed at the absurdity.

'You think this is funny, fucker?' Kraft shouted.

Melville remembered the *gon-khang*. 'He went looking for something.'

Kraft made a sound of disgust. 'Five minutes on the job and already we're running into loose ends.'

'I'm the only loose end,' Melville said.

'And a loose screw. Jesus.'

'What something?' Esposito inquired.

'I'm not sure.'

'Not sure?' Kraft said, glaring at Esposito. 'What is this hippy shit.' He glowered at Melville. 'You telling us he's gone off hunting the abominable snowman.'

'You could call it that.'

451

'Listen, pogue. Any more weird stuff and we'll toss you to the dogs.'

'I don't know where he is.'

'We'll find him,' Kraft said darkly.

'The vultures will find him first.'

'You figure he's dead?' Esposito asked.

'If he isn't, it won't be for want of trying.' Kraft snarled.

'It doesn't sound like you and him were close,' Esposito said.

Melville shook with silent laughter. Kraft slapped him out of it with a light back-hander.

'No, we weren't close,' Melville said, holding his face. 'We were about a million light years apart.'

'How come a balloon like this ever got close to a fucking Red general?' Kraft marvelled. His eyes narrowed as they fell on the portraits of the North Vietnamese leaders. 'Was it you who stuck those pictures of Charlie there? Jesus, what are you – some kind of anarchist?'

'It was Osher,' Melville told him. 'He was a patriot.'

'Let me get this straight,' Esposito said. He held a pencil at its centre, and now he slid his fingers along it until it was poised like a conductor's baton. 'Only three of you made it back to this valley. All the others were totalled, right?'

'Totalled, yes,' Melville agreed. 'Totally totalled.' He could hardly keep his eyes open for fatigue.

Esposito put down the pencil and raised his eyebrows at Kraft. He switched on the recorder again. 'Okay, Walter, from the beginning.'

The telling took much longer than it had with Captain Kamal Gurung. They kept raising queries and trying to pin him down on dates. Despite frequent drinks of water and coffee, his voice barely held out.

'What d'you use for brains, Walter?' Kraft said after the short silence that followed. His mood had softened during the testimony. Esposito's manner was case-hardened. The apprentice pulled a long face at his master. 'Any chance we can plead extenuating circumstances. I mean, if it's true Walter didn't go into Tibet off his own bat . . .'

'It is true, I swear it.'

'So what do you think?' Kraft asked Esposito.

'Son,' Esposito told him, 'I hope you're not going to turn out a big disappointment.'

Kraft pouted at Melville then examined his boots.

'There's no room for appeal,' Esposito told Melville, not shrinking from eye contact. 'It's not us who fix the price. You've upset a lot of people. They insist on their pound of flesh.' He took the spool of tape out of the recorder and slipped it into his pocket.

That's me, Melville thought, seeing his life slip away.

Captain Kamal Gurung came panting in and Esposito went over so they could talk without being overheard. Melville paid no attention.

'Sweetwater and Mr Yueh are the ones you should be going after,' he said, when the captain had left the room.

'Yueh is tucked up in fortress Taiwan,' Esposito said. 'Charlie – well, he's a hard man to nail.' Esposito shrugged. 'You're it.' He went and stared out of the window.

'The scapegoat.'

'This fucking hooch is crawling,' Kraft said, scatching his thigh.

'Give me a reason,' Melville shouted. 'China's a hostile power. This is a neutral country. We're on the same side.'

'You're not on any side,' Esposito told him. 'Far as you're concerned, it's open season.'

'Don't hand me that crap. I know how you bastards operate. You've got Liu stashed away, and when the flak has settled you'll wheel him out and claim the credit.'

'Simple asshole,' Kraft said, polishing his toecap on the cuff of his pants.

'I demand to know what you've done with Liu,' Melville cried. 'I've earned that much at least.' He put his head in his hands and began to blubber.

'This much I guarantee,' Esposito said. 'Liu's not having a nice time.'

'He was DOA the moment he set foot in this ville,' Kraft added.

Melville did not understand it even in translation. 'Dead on arrival? If he was dead, how could he have told you about Gunn? Why are you lying to me?'

'Figuratively speaking,' Esposito said. He turned and contemplated Melville. After a time he sighed. 'Alright,' he said coming back to the table, 'I guess you've earned that much.' He sat down and let another interval develop. 'First thing your Chinese general did on turning himself in was demand a ride to the Soviet embassy.'

Melville's eyes switched from one to the other. 'You're shitting me.' He was so stunned that he hardly heard the approach of another helicopter.

'Nope,' Esposito said.

'There must be some mistake.'

'Dead right,' Kraft said, and laughed.

'He was going to India,' Melville said. 'He told Gunn everything. Major Jetha was his contact.'

'Between him and the Soviet military attaché and a pair of Russian engineering consultants working on a cigarette factory outside Kathmandu.'

'No, I refuse to accept it.'

Esposito shrugged.

'You've got to hand it to him,' Kraft said. 'He wound you all up and pointed you in the wrong direction. Mr Yueh thinks he's going to outsmart him and set him up on Taiwan; you figure you'll take him to the States; but that little old general, he knows he's headed for a retirement home outside Moscow.' Kraft chortled. 'Now that's what I call devious.'

Melville became aware of the helicopter chomping air overhead. He paid it no attention. 'If that was his aim, why not go to the Russians in the first place?'

'Lack of resources,' Kraft said. 'They don't run any Tibetan guerillas that we know of.'

'They could have approached the Indians for help.'

'At worst that would have meant an outright refusal. End of story. At best, the Indians would have demanded a share. Anyway, no need; the Russians have got Mr Yueh's number from way back. They knew he'd jump at the chance to grab himself a Red general, so they told Liu to apply through the usual channels. They reckoned he'd be able to walk away from your bum outfit whenever he pleased, and then hand himself over to Jetha.' Kraft opened his hands. 'And that's exactly what he did.'

Delayed shock struck Melville cold. 'Oh my God, he's in the Soviet Union.'

'He'd like to be,' Kraft said. 'Didn't make it, though.'

'Then where the hell is he? Who's got him?' Melville turned on Kraft. 'Why are you smirking like that?'

'He's back with his own,' Esposito said, getting up. 'Back in the People's Republic.'

'Damn you,' Melville shouted, smashing his fist on the table. 'How could you let him go? You must have had time to act.'

Esposito wandered over to the window.

'A lot of good men died for the sake of that general,' Melville yelled over the roar of the helicopter.

'Listen,' Kraft told him, not unkindly, 'you could have brought Liu tied to a pole and set him down in the lobby of our embassy and we'd still have sent him back.'

'That's enough,' Esposito told his partner, craning his head to see through the opening.

'Now you know what deep water you've been pissing in,' Kraft said. 'Think yourself lucky you're not going to be strapped into the seat next to Liu.' He stretched out his legs and crossed them at the ankle.

'I said enough,' Esposito commanded, turning to stare his apprentice down. He breathed a reproachful sigh. 'Kraft by name but not by nature. And take your hand off that gun before you shoot your cock off.'

Kraft made haste to withdraw his hand from his waistband. He sat and sulked while the helicopter came in to land. Its din made further speech pointless. Esposito faced the room, hands shoved deep in his pants pockets, head bowed. At last the rotors stopped. Behind Melville the door opened. Esposito looked up and nodded, raising five fingers.

'Don't get your hopes up,' he told Melville.

Reprieve hadn't entered Melville's mind for some time. He was tired unto death. He felt a certain contempt for all the effort he'd expended trying to stay alive. 'I wasn't,' he said.

'Ours not to reason why, Walter. You know how it is.'

'I know. You do and I die.'

'I wish there was some way out, but you're the bare minimum. The people who just dropped in won't settle for anything less.'

Melville ran his hands through his hair. His fingers trapped an engorged tick. He disentangled it and held it alive, still struggling.

'What in fuck is that?' Kraft demanded, pulling in his legs and standing up so abruptly that his seat overturned.

'You want a taste of my blood? Go ahead, take it.'

'You dirty little dipstick,' Kraft said.

'Want a sample?' Melville asked Esposito, whose face looked to be carved from hickory. 'Ah, I forgot. You want something bigger to get your teeth into.' Delicately he placed the tick between his teeth. He could feel its legs waving at the centre of his demented grin. He tightened his jaws, popping the tick in a little spray of blood, and ran his tongue along his lips.

Kraft wrinkled his own lips. 'Let's do it and get out before we catch the plague or something.'

455

'Yeah, do it,' Melville jeered, 'and then fuck off in your shiny new boots and shiny new helicopter.'

'Shut up,' Esposito said. He went and stood behind Melville. 'Time to straighten it out,' he said, touching him on the shoulder.

Outside, confusion ensued. They were fenced in by soldiers. Esposito and Kraft didn't know which way to turn.

Kraft tried to break past the cordon. 'Lemme through, give us room. Hey, come on, the guy's not going to make a break. Captain, get your men back.'

After some discussion, Captain Kamal Gurung agreed that three soldiers and himself would be sufficient to prevent the prisoner from escaping. Esposito still looked uncertain.

'I know a place,' Melville told him.

'I admire the way you're standing up to it,' Esposito told him as he led the way out of the camp.

Melville had no idea how he was standing up to it. His mind was disjointed. The world was out of joint. It had the clarity of hallucination. The sun shone devotedly, the sky was immaculate, the snow pristine. He wondered if his assassins had slipped something into his coffee to lighten his last hour.

'We should have brought snowshoes,' Kraft panted.

'And a picnic hamper and barbecue,' Esposito said.

Melville witnessed Kraft's discomfiture without malice. Fifty yards adrift of them, three men in long overcoats were wading through the snow with the caution of men fording a treacherous river.

'Chinese,' Esposito said.

'Not tame ones,' Melville said.

'I told you we're not doing this out of pique.'

'I guess I know why,' Melville said. 'You've fixed up some kind of reconciliation with Peking. Mr Yueh got to know about it and decided to shoot it down. Maybe Liu heard a whisper, too.'

'Your guess is as good as mine. Like I said: deep waters.' Esposito cleared his throat with a suggestion of awkwardness. 'I managed to have a quick word, long distance, with Charlie. He's real sorry. He had no idea of the dimensions.'

'What happened? The world stop beating a path to his door?'

'You grow old, Walter. You lose touch. Your right hand loses its cunning.'

'I wouldn't know, would I? Think you might run into him again?'

'Only if he doesn't see me coming.'

456

'If you do, tell him I'm a disappointed man.'

'If I do, I'll pass it on. He would have got you off the hook if he could, but he didn't know if you were alive.'

'You told him,' Melville said, anger piercing his numbness. 'He could have done something. He could have given the story to the newspapers. United States returns defecting Red Chinese general to Peking. The readers would have loved it.'

'It doesn't work that way for an old pro like Charlie. Rules of the club.'

'Yes, of course,' Melville said, his anger dulled. 'I was forgetting you're fellow members and I don't belong.' He laughed. 'I should have paid attention to what Hubbard told me. Three is always the sum of two plus one. That's the equation to live by.'

'Walter,' Esposito said, stopping.

'I've got nothing more to say to you.'

'Just one question. Why in hell did you do it?'

Reasons were too far in the past. He gave a helpless shrug. 'It seemed like a good idea at the time.'

They walked on in silence. The mountain wall cast the gorge into deep shadow and the temperature plunged as they crossed into it. Esposito turned. Although the Chinese delegation was receiving assistance from the soldiers, they had fallen further behind. Esposito's face tightened. 'Tell the ghouls to shift their asses,' he ordered the captain. 'Sorry about this,' he said to Melville.

'Jesus, it's cold,' Kraft said, hopping from foot to foot. 'It's okay for you,' he said to Melville. 'You're used to it.'

'His first time out,' Esposito murmured by way of explanation. 'Naturally he's nervous.'

'Naturally,' Melville agreed. He strolled to the end of the rock prow.

'Hey,' Kraft called. 'Not too near the edge.' He cast a furtive glance at Esposito.

Casually, Melville craned over. Even leaning right out, he couldn't see the bottom. It was lost in the dark. He gave an involuntary shiver and turned back.

'Hey,' Kraft called again. 'Where did that fucking bird come from? Gee, it's huge.'

Melville recognised his old acquaintance the vulture. It cruised back and forth, turning in its own length, as single-minded as a shark patrolling a reef. It marked him with the same expression – or absence of it – as before. Probably it had no other.

'It's a bone vulture. It comes for the bones.'

'It's got a real shitty look about it,' Kraft said. He stamped his feet and swung his arms. 'Hurry it up,' he muttered, squinting at the Chinese.

They were bunched up, talking with animation, pointing at this and that with the relish of firemen making an on-site inspection of a small disaster.

'Fucking circus,' Kraft mumbled. 'It's not right.'

'Shut up,' Esposito said, taking out his gun.

The sight of it exploded a charge of fear in Melville's chest. He yawned so massively that his jaw nearly locked. He shook his head and stared grimly beyond his executioner. He tried to tell himself that it was for the best. With everyone else dead, it would have been a hard thing to live with. That had been Gunn's problem. On the other hand he was not Gunn.

The sun was beginning to fail, and through his tears he saw the mountain across the pit glowing the colour of a halloween pumpkin. It would be the last thing he saw, he decided, shutting his eyes as Esposito walked towards him. He had a horror that if he kept his eyes open, time would freeze as it had when he slipped trying to rescue Yonden, and that he would see the bullet leaving the muzzle on its way to his heart.

From the entrance to the place of wet skulls, Linka watched the helicopters leave one after the other. They climbed slowly, tiny against the mountains, no larger than spiders spiralling up invisible threads. At last their clatter went away, but he stayed where he was, watching the camp grow quiet.

'The soldiers will be gone in a few days,' he told Pemba.

Now that the decision to leave was firmly implanted, he knew it was the right one. By temperament he was a survivor, and survivors don't take incalculable risks.

'Tell me what the world is like,' Pemba whispered.

'Full of people,' he said, giving her arm a reassuring squeeze. 'Full of opportunity.'

And that was the truth, he thought. He understood people very well, and he possessed something they all wanted. There was always a living to be made for men like himself who had an eye on the future and who could provide charms against it.

His gaze went to the southern skyline, and then travelled across it. In his mind's eye he was already in the lowlands, impressing himself on the people. First, though, he would shave his head and make a pilgrimage. The prospect eased the weight on his heart and for a while he was able to forget the evening shadow creeping across the snow.

WINDSOR CHORLTON

CANCELEER

Published in hardcover by Hodder & Stoughton, Windsor Chorlton's second scintillating thriller is coming in September 1991.

When Digby Fox disappears somewhere in Morocco leaving a thirty-ton marijuana deal unfinished, he also leaves a lot of disgruntled and very dangerous clients who want to know where their money has gone. Pat Case, dreadlocked ex-para and master of the arcane art of falconry, is recruited by a South London gangster to find Fox and his missing millions – but the quest soon proves to be as full of twists and turns as a flight by one of his beloved hawks. And when Case runs his quarry to earth in the heat and sweat of Morocco, he finds that he too is the object of a chase in which he must use all his hunter's guile to survive . . .

Flickering between intense sunlight and deeper shadows, CANCELEER is a brilliantly authentic thriller set amidst the tensions of the Middle East, a fascinating guide to the seamy fringe between the worlds of secret intelligence and organized crime, and an extraordinary psychological drama that explores the perverse fascination between hunter and hunted, exploiter and victim.

HODDER AND STOUGHTON HARDBACKS

CHRISTIE DICKASON

THE TEARS OF THE TIGER

The reluctant inheritor of her father's opium empire, always under surveillance by her fiery lover Thu, Nina was trapped in a gilded cage.

Then she met the American, Will John, and became pregnant.

And knew she had to escape.

Enthralling, heart-stopping, utterly involving, *The Tears of the Tiger* is the epic story of a woman's passion and tenacity, leading from the mountain forts of Laos, to the steamy streets of Bangkok and the glittering diplomatic circles of Washington, where war is known only by the ghosts of the past.

'Told with a flair as vivid as a film'   *Sunday Express*

'Dickason has a considerable gift'
                    The New York Times Book Review

HODDER AND STOUGHTON PAPERBACKS